DATE DUE			6/15
10/30/15			
8/11/17			
5-12-18			
4/11/19			
9/21/19			
11/13/19			

Lincoln Peirce

MR. POPULARITY

HARPER
An Imprint of HarperCollins*Publishers*

These comic strips first appeared in newspapers
from August 10, 2009, through March 7, 2010.

Library of Congress Control Number: 2013956489
ISBN 978-0-06-208700-3 (pbk.)

Typography by Andrea Vandergrift
14 15 16 17 18 CG/RRDC 10 9 8 7 6 5 4 3 2 1
❖
First Edition

More

BIG NATE

adventures from

Lincoln Peirce

Novels:

BIG NATE: IN A CLASS BY HIMSELF

BIG NATE STRIKES AGAIN

BIG NATE ON A ROLL

BIG NATE GOES FOR BROKE

BIG NATE FLIPS OUT

BIG NATE: IN THE ZONE

Activity Books:

BIG NATE BOREDOM BUSTER

BIG NATE FUN BLASTER

BIG NATE DOODLEPALOOZA

Comic Compilations:

BIG NATE: WHAT COULD POSSIBLY GO WRONG?

BIG NATE: HERE GOES NOTHING

BIG NATE: GENIUS MODE

BIG NATE FROM THE TOP

BIG NATE OUT LOUD

BIG NATE AND FRIENDS

BIG NATE MAKES THE GRADE

BIG NATE: GAME ON!

BIG NATE: I CAN'T TAKE IT!

BIG NATE: GREAT MINDS THINK ALIKE

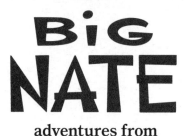

SIR STORYTIME

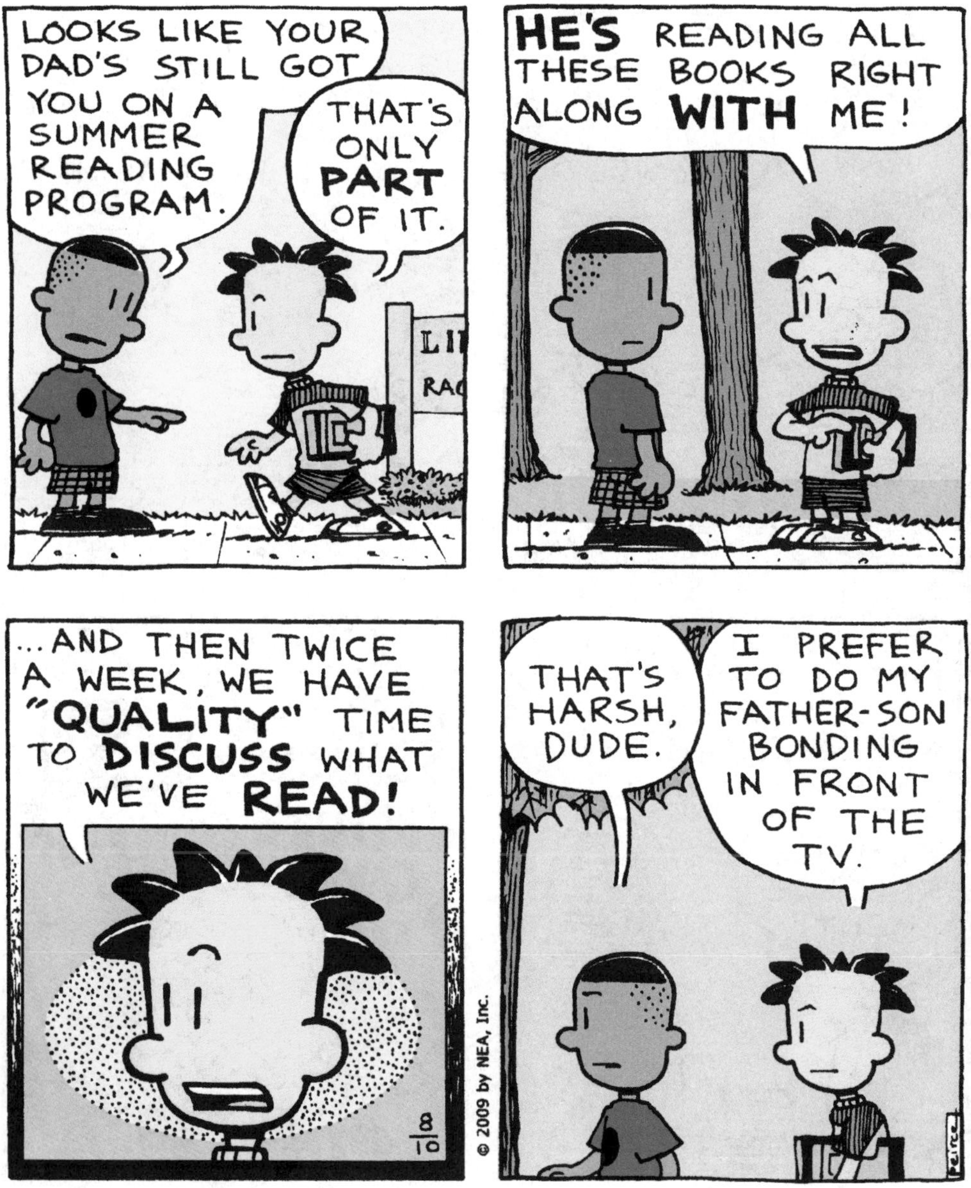
LOOKS LIKE YOUR DAD'S STILL GOT YOU ON A SUMMER READING PROGRAM.
THAT'S ONLY PART OF IT.
LI
RA
HE'S READING ALL THESE BOOKS RIGHT ALONG WITH ME!
...AND THEN TWICE A WEEK, WE HAVE "QUALITY" TIME TO DISCUSS WHAT WE'VE READ!
8/10
© 2009 by NEA, Inc.
THAT'S HARSH, DUDE.
I PREFER TO DO MY FATHER-SON BONDING IN FRONT OF THE TV.
peirce

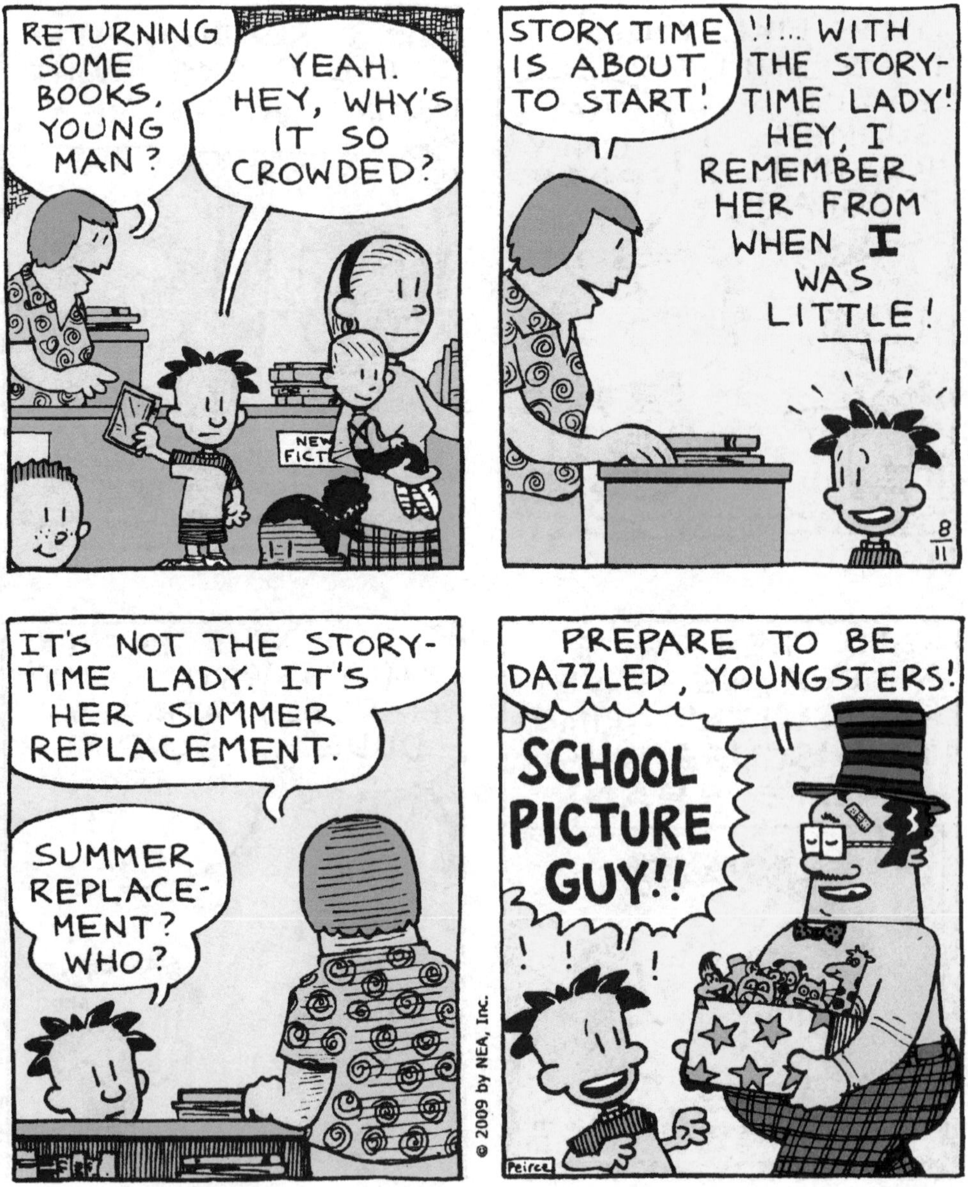
RETURNING SOME BOOKS, YOUNG MAN?
YEAH. HEY, WHY'S IT SO CROWDED?
NEW FICT
STORY TIME IS ABOUT TO START!
!!... WITH THE STORY-TIME LADY! HEY, I REMEMBER HER FROM WHEN I WAS LITTLE!
8/11
IT'S NOT THE STORY-TIME LADY. IT'S HER SUMMER REPLACEMENT.
SUMMER REPLACE-MENT? WHO?
© 2009 by NEA, Inc.
PREPARE TO BE DAZZLED, YOUNGSTERS!
SCHOOL PICTURE GUY!!
! ! !
Peirce

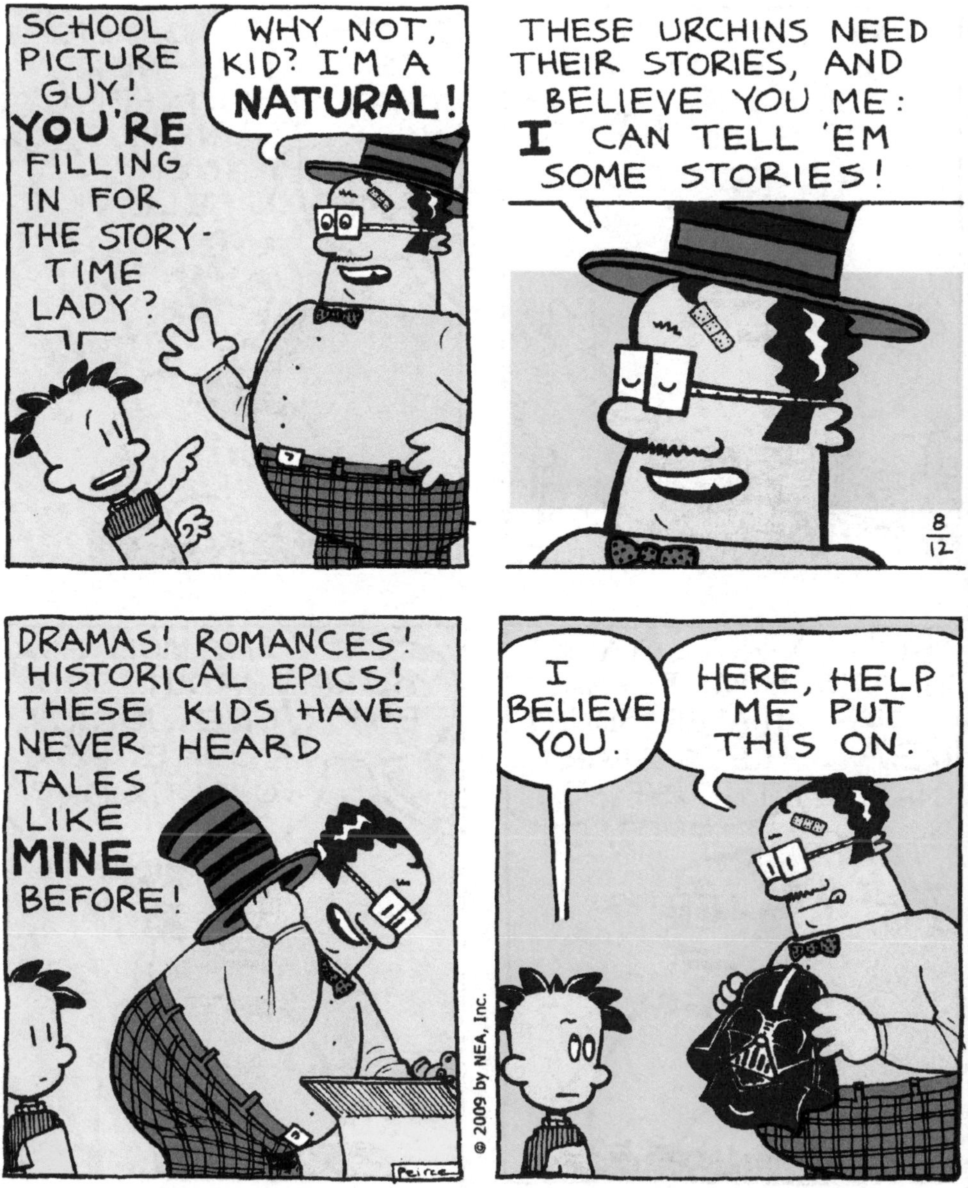
SCHOOL PICTURE GUY! YOU'RE FILLING IN FOR THE STORY-TIME LADY?
WHY NOT, KID? I'M A NATURAL!
THESE URCHINS NEED THEIR STORIES, AND BELIEVE YOU ME: I CAN TELL 'EM SOME STORIES!
8/12
DRAMAS! ROMANCES! HISTORICAL EPICS! THESE KIDS HAVE NEVER HEARD TALES LIKE MINE BEFORE!
Peirce
© 2009 by NEA, Inc.
I BELIEVE YOU.
HERE, HELP ME PUT THIS ON.

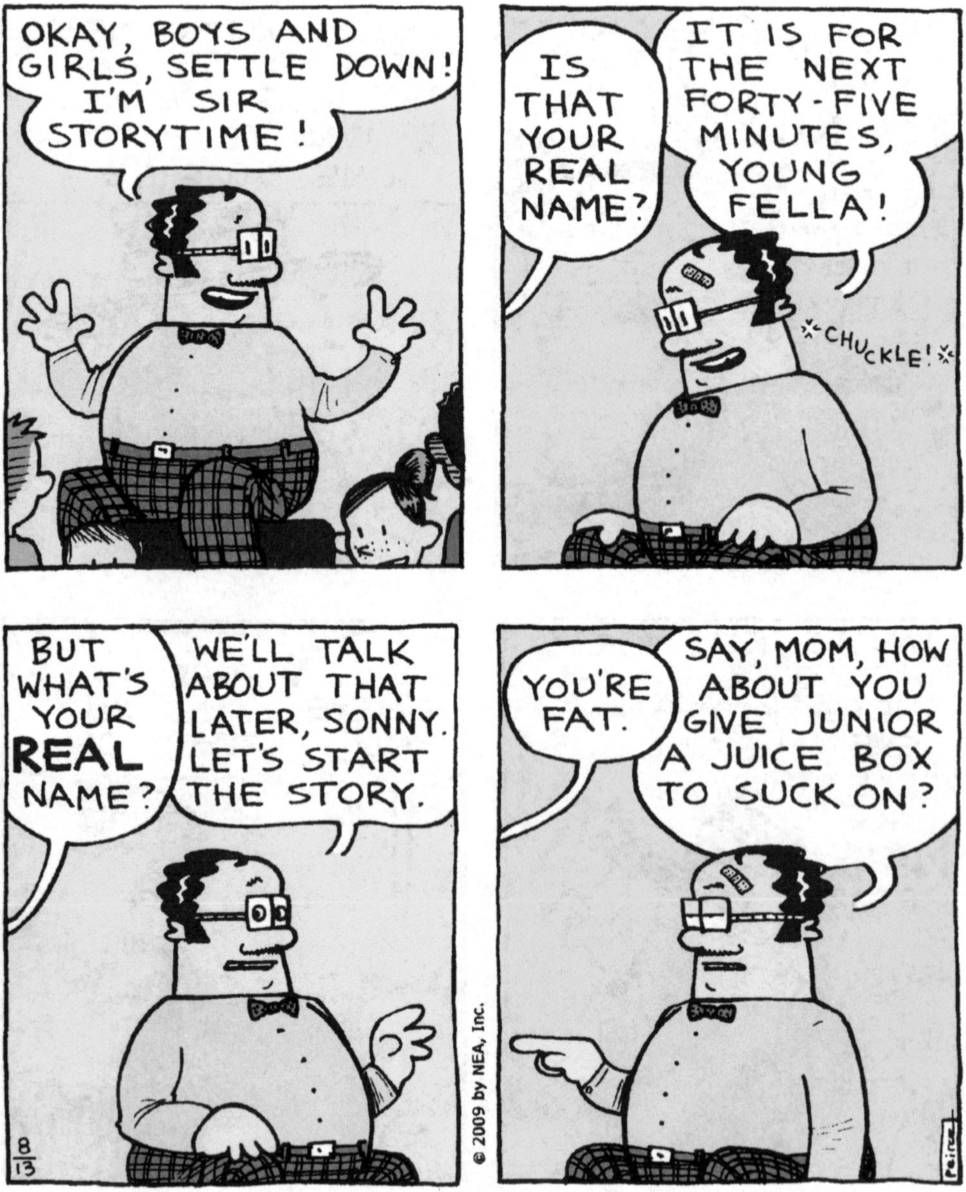
OKAY, BOYS AND GIRLS, SETTLE DOWN! I'M SIR STORYTIME!
IS THAT YOUR REAL NAME?
IT IS FOR THE NEXT FORTY-FIVE MINUTES, YOUNG FELLA!
CHUCKLE!
BUT WHAT'S YOUR **REAL** NAME?
WE'LL TALK ABOUT THAT LATER, SONNY. LET'S START THE STORY.
8/13
© 2009 by NEA, Inc.
YOU'RE FAT.
SAY, MOM, HOW ABOUT YOU GIVE JUNIOR A JUICE BOX TO SUCK ON?
Peirce

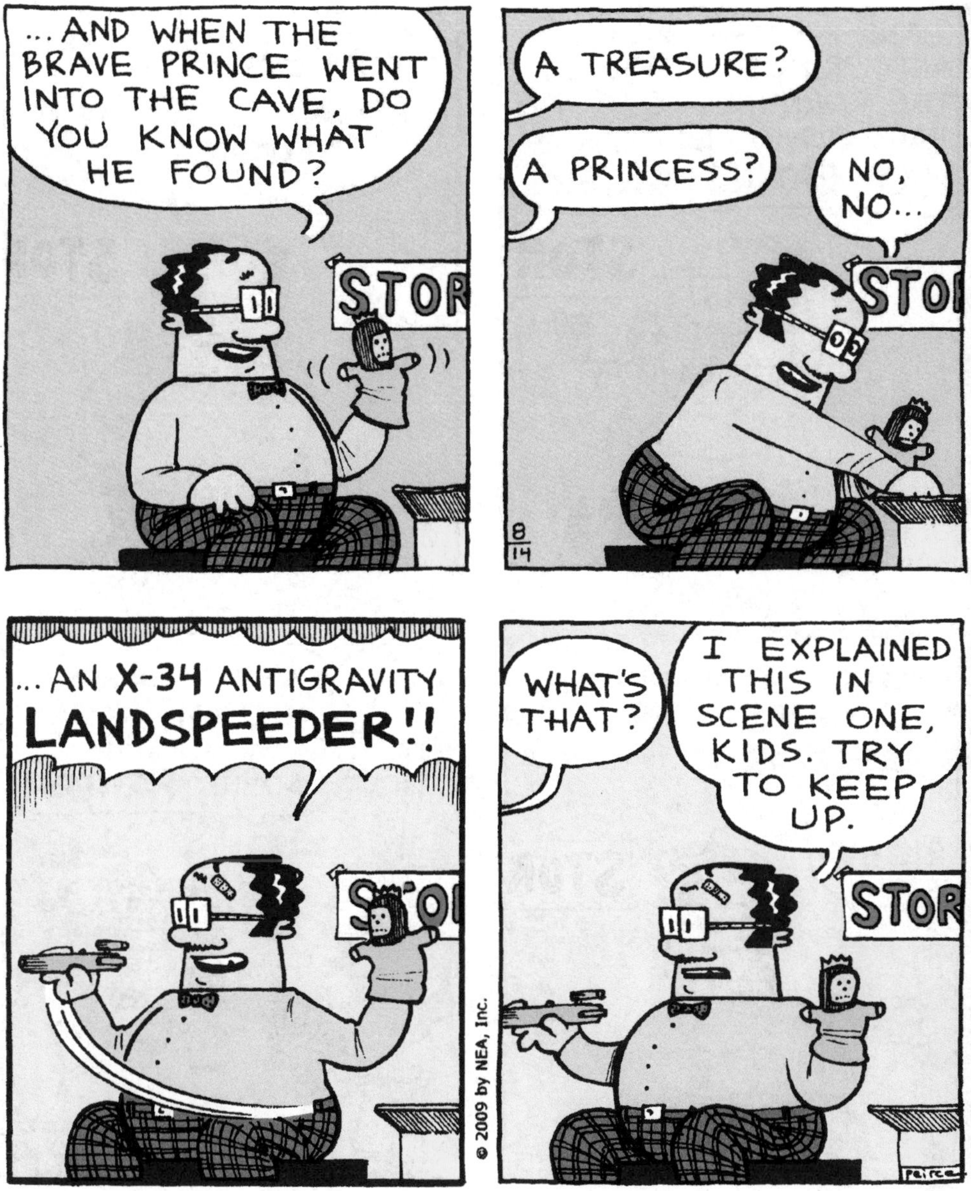
...AND WHEN THE BRAVE PRINCE WENT INTO THE CAVE, DO YOU KNOW WHAT HE FOUND?
STOR
8
14
A TREASURE?
A PRINCESS?
NO, NO...
STOR
...AN X-34 ANTIGRAVITY LANDSPEEDER!!
© 2009 by NEA, Inc.
WHAT'S THAT?
I EXPLAINED THIS IN SCENE ONE, KIDS. TRY TO KEEP UP.
STOR
peirce

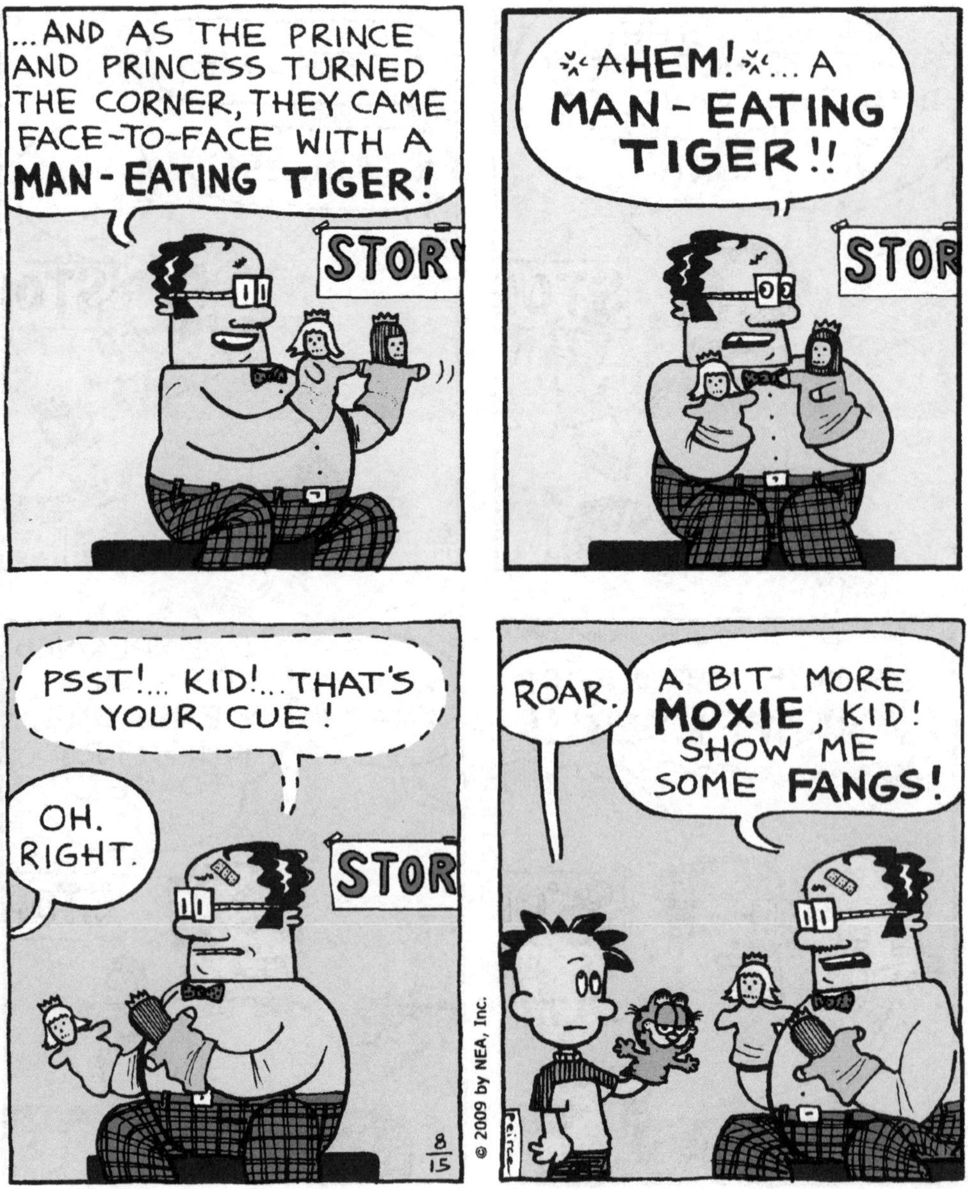
...AND AS THE PRINCE AND PRINCESS TURNED THE CORNER, THEY CAME FACE-TO-FACE WITH A **MAN-EATING TIGER!**
STORY
AHEM!... A **MAN-EATING TIGER!!**
STOR
PSST!... KID!... THAT'S YOUR CUE!
OH. RIGHT.
STOR
8/15
© 2009 by NEA, Inc.
ROAR.
A BIT MORE **MOXIE**, KID! SHOW ME SOME **FANGS!**

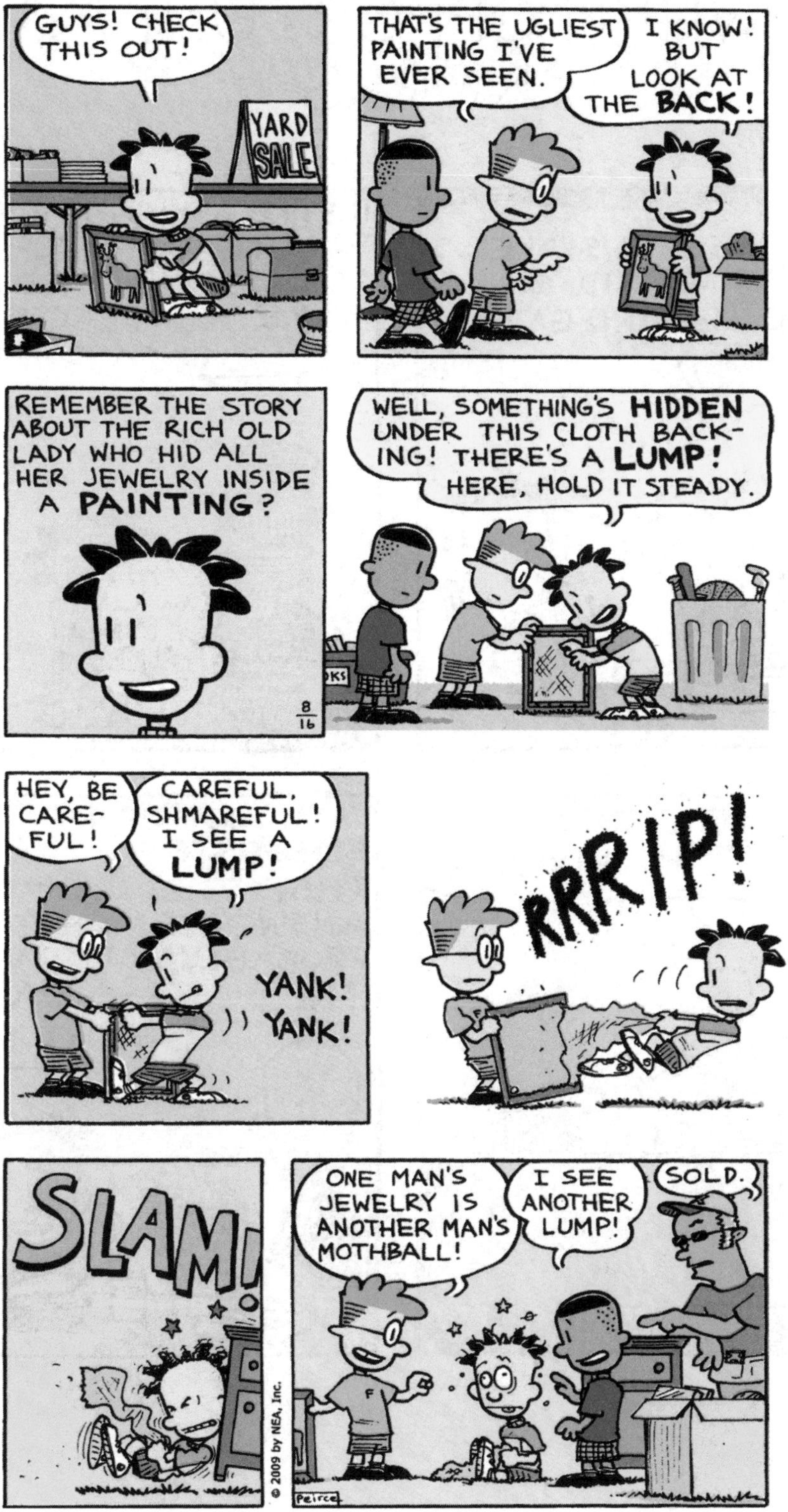
GUYS! CHECK THIS OUT!
YARD SALE
THAT'S THE UGLIEST PAINTING I'VE EVER SEEN.
I KNOW! BUT LOOK AT THE **BACK**!
REMEMBER THE STORY ABOUT THE RICH OLD LADY WHO HID ALL HER JEWELRY INSIDE A **PAINTING**?
8/16
WELL, SOMETHING'S **HIDDEN** UNDER THIS CLOTH BACKING! THERE'S A **LUMP**! HERE, HOLD IT STEADY.
HEY, BE CAREFUL!
CAREFUL, SHMAREFUL! I SEE A **LUMP**!
YANK! YANK!
RRRIP!
SLAM!
© 2009 by NEA, Inc.
ONE MAN'S JEWELRY IS ANOTHER MAN'S MOTHBALL!
I SEE ANOTHER LUMP!
SOLD.
Peirce

WHEN OPPORTUNITY KNOCKS . . .

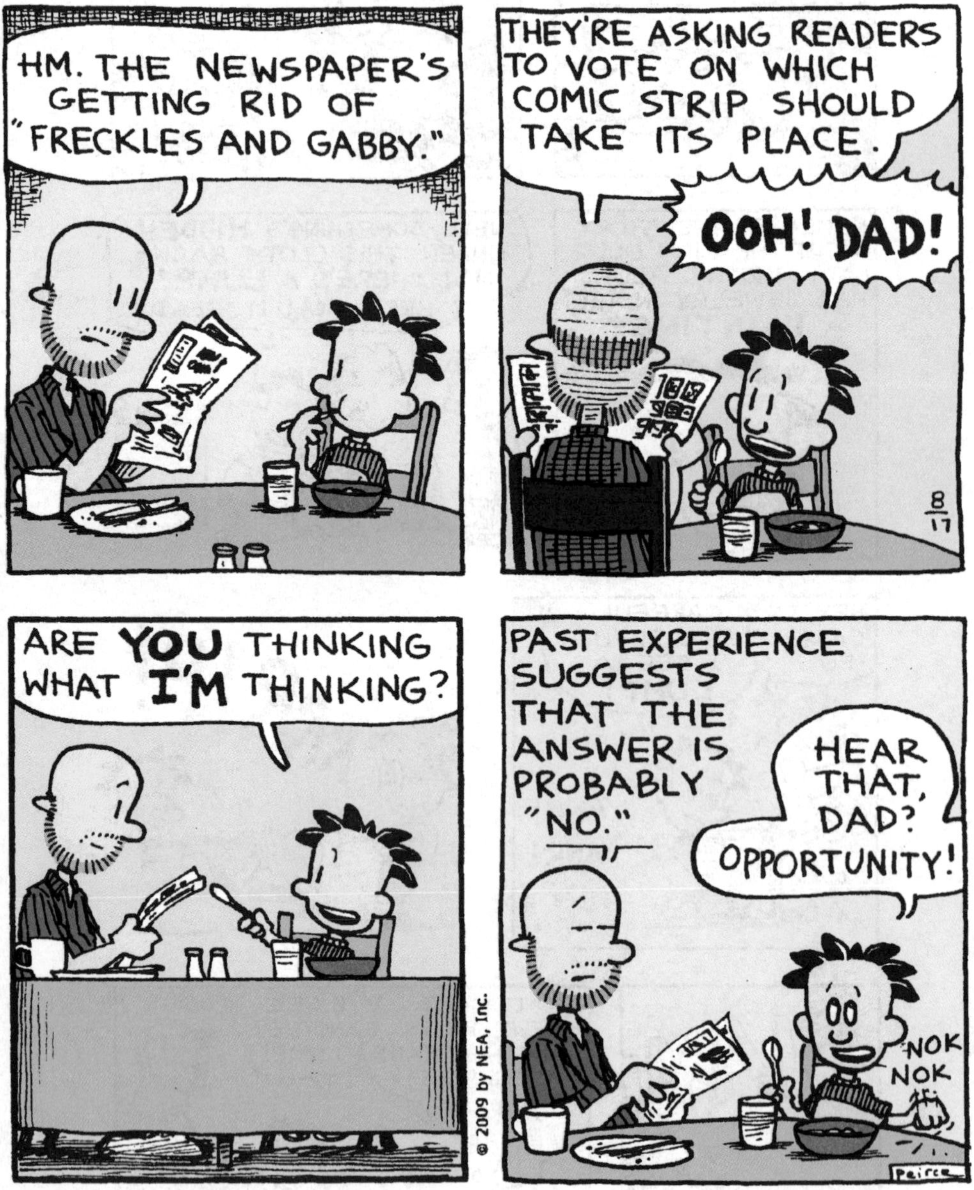
HM. THE NEWSPAPER'S GETTING RID OF "FRECKLES AND GABBY."
THEY'RE ASKING READERS TO VOTE ON WHICH COMIC STRIP SHOULD TAKE ITS PLACE.
OOH! DAD!
8/17
ARE YOU THINKING WHAT I'M THINKING?
PAST EXPERIENCE SUGGESTS THAT THE ANSWER IS PROBABLY "NO."
HEAR THAT, DAD? OPPORTUNITY!
NOK NOK
Peirce
© 2009 by NEA, Inc.

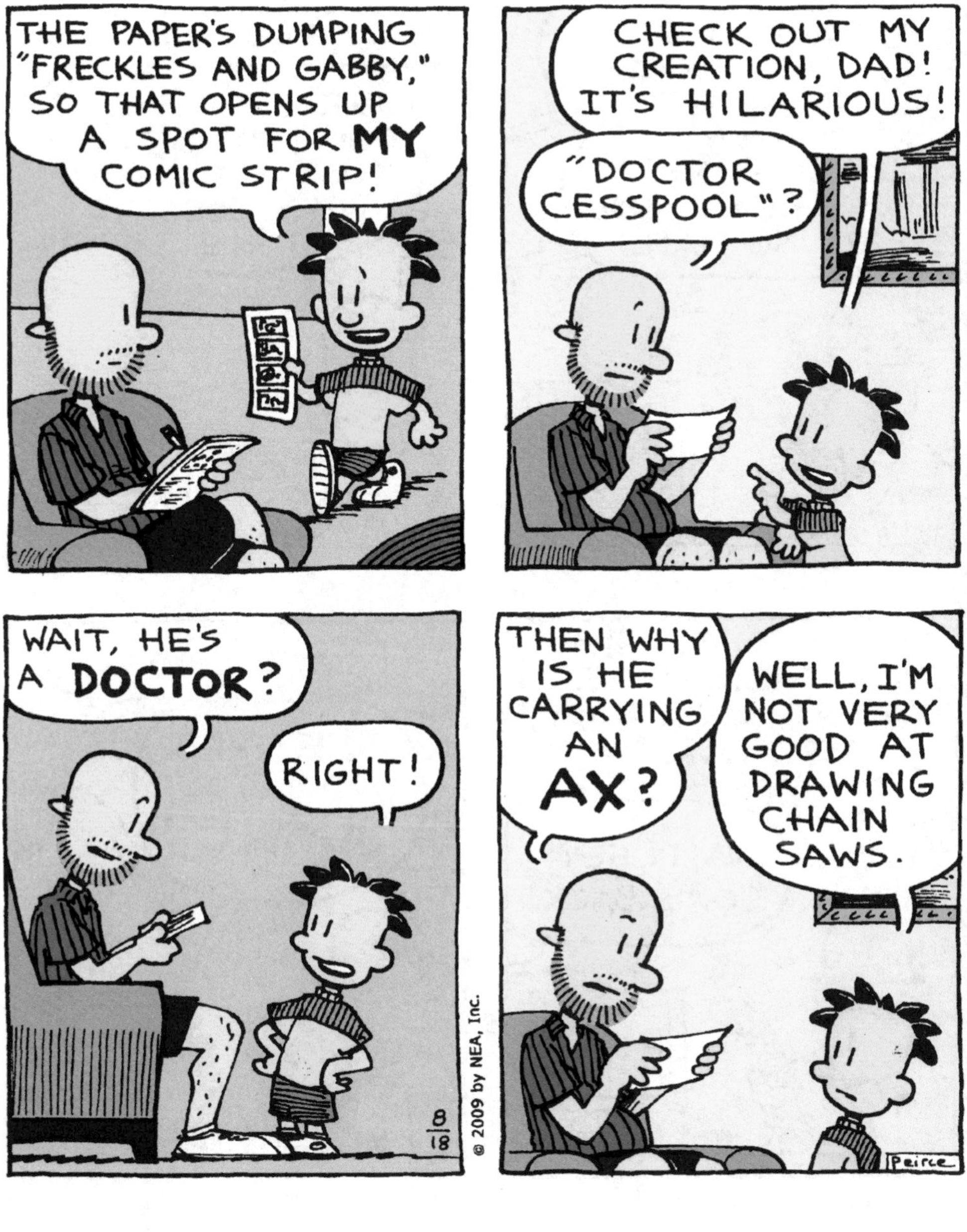
THE PAPER'S DUMPING "FRECKLES AND GABBY," SO THAT OPENS UP A SPOT FOR MY COMIC STRIP!
CHECK OUT MY CREATION, DAD! IT'S HILARIOUS!
"DOCTOR CESSPOOL"?
WAIT, HE'S A DOCTOR?
RIGHT!
THEN WHY IS HE CARRYING AN AX?
WELL, I'M NOT VERY GOOD AT DRAWING CHAIN SAWS.
8/18
© 2009 by NEA, Inc.
Peirce

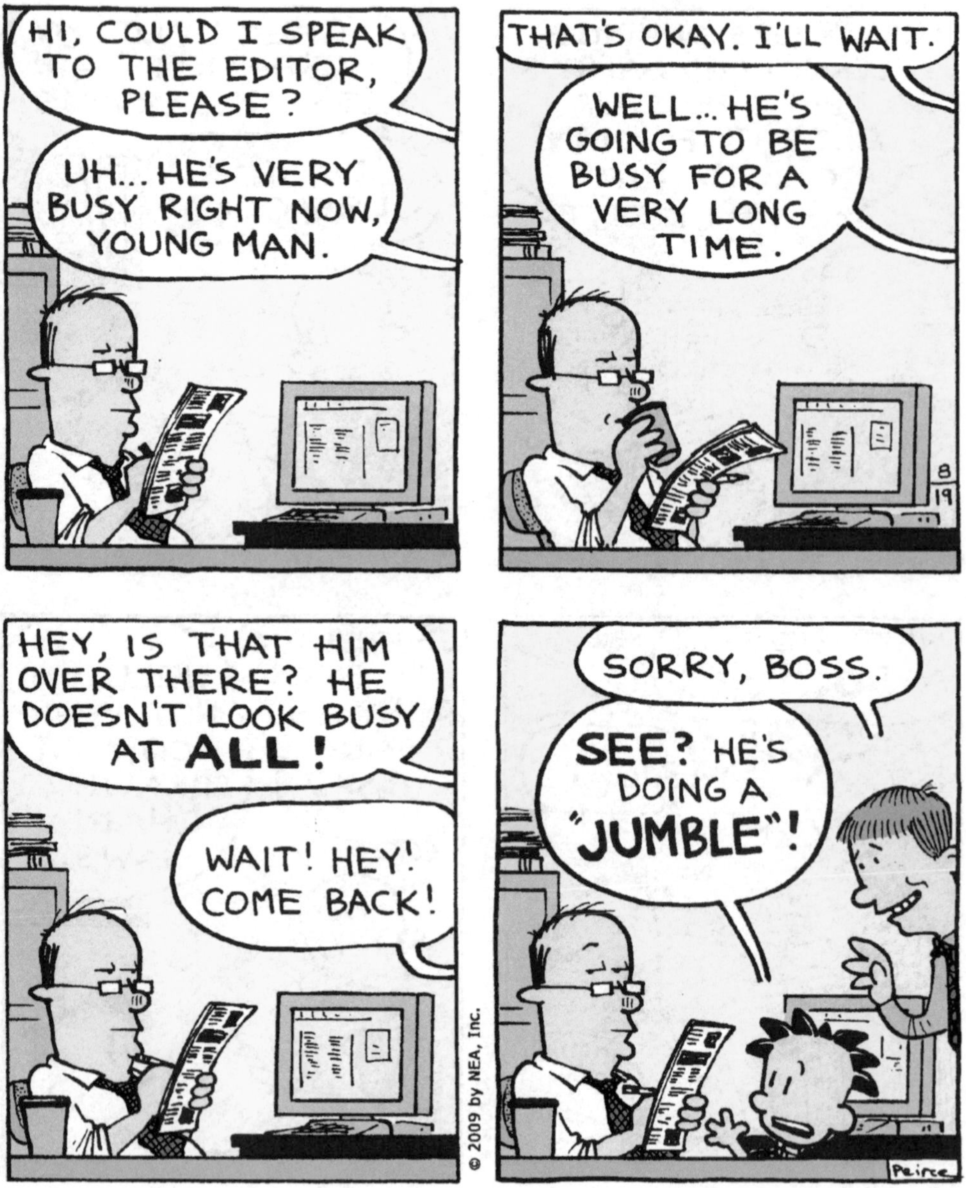
HI, COULD I SPEAK TO THE EDITOR, PLEASE?
UH... HE'S VERY BUSY RIGHT NOW, YOUNG MAN.
THAT'S OKAY. I'LL WAIT.
WELL... HE'S GOING TO BE BUSY FOR A VERY LONG TIME.
8 19
HEY, IS THAT HIM OVER THERE? HE DOESN'T LOOK BUSY AT ALL!
WAIT! HEY! COME BACK!
SORRY, BOSS.
SEE? HE'S DOING A "JUMBLE"!
Peirce

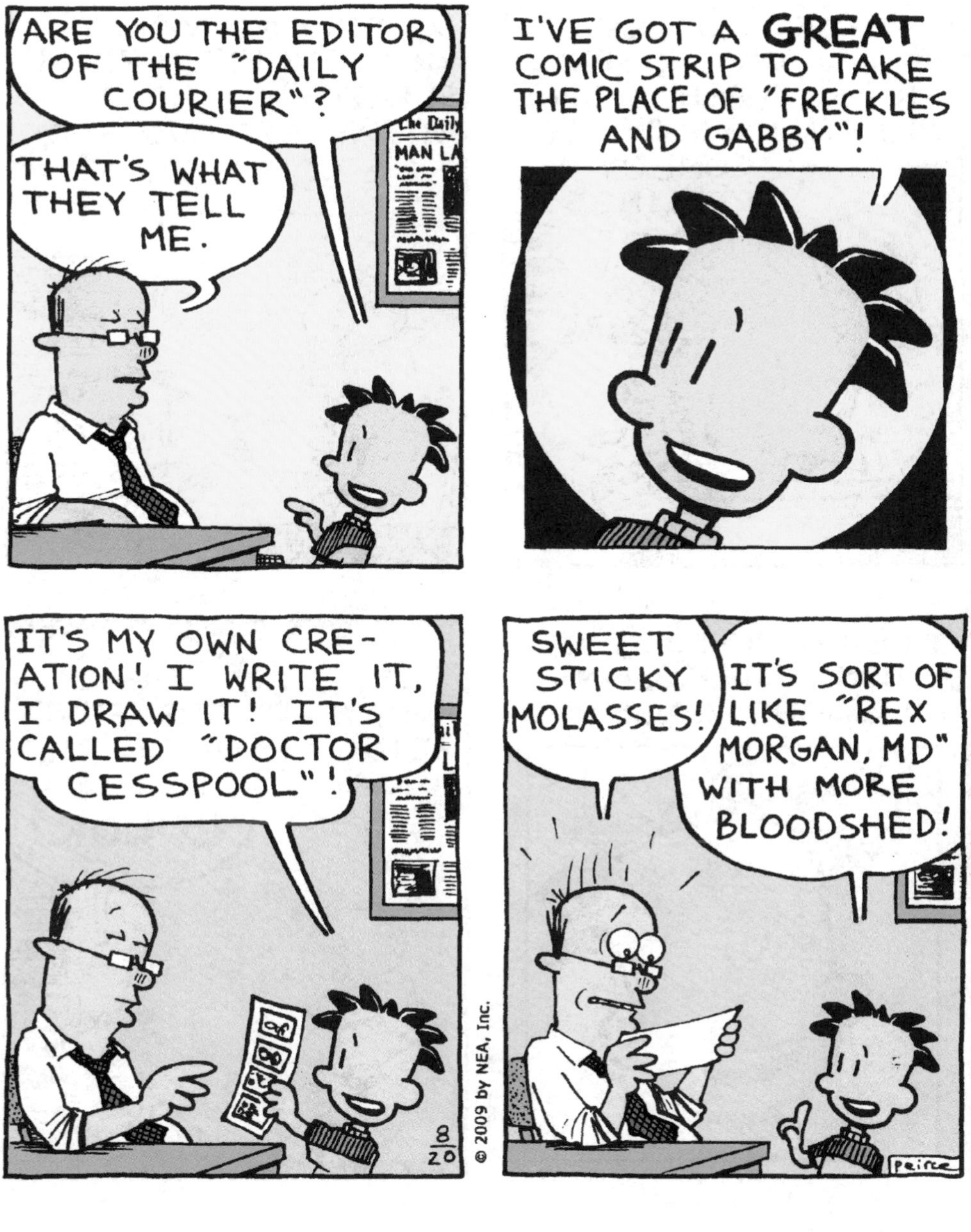
ARE YOU THE EDITOR OF THE "DAILY COURIER"?
THAT'S WHAT THEY TELL ME.
I'VE GOT A GREAT COMIC STRIP TO TAKE THE PLACE OF "FRECKLES AND GABBY"!
IT'S MY OWN CRE-ATION! I WRITE IT, I DRAW IT! IT'S CALLED "DOCTOR CESSPOOL"!
SWEET STICKY MOLASSES!
IT'S SORT OF LIKE "REX MORGAN, MD" WITH MORE BLOODSHED!
8/20
© 2009 by NEA, Inc.
peirce

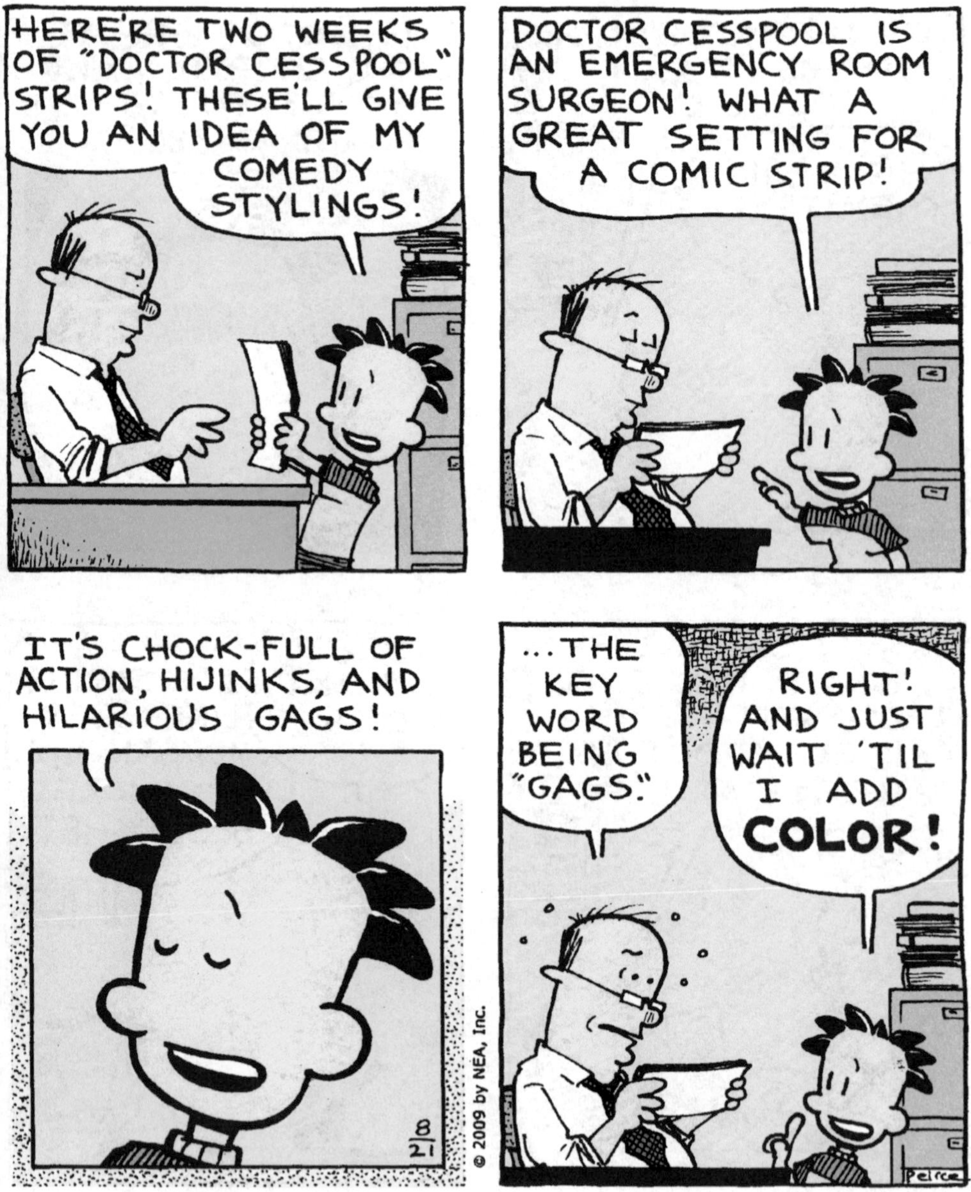
HERE'RE TWO WEEKS OF "DOCTOR CESSPOOL" STRIPS! THESE'LL GIVE YOU AN IDEA OF MY COMEDY STYLINGS!
DOCTOR CESSPOOL IS AN EMERGENCY ROOM SURGEON! WHAT A GREAT SETTING FOR A COMIC STRIP!
IT'S CHOCK-FULL OF ACTION, HIJINKS, AND HILARIOUS GAGS!
8/21
© 2009 by NEA, Inc.
...THE KEY WORD BEING "GAGS."
RIGHT! AND JUST WAIT 'TIL I ADD COLOR!
Peirce

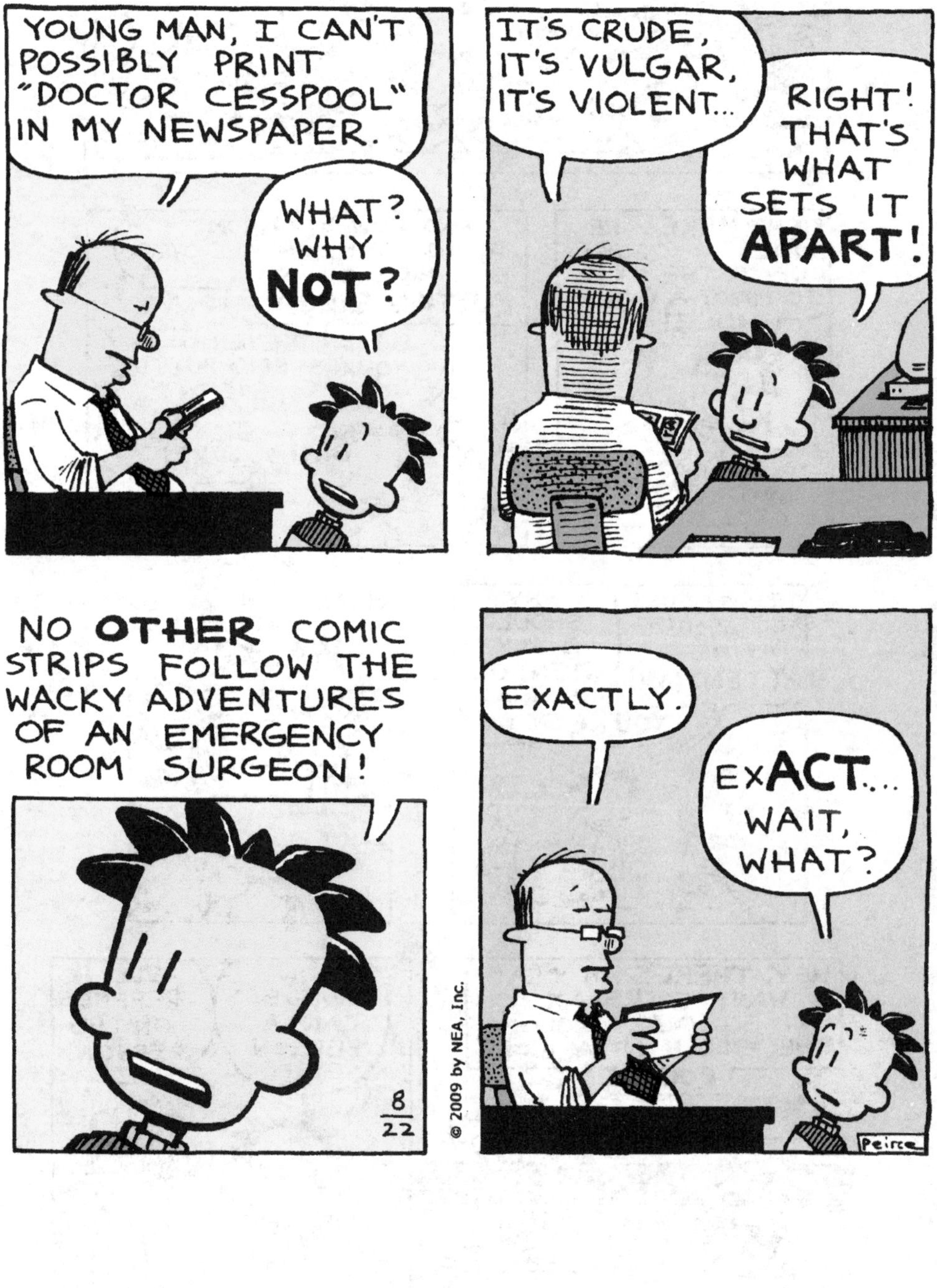
YOUNG MAN, I CAN'T POSSIBLY PRINT "DOCTOR CESSPOOL" IN MY NEWSPAPER.
WHAT? WHY NOT?
IT'S CRUDE, IT'S VULGAR, IT'S VIOLENT...
RIGHT! THAT'S WHAT SETS IT APART!
NO OTHER COMIC STRIPS FOLLOW THE WACKY ADVENTURES OF AN EMERGENCY ROOM SURGEON!
8/22
© 2009 by NEA, Inc.
EXACTLY.
ExACT... WAIT, WHAT?
Peirce

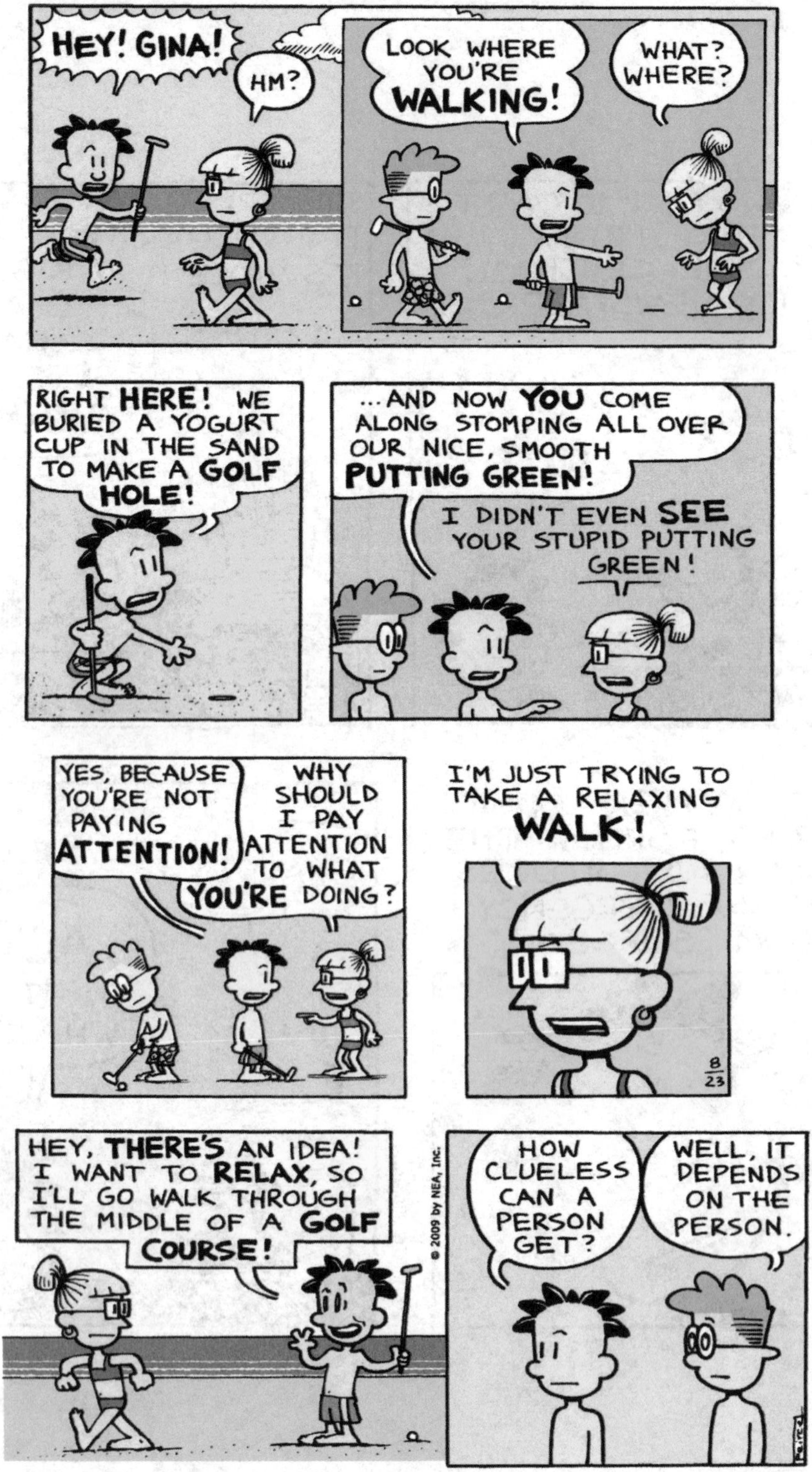
HEY! GINA!
HM?
LOOK WHERE YOU'RE WALKING!
WHAT? WHERE?
RIGHT HERE! WE BURIED A YOGURT CUP IN THE SAND TO MAKE A GOLF HOLE!
...AND NOW YOU COME ALONG STOMPING ALL OVER OUR NICE, SMOOTH PUTTING GREEN!
I DIDN'T EVEN SEE YOUR STUPID PUTTING GREEN!
YES, BECAUSE YOU'RE NOT PAYING ATTENTION!
WHY SHOULD I PAY ATTENTION TO WHAT YOU'RE DOING?
I'M JUST TRYING TO TAKE A RELAXING WALK!
8/23
HEY, THERE'S AN IDEA! I WANT TO RELAX, SO I'LL GO WALK THROUGH THE MIDDLE OF A GOLF COURSE!
© 2009 by NEA, Inc.
HOW CLUELESS CAN A PERSON GET?
WELL, IT DEPENDS ON THE PERSON.
Peirce

SHOP 'TIL YOU DROP

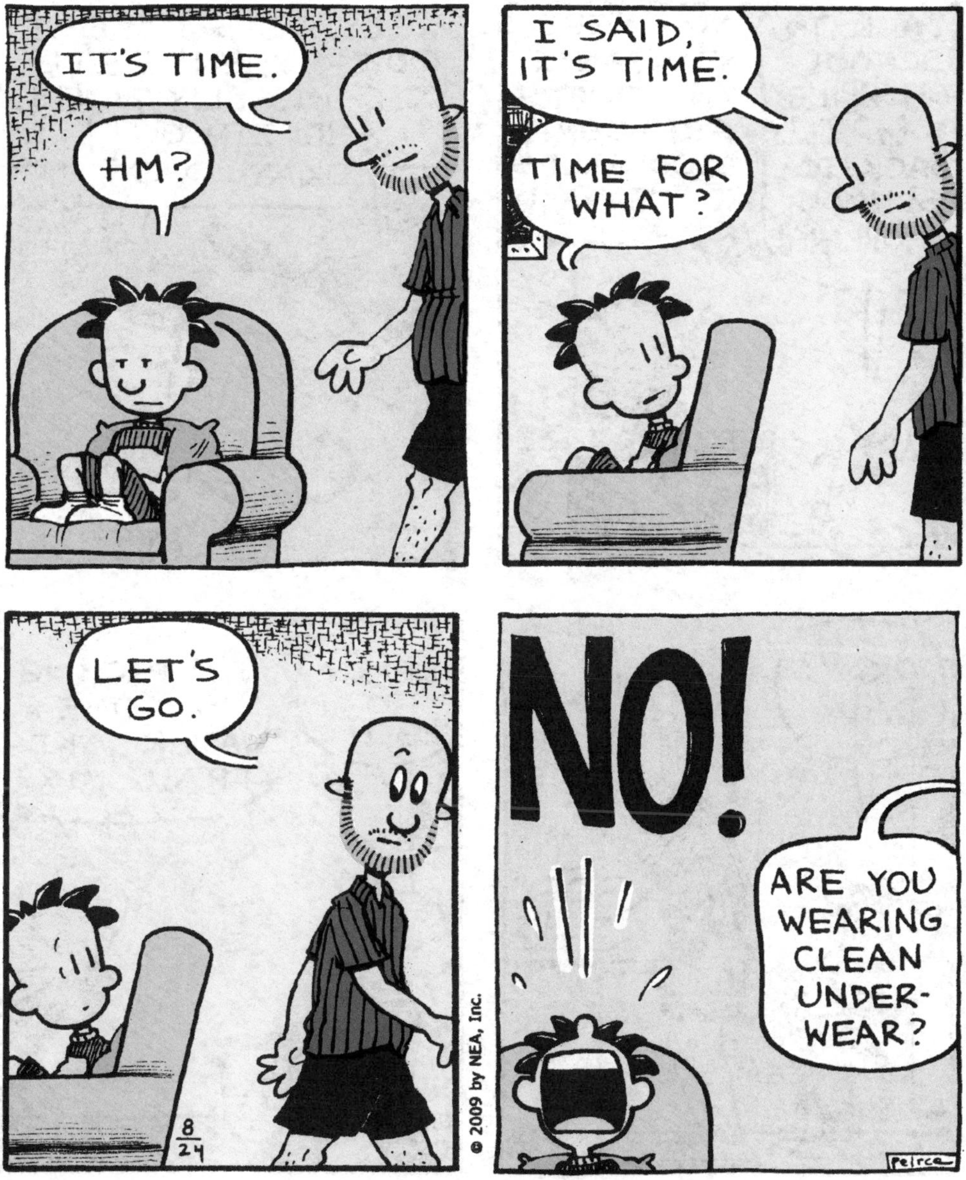
IT'S TIME.
HM?
I SAID, IT'S TIME.
TIME FOR WHAT?
LET'S GO.
8/24
© 2009 by NEA, Inc.
NO!
ARE YOU WEARING CLEAN UNDER-WEAR?
peirce

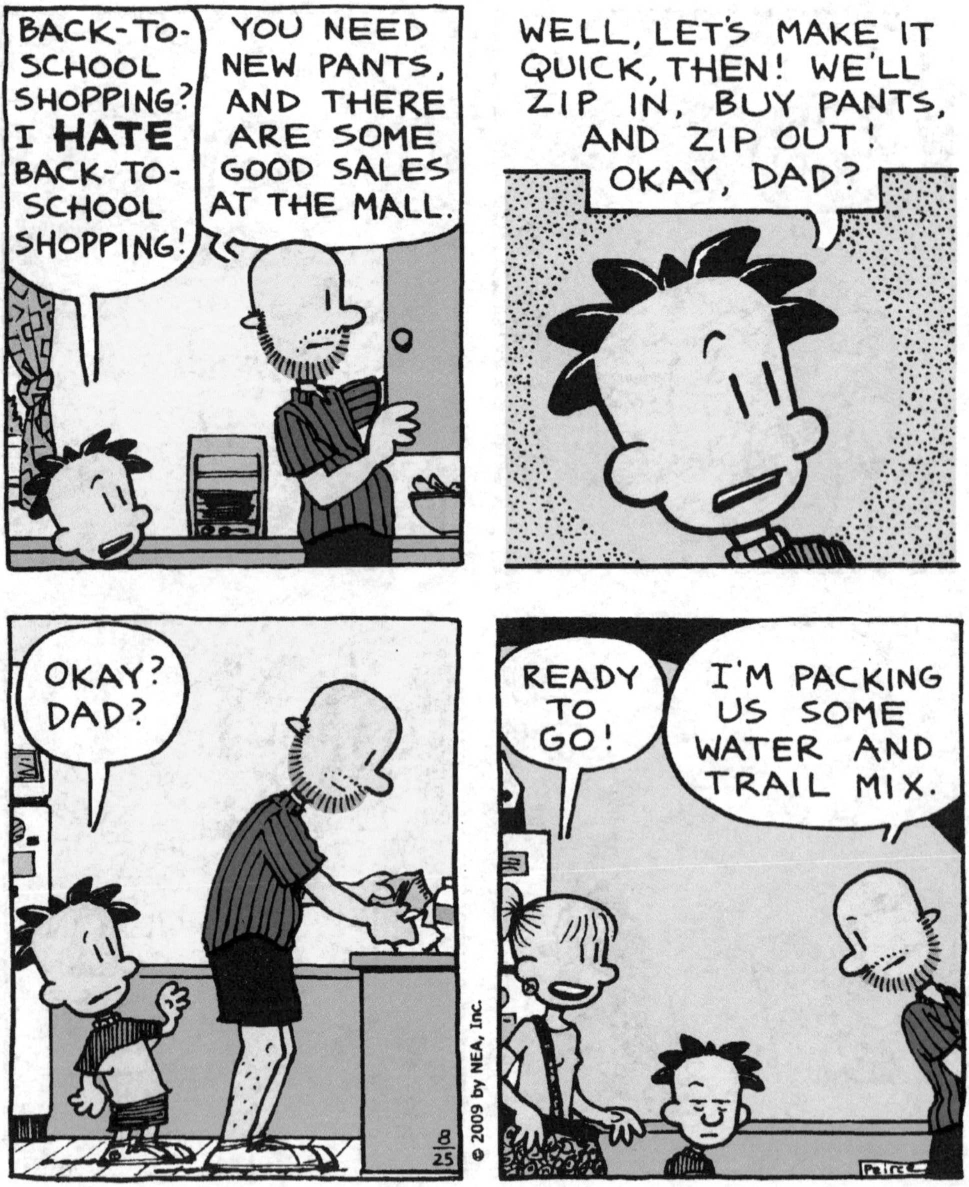
BACK-TO-SCHOOL SHOPPING? I **HATE** BACK-TO-SCHOOL SHOPPING!
YOU NEED NEW PANTS, AND THERE ARE SOME GOOD SALES AT THE MALL.
WELL, LET'S MAKE IT QUICK, THEN! WE'LL ZIP IN, BUY PANTS, AND ZIP OUT! OKAY, DAD?
OKAY? DAD?
READY TO GO!
I'M PACKING US SOME WATER AND TRAIL MIX.
8/25
© 2009 by NEA, Inc.
Peirce

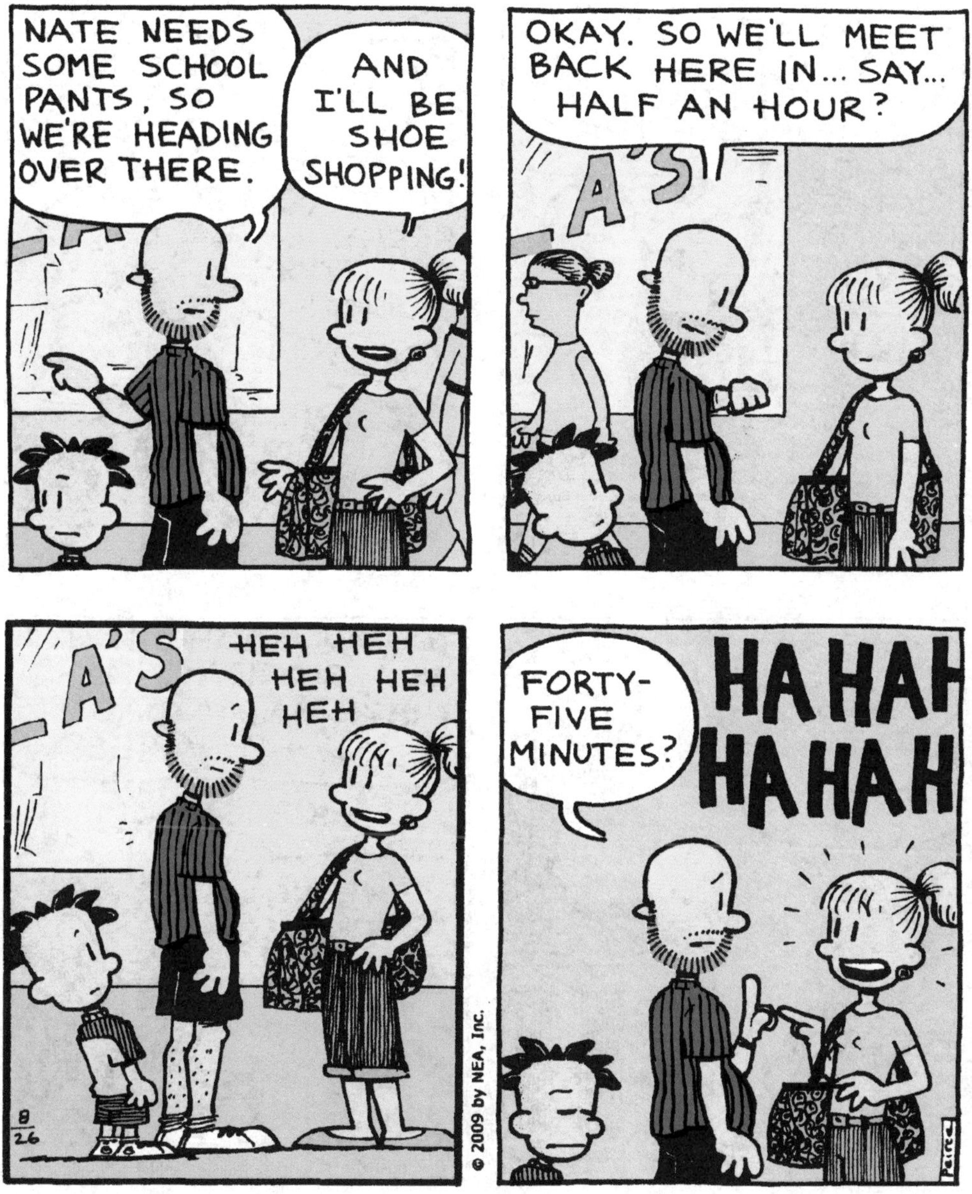
NATE NEEDS SOME SCHOOL PANTS, SO WE'RE HEADING OVER THERE.
AND I'LL BE SHOE SHOPPING!
OKAY. SO WE'LL MEET BACK HERE IN... SAY... HALF AN HOUR?
HEH HEH HEH HEH HEH
8/26
FORTY-FIVE MINUTES?
HA HAH HA HAH
Peirce

HOW COME I CAN'T BUY MY BACK-TO-SCHOOL CLOTHES ON MY **OWN**?

BECAUSE I HAVE THE MONEY, FOR ONE THING.

BOY SIZES

WELL, JUST GIVE **ME** THE MONEY! **I'LL** TAKE CARE OF THE SHOPPING WHILE **YOU** RELAX IN THE FOOD COURT!

✳SNORT!✳

COTTO SWEA

WE TRIED THAT LAST YEAR.

WE DID?

CREW-NE

8/27

© 2009 by NEA, Inc.

YOU BOUGHT TWO HOURS OF A FLORIDA TIME-SHARE AND A BAG OF "SUGAR BABIES."

I HAVE NO MEMORY OF THAT.

Peirce

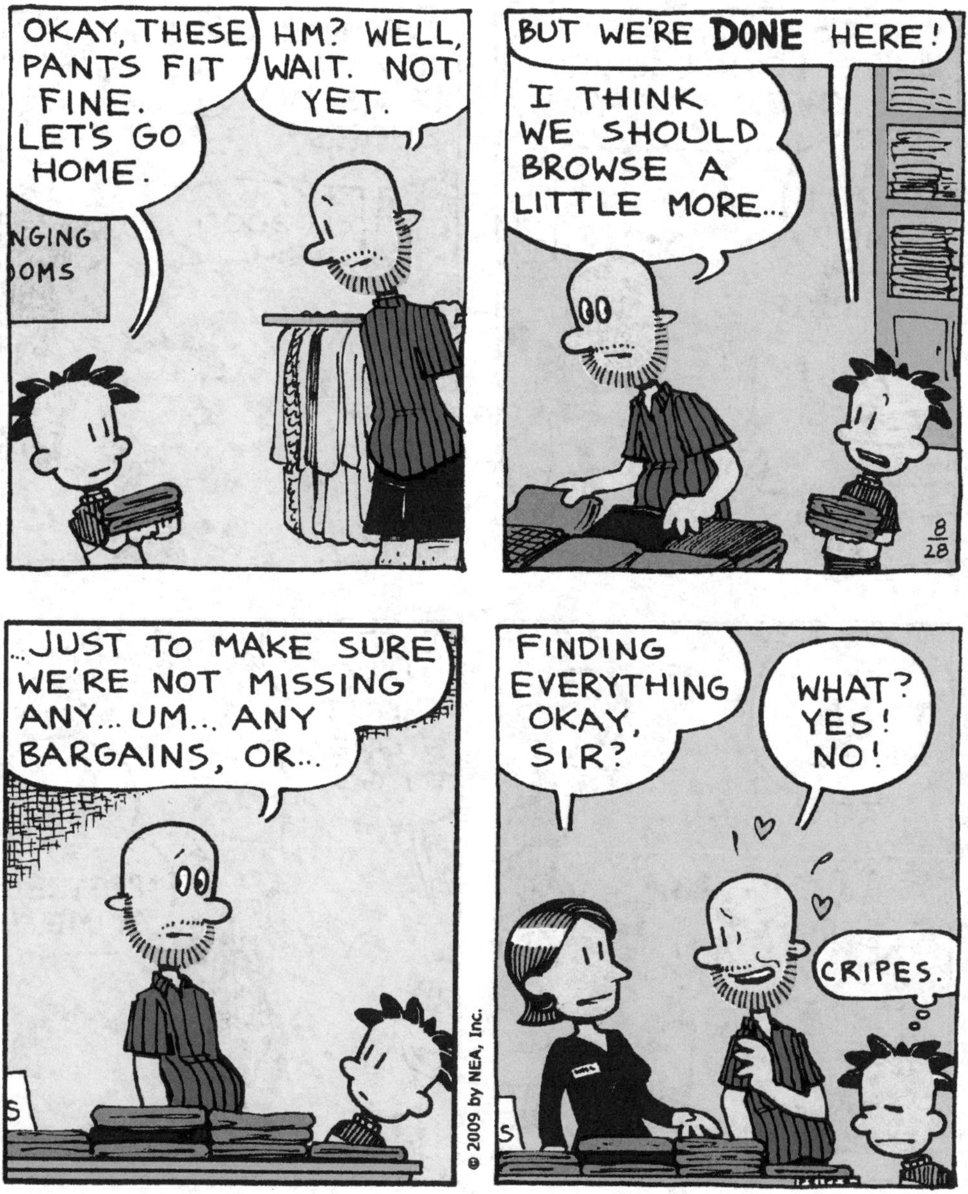
OKAY, THESE PANTS FIT FINE. LET'S GO HOME.
HM? WELL, WAIT. NOT YET.
NGING
OOMS
BUT WE'RE **DONE** HERE!
I THINK WE SHOULD BROWSE A LITTLE MORE...
8
28
...JUST TO MAKE SURE WE'RE NOT MISSING ANY... UM... ANY BARGAINS, OR...
© 2009 by NEA, Inc.
FINDING EVERYTHING OKAY, SIR?
WHAT? YES! NO!
CRIPES.

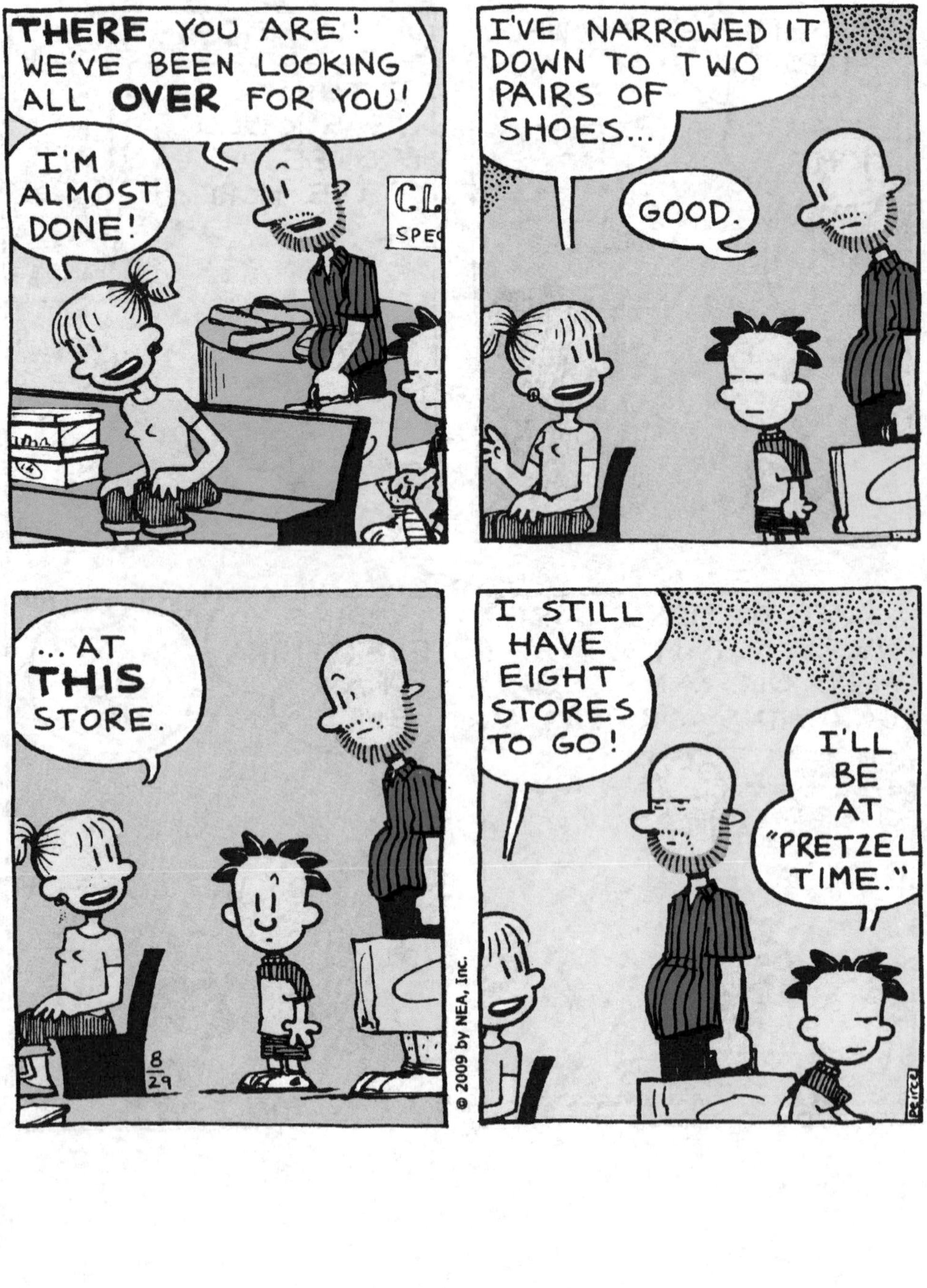
THERE YOU ARE! WE'VE BEEN LOOKING ALL OVER FOR YOU!
I'M ALMOST DONE!
I'VE NARROWED IT DOWN TO TWO PAIRS OF SHOES...
GOOD.
... AT THIS STORE.
I STILL HAVE EIGHT STORES TO GO!
I'LL BE AT "PRETZEL TIME."
8/29
© 2009 by NEA, Inc.
PEIRCE

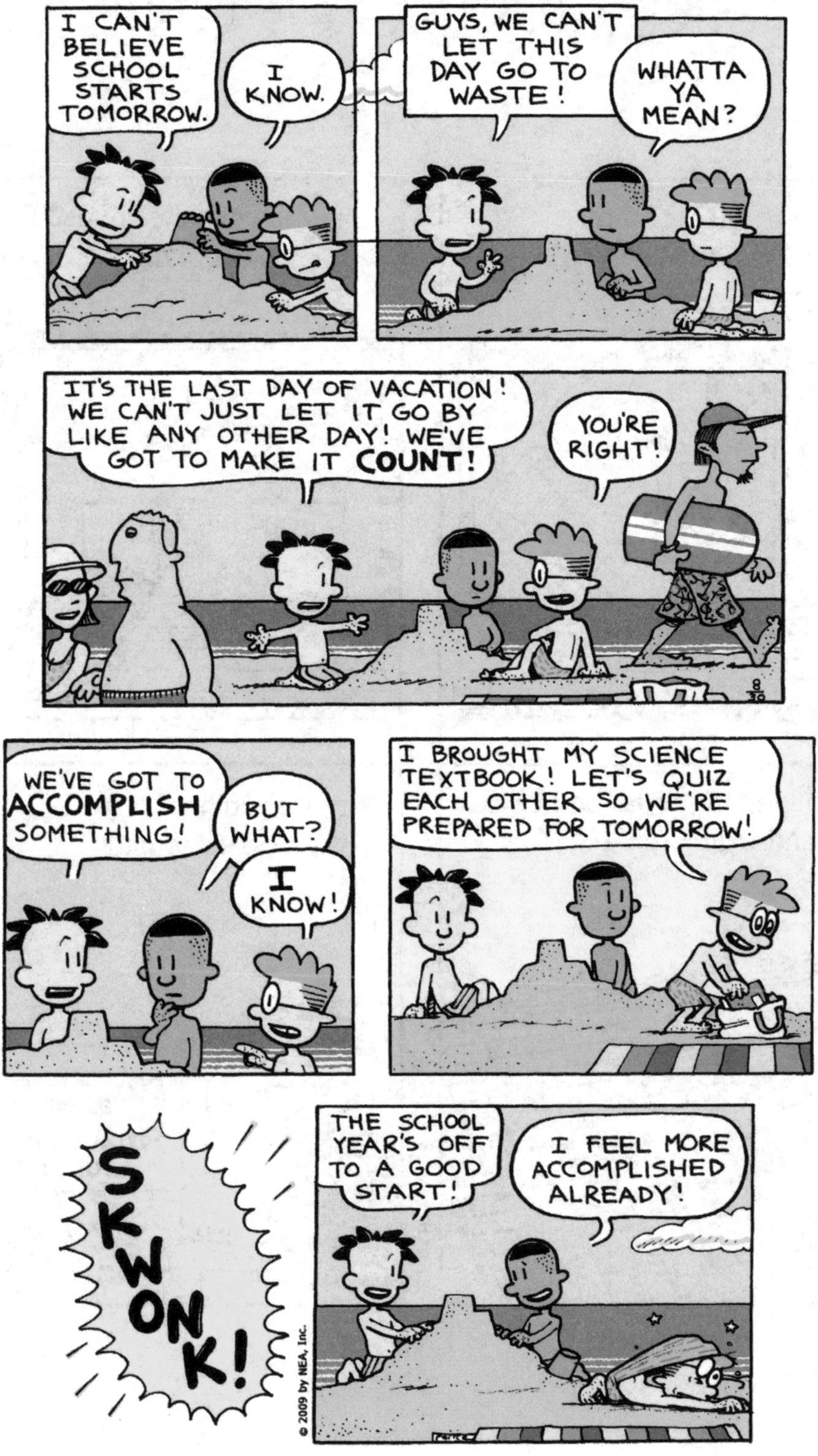
I CAN'T BELIEVE SCHOOL STARTS TOMORROW.
I KNOW.
GUYS, WE CAN'T LET THIS DAY GO TO WASTE!
WHATTA YA MEAN?
IT'S THE LAST DAY OF VACATION! WE CAN'T JUST LET IT GO BY LIKE ANY OTHER DAY! WE'VE GOT TO MAKE IT COUNT!
YOU'RE RIGHT!
8/30
WE'VE GOT TO ACCOMPLISH SOMETHING!
BUT WHAT?
I KNOW!
I BROUGHT MY SCIENCE TEXTBOOK! LET'S QUIZ EACH OTHER SO WE'RE PREPARED FOR TOMORROW!
SKWONK!
THE SCHOOL YEAR'S OFF TO A GOOD START!
I FEEL MORE ACCOMPLISHED ALREADY!
© 2009 by NEA, Inc.

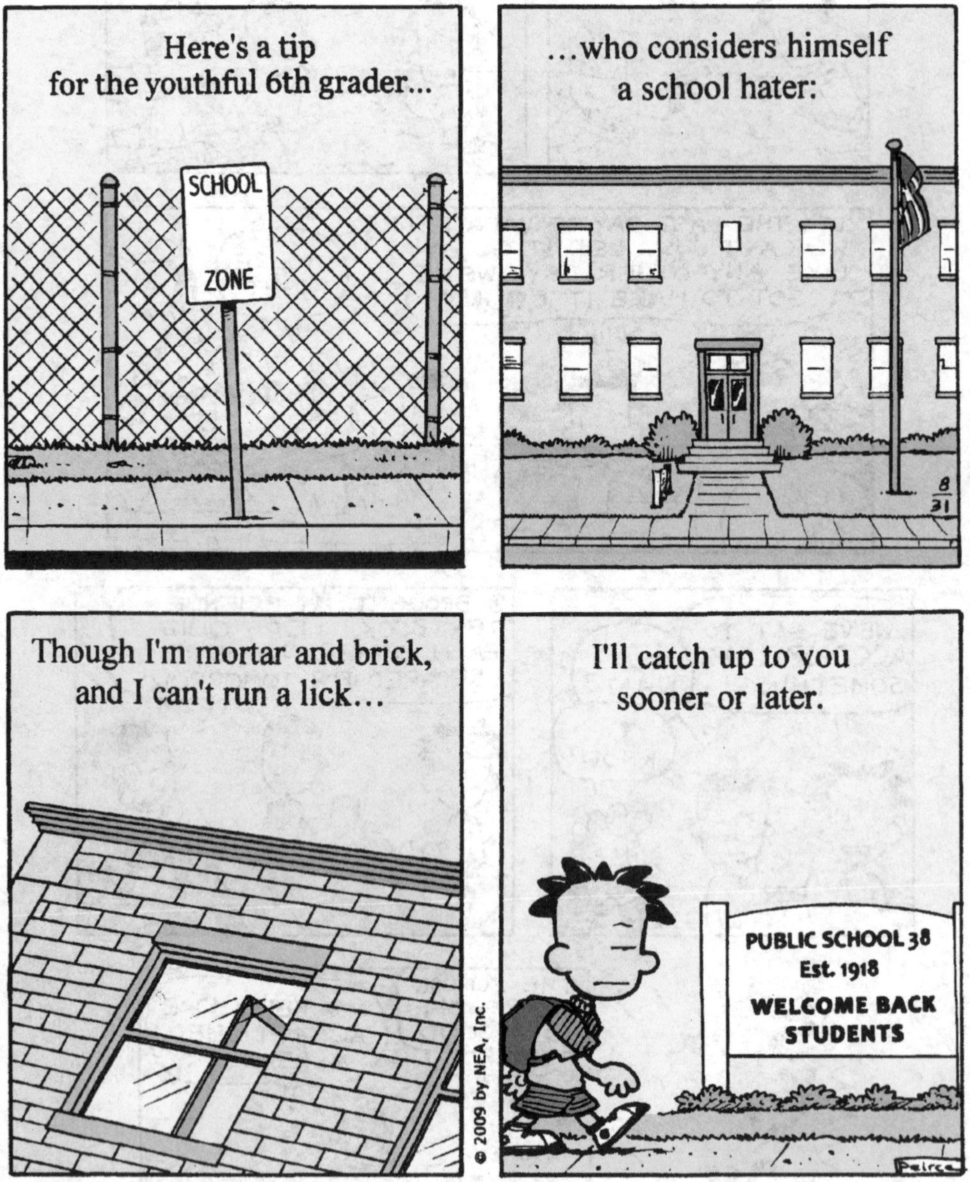
Here's a tip
for the youthful 6th grader...
SCHOOL
ZONE
...who considers himself
a school hater:
8
31
Though I'm mortar and brick,
and I can't run a lick...
I'll catch up to you
sooner or later.
PUBLIC SCHOOL 38
Est. 1918
WELCOME BACK
STUDENTS
© 2009 by NEA, Inc.
Peirce

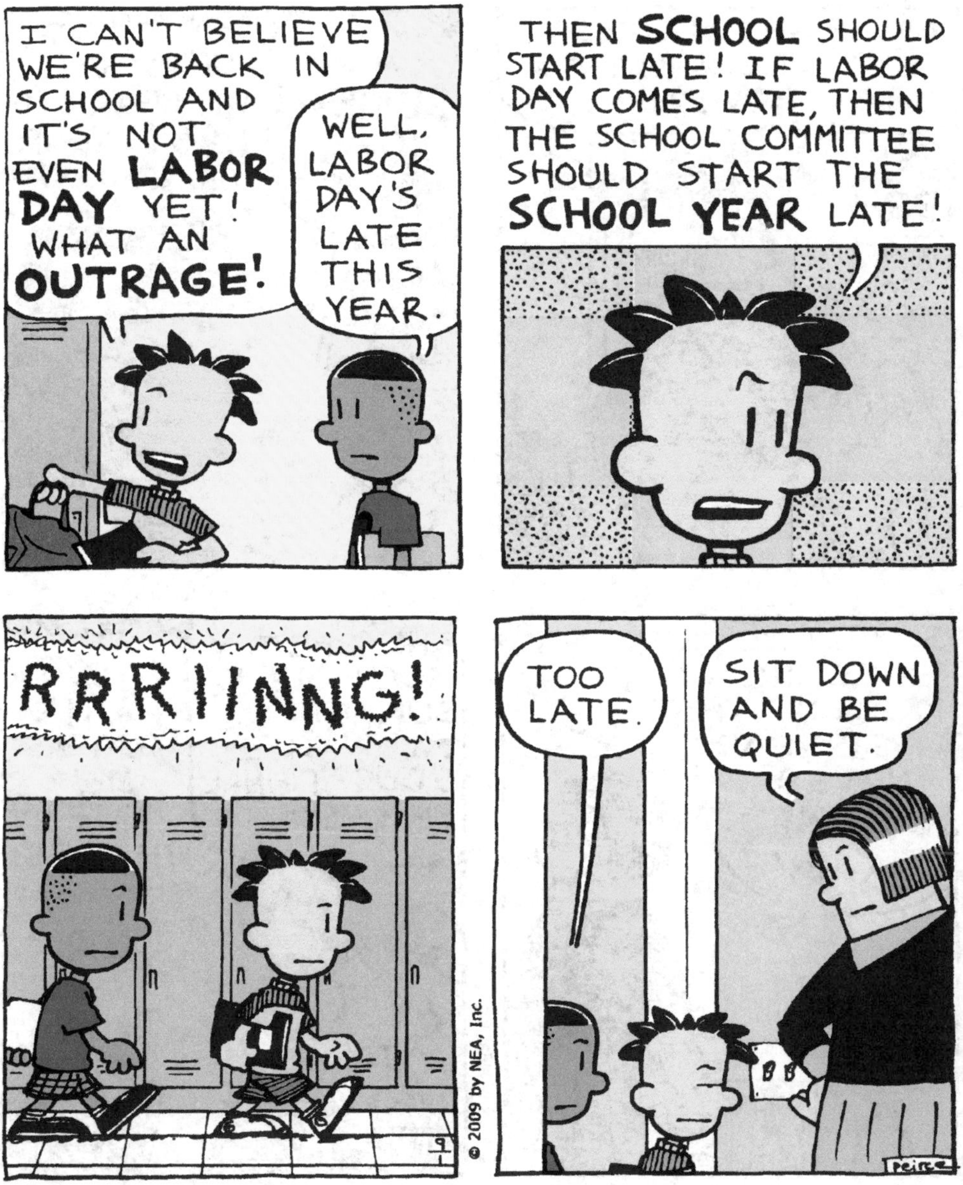
I CAN'T BELIEVE WE'RE BACK IN SCHOOL AND IT'S NOT EVEN LABOR DAY YET! WHAT AN OUTRAGE!
WELL, LABOR DAY'S LATE THIS YEAR.
THEN SCHOOL SHOULD START LATE! IF LABOR DAY COMES LATE, THEN THE SCHOOL COMMITTEE SHOULD START THE SCHOOL YEAR LATE!
RRRIINNG!
© 2009 by NEA, Inc.
TOO LATE.
SIT DOWN AND BE QUIET.
peirce

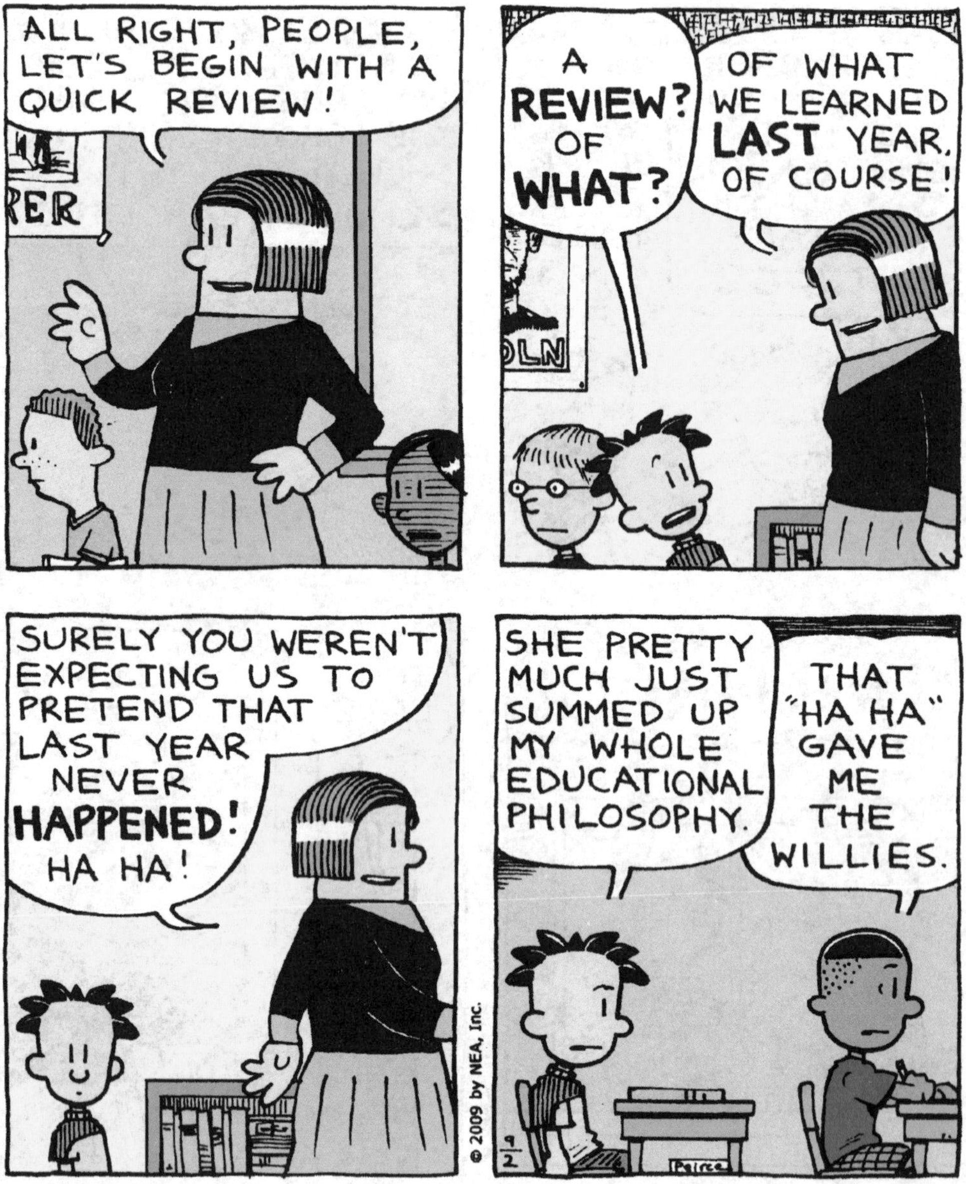
ALL RIGHT, PEOPLE, LET'S BEGIN WITH A QUICK REVIEW!
A REVIEW? OF WHAT?
OF WHAT WE LEARNED LAST YEAR, OF COURSE!
SURELY YOU WEREN'T EXPECTING US TO PRETEND THAT LAST YEAR NEVER HAPPENED! HA HA!
SHE PRETTY MUCH JUST SUMMED UP MY WHOLE EDUCATIONAL PHILOSOPHY.
THAT "HA HA" GAVE ME THE WILLIES.
© 2009 by NEA, Inc.

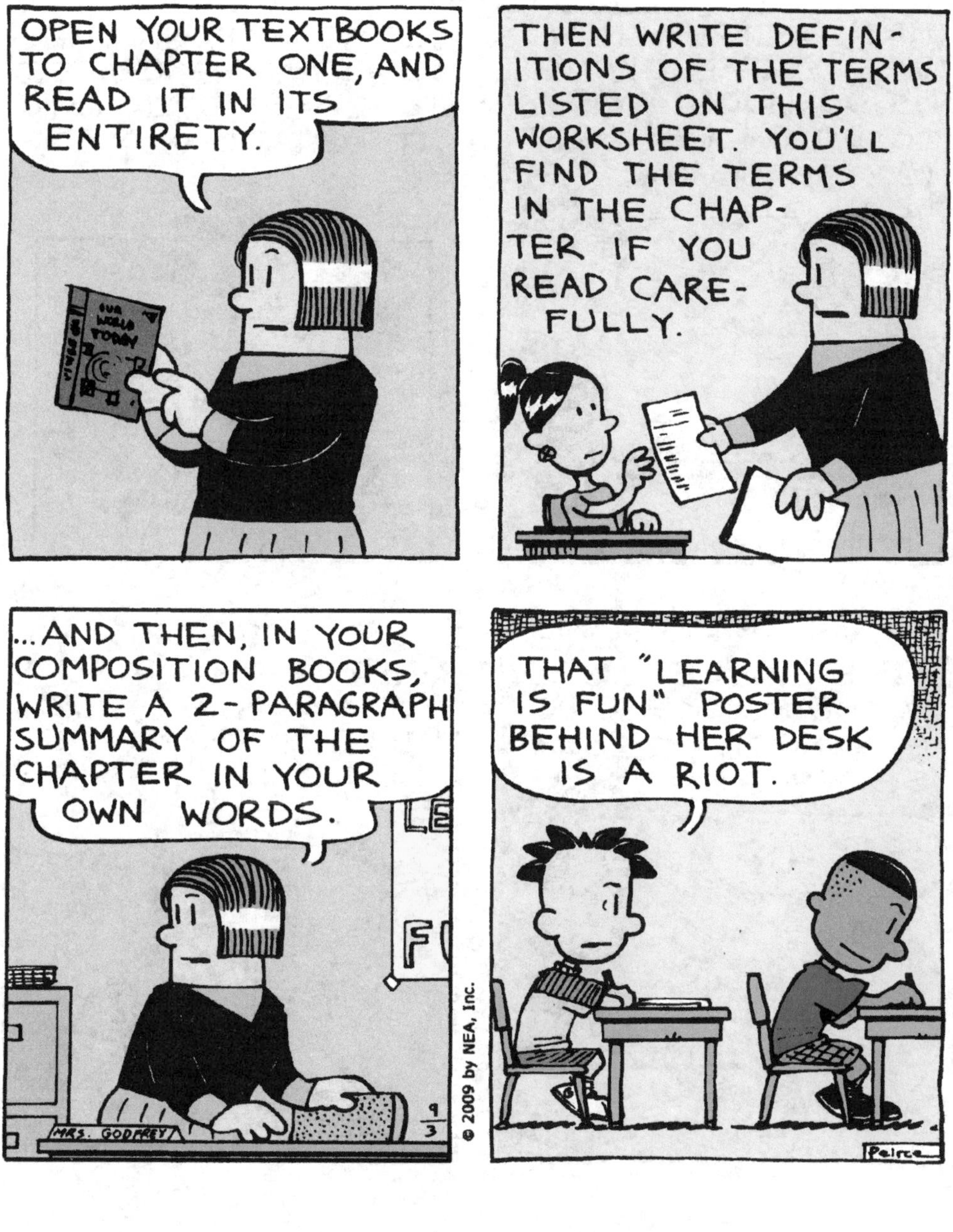
OPEN YOUR TEXTBOOKS TO CHAPTER ONE, AND READ IT IN ITS ENTIRETY.
OUR WORLD TODAY
THEN WRITE DEFINITIONS OF THE TERMS LISTED ON THIS WORKSHEET. YOU'LL FIND THE TERMS IN THE CHAPTER IF YOU READ CAREFULLY.
...AND THEN, IN YOUR COMPOSITION BOOKS, WRITE A 2-PARAGRAPH SUMMARY OF THE CHAPTER IN YOUR OWN WORDS.
MRS. GODFREY
9/3
© 2009 by NEA, Inc.
THAT "LEARNING IS FUN" POSTER BEHIND HER DESK IS A RIOT.
Peirce

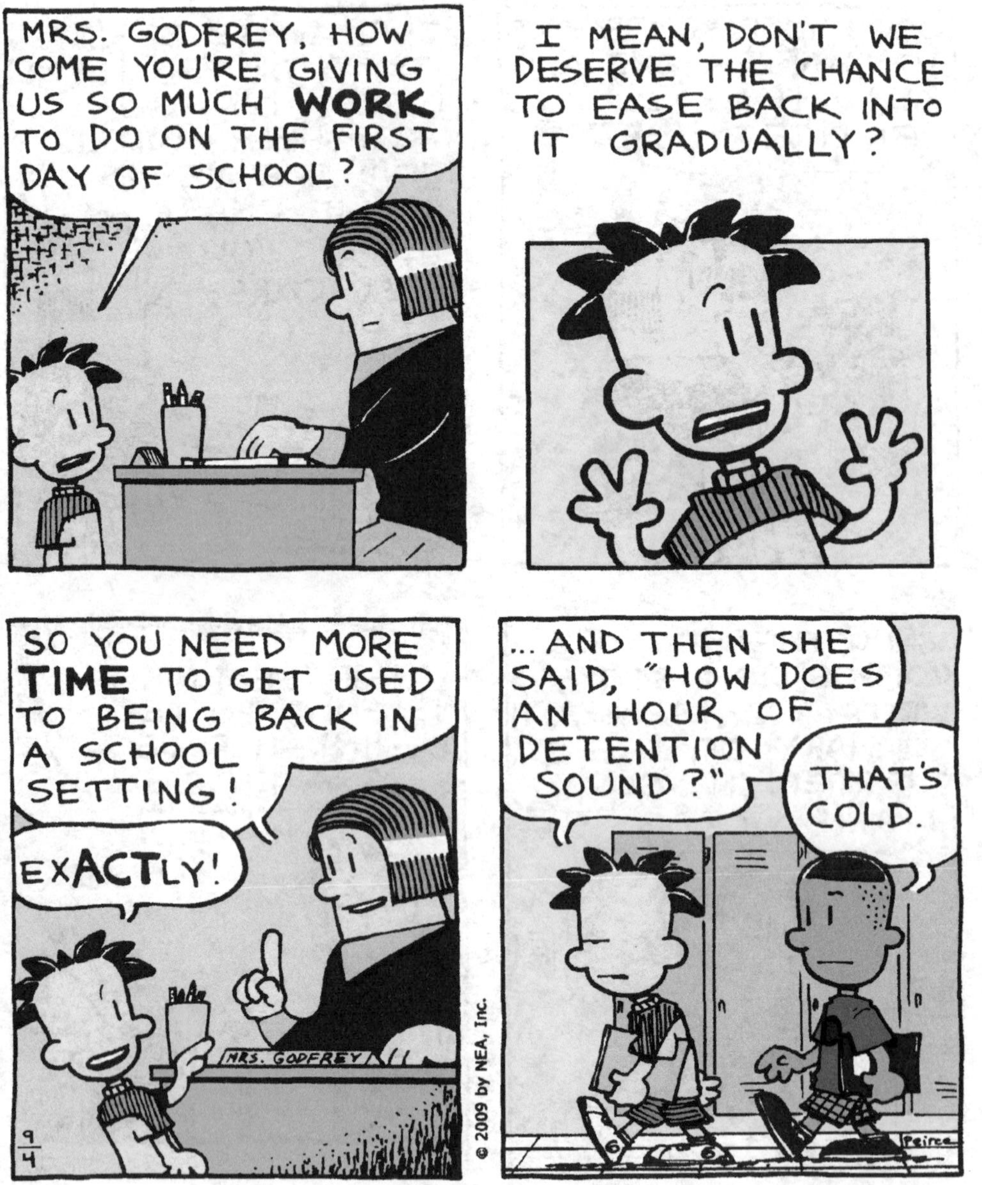
MRS. GODFREY, HOW COME YOU'RE GIVING US SO MUCH **WORK** TO DO ON THE FIRST DAY OF SCHOOL?
I MEAN, DON'T WE DESERVE THE CHANCE TO EASE BACK INTO IT GRADUALLY?
SO YOU NEED MORE **TIME** TO GET USED TO BEING BACK IN A SCHOOL SETTING!
ExACTly!
MRS. GODFREY
9/4
... AND THEN SHE SAID, "HOW DOES AN HOUR OF DETENTION SOUND?"
THAT'S COLD.
Peirce

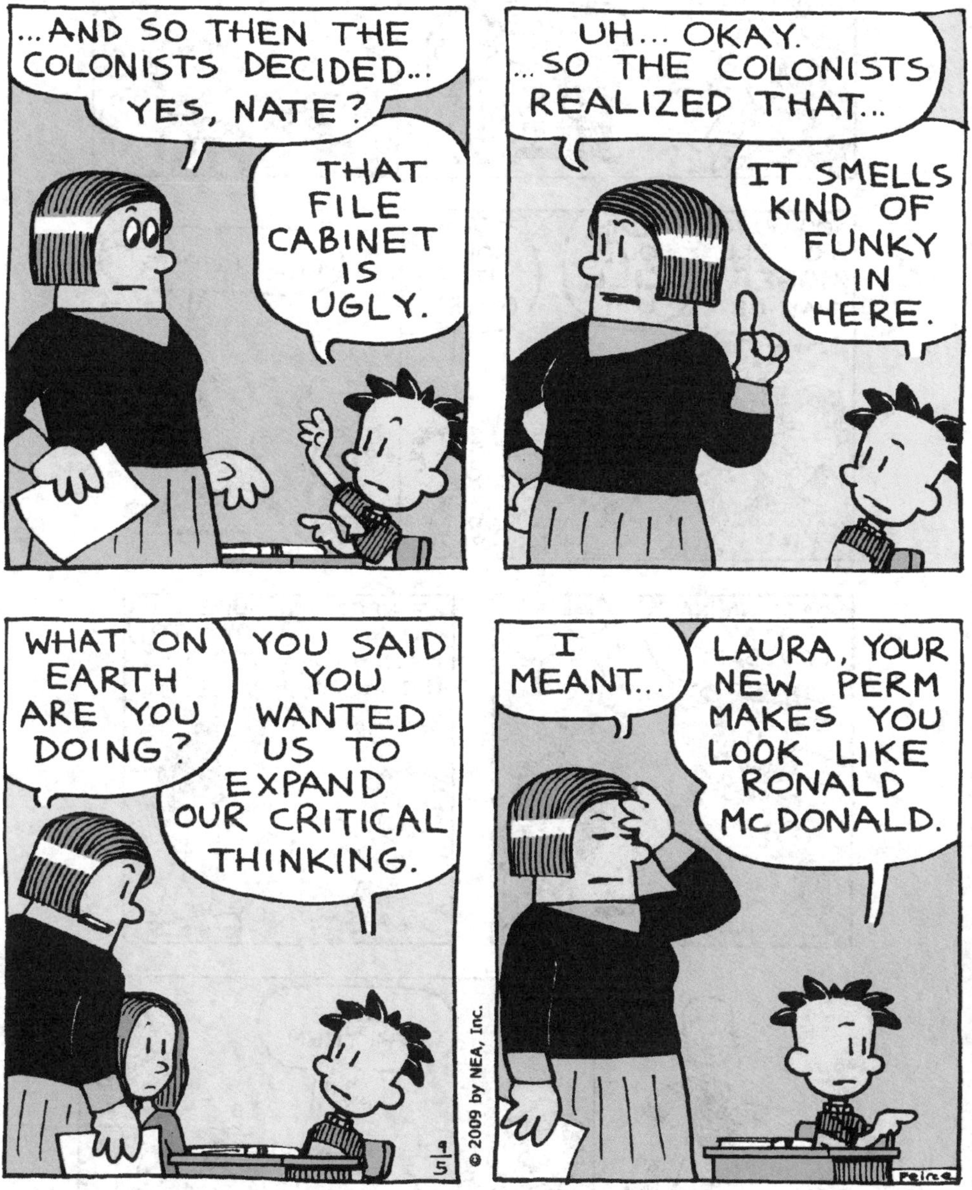
...AND SO THEN THE COLONISTS DECIDED... YES, NATE?
THAT FILE CABINET IS UGLY.
UH... OKAY. ...SO THE COLONISTS REALIZED THAT...
IT SMELLS KIND OF FUNKY IN HERE.
WHAT ON EARTH ARE YOU DOING?
YOU SAID YOU WANTED US TO EXPAND OUR CRITICAL THINKING.
I MEANT...
LAURA, YOUR NEW PERM MAKES YOU LOOK LIKE RONALD McDONALD.
9/5
© 2009 by NEA, Inc.

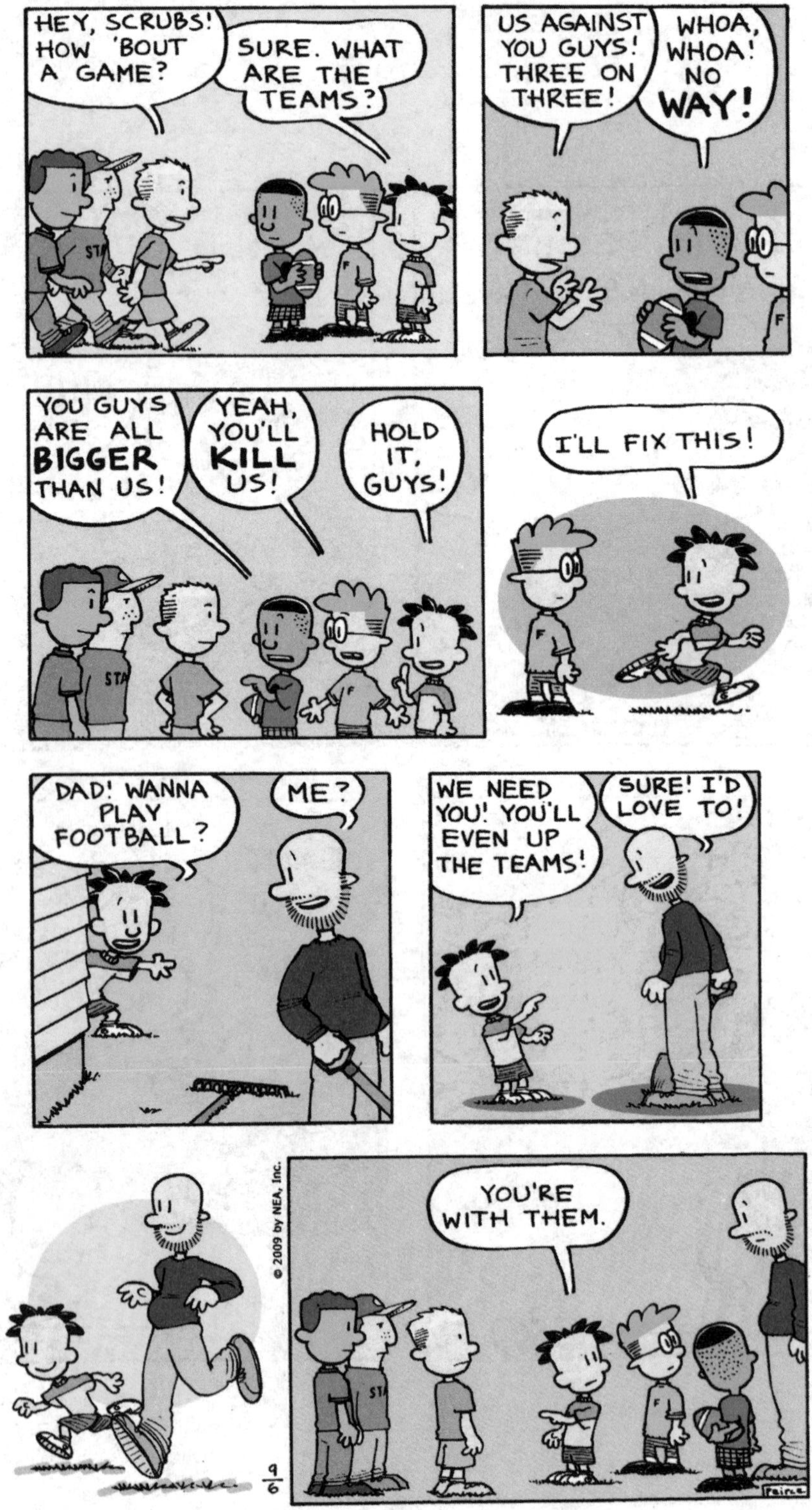
HEY, SCRUBS! HOW 'BOUT A GAME?
SURE. WHAT ARE THE TEAMS?
US AGAINST YOU GUYS! THREE ON THREE!
WHOA, WHOA! NO WAY!
YOU GUYS ARE ALL BIGGER THAN US!
YEAH, YOU'LL KILL US!
HOLD IT, GUYS!
I'LL FIX THIS!
DAD! WANNA PLAY FOOTBALL?
ME?
WE NEED YOU! YOU'LL EVEN UP THE TEAMS!
SURE! I'D LOVE TO!
© 2009 by NEA, Inc.
YOU'RE WITH THEM.
9/6
Peirce

GOOD SUB, BAD SUB

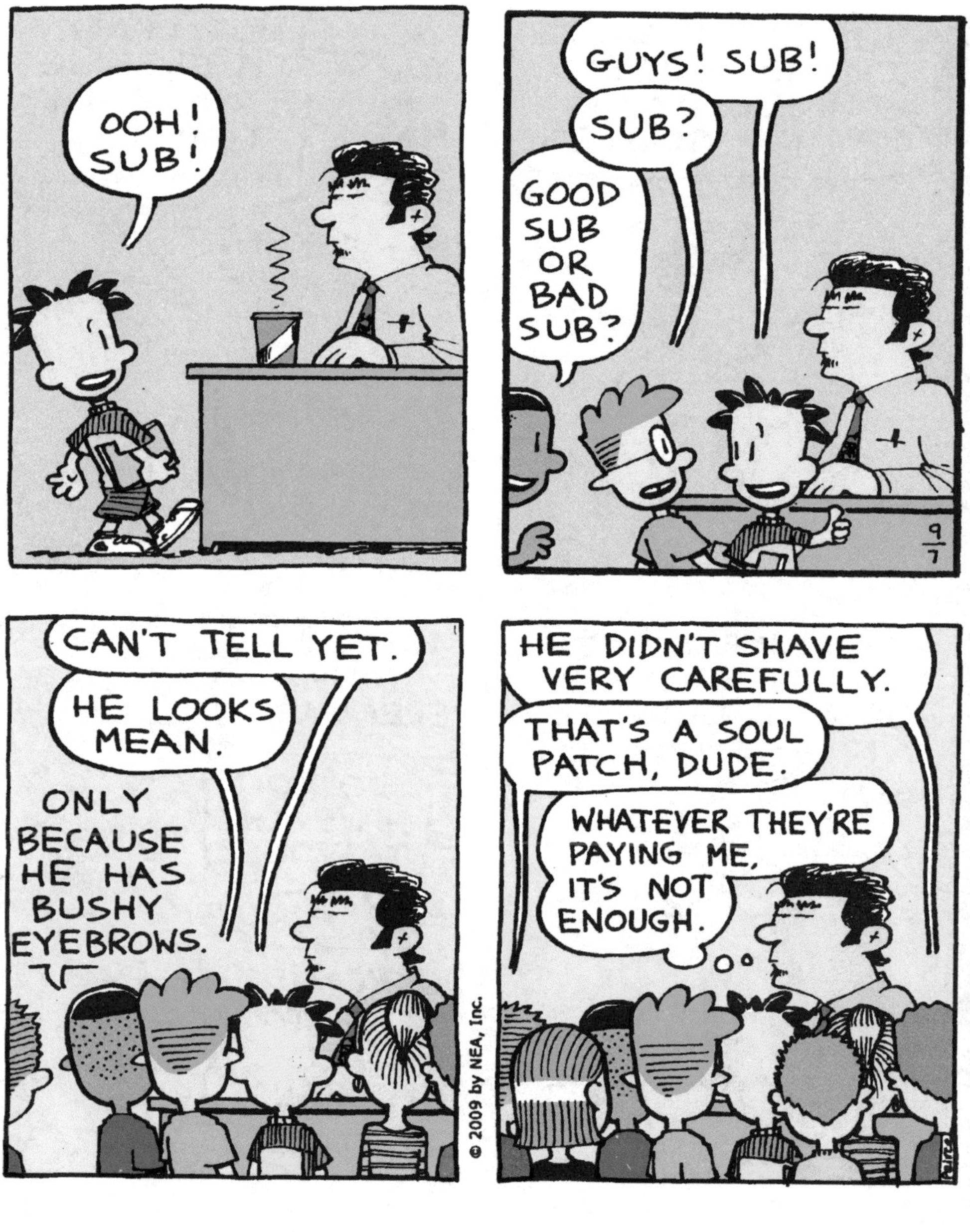
OOH! SUB!
GUYS! SUB!
SUB?
GOOD SUB OR BAD SUB?
9/7
CAN'T TELL YET.
HE LOOKS MEAN.
ONLY BECAUSE HE HAS BUSHY EYEBROWS.
© 2009 by NEA, Inc.
HE DIDN'T SHAVE VERY CAREFULLY.
THAT'S A SOUL PATCH, DUDE.
WHATEVER THEY'RE PAYING ME, IT'S NOT ENOUGH.
PEIRCE

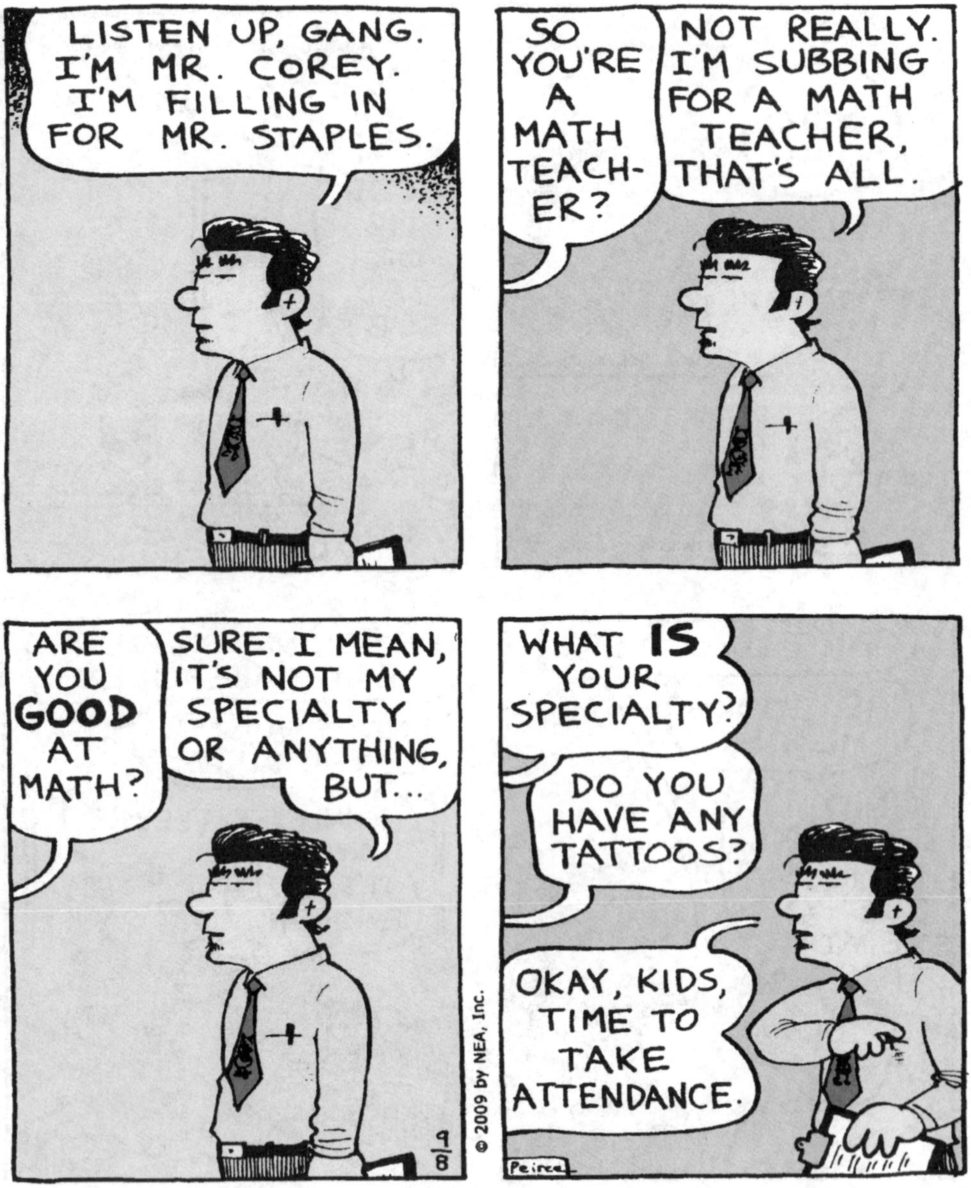
LISTEN UP, GANG. I'M MR. COREY. I'M FILLING IN FOR MR. STAPLES.
SO YOU'RE A MATH TEACH-ER?
NOT REALLY. I'M SUBBING FOR A MATH TEACHER, THAT'S ALL.
ARE YOU **GOOD** AT MATH?
SURE. I MEAN, IT'S NOT MY SPECIALTY OR ANYTHING, BUT...
9/8
© 2009 by NEA, Inc.
WHAT **IS** YOUR SPECIALTY?
DO YOU HAVE ANY TATTOOS?
OKAY, KIDS, TIME TO TAKE ATTENDANCE.
Peirce

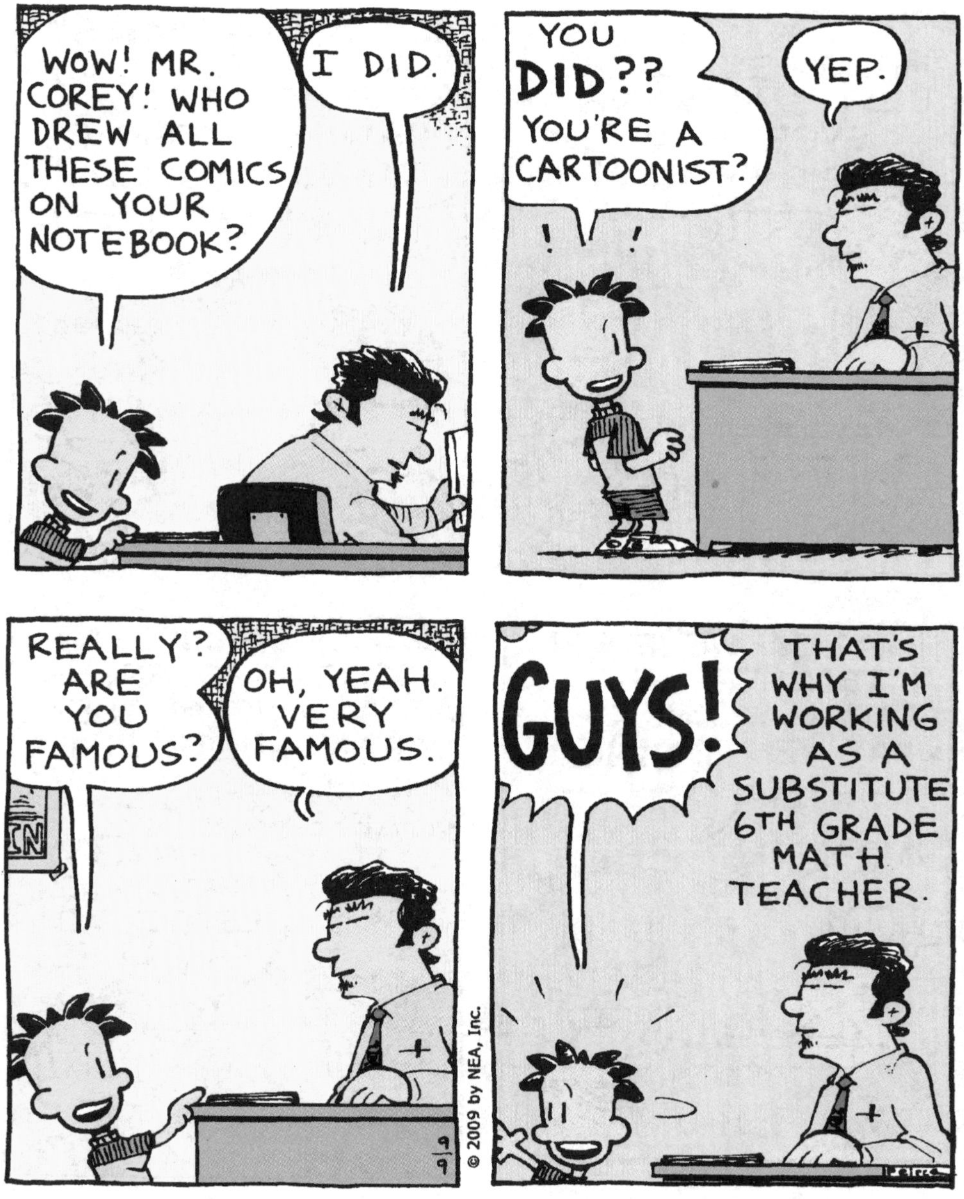
WOW! MR. COREY! WHO DREW ALL THESE COMICS ON YOUR NOTEBOOK?
I DID.
YOU DID?? YOU'RE A CARTOONIST?
YEP.
REALLY? ARE YOU FAMOUS?
OH, YEAH. VERY FAMOUS.
© 2009 by NEA, Inc.
GUYS!
THAT'S WHY I'M WORKING AS A SUBSTITUTE 6TH GRADE MATH TEACHER.

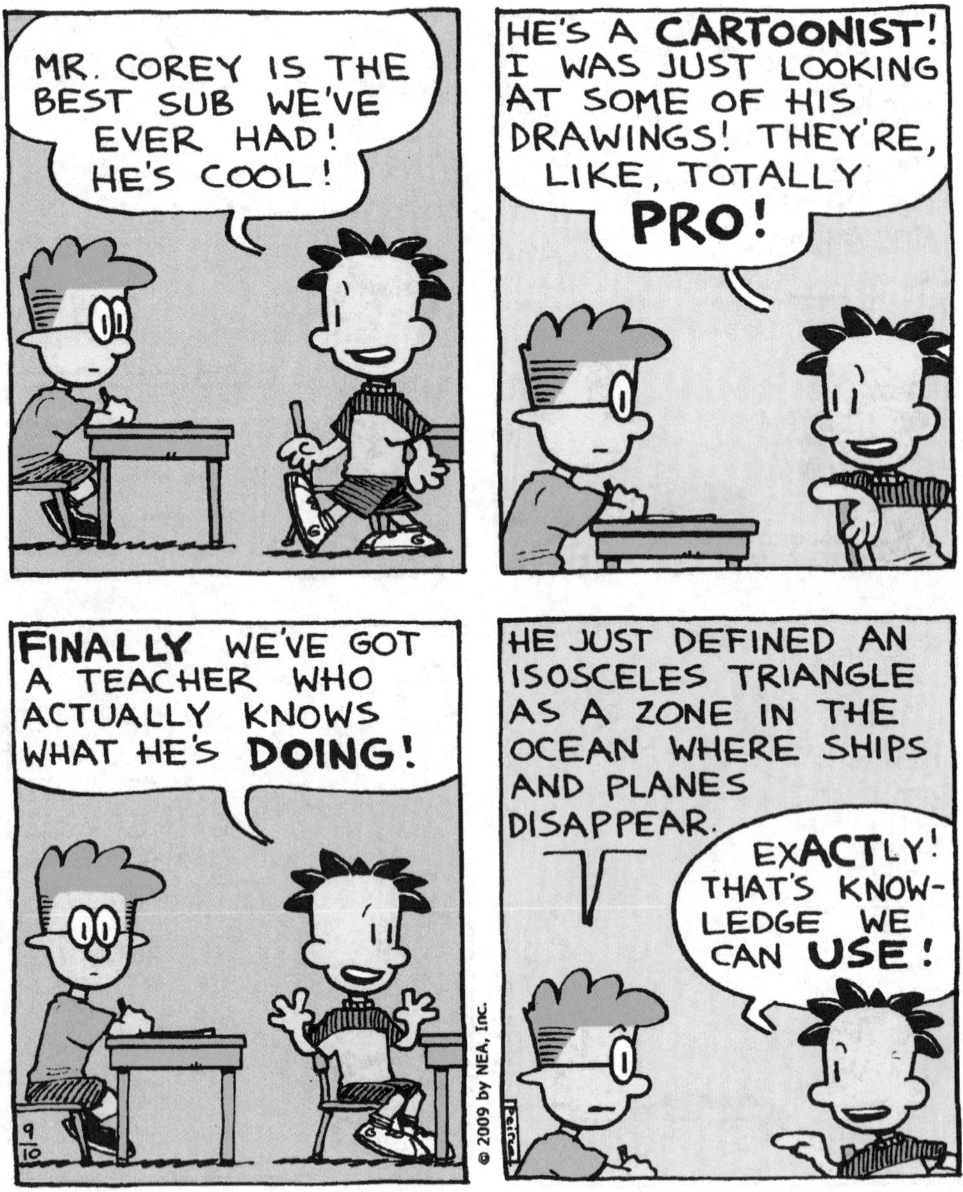
MR. COREY IS THE BEST SUB WE'VE EVER HAD! HE'S COOL!
HE'S A **CARTOONIST**! I WAS JUST LOOKING AT SOME OF HIS DRAWINGS! THEY'RE, LIKE, TOTALLY **PRO**!
FINALLY WE'VE GOT A TEACHER WHO ACTUALLY KNOWS WHAT HE'S **DOING**!
HE JUST DEFINED AN ISOSCELES TRIANGLE AS A ZONE IN THE OCEAN WHERE SHIPS AND PLANES DISAPPEAR.
EXACTLY! THAT'S KNOW-LEDGE WE CAN **USE**!
9/10
© 2009 by NEA, Inc.
Peirce

I WISH YOU COULD BE OUR TEACHER **PERMANENTLY**, MR. COREY.

THAT'S KIND OF YOU TO SAY.

YOU'RE **WAY** BETTER THAN MR. STAPLES!

OH, I DOUBT THAT.

IT'S **TRUE!** HE CAN'T DRAW AWESOME CARTOONS LIKE **YOU** CAN! HE CAN'T DRAW **ANYTHING!**

9/11

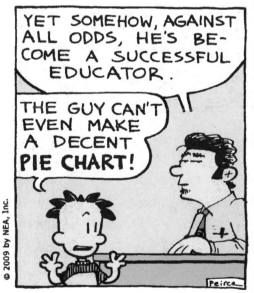

YET SOMEHOW, AGAINST ALL ODDS, HE'S BECOME A SUCCESSFUL EDUCATOR.

THE GUY CAN'T EVEN MAKE A DECENT **PIE CHART!**

Peirce

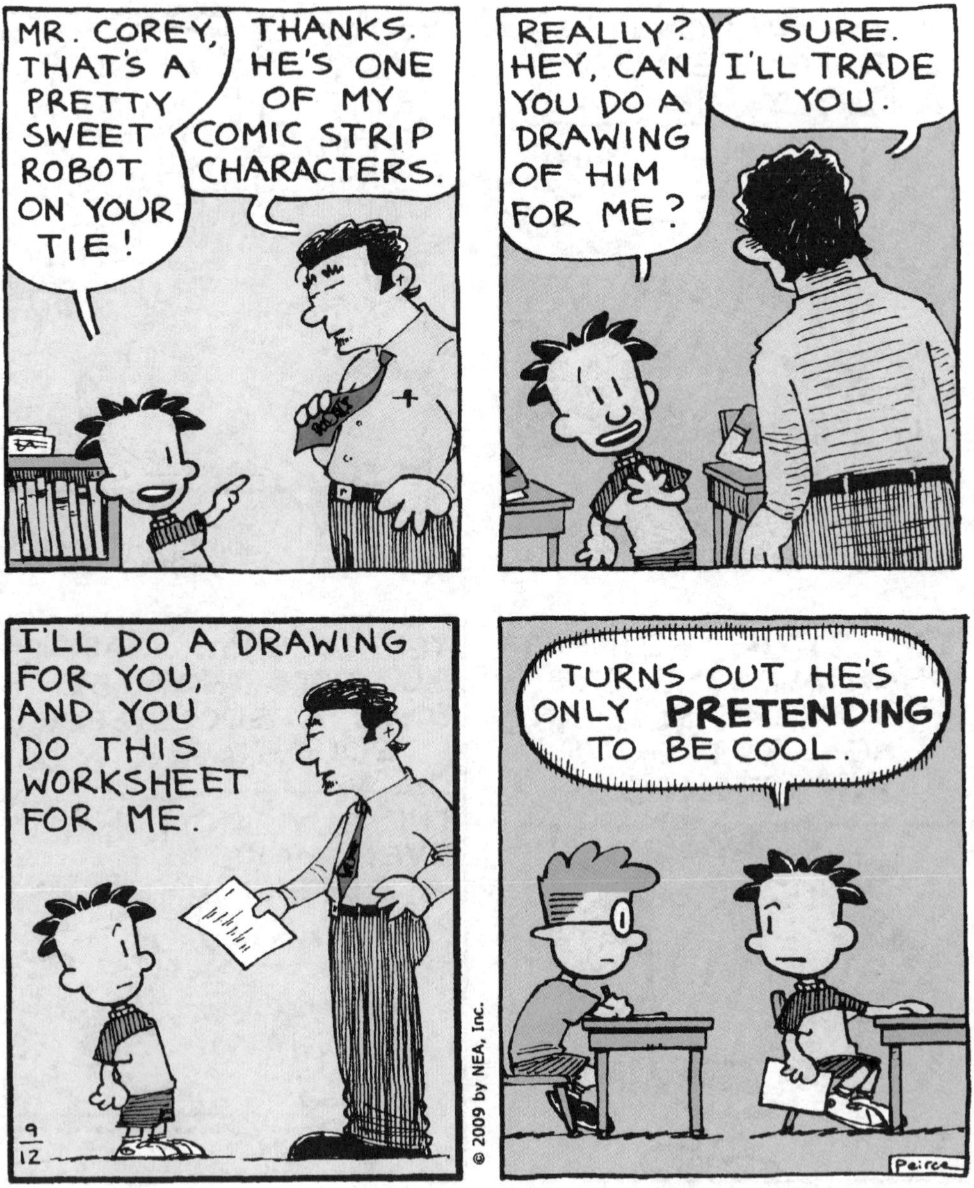
MR. COREY, THAT'S A PRETTY SWEET ROBOT ON YOUR TIE!
THANKS. HE'S ONE OF MY COMIC STRIP CHARACTERS.
REALLY? HEY, CAN YOU DO A DRAWING OF HIM FOR ME?
SURE. I'LL TRADE YOU.
I'LL DO A DRAWING FOR YOU, AND YOU DO THIS WORKSHEET FOR ME.
TURNS OUT HE'S ONLY **PRETENDING** TO BE COOL.
9/12
© 2009 by NEA, Inc.
Peirce

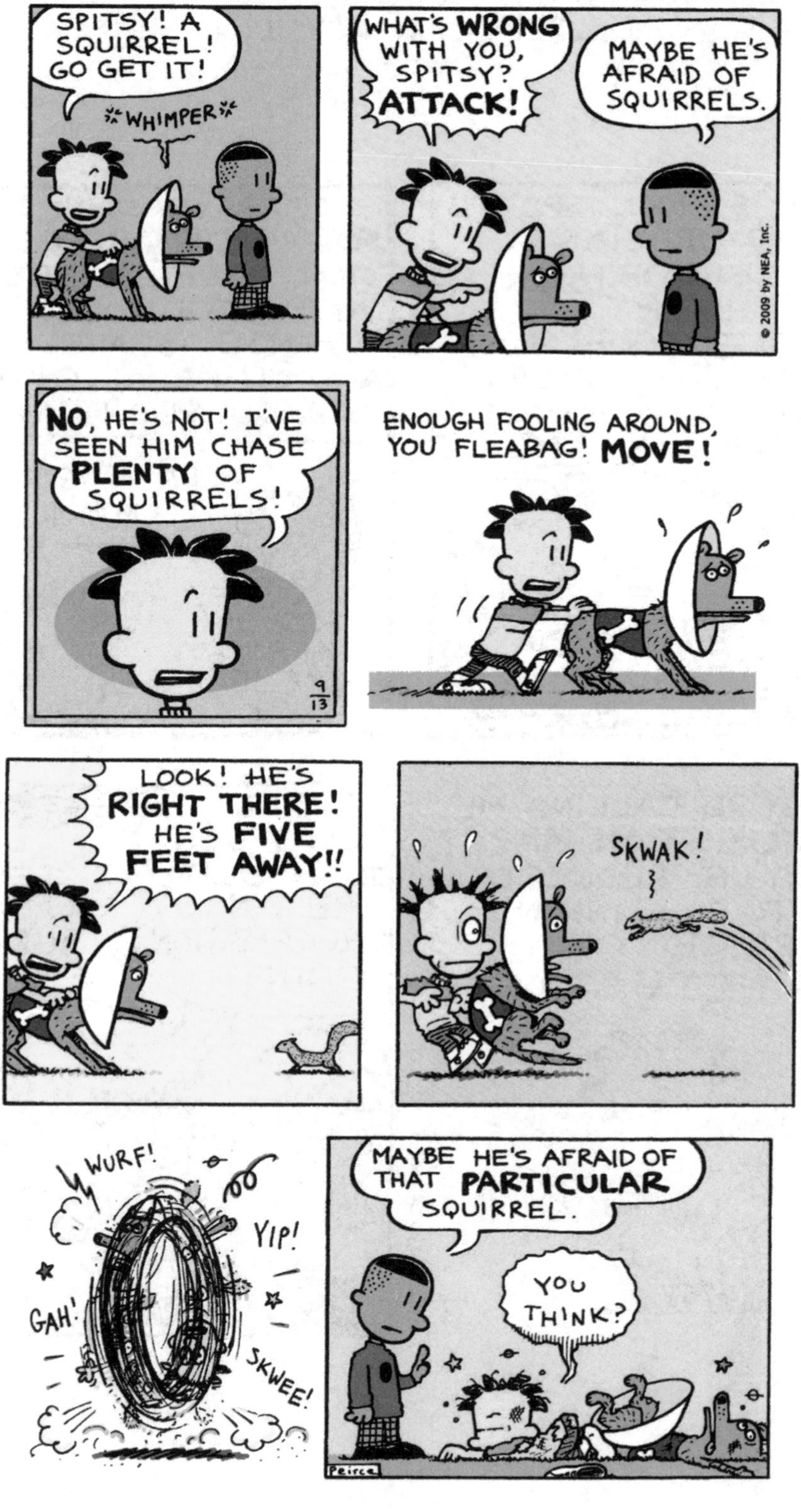
SPITSY! A SQUIRREL! GO GET IT!
WHIMPER
WHAT'S WRONG WITH YOU, SPITSY? ATTACK!
MAYBE HE'S AFRAID OF SQUIRRELS.
© 2009 by NEA, Inc.
NO, HE'S NOT! I'VE SEEN HIM CHASE PLENTY OF SQUIRRELS!
9/13
ENOUGH FOOLING AROUND, YOU FLEABAG! MOVE!
LOOK! HE'S RIGHT THERE! HE'S FIVE FEET AWAY!!
SKWAK!
WURF!
YIP!
GAH!
SKWEE!
MAYBE HE'S AFRAID OF THAT PARTICULAR SQUIRREL.
YOU THINK?
Peirce

ZEROING IN

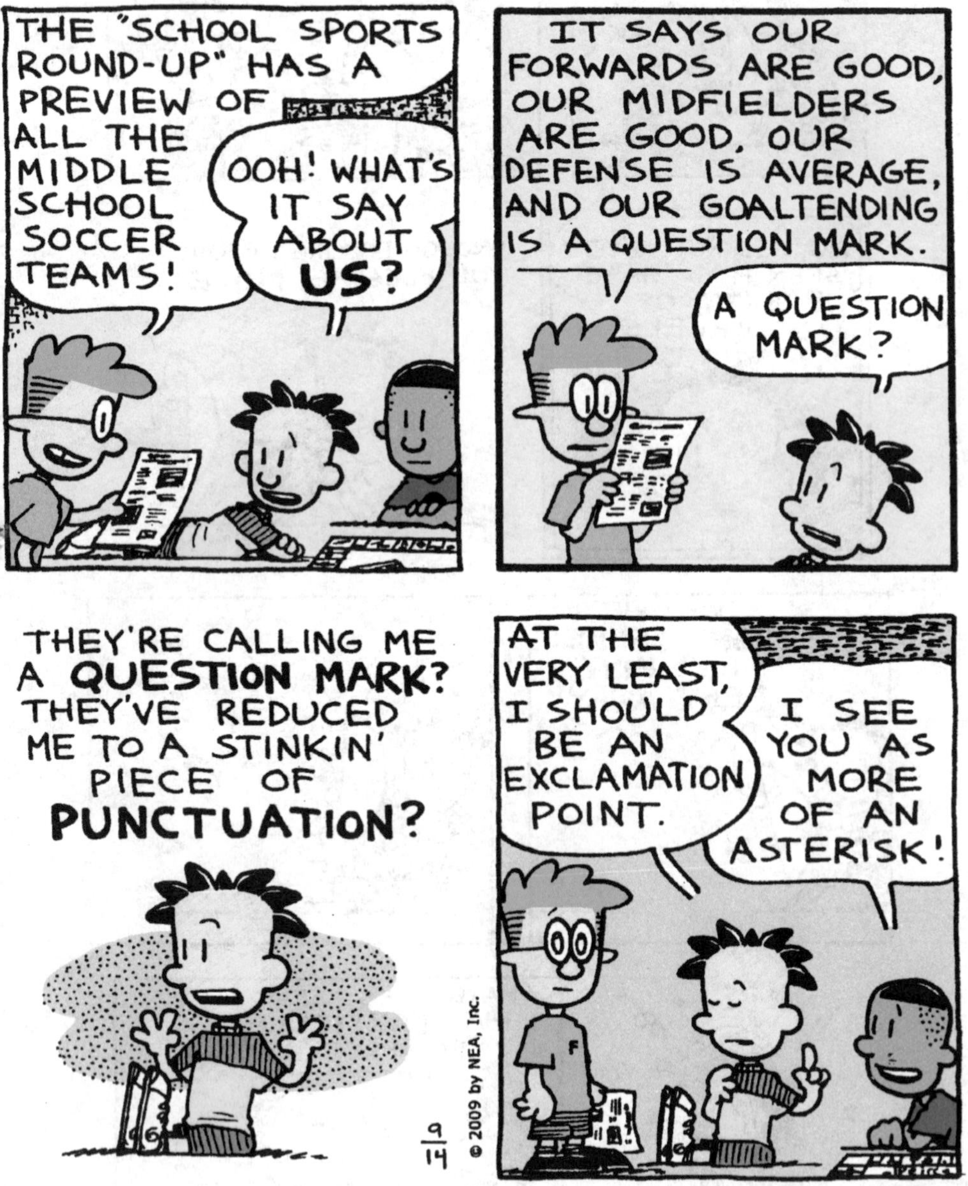
THE "SCHOOL SPORTS ROUND-UP" HAS A PREVIEW OF ALL THE MIDDLE SCHOOL SOCCER TEAMS!
OOH! WHAT'S IT SAY ABOUT **US**?
IT SAYS OUR FORWARDS ARE GOOD, OUR MIDFIELDERS ARE GOOD, OUR DEFENSE IS AVERAGE, AND OUR GOALTENDING IS A QUESTION MARK.
A QUESTION MARK?
THEY'RE CALLING ME A **QUESTION MARK**? THEY'VE REDUCED ME TO A STINKIN' PIECE OF **PUNCTUATION**?
AT THE VERY LEAST, I SHOULD BE AN EXCLAMATION POINT.
I SEE YOU AS MORE OF AN ASTERISK!
9/14
© 2009 by NEA, Inc.

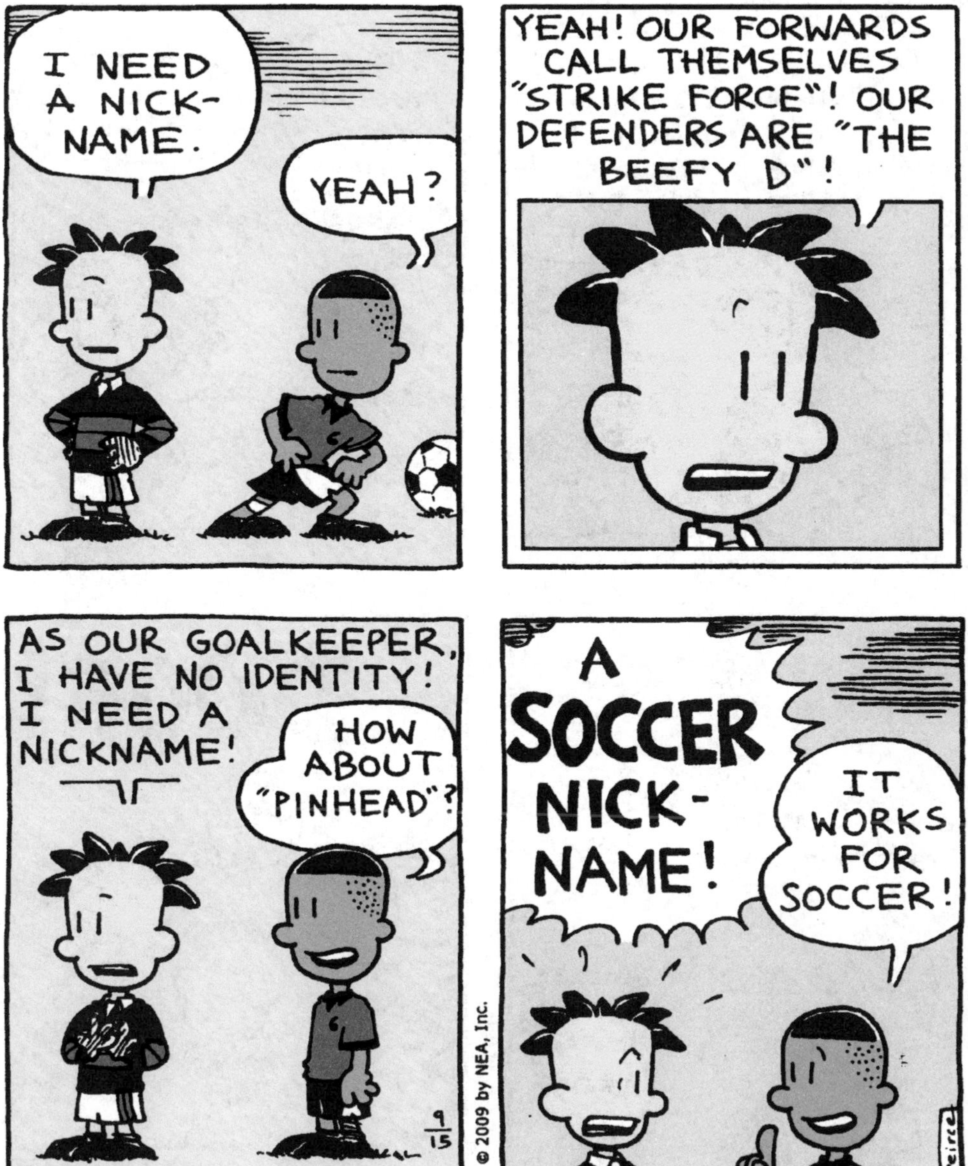
I NEED A NICK-NAME.
YEAH?
YEAH! OUR FORWARDS CALL THEMSELVES "STRIKE FORCE"! OUR DEFENDERS ARE "THE BEEFY D"!
AS OUR GOALKEEPER, I HAVE NO IDENTITY! I NEED A NICKNAME!
HOW ABOUT "PINHEAD"?
A SOCCER NICK-NAME!
IT WORKS FOR SOCCER!
9/15
PEIRCE

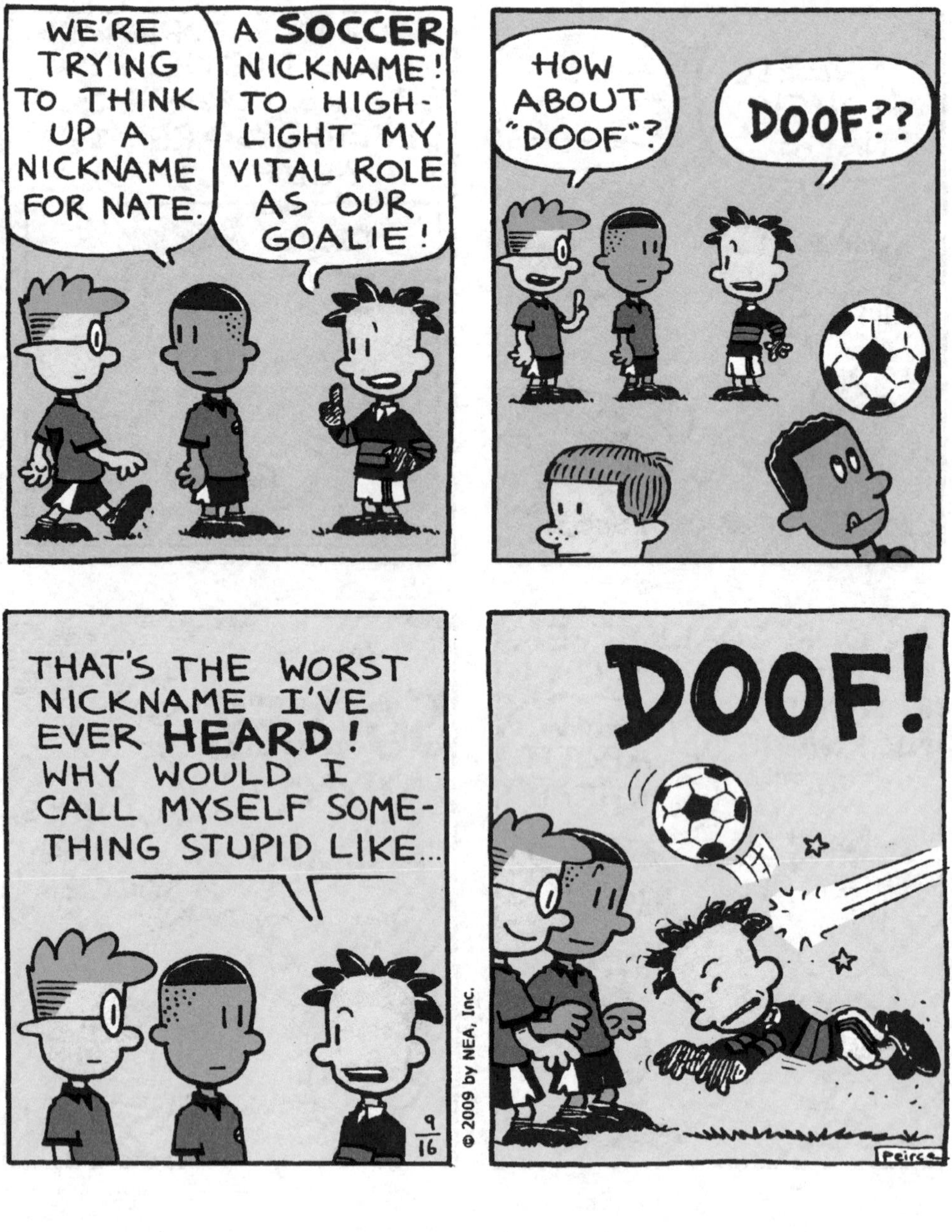
WE'RE TRYING TO THINK UP A NICKNAME FOR NATE.
A **SOCCER** NICKNAME! TO HIGHLIGHT MY VITAL ROLE AS OUR GOALIE!
HOW ABOUT "DOOF"?
DOOF??
THAT'S THE WORST NICKNAME I'VE EVER **HEARD**! WHY WOULD I CALL MYSELF SOMETHING STUPID LIKE...
DOOF!
9/16
© 2009 by NEA, Inc.
Peirce

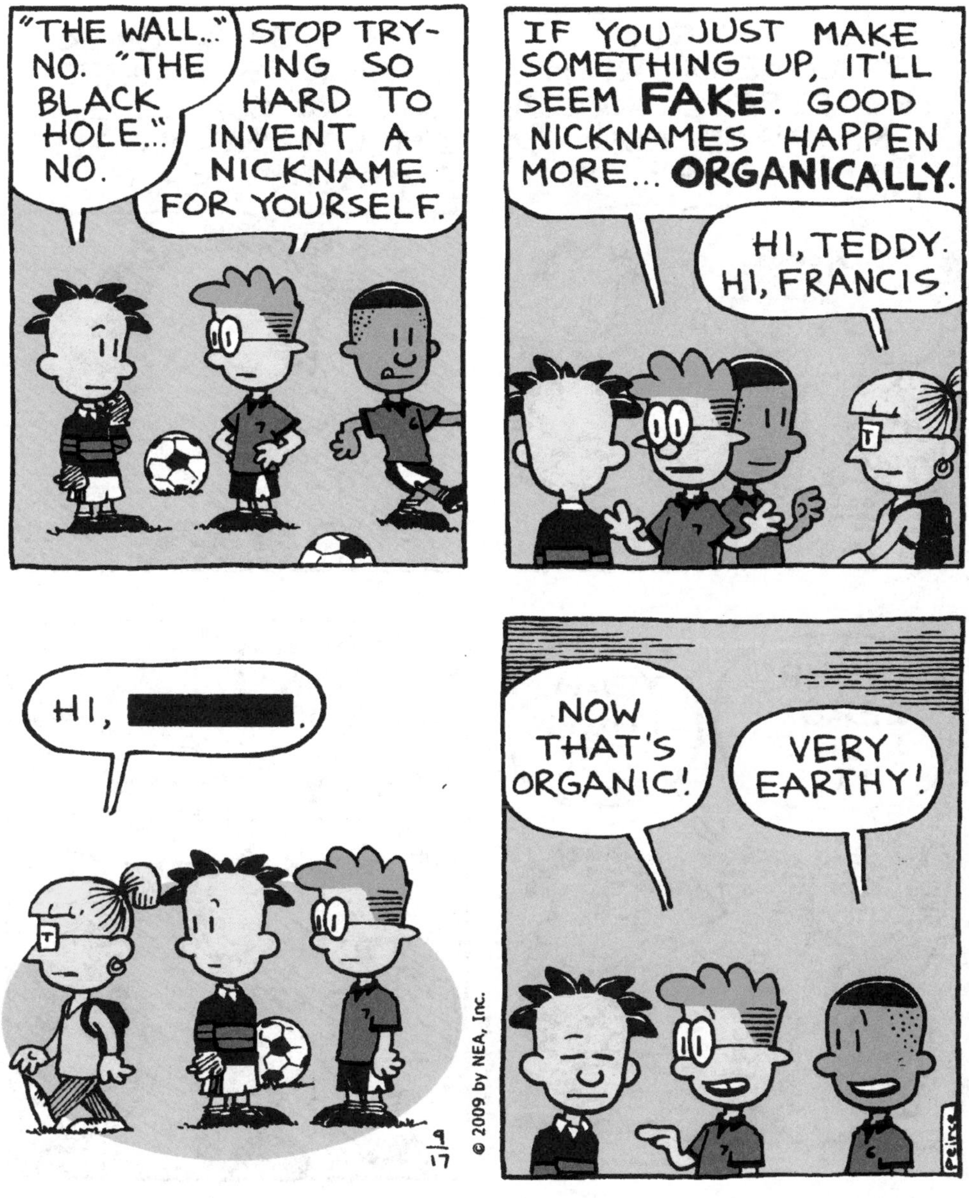
"THE WALL..." NO. "THE BLACK HOLE..." NO.
STOP TRYING SO HARD TO INVENT A NICKNAME FOR YOURSELF.
IF YOU JUST MAKE SOMETHING UP, IT'LL SEEM **FAKE**. GOOD NICKNAMES HAPPEN MORE... **ORGANICALLY**.
HI, TEDDY. HI, FRANCIS.
HI, [redacted].
NOW THAT'S ORGANIC!
VERY EARTHY!

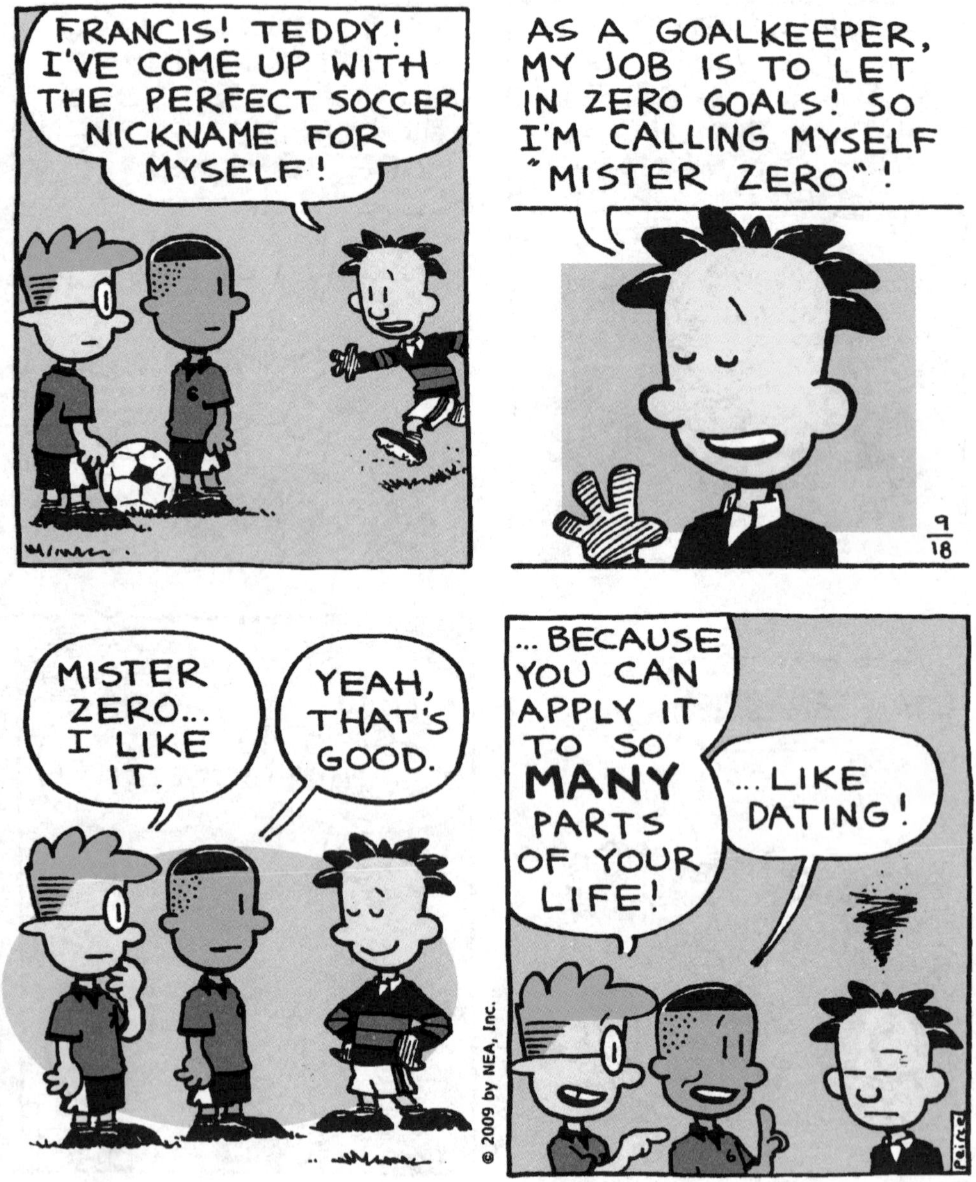
FRANCIS! TEDDY! I'VE COME UP WITH THE PERFECT SOCCER NICKNAME FOR MYSELF!
AS A GOALKEEPER, MY JOB IS TO LET IN ZERO GOALS! SO I'M CALLING MYSELF "MISTER ZERO"!
9/18
MISTER ZERO... I LIKE IT.
YEAH, THAT'S GOOD.
© 2009 by NEA, Inc.
...BECAUSE YOU CAN APPLY IT TO SO MANY PARTS OF YOUR LIFE!
...LIKE DATING!
Peirce

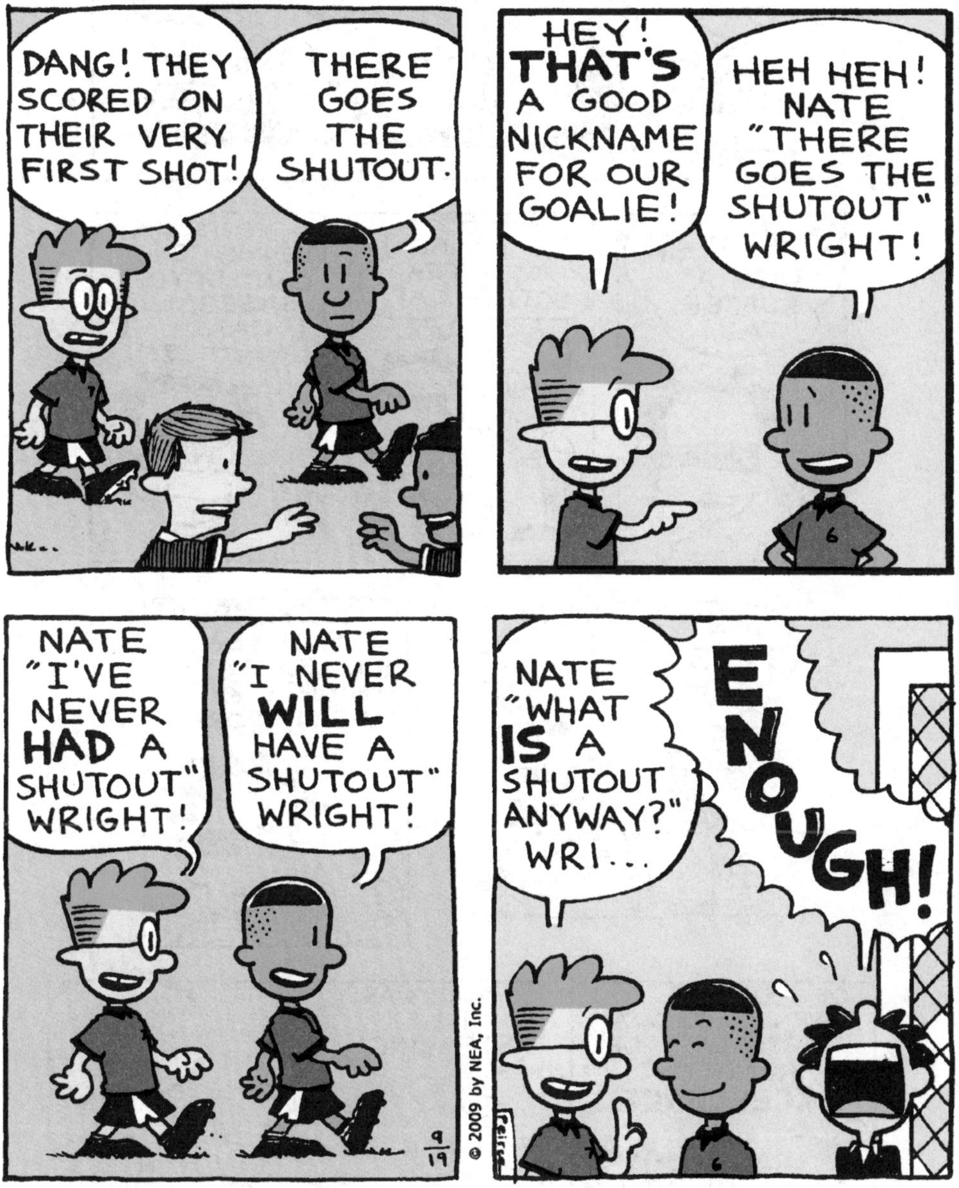
DANG! THEY SCORED ON THEIR VERY FIRST SHOT!
THERE GOES THE SHUTOUT.
HEY! **THAT'S** A GOOD NICKNAME FOR OUR GOALIE!
HEH HEH! NATE "THERE GOES THE SHUTOUT" WRIGHT!
NATE "I'VE NEVER **HAD** A SHUTOUT" WRIGHT!
NATE "I NEVER **WILL** HAVE A SHUTOUT" WRIGHT!
NATE "WHAT **IS** A SHUTOUT ANYWAY?" WRI...
ENOUGH!
9/19
© 2009 by NEA, Inc.
Peirce

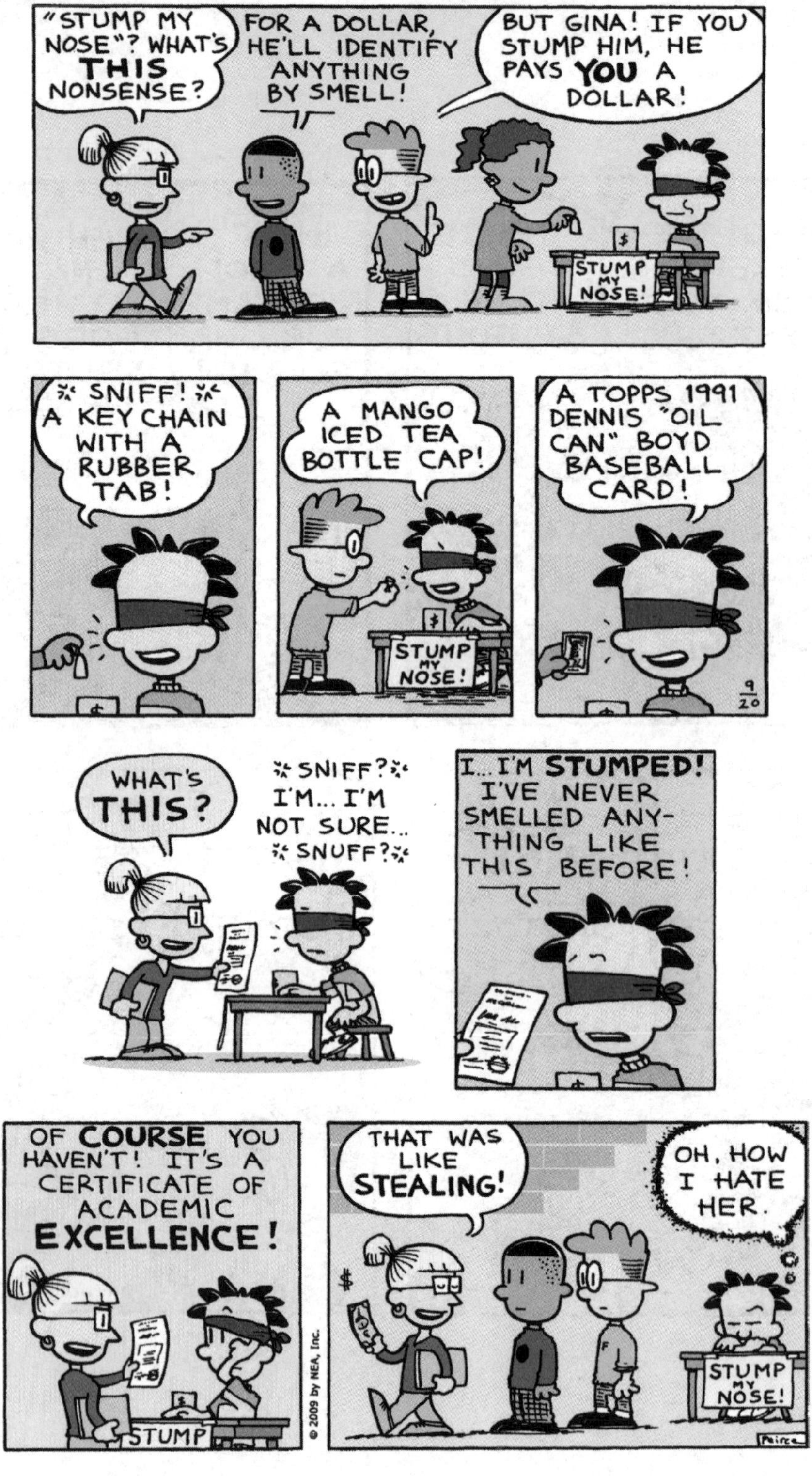
"STUMP MY NOSE"? WHAT'S THIS NONSENSE?
FOR A DOLLAR, HE'LL IDENTIFY ANYTHING BY SMELL!
BUT GINA! IF YOU STUMP HIM, HE PAYS YOU A DOLLAR!
$
STUMP MY NOSE!
SNIFF! A KEY CHAIN WITH A RUBBER TAB!
A MANGO ICED TEA BOTTLE CAP!
STUMP MY NOSE!
A TOPPS 1991 DENNIS "OIL CAN" BOYD BASEBALL CARD!
9/20
WHAT'S THIS?
SNIFF? I'M... I'M NOT SURE... SNUFF?
I... I'M STUMPED! I'VE NEVER SMELLED ANYTHING LIKE THIS BEFORE!
OF COURSE YOU HAVEN'T! IT'S A CERTIFICATE OF ACADEMIC EXCELLENCE!
STUMP
© 2009 by NEA, Inc.
THAT WAS LIKE STEALING!
OH, HOW I HATE HER.
STUMP MY NOSE!
Peirce

MR. POPULARITY

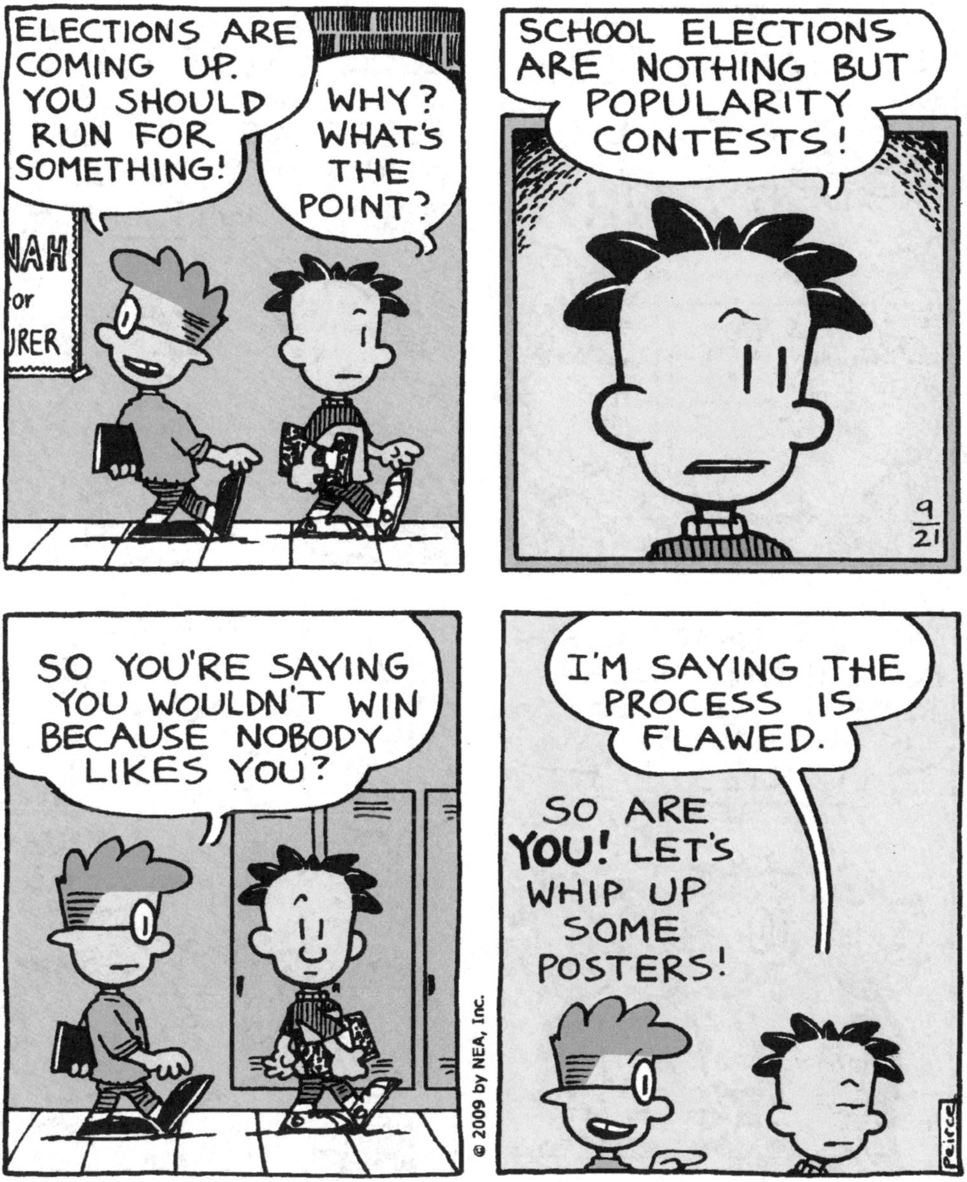
ELECTIONS ARE COMING UP. YOU SHOULD RUN FOR SOMETHING!
WHY? WHAT'S THE POINT?
NAH
or
RER
SCHOOL ELECTIONS ARE NOTHING BUT POPULARITY CONTESTS!
9/21
SO YOU'RE SAYING YOU WOULDN'T WIN BECAUSE NOBODY LIKES YOU?
© 2009 by NEA, Inc.
I'M SAYING THE PROCESS IS FLAWED.
SO ARE **YOU!** LET'S WHIP UP SOME POSTERS!
Peirce

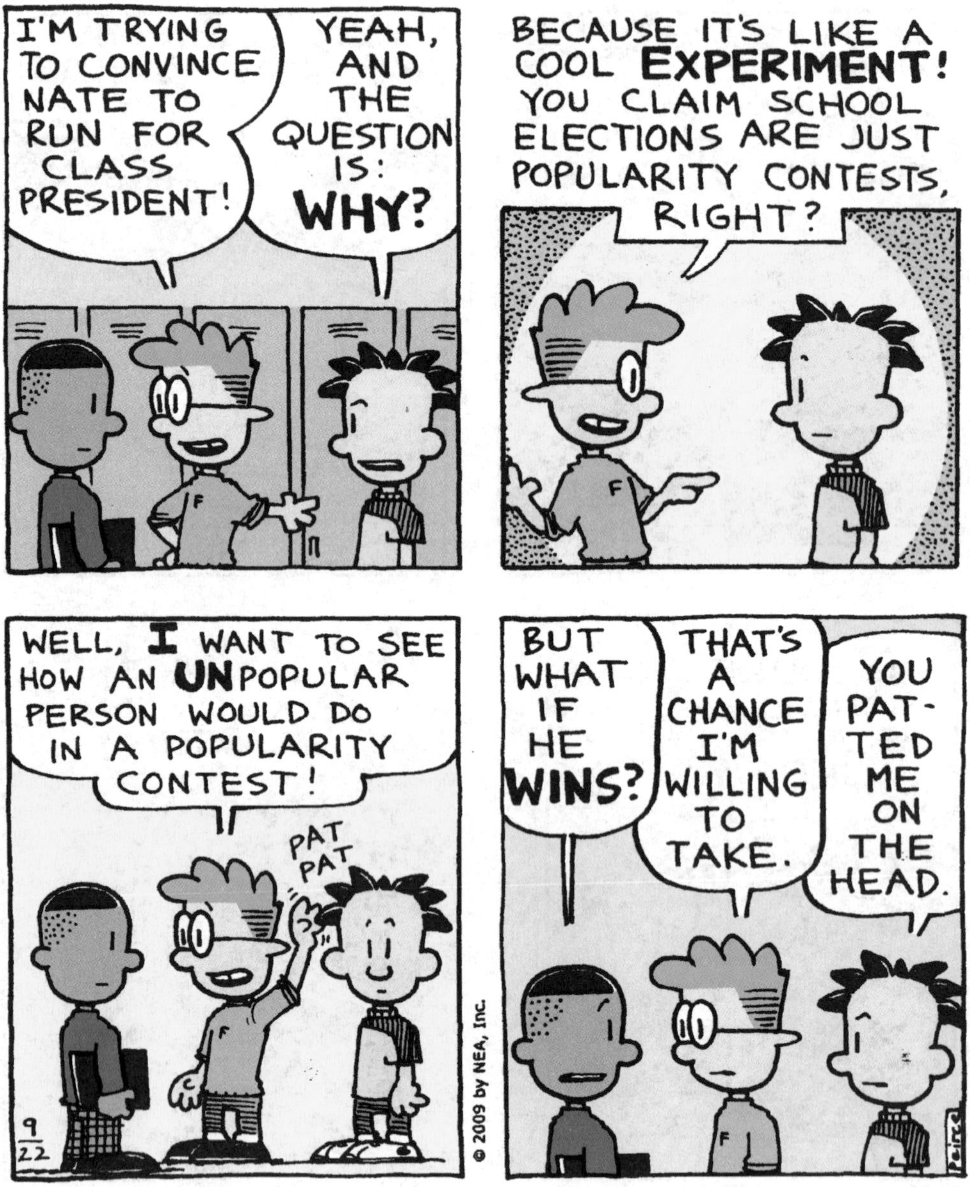
I'M TRYING TO CONVINCE NATE TO RUN FOR CLASS PRESIDENT!
YEAH, AND THE QUESTION IS: WHY?
BECAUSE IT'S LIKE A COOL EXPERIMENT! YOU CLAIM SCHOOL ELECTIONS ARE JUST POPULARITY CONTESTS, RIGHT?
WELL, I WANT TO SEE HOW AN UNPOPULAR PERSON WOULD DO IN A POPULARITY CONTEST!
PAT PAT
9/22
BUT WHAT IF HE WINS?
THAT'S A CHANCE I'M WILLING TO TAKE.
YOU PATTED ME ON THE HEAD.

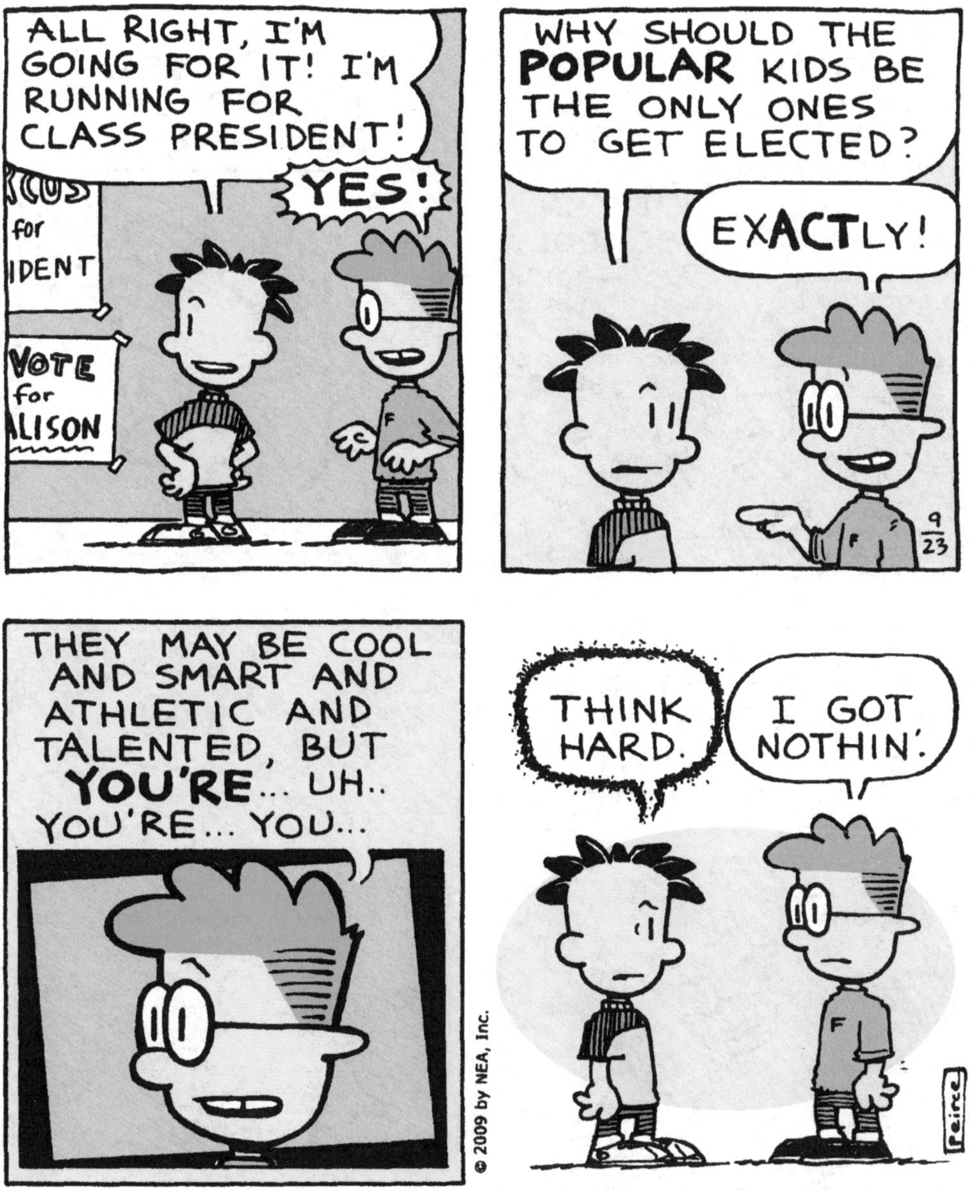
ALL RIGHT, I'M GOING FOR IT! I'M RUNNING FOR CLASS PRESIDENT!
YES!
for
IDENT
VOTE for ALISON
WHY SHOULD THE **POPULAR** KIDS BE THE ONLY ONES TO GET ELECTED?
EXACTLY!
9/23
THEY MAY BE COOL AND SMART AND ATHLETIC AND TALENTED, BUT **YOU'RE**... UH.. YOU'RE... YOU...
© 2009 by NEA, Inc.
THINK HARD.
I GOT NOTHIN'.
Peirce

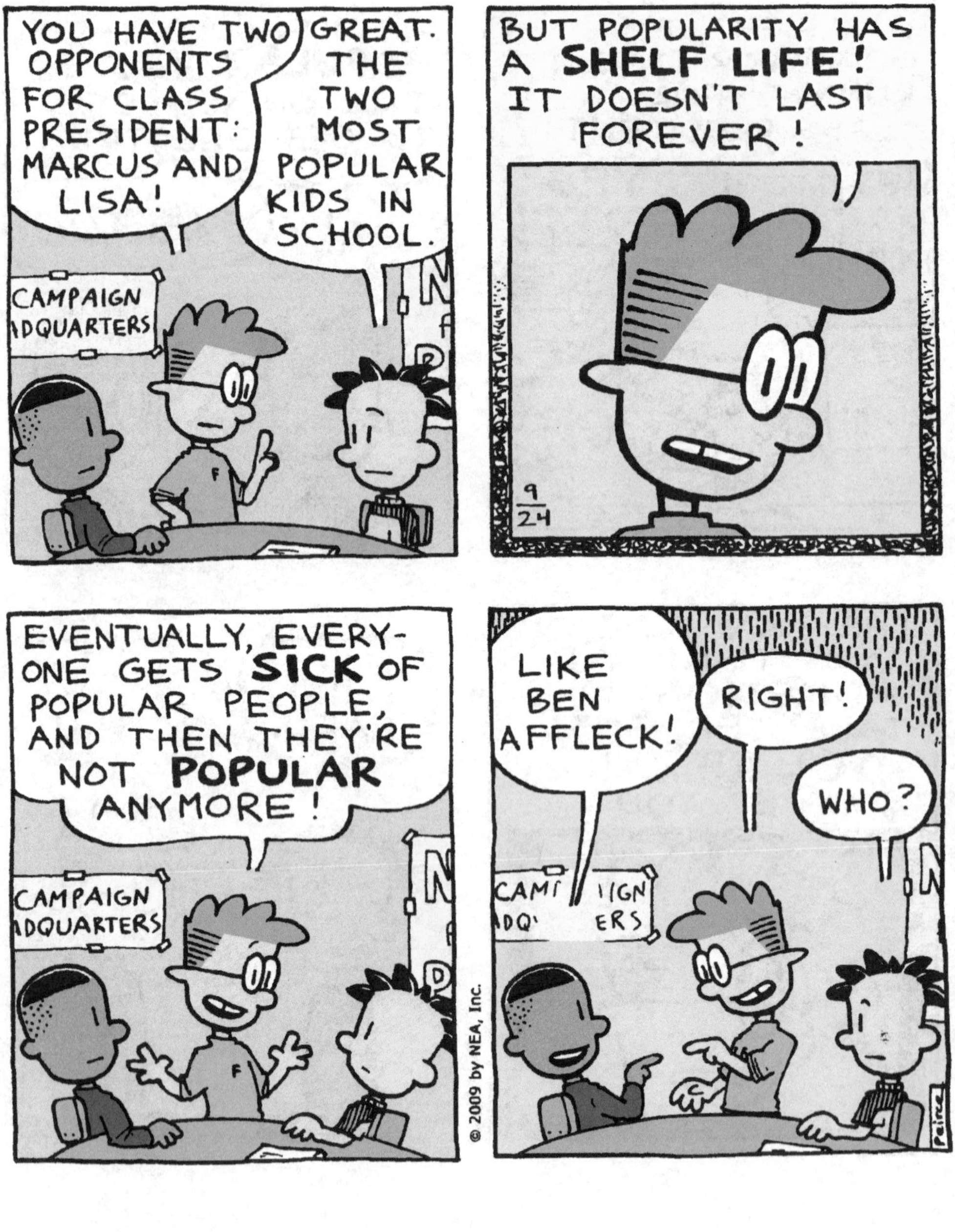
YOU HAVE TWO OPPONENTS FOR CLASS PRESIDENT: MARCUS AND LISA!
GREAT. THE TWO MOST POPULAR KIDS IN SCHOOL.
CAMPAIGN HEADQUARTERS
BUT POPULARITY HAS A SHELF LIFE! IT DOESN'T LAST FOREVER!
9/24
EVENTUALLY, EVERYONE GETS SICK OF POPULAR PEOPLE, AND THEN THEY'RE NOT POPULAR ANYMORE!
LIKE BEN AFFLECK!
RIGHT!
WHO?
© 2009 by NEA, Inc.
Peirce

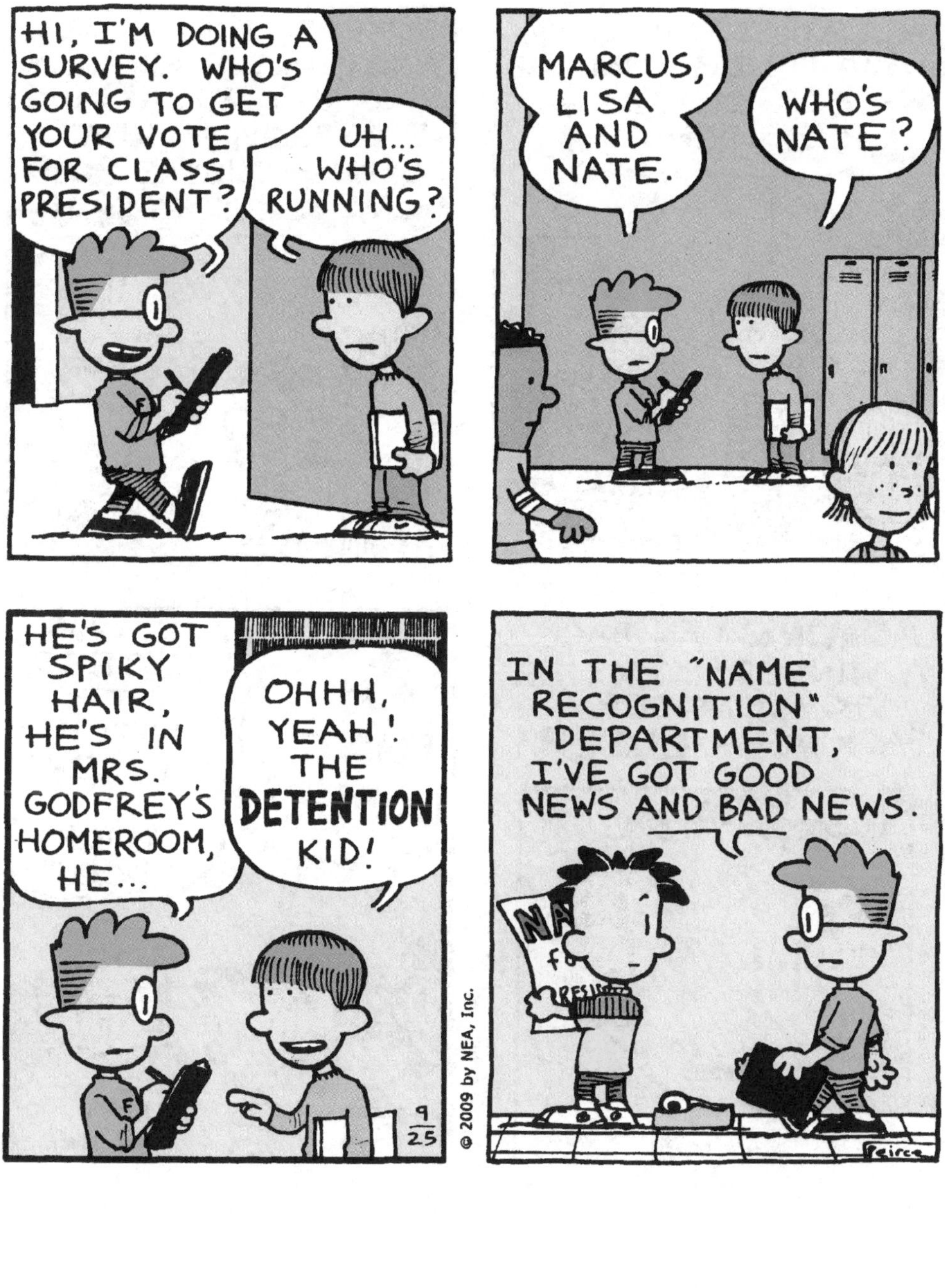
HI, I'M DOING A SURVEY. WHO'S GOING TO GET YOUR VOTE FOR CLASS PRESIDENT?
UH... WHO'S RUNNING?
MARCUS, LISA AND NATE.
WHO'S NATE?
HE'S GOT SPIKY HAIR, HE'S IN MRS. GODFREY'S HOMEROOM, HE...
OHHH, YEAH! THE DETENTION KID!
9/25
© 2009 by NEA, Inc.
IN THE "NAME RECOGNITION" DEPARTMENT, I'VE GOT GOOD NEWS AND BAD NEWS.
Peirce

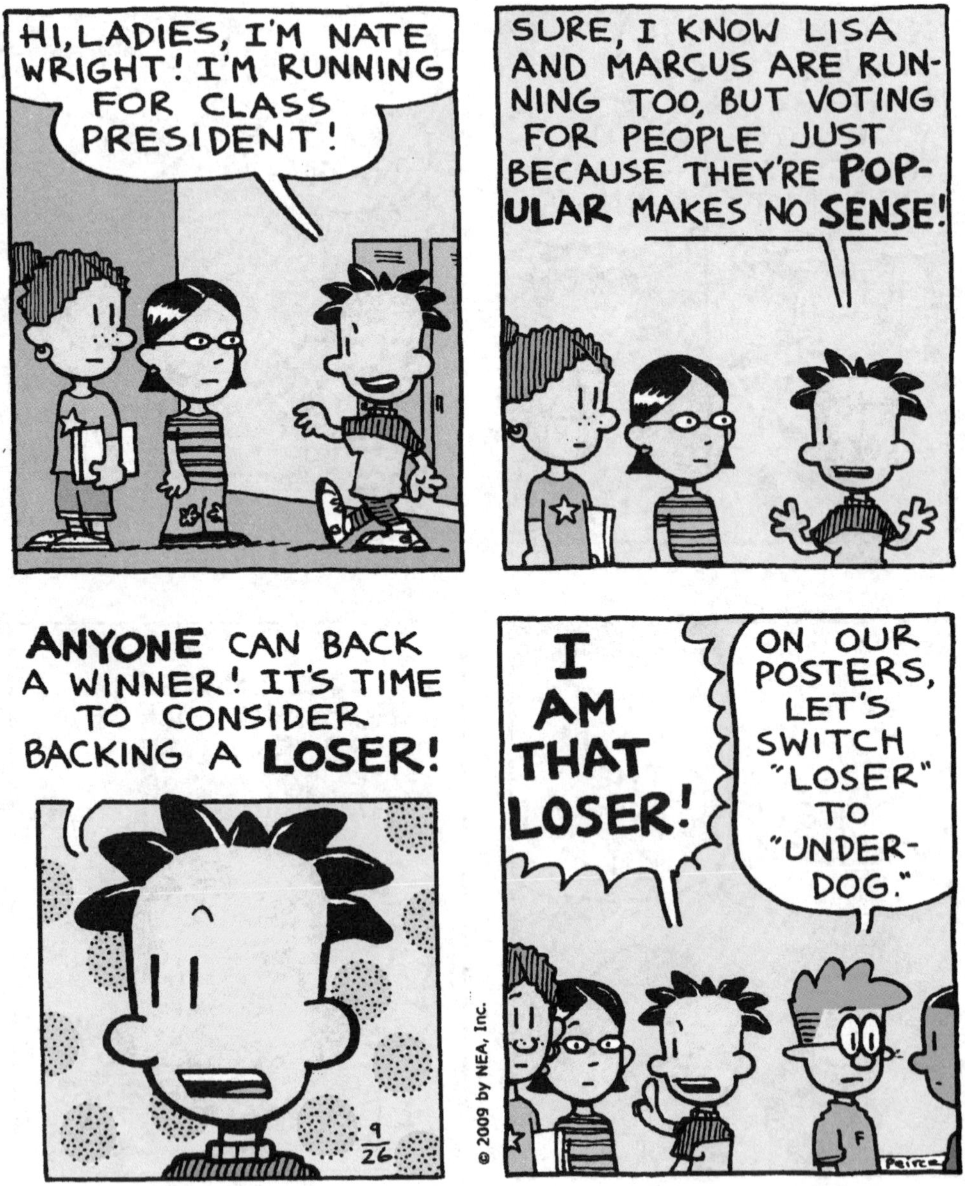
HI, LADIES, I'M NATE WRIGHT! I'M RUNNING FOR CLASS PRESIDENT!
SURE, I KNOW LISA AND MARCUS ARE RUNNING TOO, BUT VOTING FOR PEOPLE JUST BECAUSE THEY'RE POPULAR MAKES NO SENSE!
ANYONE CAN BACK A WINNER! IT'S TIME TO CONSIDER BACKING A LOSER!
9/26
© 2009 by NEA, Inc.
I AM THAT LOSER!
ON OUR POSTERS, LET'S SWITCH "LOSER" TO "UNDERDOG."
Peirce

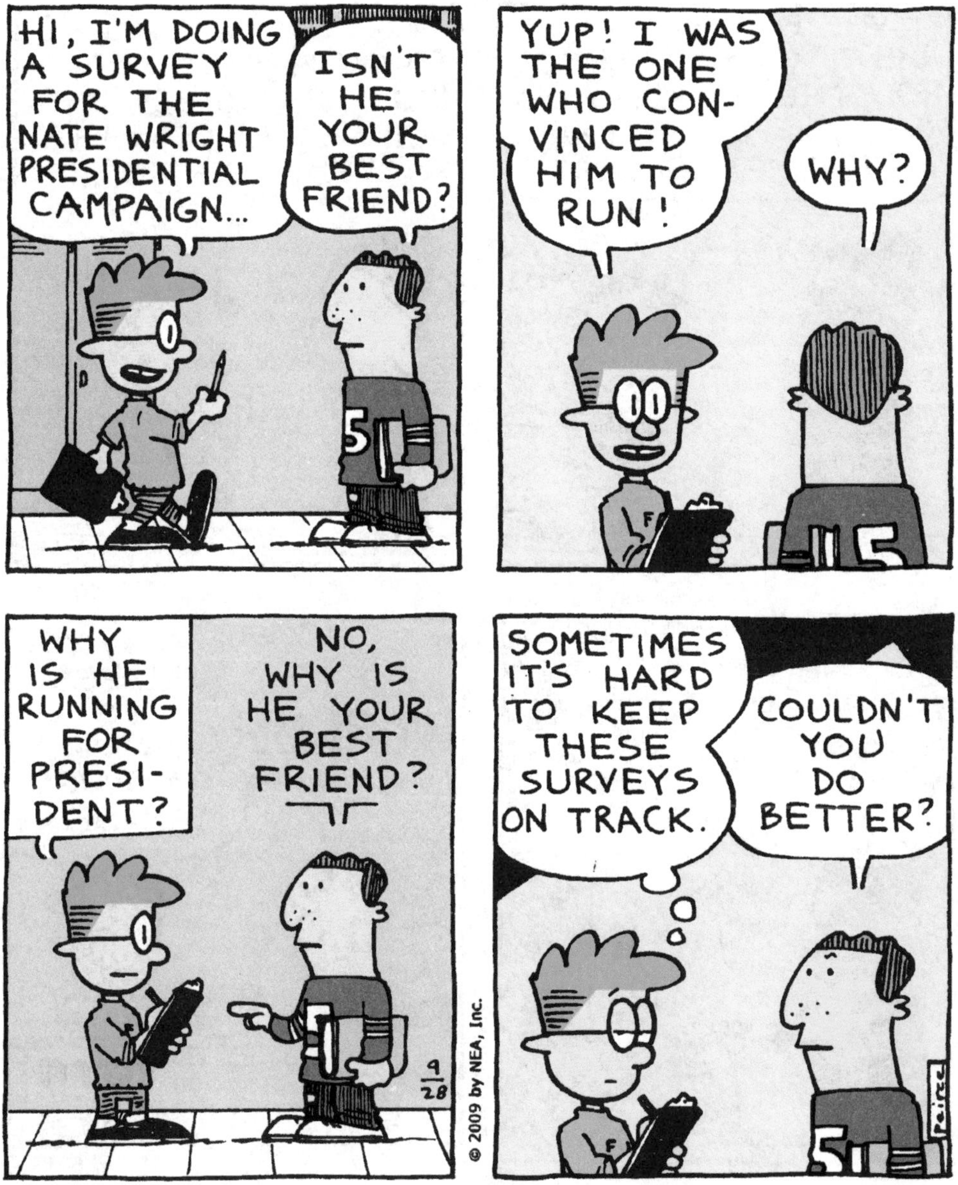
HI, I'M DOING A SURVEY FOR THE NATE WRIGHT PRESIDENTIAL CAMPAIGN...
ISN'T HE YOUR BEST FRIEND?
YUP! I WAS THE ONE WHO CONVINCED HIM TO RUN!
WHY?
WHY IS HE RUNNING FOR PRESIDENT?
NO, WHY IS HE YOUR BEST FRIEND?
9/28
© 2009 by NEA, Inc.
SOMETIMES IT'S HARD TO KEEP THESE SURVEYS ON TRACK.
COULDN'T YOU DO BETTER?
Peirce

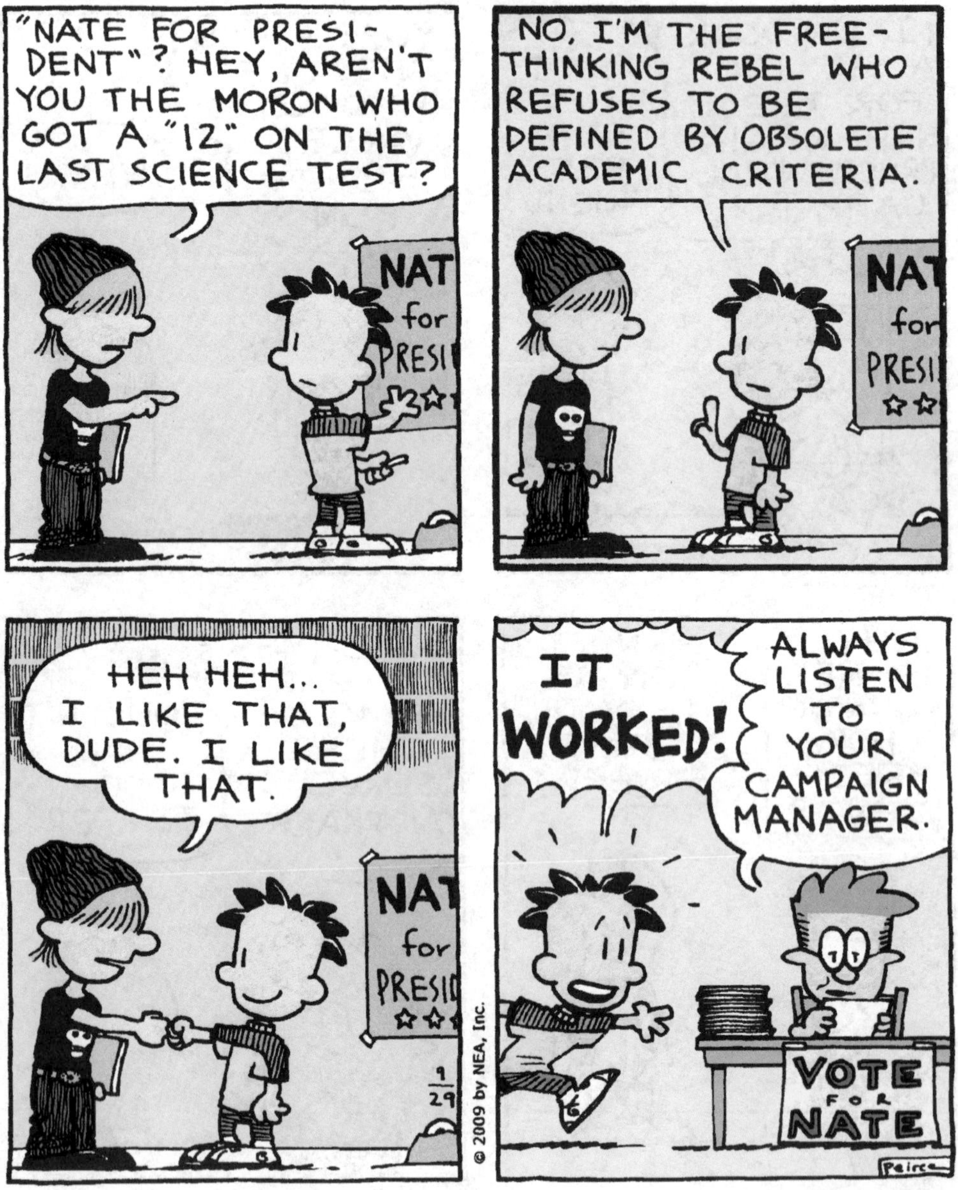
"NATE FOR PRESI-DENT"? HEY, AREN'T YOU THE MORON WHO GOT A "12" ON THE LAST SCIENCE TEST?
NATE for PRESI
NO, I'M THE FREE-THINKING REBEL WHO REFUSES TO BE DEFINED BY OBSOLETE ACADEMIC CRITERIA.
HEH HEH... I LIKE THAT, DUDE. I LIKE THAT.
9/29
© 2009 by NEA, Inc.
IT WORKED!
ALWAYS LISTEN TO YOUR CAMPAIGN MANAGER.
VOTE FOR NATE
Peirce

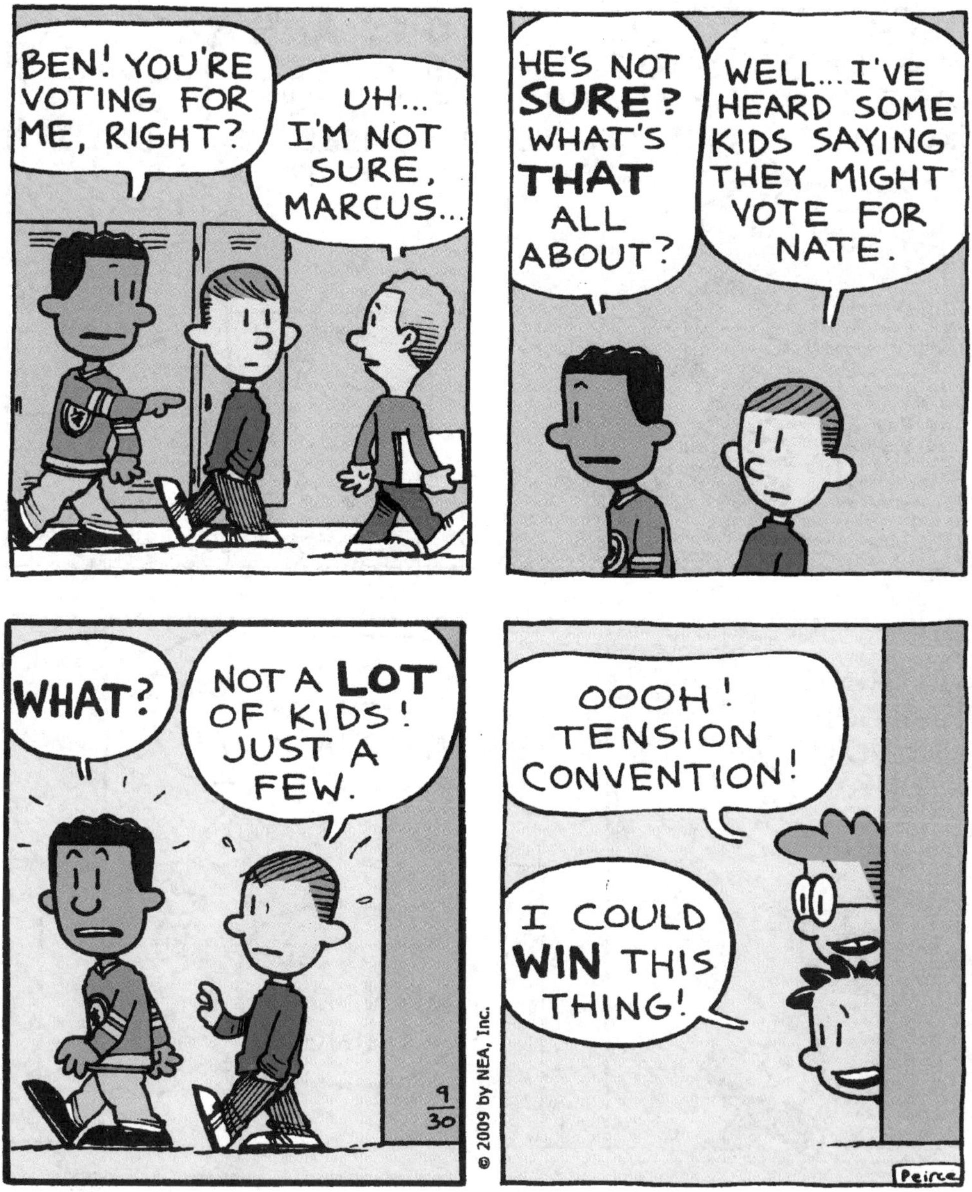
BEN! YOU'RE VOTING FOR ME, RIGHT?
UH... I'M NOT SURE, MARCUS...
HE'S NOT **SURE**? WHAT'S **THAT** ALL ABOUT?
WELL... I'VE HEARD SOME KIDS SAYING THEY MIGHT VOTE FOR NATE.
WHAT?
NOT A **LOT** OF KIDS! JUST A FEW.
9/30
© 2009 by NEA, Inc.
OOOH! TENSION CONVENTION!
I COULD **WIN** THIS THING!
Peirce

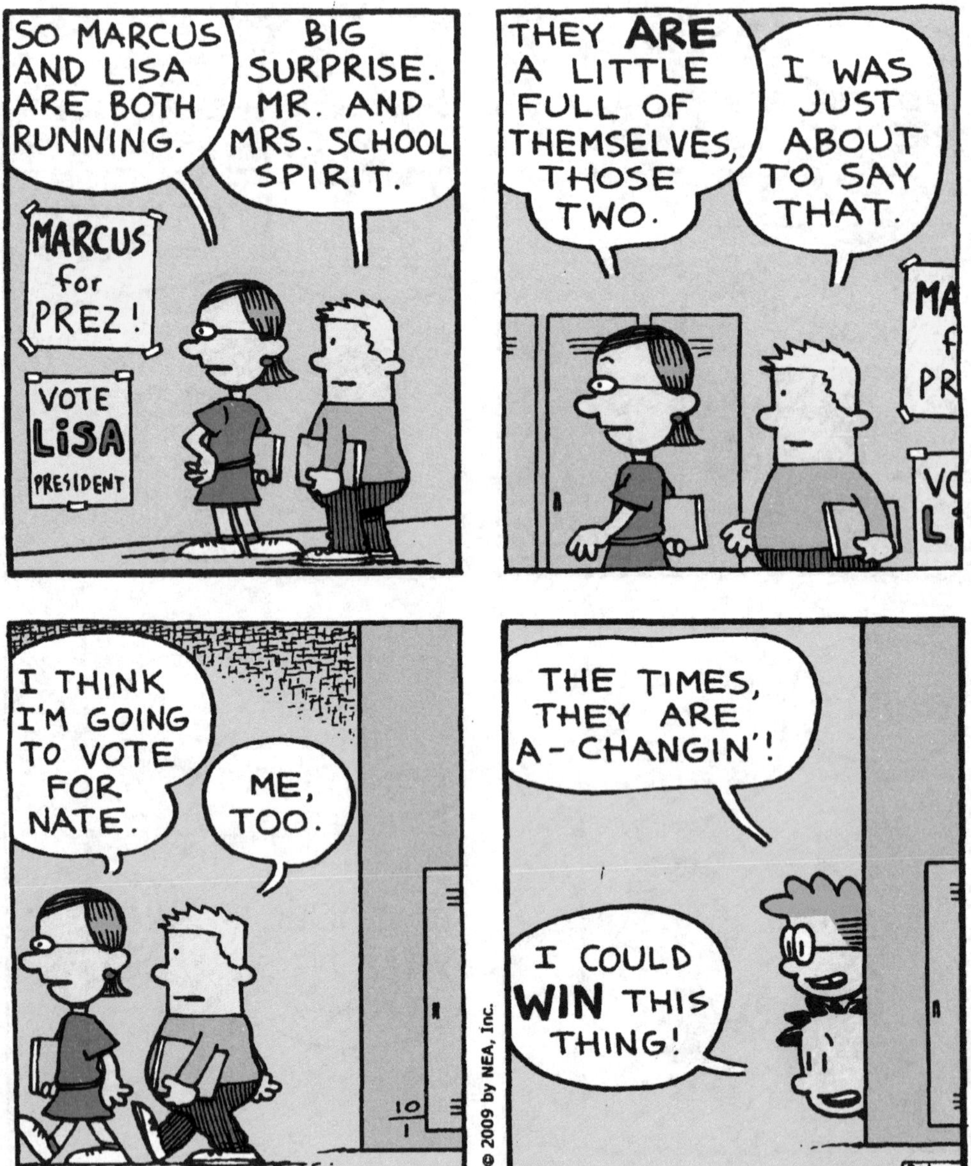
SO MARCUS AND LISA ARE BOTH RUNNING.
BIG SURPRISE. MR. AND MRS. SCHOOL SPIRIT.
MARCUS for PREZ!
VOTE LiSA PRESIDENT
THEY ARE A LITTLE FULL OF THEMSELVES, THOSE TWO.
I WAS JUST ABOUT TO SAY THAT.
I THINK I'M GOING TO VOTE FOR NATE.
ME, TOO.
THE TIMES, THEY ARE A-CHANGIN'!
I COULD WIN THIS THING!
© 2009 by NEA, Inc.

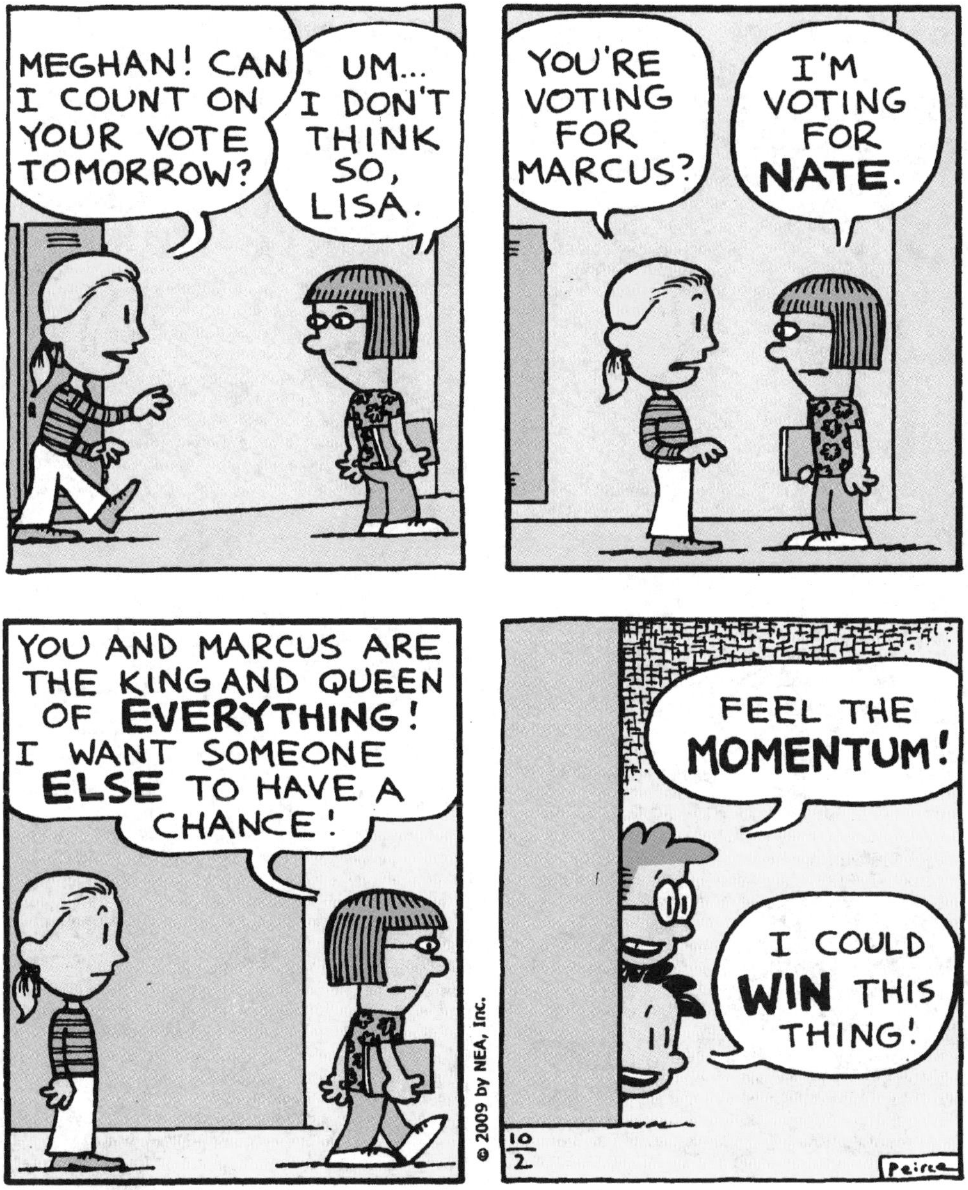
MEGHAN! CAN I COUNT ON YOUR VOTE TOMORROW?
UM... I DON'T THINK SO, LISA.
YOU'RE VOTING FOR MARCUS?
I'M VOTING FOR NATE.
YOU AND MARCUS ARE THE KING AND QUEEN OF EVERYTHING! I WANT SOMEONE ELSE TO HAVE A CHANCE!
FEEL THE MOMENTUM!
I COULD WIN THIS THING!
© 2009 by NEA, Inc.
10/2
Peirce

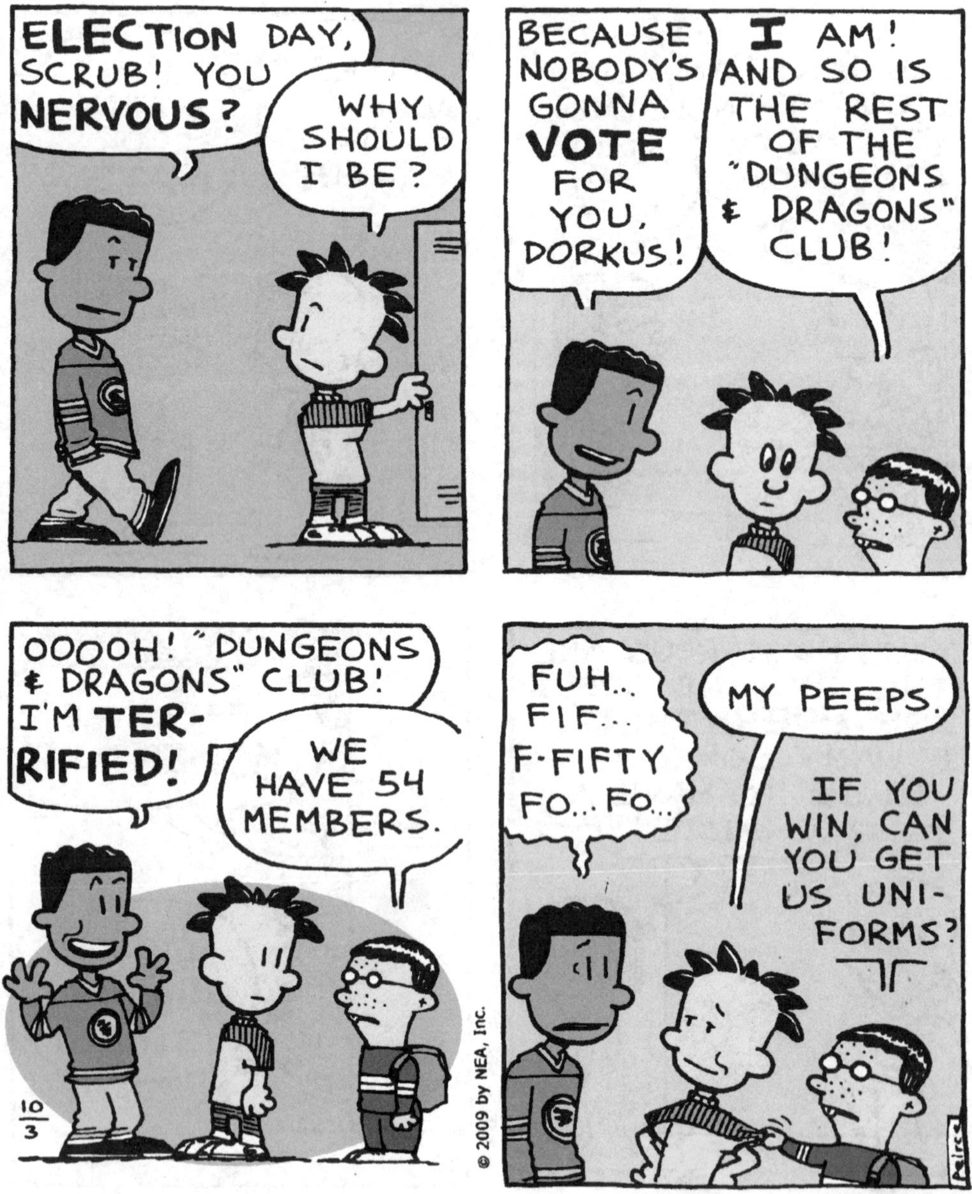
ELECTION DAY, SCRUB! YOU NERVOUS?
WHY SHOULD I BE?
BECAUSE NOBODY'S GONNA VOTE FOR YOU, DORKUS!
I AM! AND SO IS THE REST OF THE "DUNGEONS & DRAGONS" CLUB!
OOOOH! "DUNGEONS & DRAGONS" CLUB! I'M TER-RIFIED!
WE HAVE 54 MEMBERS.
10/3
© 2009 by NEA, Inc.
FUH... FIF... F-FIFTY FO... FO...
MY PEEPS.
IF YOU WIN, CAN YOU GET US UNI-FORMS?
Peirce

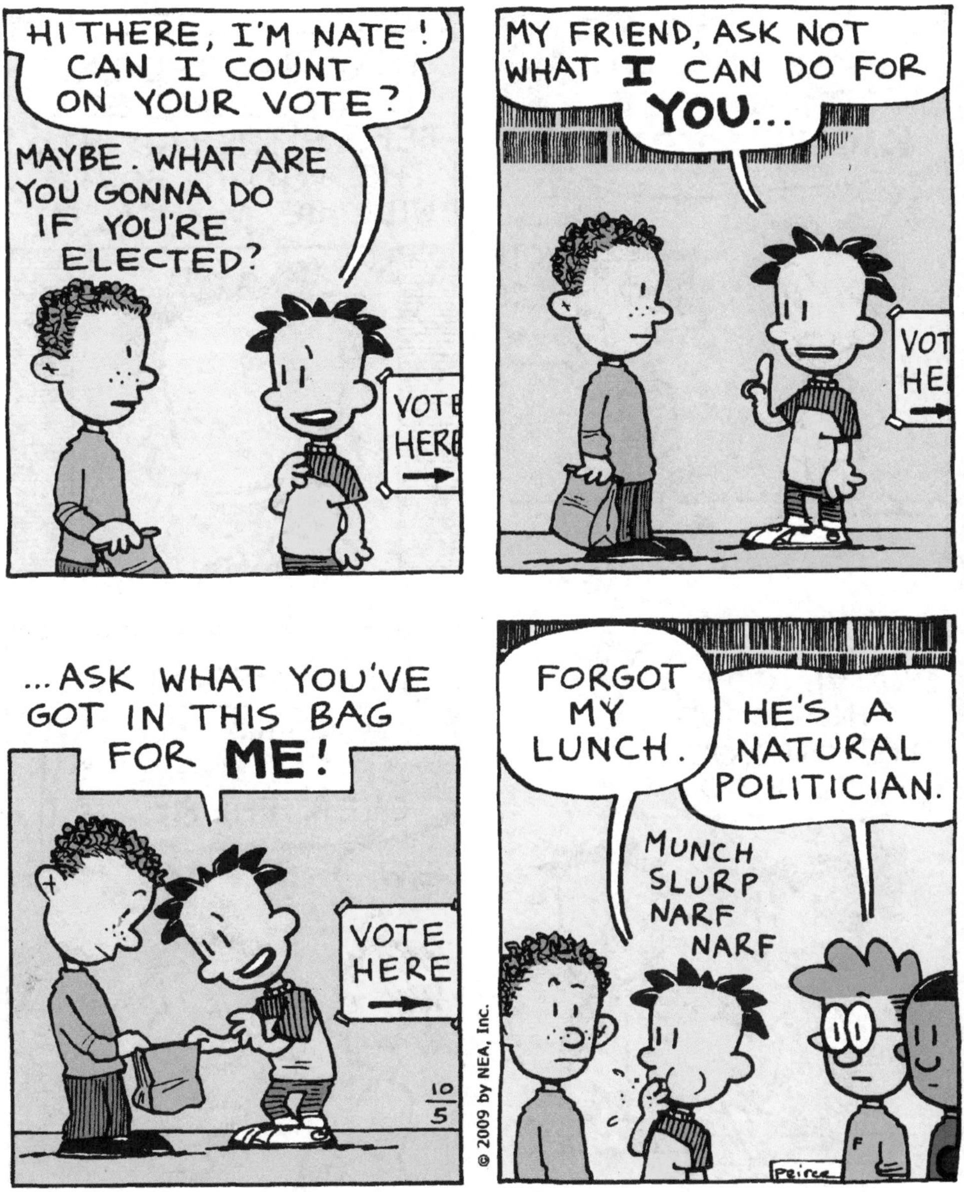
HI THERE, I'M NATE! CAN I COUNT ON YOUR VOTE?
MAYBE. WHAT ARE YOU GONNA DO IF YOU'RE ELECTED?
VOTE HERE
MY FRIEND, ASK NOT WHAT I CAN DO FOR YOU...
...ASK WHAT YOU'VE GOT IN THIS BAG FOR ME!
VOTE HERE
10/5
© 2009 by NEA, Inc.
FORGOT MY LUNCH.
HE'S A NATURAL POLITICIAN.
MUNCH SLURP NARF NARF
Peirce

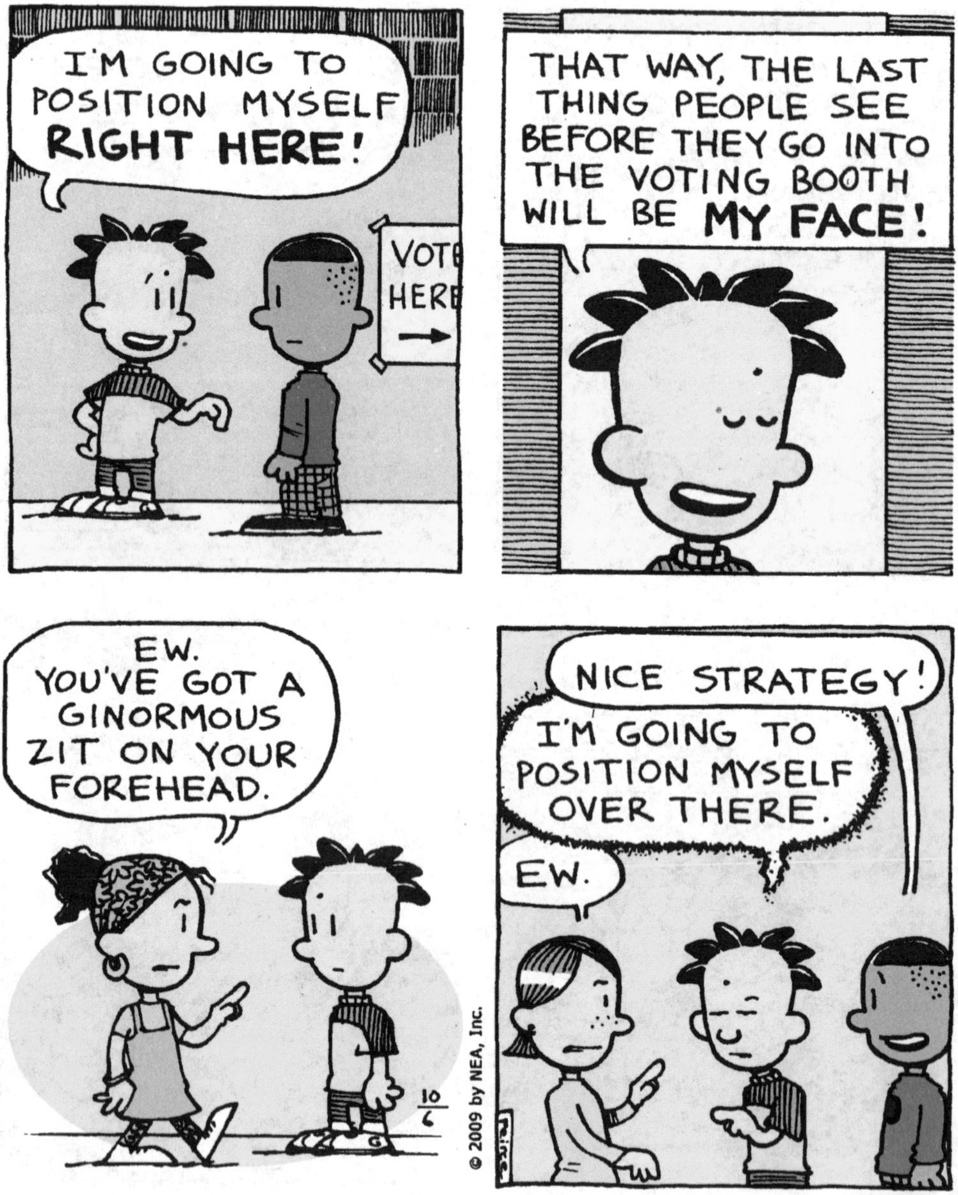
I'M GOING TO POSITION MYSELF RIGHT HERE!
VOTE HERE
THAT WAY, THE LAST THING PEOPLE SEE BEFORE THEY GO INTO THE VOTING BOOTH WILL BE MY FACE!
EW. YOU'VE GOT A GINORMOUS ZIT ON YOUR FOREHEAD.
NICE STRATEGY!
I'M GOING TO POSITION MYSELF OVER THERE.
EW.
10
6
Peirce

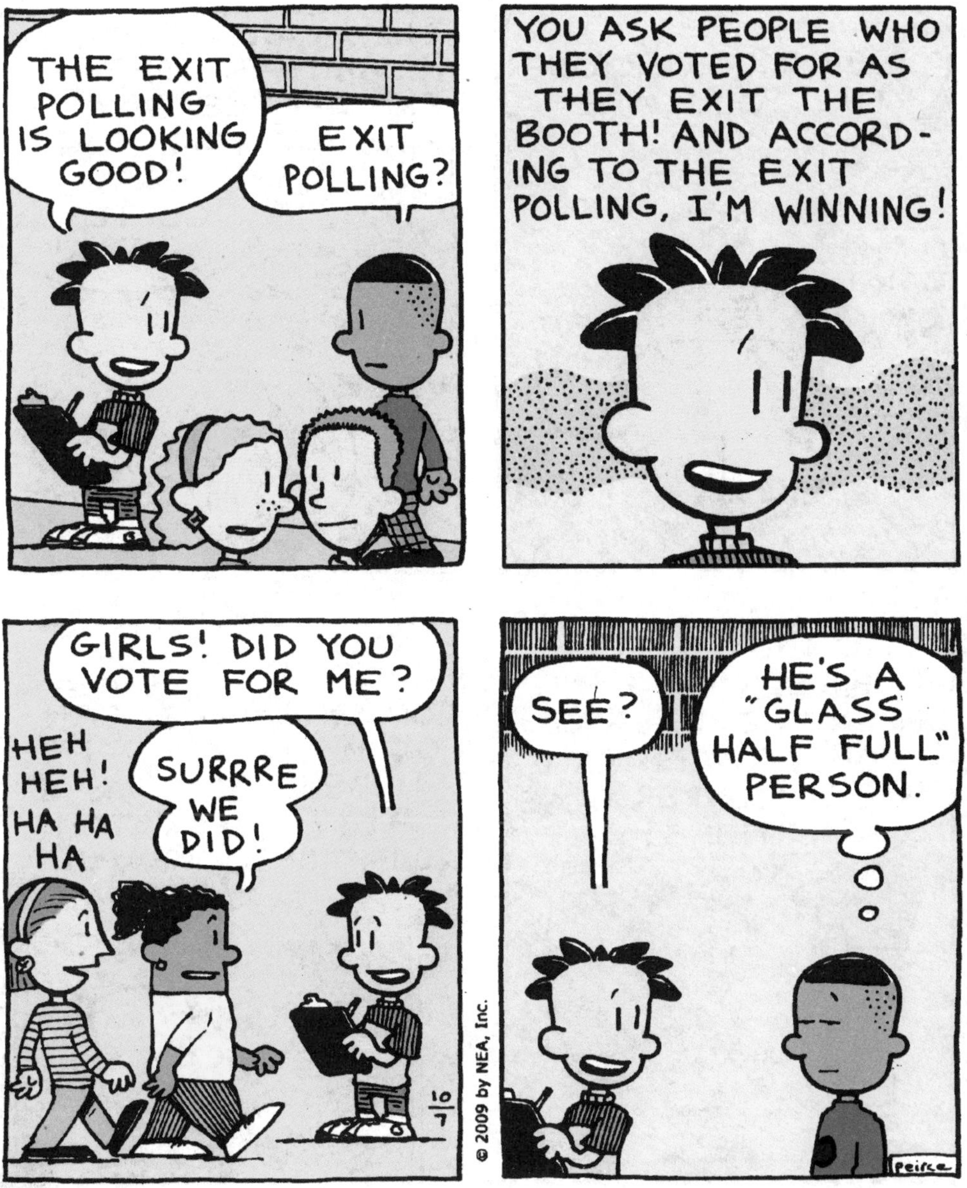
THE EXIT POLLING IS LOOKING GOOD!
EXIT POLLING?
YOU ASK PEOPLE WHO THEY VOTED FOR AS THEY EXIT THE BOOTH! AND ACCORDING TO THE EXIT POLLING, I'M WINNING!
GIRLS! DID YOU VOTE FOR ME?
HEH HEH! HA HA HA
SURRRE WE DID!
10/7
© 2009 by NEA, Inc.
SEE?
HE'S A "GLASS HALF FULL" PERSON.
Peirce

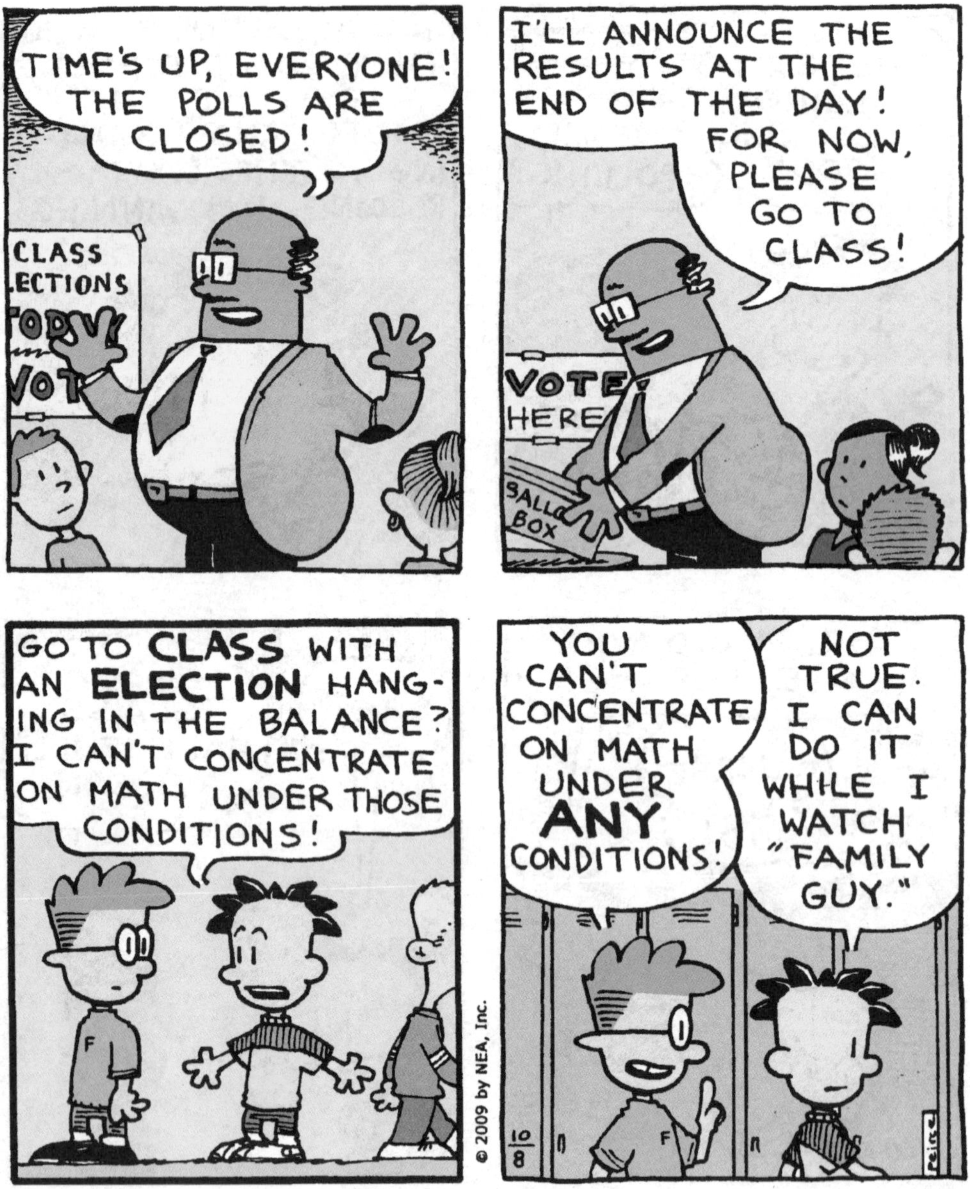
TIME'S UP, EVERYONE! THE POLLS ARE CLOSED!
CLASS ELECTIONS
VOTE HERE
I'LL ANNOUNCE THE RESULTS AT THE END OF THE DAY! FOR NOW, PLEASE GO TO CLASS!
GO TO CLASS WITH AN ELECTION HANGING IN THE BALANCE? I CAN'T CONCENTRATE ON MATH UNDER THOSE CONDITIONS!
YOU CAN'T CONCENTRATE ON MATH UNDER ANY CONDITIONS!
NOT TRUE. I CAN DO IT WHILE I WATCH "FAMILY GUY."
© 2009 by NEA, Inc.
10/8

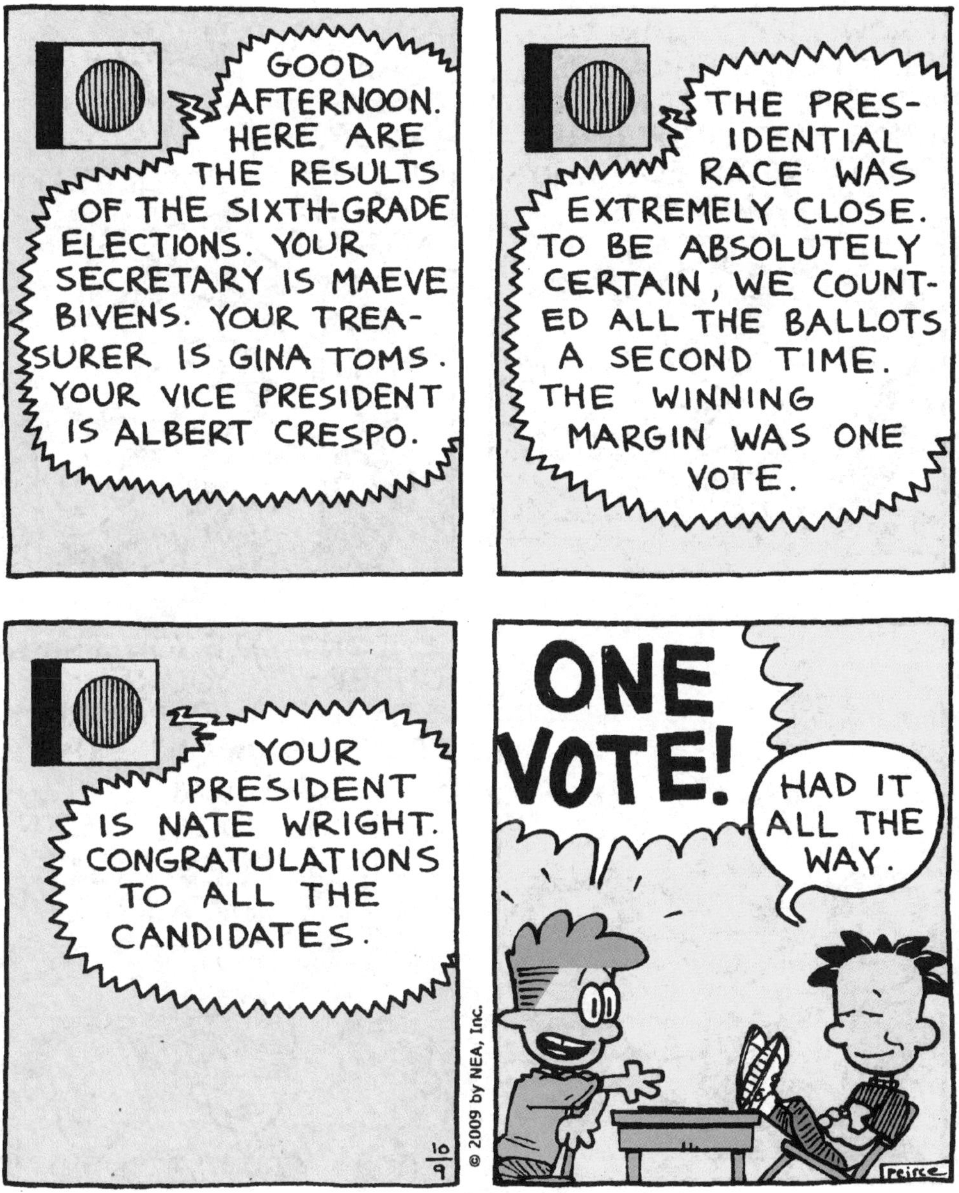
GOOD AFTERNOON. HERE ARE THE RESULTS OF THE SIXTH-GRADE ELECTIONS. YOUR SECRETARY IS MAEVE BIVENS. YOUR TREASURER IS GINA TOMS. YOUR VICE PRESIDENT IS ALBERT CRESPO.
THE PRESIDENTIAL RACE WAS EXTREMELY CLOSE. TO BE ABSOLUTELY CERTAIN, WE COUNTED ALL THE BALLOTS A SECOND TIME. THE WINNING MARGIN WAS ONE VOTE.
YOUR PRESIDENT IS NATE WRIGHT. CONGRATULATIONS TO ALL THE CANDIDATES.
ONE VOTE!
HAD IT ALL THE WAY.
10/9
© 2009 by NEA, Inc.
PEIRCE

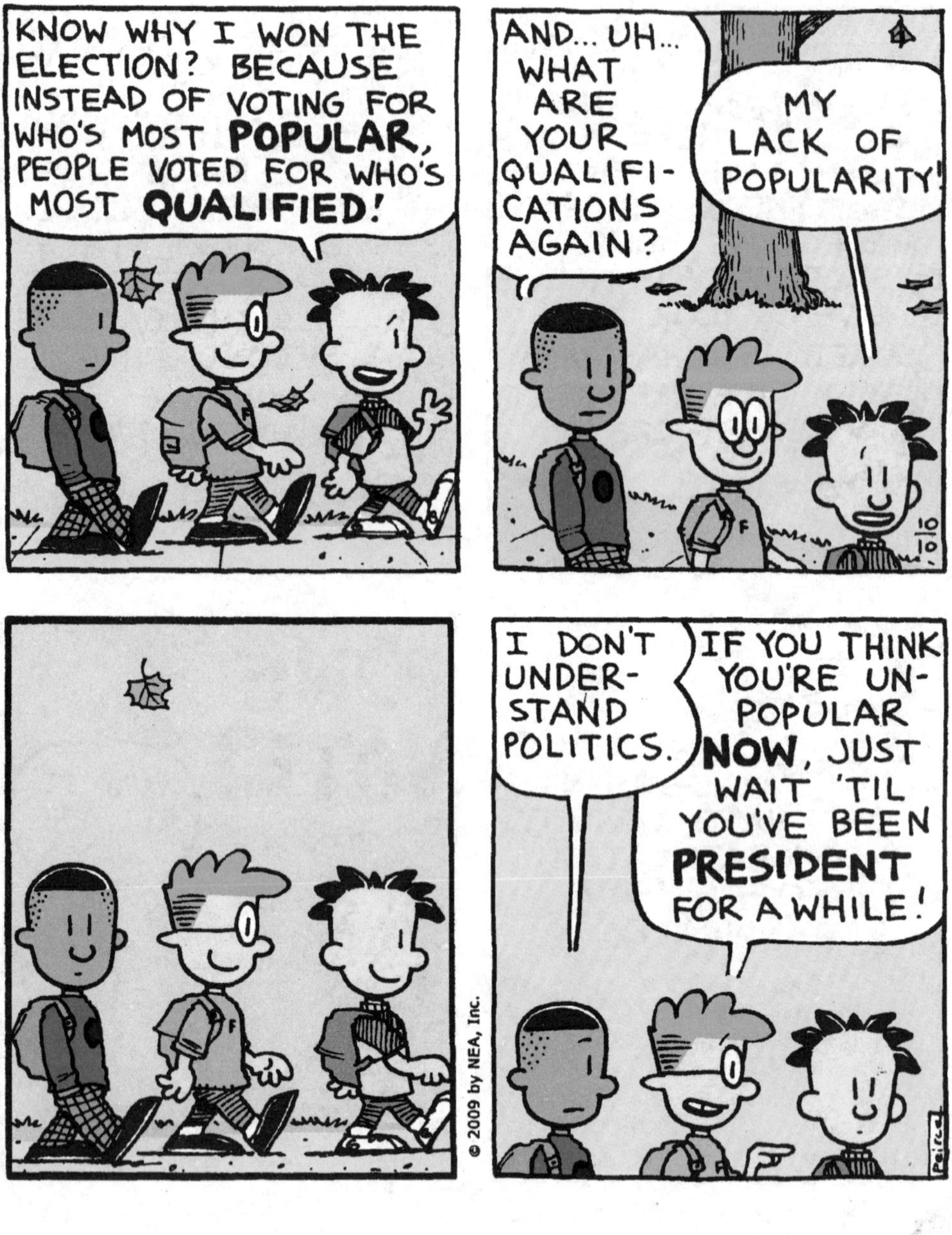
KNOW WHY I WON THE ELECTION? BECAUSE INSTEAD OF VOTING FOR WHO'S MOST **POPULAR**, PEOPLE VOTED FOR WHO'S MOST **QUALIFIED**!
AND... UH... WHAT ARE YOUR QUALIFI-CATIONS AGAIN?
MY LACK OF POPULARITY!
10/10
I DON'T UNDER-STAND POLITICS.
IF YOU THINK YOU'RE UN-POPULAR **NOW**, JUST WAIT 'TIL YOU'VE BEEN **PRESIDENT** FOR A WHILE!
© 2009 by NEA, Inc.
PEIRCE

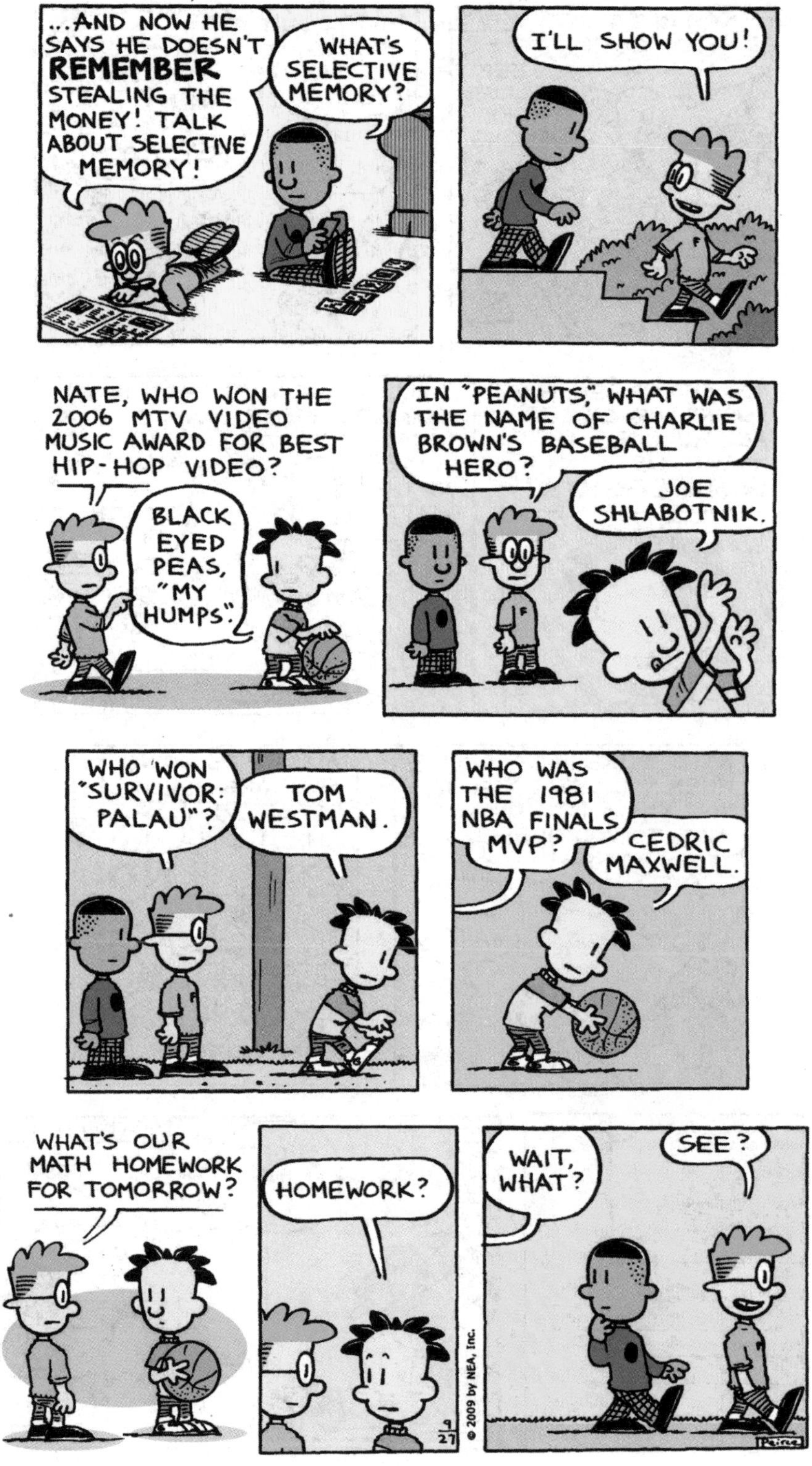
...AND NOW HE SAYS HE DOESN'T **REMEMBER** STEALING THE MONEY! TALK ABOUT SELECTIVE MEMORY!
WHAT'S SELECTIVE MEMORY?
I'LL SHOW YOU!
NATE, WHO WON THE 2006 MTV VIDEO MUSIC AWARD FOR BEST HIP-HOP VIDEO?
BLACK EYED PEAS, "MY HUMPS."
IN "PEANUTS," WHAT WAS THE NAME OF CHARLIE BROWN'S BASEBALL HERO?
JOE SHLABOTNIK.
WHO WON "SURVIVOR: PALAU"?
TOM WESTMAN.
WHO WAS THE 1981 NBA FINALS MVP?
CEDRIC MAXWELL.
WHAT'S OUR MATH HOMEWORK FOR TOMORROW?
HOMEWORK?
9/27
© 2009 by NEA, Inc.
WAIT, WHAT?
SEE?
Peirce

SAY, ISN'T THAT ONE OF YOUR COACHES?

KEEP WALKING. KEEP WALKING.

HM? DON'T YOU WANT TO SAY HELLO?

SAY HELLO TO **COACH JOHN**? THE MAN'S A **PSYCHO**!

YOU SHOULD SEE HIM DURING PRACTICE! ALL HE DOES IS MAKE US RUN **WIND SPRINTS**!

WELL... ※CHUCKLE!※... HE'S NOT GOING TO BE IN "COACH MODE" AT THE **MALL**!

HE'S **ALWAYS** IN "COACH MODE."

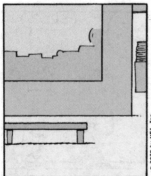

NATE, YOU'RE BEING RUDE. WHEN YOU SEE SOMEONE YOU KNOW, IT'S IMPOLITE NOT TO ACKNOWLEDGE THEM!

DAD! WAIT!

ALL WE'RE DOING IS SAYING HELLO!

NO! NO!

EIGHT... NINE... TEN...

HAPPY?

© 2009 by NEA, Inc.

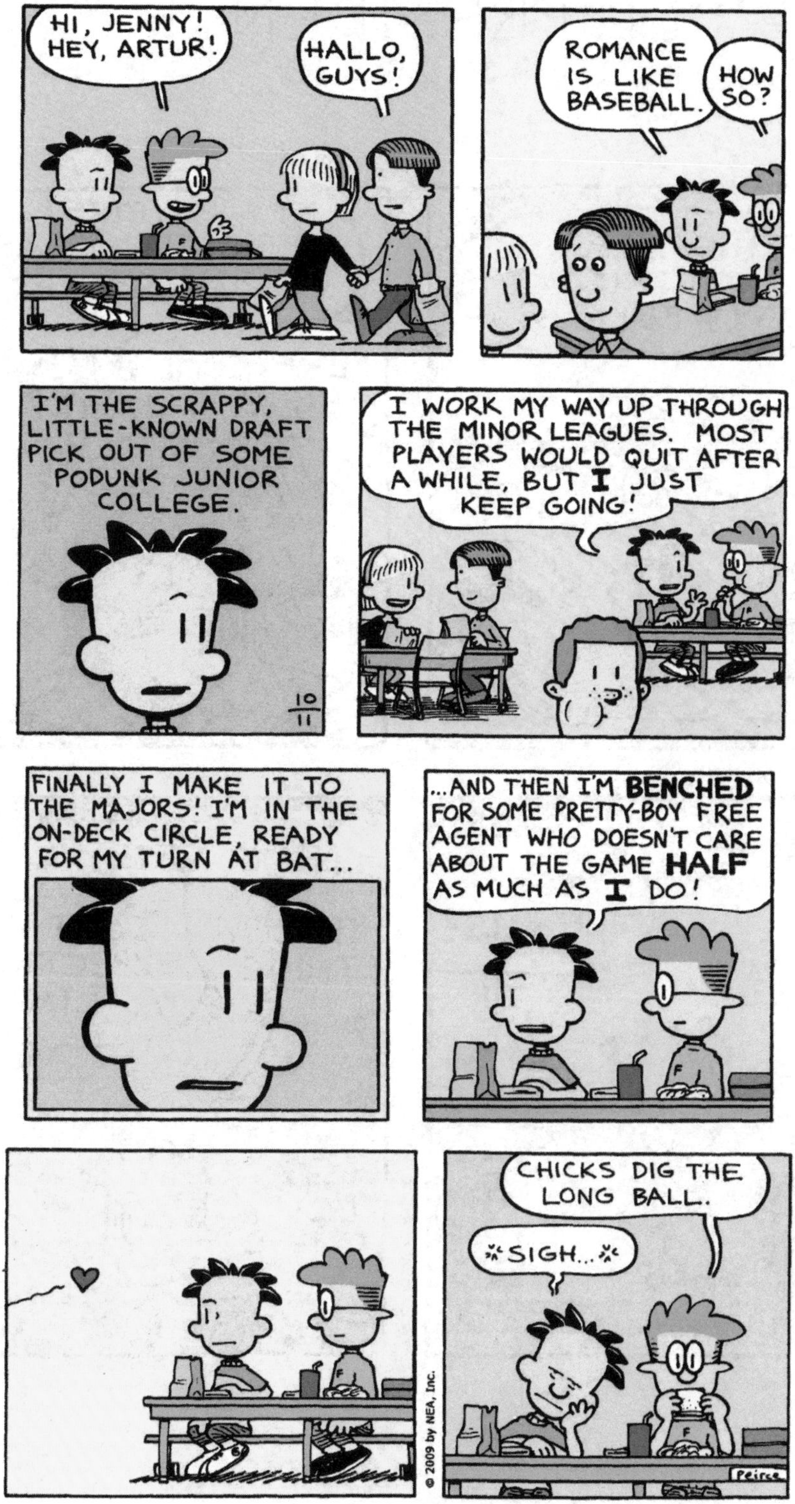
HI, JENNY! HEY, ARTUR!
HALLO, GUYS!
ROMANCE IS LIKE BASEBALL.
HOW SO?
I'M THE SCRAPPY, LITTLE-KNOWN DRAFT PICK OUT OF SOME PODUNK JUNIOR COLLEGE.
10/11
I WORK MY WAY UP THROUGH THE MINOR LEAGUES. MOST PLAYERS WOULD QUIT AFTER A WHILE, BUT I JUST KEEP GOING!
FINALLY I MAKE IT TO THE MAJORS! I'M IN THE ON-DECK CIRCLE, READY FOR MY TURN AT BAT...
...AND THEN I'M BENCHED FOR SOME PRETTY-BOY FREE AGENT WHO DOESN'T CARE ABOUT THE GAME HALF AS MUCH AS I DO!
© 2009 by NEA, Inc.
CHICKS DIG THE LONG BALL.
SIGH...
Peirce

EL PRESIDENTE

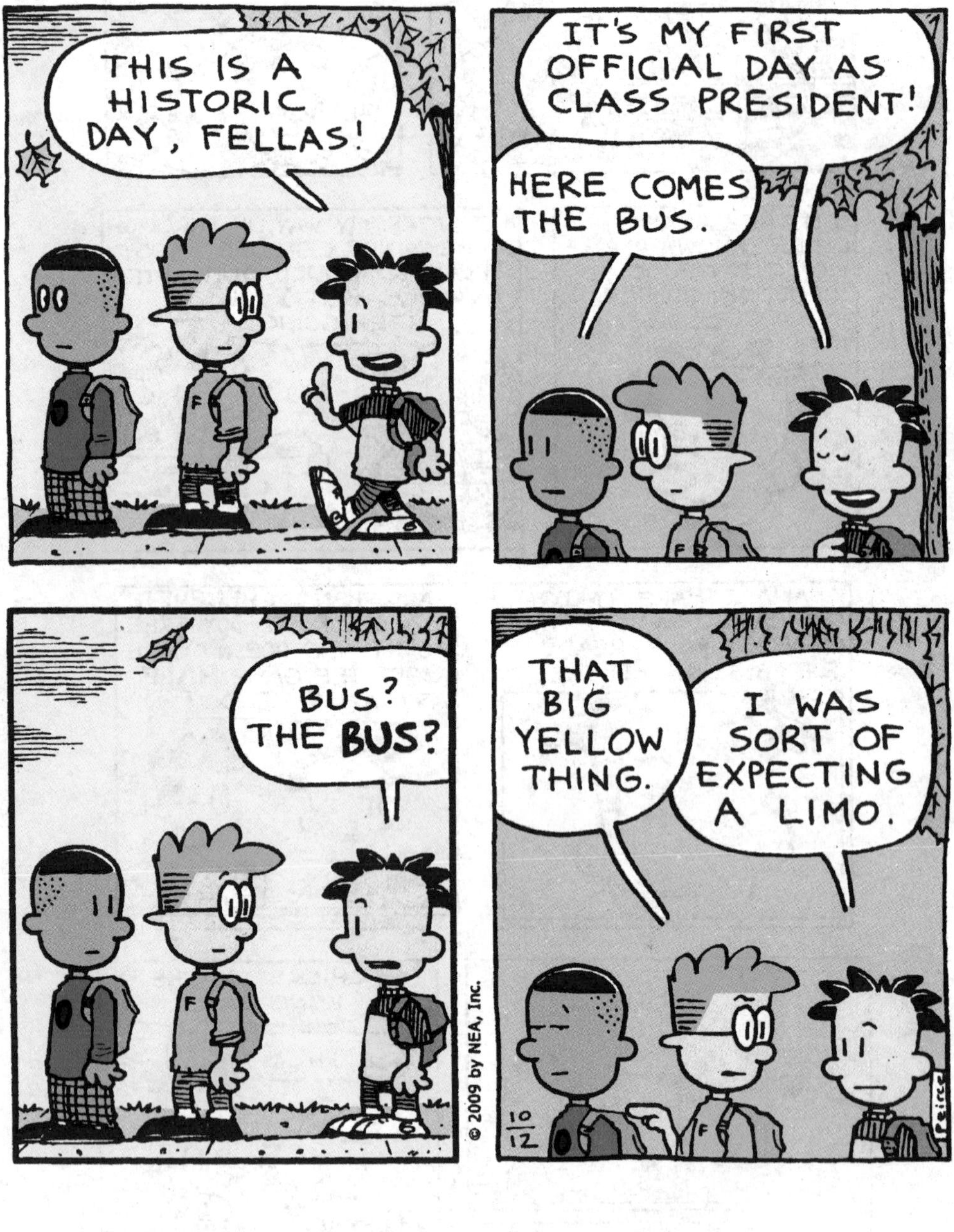
THIS IS A HISTORIC DAY, FELLAS!
IT'S MY FIRST OFFICIAL DAY AS CLASS PRESIDENT!
HERE COMES THE BUS.
BUS? THE **BUS**?
THAT BIG YELLOW THING.
I WAS SORT OF EXPECTING A LIMO.
© 2009 by NEA, Inc.
10 12
Peirce

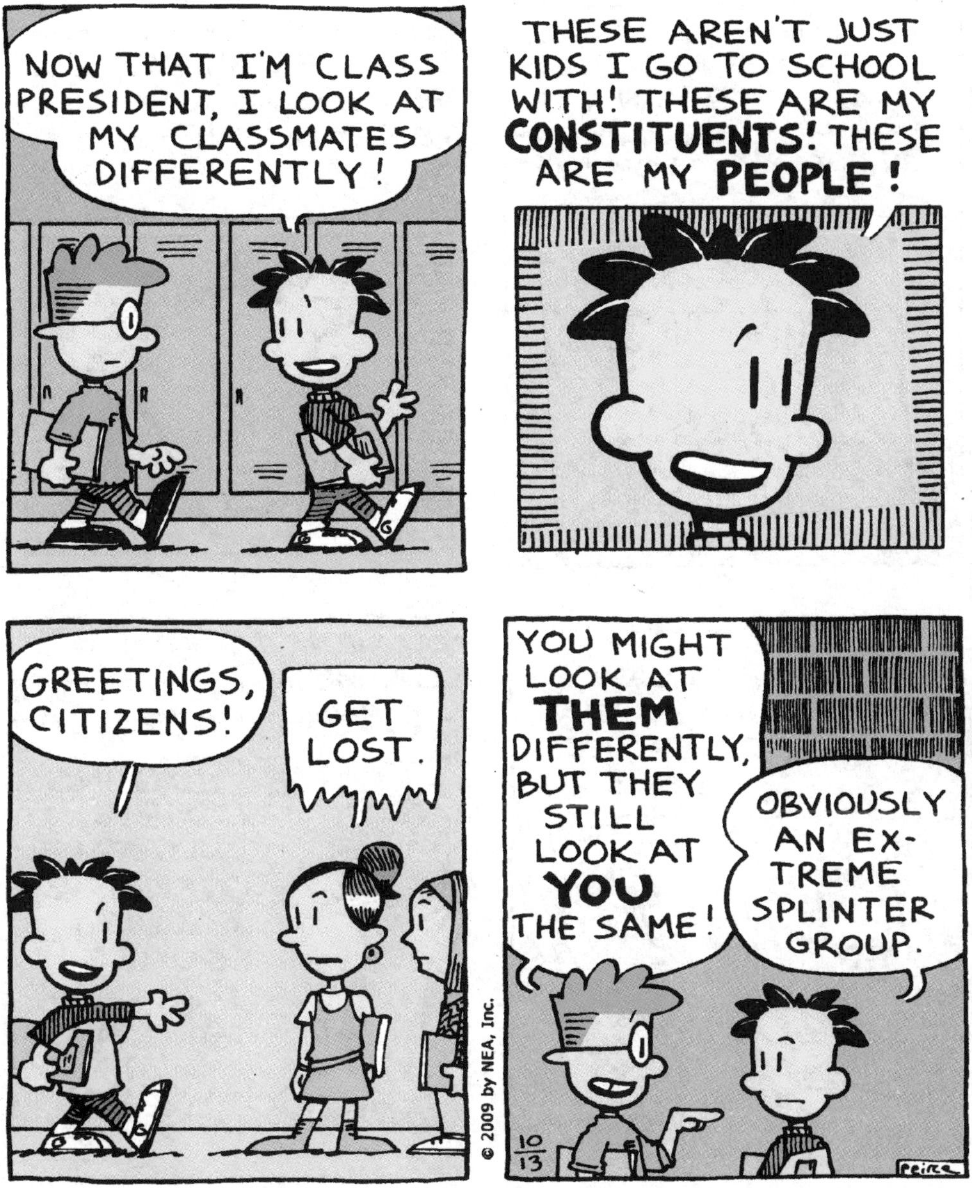
NOW THAT I'M CLASS PRESIDENT, I LOOK AT MY CLASSMATES DIFFERENTLY!
THESE AREN'T JUST KIDS I GO TO SCHOOL WITH! THESE ARE MY CONSTITUENTS! THESE ARE MY PEOPLE!
GREETINGS, CITIZENS!
GET LOST.
YOU MIGHT LOOK AT THEM DIFFERENTLY, BUT THEY STILL LOOK AT YOU THE SAME!
OBVIOUSLY AN EX-TREME SPLINTER GROUP.
© 2009 by NEA, Inc.
10/13
PEIRCE

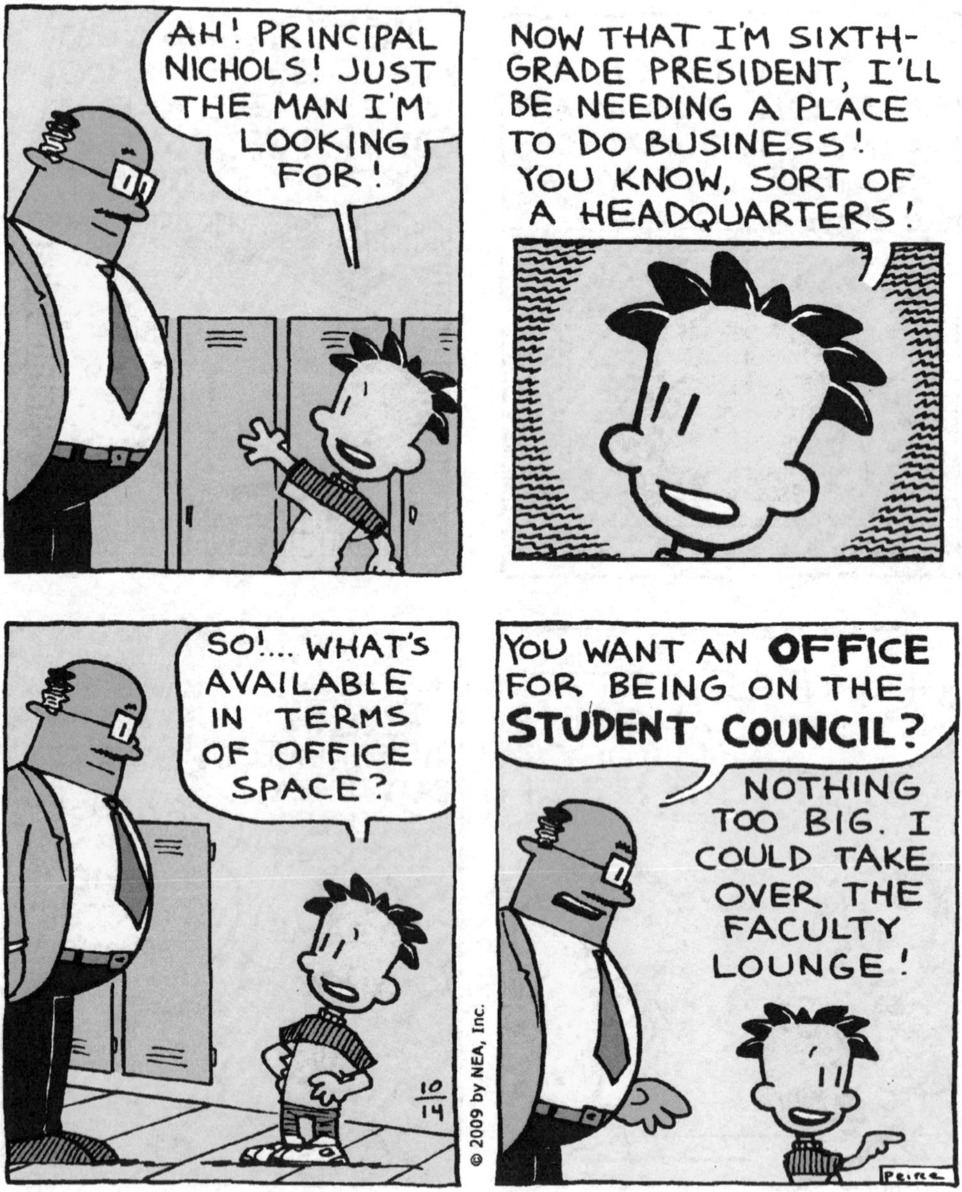
AH! PRINCIPAL NICHOLS! JUST THE MAN I'M LOOKING FOR!
NOW THAT I'M SIXTH-GRADE PRESIDENT, I'LL BE NEEDING A PLACE TO DO BUSINESS! YOU KNOW, SORT OF A HEADQUARTERS!
SO!... WHAT'S AVAILABLE IN TERMS OF OFFICE SPACE?
10/14
© 2009 by NEA, Inc.
YOU WANT AN **OFFICE** FOR BEING ON THE **STUDENT COUNCIL**?
NOTHING TOO BIG. I COULD TAKE OVER THE FACULTY LOUNGE!
PEIRCE

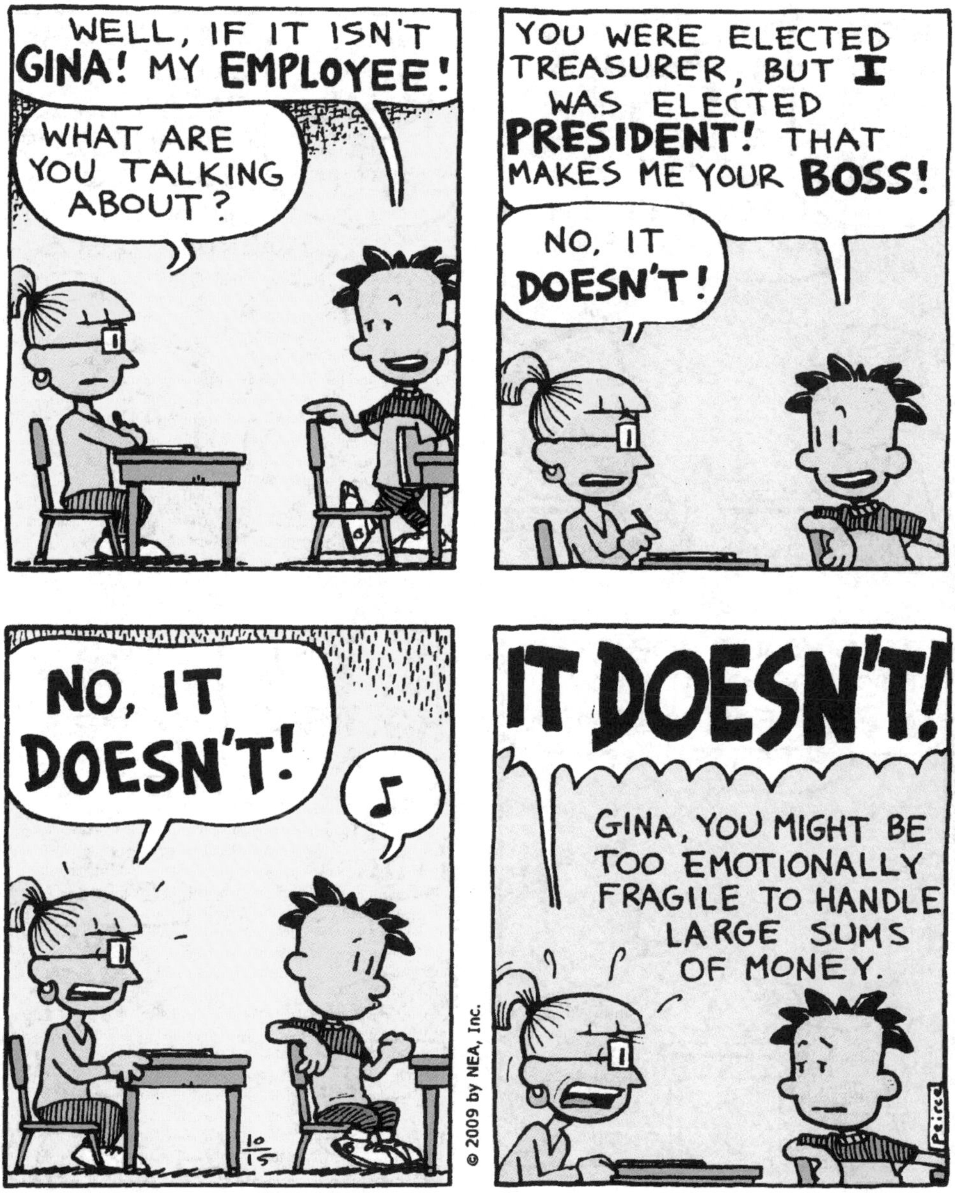
WELL, IF IT ISN'T GINA! MY EMPLOYEE!
WHAT ARE YOU TALKING ABOUT?
YOU WERE ELECTED TREASURER, BUT I WAS ELECTED PRESIDENT! THAT MAKES ME YOUR BOSS!
NO, IT DOESN'T!
NO, IT DOESN'T!
♪
IT DOESN'T!
GINA, YOU MIGHT BE TOO EMOTIONALLY FRAGILE TO HANDLE LARGE SUMS OF MONEY.

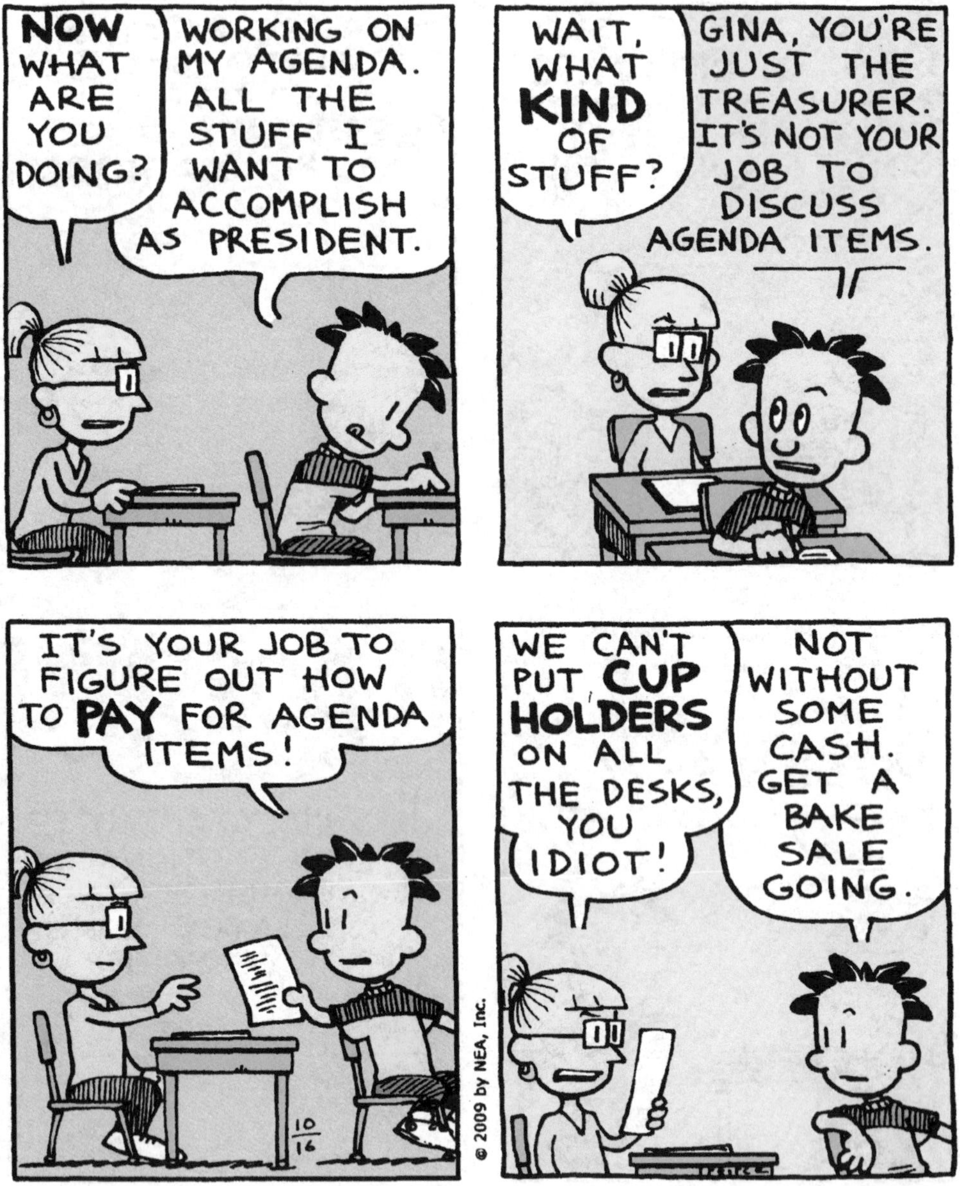
NOW WHAT ARE YOU DOING?
WORKING ON MY AGENDA. ALL THE STUFF I WANT TO ACCOMPLISH AS PRESIDENT.
WAIT, WHAT KIND OF STUFF?
GINA, YOU'RE JUST THE TREASURER. IT'S NOT YOUR JOB TO DISCUSS AGENDA ITEMS.
IT'S YOUR JOB TO FIGURE OUT HOW TO PAY FOR AGENDA ITEMS!
WE CAN'T PUT CUP HOLDERS ON ALL THE DESKS, YOU IDIOT!
NOT WITHOUT SOME CASH. GET A BAKE SALE GOING.
10/16
© 2009 by NEA, Inc.

I HATE TO BREAK THIS TO YOU, BRAINLESS, BUT BEING SIXTH-GRADE CLASS PRESIDENT IS **NOT** THAT BIG A DEAL!

IT'S NOT LIKE YOU HAVE ANY **POWER!** IT DOESN'T EVEN **MATTER** WHO'S PRESIDENT!

PEOPLE AREN'T STANDING AROUND WONDERING "OOOH, WHAT DOES THE **PRESIDENT** HAVE TO SAY?"

SO WHAT'S SHE SAYING?

LOSE THE PODIUM.

PREZ

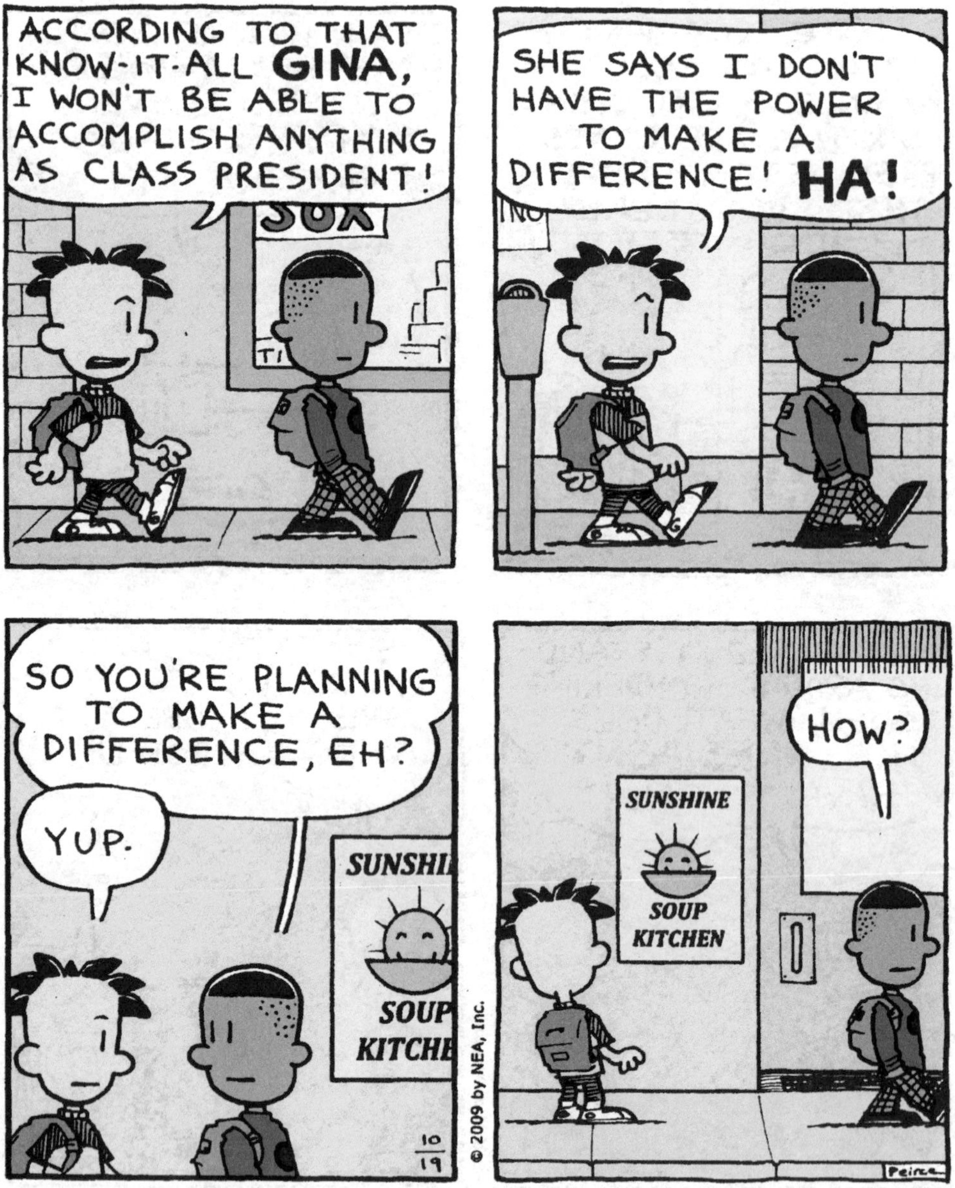
ACCORDING TO THAT KNOW-IT-ALL GINA, I WON'T BE ABLE TO ACCOMPLISH ANYTHING AS CLASS PRESIDENT!
SHE SAYS I DON'T HAVE THE POWER TO MAKE A DIFFERENCE! HA!
SO YOU'RE PLANNING TO MAKE A DIFFERENCE, EH?
YUP.
SUNSHI
SOUP
KITCHE
10
19
© 2009 by NEA, Inc.
SUNSHINE
SOUP
KITCHEN
HOW?
Peirce

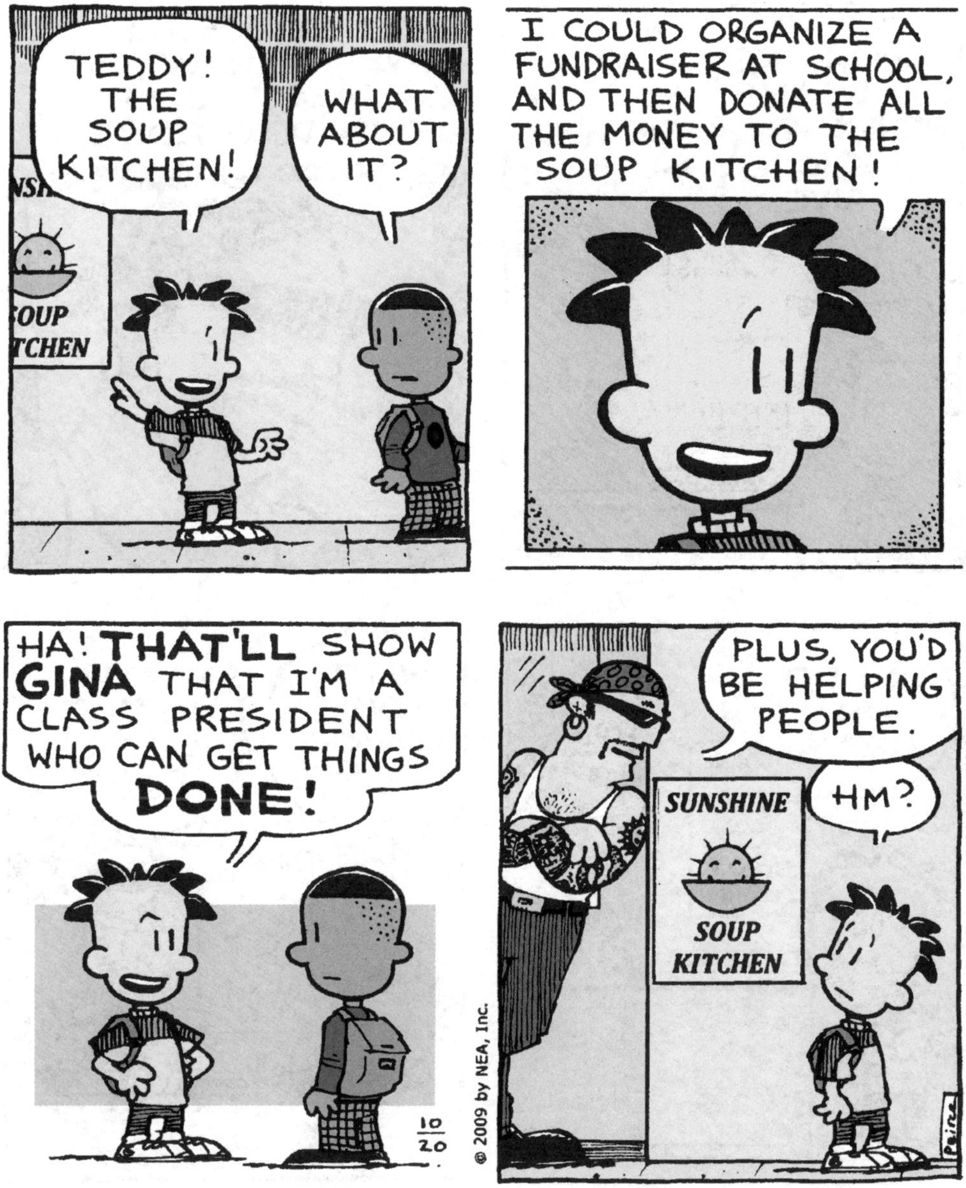
TEDDY! THE SOUP KITCHEN!
WHAT ABOUT IT?
SOUP
KITCHEN
I COULD ORGANIZE A FUNDRAISER AT SCHOOL, AND THEN DONATE ALL THE MONEY TO THE SOUP KITCHEN!
HA! **THAT'LL** SHOW **GINA** THAT I'M A CLASS PRESIDENT WHO CAN GET THINGS **DONE**!
10/20
© 2009 by NEA, Inc.
PLUS, YOU'D BE HELPING PEOPLE.
HM?
SUNSHINE
SOUP
KITCHEN
Peirce

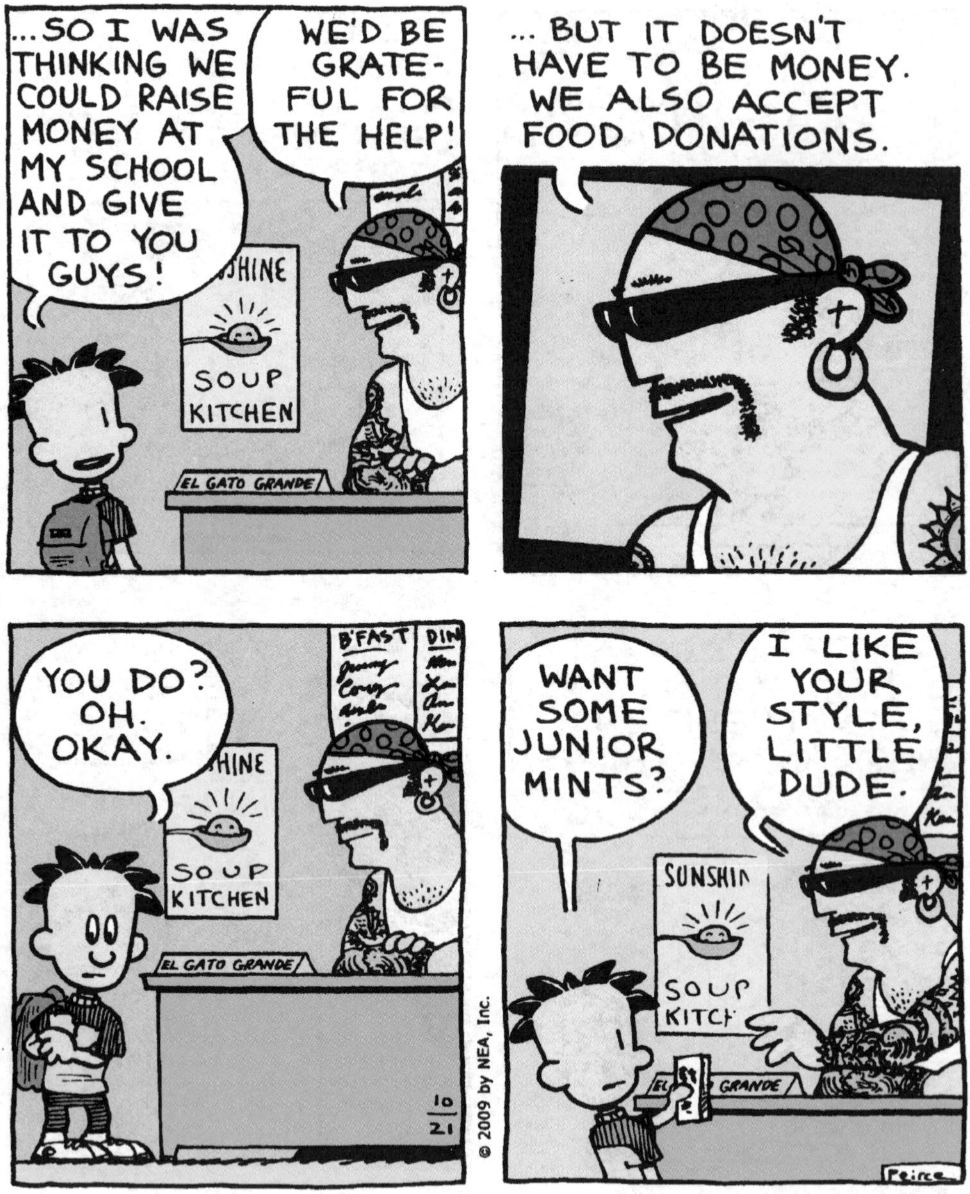
...SO I WAS THINKING WE COULD RAISE MONEY AT MY SCHOOL AND GIVE IT TO YOU GUYS!
WE'D BE GRATE-FUL FOR THE HELP!
SOUP KITCHEN
EL GATO GRANDE
... BUT IT DOESN'T HAVE TO BE MONEY. WE ALSO ACCEPT FOOD DONATIONS.
B'FAST
DIN
YOU DO? OH. OKAY.
SOUP KITCHEN
EL GATO GRANDE
10 21
© 2009 by NEA, Inc.
WANT SOME JUNIOR MINTS?
I LIKE YOUR STYLE, LITTLE DUDE.
SUNSHIN
SOUP KITCH
GRANDE
Peirce

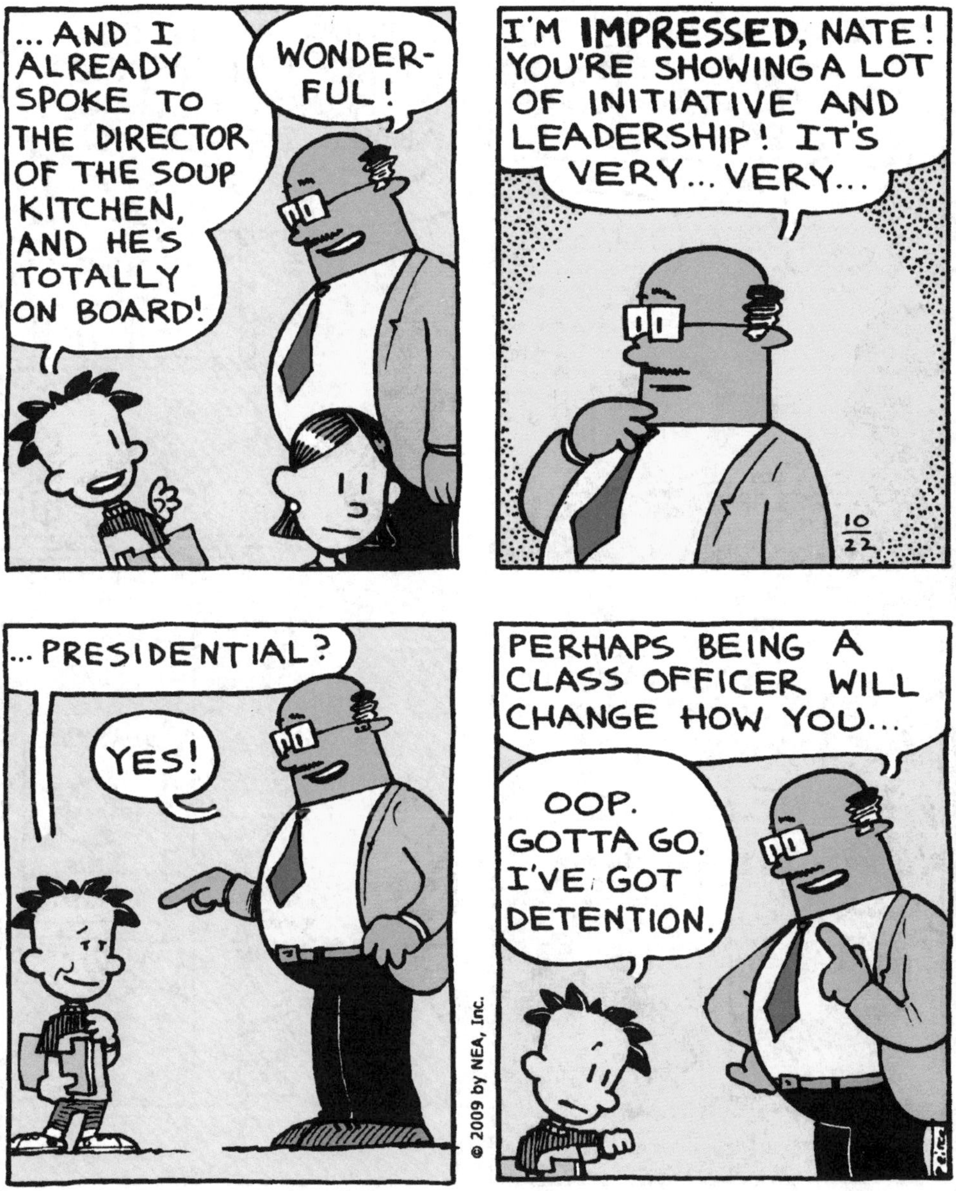
...AND I ALREADY SPOKE TO THE DIRECTOR OF THE SOUP KITCHEN, AND HE'S TOTALLY ON BOARD!
WONDER-FUL!
I'M IMPRESSED, NATE! YOU'RE SHOWING A LOT OF INITIATIVE AND LEADERSHIP! IT'S VERY... VERY...
10/22
...PRESIDENTIAL?
YES!
PERHAPS BEING A CLASS OFFICER WILL CHANGE HOW YOU...
OOP. GOTTA GO. I'VE GOT DETENTION.

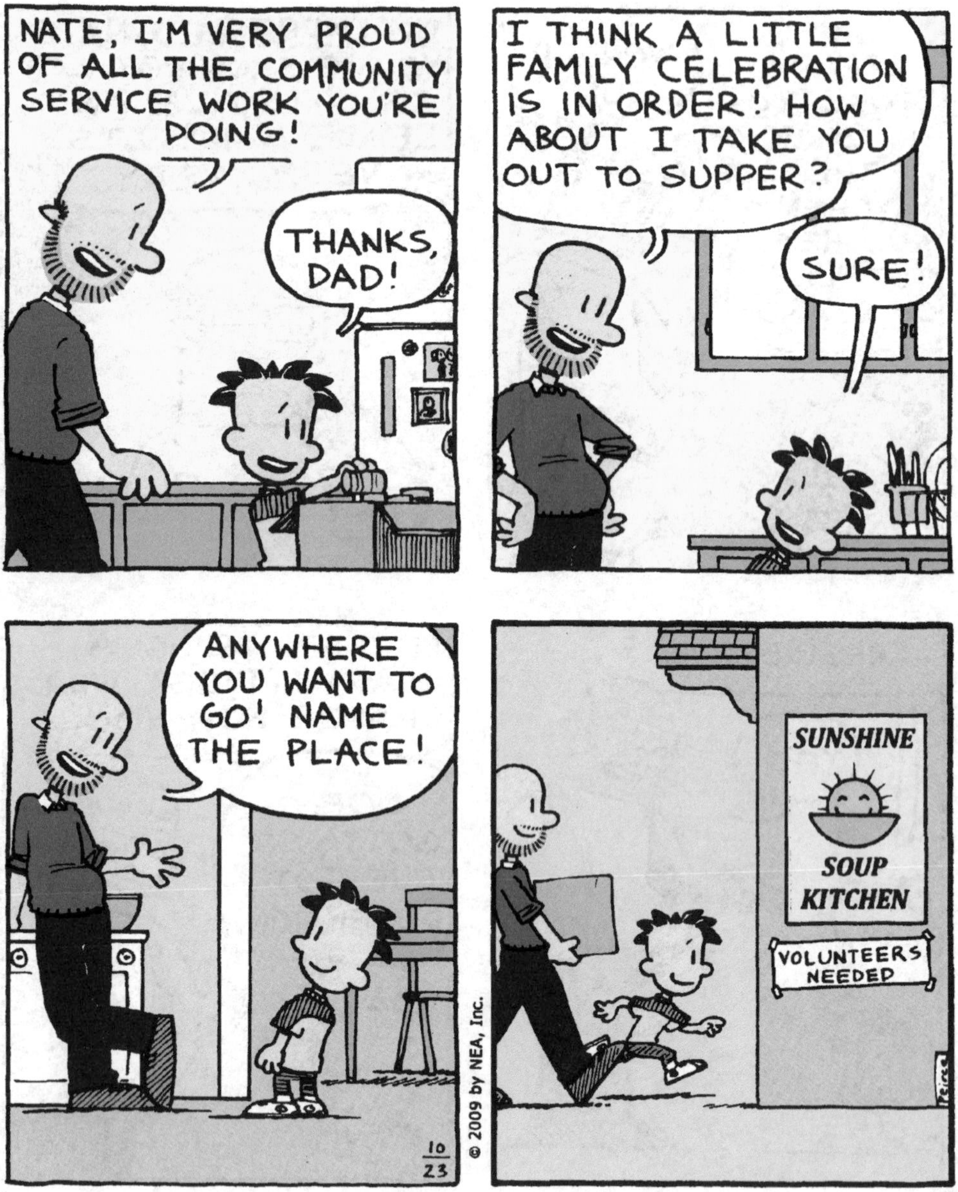
NATE, I'M VERY PROUD OF ALL THE COMMUNITY SERVICE WORK YOU'RE DOING!
THANKS, DAD!
I THINK A LITTLE FAMILY CELEBRATION IS IN ORDER! HOW ABOUT I TAKE YOU OUT TO SUPPER?
SURE!
ANYWHERE YOU WANT TO GO! NAME THE PLACE!
10 23
© 2009 by NEA, Inc.
SUNSHINE
SOUP KITCHEN
VOLUNTEERS NEEDED
Peirce

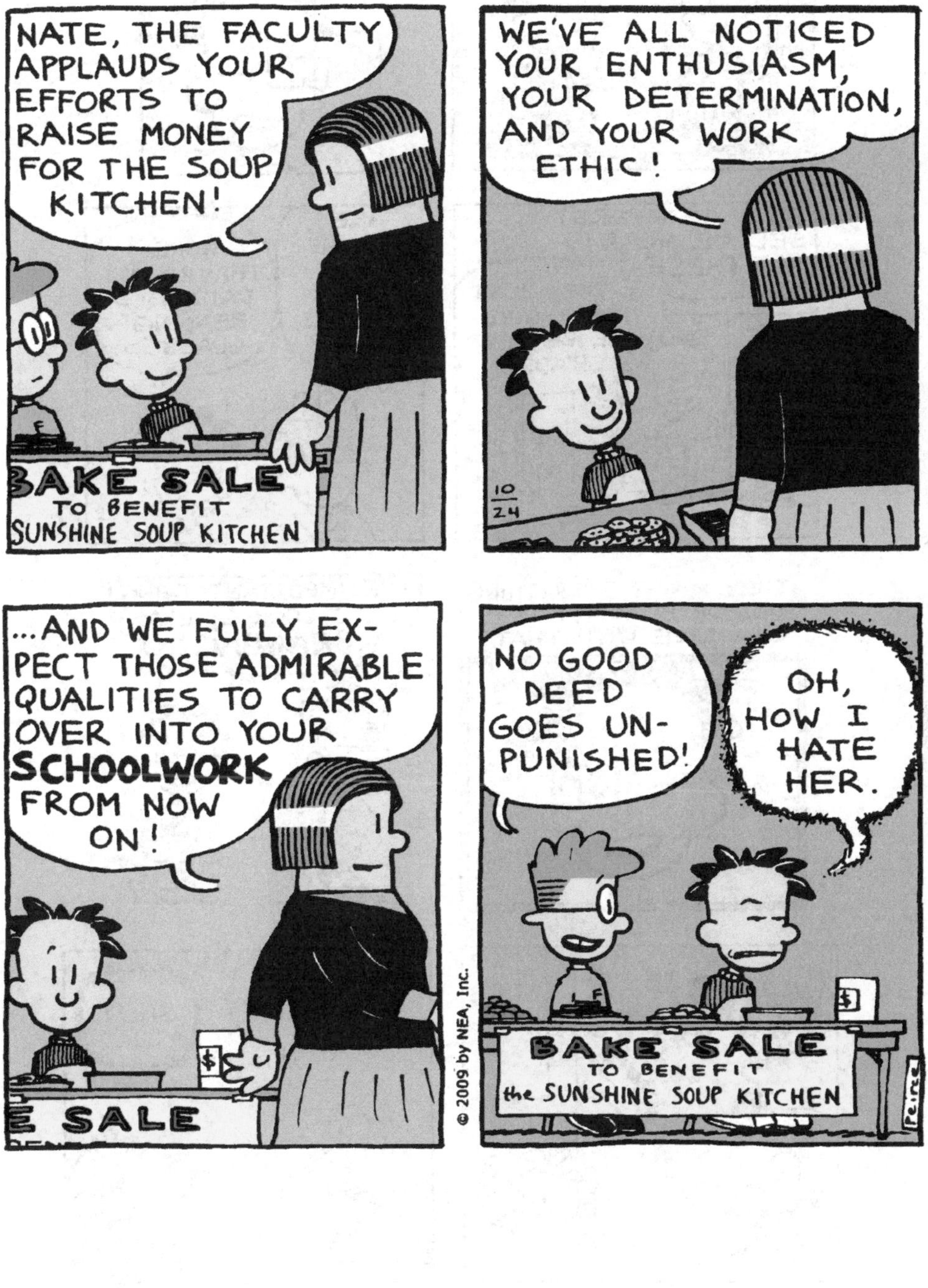
NATE, THE FACULTY APPLAUDS YOUR EFFORTS TO RAISE MONEY FOR THE SOUP KITCHEN!
BAKE SALE TO BENEFIT SUNSHINE SOUP KITCHEN
WE'VE ALL NOTICED YOUR ENTHUSIASM, YOUR DETERMINATION, AND YOUR WORK ETHIC!
10 24
...AND WE FULLY EXPECT THOSE ADMIRABLE QUALITIES TO CARRY OVER INTO YOUR **SCHOOLWORK** FROM NOW ON!
$
E SALE
© 2009 by NEA, Inc.
NO GOOD DEED GOES UNPUNISHED!
OH, HOW I HATE HER.
$
BAKE SALE TO BENEFIT the SUNSHINE SOUP KITCHEN
Peirce

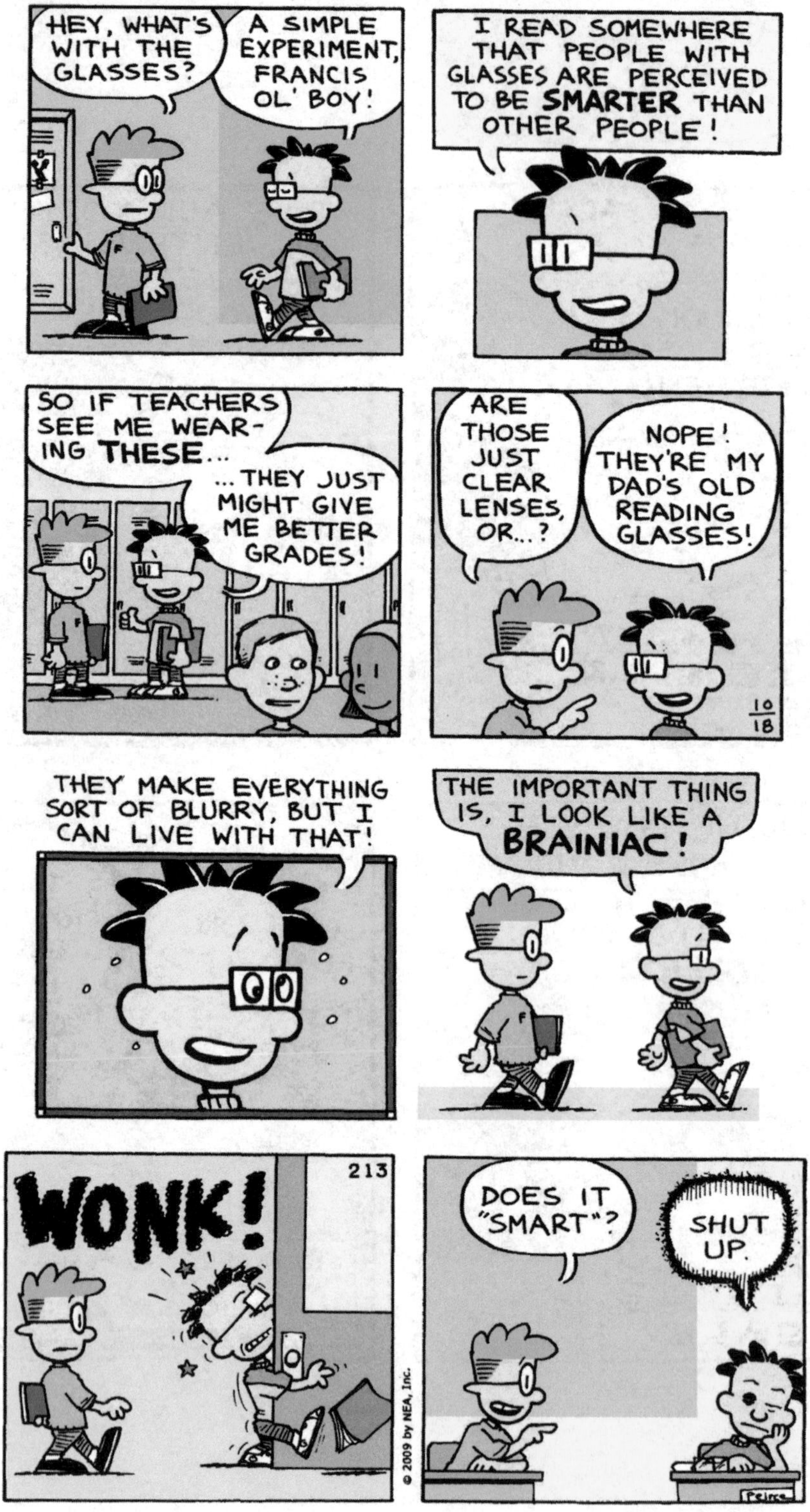
HEY, WHAT'S WITH THE GLASSES?
A SIMPLE EXPERIMENT, FRANCIS OL' BOY!
I READ SOMEWHERE THAT PEOPLE WITH GLASSES ARE PERCEIVED TO BE **SMARTER** THAN OTHER PEOPLE!
SO IF TEACHERS SEE ME WEARING **THESE**...
...THEY JUST MIGHT GIVE ME BETTER GRADES!
ARE THOSE JUST CLEAR LENSES, OR...?
NOPE! THEY'RE MY DAD'S OLD READING GLASSES!
10/18
THEY MAKE EVERYTHING SORT OF BLURRY, BUT I CAN LIVE WITH THAT!
THE IMPORTANT THING IS, I LOOK LIKE A **BRAINIAC**!
WONK!
213
© 2009 by NEA, Inc.
DOES IT "SMART"?
SHUT UP.
Peirce

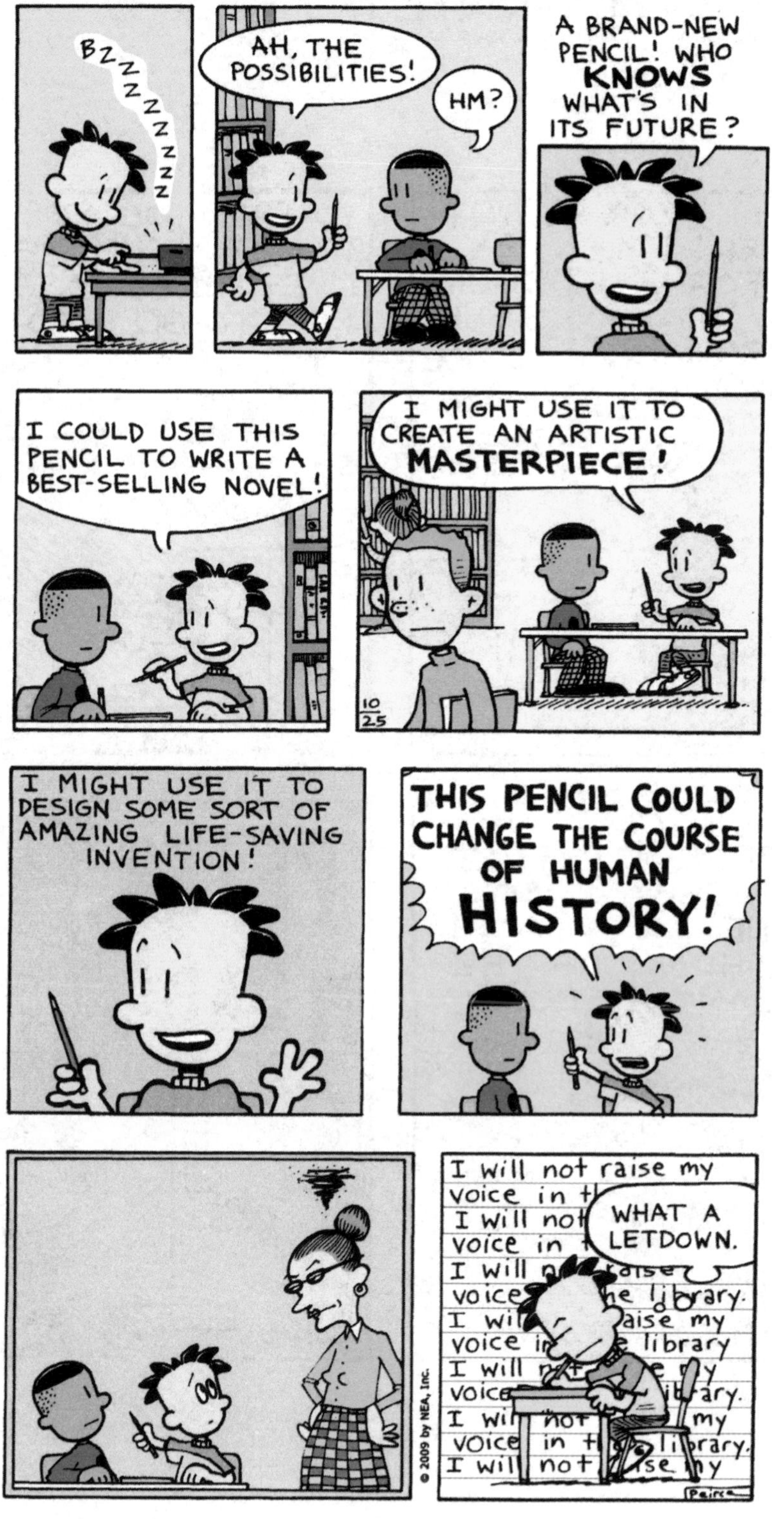
BZZZZZZZZZ
AH, THE POSSIBILITIES!
HM?
A BRAND-NEW PENCIL! WHO KNOWS WHAT'S IN ITS FUTURE?
I COULD USE THIS PENCIL TO WRITE A BEST-SELLING NOVEL!
I MIGHT USE IT TO CREATE AN ARTISTIC MASTERPIECE!
10 25
I MIGHT USE IT TO DESIGN SOME SORT OF AMAZING LIFE-SAVING INVENTION!
THIS PENCIL COULD CHANGE THE COURSE OF HUMAN HISTORY!
© 2009 by NEA, Inc.
I will not raise my voice in the library.
WHAT A LETDOWN.
Peirce

TRICKED OUT

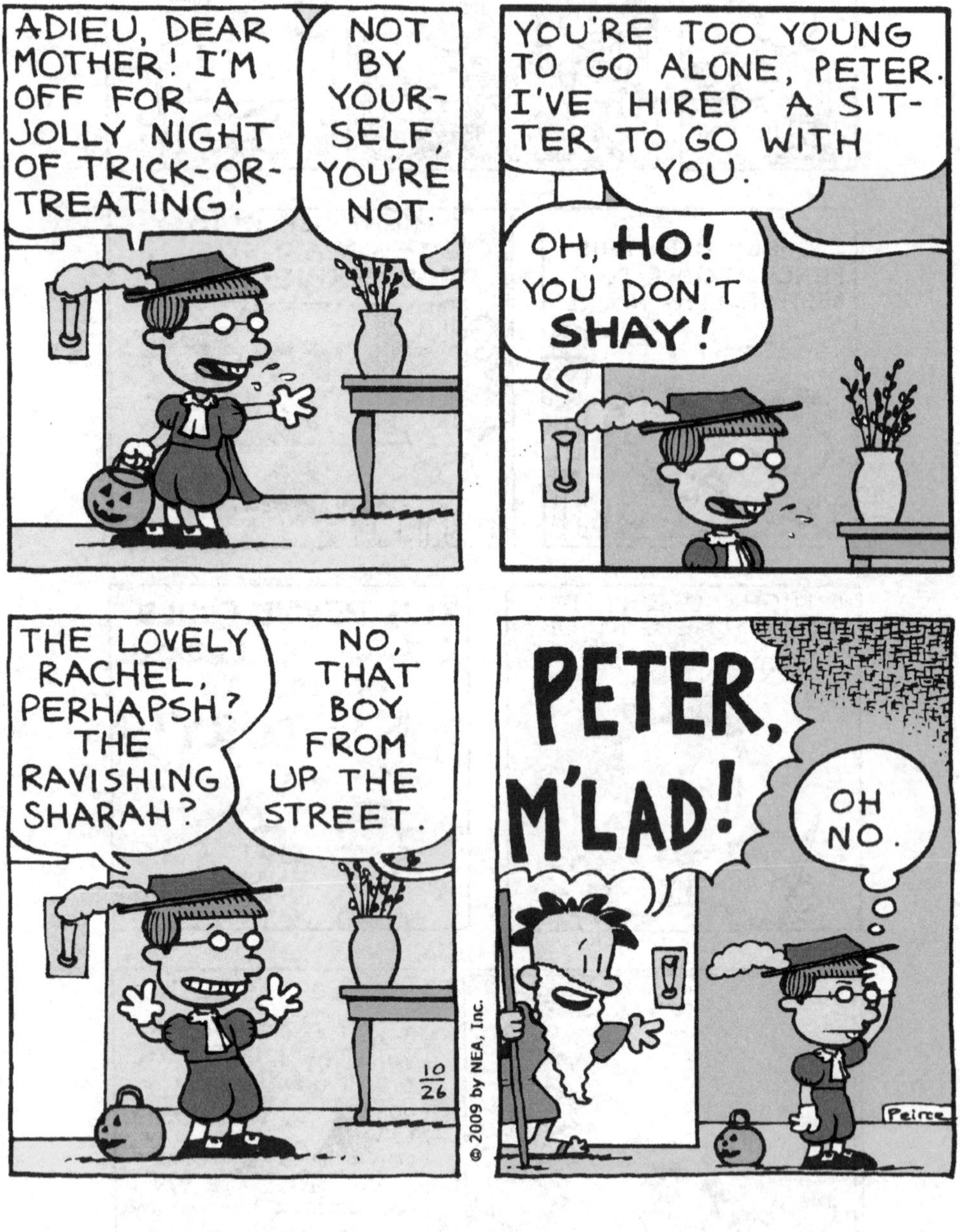
ADIEU, DEAR MOTHER! I'M OFF FOR A JOLLY NIGHT OF TRICK-OR-TREATING!
NOT BY YOUR-SELF, YOU'RE NOT.
YOU'RE TOO YOUNG TO GO ALONE, PETER. I'VE HIRED A SIT-TER TO GO WITH YOU.
OH, HO! YOU DON'T SHAY!
THE LOVELY RACHEL, PERHAPSH? THE RAVISHING SHARAH?
NO, THAT BOY FROM UP THE STREET.
PETER, M'LAD!
OH NO.
10/26
© 2009 by NEA, Inc.
Peirce

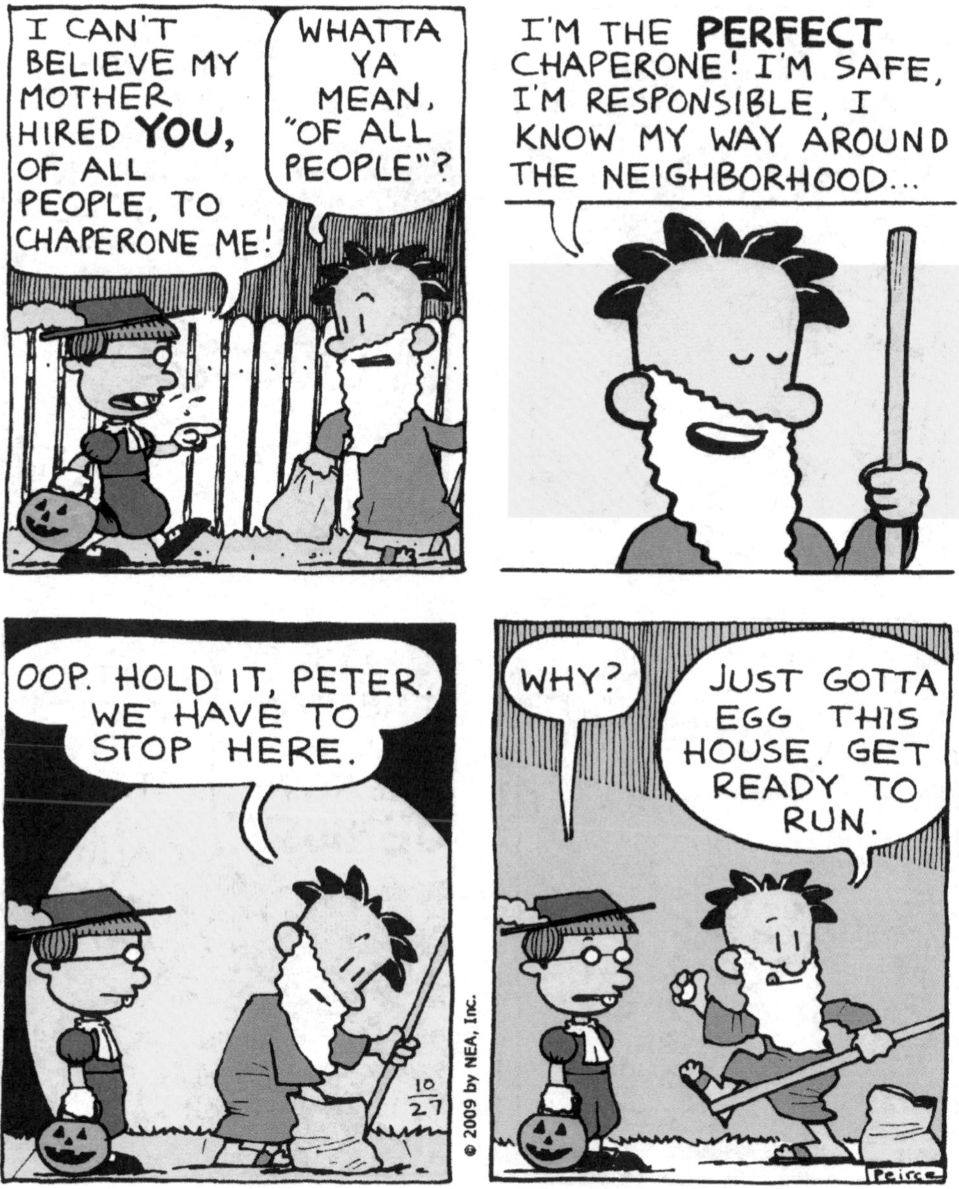
I CAN'T BELIEVE MY MOTHER HIRED **YOU**, OF ALL PEOPLE, TO CHAPERONE ME!
WHATTA YA MEAN, "OF ALL PEOPLE"?
I'M THE **PERFECT** CHAPERONE! I'M SAFE, I'M RESPONSIBLE, I KNOW MY WAY AROUND THE NEIGHBORHOOD...
OOP. HOLD IT, PETER. WE HAVE TO STOP HERE.
10 27
© 2009 by NEA, Inc.
WHY?
JUST GOTTA EGG THIS HOUSE. GET READY TO RUN.
Peirce

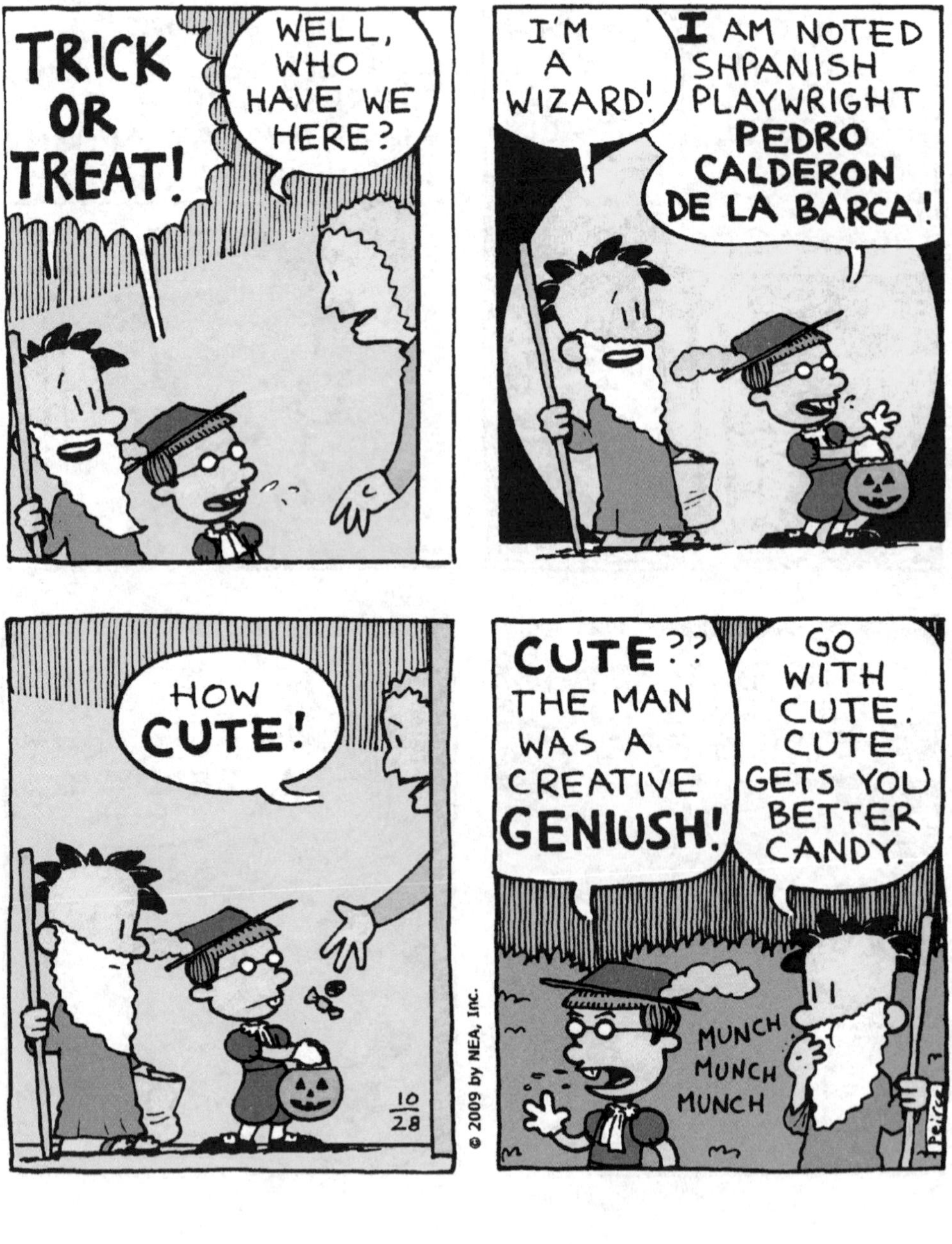
TRICK OR TREAT!
WELL, WHO HAVE WE HERE?
I'M A WIZARD!
I AM NOTED SHPANISH PLAYWRIGHT PEDRO CALDERON DE LA BARCA!
HOW CUTE!
10 28
CUTE?? THE MAN WAS A CREATIVE GENIUSH!
GO WITH CUTE. CUTE GETS YOU BETTER CANDY.
MUNCH MUNCH MUNCH
Peirce

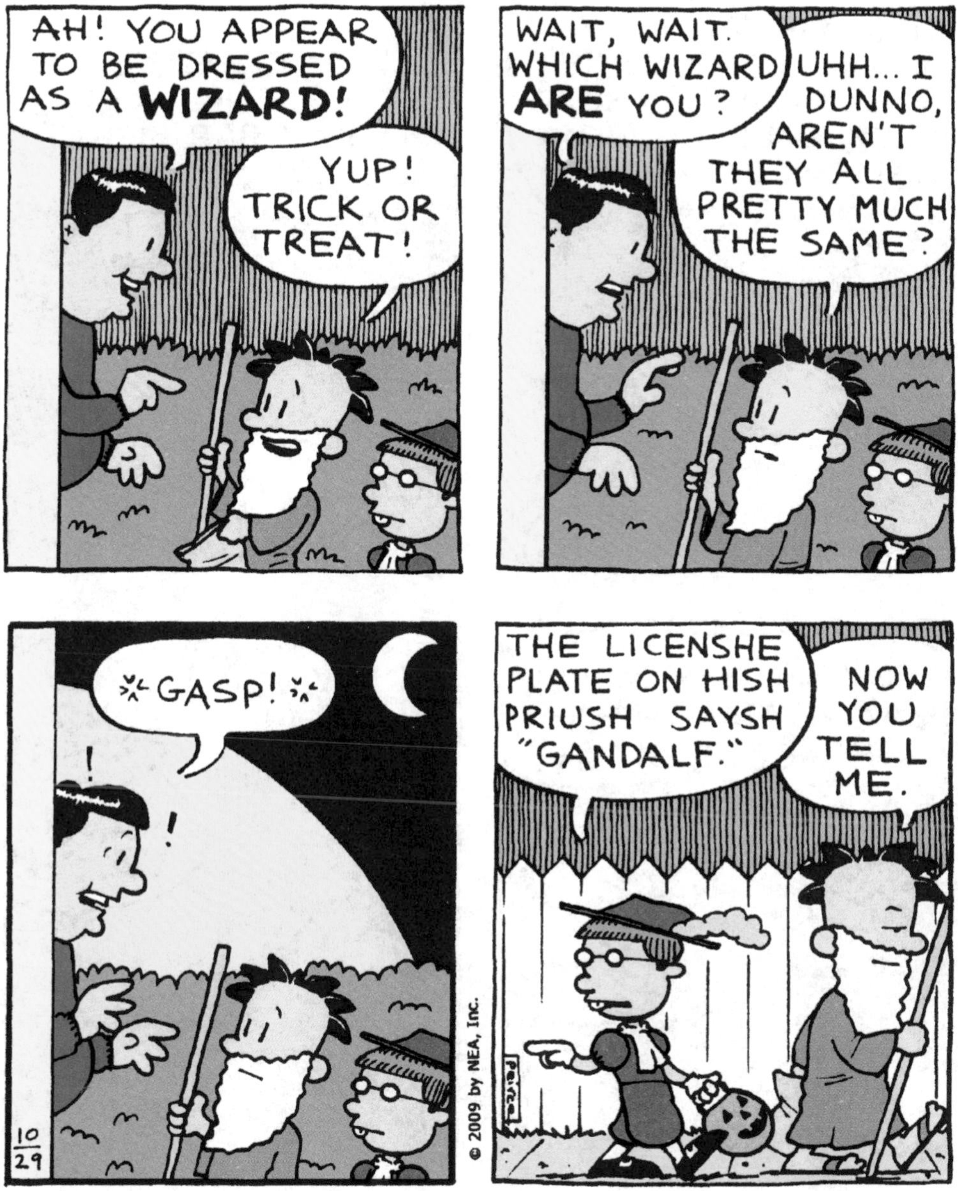
AH! YOU APPEAR TO BE DRESSED AS A **WIZARD**!
YUP! TRICK OR TREAT!
WAIT, WAIT. WHICH WIZARD **ARE** YOU?
UHH... I DUNNO, AREN'T THEY ALL PRETTY MUCH THE SAME?
GASP!
!
!
THE LICENSHE PLATE ON HISH PRIUSH SAYSH "GANDALF."
NOW YOU TELL ME.
10/29
© 2009 by NEA, Inc.
Peirce

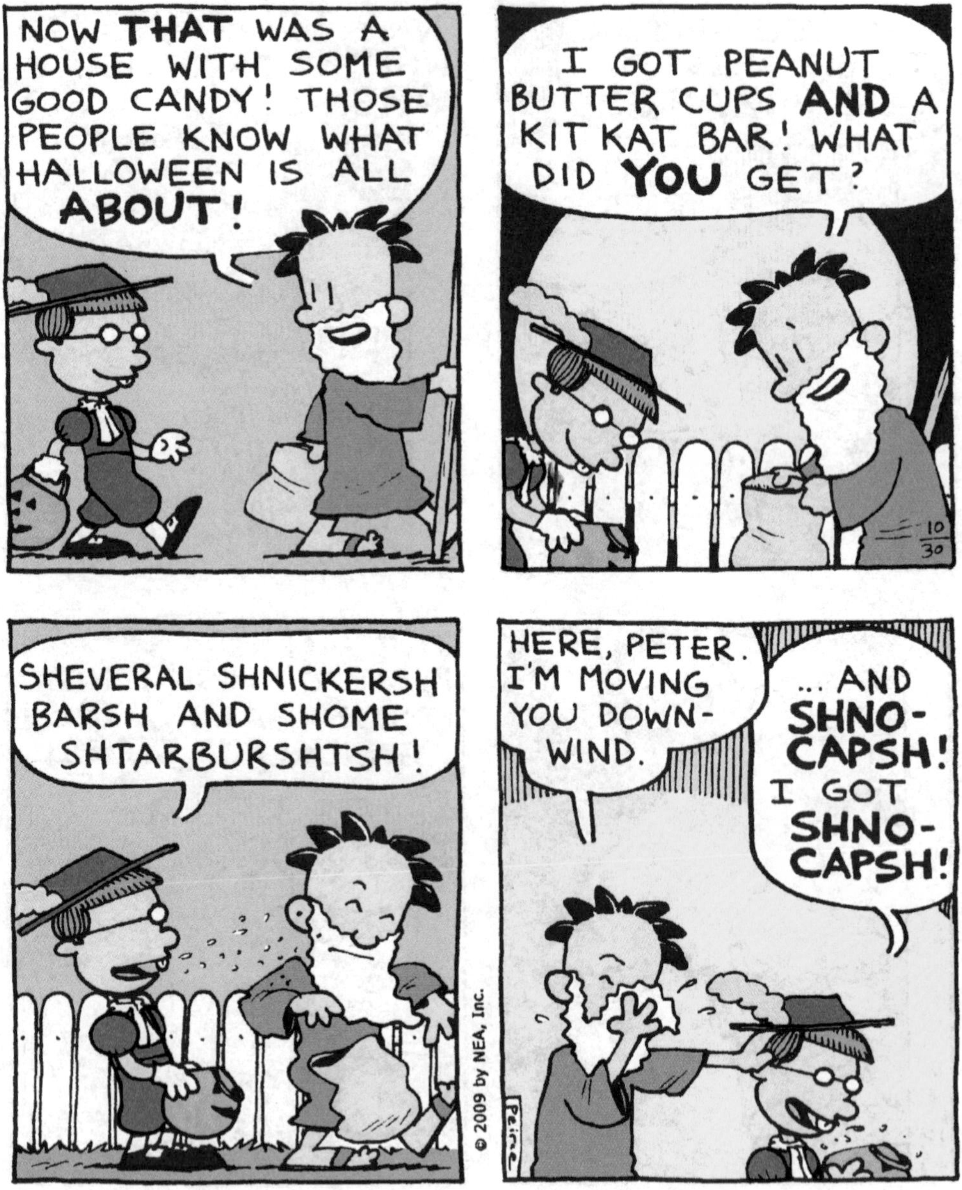
NOW THAT WAS A HOUSE WITH SOME GOOD CANDY! THOSE PEOPLE KNOW WHAT HALLOWEEN IS ALL ABOUT!
I GOT PEANUT BUTTER CUPS AND A KIT KAT BAR! WHAT DID YOU GET?
10/30
SHEVERAL SHNICKERSH BARSH AND SHOME SHTARBURSHTSH!
© 2009 by NEA, Inc.
Peirce
HERE, PETER. I'M MOVING YOU DOWN-WIND.
... AND SHNO-CAPSH! I GOT SHNO-CAPSH!

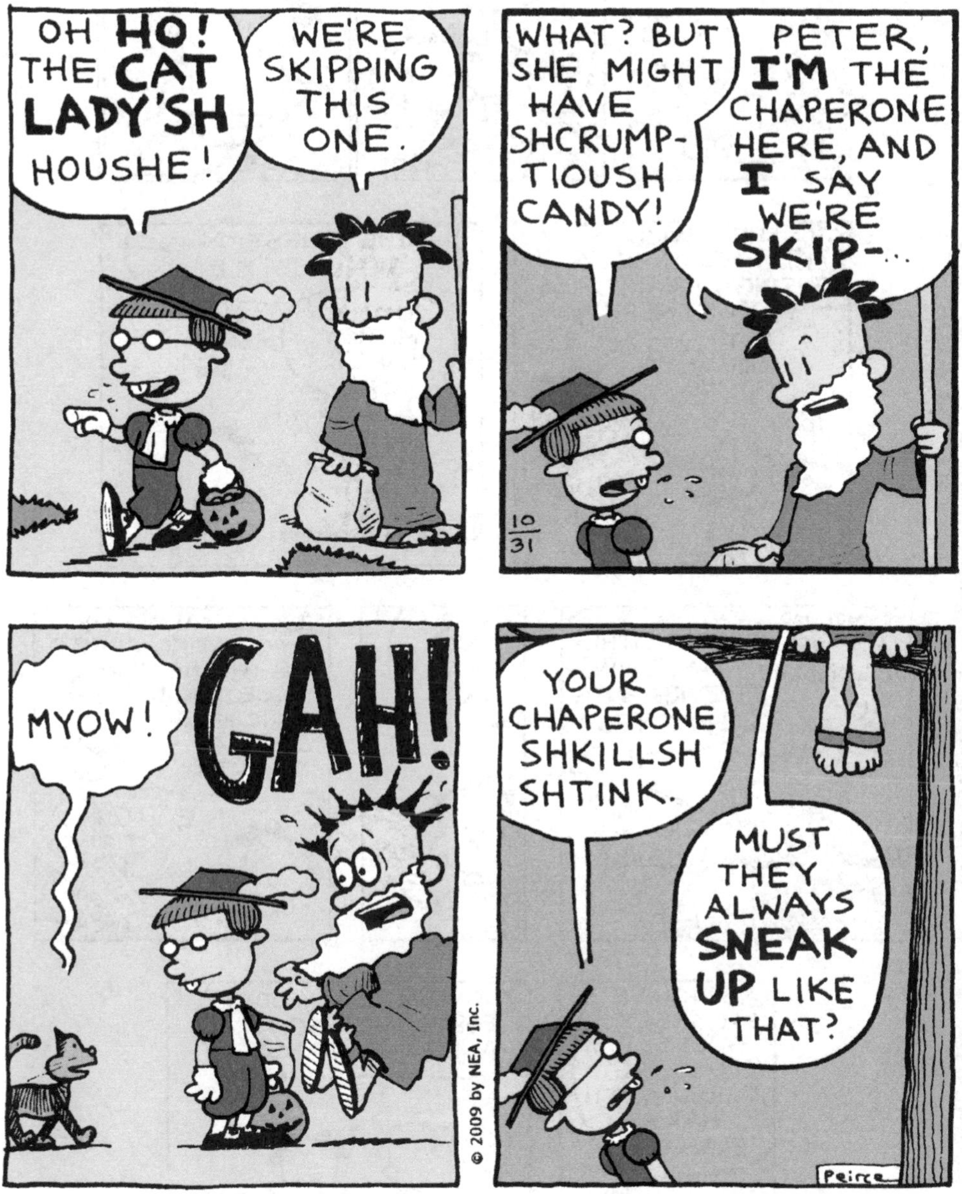

OH HO! THE CAT LADY'SH HOUSHE!
WE'RE SKIPPING THIS ONE.
WHAT? BUT SHE MIGHT HAVE SHCRUMP-TIOUSH CANDY!
PETER, I'M THE CHAPERONE HERE, AND I SAY WE'RE SKIP-...
10/31
MYOW!
GAH!
YOUR CHAPERONE SHKILLSH SHTINK.
MUST THEY ALWAYS SNEAK UP LIKE THAT?
Peirce

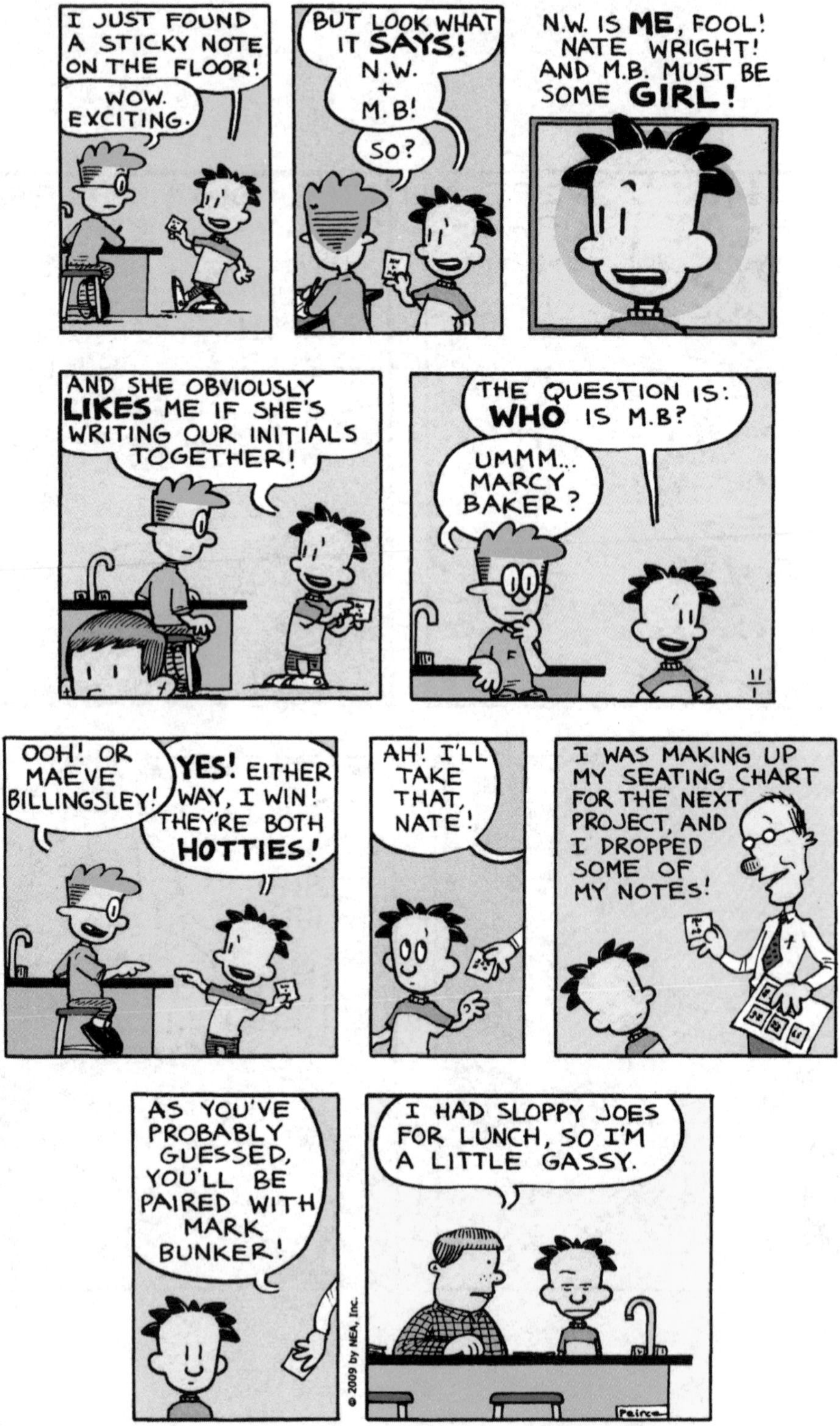
I JUST FOUND A STICKY NOTE ON THE FLOOR!
WOW. EXCITING.
BUT LOOK WHAT IT SAYS! N.W. + M.B!
SO?
N.W. IS ME, FOOL! NATE WRIGHT! AND M.B. MUST BE SOME GIRL!
AND SHE OBVIOUSLY LIKES ME IF SHE'S WRITING OUR INITIALS TOGETHER!
THE QUESTION IS: WHO IS M.B?
UMMM... MARCY BAKER?
OOH! OR MAEVE BILLINGSLEY!
YES! EITHER WAY, I WIN! THEY'RE BOTH HOTTIES!
AH! I'LL TAKE THAT, NATE!
I WAS MAKING UP MY SEATING CHART FOR THE NEXT PROJECT, AND I DROPPED SOME OF MY NOTES!
AS YOU'VE PROBABLY GUESSED, YOU'LL BE PAIRED WITH MARK BUNKER!
© 2009 by NEA, Inc.
I HAD SLOPPY JOES FOR LUNCH, SO I'M A LITTLE GASSY.
Peirce

MR. FANCY-PANTS

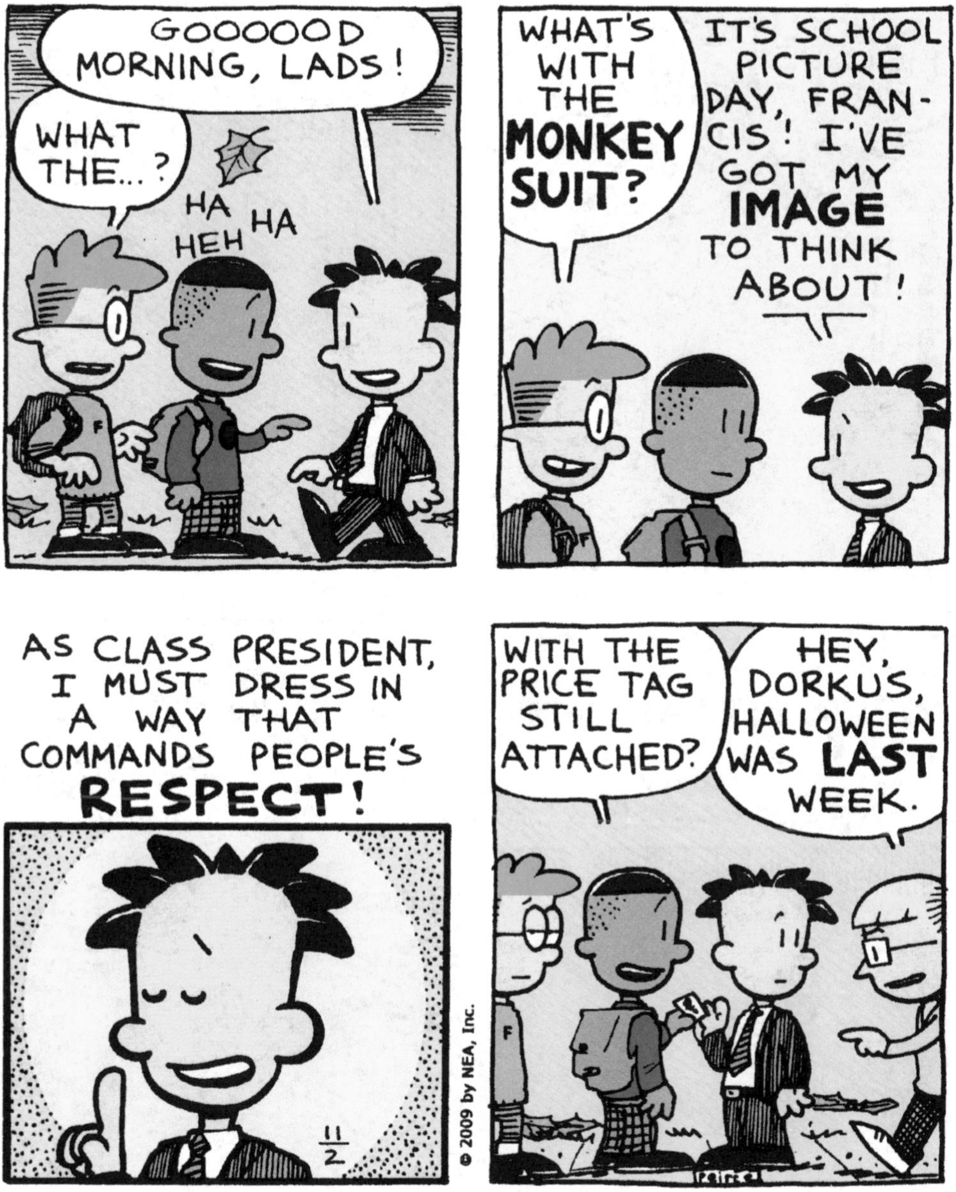
GOOOOOD MORNING, LADS!
WHAT THE...?
HA HEH HA
WHAT'S WITH THE **MONKEY SUIT**?
IT'S SCHOOL PICTURE DAY, FRANCIS! I'VE GOT MY **IMAGE** TO THINK ABOUT!
AS CLASS PRESIDENT, I MUST DRESS IN A WAY THAT COMMANDS PEOPLE'S **RESPECT**!
11/2
© 2009 by NEA, Inc.
WITH THE PRICE TAG STILL ATTACHED?
HEY, DORKUS, HALLOWEEN WAS **LAST** WEEK.

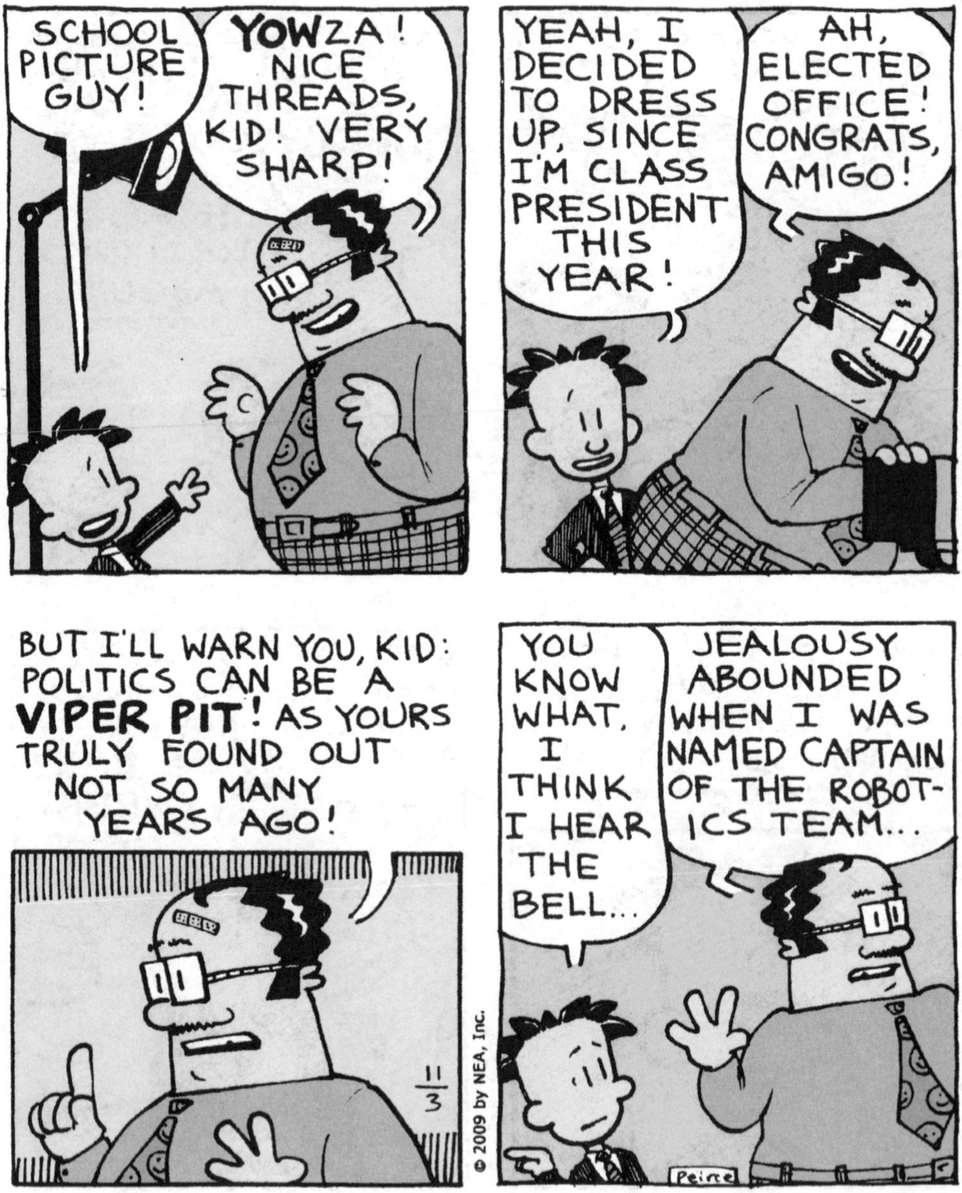
SCHOOL PICTURE GUY!
YOWZA! NICE THREADS, KID! VERY SHARP!
YEAH, I DECIDED TO DRESS UP, SINCE I'M CLASS PRESIDENT THIS YEAR!
AH, ELECTED OFFICE! CONGRATS, AMIGO!
BUT I'LL WARN YOU, KID: POLITICS CAN BE A VIPER PIT! AS YOURS TRULY FOUND OUT NOT SO MANY YEARS AGO!
JEALOUSY ABOUNDED WHEN I WAS NAMED CAPTAIN OF THE ROBOTICS TEAM...
YOU KNOW WHAT, I THINK I HEAR THE BELL...
11/3
© 2009 by NEA, Inc.
Peirce

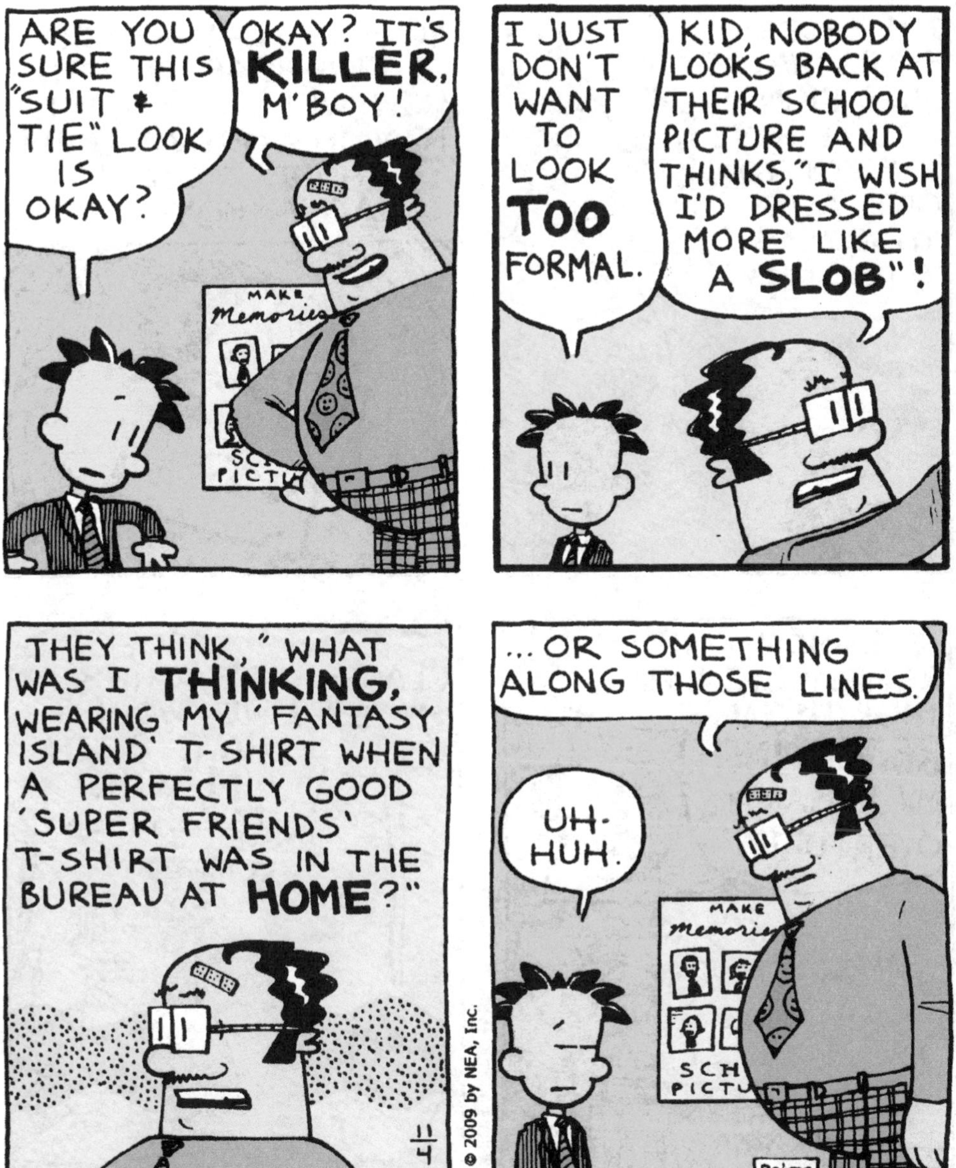
ARE YOU SURE THIS "SUIT & TIE" LOOK IS OKAY?
OKAY? IT'S KILLER, M'BOY!
I JUST DON'T WANT TO LOOK TOO FORMAL.
KID, NOBODY LOOKS BACK AT THEIR SCHOOL PICTURE AND THINKS, "I WISH I'D DRESSED MORE LIKE A SLOB"!
THEY THINK, "WHAT WAS I THINKING, WEARING MY 'FANTASY ISLAND' T-SHIRT WHEN A PERFECTLY GOOD 'SUPER FRIENDS' T-SHIRT WAS IN THE BUREAU AT HOME?"
...OR SOMETHING ALONG THOSE LINES.
UH-HUH.
MAKE Memories
SCH PICTU
11/4
Peirce

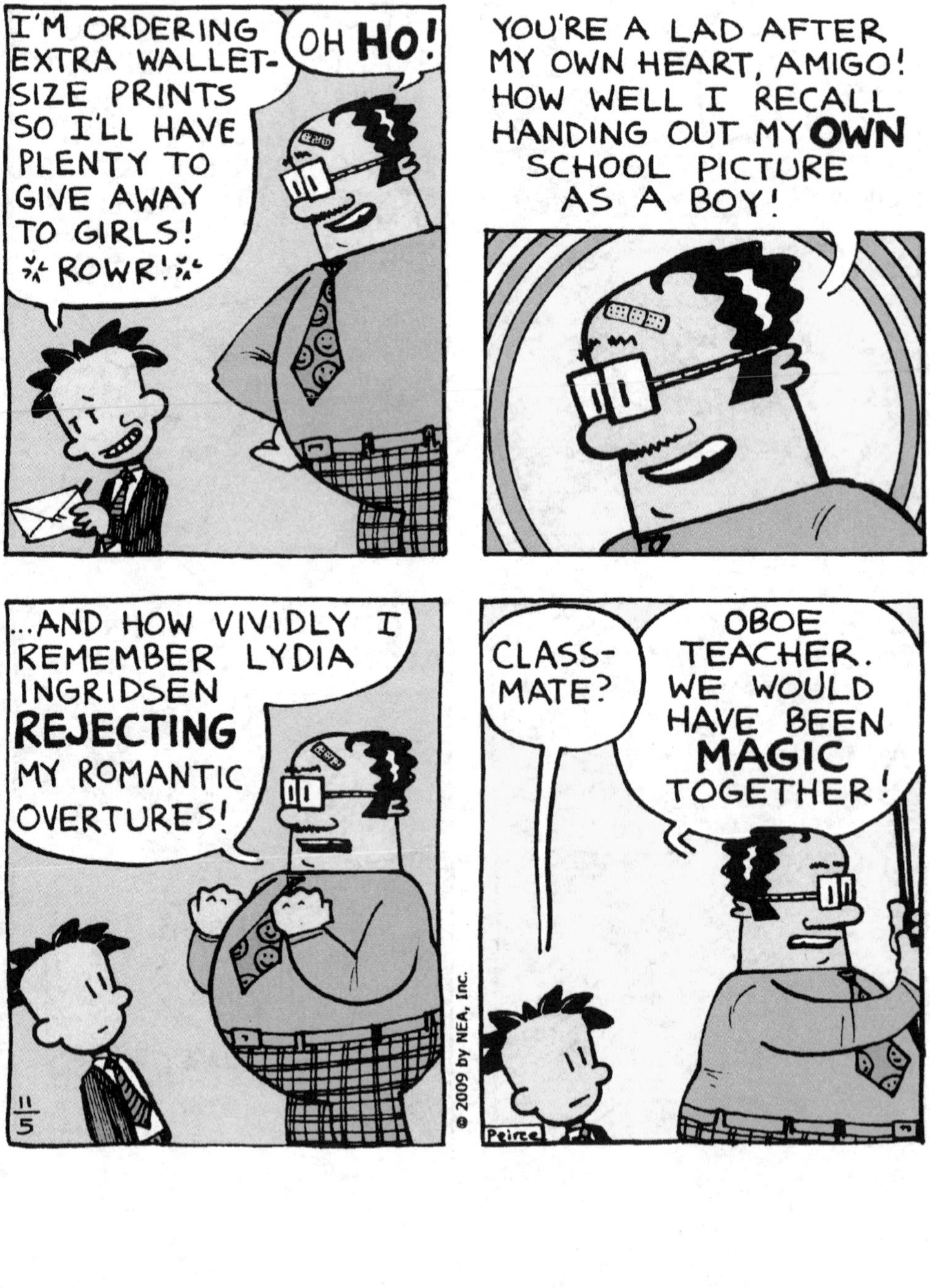
I'M ORDERING EXTRA WALLET-SIZE PRINTS SO I'LL HAVE PLENTY TO GIVE AWAY TO GIRLS! ROWR!
OH HO!
YOU'RE A LAD AFTER MY OWN HEART, AMIGO! HOW WELL I RECALL HANDING OUT MY OWN SCHOOL PICTURE AS A BOY!
...AND HOW VIVIDLY I REMEMBER LYDIA INGRIDSEN REJECTING MY ROMANTIC OVERTURES!
11/5
© 2009 by NEA, Inc.
CLASS-MATE?
OBOE TEACHER. WE WOULD HAVE BEEN MAGIC TOGETHER!
Peirce

NO-MAN'S-LAND

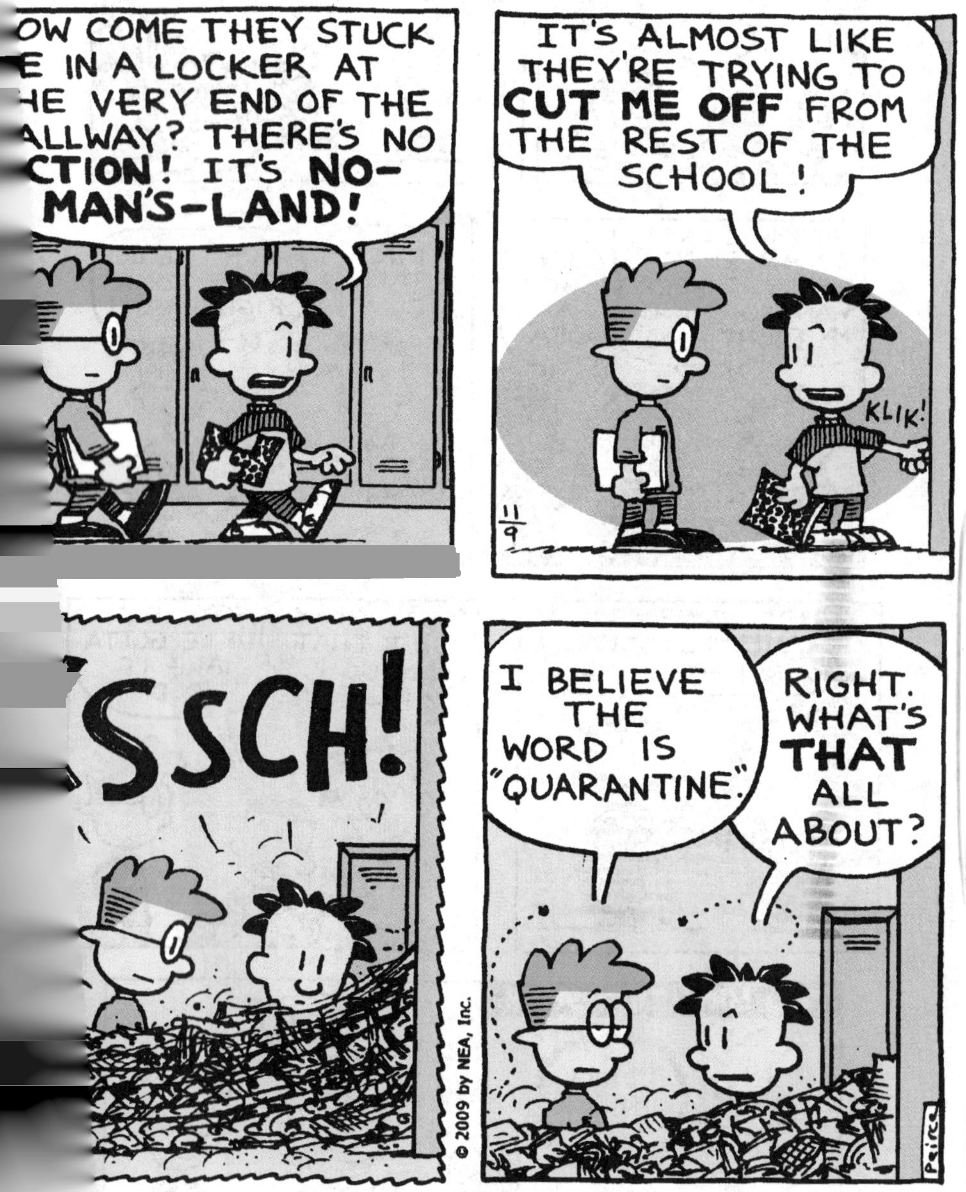
OW COME THEY STUCK
E IN A LOCKER AT
HE VERY END OF THE
ALLWAY? THERE'S NO
CTION! IT'S **NO-
MAN'S-LAND!**
IT'S ALMOST LIKE THEY'RE TRYING TO **CUT ME OFF** FROM THE REST OF THE SCHOOL!
KLIK!
11/9
SSCH!
I BELIEVE THE WORD IS "QUARANTINE".
RIGHT. WHAT'S **THAT** ALL ABOUT?
© 2009 by NEA, Inc.
Peirce

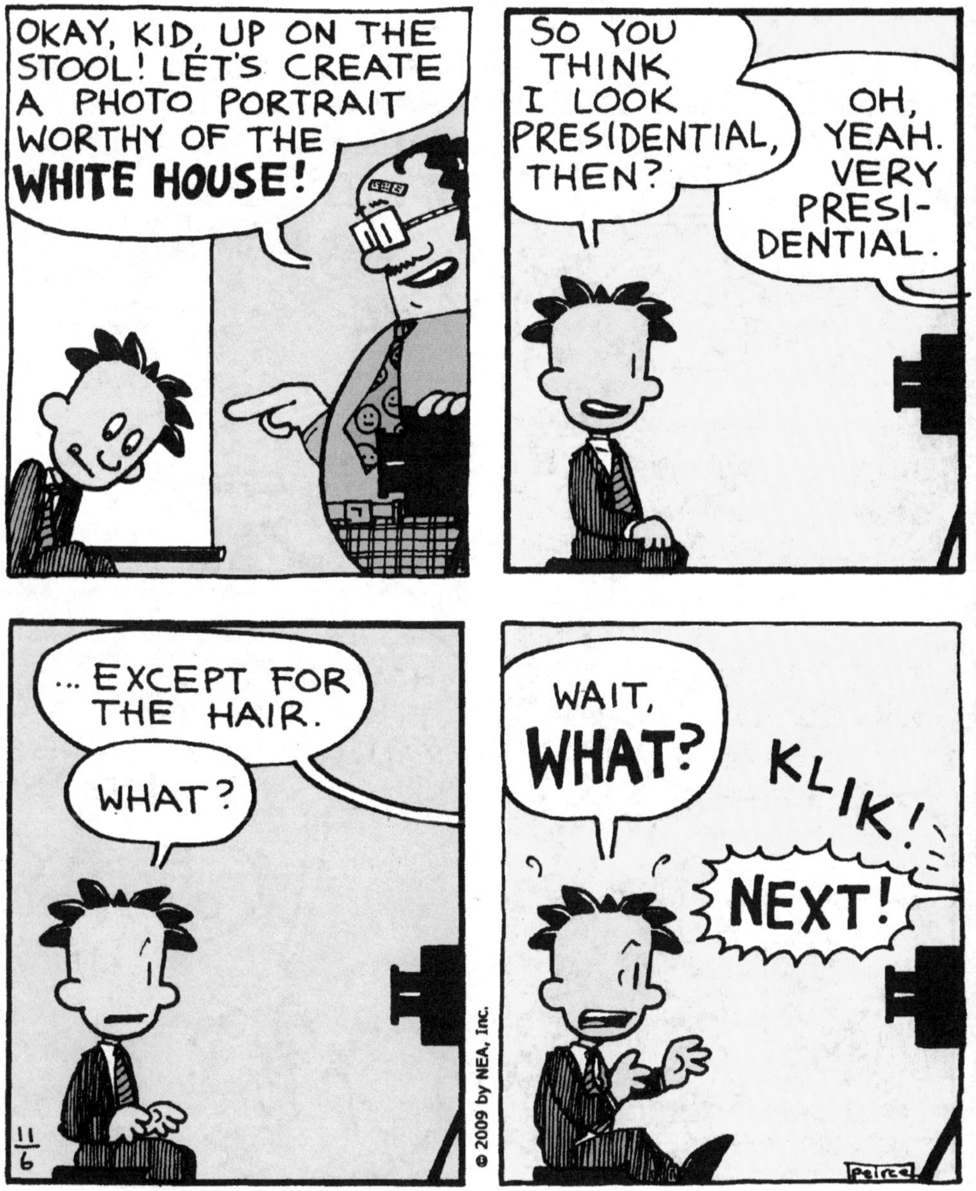
OKAY, KID, UP ON THE STOOL! LET'S CREATE A PHOTO PORTRAIT WORTHY OF THE **WHITE HOUSE!**
SO YOU THINK I LOOK PRESIDENTIAL, THEN?
OH, YEAH. VERY PRESI- DENTIAL.
... EXCEPT FOR THE HAIR.
WHAT?
11/6
WAIT, **WHAT?**
KLIK!
NEXT!
© 2009 by NEA, Inc.
Peirce

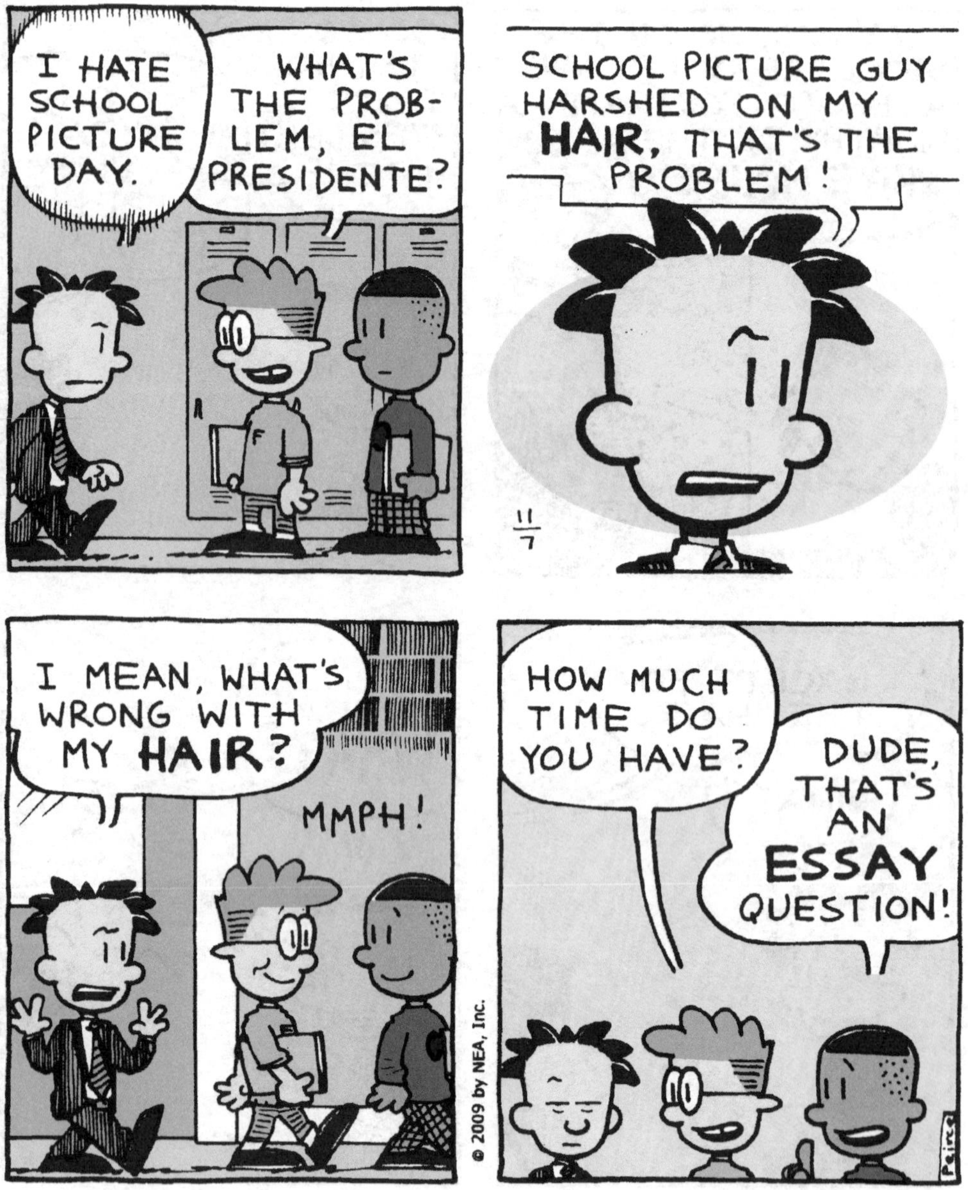
I HATE SCHOOL PICTURE DAY.
WHAT'S THE PROBLEM, EL PRESIDENTE?
SCHOOL PICTURE GUY HARSHED ON MY **HAIR,** THAT'S THE PROBLEM!
11/7
I MEAN, WHAT'S WRONG WITH MY **HAIR?**
MMPH!
HOW MUCH TIME DO YOU HAVE?
DUDE, THAT'S AN **ESSAY** QUESTION!
Peirce

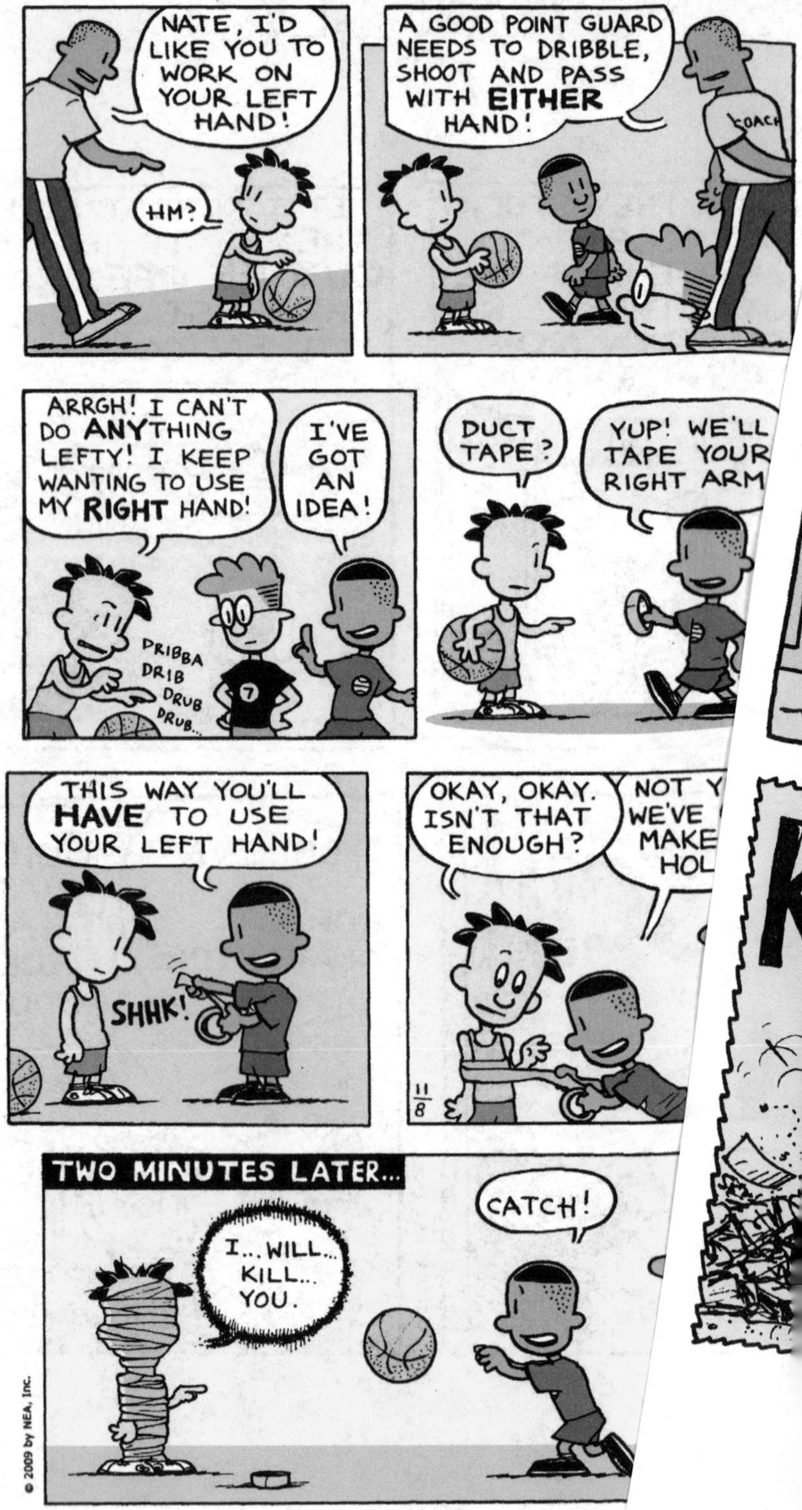
NATE, I'D LIKE YOU TO WORK ON YOUR LEFT HAND!
HM?
A GOOD POINT GUARD NEEDS TO DRIBBLE, SHOOT AND PASS WITH **EITHER** HAND!
COACH
ARRGH! I CAN'T DO **ANY**THING LEFTY! I KEEP WANTING TO USE MY **RIGHT** HAND!
I'VE GOT AN IDEA!
DRIBBA DRIB DRUB DRUB...
DUCT TAPE?
YUP! WE'LL TAPE YOUR RIGHT ARM
THIS WAY YOU'LL **HAVE** TO USE YOUR LEFT HAND!
SHHK!
OKAY, OKAY. ISN'T THAT ENOUGH?
11/8
TWO MINUTES LATER...
I... WILL... KILL... YOU.
CATCH!

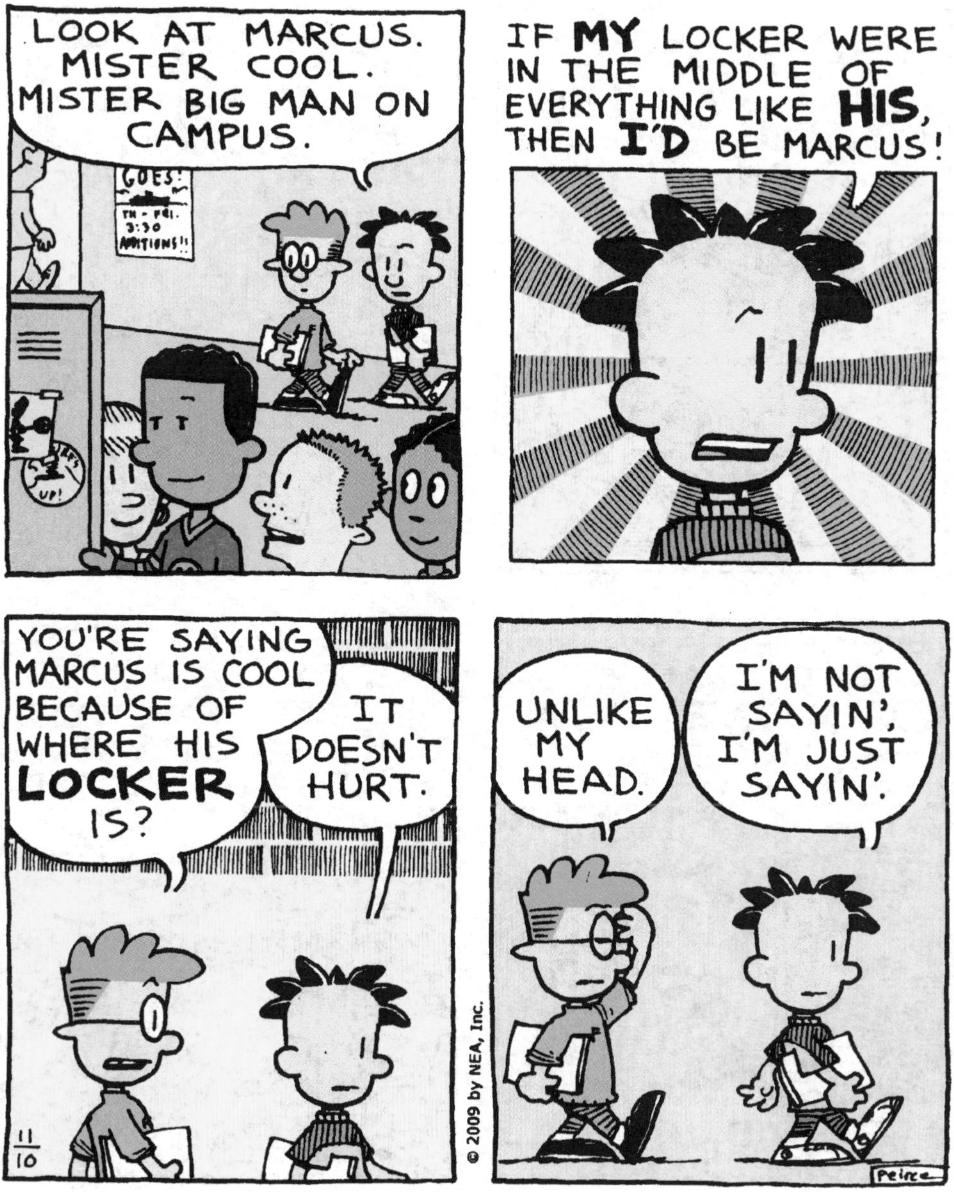
LOOK AT MARCUS. MISTER COOL. MISTER BIG MAN ON CAMPUS.
TH - FRI. 3:30 AUDITIONS!!
IF MY LOCKER WERE IN THE MIDDLE OF EVERYTHING LIKE HIS, THEN I'D BE MARCUS!
YOU'RE SAYING MARCUS IS COOL BECAUSE OF WHERE HIS LOCKER IS?
IT DOESN'T HURT.
11/10
© 2009 by NEA, Inc.
UNLIKE MY HEAD.
I'M NOT SAYIN', I'M JUST SAYIN'.
Peirce

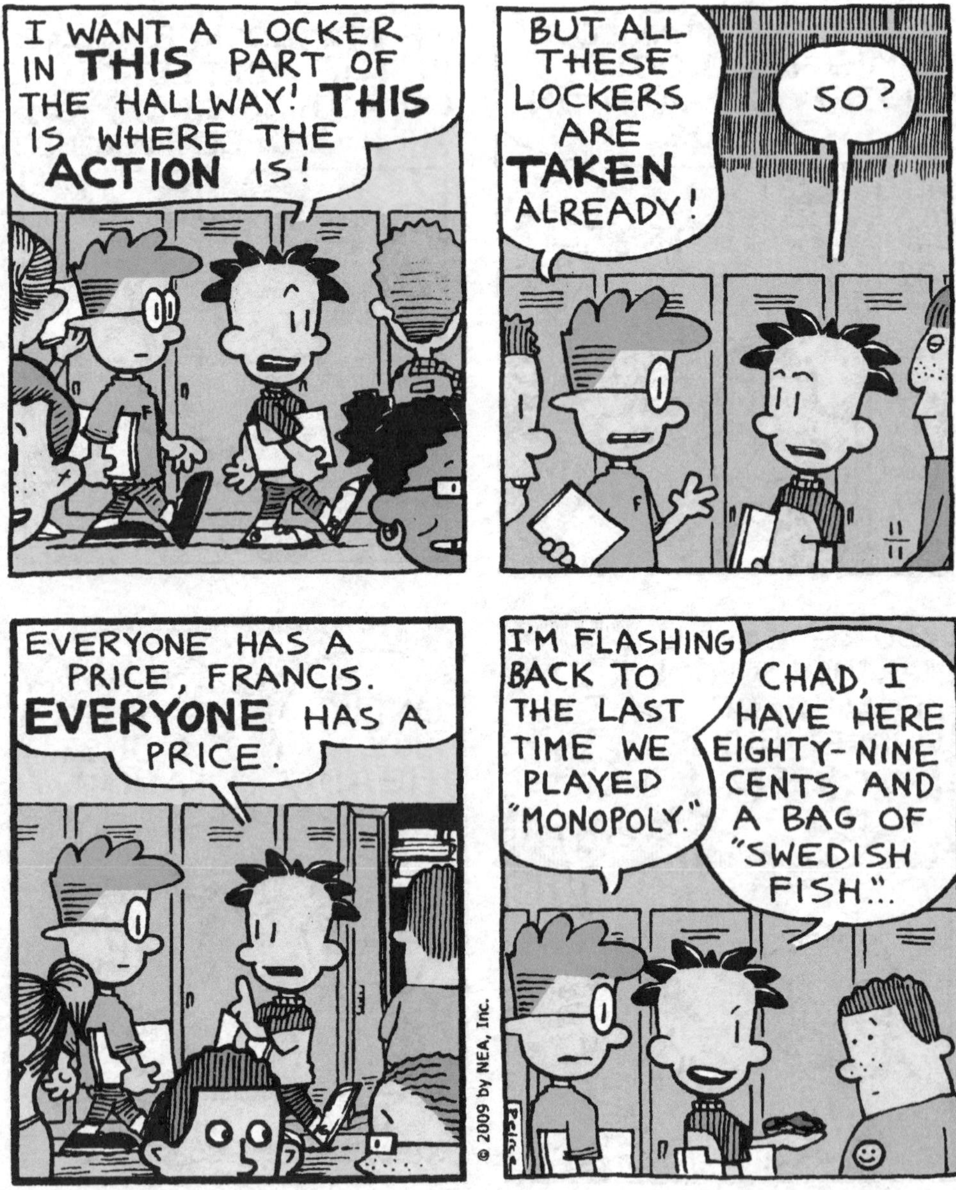
I WANT A LOCKER IN THIS PART OF THE HALLWAY! THIS IS WHERE THE ACTION IS!
BUT ALL THESE LOCKERS ARE TAKEN ALREADY!
SO?
EVERYONE HAS A PRICE, FRANCIS. EVERYONE HAS A PRICE.
I'M FLASHING BACK TO THE LAST TIME WE PLAYED "MONOPOLY."
CHAD, I HAVE HERE EIGHTY-NINE CENTS AND A BAG OF "SWEDISH FISH."
© 2009 by NEA, Inc.

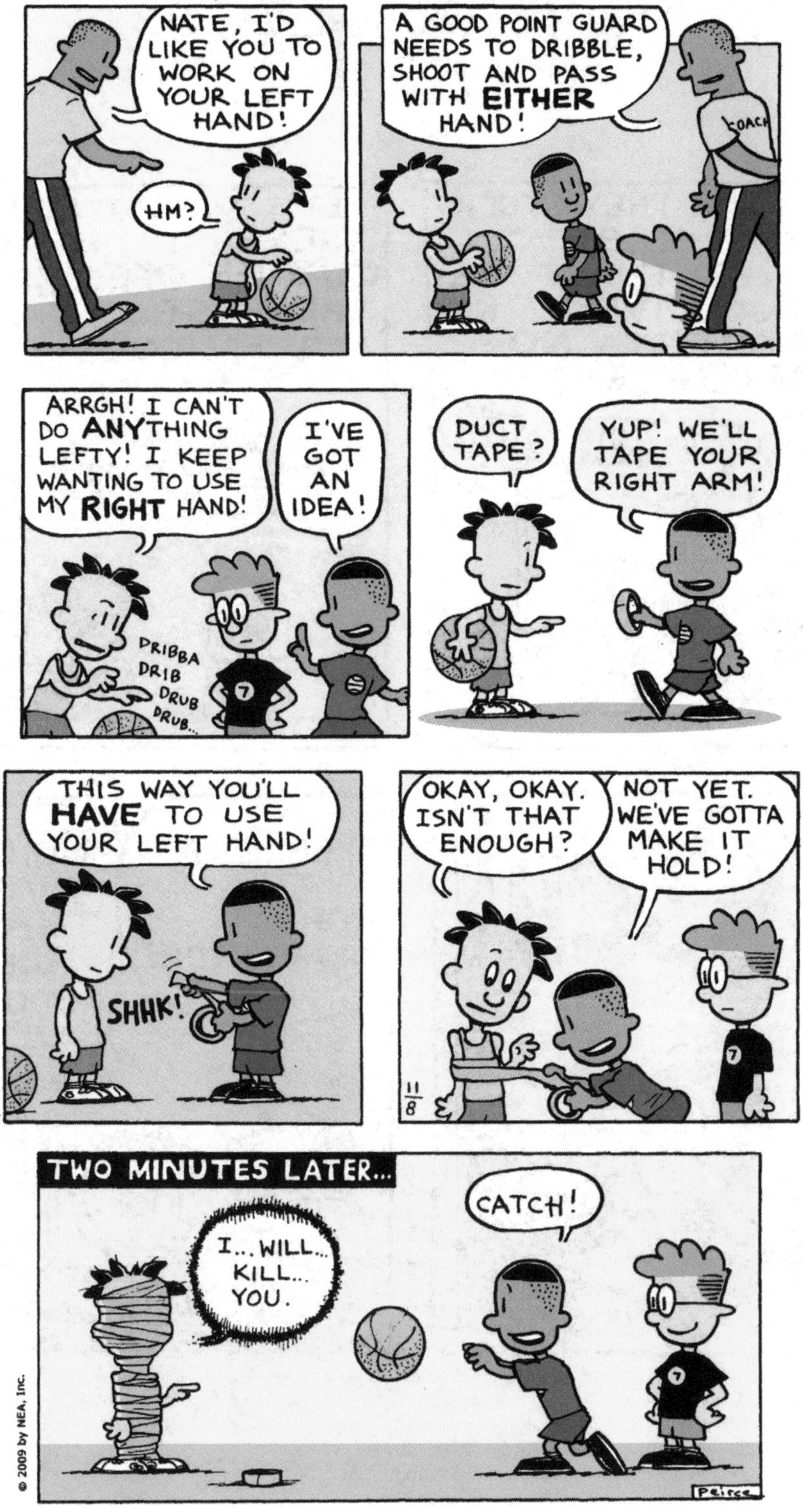
NATE, I'D LIKE YOU TO WORK ON YOUR LEFT HAND!
HM?
A GOOD POINT GUARD NEEDS TO DRIBBLE, SHOOT AND PASS WITH EITHER HAND!
COACH
ARRGH! I CAN'T DO ANYTHING LEFTY! I KEEP WANTING TO USE MY RIGHT HAND!
I'VE GOT AN IDEA!
DRIBBA DRIB DRUB DRUB...
DUCT TAPE?
YUP! WE'LL TAPE YOUR RIGHT ARM!
THIS WAY YOU'LL HAVE TO USE YOUR LEFT HAND!
SHHK!
OKAY, OKAY. ISN'T THAT ENOUGH?
NOT YET. WE'VE GOTTA MAKE IT HOLD!
11/8
TWO MINUTES LATER...
I... WILL... KILL... YOU.
CATCH!
PEIRCE

NO-MAN'S-LAND

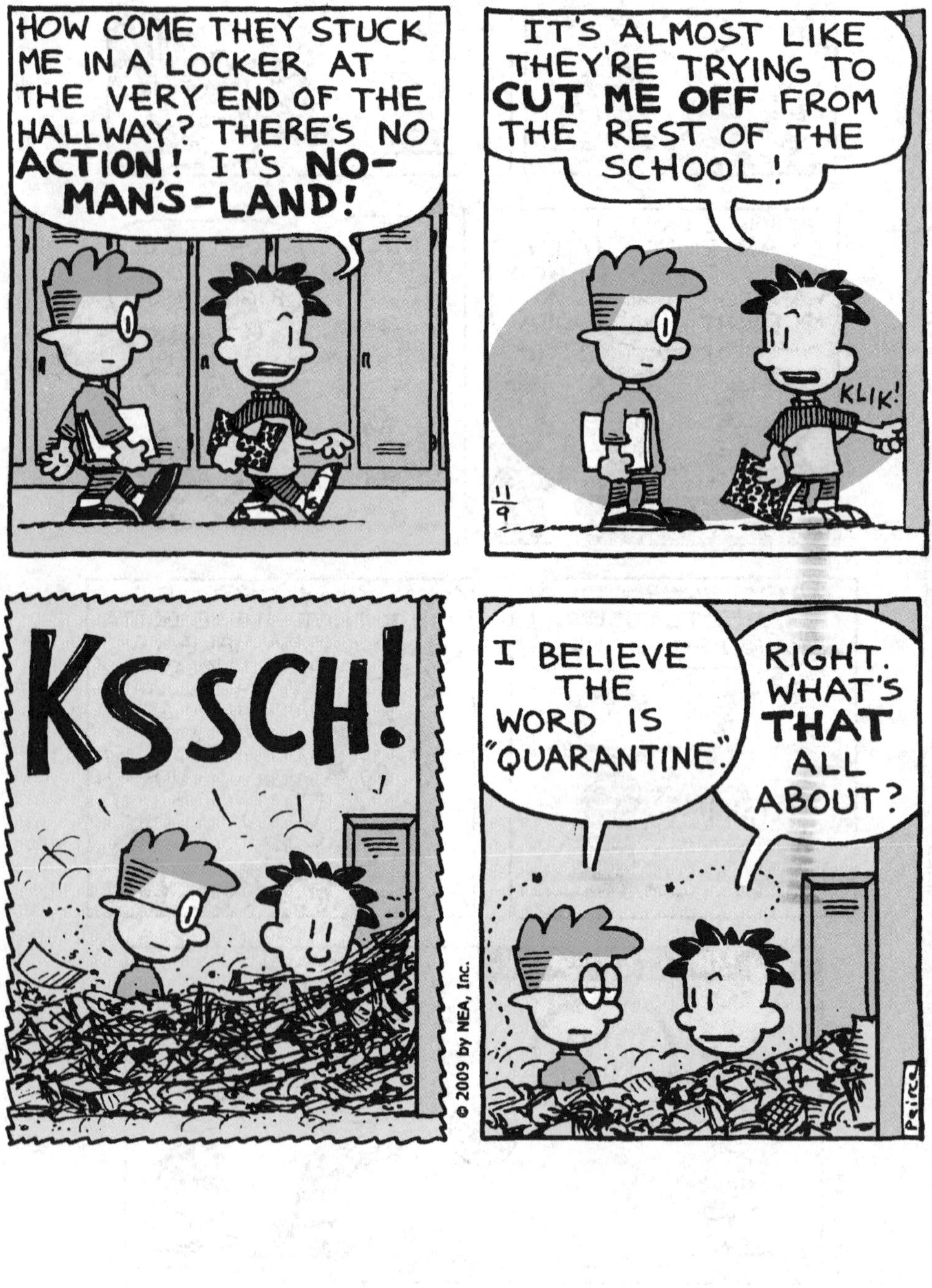
HOW COME THEY STUCK ME IN A LOCKER AT THE VERY END OF THE HALLWAY? THERE'S NO ACTION! IT'S NO-MAN'S-LAND!
IT'S ALMOST LIKE THEY'RE TRYING TO CUT ME OFF FROM THE REST OF THE SCHOOL!
KLIK!
11/9
KSSCH!
© 2009 by NEA, Inc.
I BELIEVE THE WORD IS "QUARANTINE".
RIGHT. WHAT'S THAT ALL ABOUT?
Peirce

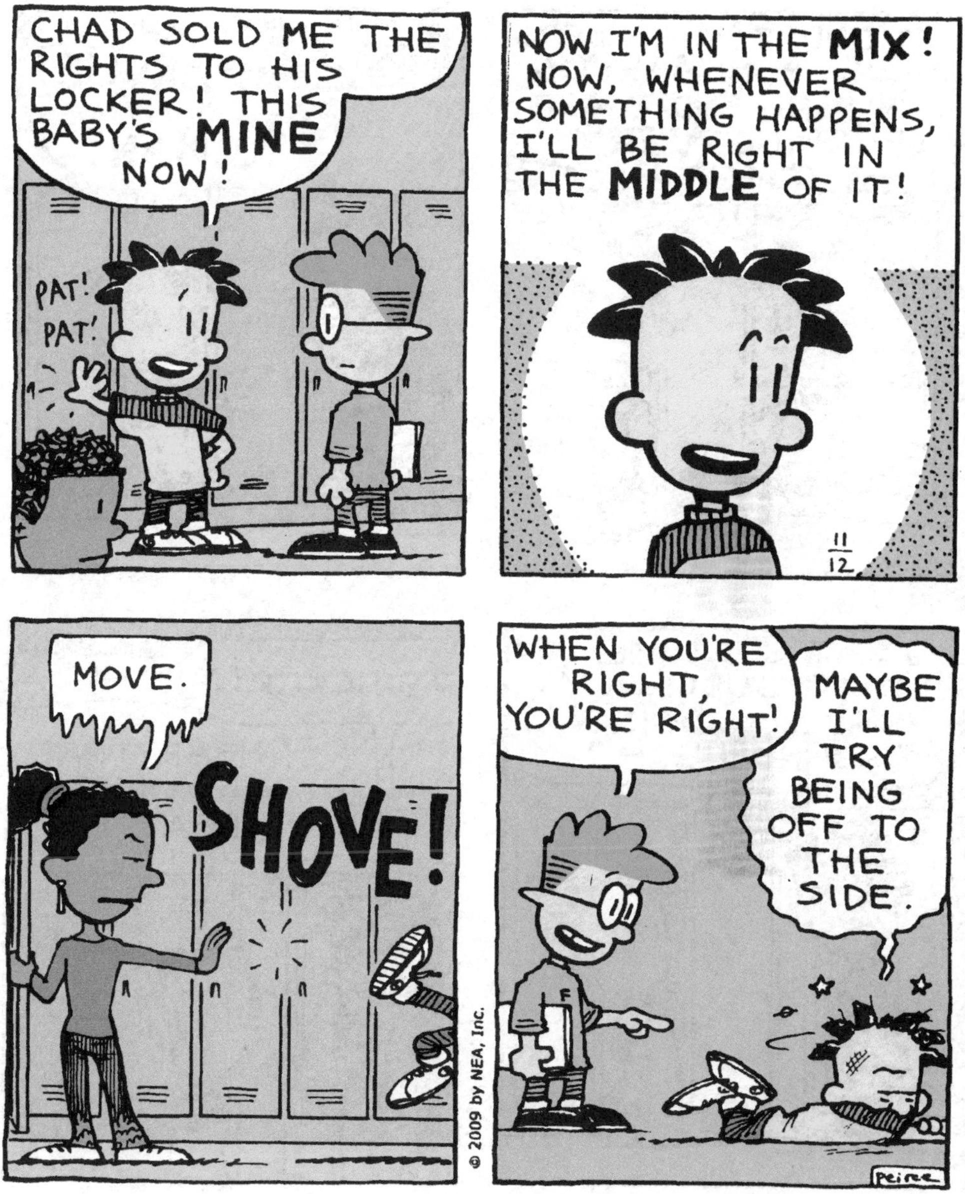
CHAD SOLD ME THE RIGHTS TO HIS LOCKER! THIS BABY'S MINE NOW!
PAT! PAT!
NOW I'M IN THE MIX! NOW, WHENEVER SOMETHING HAPPENS, I'LL BE RIGHT IN THE MIDDLE OF IT!
11/12
MOVE.
SHOVE!
© 2009 by NEA, Inc.
WHEN YOU'RE RIGHT, YOU'RE RIGHT!
MAYBE I'LL TRY BEING OFF TO THE SIDE.
peirce

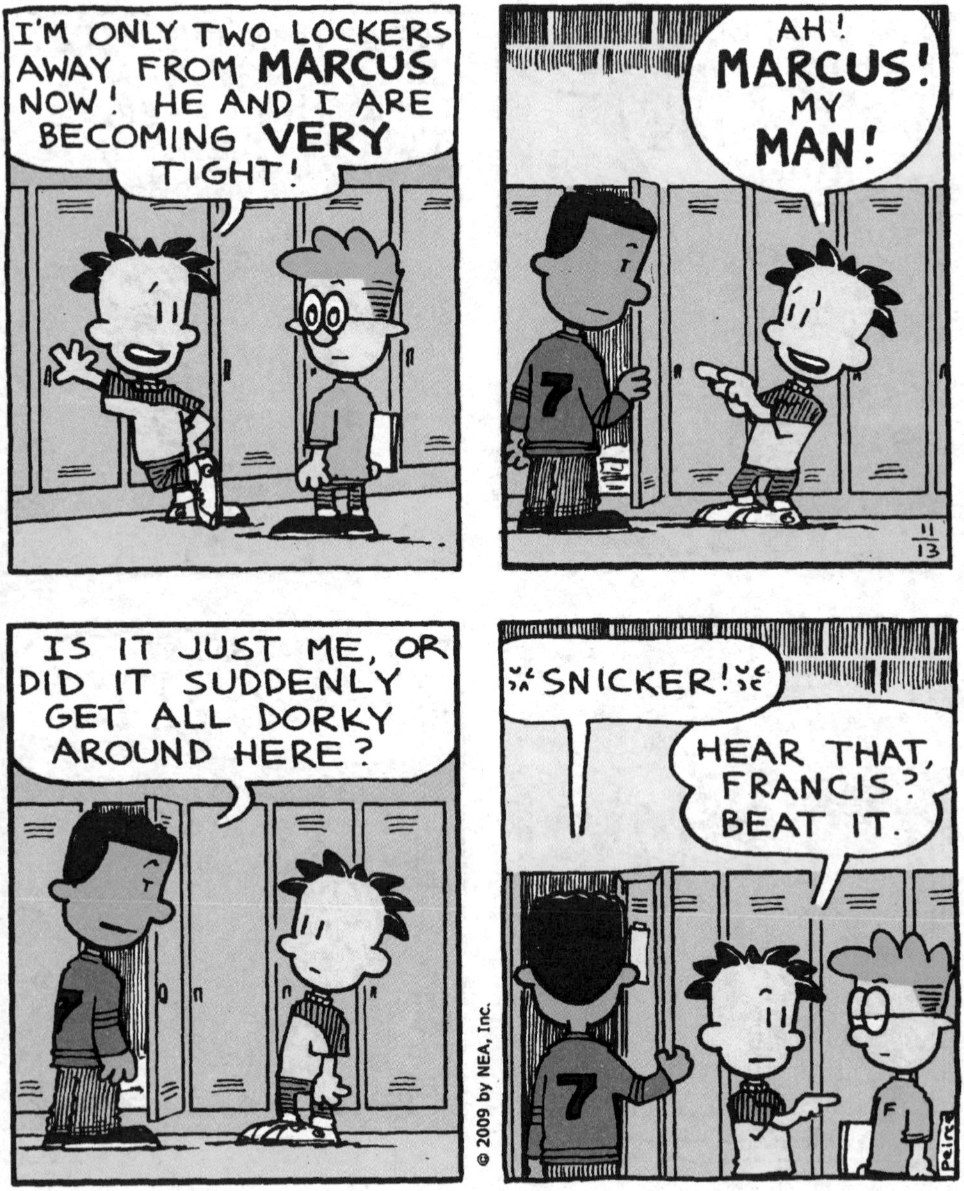
I'M ONLY TWO LOCKERS AWAY FROM **MARCUS** NOW! HE AND I ARE BECOMING **VERY** TIGHT!
AH! **MARCUS!** MY **MAN!**
11 13
IS IT JUST ME, OR DID IT SUDDENLY GET ALL DORKY AROUND HERE?
SNICKER!
HEAR THAT, FRANCIS? BEAT IT.
© 2009 by NEA, Inc.
Peirce

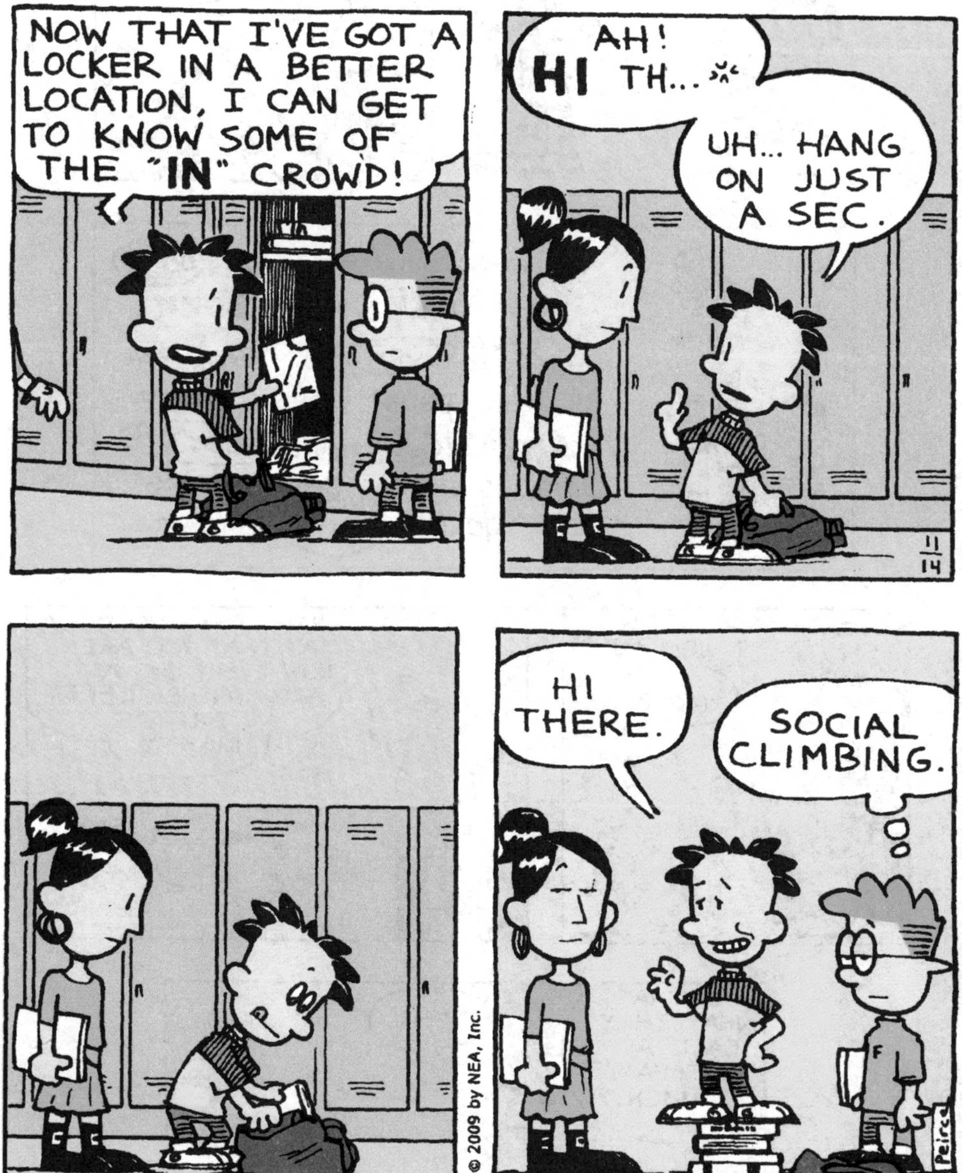
NOW THAT I'VE GOT A LOCKER IN A BETTER LOCATION, I CAN GET TO KNOW SOME OF THE "IN" CROWD!
AH! HI TH...
UH... HANG ON JUST A SEC.
11
14
© 2009 by NEA, Inc.
HI THERE.
SOCIAL CLIMBING.
Peirce

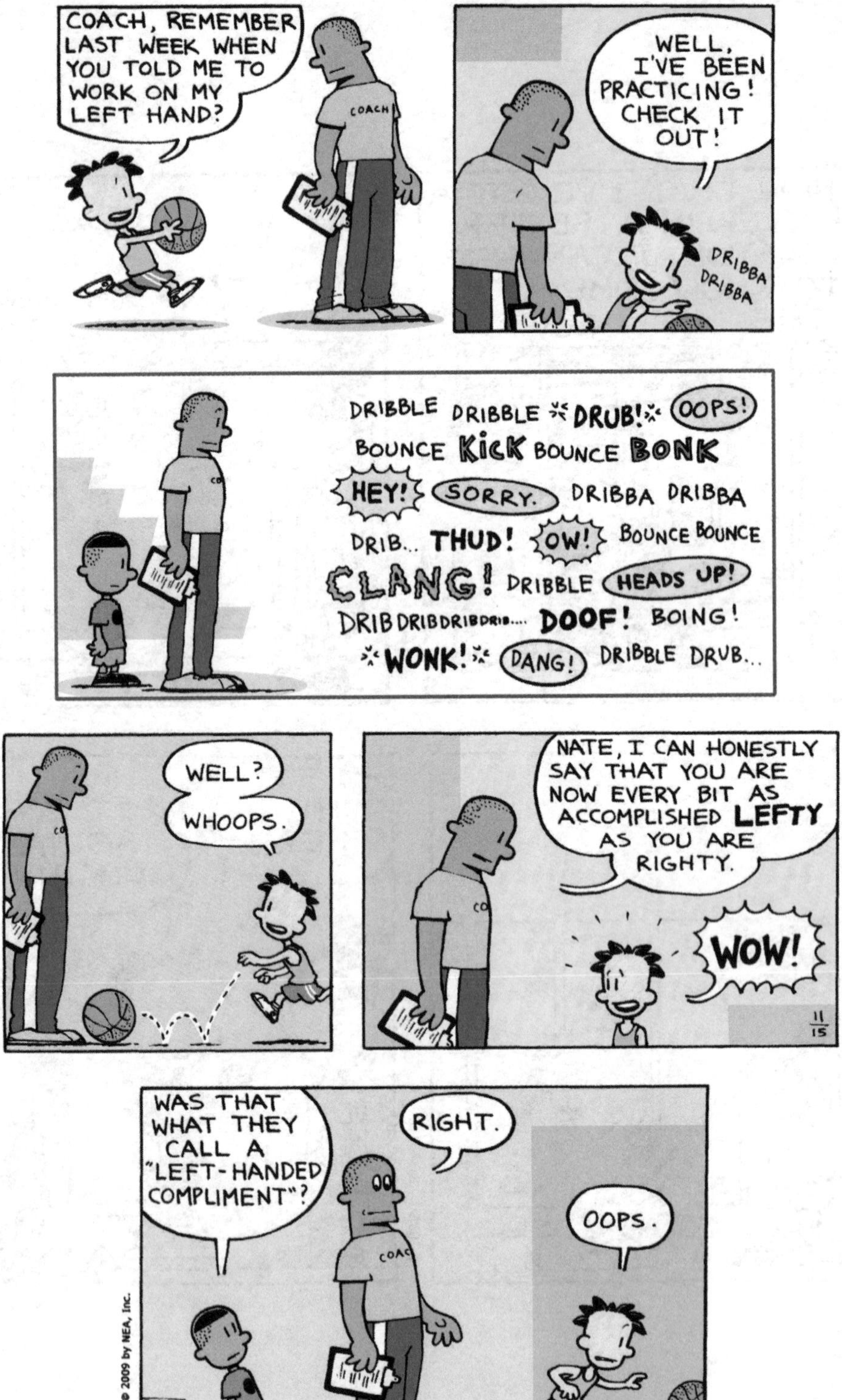
COACH, REMEMBER LAST WEEK WHEN YOU TOLD ME TO WORK ON MY LEFT HAND?
COACH
WELL, I'VE BEEN PRACTICING! CHECK IT OUT!
DRIBBA DRIBBA
DRIBBLE DRIBBLE DRUB! OOPS!
BOUNCE KICK BOUNCE BONK
HEY! SORRY. DRIBBA DRIBBA
DRIB... THUD! OW! BOUNCE BOUNCE
CLANG! DRIBBLE HEADS UP!
DRIB DRIBDRIBDRIB.... DOOF! BOING!
WONK! DANG! DRIBBLE DRUB...
WELL?
WHOOPS.
NATE, I CAN HONESTLY SAY THAT YOU ARE NOW EVERY BIT AS ACCOMPLISHED LEFTY AS YOU ARE RIGHTY.
WOW!
11/15
WAS THAT WHAT THEY CALL A "LEFT-HANDED COMPLIMENT"?
RIGHT.
OOPS.
COACH
© 2009 by NEA, Inc.
Peirce

SWISH

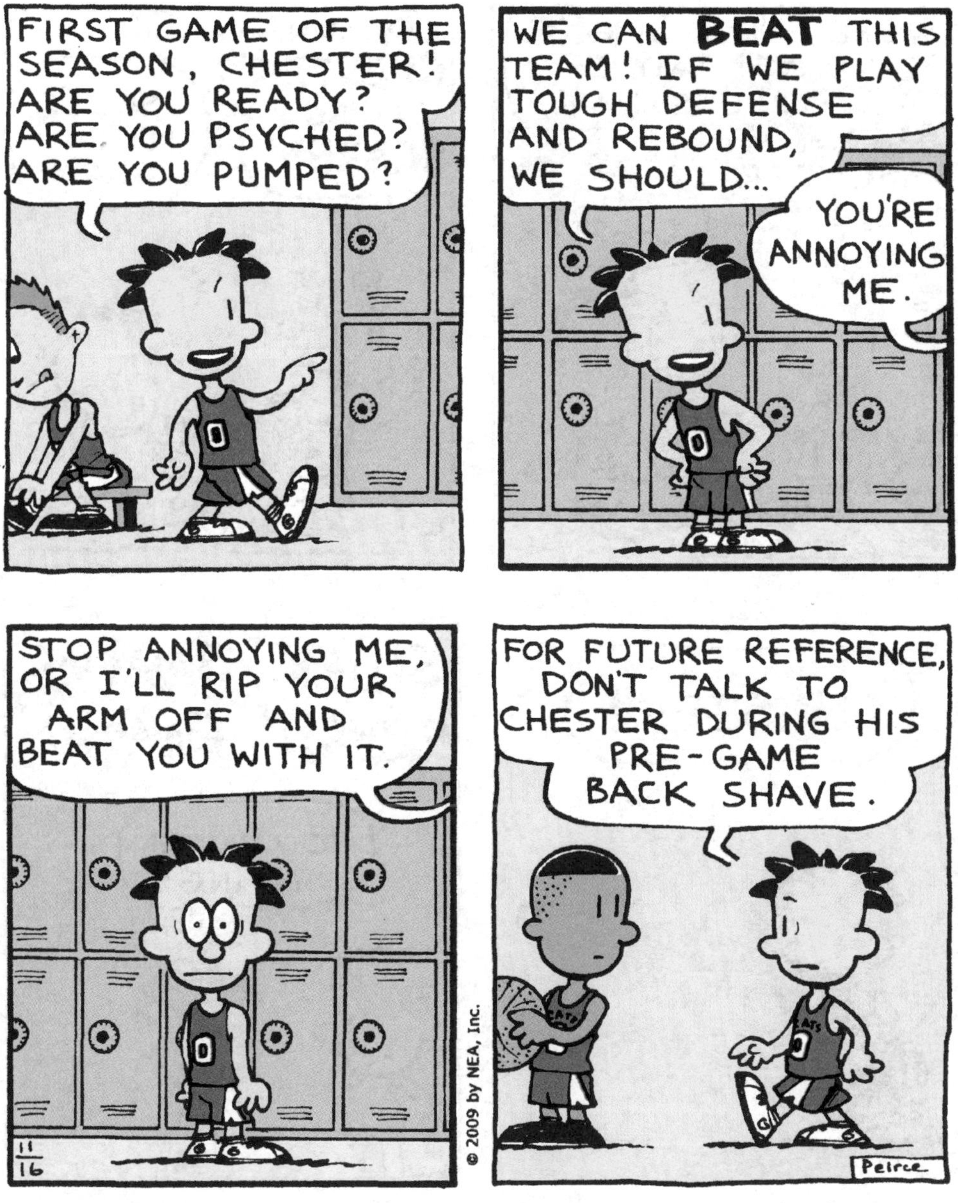
FIRST GAME OF THE SEASON, CHESTER! ARE YOU READY? ARE YOU PSYCHED? ARE YOU PUMPED?
WE CAN **BEAT** THIS TEAM! IF WE PLAY TOUGH DEFENSE AND REBOUND, WE SHOULD...
YOU'RE ANNOYING ME.
STOP ANNOYING ME, OR I'LL RIP YOUR ARM OFF AND BEAT YOU WITH IT.
FOR FUTURE REFERENCE, DON'T TALK TO CHESTER DURING HIS PRE-GAME BACK SHAVE.
11/16
© 2009 by NEA, Inc.
Peirce

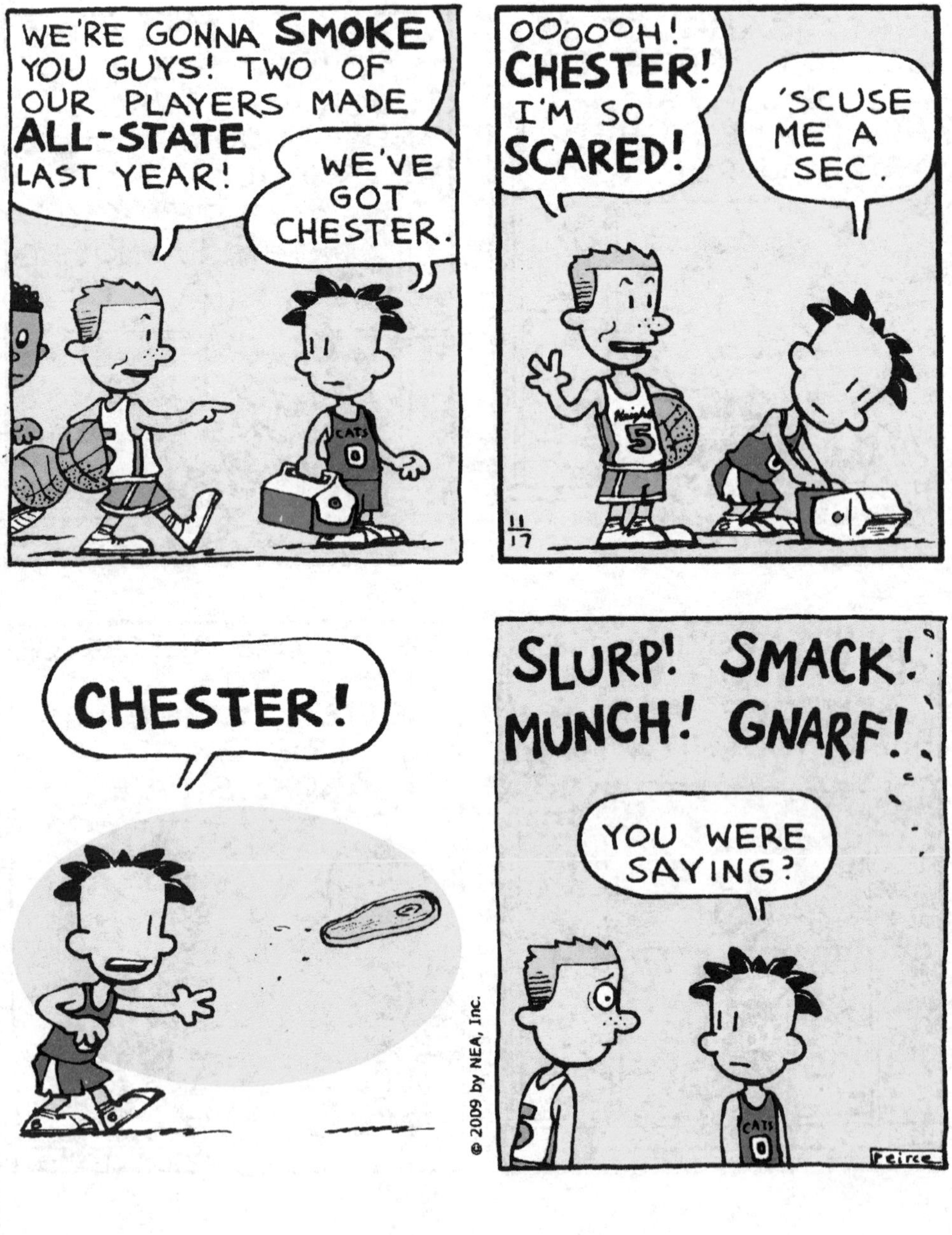
WE'RE GONNA SMOKE YOU GUYS! TWO OF OUR PLAYERS MADE ALL-STATE LAST YEAR!
WE'VE GOT CHESTER.
OOOOOOH! CHESTER! I'M SO SCARED!
'SCUSE ME A SEC.
11/17
CHESTER!
SLURP! SMACK! MUNCH! GNARF!
YOU WERE SAYING?
© 2009 by NEA, Inc.
Peirce

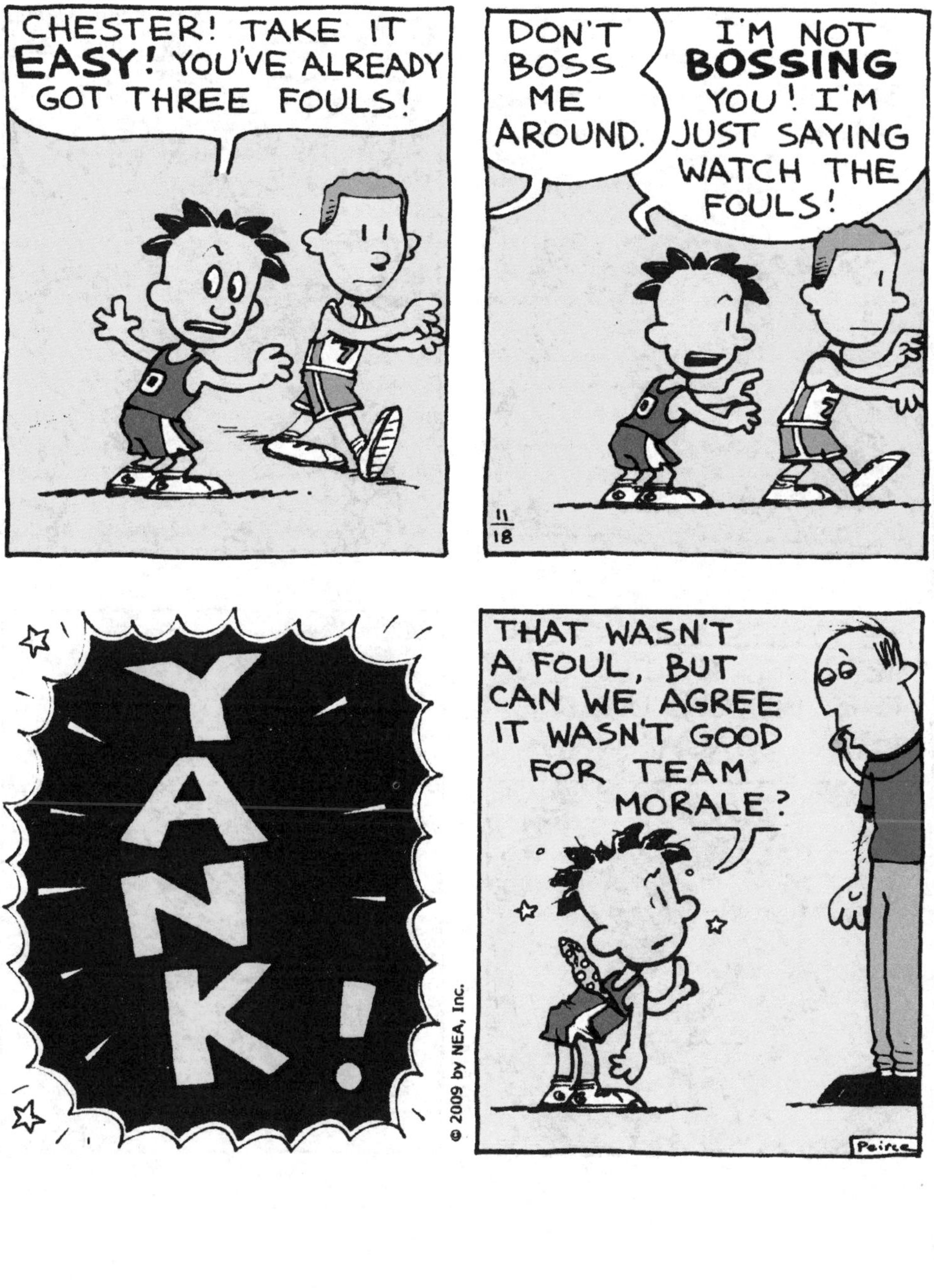
CHESTER! TAKE IT EASY! YOU'VE ALREADY GOT THREE FOULS!
DON'T BOSS ME AROUND.
I'M NOT BOSSING YOU! I'M JUST SAYING WATCH THE FOULS!
11/18
YANK!
© 2009 by NEA, Inc.
THAT WASN'T A FOUL, BUT CAN WE AGREE IT WASN'T GOOD FOR TEAM MORALE?
Peirce

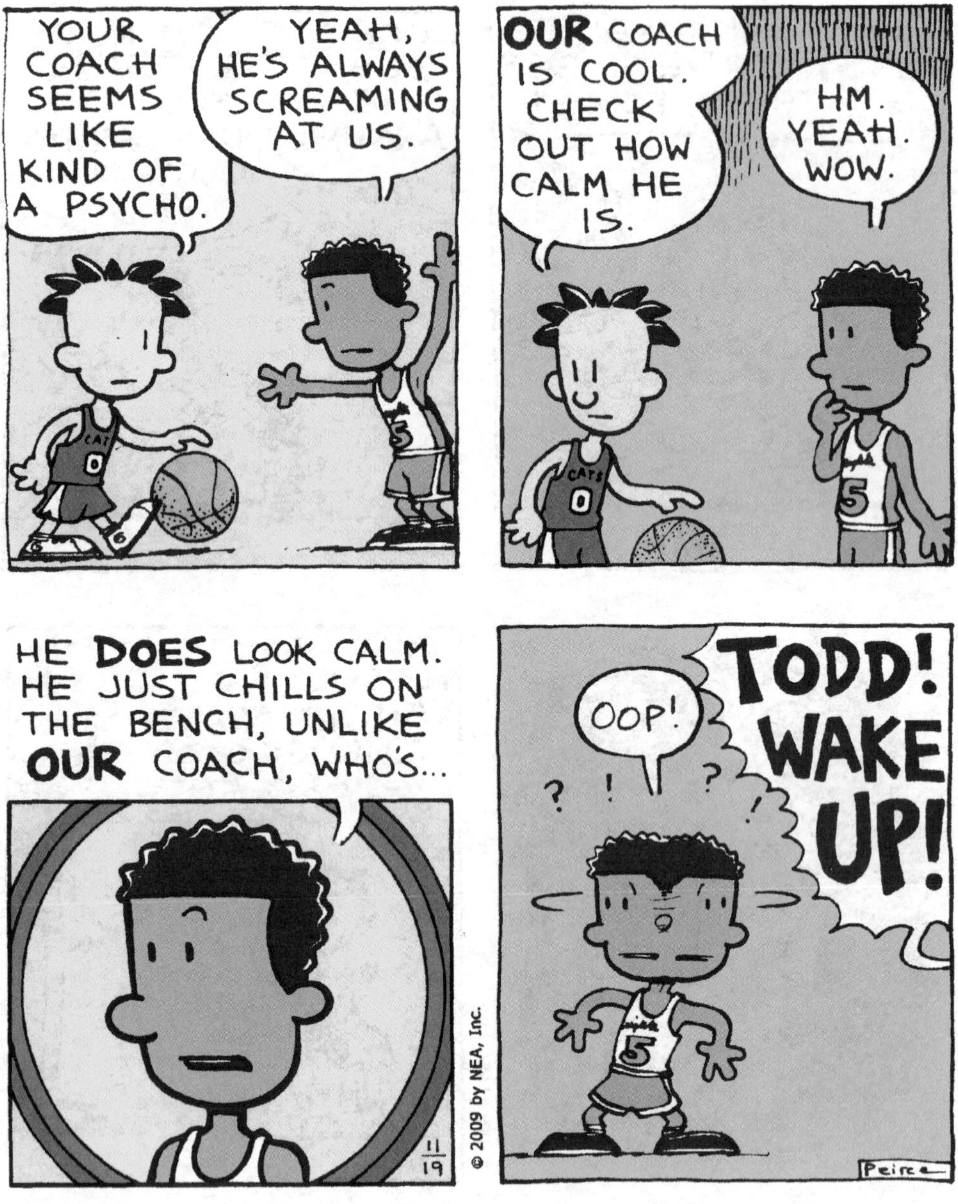
YOUR COACH SEEMS LIKE KIND OF A PSYCHO.
YEAH, HE'S ALWAYS SCREAMING AT US.
OUR COACH IS COOL. CHECK OUT HOW CALM HE IS.
HM. YEAH. WOW.
HE DOES LOOK CALM. HE JUST CHILLS ON THE BENCH, UNLIKE OUR COACH, WHO'S...
11/19
© 2009 by NEA, Inc.
OOP!
TODD! WAKE UP!
Peirce

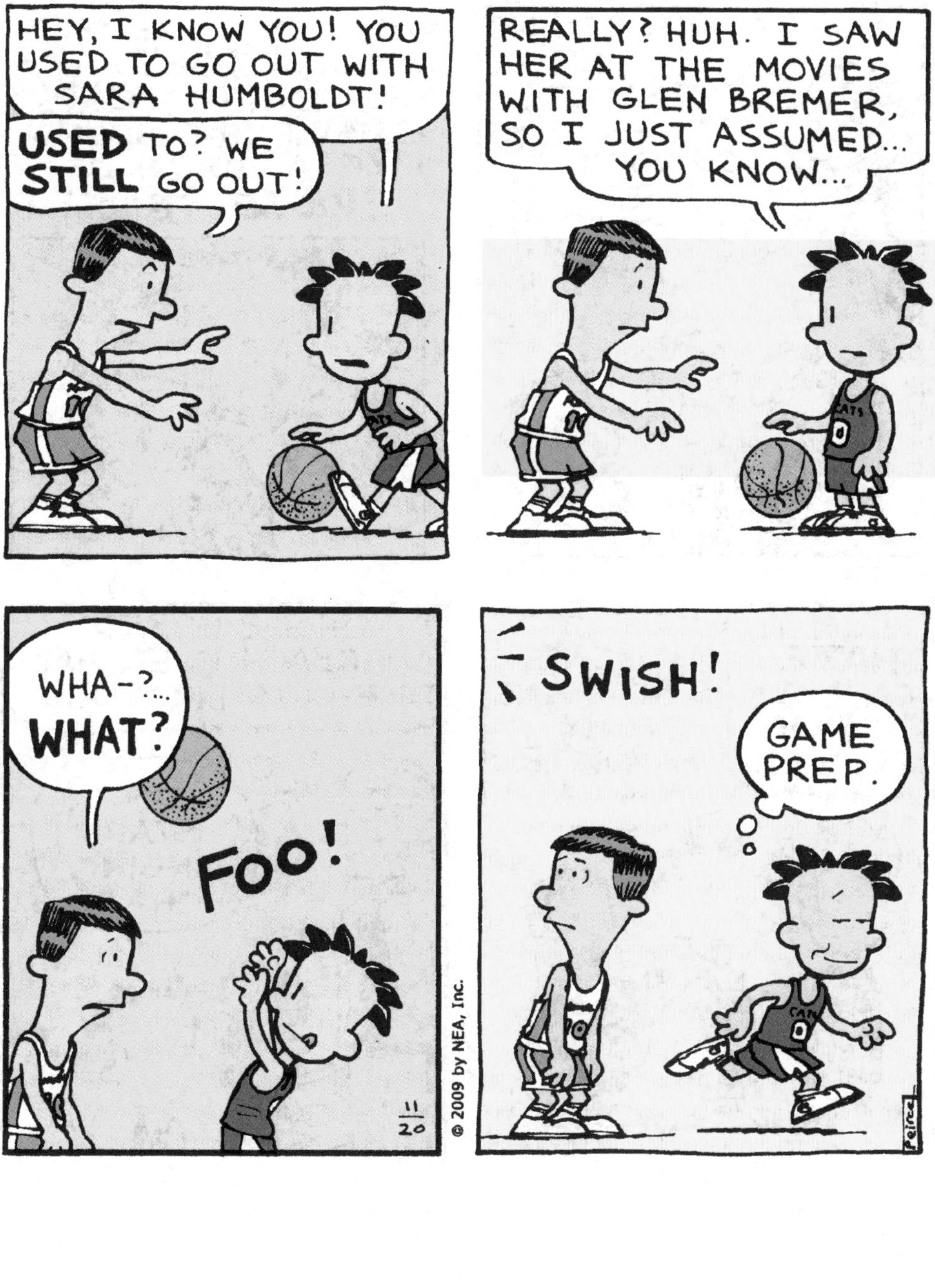
HEY, I KNOW YOU! YOU USED TO GO OUT WITH SARA HUMBOLDT!
USED TO? WE STILL GO OUT!
REALLY? HUH. I SAW HER AT THE MOVIES WITH GLEN BREMER, SO I JUST ASSUMED... YOU KNOW...
WHA-?... WHAT?
FOO!
11 20
© 2009 by NEA, Inc.
SWISH!
GAME PREP.
Peirce

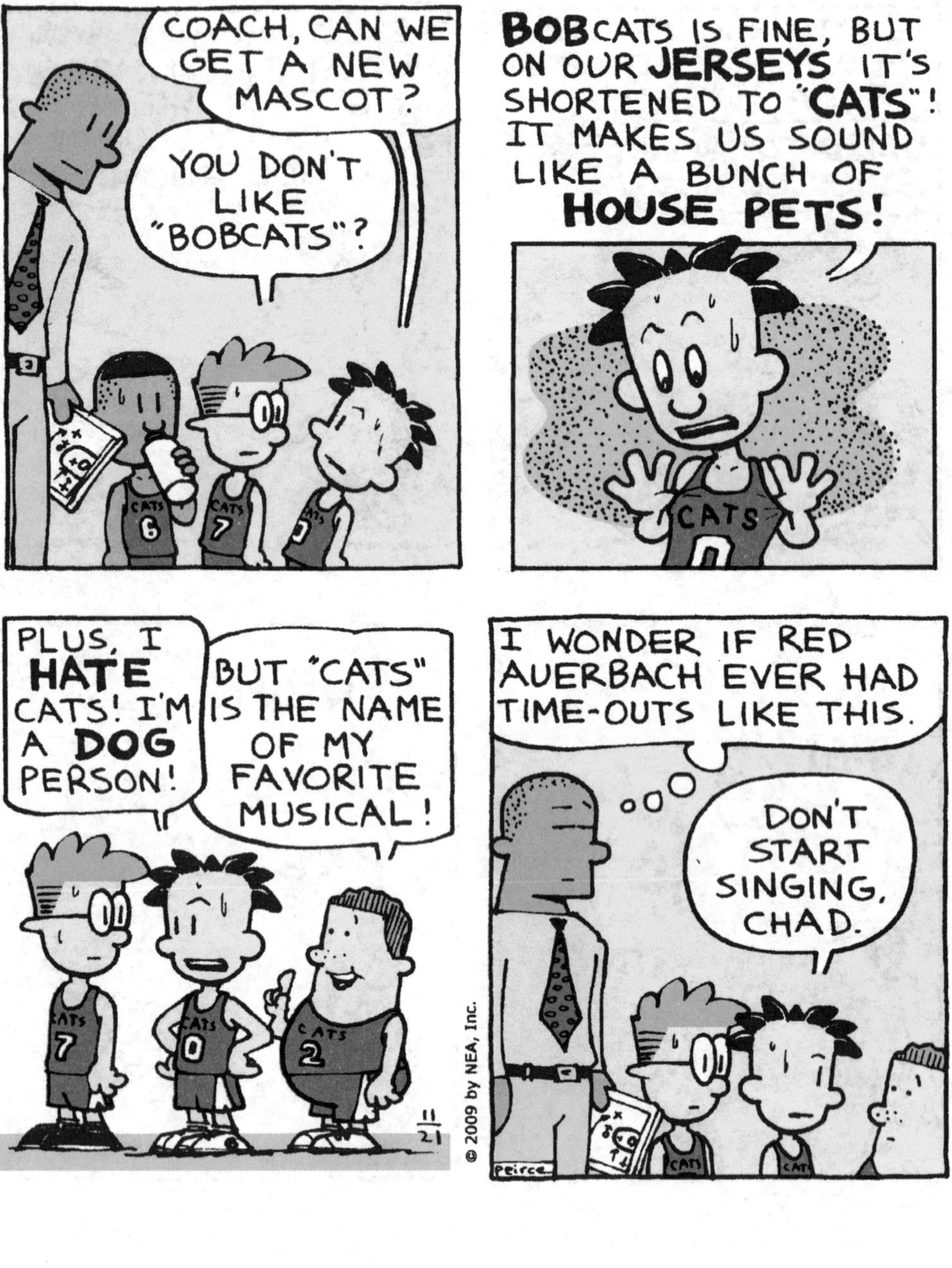
COACH, CAN WE GET A NEW MASCOT?
YOU DON'T LIKE "BOBCATS"?
CATS
6
CATS
7
BOBCATS IS FINE, BUT ON OUR JERSEYS IT'S SHORTENED TO "CATS"! IT MAKES US SOUND LIKE A BUNCH OF HOUSE PETS!
CATS
PLUS, I HATE CATS! I'M A DOG PERSON!
BUT "CATS" IS THE NAME OF MY FAVORITE MUSICAL!
CATS
7
CATS
0
CATS
2
11/21
© 2009 by NEA, Inc.
I WONDER IF RED AUERBACH EVER HAD TIME-OUTS LIKE THIS.
DON'T START SINGING, CHAD.
Peirce

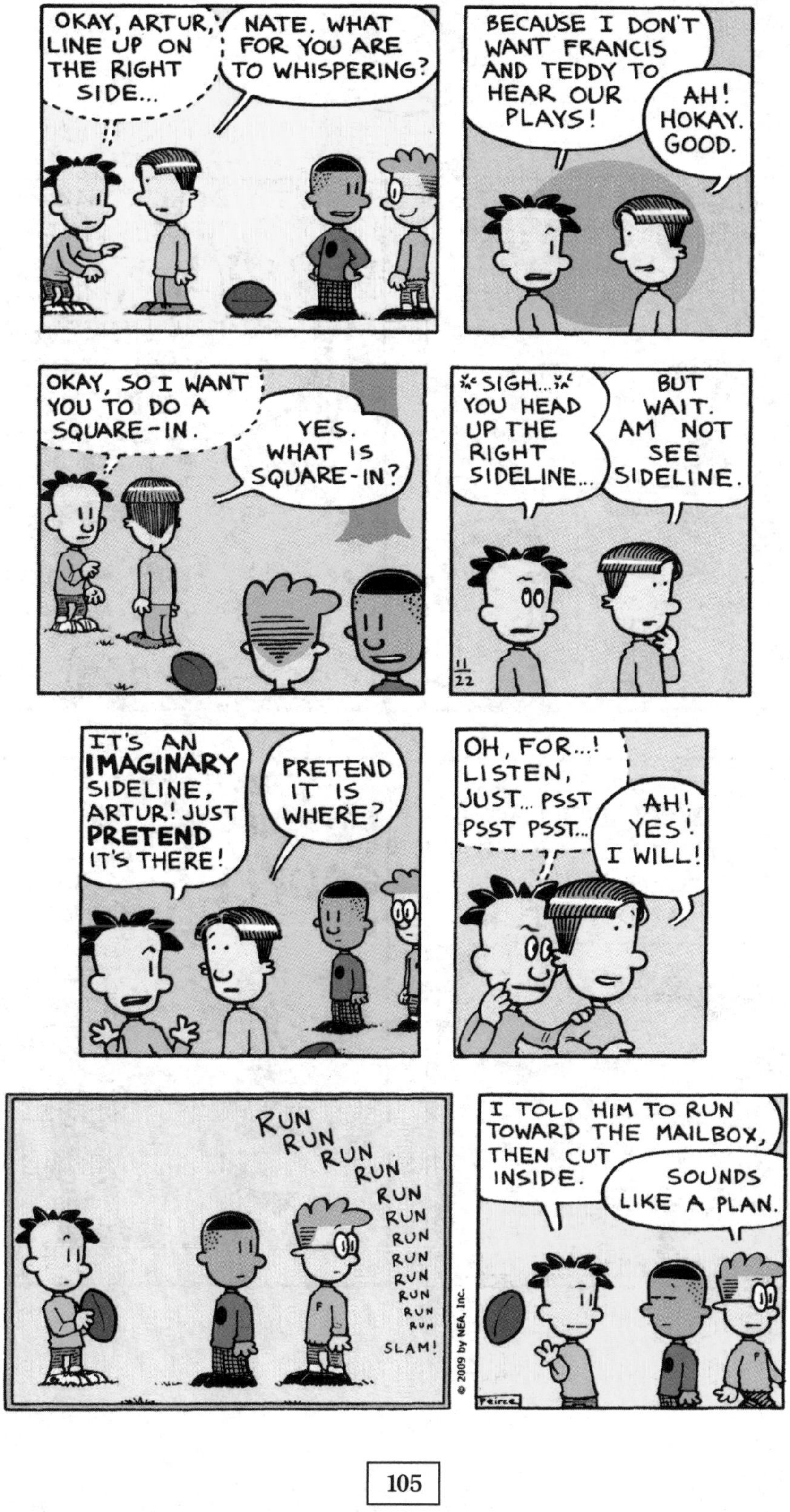
OKAY, ARTUR, LINE UP ON THE RIGHT SIDE...
NATE. WHAT FOR YOU ARE TO WHISPERING?
BECAUSE I DON'T WANT FRANCIS AND TEDDY TO HEAR OUR PLAYS!
AH! HOKAY. GOOD.
OKAY, SO I WANT YOU TO DO A SQUARE-IN.
YES. WHAT IS SQUARE-IN?
SIGH... YOU HEAD UP THE RIGHT SIDELINE...
BUT WAIT. AM NOT SEE SIDELINE.
11/22
IT'S AN **IMAGINARY** SIDELINE, ARTUR! JUST **PRETEND** IT'S THERE!
PRETEND IT IS WHERE?
OH, FOR...! LISTEN, JUST... PSST PSST PSST...
AH! YES! I WILL!
RUN RUN RUN RUN RUN RUN RUN RUN RUN RUN RUN RUN
SLAM!
© 2009 by NEA, Inc.
I TOLD HIM TO RUN TOWARD THE MAILBOX, THEN CUT INSIDE.
SOUNDS LIKE A PLAN.
Peirce

P.D.A.

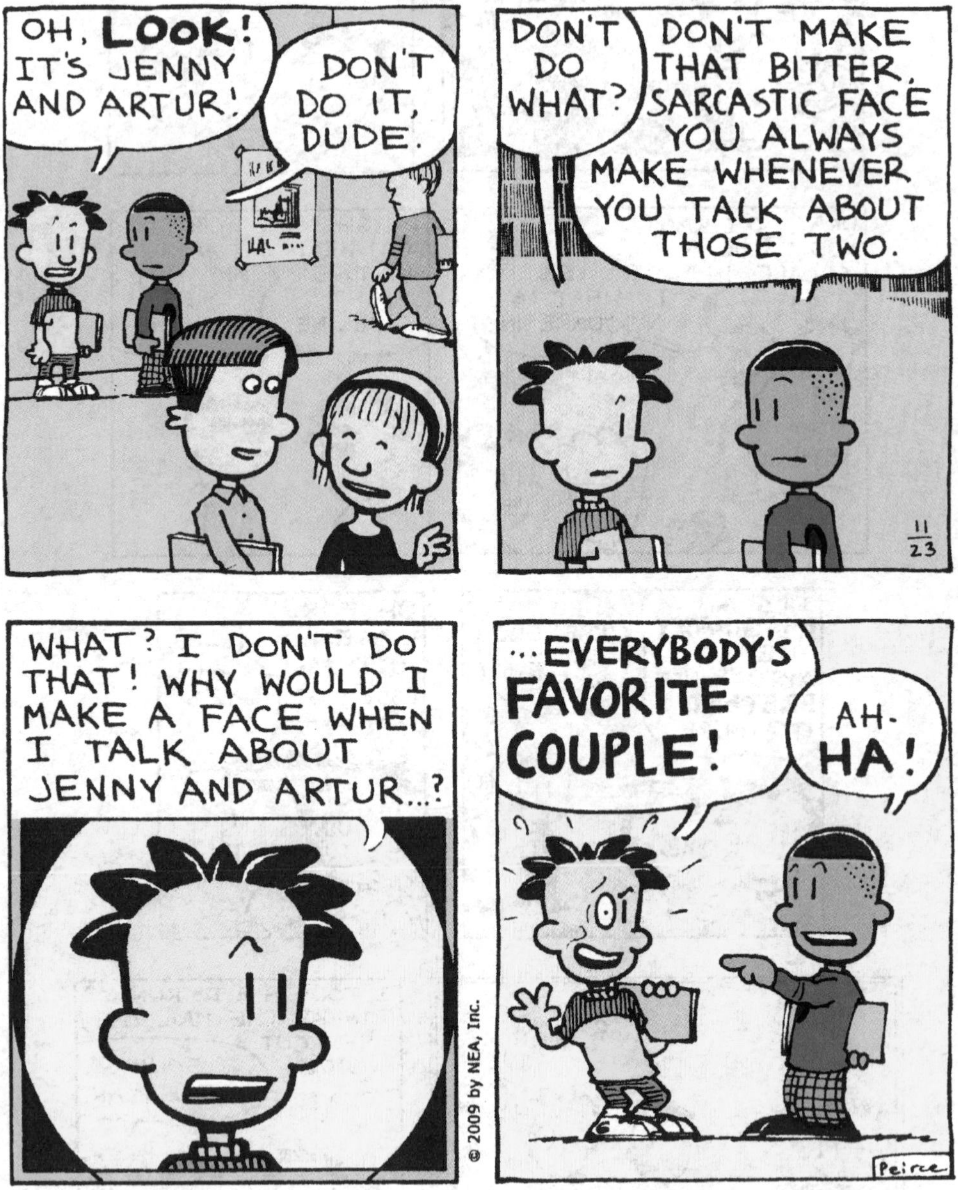
OH, **LOOK**! IT'S JENNY AND ARTUR!
DON'T DO IT, DUDE.
DON'T DO WHAT?
DON'T MAKE THAT BITTER, SARCASTIC FACE YOU ALWAYS MAKE WHENEVER YOU TALK ABOUT THOSE TWO.
11 23
WHAT? I DON'T DO THAT! WHY WOULD I MAKE A FACE WHEN I TALK ABOUT JENNY AND ARTUR...?
...**EVERYBODY'S FAVORITE COUPLE!**
AH-HA!
Peirce

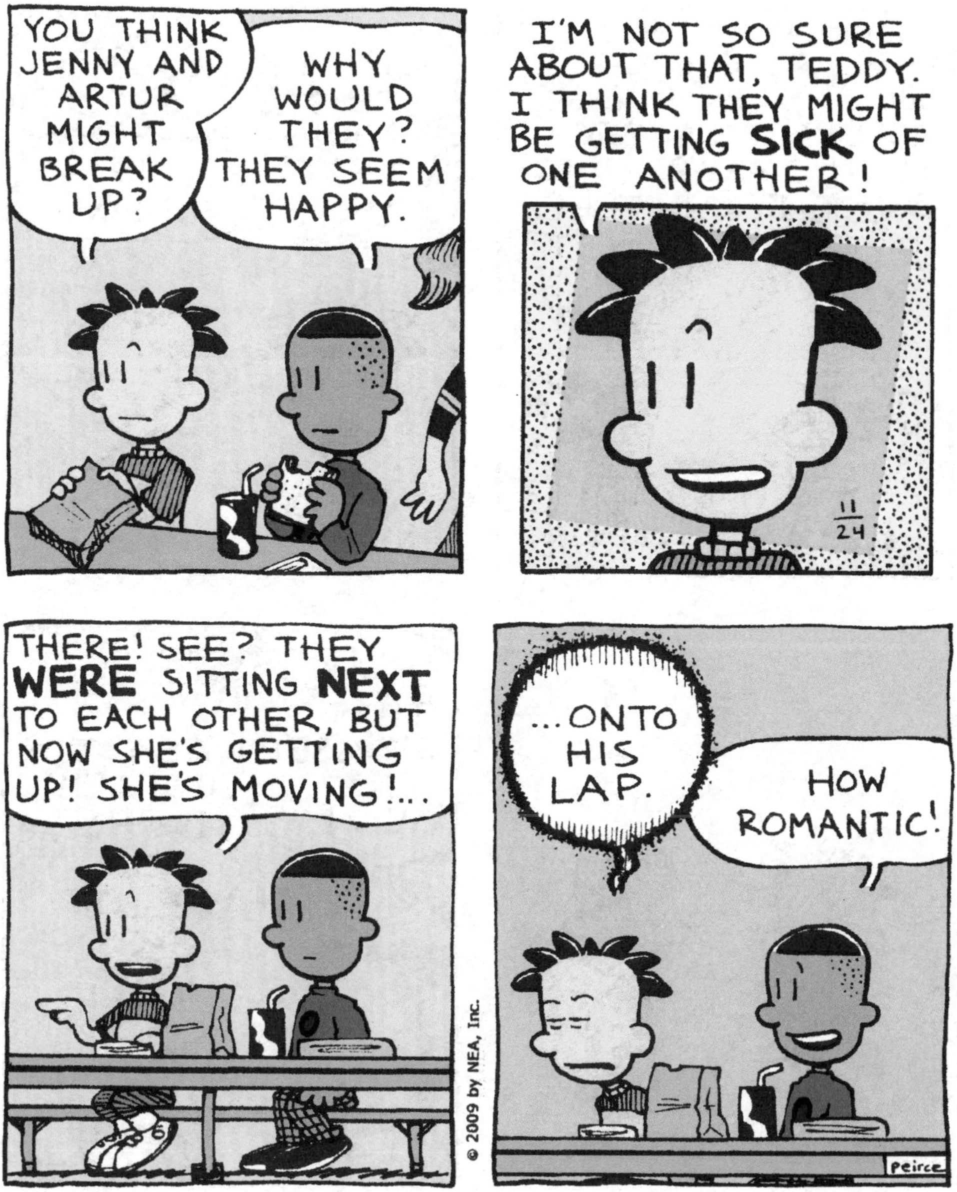
YOU THINK JENNY AND ARTUR MIGHT BREAK UP?
WHY WOULD THEY? THEY SEEM HAPPY.
I'M NOT SO SURE ABOUT THAT, TEDDY. I THINK THEY MIGHT BE GETTING SICK OF ONE ANOTHER!
11 24
THERE! SEE? THEY WERE SITTING NEXT TO EACH OTHER, BUT NOW SHE'S GETTING UP! SHE'S MOVING!...
© 2009 by NEA, Inc.
...ONTO HIS LAP.
HOW ROMANTIC!
peirce

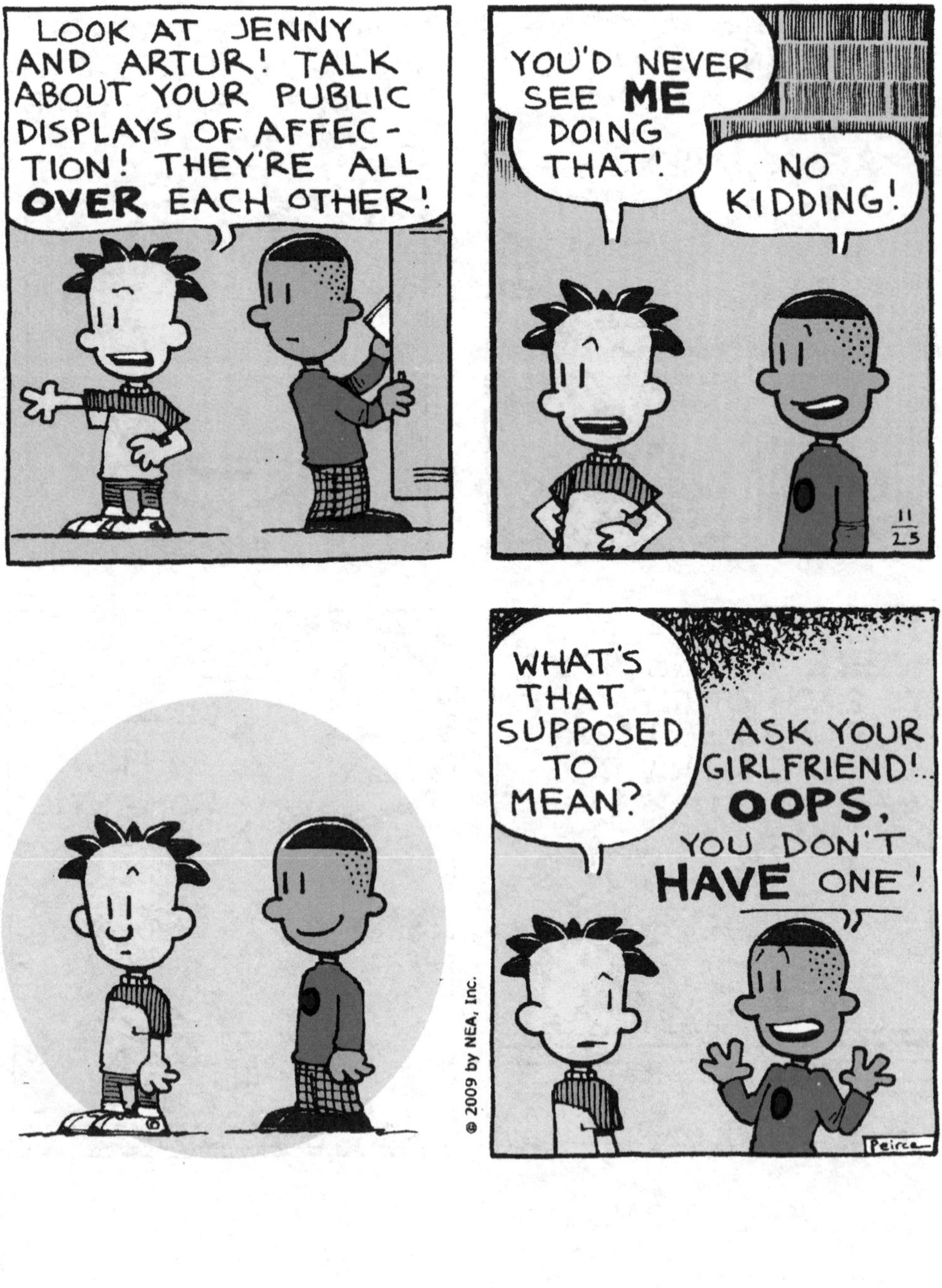
LOOK AT JENNY AND ARTUR! TALK ABOUT YOUR PUBLIC DISPLAYS OF AFFECTION! THEY'RE ALL **OVER** EACH OTHER!
YOU'D NEVER SEE **ME** DOING THAT!
NO KIDDING!
11/25
WHAT'S THAT SUPPOSED TO MEAN?
ASK YOUR GIRLFRIEND!.. **OOPS**, YOU DON'T **HAVE** ONE!
Peirce

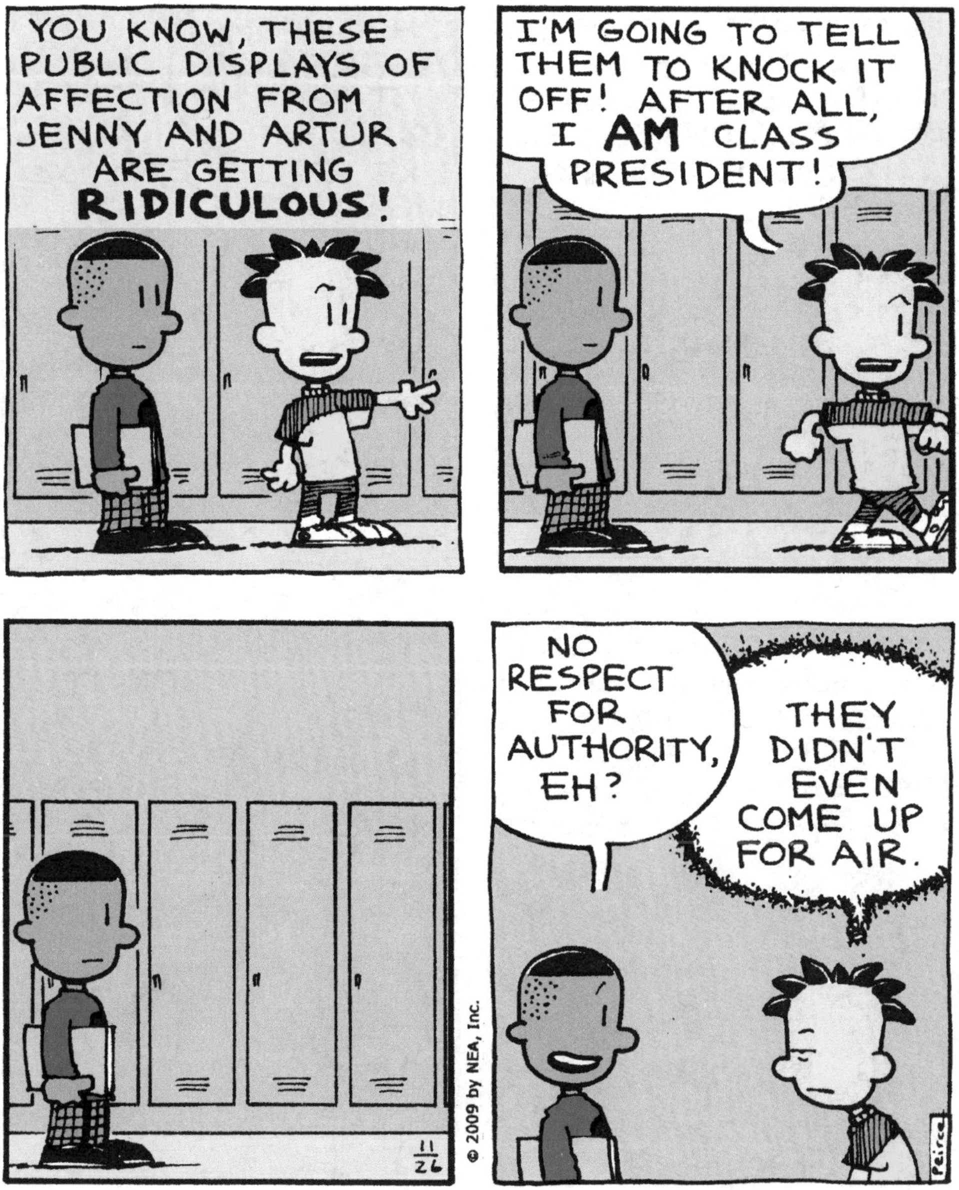
YOU KNOW, THESE PUBLIC DISPLAYS OF AFFECTION FROM JENNY AND ARTUR ARE GETTING **RIDICULOUS!**
I'M GOING TO TELL THEM TO KNOCK IT OFF! AFTER ALL, I **AM** CLASS PRESIDENT!
11/26
© 2009 by NEA, Inc.
NO RESPECT FOR AUTHORITY, EH?
THEY DIDN'T EVEN COME UP FOR AIR.
Peirce

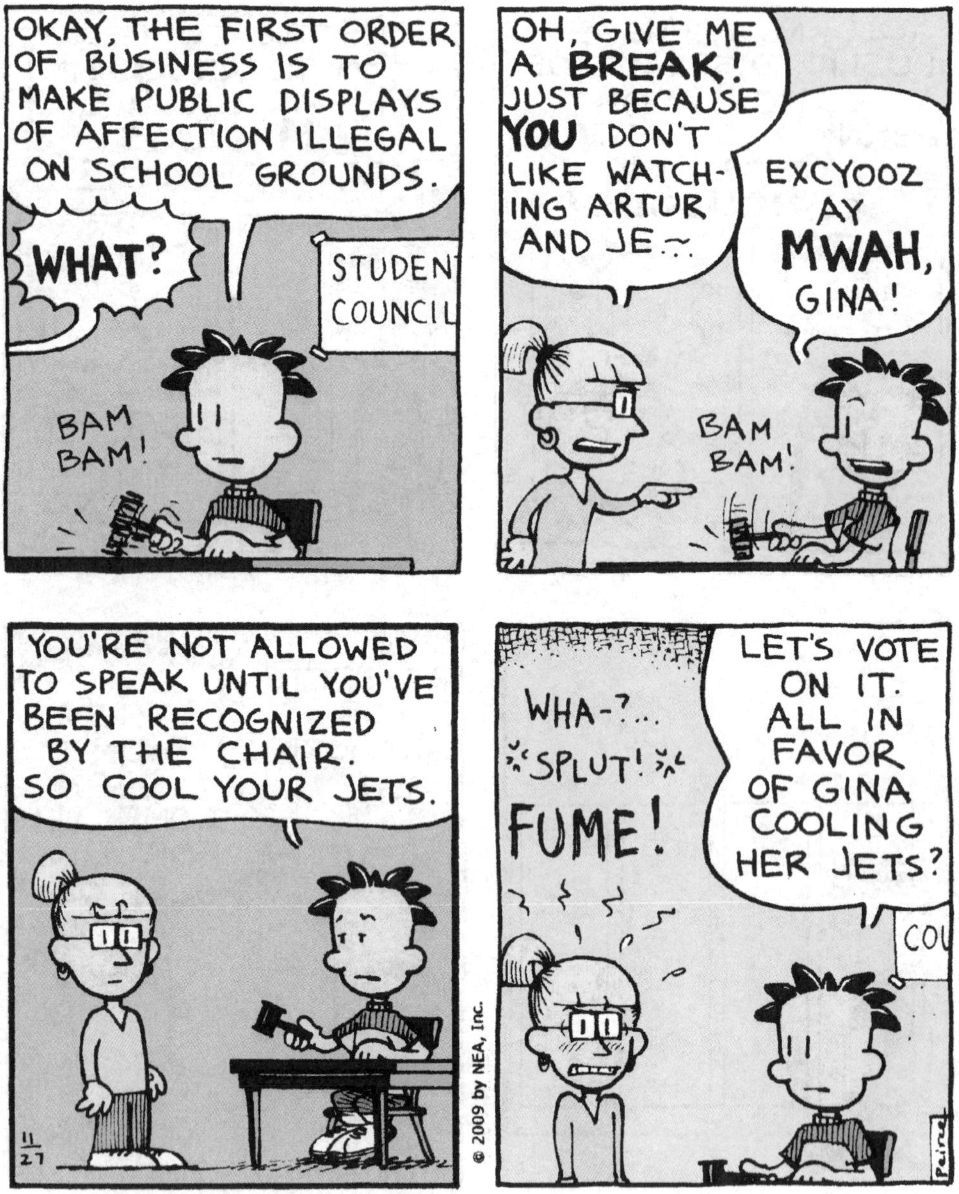
OKAY, THE FIRST ORDER OF BUSINESS IS TO MAKE PUBLIC DISPLAYS OF AFFECTION ILLEGAL ON SCHOOL GROUNDS.
WHAT?
STUDENT COUNCIL
BAM BAM!
OH, GIVE ME A BREAK! JUST BECAUSE YOU DON'T LIKE WATCHING ARTUR AND JE~
EXCYOOZ AY MWAH, GINA!
BAM BAM!
YOU'RE NOT ALLOWED TO SPEAK UNTIL YOU'VE BEEN RECOGNIZED BY THE CHAIR. SO COOL YOUR JETS.
11/27
© 2009 by NEA, Inc.
WHA-?...
SPLUT!
FUME!
LET'S VOTE ON IT. ALL IN FAVOR OF GINA COOLING HER JETS?
COU
Peirce

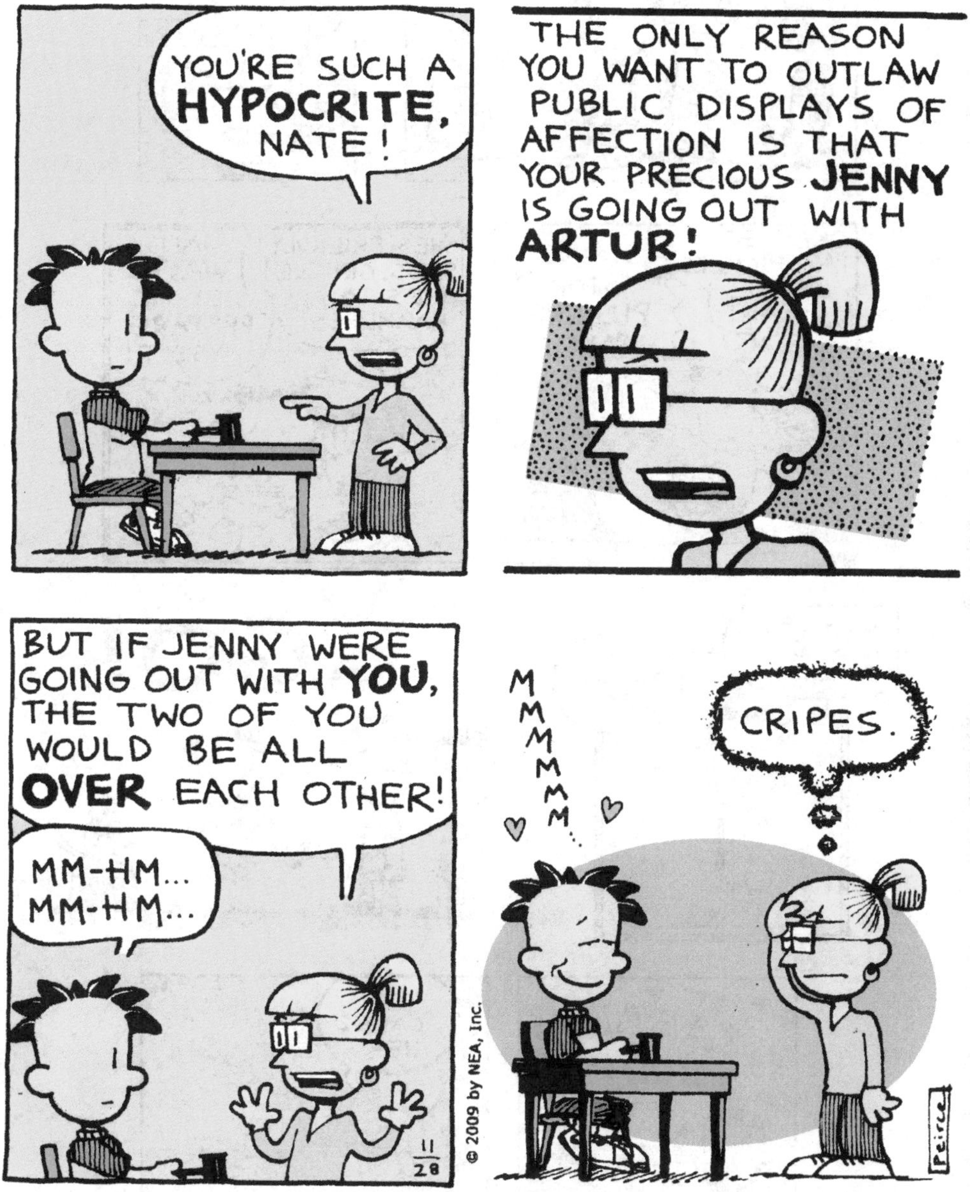
YOU'RE SUCH A **HYPOCRITE**, NATE!
THE ONLY REASON YOU WANT TO OUTLAW PUBLIC DISPLAYS OF AFFECTION IS THAT YOUR PRECIOUS **JENNY** IS GOING OUT WITH **ARTUR**!
BUT IF JENNY WERE GOING OUT WITH **YOU**, THE TWO OF YOU WOULD BE ALL **OVER** EACH OTHER!
MM-HM... MM-HM...
11 28
© 2009 by NEA, Inc.
MMMMMMM...
CRIPES.
Peirce

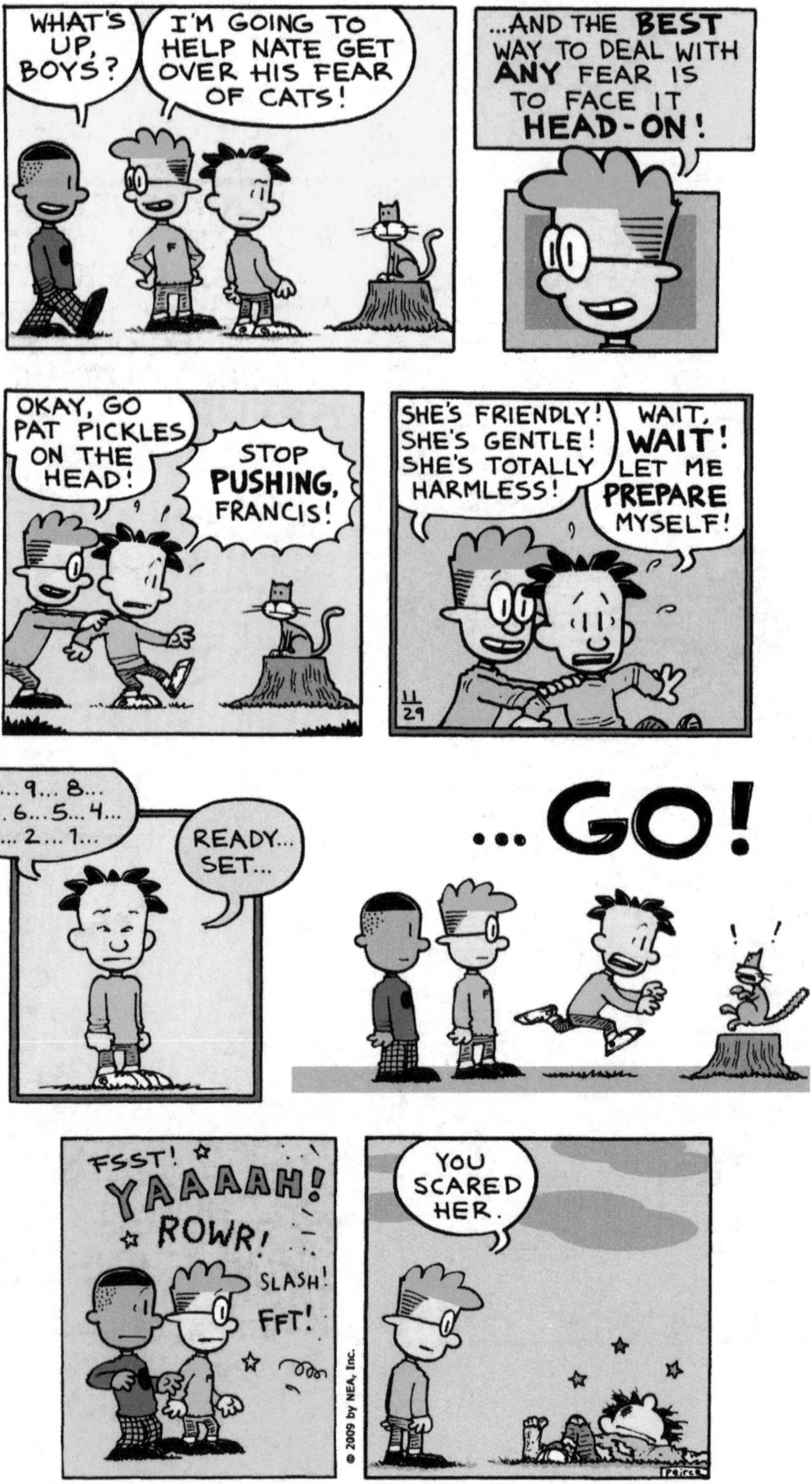
WHAT'S UP, BOYS?
I'M GOING TO HELP NATE GET OVER HIS FEAR OF CATS!
...AND THE BEST WAY TO DEAL WITH ANY FEAR IS TO FACE IT HEAD-ON!
OKAY, GO PAT PICKLES ON THE HEAD!
STOP PUSHING, FRANCIS!
SHE'S FRIENDLY! SHE'S GENTLE! SHE'S TOTALLY HARMLESS!
WAIT, WAIT! LET ME PREPARE MYSELF!
11 29
10... 9... 8... 7... 6... 5... 4... 3... 2... 1...
READY... SET...
...GO!
FSST!
YAAAAH!
ROWR!
SLASH!
FFT!
© 2009 by NEA, Inc.
YOU SCARED HER.
Peirce

BON VOYAGE!

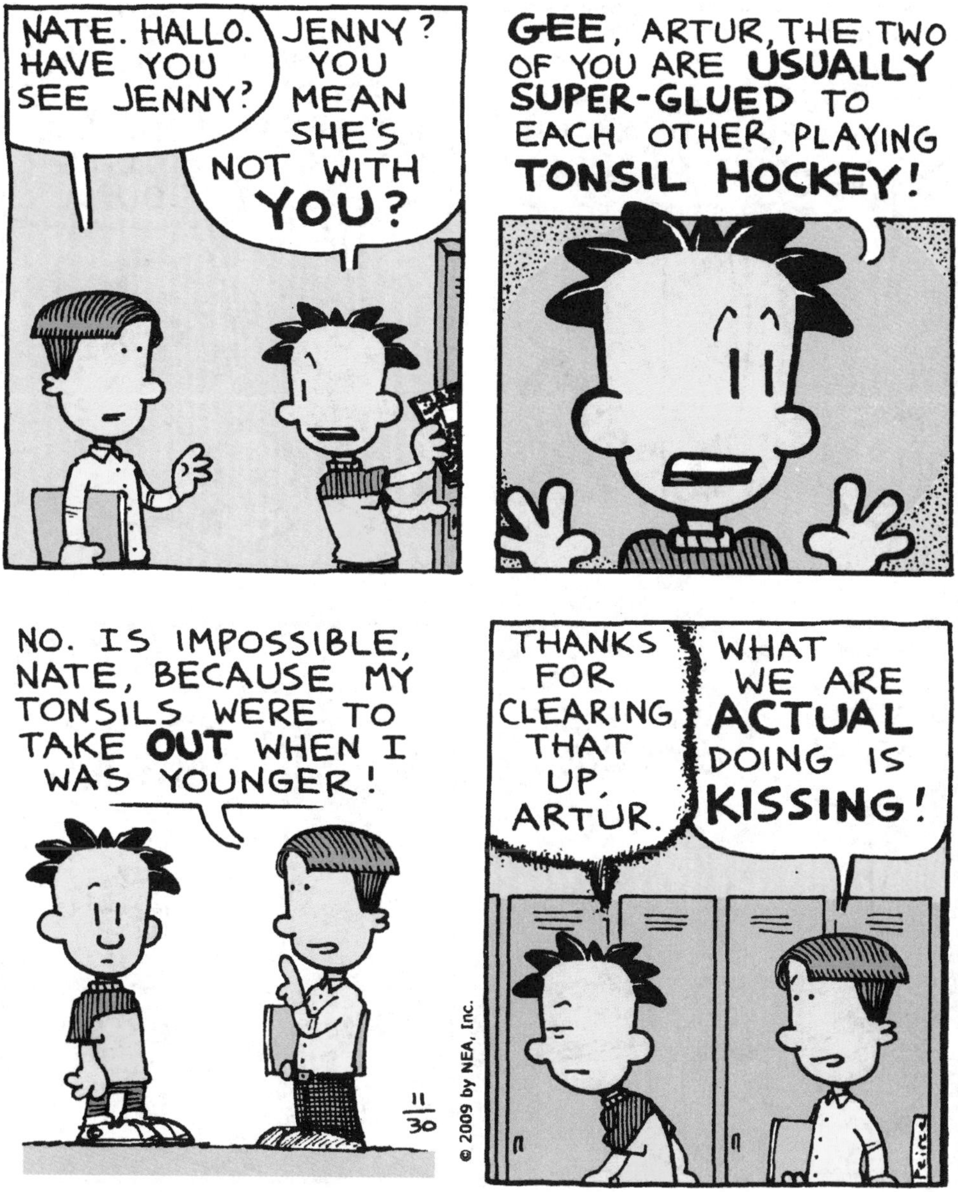
NATE. HALLO. HAVE YOU SEE JENNY?
JENNY? YOU MEAN SHE'S NOT WITH **YOU**?
GEE, ARTUR, THE TWO OF YOU ARE **USUALLY SUPER-GLUED** TO EACH OTHER, PLAYING **TONSIL HOCKEY**!
NO. IS IMPOSSIBLE, NATE, BECAUSE MY TONSILS WERE TO TAKE **OUT** WHEN I WAS YOUNGER!
11/30
© 2009 by NEA, Inc.
THANKS FOR CLEARING THAT UP, ARTUR.
WHAT WE ARE **ACTUAL** DOING IS **KISSING**!
Peirce

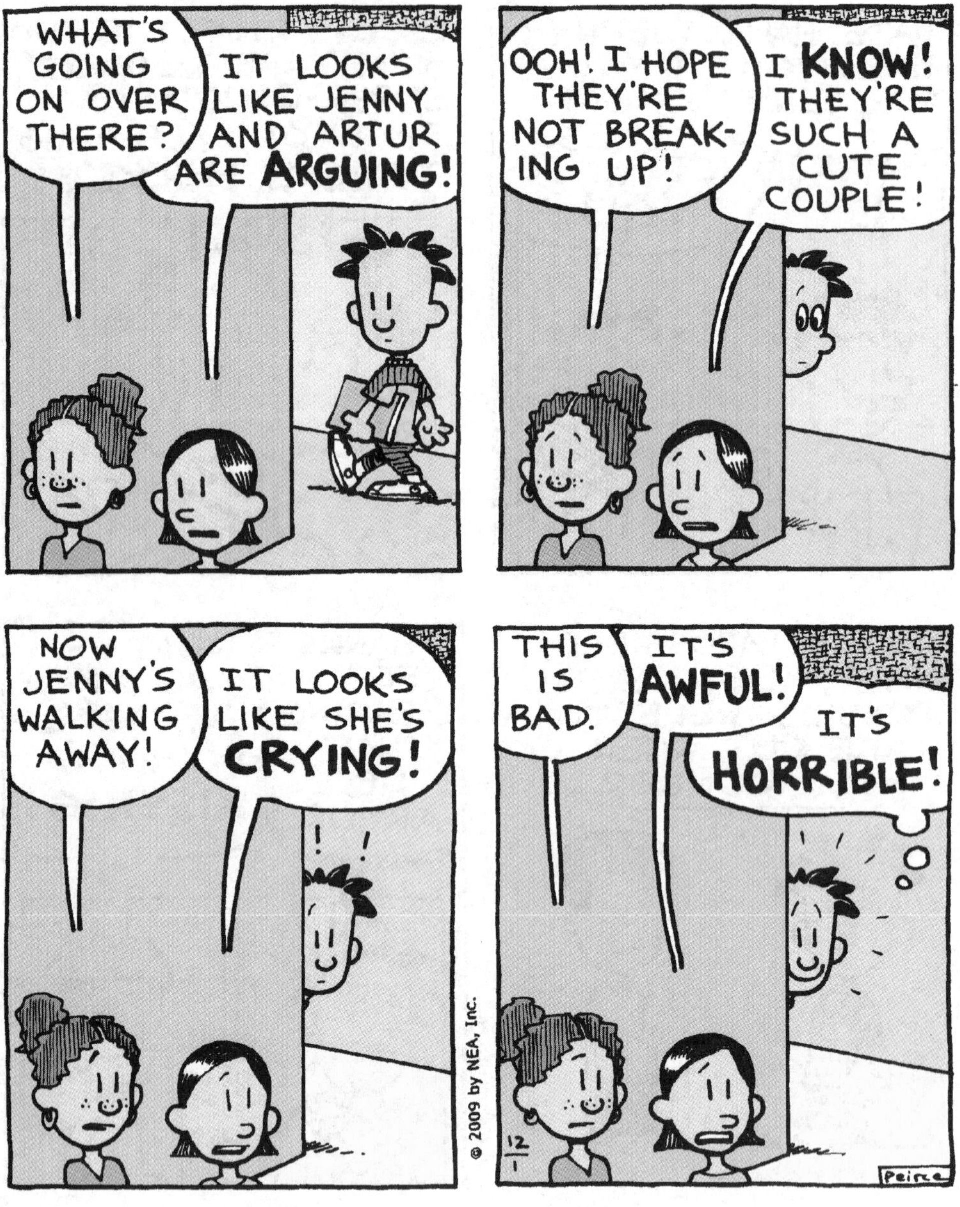
WHAT'S GOING ON OVER THERE?
IT LOOKS LIKE JENNY AND ARTUR ARE ARGUING!
OOH! I HOPE THEY'RE NOT BREAKING UP!
I KNOW! THEY'RE SUCH A CUTE COUPLE!
NOW JENNY'S WALKING AWAY!
IT LOOKS LIKE SHE'S CRYING!
! !
THIS IS BAD.
IT'S AWFUL!
IT'S HORRIBLE!
© 2009 by NEA, Inc.
12/1
Peirce

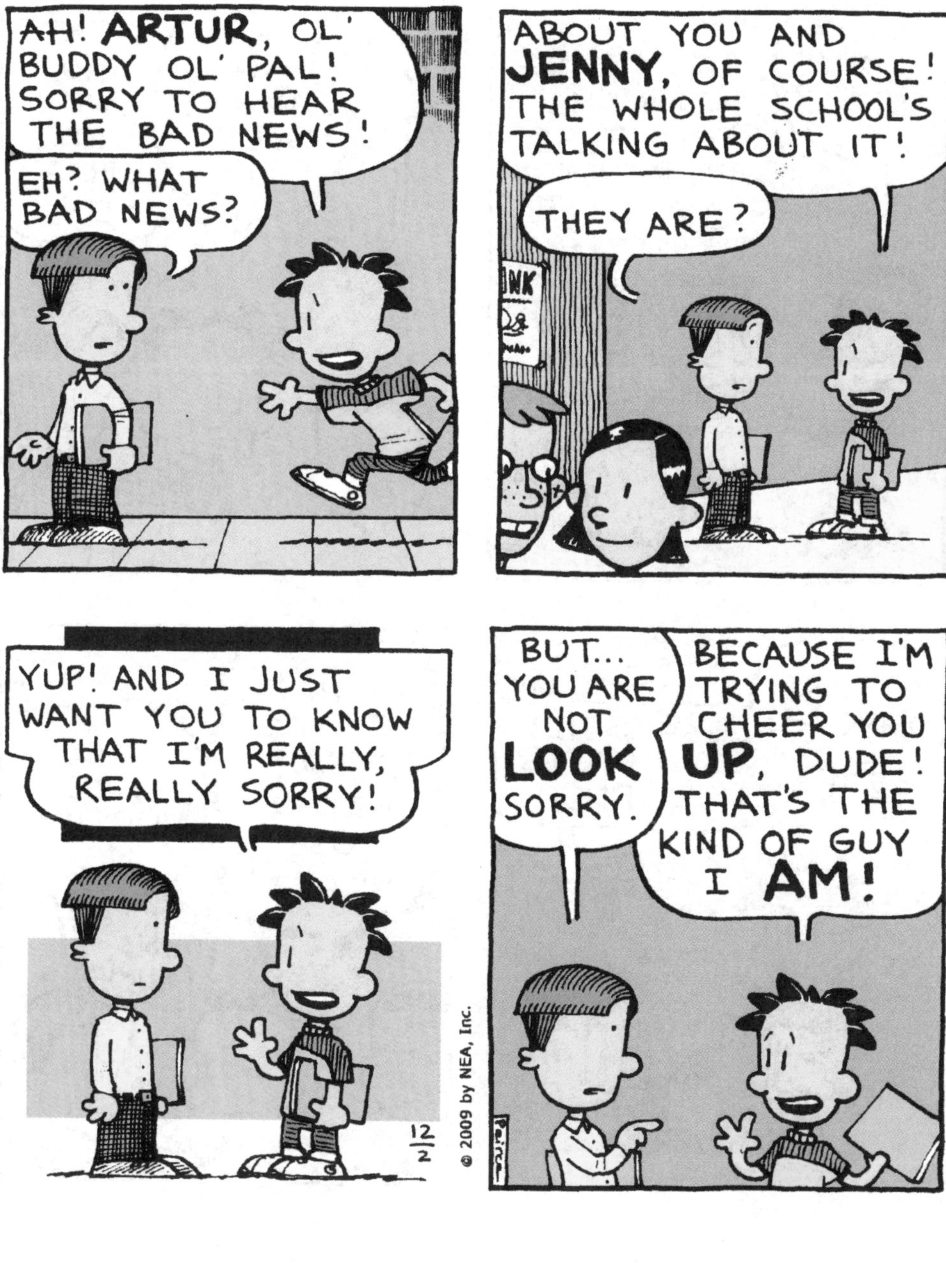
AH! ARTUR, OL' BUDDY OL' PAL! SORRY TO HEAR THE BAD NEWS!
EH? WHAT BAD NEWS?
ABOUT YOU AND JENNY, OF COURSE! THE WHOLE SCHOOL'S TALKING ABOUT IT!
THEY ARE?
YUP! AND I JUST WANT YOU TO KNOW THAT I'M REALLY, REALLY SORRY!
12/2
© 2009 by NEA, Inc.
BUT... YOU ARE NOT LOOK SORRY.
BECAUSE I'M TRYING TO CHEER YOU UP, DUDE! THAT'S THE KIND OF GUY I AM!

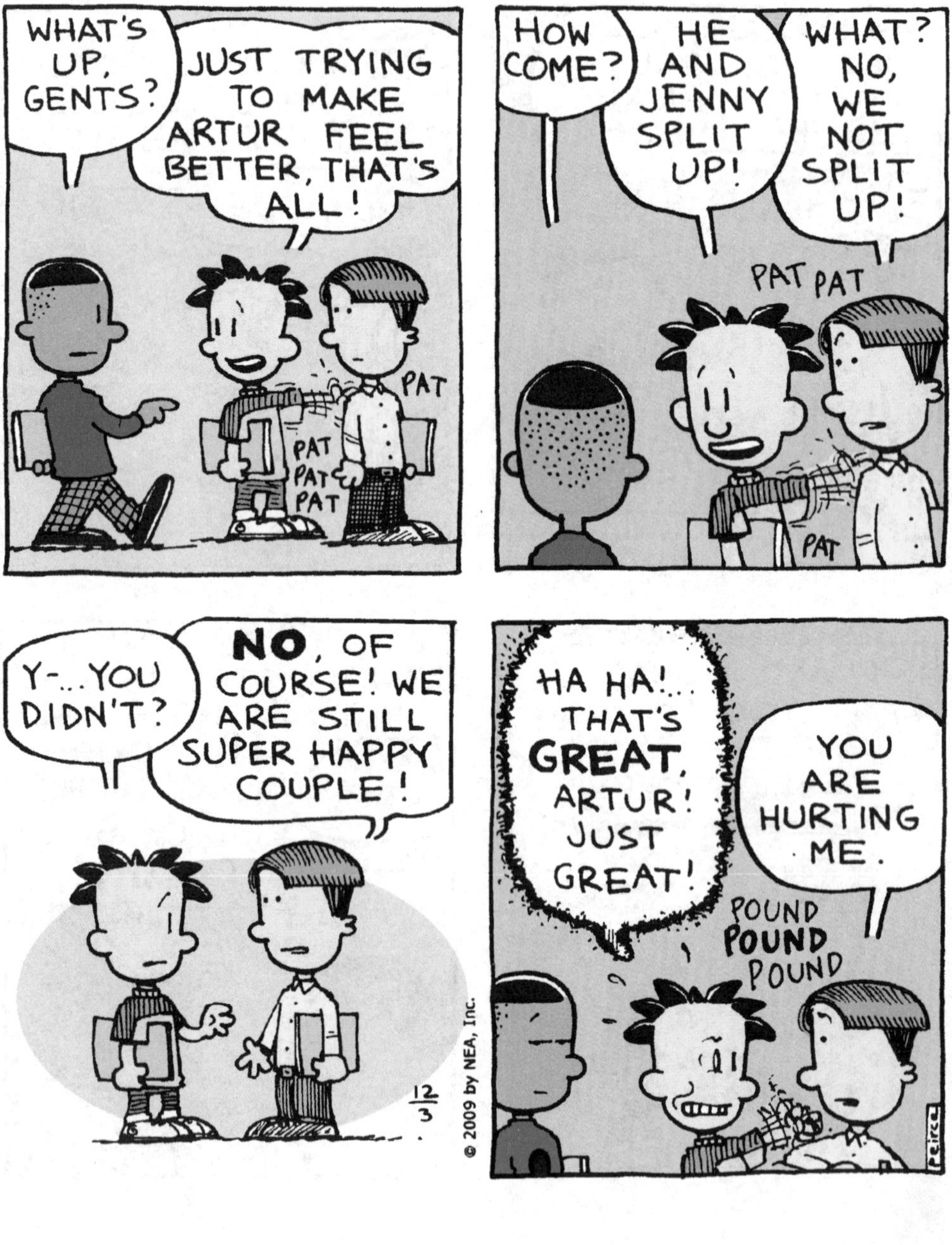
WHAT'S UP, GENTS?
JUST TRYING TO MAKE ARTUR FEEL BETTER, THAT'S ALL!
PAT
PAT PAT PAT
HOW COME?
HE AND JENNY SPLIT UP!
WHAT? NO, WE NOT SPLIT UP!
PAT PAT
PAT
Y-... YOU DIDN'T?
NO, OF COURSE! WE ARE STILL SUPER HAPPY COUPLE!
12
3
© 2009 by NEA, Inc.
HA HA!... THAT'S GREAT, ARTUR! JUST GREAT!
YOU ARE HURTING ME.
POUND POUND POUND
Peirce

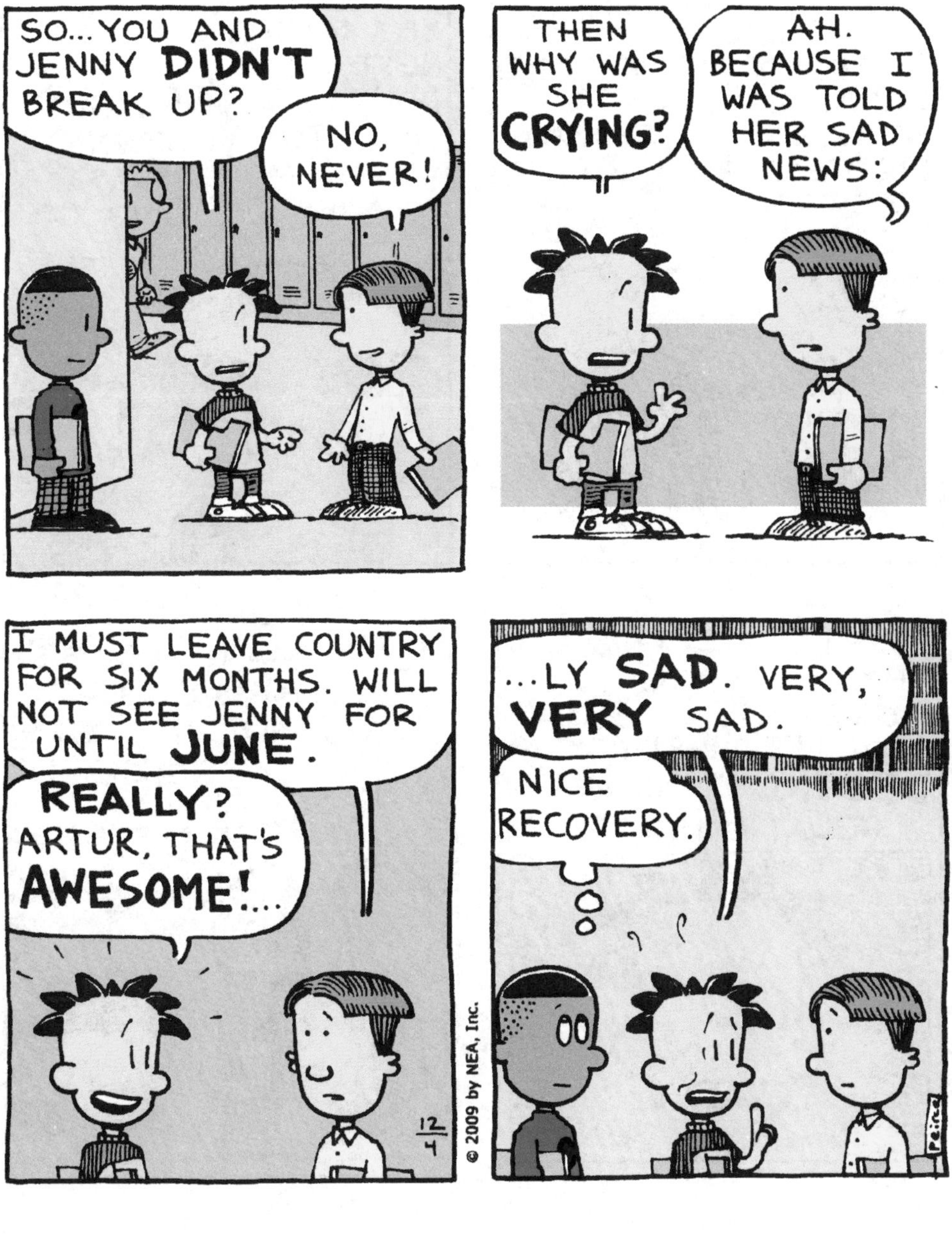
SO... YOU AND JENNY DIDN'T BREAK UP?
NO, NEVER!
THEN WHY WAS SHE CRYING?
AH. BECAUSE I WAS TOLD HER SAD NEWS:
I MUST LEAVE COUNTRY FOR SIX MONTHS. WILL NOT SEE JENNY FOR UNTIL JUNE.
REALLY? ARTUR, THAT'S AWESOME!...
12 4
© 2009 by NEA, Inc.
...LY SAD. VERY, VERY SAD.
NICE RECOVERY.
Peirce

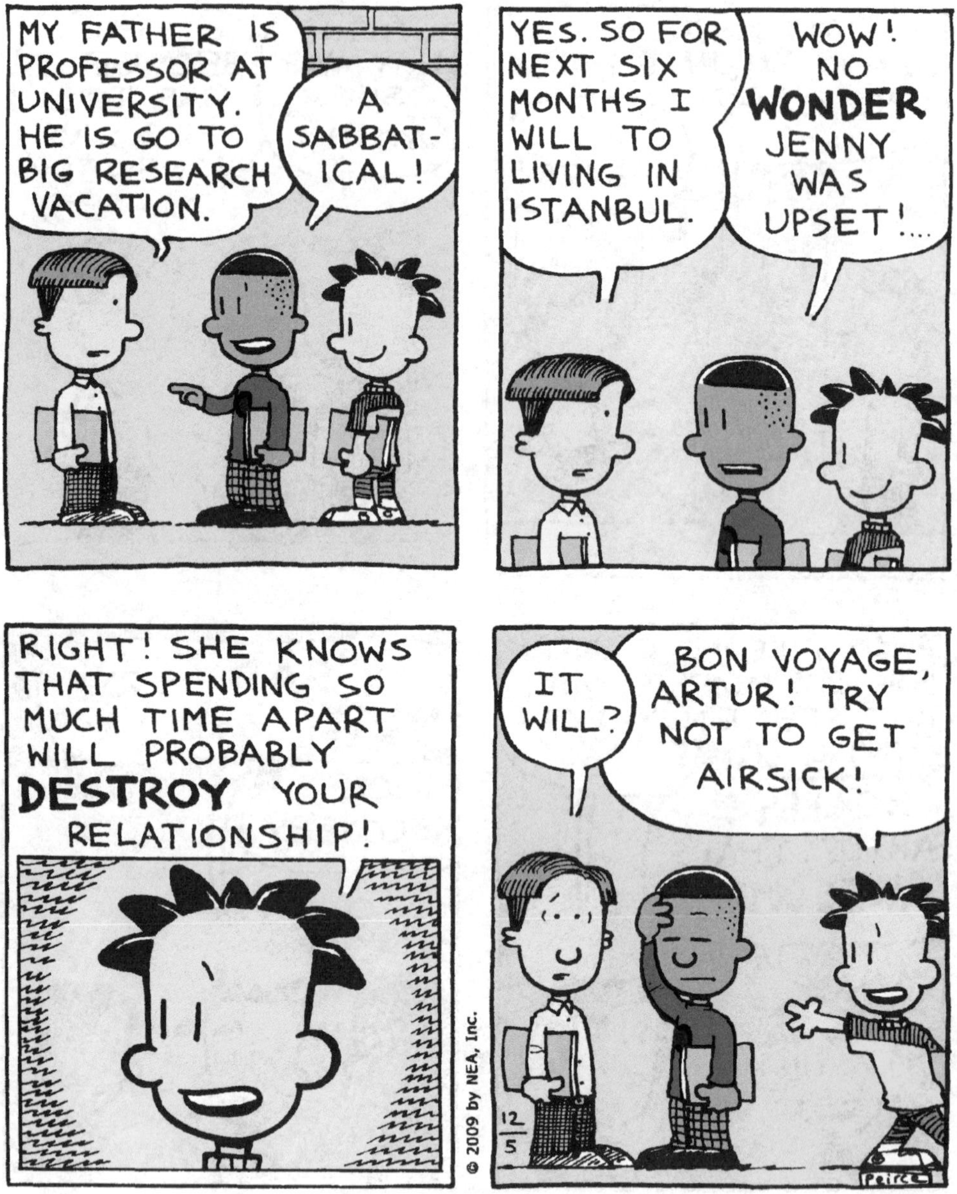

MY FATHER IS PROFESSOR AT UNIVERSITY. HE IS GO TO BIG RESEARCH VACATION.
A SABBATICAL!
YES. SO FOR NEXT SIX MONTHS I WILL TO LIVING IN ISTANBUL.
WOW! NO **WONDER** JENNY WAS UPSET!...
RIGHT! SHE KNOWS THAT SPENDING SO MUCH TIME APART WILL PROBABLY **DESTROY** YOUR RELATIONSHIP!
IT WILL?
BON VOYAGE, ARTUR! TRY NOT TO GET AIRSICK!
© 2009 by NEA, Inc.
12/5
Peirce

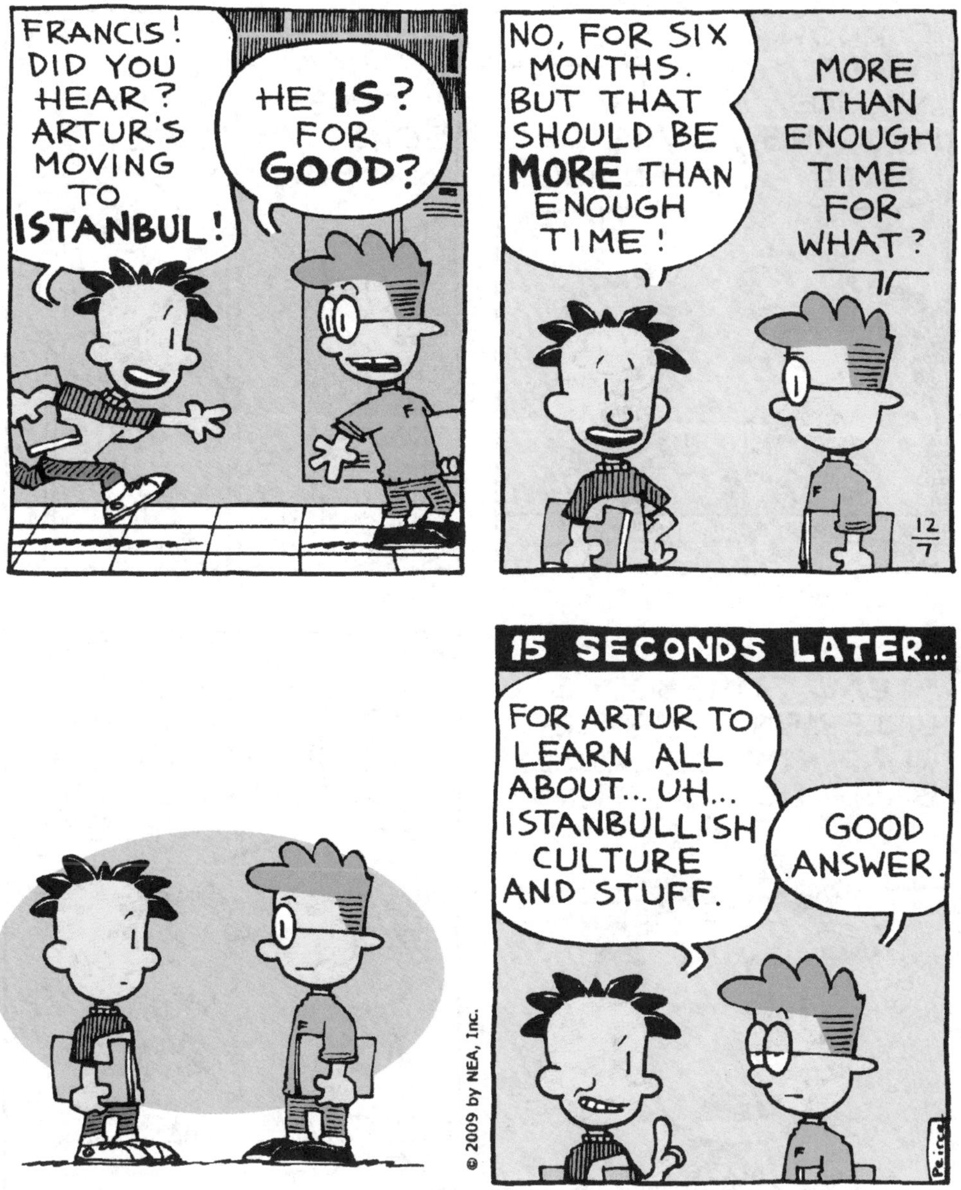
FRANCIS! DID YOU HEAR? ARTUR'S MOVING TO ISTANBUL!
HE IS? FOR GOOD?
NO, FOR SIX MONTHS. BUT THAT SHOULD BE MORE THAN ENOUGH TIME!
MORE THAN ENOUGH TIME FOR WHAT?
12/7
15 SECONDS LATER...
FOR ARTUR TO LEARN ALL ABOUT... UH... ISTANBULLISH CULTURE AND STUFF.
GOOD ANSWER.
© 2009 by NEA, Inc.
Peirce

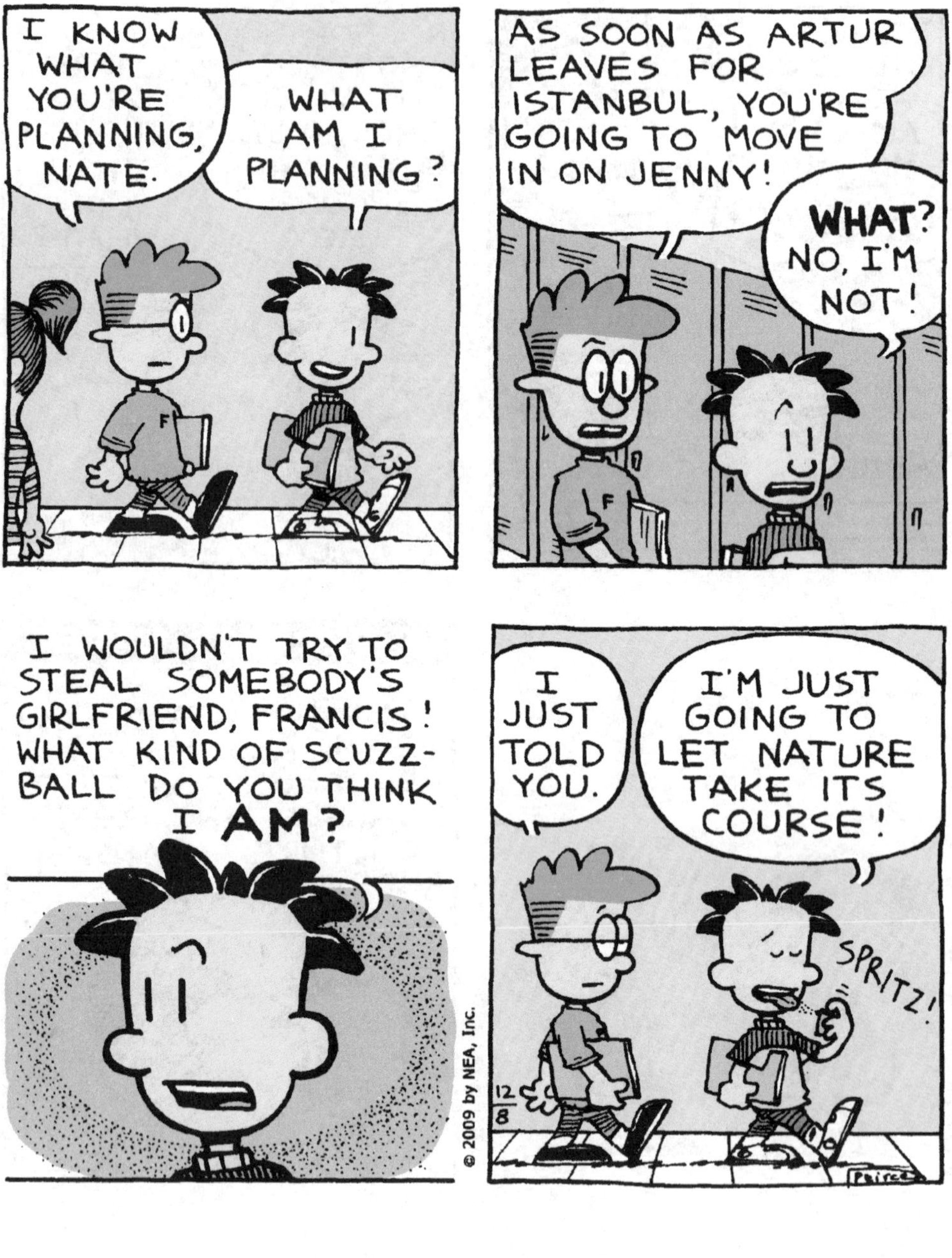
I KNOW WHAT YOU'RE PLANNING, NATE.
WHAT AM I PLANNING?
AS SOON AS ARTUR LEAVES FOR ISTANBUL, YOU'RE GOING TO MOVE IN ON JENNY!
WHAT? NO, I'M NOT!
I WOULDN'T TRY TO STEAL SOMEBODY'S GIRLFRIEND, FRANCIS! WHAT KIND OF SCUZZ-BALL DO YOU THINK I AM?
I JUST TOLD YOU.
I'M JUST GOING TO LET NATURE TAKE ITS COURSE!
SPRITZ!
12/8
© 2009 by NEA, Inc.
PEIRCE

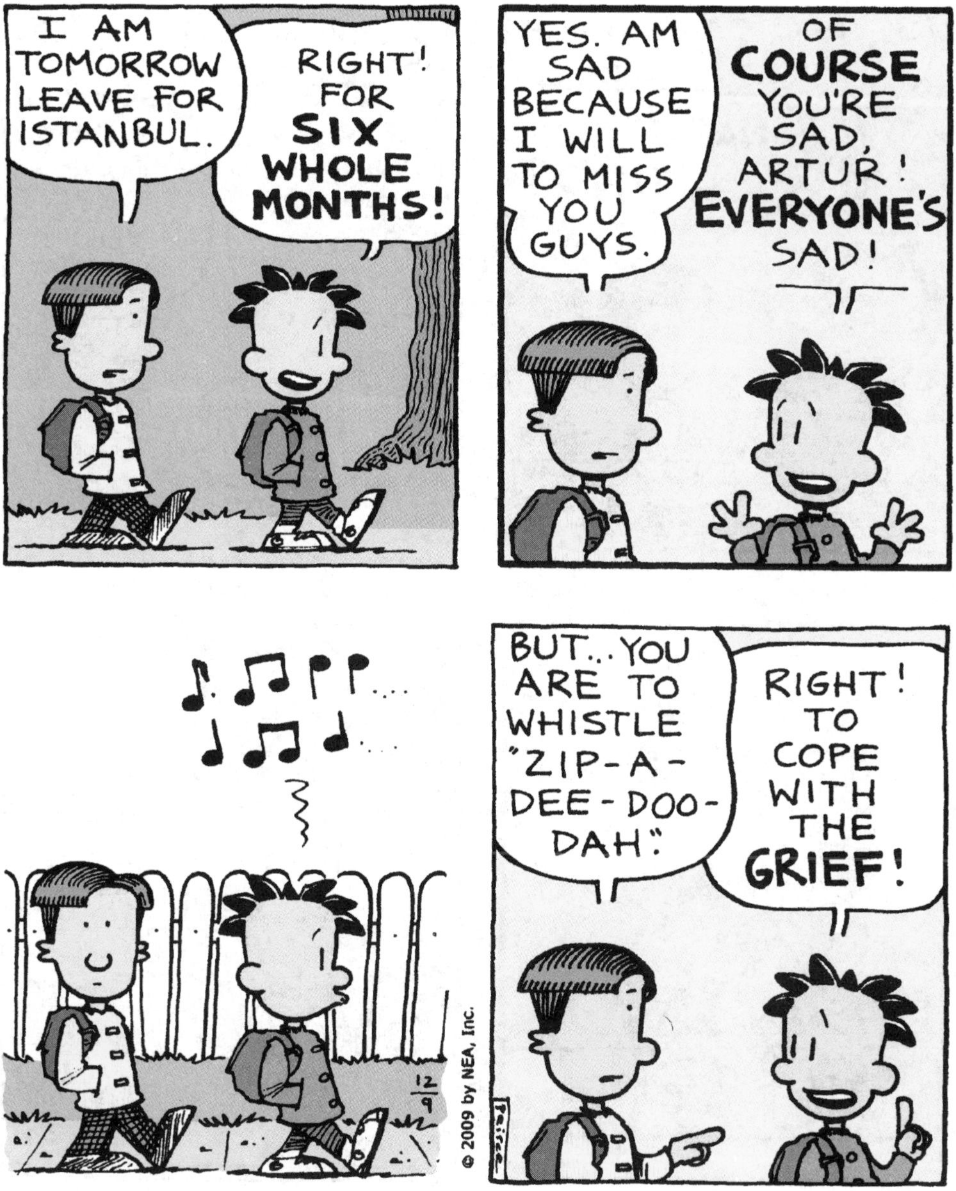

I AM TOMORROW LEAVE FOR ISTANBUL.
RIGHT! FOR SIX WHOLE MONTHS!
YES. AM SAD BECAUSE I WILL TO MISS YOU GUYS.
OF COURSE YOU'RE SAD, ARTUR! EVERYONE'S SAD!
BUT... YOU ARE TO WHISTLE "ZIP-A-DEE-DOO-DAH".
RIGHT! TO COPE WITH THE GRIEF!
12/9
© 2009 by NEA, Inc.
Peirce

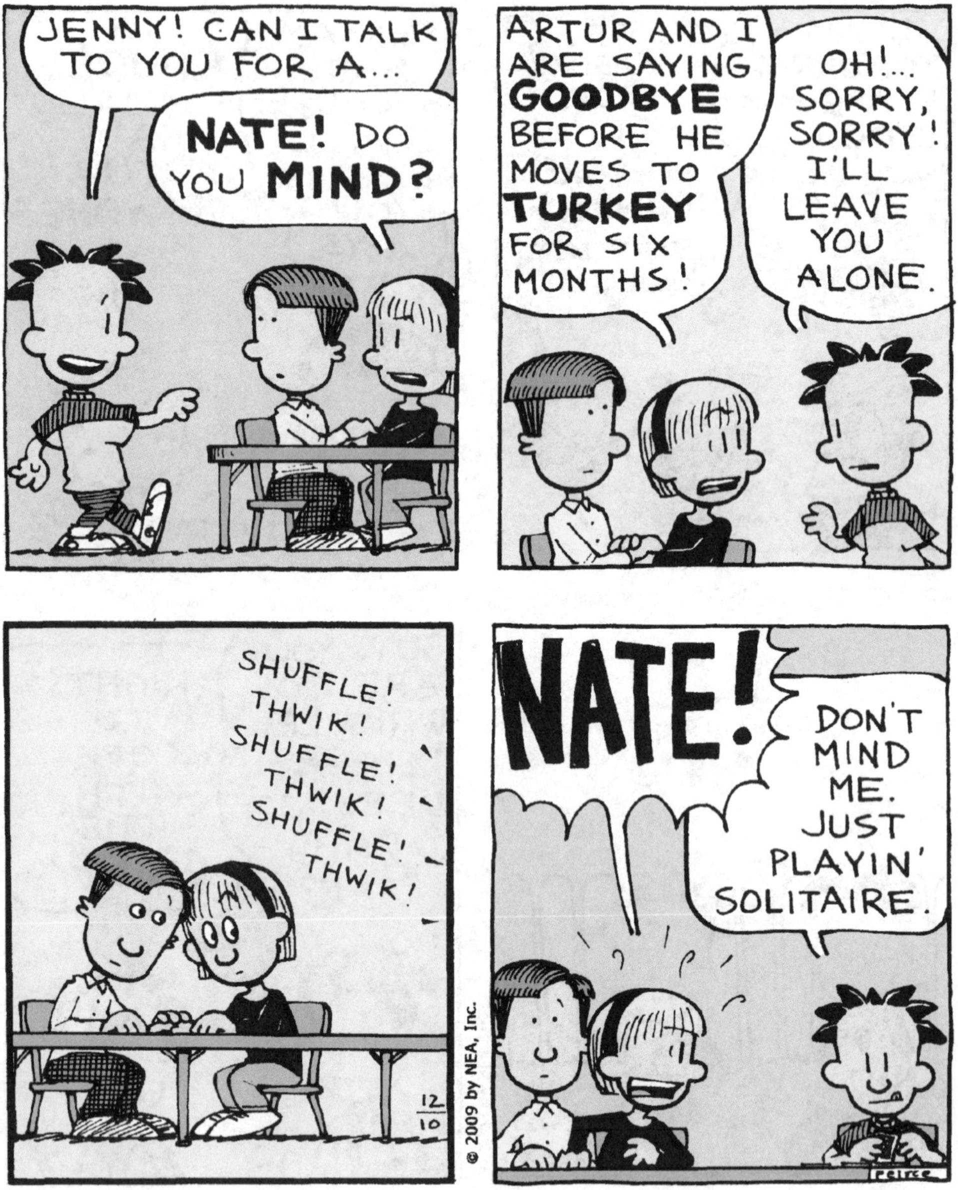
JENNY! CAN I TALK TO YOU FOR A...
NATE! DO YOU MIND?
ARTUR AND I ARE SAYING GOODBYE BEFORE HE MOVES TO TURKEY FOR SIX MONTHS!
OH!... SORRY, SORRY! I'LL LEAVE YOU ALONE.
SHUFFLE! THWIK! SHUFFLE! THWIK! SHUFFLE! THWIK!
12/10
© 2009 by NEA, Inc.
NATE!
DON'T MIND ME. JUST PLAYIN' SOLITAIRE.
peirce

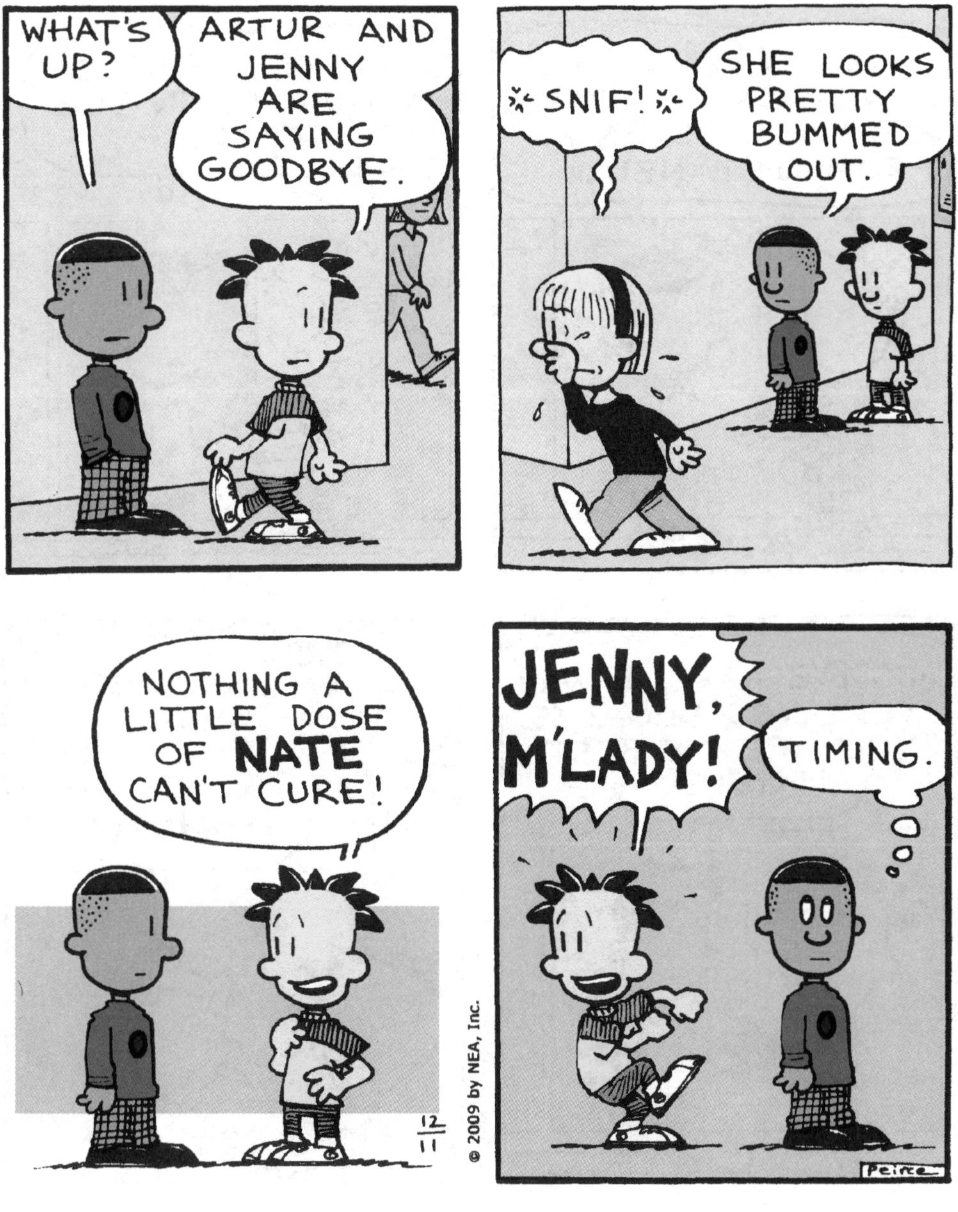
WHAT'S UP?
ARTUR AND JENNY ARE SAYING GOODBYE.
SNIF!
SHE LOOKS PRETTY BUMMED OUT.
NOTHING A LITTLE DOSE OF **NATE** CAN'T CURE!
12/11
© 2009 by NEA, Inc.
JENNY, M'LADY!
TIMING.
Peirce

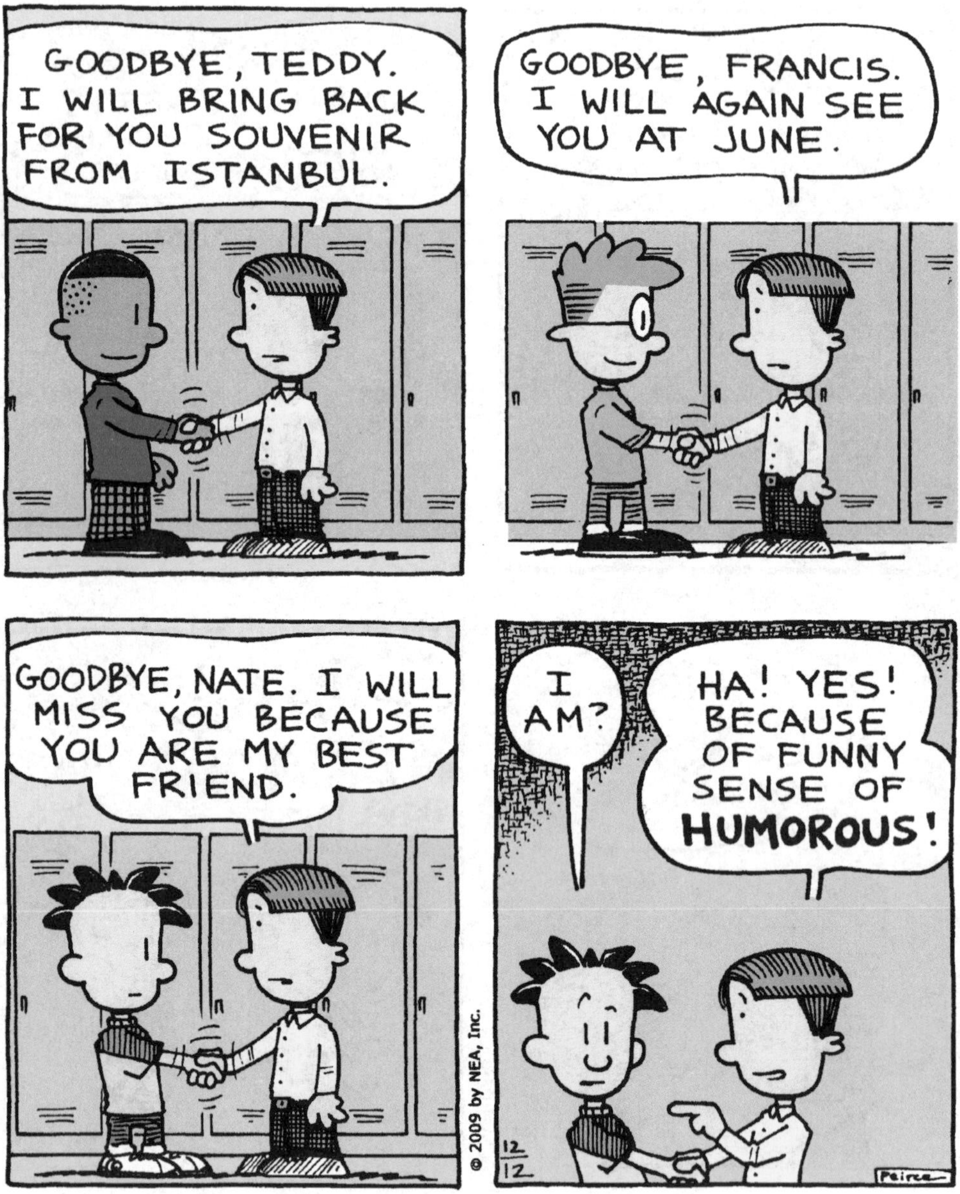
GOODBYE, TEDDY. I WILL BRING BACK FOR YOU SOUVENIR FROM ISTANBUL.
GOODBYE, FRANCIS. I WILL AGAIN SEE YOU AT JUNE.
GOODBYE, NATE. I WILL MISS YOU BECAUSE YOU ARE MY BEST FRIEND.
I AM?
HA! YES! BECAUSE OF FUNNY SENSE OF HUMOROUS!
© 2009 by NEA, Inc.
12/12
Peirce

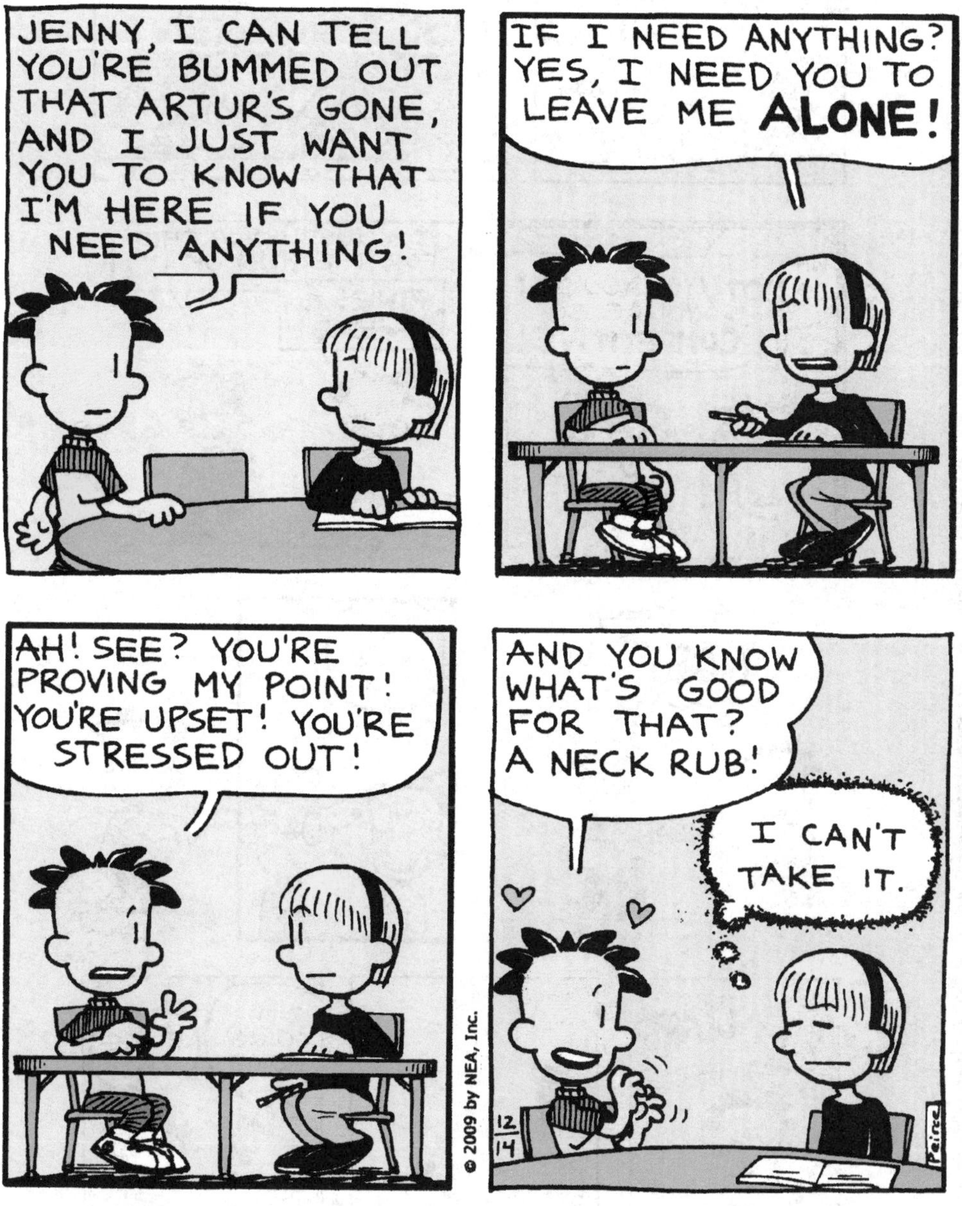
JENNY, I CAN TELL YOU'RE BUMMED OUT THAT ARTUR'S GONE, AND I JUST WANT YOU TO KNOW THAT I'M HERE IF YOU NEED ANYTHING!
IF I NEED ANYTHING? YES, I NEED YOU TO LEAVE ME ALONE!
AH! SEE? YOU'RE PROVING MY POINT! YOU'RE UPSET! YOU'RE STRESSED OUT!
AND YOU KNOW WHAT'S GOOD FOR THAT? A NECK RUB!
I CAN'T TAKE IT.
© 2009 by NEA, Inc.
12/14
Peirce

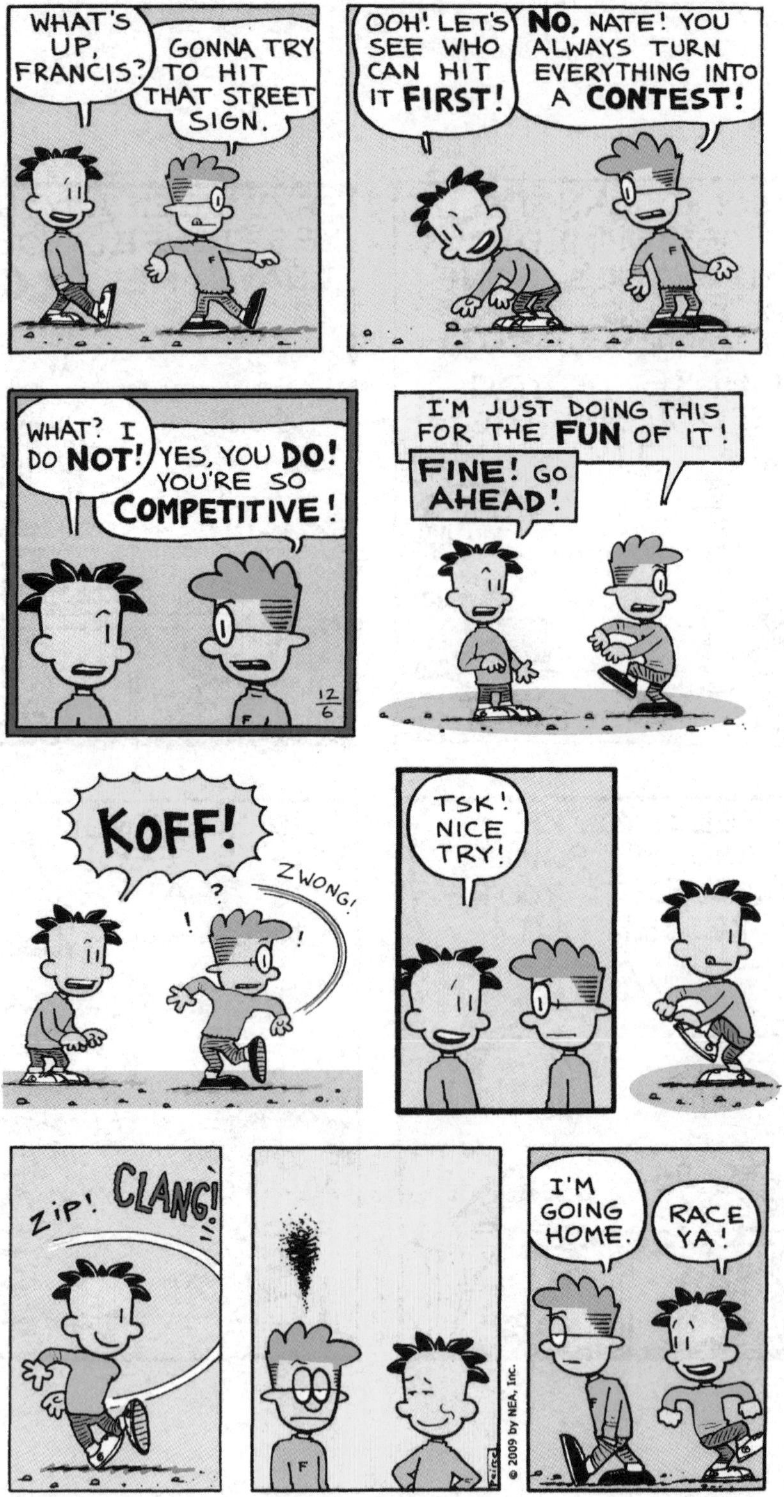
WHAT'S UP, FRANCIS?
GONNA TRY TO HIT THAT STREET SIGN.
OOH! LET'S SEE WHO CAN HIT IT FIRST!
NO, NATE! YOU ALWAYS TURN EVERYTHING INTO A CONTEST!
WHAT? I DO NOT!
YES, YOU DO! YOU'RE SO COMPETITIVE!
12/6
I'M JUST DOING THIS FOR THE FUN OF IT!
FINE! GO AHEAD!
KOFF!
?
! !
ZWONG!
TSK! NICE TRY!
ZIP! CLANG!
© 2009 by NEA, Inc.
I'M GOING HOME.
RACE YA!

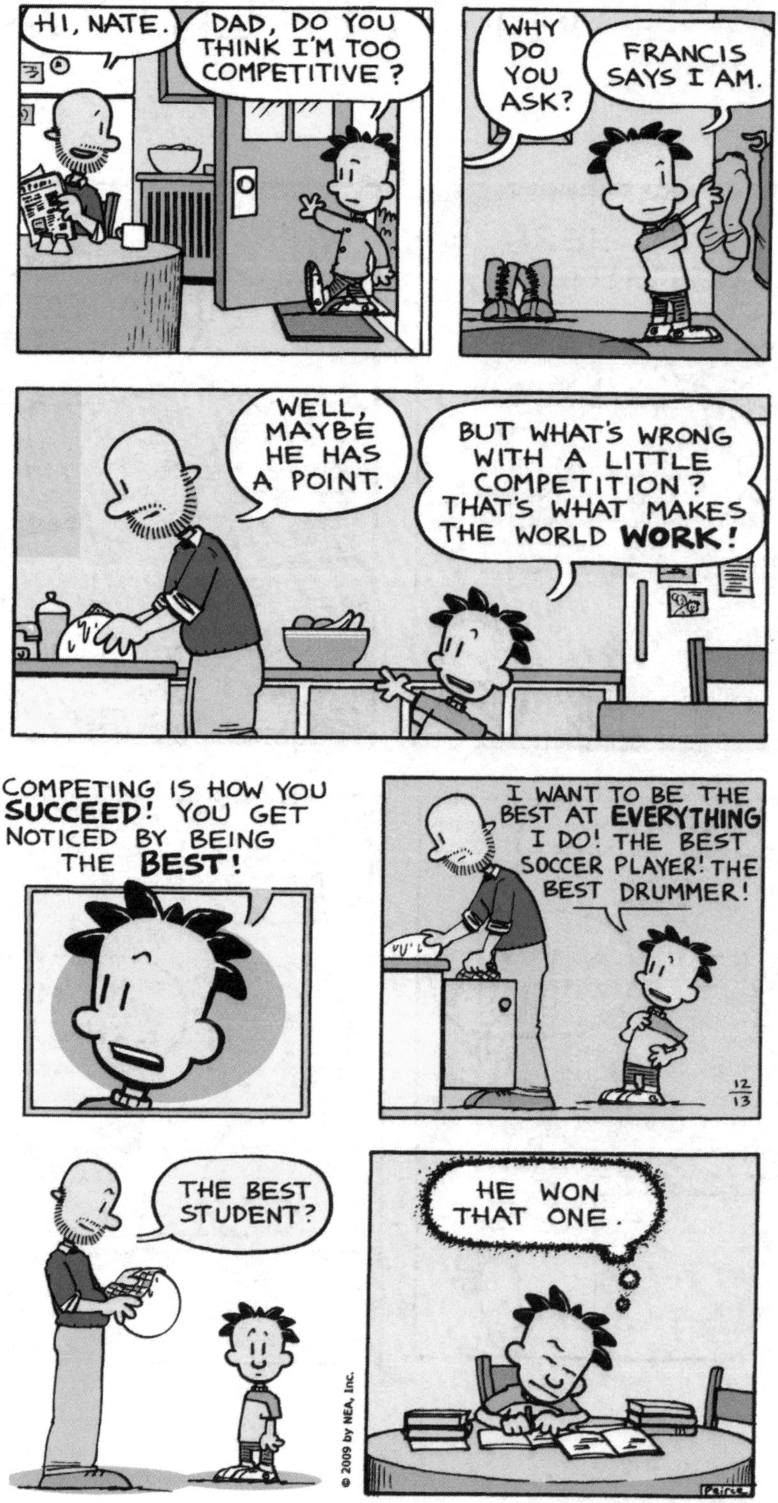
HI, NATE.
DAD, DO YOU THINK I'M TOO COMPETITIVE?
WHY DO YOU ASK?
FRANCIS SAYS I AM.
WELL, MAYBE HE HAS A POINT.
BUT WHAT'S WRONG WITH A LITTLE COMPETITION? THAT'S WHAT MAKES THE WORLD **WORK**!
COMPETING IS HOW YOU **SUCCEED**! YOU GET NOTICED BY BEING THE **BEST**!
I WANT TO BE THE BEST AT **EVERYTHING** I DO! THE BEST SOCCER PLAYER! THE BEST DRUMMER!
12/13
THE BEST STUDENT?
© 2009 by NEA, Inc.
HE WON THAT ONE.
Peirce

DATE WITH DETENTION

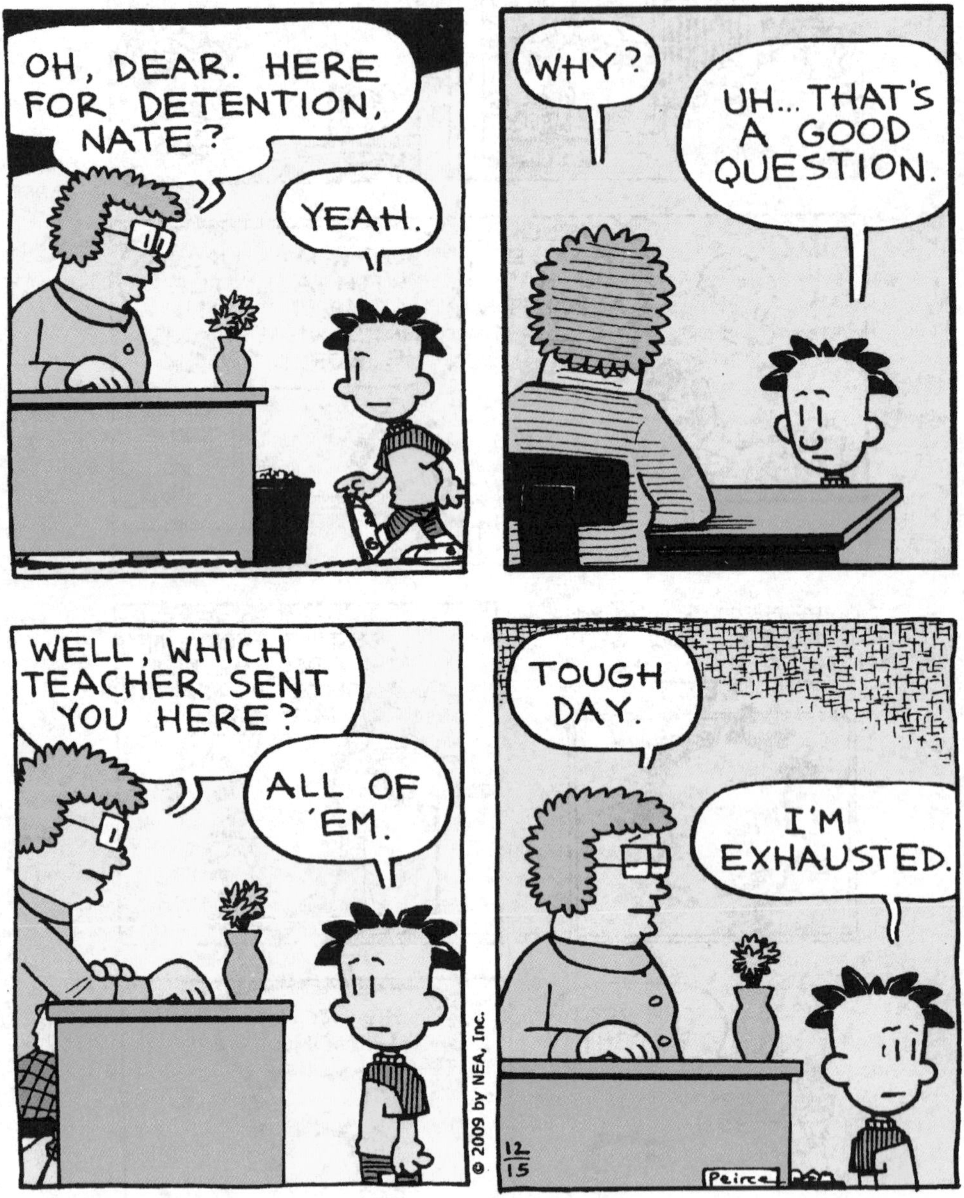
OH, DEAR. HERE FOR DETENTION, NATE?
YEAH.
WHY?
UH... THAT'S A GOOD QUESTION.
WELL, WHICH TEACHER SENT YOU HERE?
ALL OF 'EM.
© 2009 by NEA, Inc.
TOUGH DAY.
I'M EXHAUSTED.
12/15
Peirce

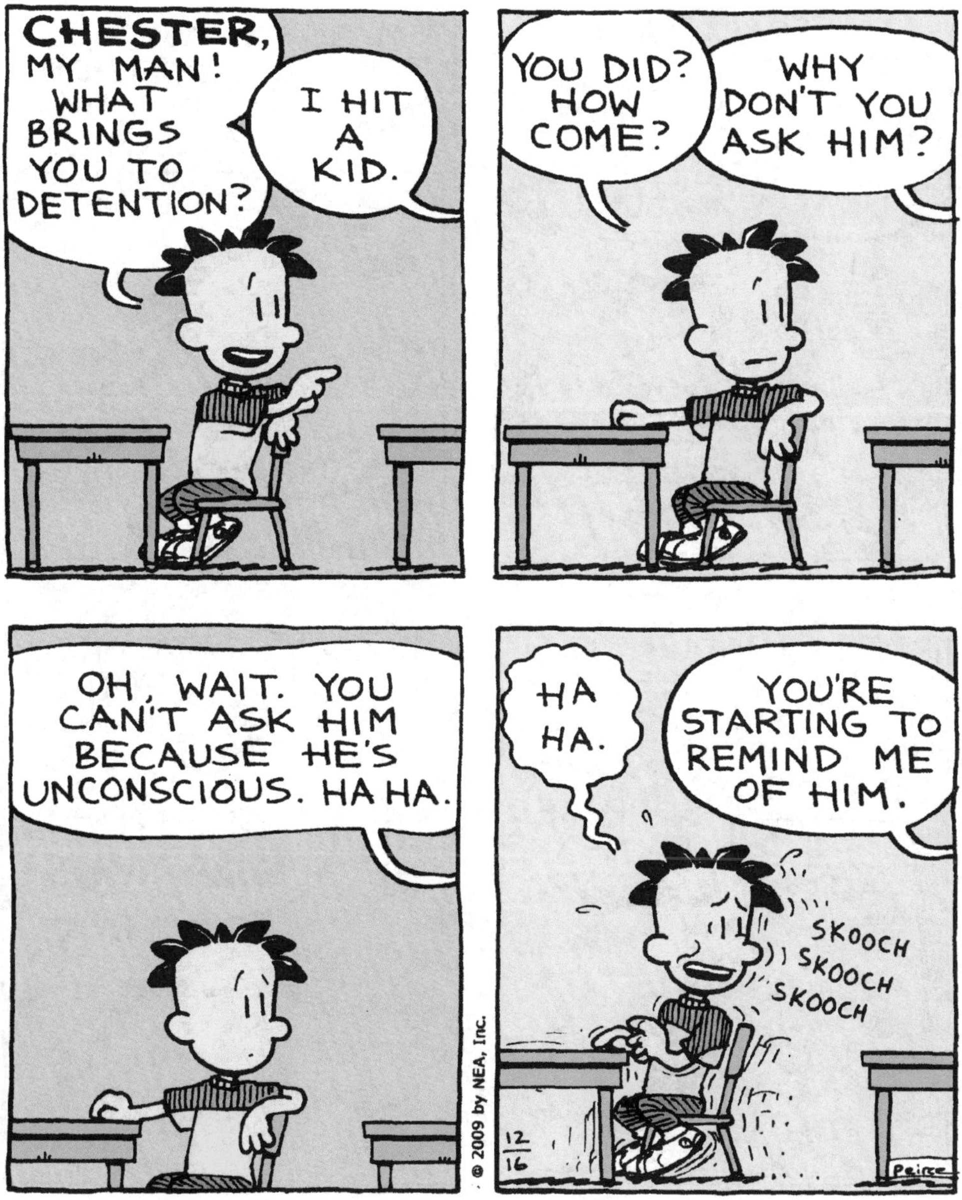
CHESTER, MY MAN! WHAT BRINGS YOU TO DETENTION?
I HIT A KID.
YOU DID? HOW COME?
WHY DON'T YOU ASK HIM?
OH, WAIT. YOU CAN'T ASK HIM BECAUSE HE'S UNCONSCIOUS. HA HA.
HA HA.
YOU'RE STARTING TO REMIND ME OF HIM.
SKOOCH
SKOOCH
SKOOCH
© 2009 by NEA, Inc.
12/16
Peirce

FAIR-WEATHER FRIENDS

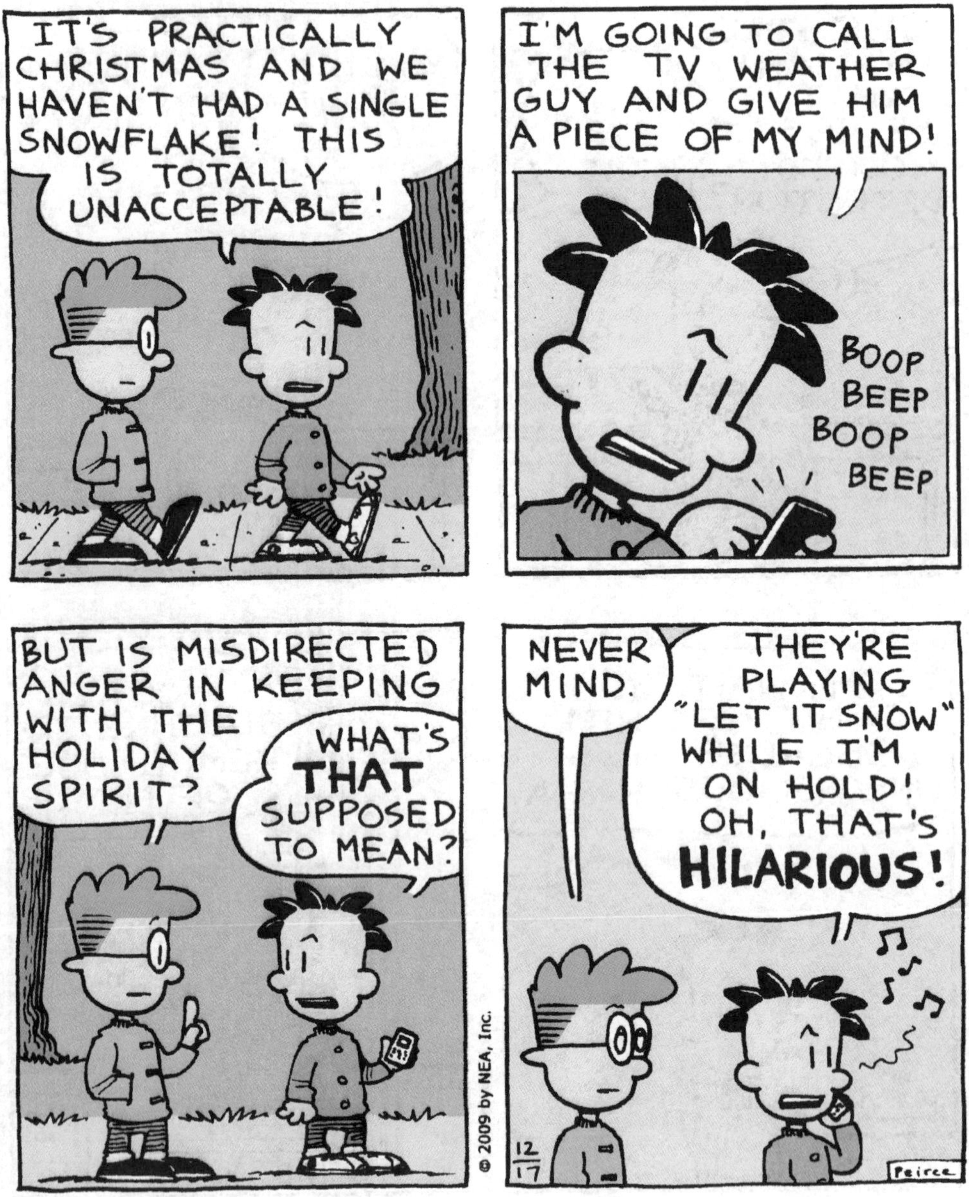

IT'S PRACTICALLY CHRISTMAS AND WE HAVEN'T HAD A SINGLE SNOWFLAKE! THIS IS TOTALLY UNACCEPTABLE!
I'M GOING TO CALL THE TV WEATHER GUY AND GIVE HIM A PIECE OF MY MIND!
BOOP BEEP BOOP BEEP
BUT IS MISDIRECTED ANGER IN KEEPING WITH THE HOLIDAY SPIRIT?
WHAT'S **THAT** SUPPOSED TO MEAN?
NEVER MIND.
THEY'RE PLAYING "LET IT SNOW" WHILE I'M ON HOLD! OH, THAT'S **HILARIOUS!**
© 2009 by NEA, Inc.
12/17
Peirce

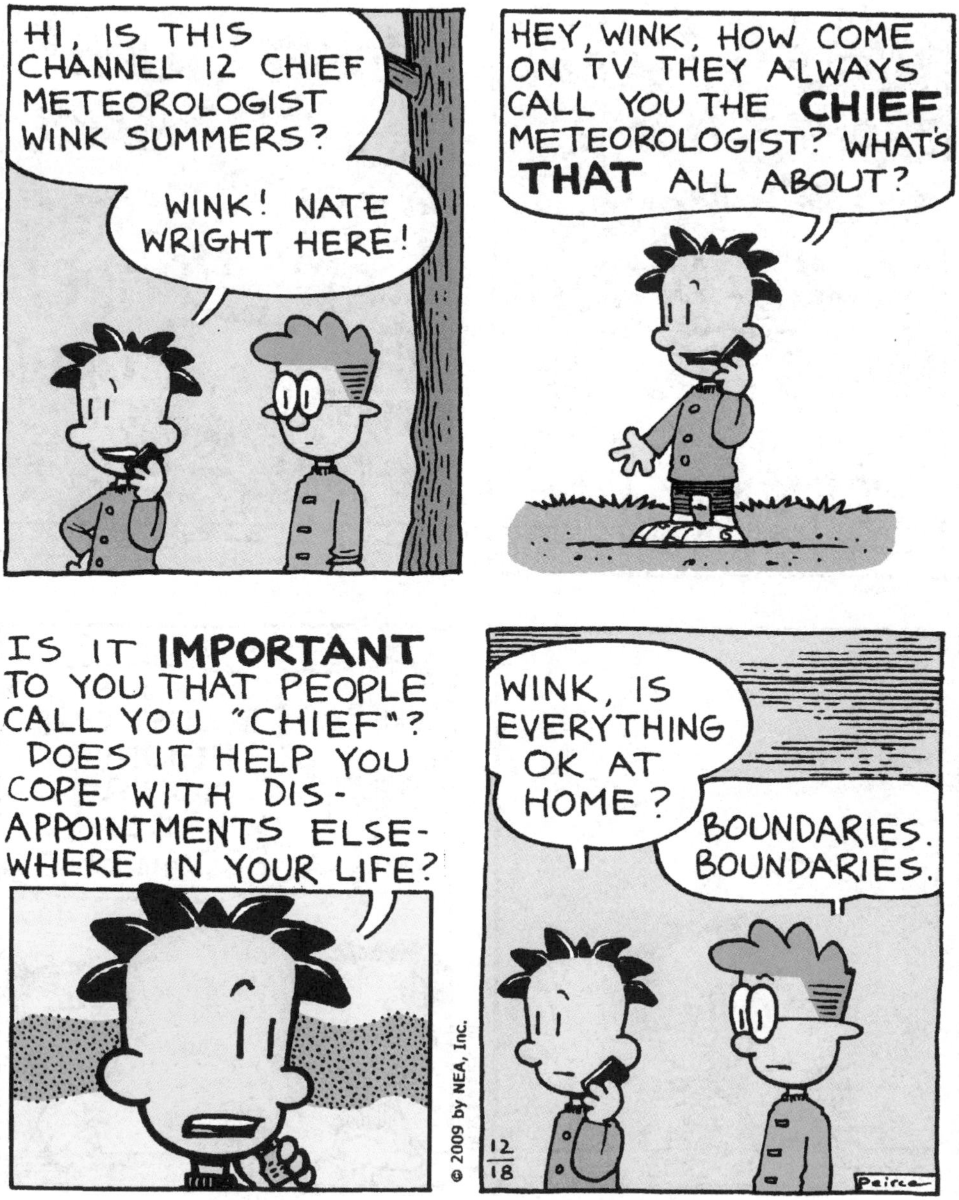
HI, IS THIS CHANNEL 12 CHIEF METEOROLOGIST WINK SUMMERS?
WINK! NATE WRIGHT HERE!
HEY, WINK, HOW COME ON TV THEY ALWAYS CALL YOU THE **CHIEF** METEOROLOGIST? WHAT'S **THAT** ALL ABOUT?
IS IT **IMPORTANT** TO YOU THAT PEOPLE CALL YOU "CHIEF"? DOES IT HELP YOU COPE WITH DIS-APPOINTMENTS ELSE-WHERE IN YOUR LIFE?
© 2009 by NEA, Inc.
12/18
WINK, IS EVERYTHING OK AT HOME?
BOUNDARIES. BOUNDARIES.
Peirce

HOW 'BOUT A NAPKIN

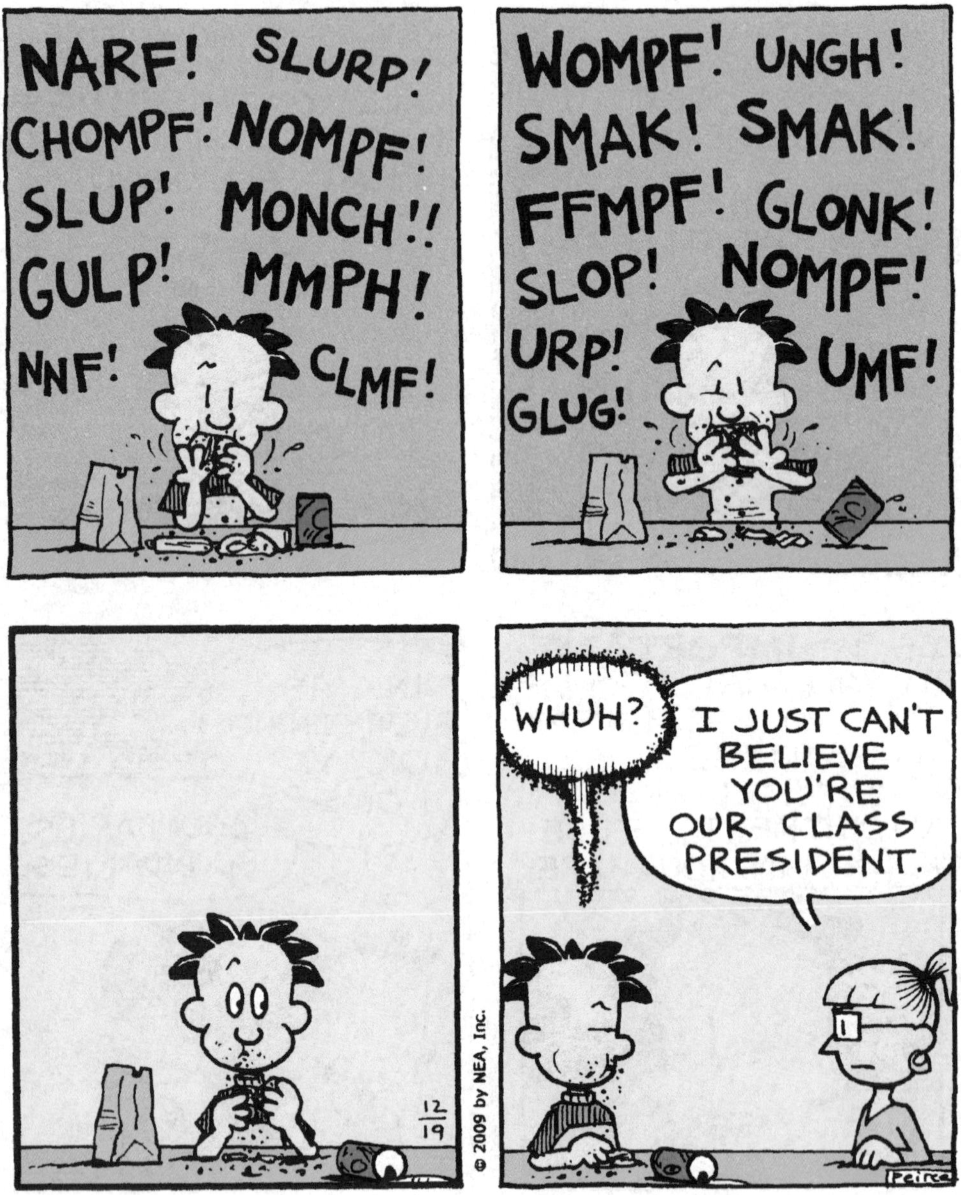
NARF! SLURP!
CHOMPF! NOMPF!
SLUP! MONCH!!
GULP! MMPH!
NNF! CLMF!
WOMPF! UNGH!
SMAK! SMAK!
FFMPF! GLONK!
SLOP! NOMPF!
URP! UMF!
GLUG!
12/19
© 2009 by NEA, Inc.
WHUH?
I JUST CAN'T BELIEVE YOU'RE OUR CLASS PRESIDENT.
Peirce

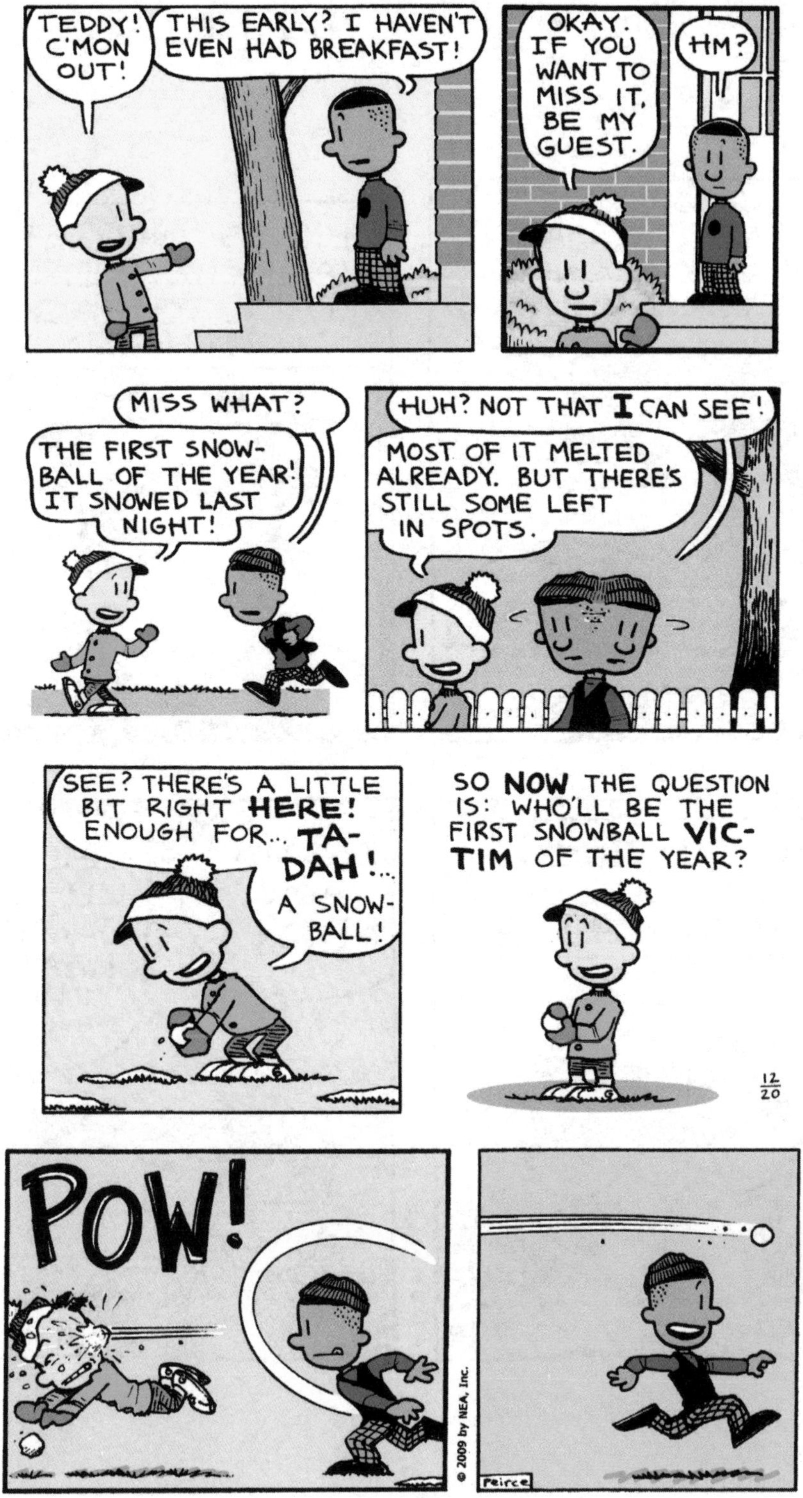
TEDDY! C'MON OUT!
THIS EARLY? I HAVEN'T EVEN HAD BREAKFAST!
OKAY. IF YOU WANT TO MISS IT, BE MY GUEST.
HM?
MISS WHAT?
THE FIRST SNOW-BALL OF THE YEAR! IT SNOWED LAST NIGHT!
HUH? NOT THAT I CAN SEE!
MOST OF IT MELTED ALREADY. BUT THERE'S STILL SOME LEFT IN SPOTS.
SEE? THERE'S A LITTLE BIT RIGHT HERE! ENOUGH FOR... TA-DAH!... A SNOW-BALL!
SO NOW THE QUESTION IS: WHO'LL BE THE FIRST SNOWBALL VIC-TIM OF THE YEAR?
12/20
POW!
© 2009 by NEA, Inc.
Peirce

REALITY BITES

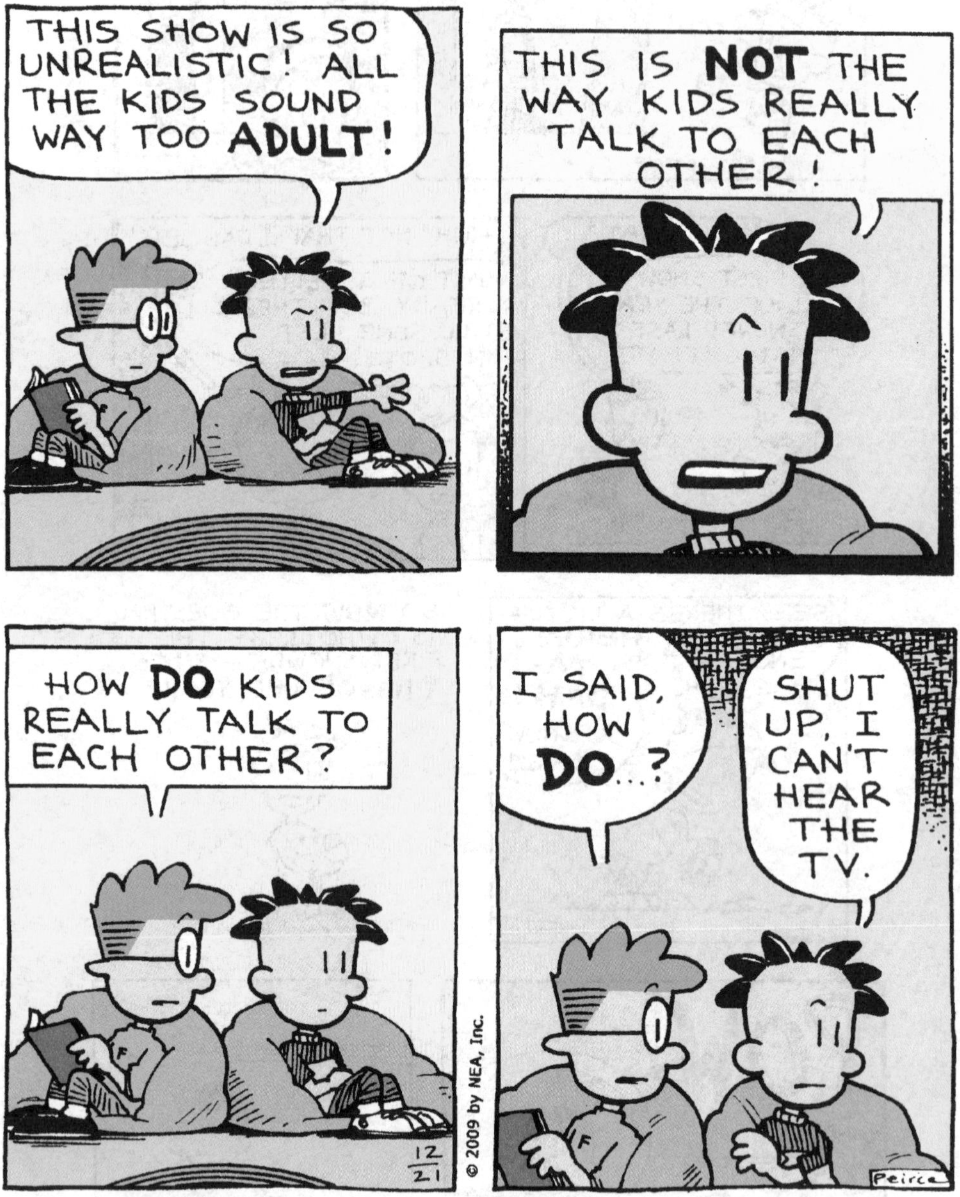

THIS SHOW IS SO UNREALISTIC! ALL THE KIDS SOUND WAY TOO **ADULT**!
THIS IS **NOT** THE WAY KIDS REALLY TALK TO EACH OTHER!
HOW **DO** KIDS REALLY TALK TO EACH OTHER?
12 21
© 2009 by NEA, Inc.
I SAID, HOW **DO**...?
SHUT UP, I CAN'T HEAR THE TV.
Peirce

'TWAS THE NATE BEFORE CHRISTMAS

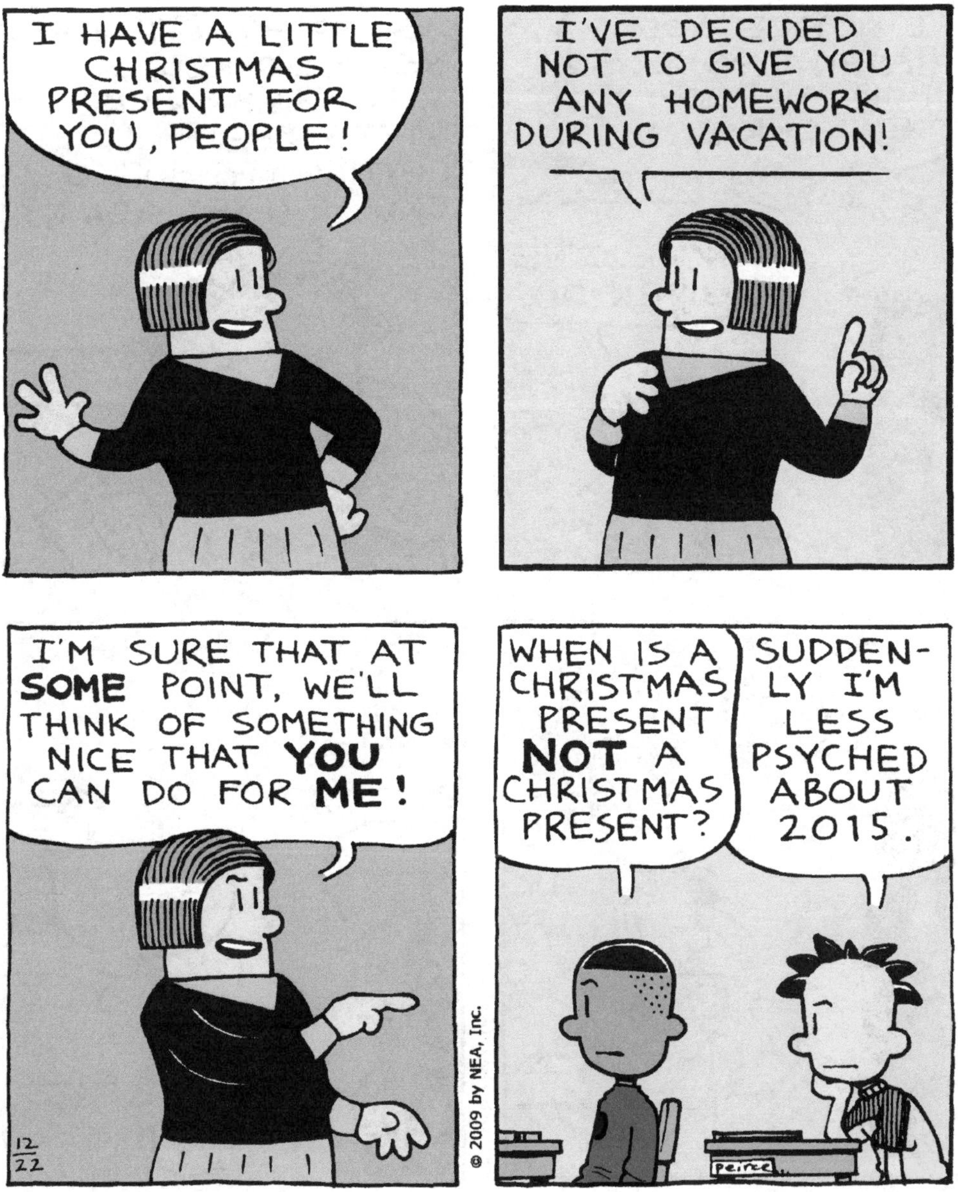
I HAVE A LITTLE CHRISTMAS PRESENT FOR YOU, PEOPLE!
I'VE DECIDED NOT TO GIVE YOU ANY HOMEWORK DURING VACATION!
I'M SURE THAT AT **SOME** POINT, WE'LL THINK OF SOMETHING NICE THAT **YOU** CAN DO FOR **ME**!
12/22
© 2009 by NEA, Inc.
WHEN IS A CHRISTMAS PRESENT **NOT** A CHRISTMAS PRESENT?
SUDDEN-LY I'M LESS PSYCHED ABOUT 2015.
peirce

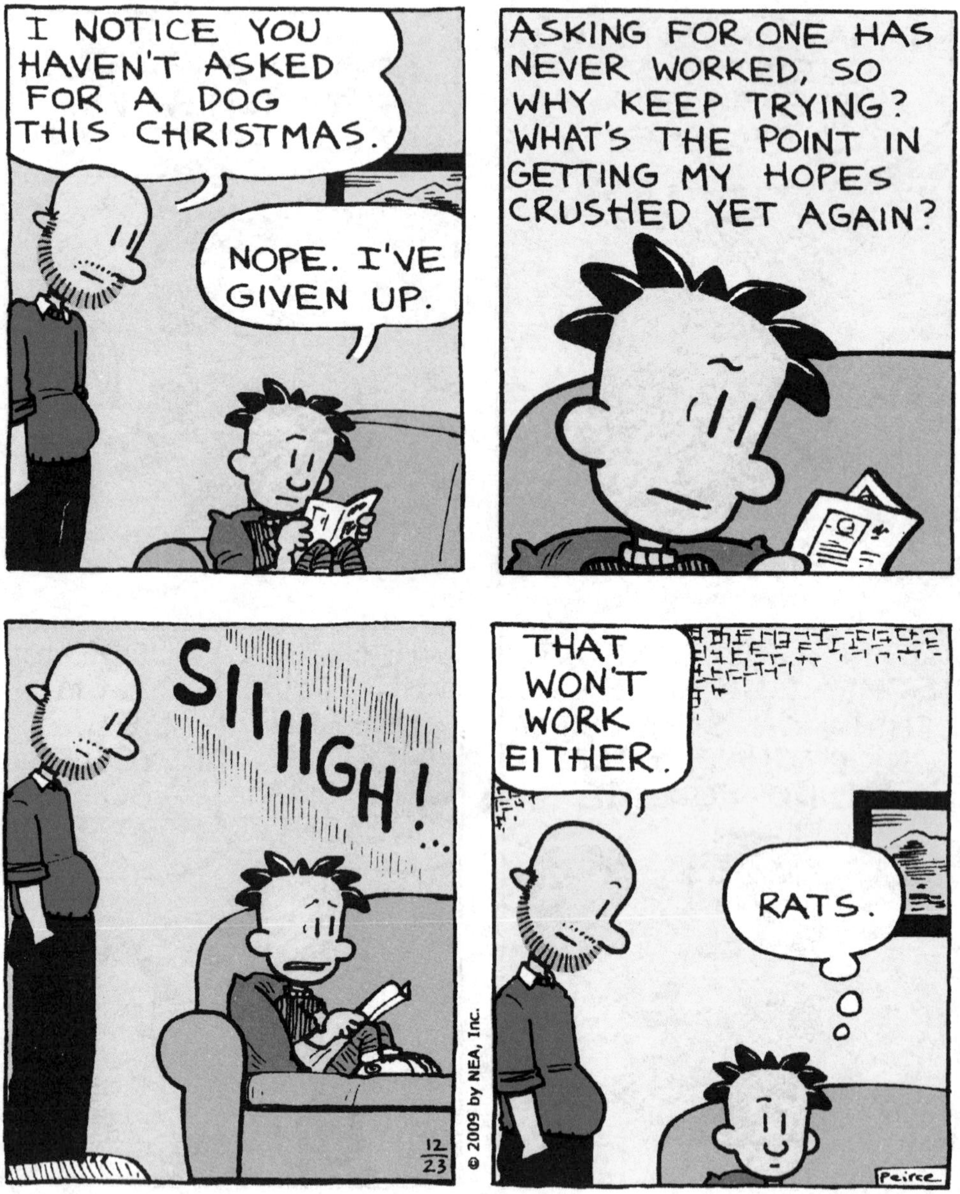
I NOTICE YOU HAVEN'T ASKED FOR A DOG THIS CHRISTMAS.
NOPE. I'VE GIVEN UP.
ASKING FOR ONE HAS NEVER WORKED, SO WHY KEEP TRYING? WHAT'S THE POINT IN GETTING MY HOPES CRUSHED YET AGAIN?
SIIIIGH!...
12/23
© 2009 by NEA, Inc.
THAT WON'T WORK EITHER.
RATS.
Peirce

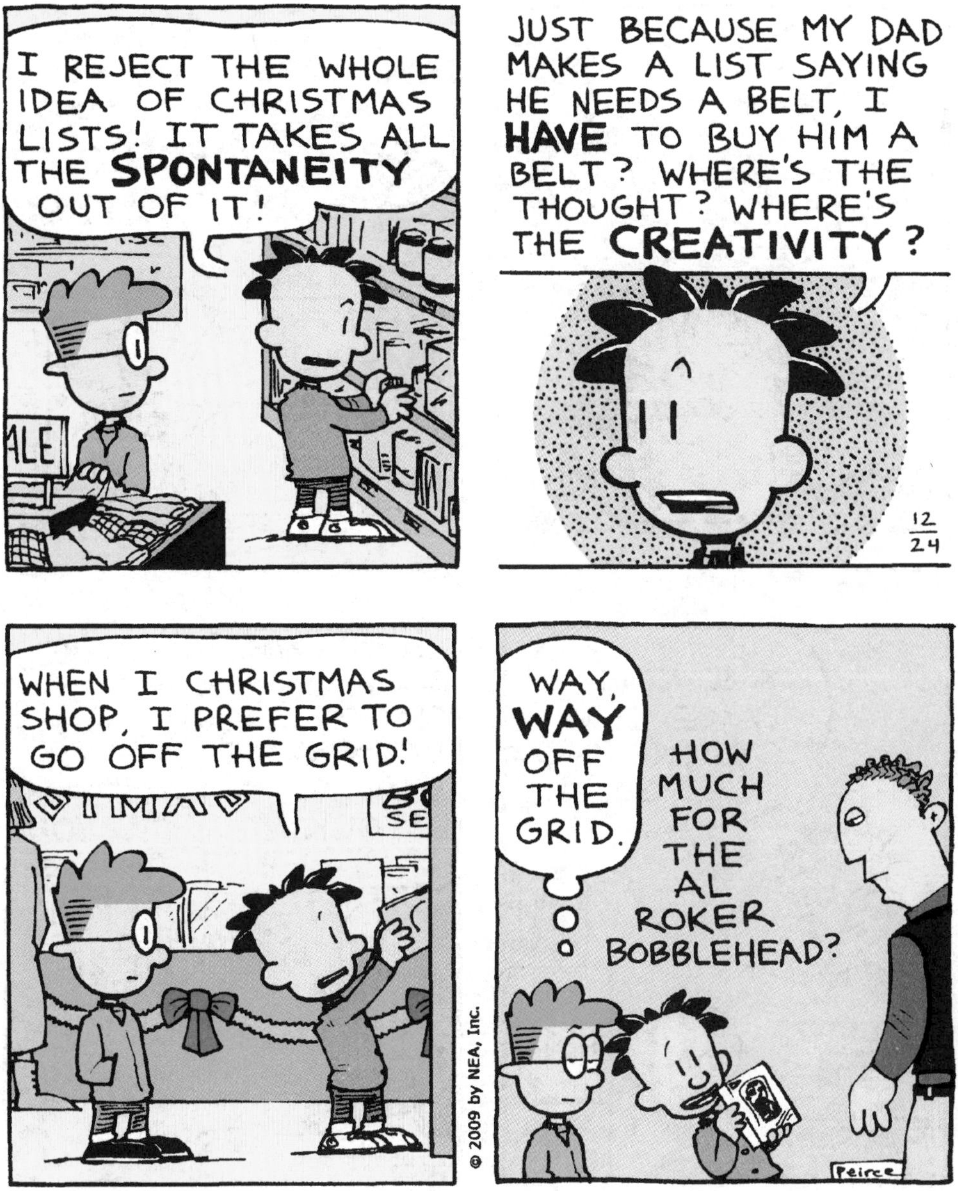
I REJECT THE WHOLE IDEA OF CHRISTMAS LISTS! IT TAKES ALL THE SPONTANEITY OUT OF IT!
JUST BECAUSE MY DAD MAKES A LIST SAYING HE NEEDS A BELT, I HAVE TO BUY HIM A BELT? WHERE'S THE THOUGHT? WHERE'S THE CREATIVITY?
12/24
WHEN I CHRISTMAS SHOP, I PREFER TO GO OFF THE GRID!
WAY, WAY OFF THE GRID.
HOW MUCH FOR THE AL ROKER BOBBLEHEAD?
Peirce
© 2009 by NEA, Inc.

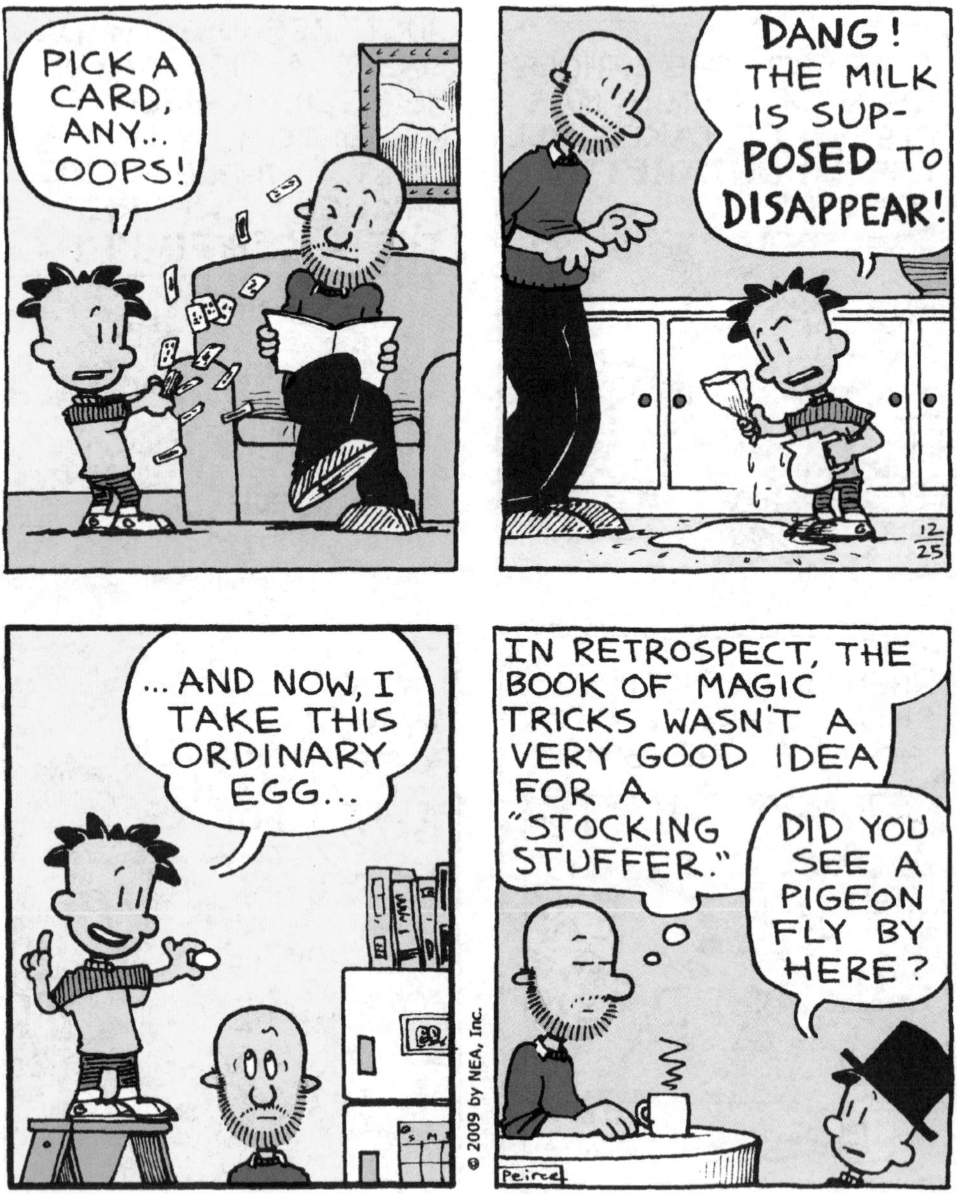
PICK A CARD, ANY... OOPS!
DANG! THE MILK IS SUP-POSED TO DISAPPEAR!
12/25
... AND NOW, I TAKE THIS ORDINARY EGG...
© 2009 by NEA, Inc.
IN RETROSPECT, THE BOOK OF MAGIC TRICKS WASN'T A VERY GOOD IDEA FOR A "STOCKING STUFFER."
DID YOU SEE A PIGEON FLY BY HERE?
Peirce

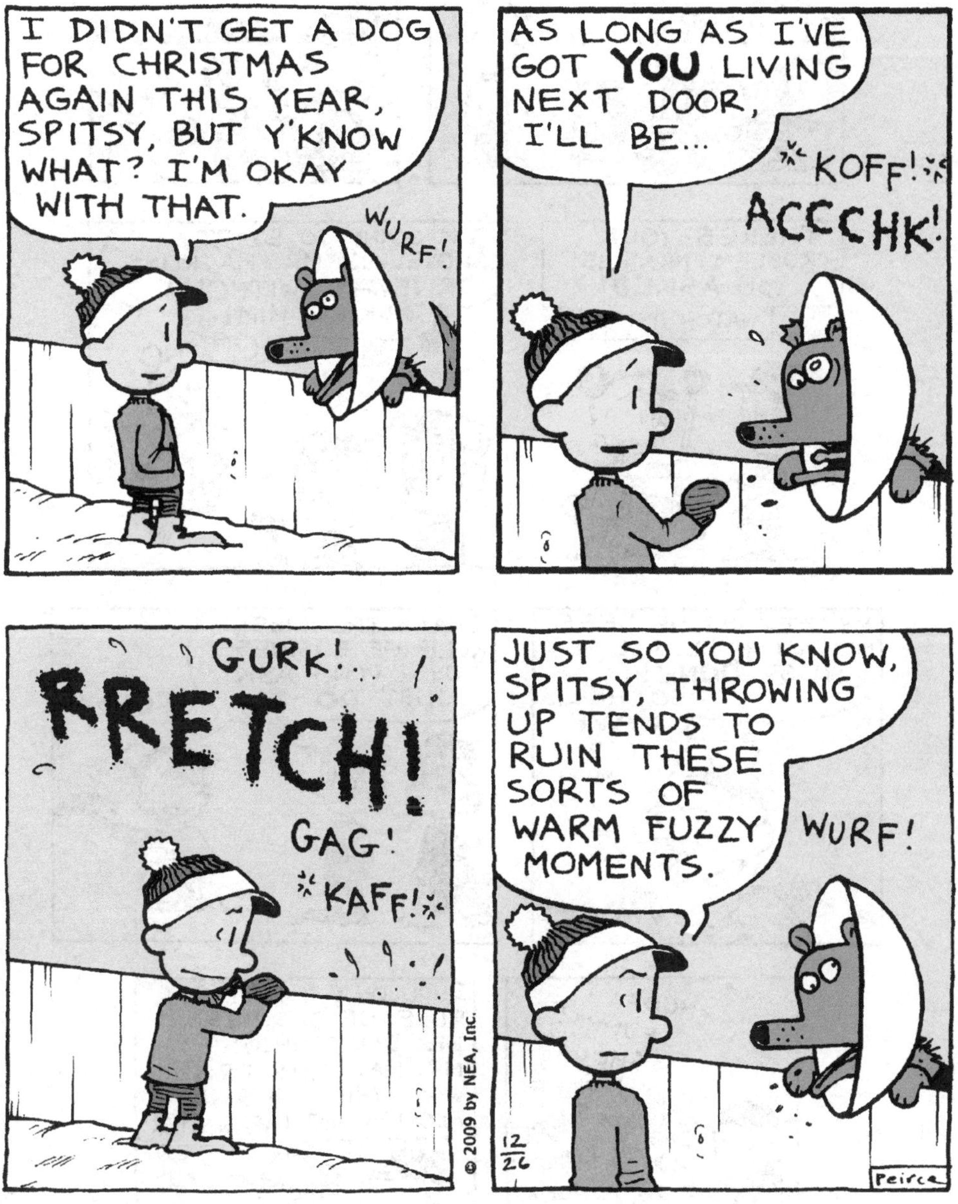
I DIDN'T GET A DOG FOR CHRISTMAS AGAIN THIS YEAR, SPITSY, BUT Y'KNOW WHAT? I'M OKAY WITH THAT.
WURF!
AS LONG AS I'VE GOT **YOU** LIVING NEXT DOOR, I'LL BE...
KOFF!
ACCCHK!
GURK!..
RRETCH!
GAG!
KAFF!
© 2009 by NEA, Inc.
JUST SO YOU KNOW, SPITSY, THROWING UP TENDS TO RUIN THESE SORTS OF WARM FUZZY MOMENTS.
WURF!
12/26
Peirce

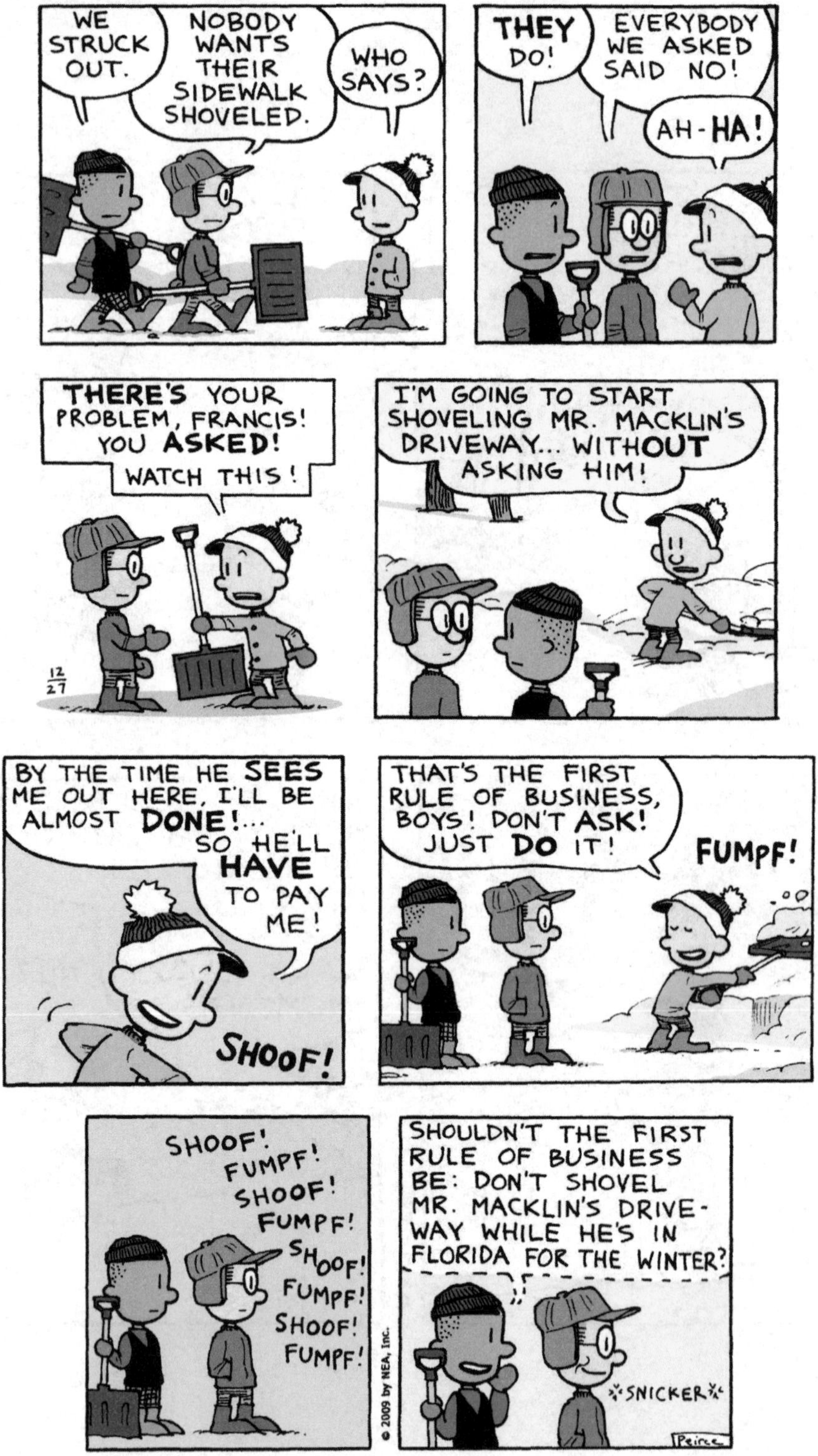
WE STRUCK OUT.
NOBODY WANTS THEIR SIDEWALK SHOVELED.
WHO SAYS?
THEY DO!
EVERYBODY WE ASKED SAID NO!
AH-HA!
THERE'S YOUR PROBLEM, FRANCIS! YOU ASKED!
WATCH THIS!
12 27
I'M GOING TO START SHOVELING MR. MACKLIN'S DRIVEWAY... WITHOUT ASKING HIM!
BY THE TIME HE SEES ME OUT HERE, I'LL BE ALMOST DONE!...
SO HE'LL HAVE TO PAY ME!
SHOOF!
THAT'S THE FIRST RULE OF BUSINESS, BOYS! DON'T ASK! JUST DO IT!
FUMPF!
SHOOF! FUMPF! SHOOF! FUMPF! SHOOF! FUMPF! SHOOF! FUMPF!
© 2009 by NEA, Inc.
SHOULDN'T THE FIRST RULE OF BUSINESS BE: DON'T SHOVEL MR. MACKLIN'S DRIVEWAY WHILE HE'S IN FLORIDA FOR THE WINTER?
SNICKER
Peirce

SNOW BUSINESS

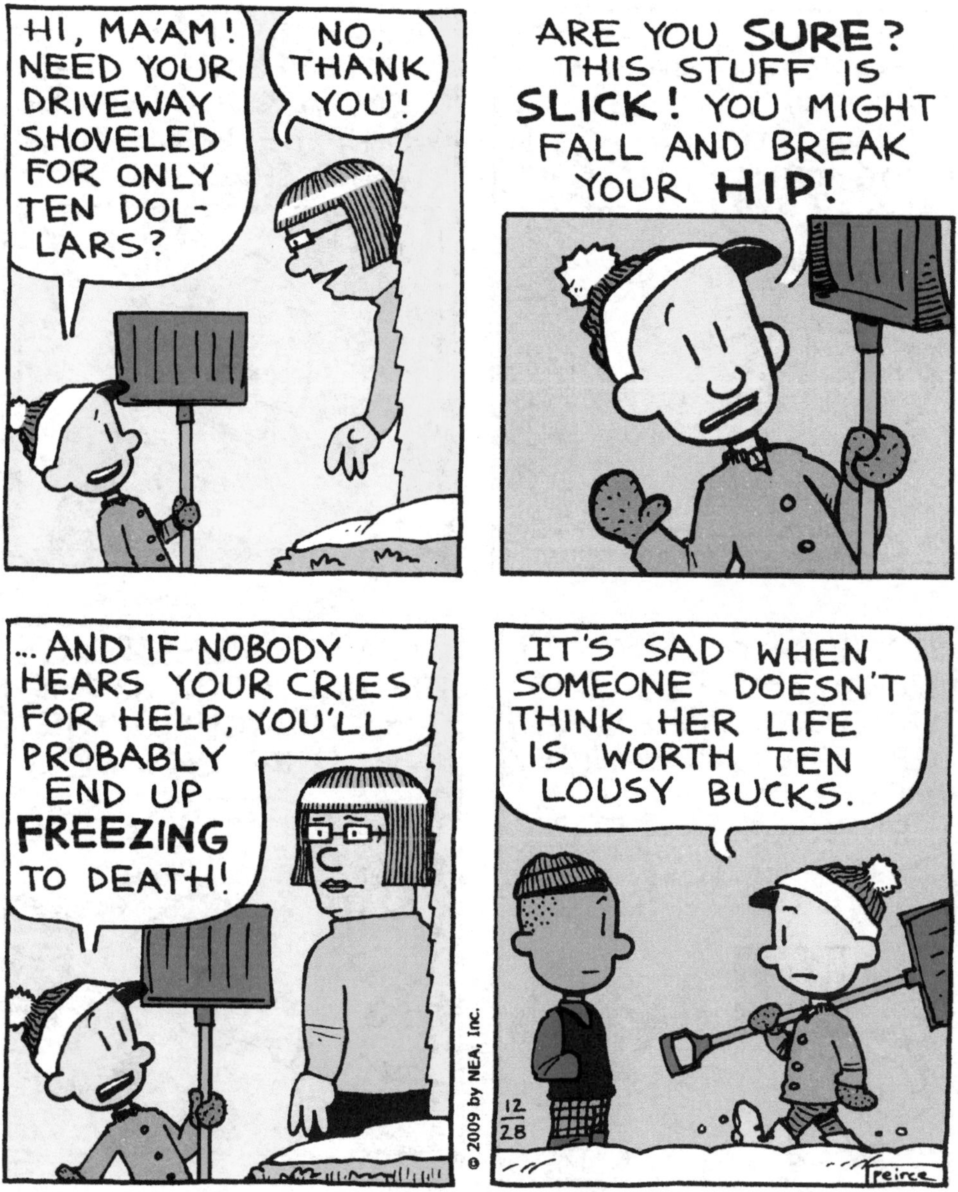
HI, MA'AM! NEED YOUR DRIVEWAY SHOVELED FOR ONLY TEN DOL-LARS?
NO, THANK YOU!
ARE YOU **SURE**? THIS STUFF IS **SLICK!** YOU MIGHT FALL AND BREAK YOUR **HIP!**
...AND IF NOBODY HEARS YOUR CRIES FOR HELP, YOU'LL PROBABLY END UP **FREEZING** TO DEATH!
IT'S SAD WHEN SOMEONE DOESN'T THINK HER LIFE IS WORTH TEN LOUSY BUCKS.
© 2009 by NEA, Inc.
12/28
peirce

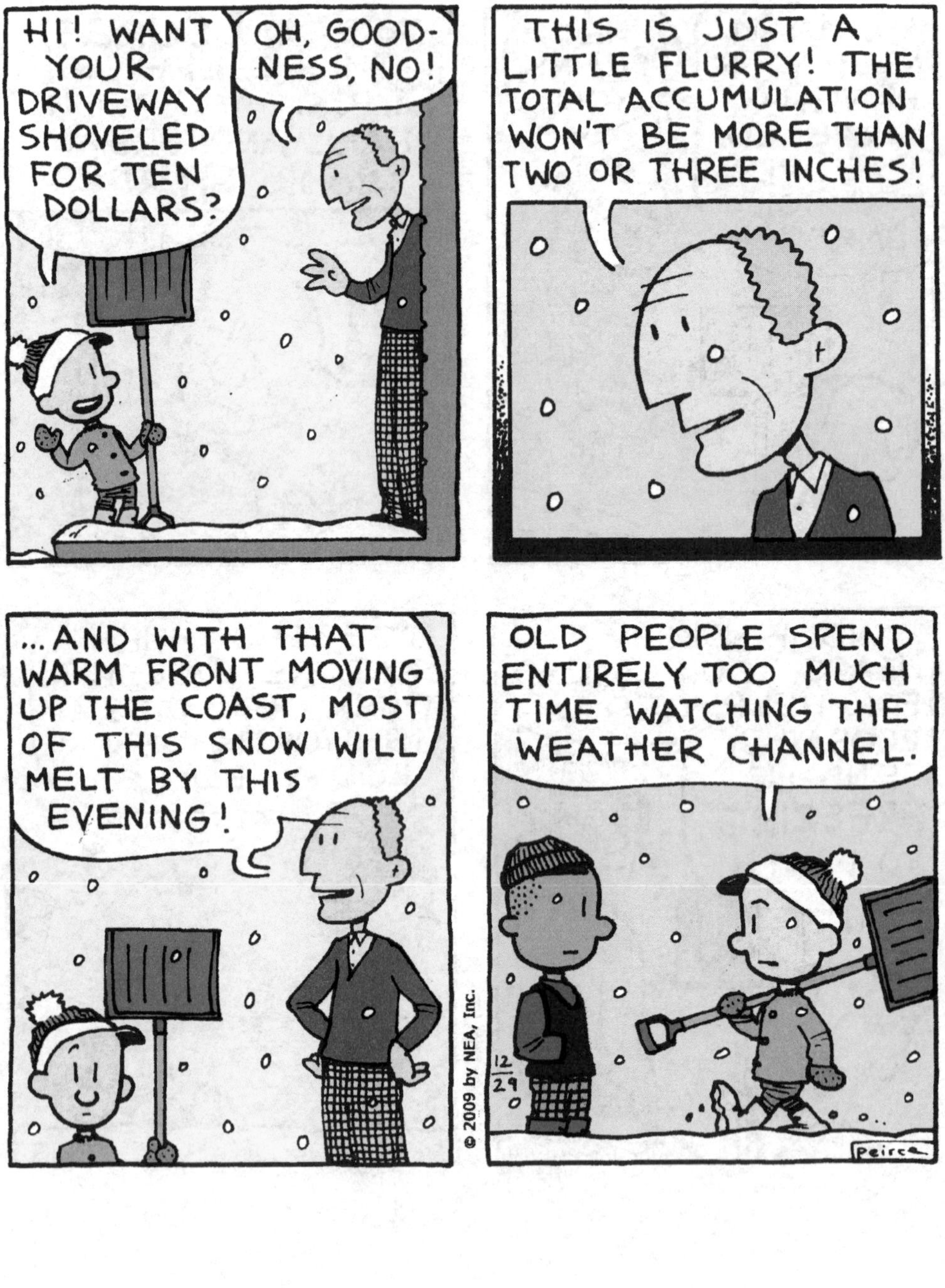
HI! WANT YOUR DRIVEWAY SHOVELED FOR TEN DOLLARS?
OH, GOODNESS, NO!
THIS IS JUST A LITTLE FLURRY! THE TOTAL ACCUMULATION WON'T BE MORE THAN TWO OR THREE INCHES!
...AND WITH THAT WARM FRONT MOVING UP THE COAST, MOST OF THIS SNOW WILL MELT BY THIS EVENING!
© 2009 by NEA, Inc.
OLD PEOPLE SPEND ENTIRELY TOO MUCH TIME WATCHING THE WEATHER CHANNEL.
12/29
Peirce

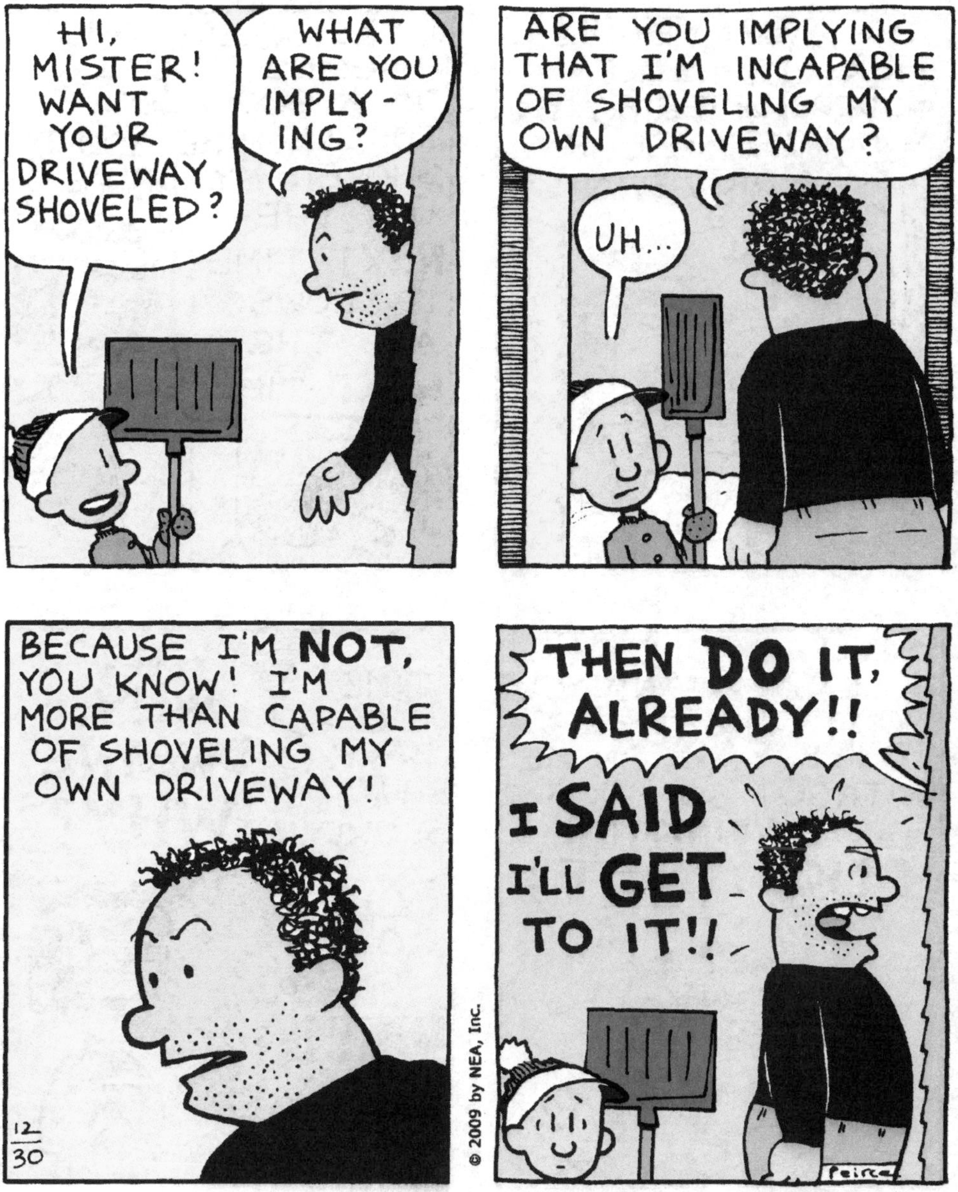
HI, MISTER! WANT YOUR DRIVEWAY SHOVELED?
WHAT ARE YOU IMPLYING?
ARE YOU IMPLYING THAT I'M INCAPABLE OF SHOVELING MY OWN DRIVEWAY?
UH...
BECAUSE I'M NOT, YOU KNOW! I'M MORE THAN CAPABLE OF SHOVELING MY OWN DRIVEWAY!
12/30
THEN DO IT, ALREADY!!
I SAID I'LL GET TO IT!!
© 2009 by NEA, Inc.
Peirce

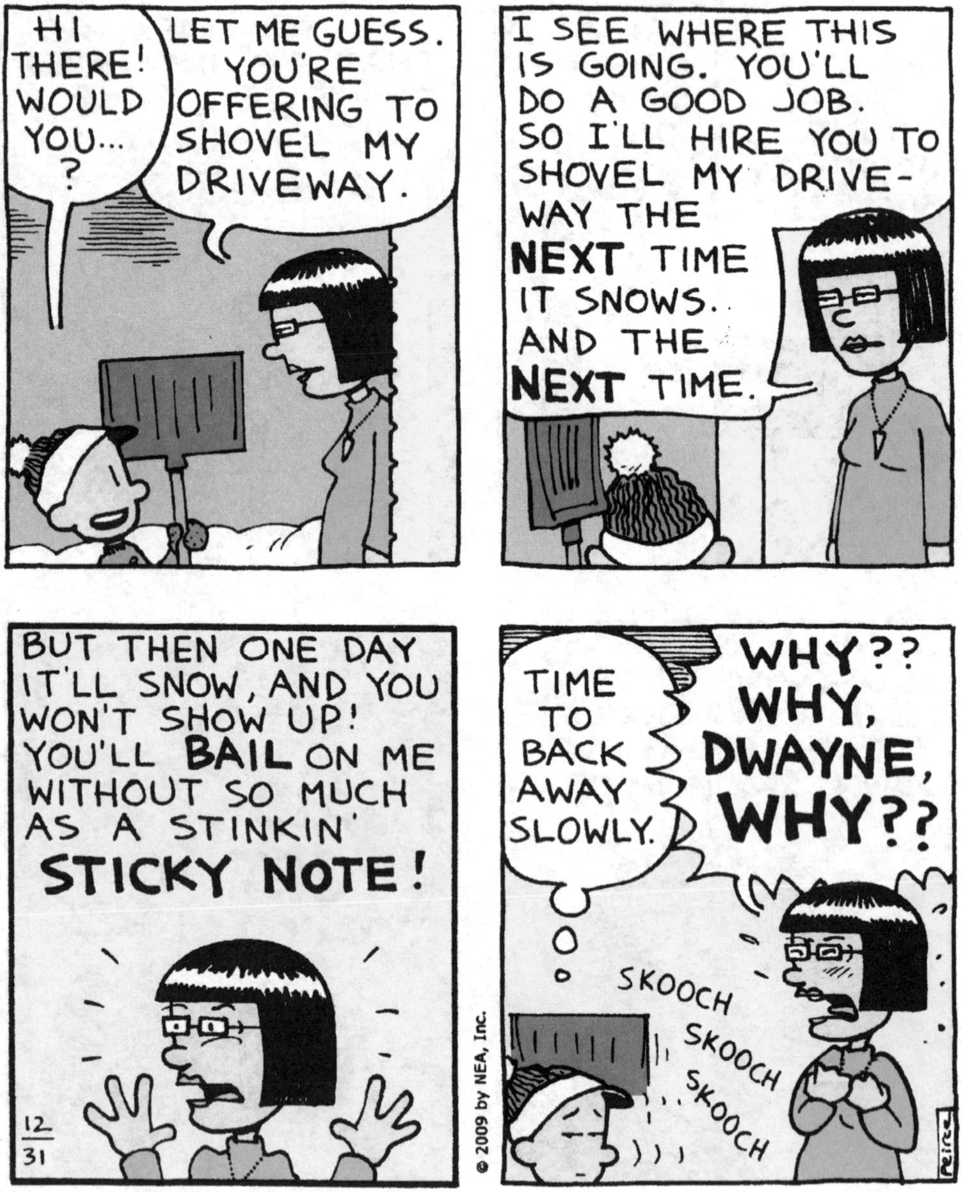
HI THERE! WOULD YOU... ?
LET ME GUESS. YOU'RE OFFERING TO SHOVEL MY DRIVEWAY.
I SEE WHERE THIS IS GOING. YOU'LL DO A GOOD JOB. SO I'LL HIRE YOU TO SHOVEL MY DRIVEWAY THE **NEXT** TIME IT SNOWS. AND THE **NEXT** TIME.
BUT THEN ONE DAY IT'LL SNOW, AND YOU WON'T SHOW UP! YOU'LL **BAIL** ON ME WITHOUT SO MUCH AS A STINKIN' **STICKY NOTE!**
12/31
© 2009 by NEA, Inc.
TIME TO BACK AWAY SLOWLY.
WHY?? **WHY, DWAYNE, WHY??**
SKOOCH
SKOOCH
SKOOCH
PEIRCE

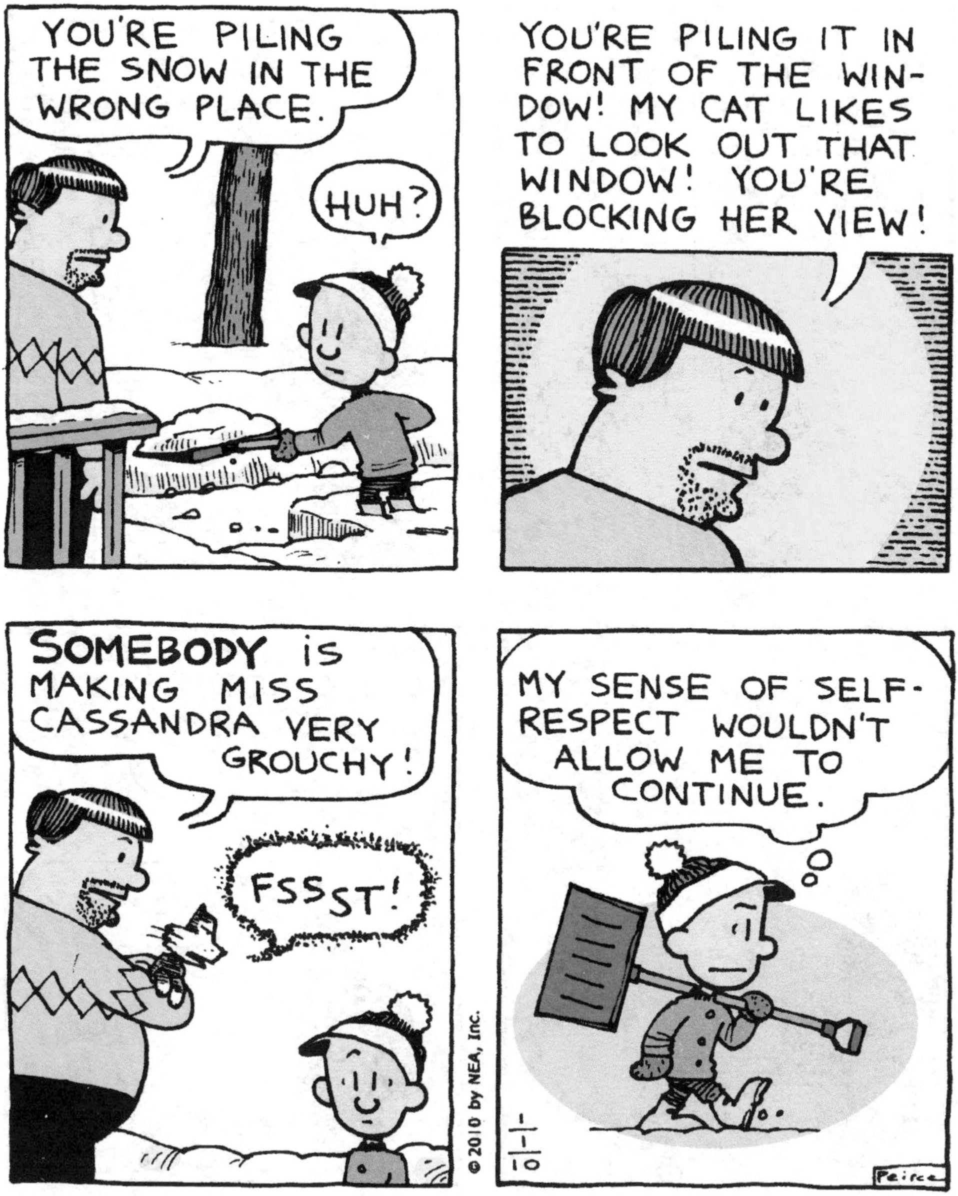

YOU'RE PILING THE SNOW IN THE WRONG PLACE.
HUH?
YOU'RE PILING IT IN FRONT OF THE WINDOW! MY CAT LIKES TO LOOK OUT THAT WINDOW! YOU'RE BLOCKING HER VIEW!
SOMEBODY is MAKING MISS CASSANDRA VERY GROUCHY!
FSSST!
MY SENSE OF SELF-RESPECT WOULDN'T ALLOW ME TO CONTINUE.
1-1-10
Peirce

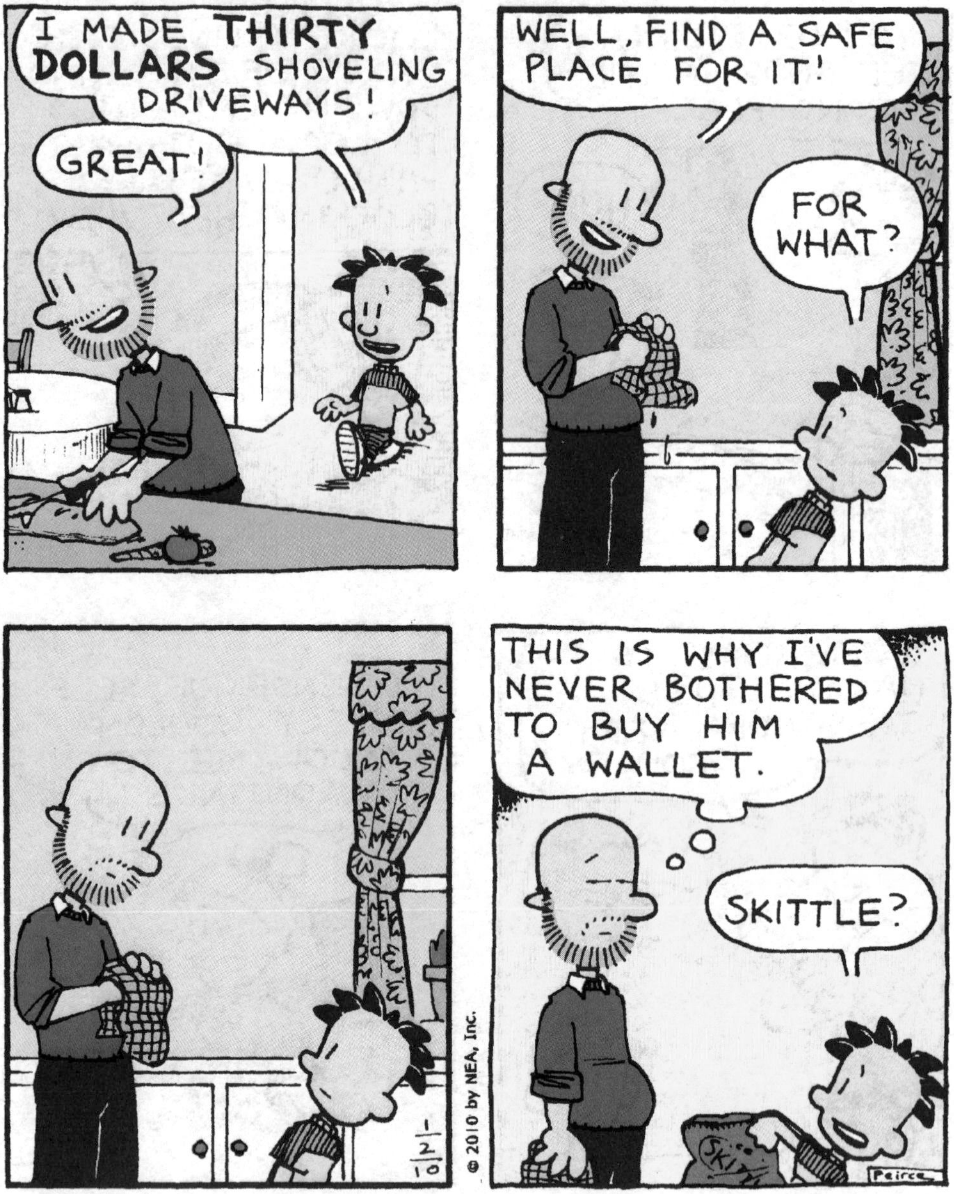
I MADE **THIRTY DOLLARS** SHOVELING DRIVEWAYS!
GREAT!
WELL, FIND A SAFE PLACE FOR IT!
FOR WHAT?
THIS IS WHY I'VE NEVER BOTHERED TO BUY HIM A WALLET.
SKITTLE?
1/2/10
Peirce

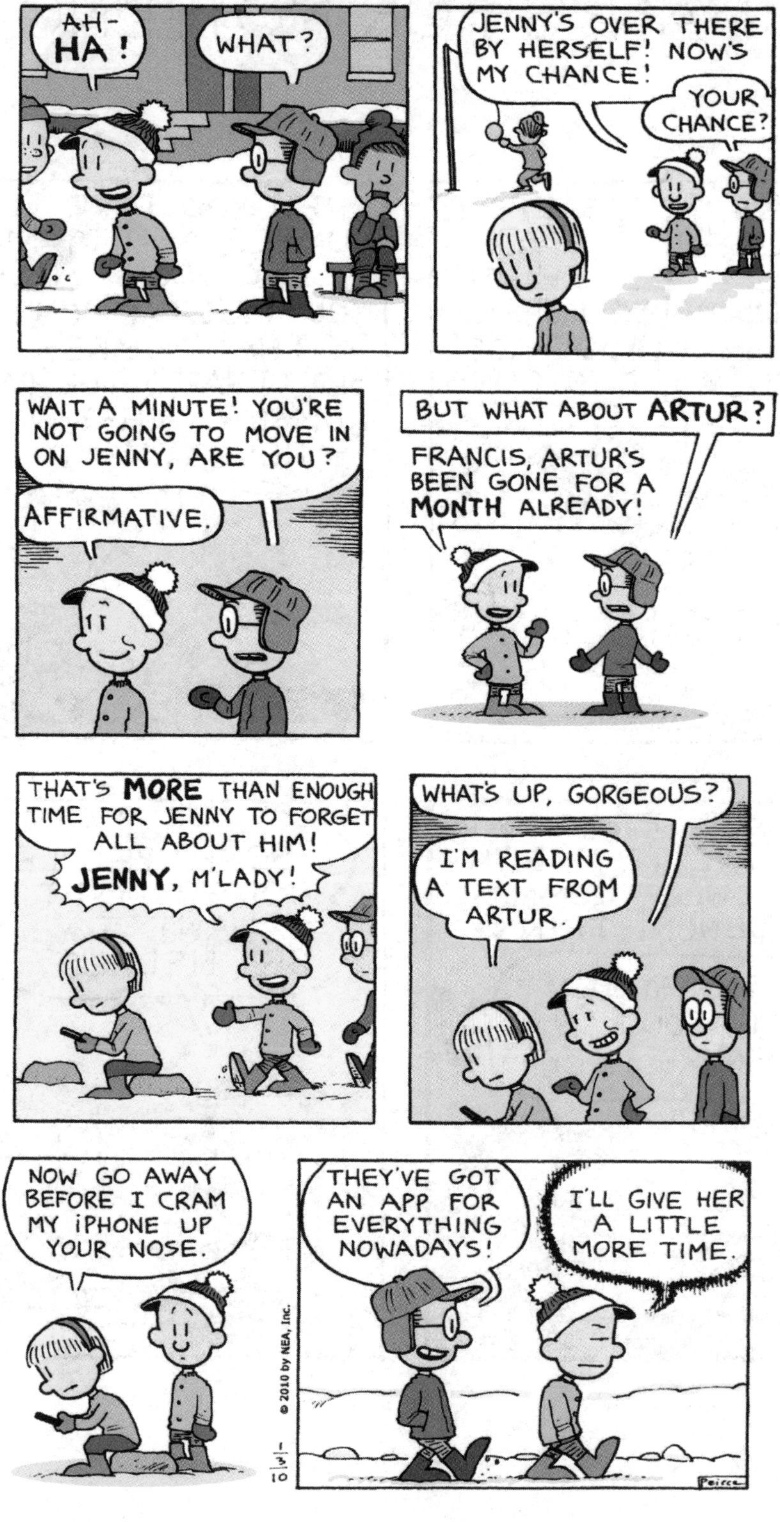
AH-HA!
WHAT?
JENNY'S OVER THERE BY HERSELF! NOW'S MY CHANCE!
YOUR CHANCE?
WAIT A MINUTE! YOU'RE NOT GOING TO MOVE IN ON JENNY, ARE YOU?
AFFIRMATIVE.
BUT WHAT ABOUT ARTUR?
FRANCIS, ARTUR'S BEEN GONE FOR A MONTH ALREADY!
THAT'S MORE THAN ENOUGH TIME FOR JENNY TO FORGET ALL ABOUT HIM!
JENNY, M'LADY!
WHAT'S UP, GORGEOUS?
I'M READING A TEXT FROM ARTUR.
NOW GO AWAY BEFORE I CRAM MY iPHONE UP YOUR NOSE.
© 2010 by NEA, Inc.
THEY'VE GOT AN APP FOR EVERYTHING NOWADAYS!
I'LL GIVE HER A LITTLE MORE TIME.
Peirce

THANKS FOR NOTHING

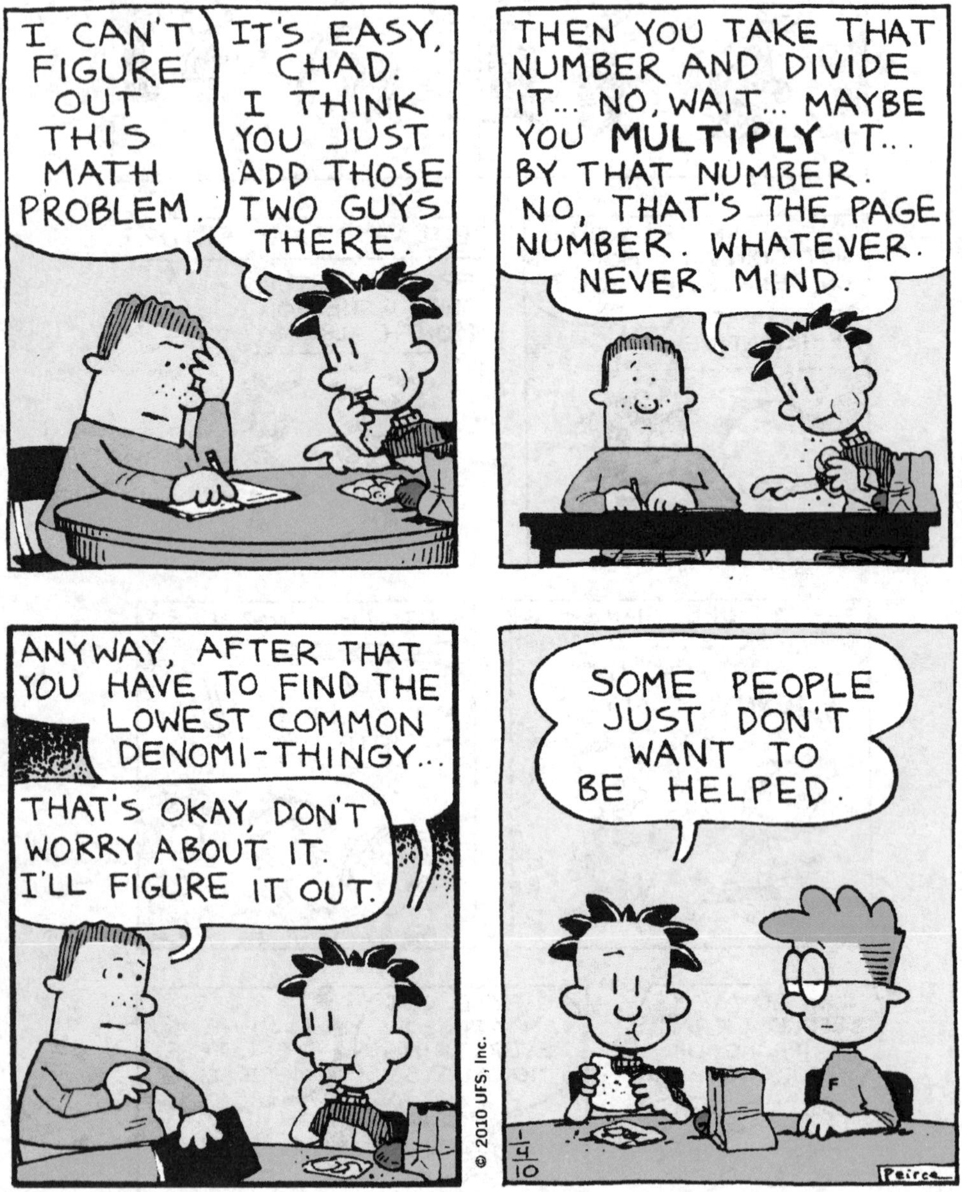
I CAN'T FIGURE OUT THIS MATH PROBLEM.
IT'S EASY, CHAD. I THINK YOU JUST ADD THOSE TWO GUYS THERE.
THEN YOU TAKE THAT NUMBER AND DIVIDE IT... NO, WAIT... MAYBE YOU MULTIPLY IT... BY THAT NUMBER. NO, THAT'S THE PAGE NUMBER. WHATEVER. NEVER MIND.
ANYWAY, AFTER THAT YOU HAVE TO FIND THE LOWEST COMMON DENOMI-THINGY...
THAT'S OKAY, DON'T WORRY ABOUT IT. I'LL FIGURE IT OUT.
SOME PEOPLE JUST DON'T WANT TO BE HELPED.
© 2010 UFS, Inc.
1-4-10
Peirce

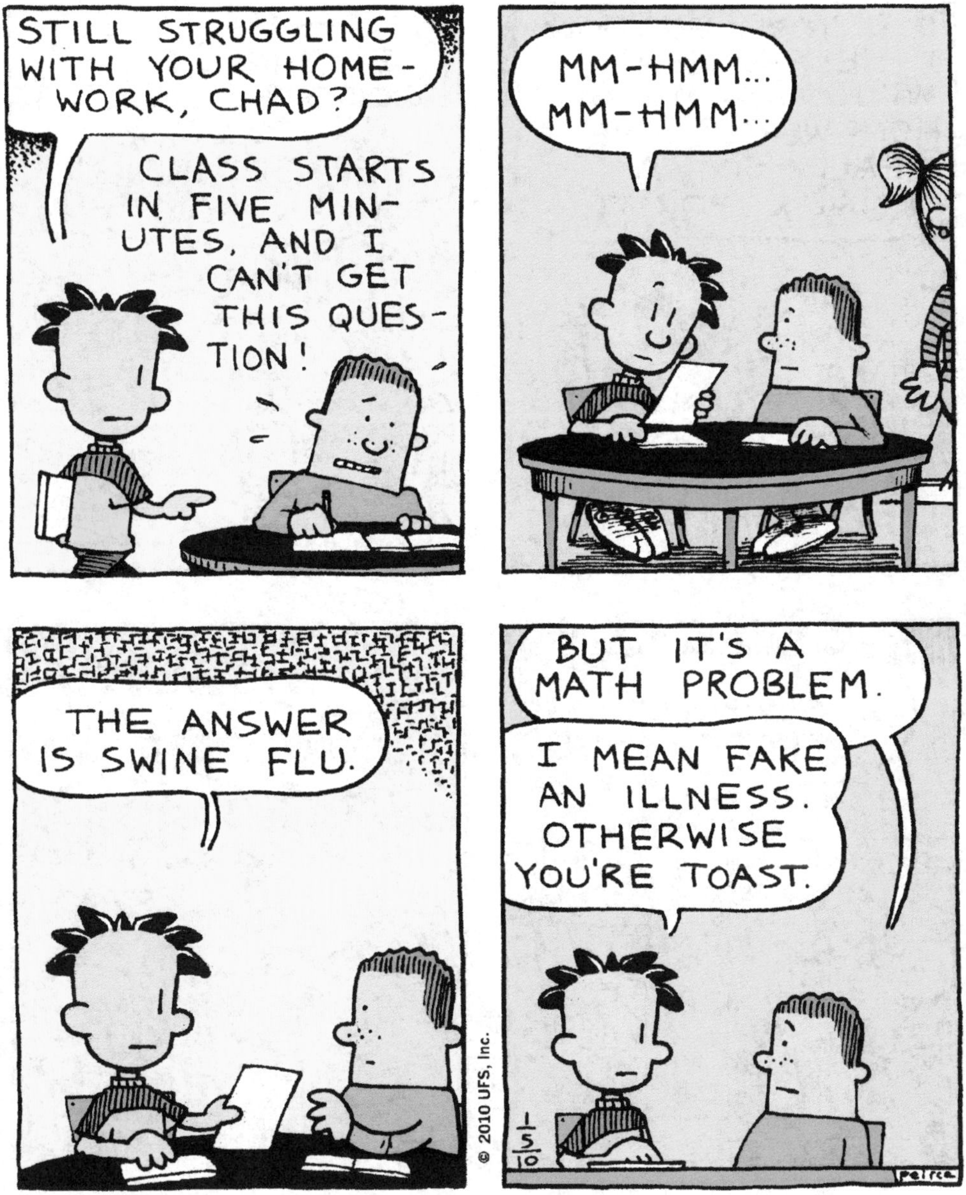
STILL STRUGGLING WITH YOUR HOME-WORK, CHAD?
CLASS STARTS IN FIVE MIN-UTES, AND I CAN'T GET THIS QUES-TION!
MM-HMM... MM-HMM...
THE ANSWER IS SWINE FLU.
BUT IT'S A MATH PROBLEM.
I MEAN FAKE AN ILLNESS. OTHERWISE YOU'RE TOAST.
1/5/10
peirce

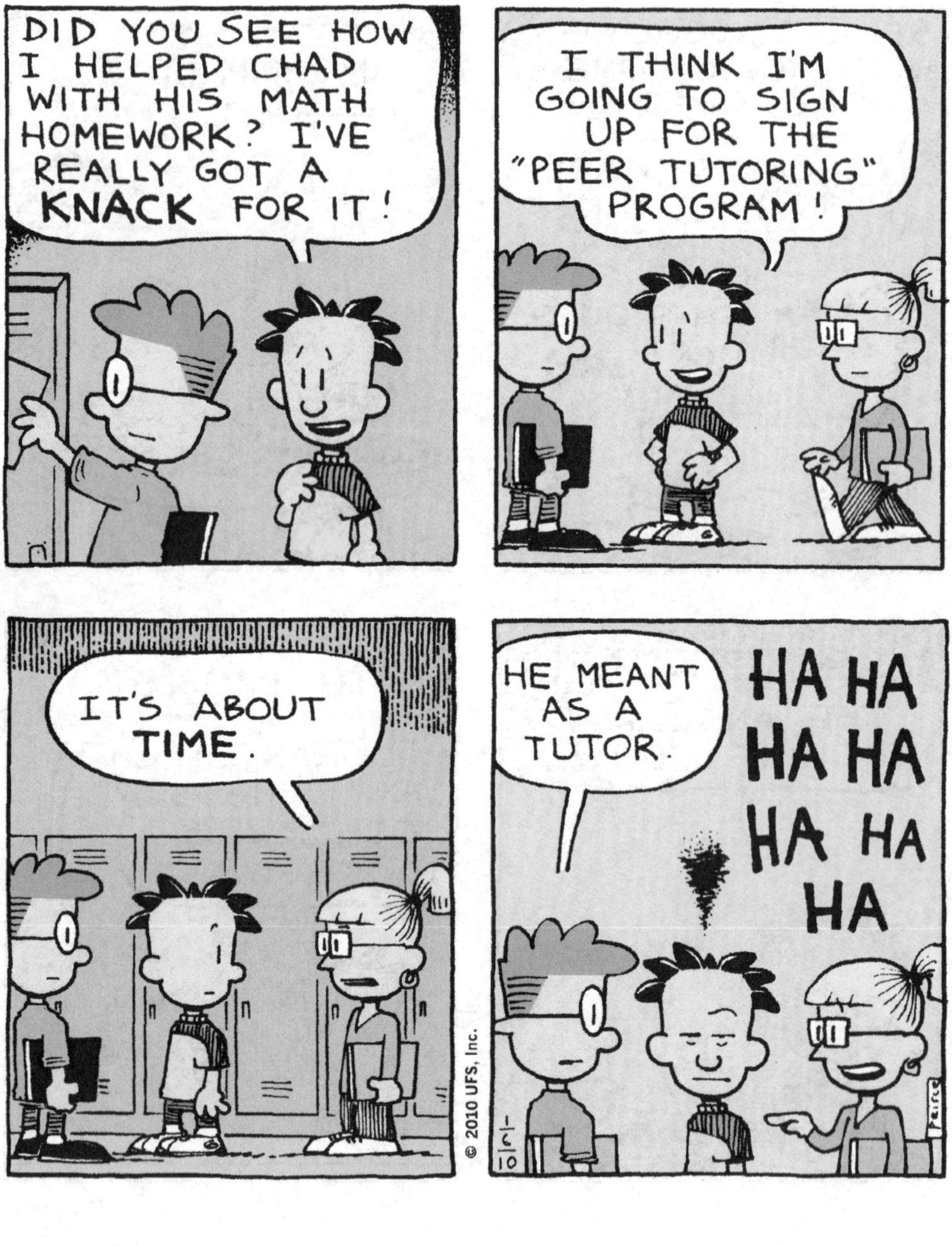
DID YOU SEE HOW I HELPED CHAD WITH HIS MATH HOMEWORK? I'VE REALLY GOT A KNACK FOR IT!
I THINK I'M GOING TO SIGN UP FOR THE "PEER TUTORING" PROGRAM!
IT'S ABOUT TIME.
HE MEANT AS A TUTOR.
HA HA HA HA HA HA HA
© 2010 UFS, Inc.
1/6/10
Peirce

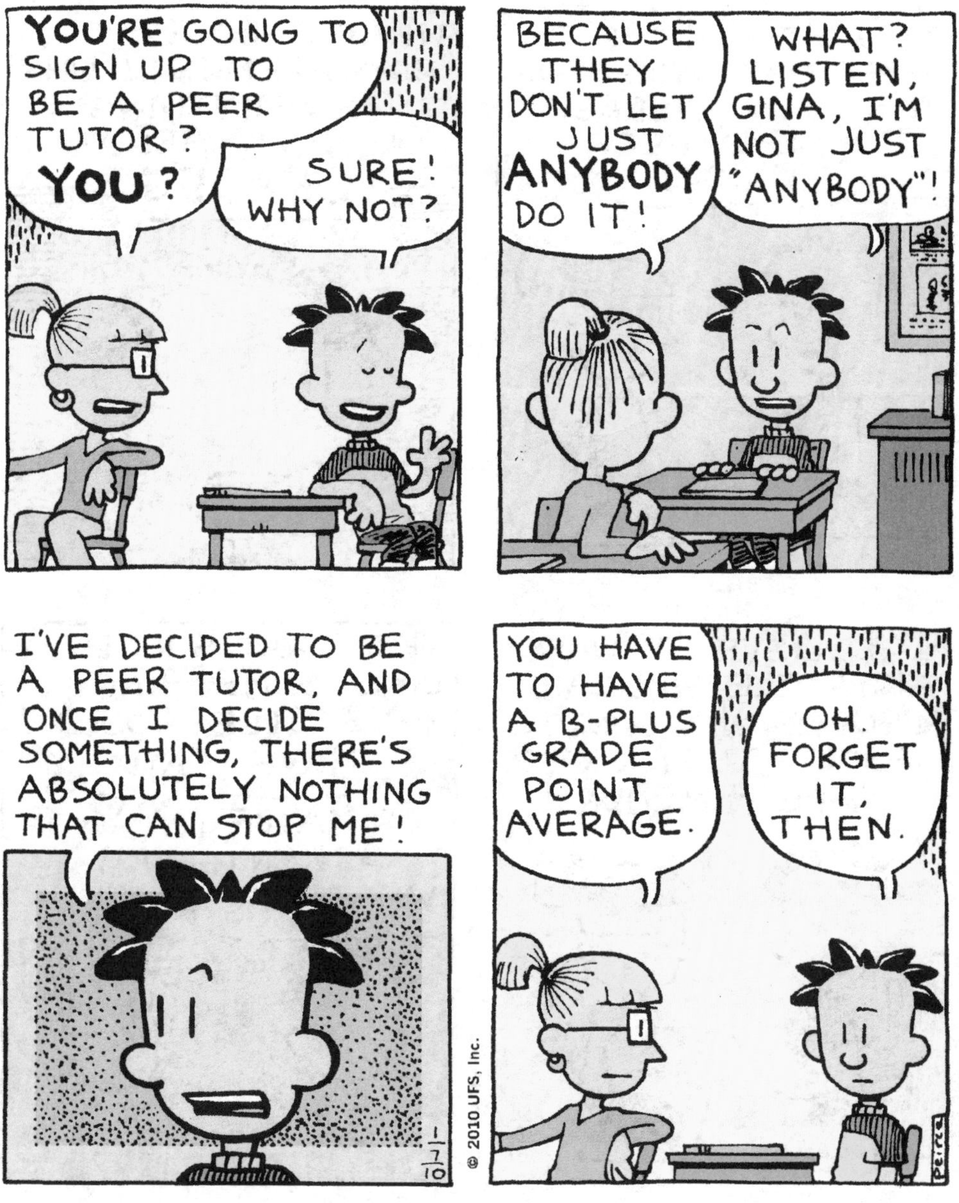
YOU'RE GOING TO SIGN UP TO BE A PEER TUTOR? YOU?
SURE! WHY NOT?
BECAUSE THEY DON'T LET JUST ANYBODY DO IT!
WHAT? LISTEN, GINA, I'M NOT JUST "ANYBODY"!
I'VE DECIDED TO BE A PEER TUTOR, AND ONCE I DECIDE SOMETHING, THERE'S ABSOLUTELY NOTHING THAT CAN STOP ME!
1/7/10
© 2010 UFS, Inc.
YOU HAVE TO HAVE A B-PLUS GRADE POINT AVERAGE.
OH. FORGET IT, THEN.
PEIRCE

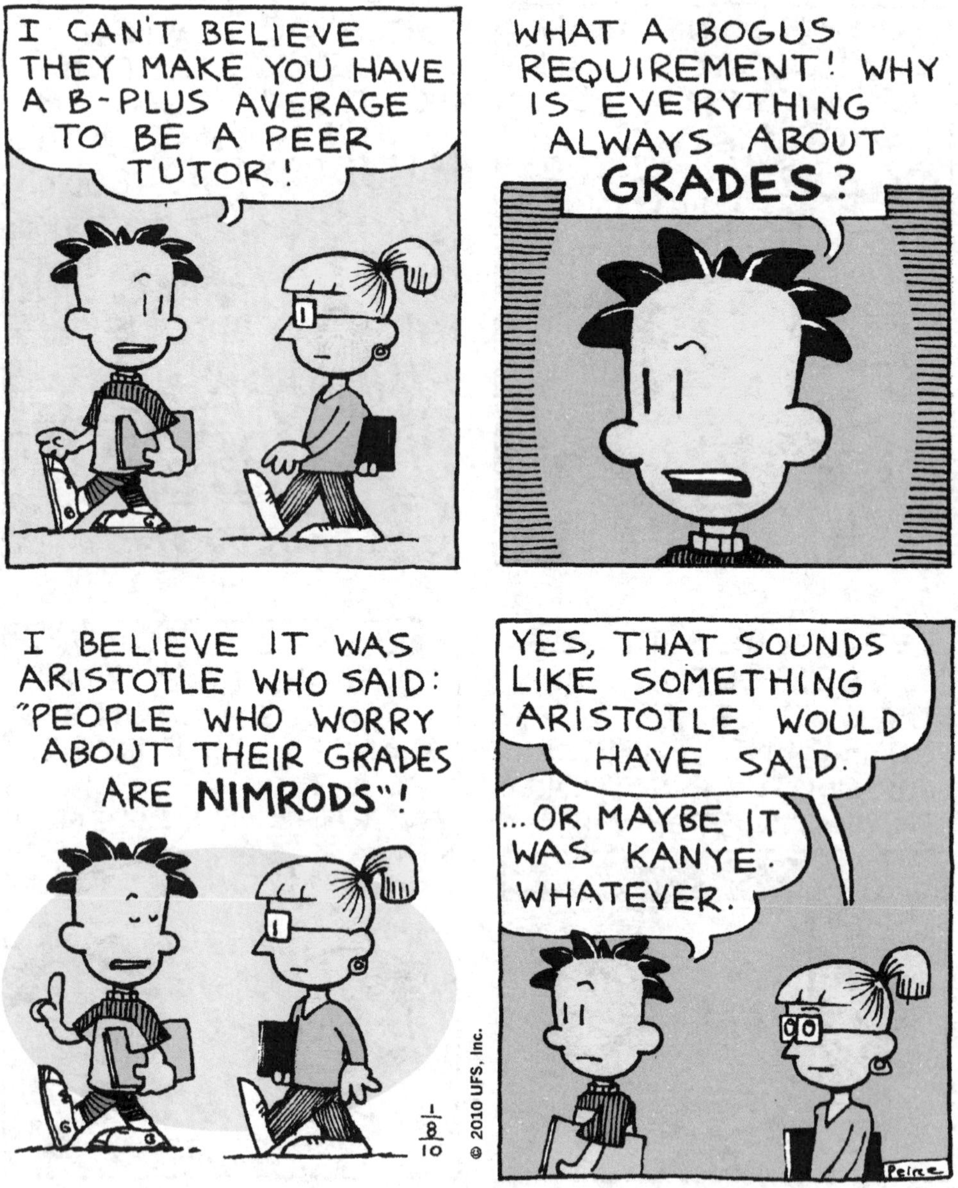
I CAN'T BELIEVE THEY MAKE YOU HAVE A B-PLUS AVERAGE TO BE A PEER TUTOR!
WHAT A BOGUS REQUIREMENT! WHY IS EVERYTHING ALWAYS ABOUT **GRADES**?
I BELIEVE IT WAS ARISTOTLE WHO SAID: "PEOPLE WHO WORRY ABOUT THEIR GRADES ARE **NIMRODS**"!
YES, THAT SOUNDS LIKE SOMETHING ARISTOTLE WOULD HAVE SAID.
...OR MAYBE IT WAS KANYE. WHATEVER.
1/8/10
© 2010 UFS, Inc.
Peirce

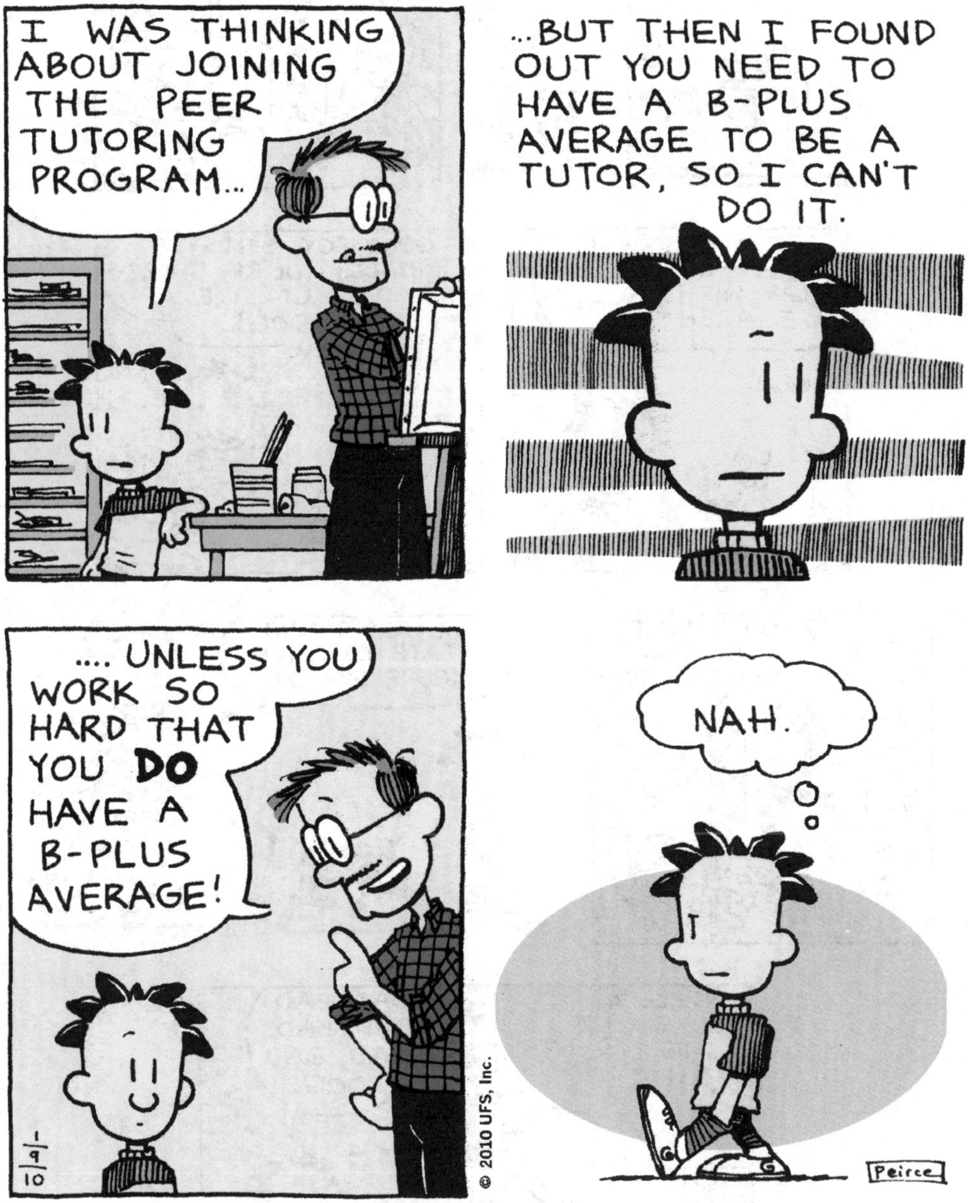
I WAS THINKING ABOUT JOINING THE PEER TUTORING PROGRAM...
...BUT THEN I FOUND OUT YOU NEED TO HAVE A B-PLUS AVERAGE TO BE A TUTOR, SO I CAN'T DO IT.
.... UNLESS YOU WORK SO HARD THAT YOU **DO** HAVE A B-PLUS AVERAGE!
NAH.
1/9/10
© 2010 UFS, Inc.
Peirce

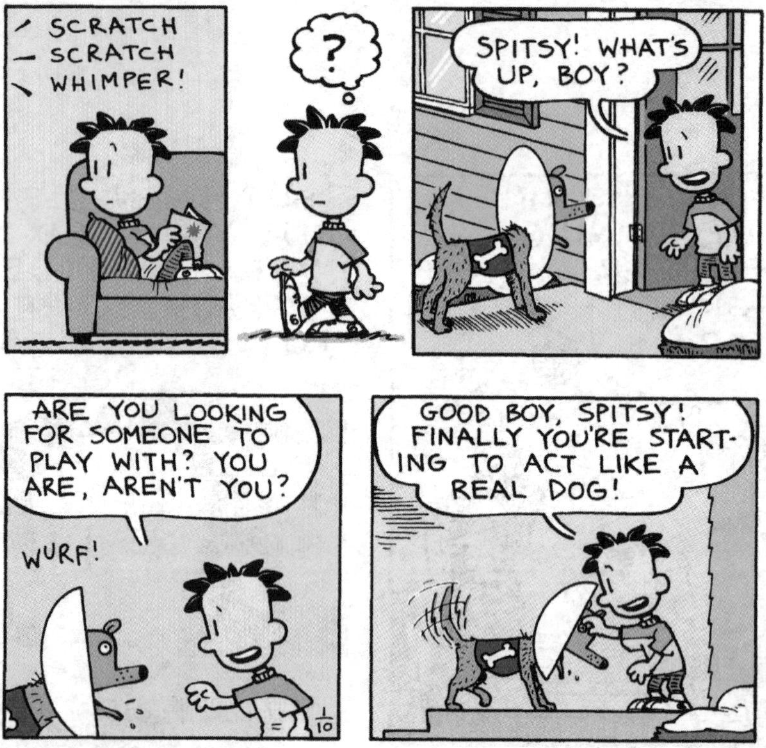
SCRATCH
SCRATCH
WHIMPER!
?
SPITSY! WHAT'S UP, BOY?
ARE YOU LOOKING FOR SOMEONE TO PLAY WITH? YOU ARE, AREN'T YOU?
WURF!
1/10
GOOD BOY, SPITSY! FINALLY YOU'RE STARTING TO ACT LIKE A REAL DOG!

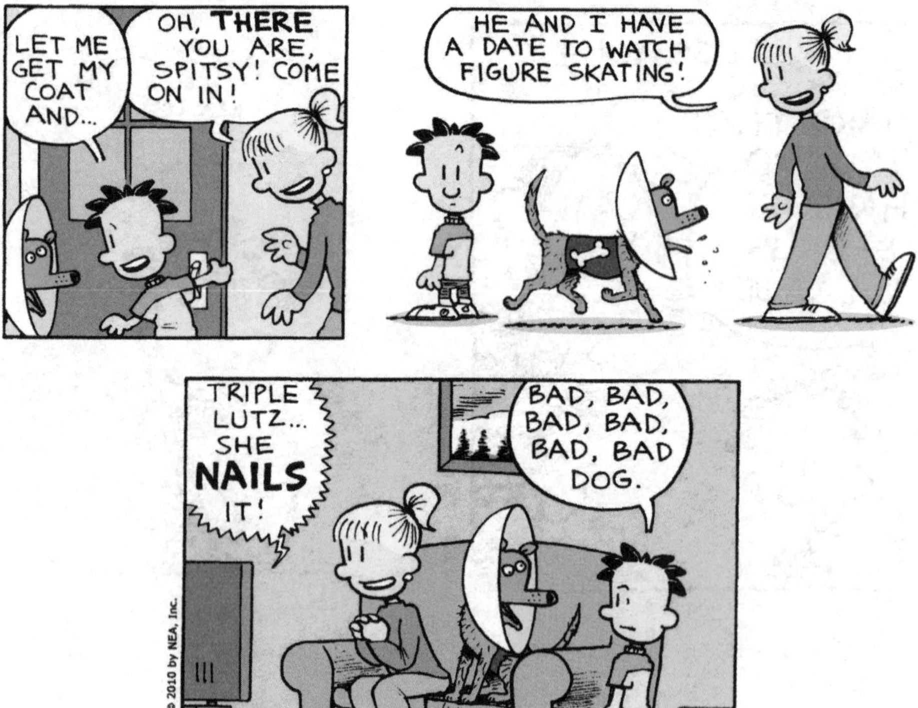
LET ME GET MY COAT AND...
OH, **THERE** YOU ARE, SPITSY! COME ON IN!
HE AND I HAVE A DATE TO WATCH FIGURE SKATING!
TRIPLE LUTZ... SHE **NAILS** IT!
BAD, BAD, BAD, BAD, BAD, BAD DOG.
© 2010 by NEA, Inc.
Peirce

NATE WRIGHT, VIBE CONSULTANT

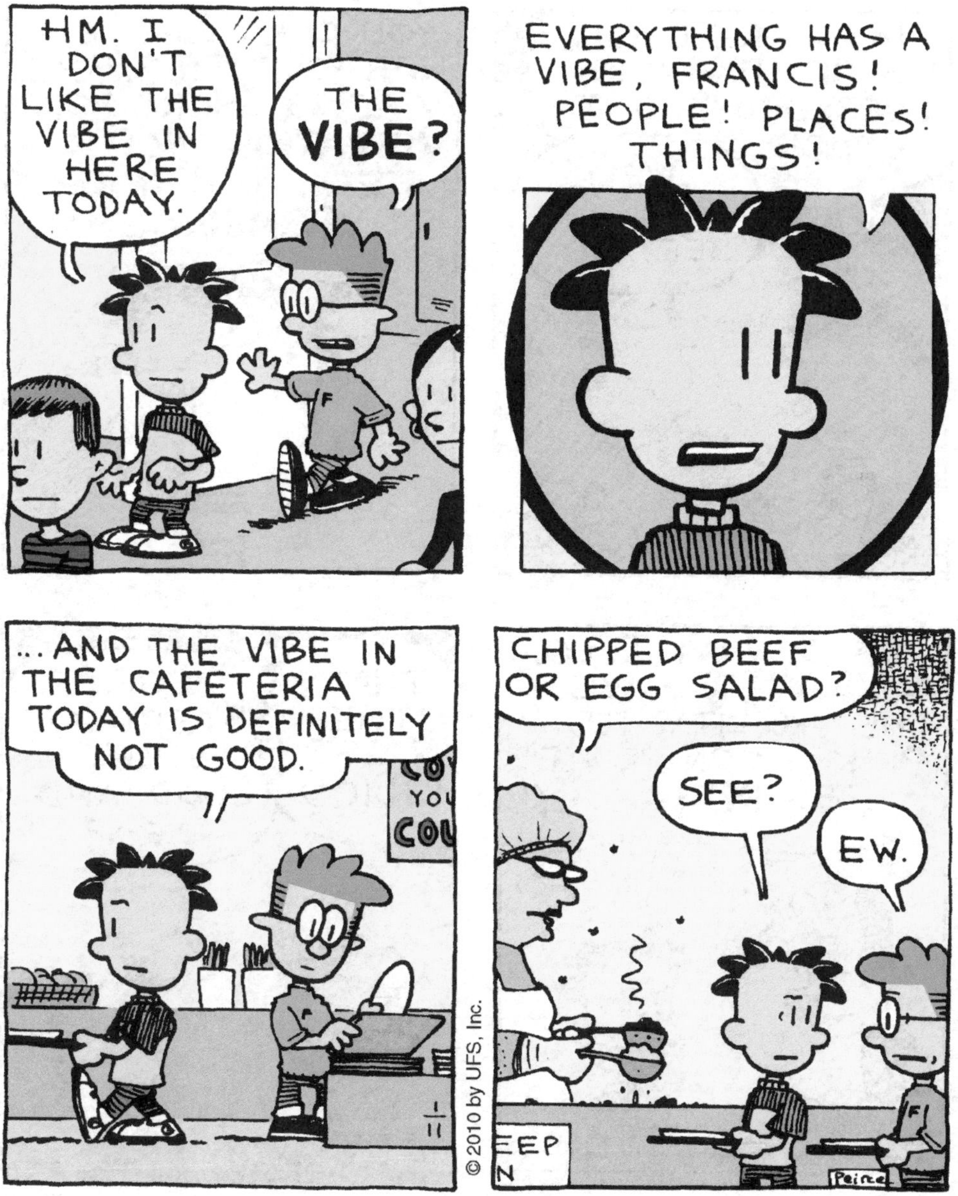
HM. I DON'T LIKE THE VIBE IN HERE TODAY.
THE VIBE?
EVERYTHING HAS A VIBE, FRANCIS! PEOPLE! PLACES! THINGS!
...AND THE VIBE IN THE CAFETERIA TODAY IS DEFINITELY NOT GOOD.
CHIPPED BEEF OR EGG SALAD?
SEE?
EW.
© 2010 by UFS, Inc.
Peirce

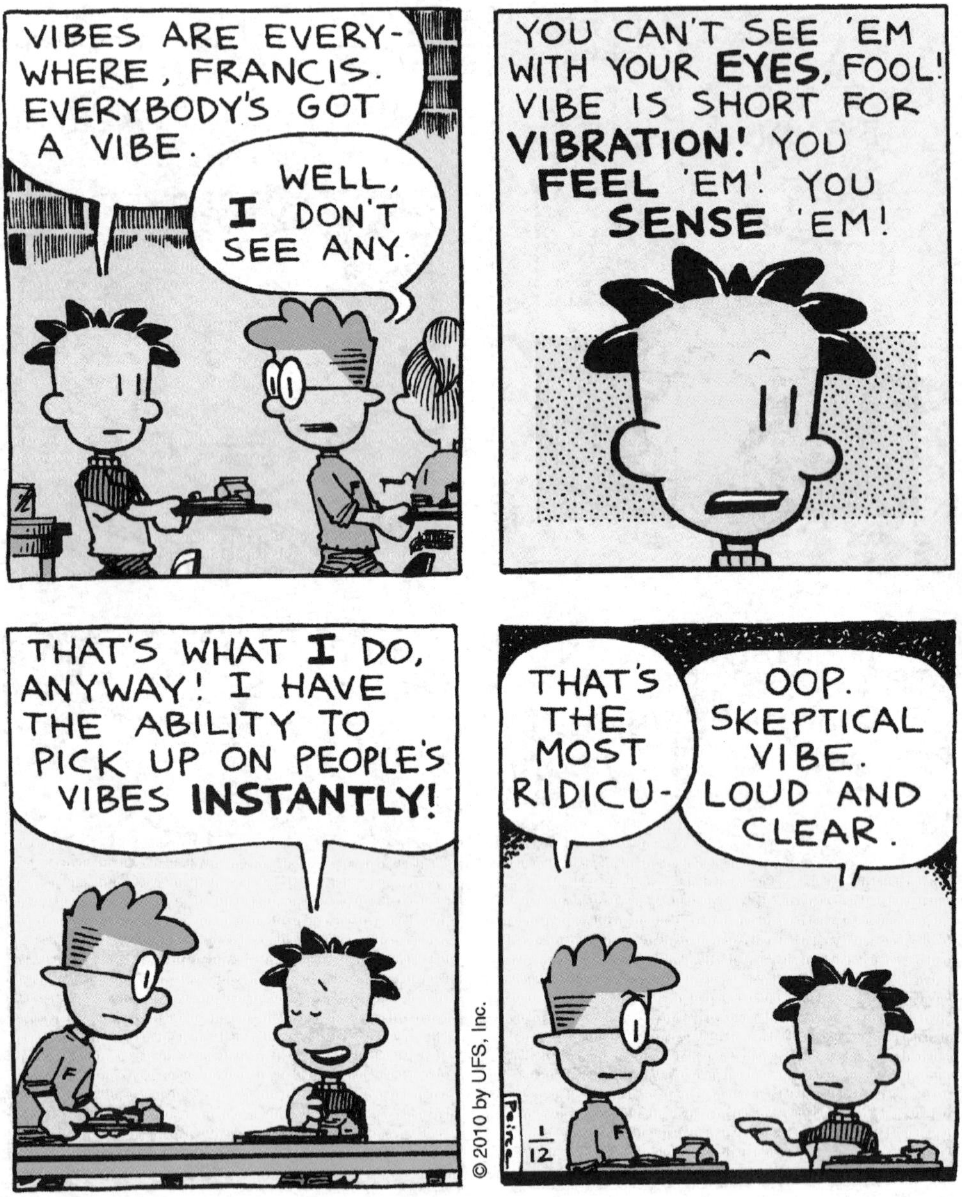
VIBES ARE EVERYWHERE, FRANCIS. EVERYBODY'S GOT A VIBE.
WELL, I DON'T SEE ANY.
YOU CAN'T SEE 'EM WITH YOUR EYES, FOOL! VIBE IS SHORT FOR VIBRATION! YOU FEEL 'EM! YOU SENSE 'EM!
THAT'S WHAT I DO, ANYWAY! I HAVE THE ABILITY TO PICK UP ON PEOPLE'S VIBES INSTANTLY!
THAT'S THE MOST RIDICU-
OOP. SKEPTICAL VIBE. LOUD AND CLEAR.
Peirce
1/12
© 2010 by UFS, Inc.

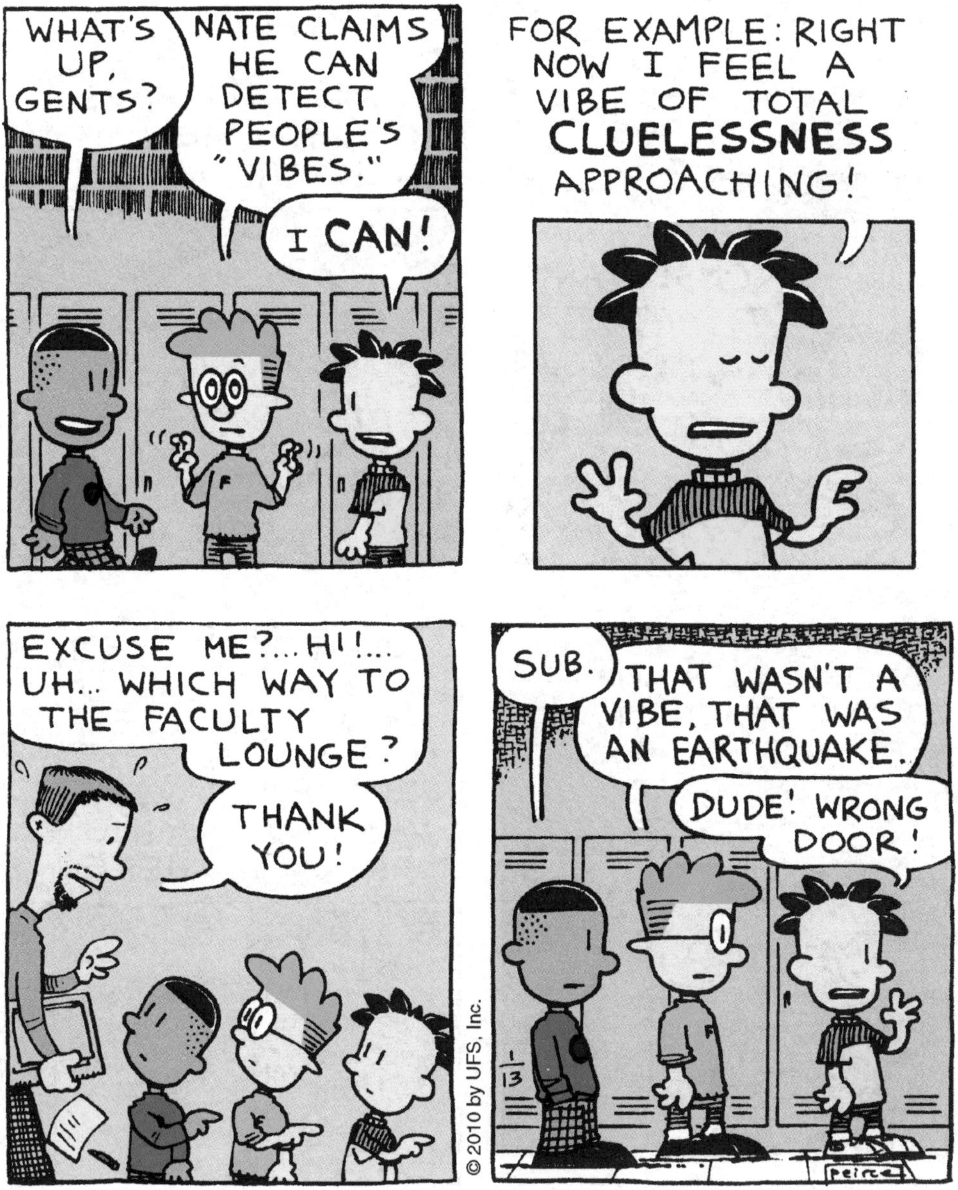
WHAT'S UP, GENTS?
NATE CLAIMS HE CAN DETECT PEOPLE'S "VIBES."
I CAN!
FOR EXAMPLE: RIGHT NOW I FEEL A VIBE OF TOTAL CLUELESSNESS APPROACHING!
EXCUSE ME?... HI!... UH... WHICH WAY TO THE FACULTY LOUNGE?
THANK YOU!
SUB.
THAT WASN'T A VIBE, THAT WAS AN EARTHQUAKE.
DUDE! WRONG DOOR!
1/13
peirce

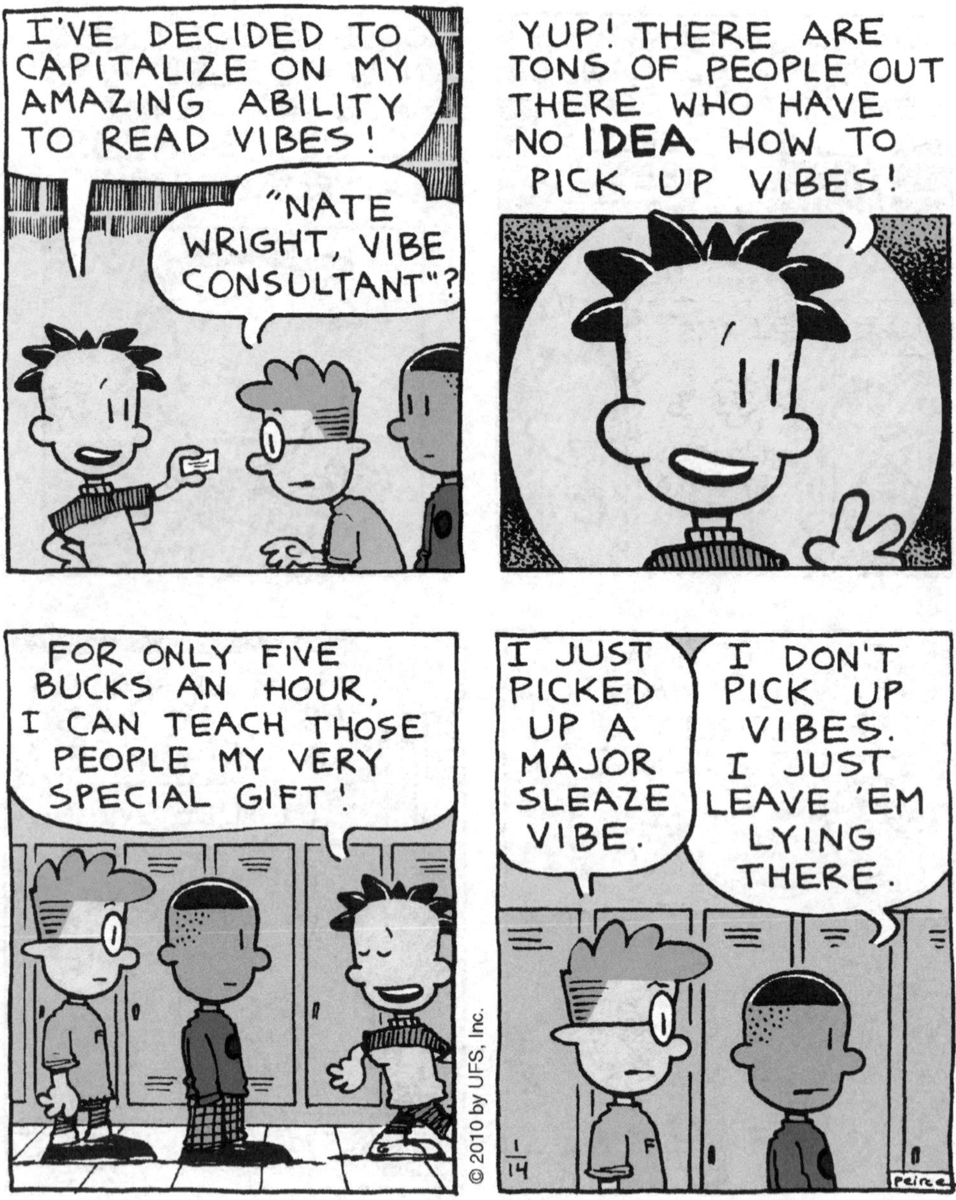
I'VE DECIDED TO CAPITALIZE ON MY AMAZING ABILITY TO READ VIBES!
"NATE WRIGHT, VIBE CONSULTANT"?
YUP! THERE ARE TONS OF PEOPLE OUT THERE WHO HAVE NO **IDEA** HOW TO PICK UP VIBES!
FOR ONLY FIVE BUCKS AN HOUR, I CAN TEACH THOSE PEOPLE MY VERY SPECIAL GIFT!
I JUST PICKED UP A MAJOR SLEAZE VIBE.
I DON'T PICK UP VIBES. I JUST LEAVE 'EM LYING THERE.
1 14
Peirce

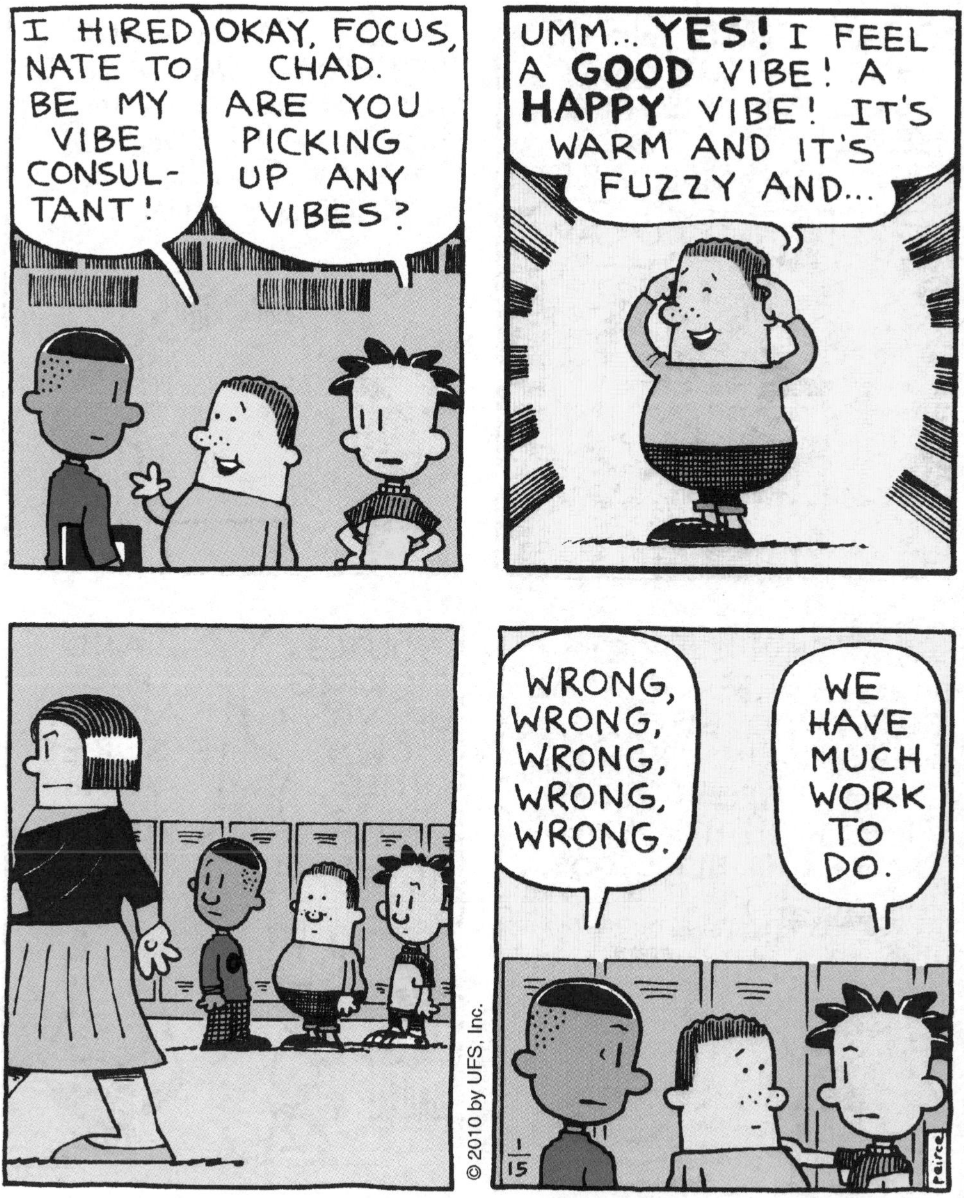
I HIRED NATE TO BE MY VIBE CONSUL-TANT!
OKAY, FOCUS, CHAD. ARE YOU PICKING UP ANY VIBES?
UMM... YES! I FEEL A GOOD VIBE! A HAPPY VIBE! IT'S WARM AND IT'S FUZZY AND...
WRONG, WRONG, WRONG, WRONG, WRONG.
WE HAVE MUCH WORK TO DO.
1/15
PEIRCE

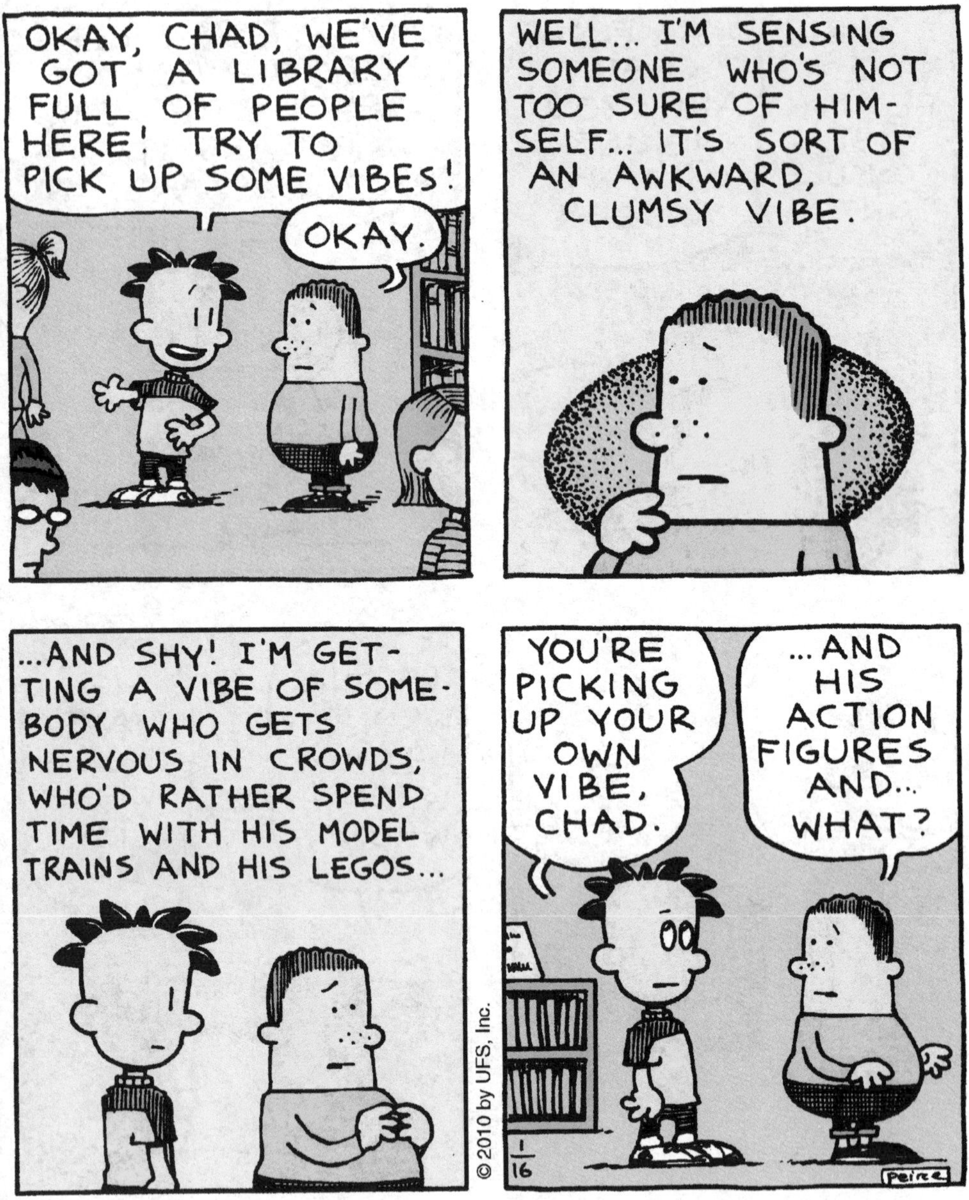
OKAY, CHAD, WE'VE GOT A LIBRARY FULL OF PEOPLE HERE! TRY TO PICK UP SOME VIBES!
OKAY.
WELL... I'M SENSING SOMEONE WHO'S NOT TOO SURE OF HIM-SELF... IT'S SORT OF AN AWKWARD, CLUMSY VIBE.
...AND SHY! I'M GET-TING A VIBE OF SOME-BODY WHO GETS NERVOUS IN CROWDS, WHO'D RATHER SPEND TIME WITH HIS MODEL TRAINS AND HIS LEGOS...
YOU'RE PICKING UP YOUR OWN VIBE, CHAD.
...AND HIS ACTION FIGURES AND... WHAT?
1/16
peirce

THOMAS JEFFERSON, FOUNDING FATHER
By Nate Wright

Thomas Jefferson, a great American, was born on the historic day of April 13, 1743 in the sleepy little village of Shadwell, Virginia. Tom's dad was named Peter and his mom was Jane. When Tom was fourteen years old, his dad (Peter) died, so from then on Tom was in charge because his father was dead. Tom decided he wanted to go to college, but apparently there weren't many colleges around back then because the only one he could find had the very strange name of William and Mary. But he went there anyway. Also, during this time he learned how to play the violin. After college Tom got married. His wife was named Martha, which by coincidence was also the name of George Washington's wife Martha.

Anyway, married life must have been kind of boring, because Tom decided to get into politics. He was in the Virginia House of Burgesses and also was a member of the second Continental Congress. Tom drafted (which is a fancy word for "wrote") the Declaration of Independence, which was when the colonial guys told the British to give them their freedom. Writing the Declaration of Independence was the reason Tom was one of the founding fathers, which is why I called this essay "Thomas Jefferson, Founding Father." During the whole American Revolution thing, Tom was elected governor of Virginia. Then his wife died. What she died from, I have no idea. But obviously Tom got on with his life, because pretty soon after that he became a congressman. Then he became minister to France, so he spent a lot of time hanging around in Paris. And then George Washington, who was president at the time, hired Tom to be the secretary of state.

Tom ran for president in 1796, but he lost the election to John Adams, so he became vice president instead. Then in 1800 Tom ran again, and this time he won. So then he was president. He was the third president in United States history. Some of his major accomplishments that he did while he was president were the Louisiana Purchase and the Embargo Act. He also invented the University of Virginia.

After that, Tom just hung out and got old, and he died on July 4th, 1826, which is an amazing coincidence because that was the 50th anniversary of the Declaration of Independence, which Tom wrote as we all remember so well. So, to sum up the life and career of Thomas Jefferson, founding father (which is also the title of this essay): he was a congressman, a governor, a secretary of state, a vice president, and a president. Wow, that is truly incredible. Oh, and also Tom's picture is on a nickel. Thomas Jefferson will never be forgotten. It is so, so, so, so, so, so, so, so, so, so, so, so, so important that today's American citizens understand how very, very, very, very, very, very important he was.

THE END

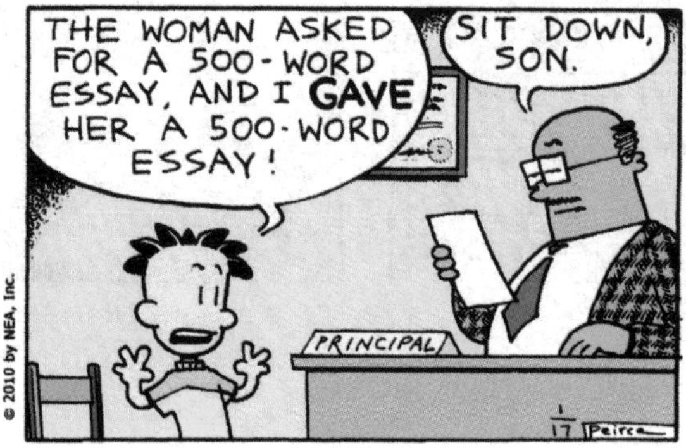
THE WOMAN ASKED FOR A 500-WORD ESSAY, AND I GAVE HER A 500-WORD ESSAY!
SIT DOWN, SON.
PRINCIPAL
1/17
Peirce
© 2010 by NEA, Inc.

MOUSE!

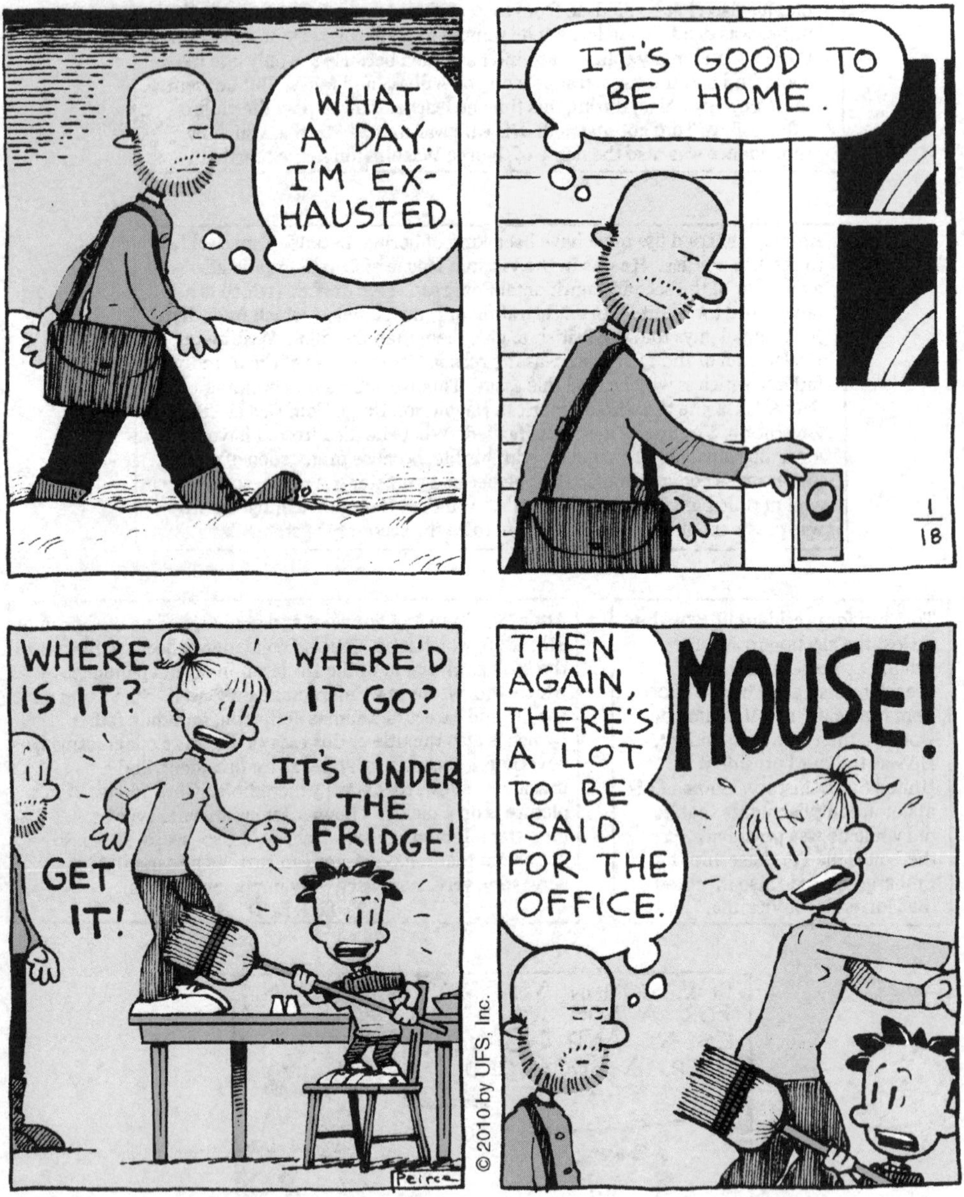
WHAT A DAY. I'M EX- HAUSTED.
IT'S GOOD TO BE HOME.
1/18
WHERE IS IT?
WHERE'D IT GO?
IT'S UNDER THE FRIDGE!
GET IT!
Peirce
© 2010 by UFS, Inc.
THEN AGAIN, THERE'S A LOT TO BE SAID FOR THE OFFICE.
MOUSE!

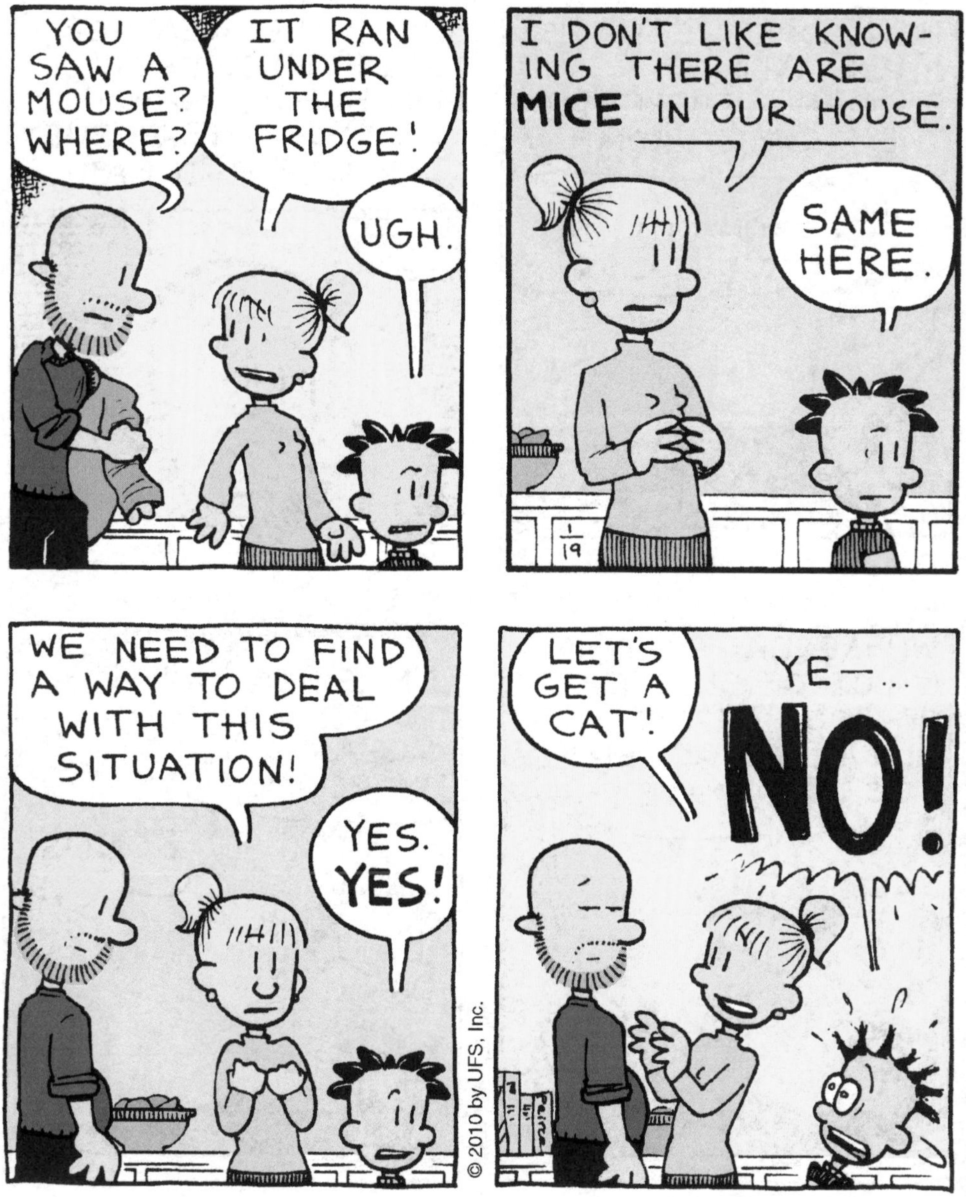
YOU SAW A MOUSE? WHERE?
IT RAN UNDER THE FRIDGE!
UGH.
I DON'T LIKE KNOWING THERE ARE **MICE** IN OUR HOUSE.
SAME HERE.
1/19
WE NEED TO FIND A WAY TO DEAL WITH THIS SITUATION!
YES. **YES!**
LET'S GET A CAT!
YE— ...
NO!
© 2010 by UFS, Inc.

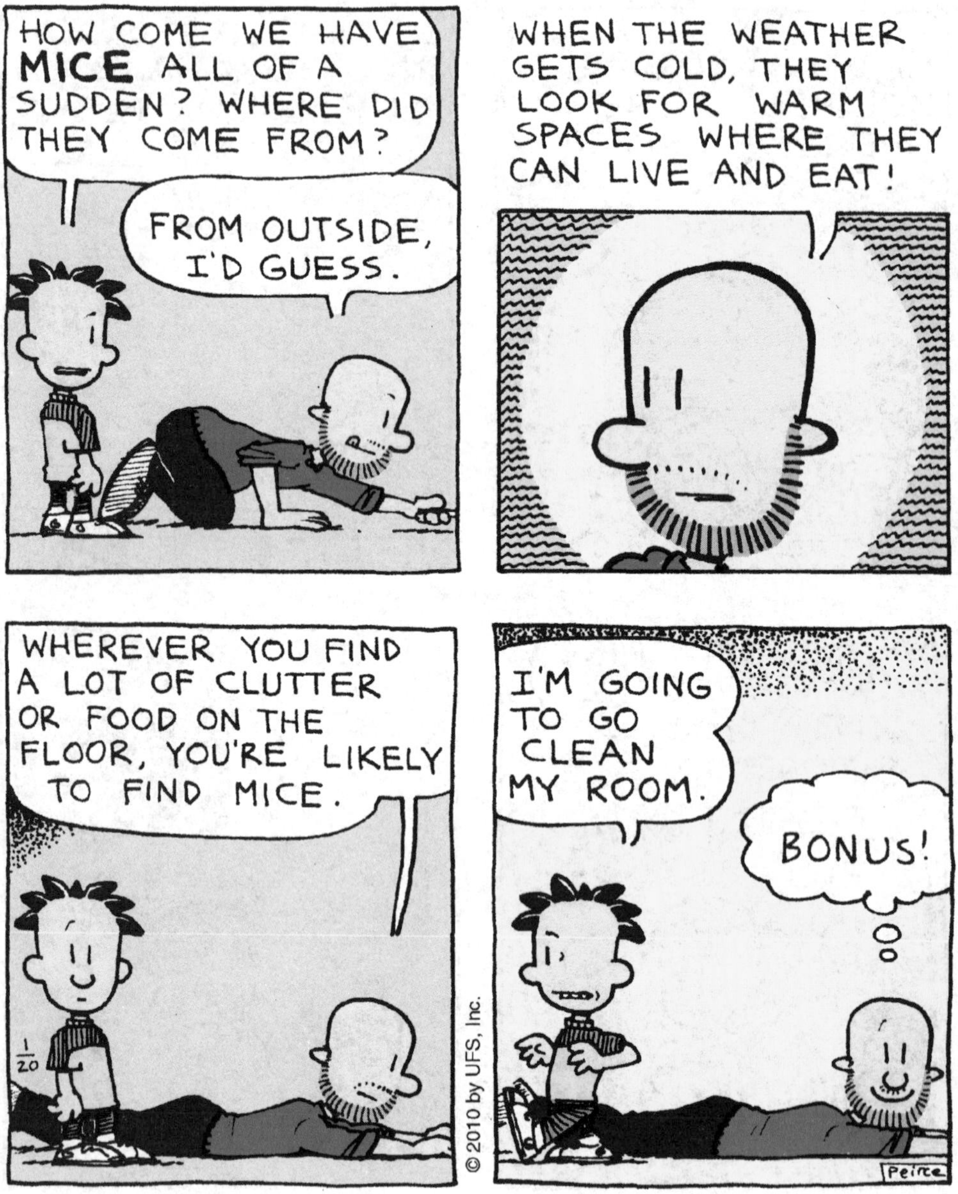
HOW COME WE HAVE **MICE** ALL OF A SUDDEN? WHERE DID THEY COME FROM?
FROM OUTSIDE, I'D GUESS.
WHEN THE WEATHER GETS COLD, THEY LOOK FOR WARM SPACES WHERE THEY CAN LIVE AND EAT!
WHEREVER YOU FIND A LOT OF CLUTTER OR FOOD ON THE FLOOR, YOU'RE LIKELY TO FIND MICE.
1/20
I'M GOING TO GO CLEAN MY ROOM.
BONUS!
Peirce

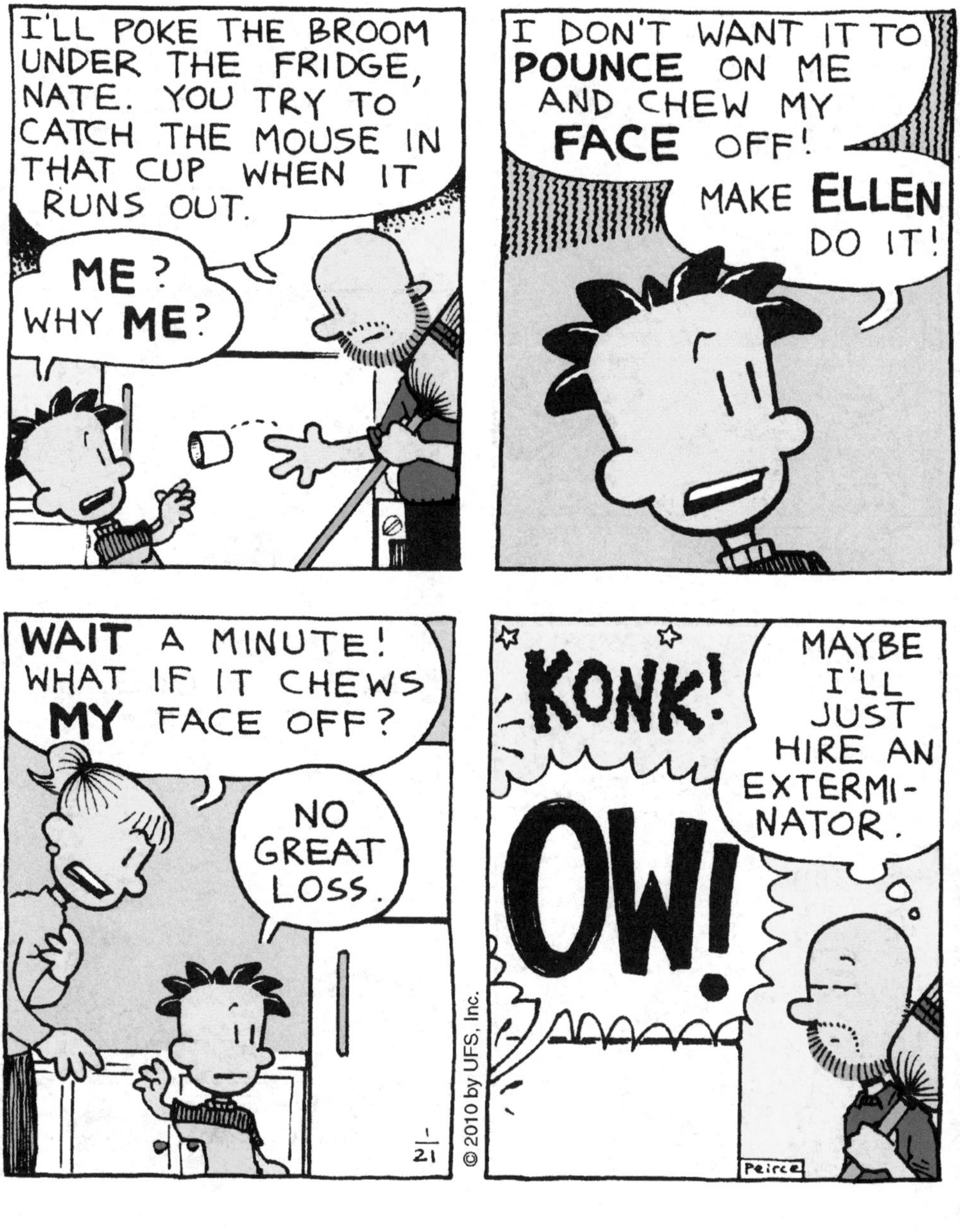
I'LL POKE THE BROOM UNDER THE FRIDGE, NATE. YOU TRY TO CATCH THE MOUSE IN THAT CUP WHEN IT RUNS OUT.
ME? WHY ME?
I DON'T WANT IT TO POUNCE ON ME AND CHEW MY FACE OFF!
MAKE ELLEN DO IT!
WAIT A MINUTE! WHAT IF IT CHEWS MY FACE OFF?
NO GREAT LOSS.
1/21
KONK!
OW!
MAYBE I'LL JUST HIRE AN EXTERMI-NATOR.
Peirce

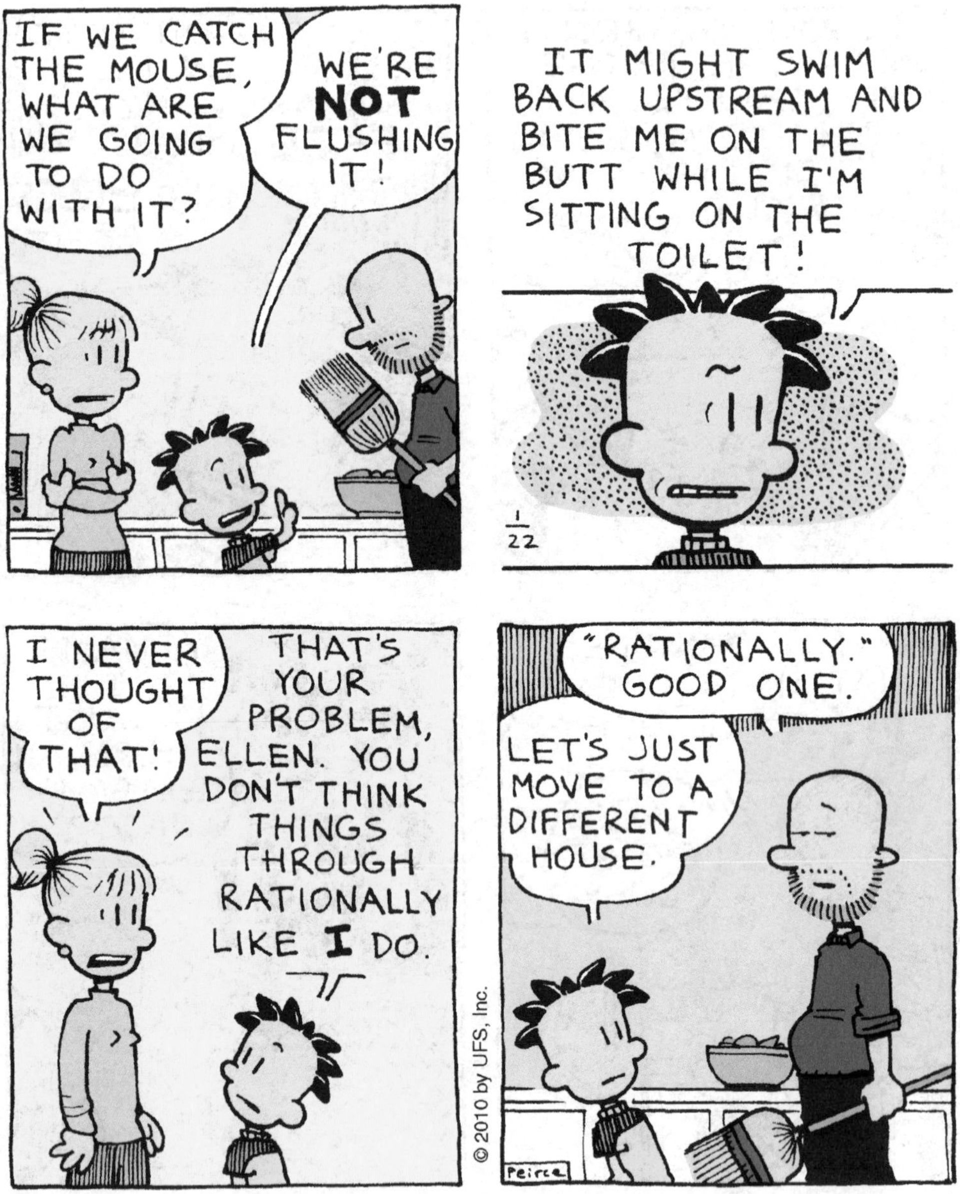

IF WE CATCH THE MOUSE, WHAT ARE WE GOING TO DO WITH IT?
WE'RE **NOT** FLUSHING IT!
IT MIGHT SWIM BACK UPSTREAM AND BITE ME ON THE BUTT WHILE I'M SITTING ON THE TOILET!
1/22
I NEVER THOUGHT OF THAT!
THAT'S YOUR PROBLEM, ELLEN. YOU DON'T THINK THINGS THROUGH RATIONALLY LIKE **I** DO.
"RATIONALLY." GOOD ONE.
LET'S JUST MOVE TO A DIFFERENT HOUSE.
Peirce

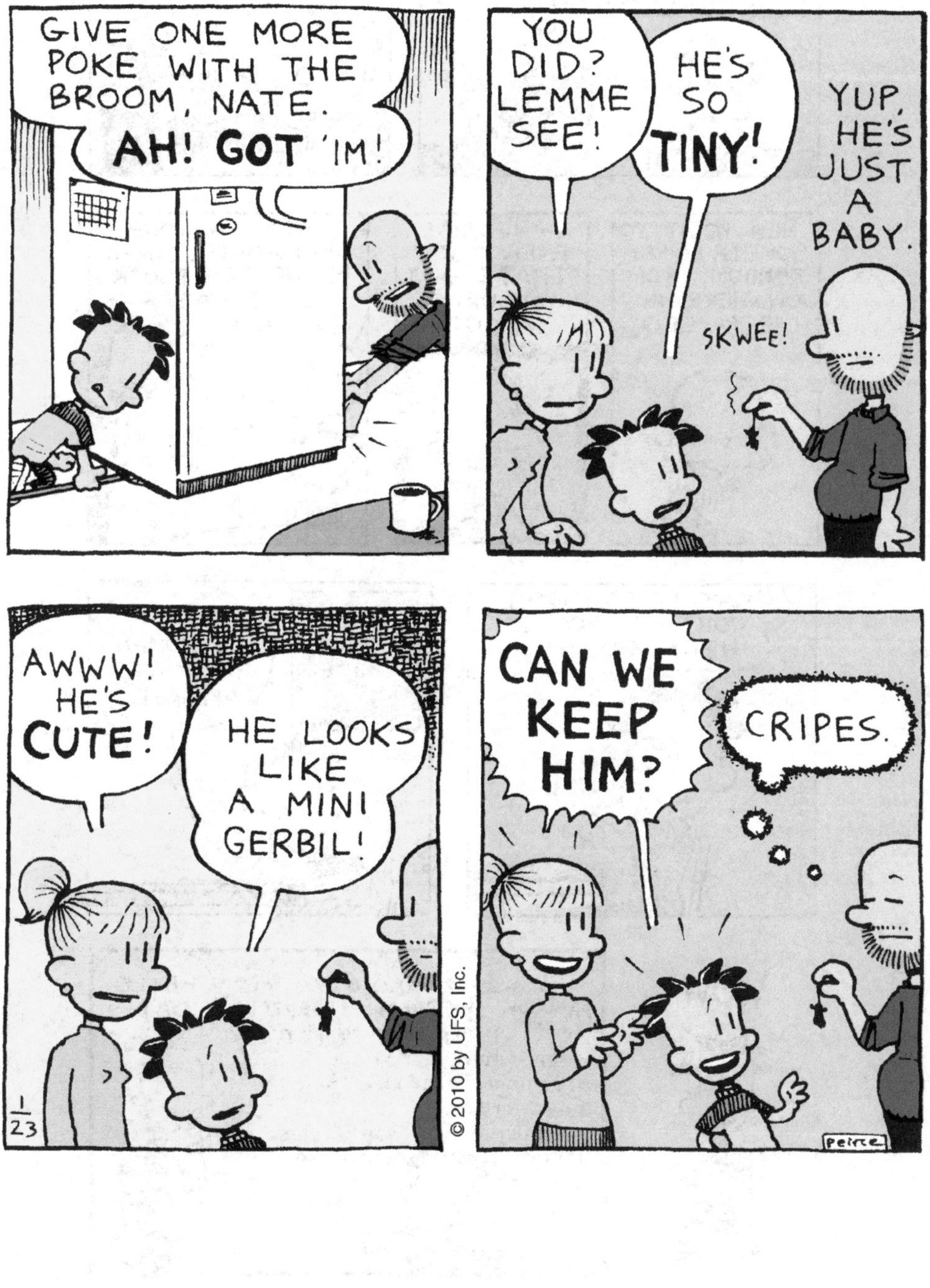
GIVE ONE MORE POKE WITH THE BROOM, NATE.
AH! GOT 'IM!
YOU DID? LEMME SEE!
HE'S SO TINY!
YUP, HE'S JUST A BABY.
SKWEE!
AWWW! HE'S CUTE!
HE LOOKS LIKE A MINI GERBIL!
1
23
© 2010 by UFS, Inc.
CAN WE KEEP HIM?
CRIPES.
peirce

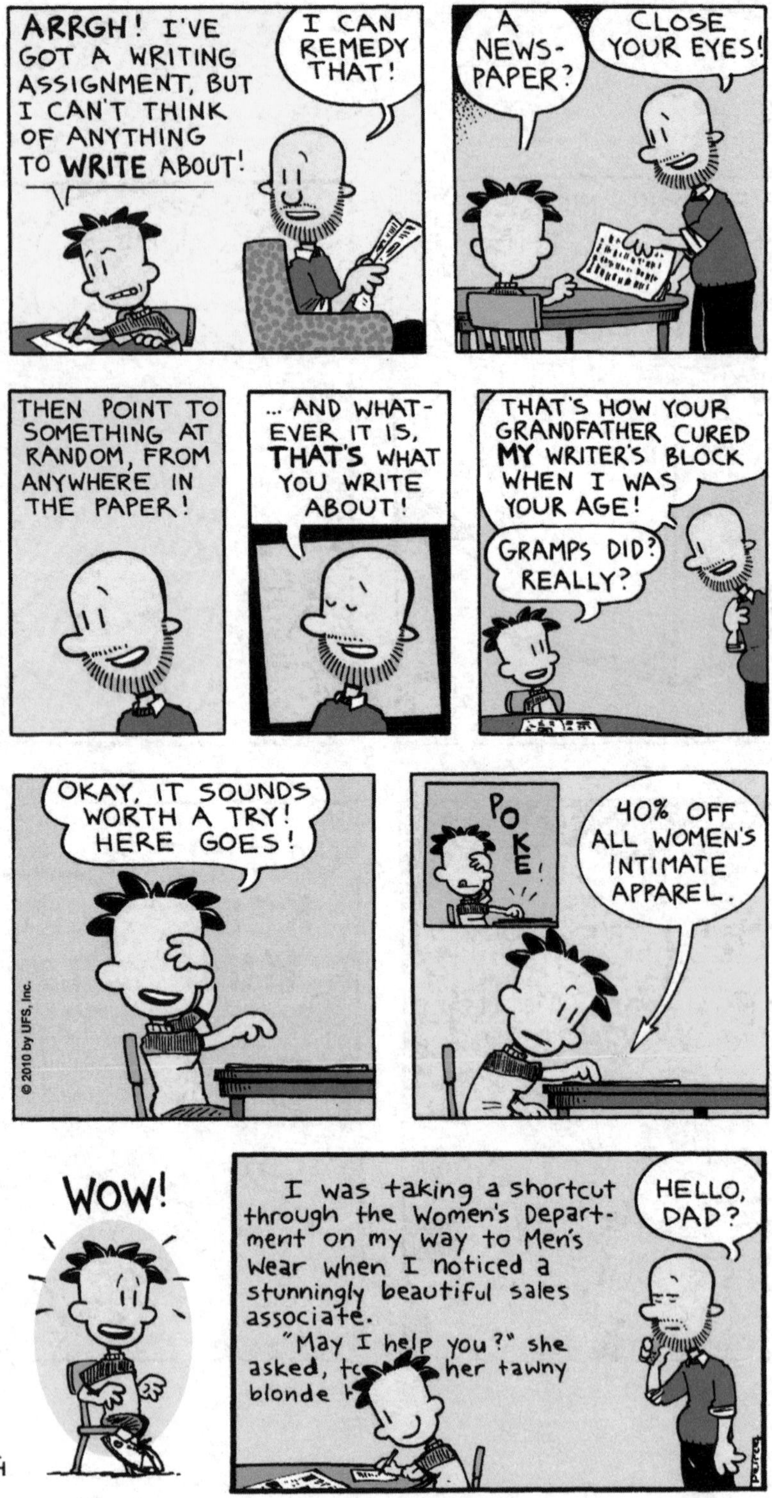

ARRGH! I'VE GOT A WRITING ASSIGNMENT, BUT I CAN'T THINK OF ANYTHING TO WRITE ABOUT!
I CAN REMEDY THAT!
A NEWS-PAPER?
CLOSE YOUR EYES!
THEN POINT TO SOMETHING AT RANDOM, FROM ANYWHERE IN THE PAPER!
... AND WHATEVER IT IS, THAT'S WHAT YOU WRITE ABOUT!
THAT'S HOW YOUR GRANDFATHER CURED MY WRITER'S BLOCK WHEN I WAS YOUR AGE!
GRAMPS DID? REALLY?
OKAY, IT SOUNDS WORTH A TRY! HERE GOES!
© 2010 by UFS, Inc.
POKE!
40% OFF ALL WOMEN'S INTIMATE APPAREL.
WOW!
1
24
I was taking a shortcut through the Women's Department on my way to Men's Wear when I noticed a stunningly beautiful sales associate.
"May I help you?" she asked, tc her tawny blonde h
HELLO, DAD?
PEIRCE

ARTUR ISSUES

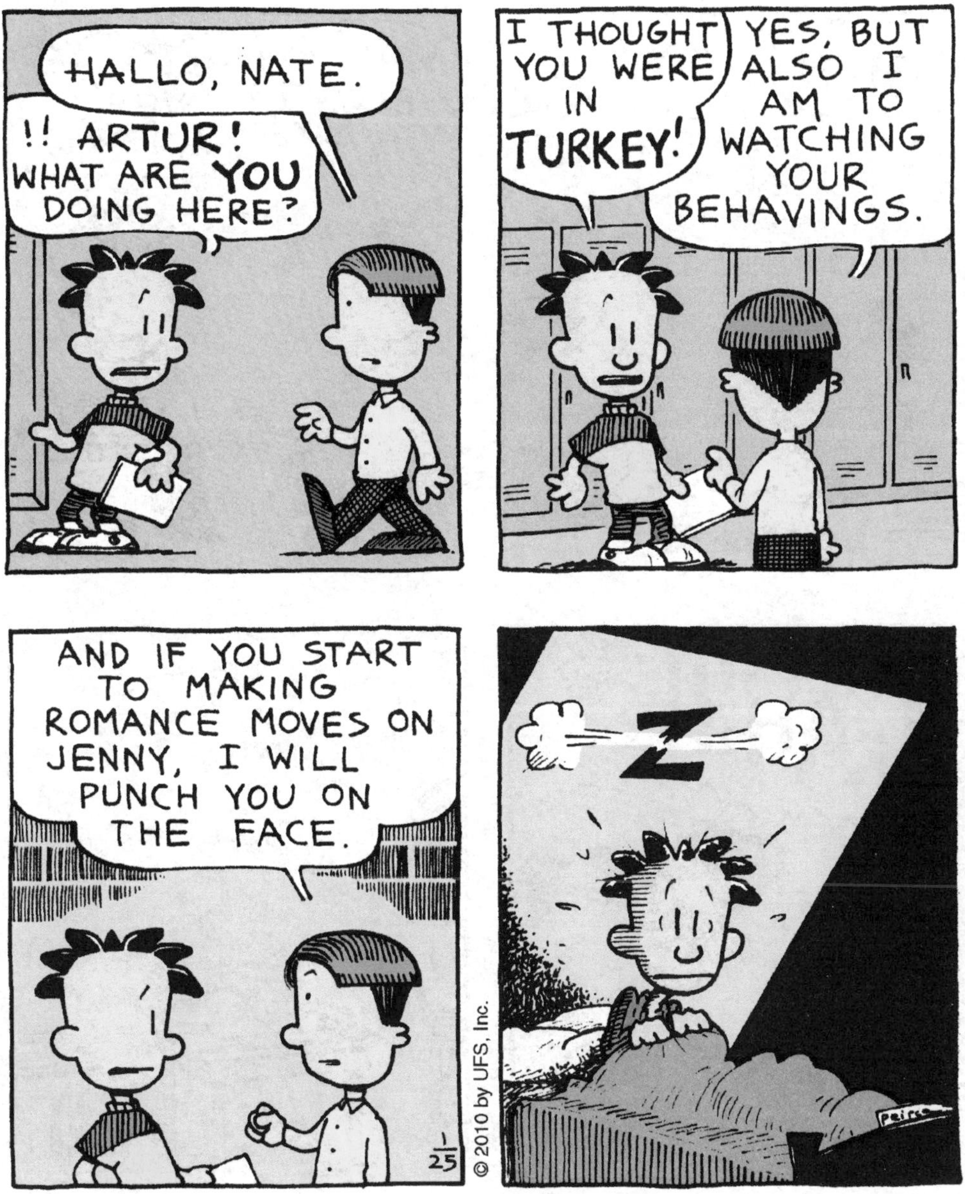

HALLO, NATE.
!! ARTUR! WHAT ARE YOU DOING HERE?
I THOUGHT YOU WERE IN TURKEY!
YES, BUT ALSO I AM TO WATCHING YOUR BEHAVINGS.
AND IF YOU START TO MAKING ROMANCE MOVES ON JENNY, I WILL PUNCH YOU ON THE FACE.
1 25
© 2010 by UFS, Inc.
Z

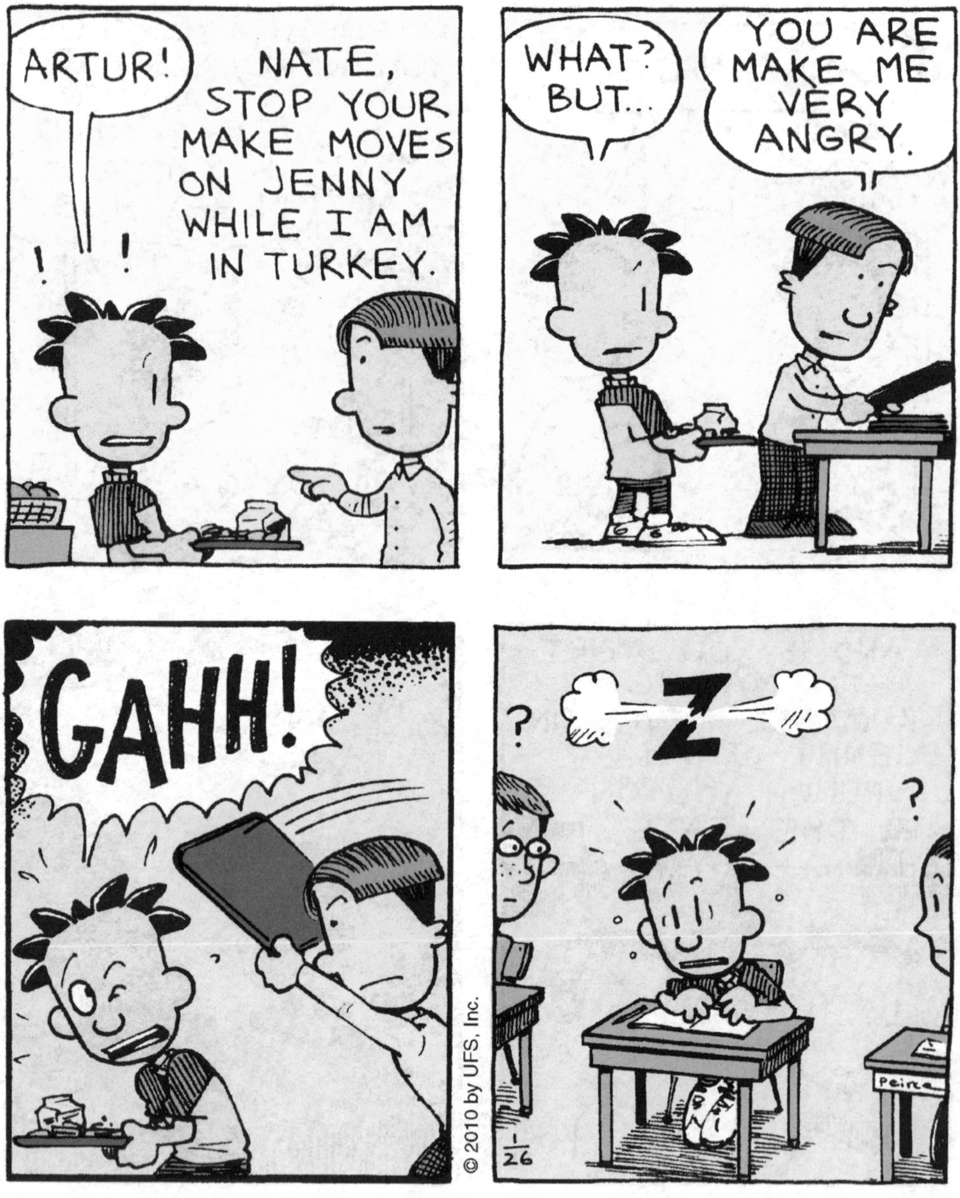
ARTUR!
NATE, STOP YOUR MAKE MOVES ON JENNY WHILE I AM IN TURKEY.
! !
WHAT? BUT...
YOU ARE MAKE ME VERY ANGRY.
GAHH!
?
?
Peirce
1
26

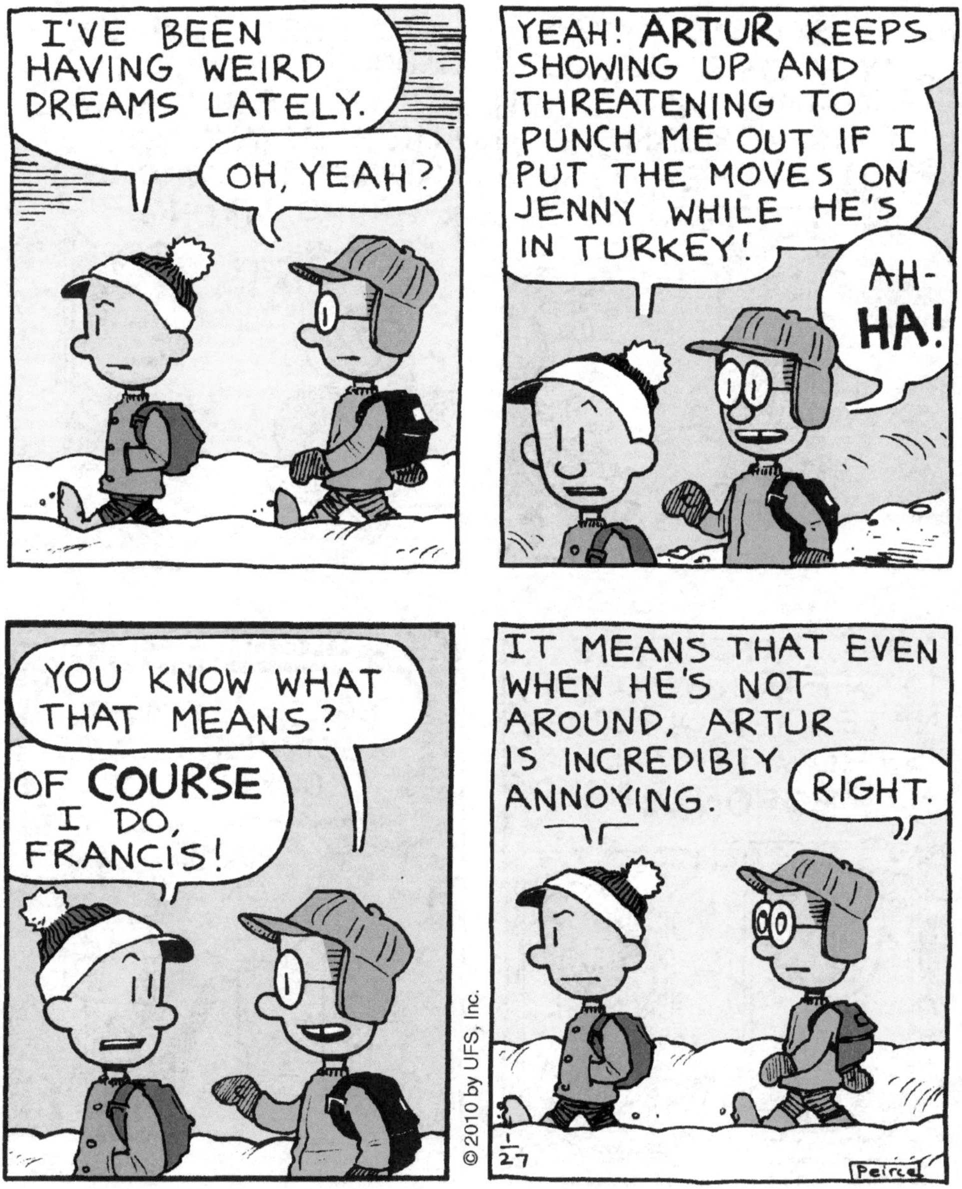
I'VE BEEN HAVING WEIRD DREAMS LATELY.
OH, YEAH?
YEAH! ARTUR KEEPS SHOWING UP AND THREATENING TO PUNCH ME OUT IF I PUT THE MOVES ON JENNY WHILE HE'S IN TURKEY!
AH-HA!
YOU KNOW WHAT THAT MEANS?
OF COURSE I DO, FRANCIS!
IT MEANS THAT EVEN WHEN HE'S NOT AROUND, ARTUR IS INCREDIBLY ANNOYING.
RIGHT.
© 2010 by UFS, Inc.
1 27
Peirce

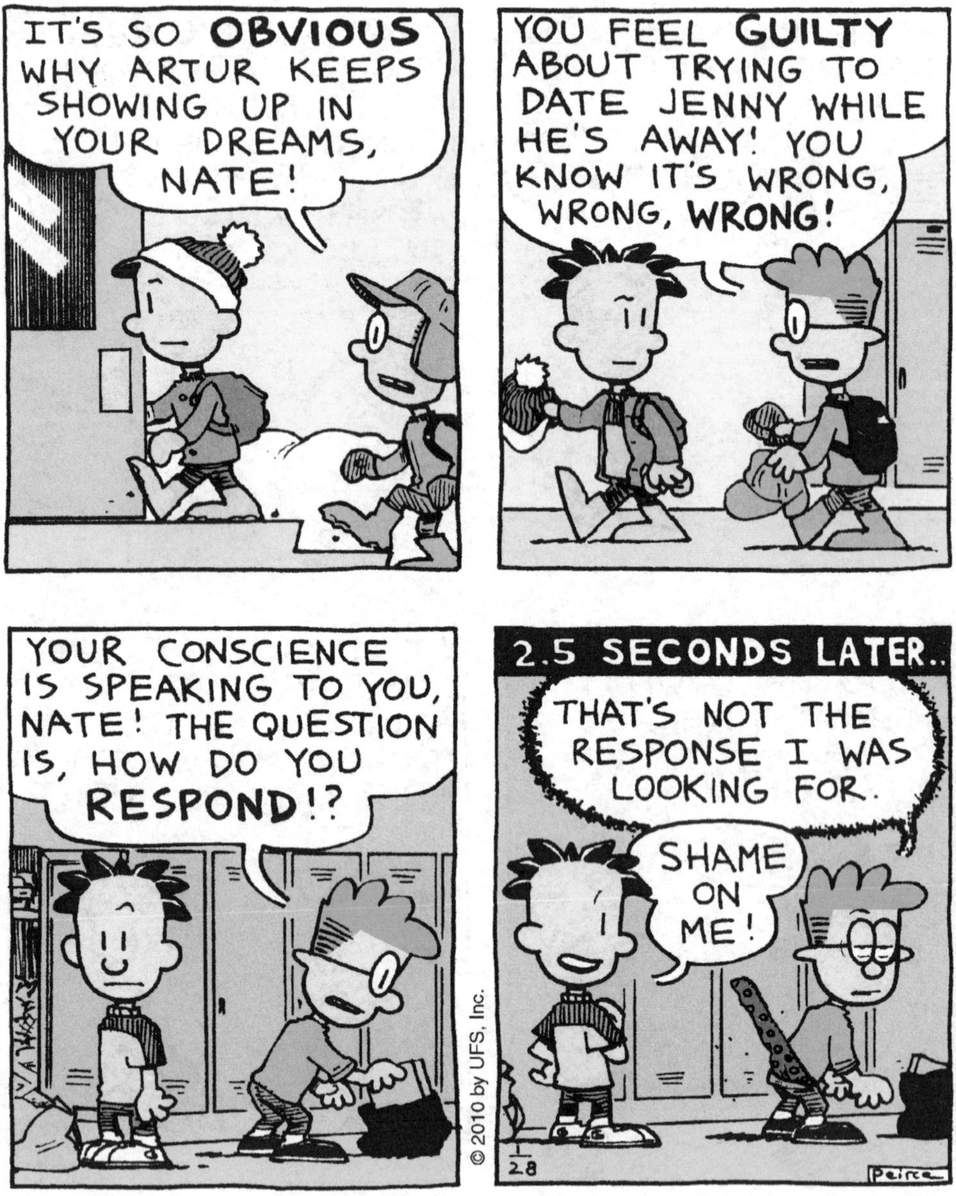
IT'S SO OBVIOUS WHY ARTUR KEEPS SHOWING UP IN YOUR DREAMS, NATE!
YOU FEEL GUILTY ABOUT TRYING TO DATE JENNY WHILE HE'S AWAY! YOU KNOW IT'S WRONG, WRONG, WRONG!
YOUR CONSCIENCE IS SPEAKING TO YOU, NATE! THE QUESTION IS, HOW DO YOU RESPOND!?
2.5 SECONDS LATER..
THAT'S NOT THE RESPONSE I WAS LOOKING FOR.
SHAME ON ME!
1 28
Peirce

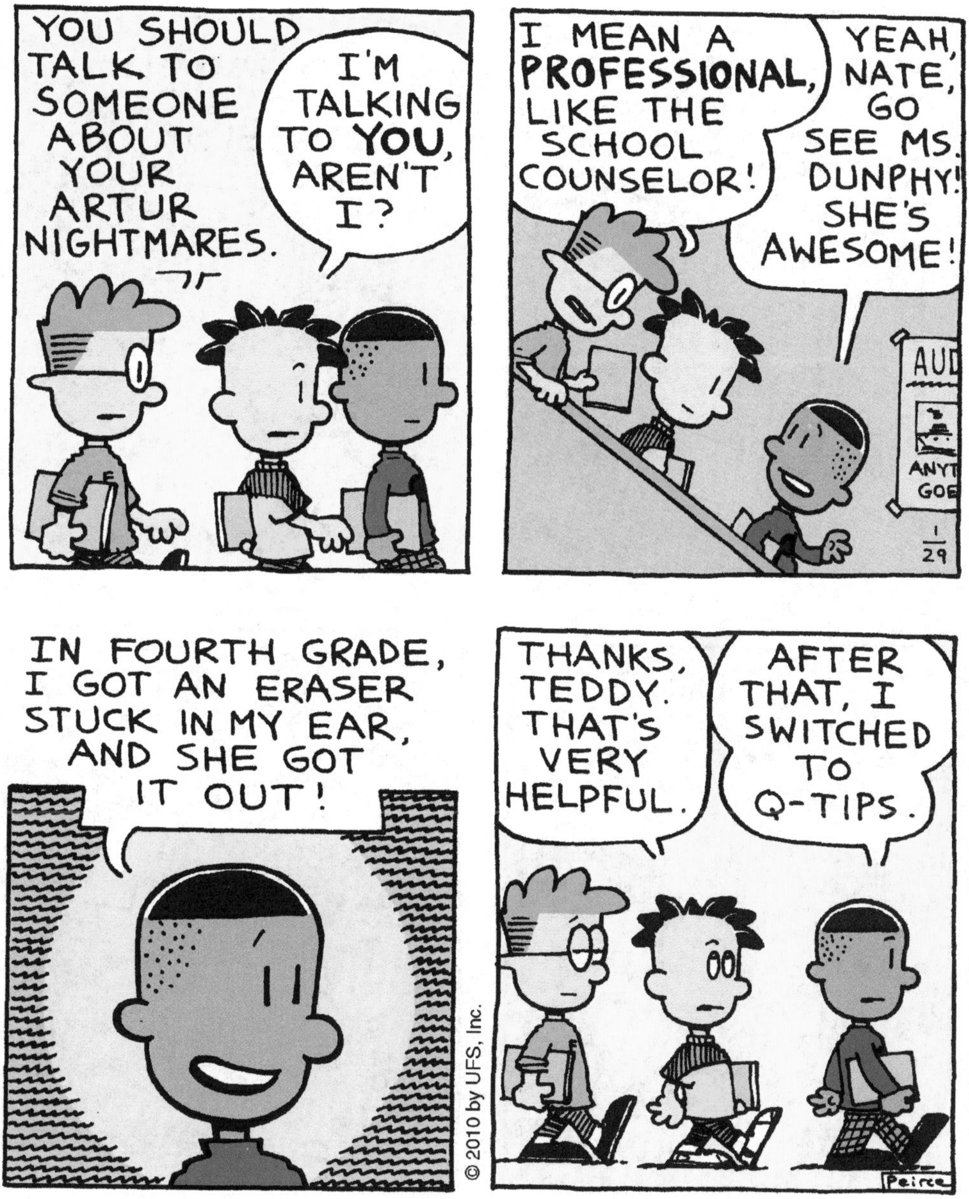
YOU SHOULD TALK TO SOMEONE ABOUT YOUR ARTUR NIGHTMARES.
I'M TALKING TO **YOU**, AREN'T I?
I MEAN A **PROFESSIONAL**, LIKE THE SCHOOL COUNSELOR!
YEAH, NATE, GO SEE MS. DUNPHY! SHE'S AWESOME!
AUD
ANYT
GOE
1/29
IN FOURTH GRADE, I GOT AN ERASER STUCK IN MY EAR, AND SHE GOT IT OUT!
THANKS, TEDDY. THAT'S VERY HELPFUL.
AFTER THAT, I SWITCHED TO Q-TIPS.
Peirce

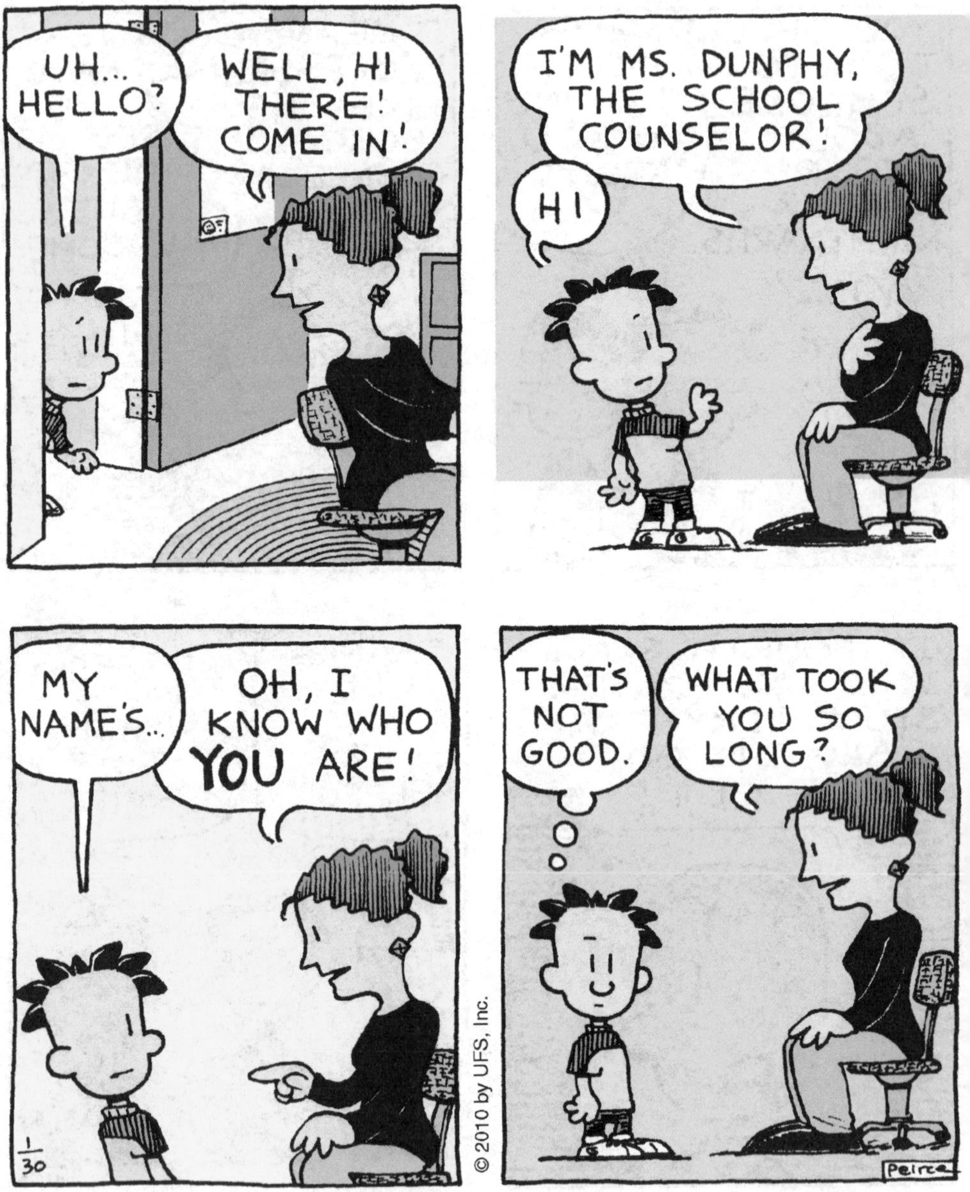
UH... HELLO?
WELL, HI THERE! COME IN!
I'M MS. DUNPHY, THE SCHOOL COUNSELOR!
HI
MY NAME'S...
OH, I KNOW WHO **YOU** ARE!
1/30
THAT'S NOT GOOD.
WHAT TOOK YOU SO LONG?
PEIRCE

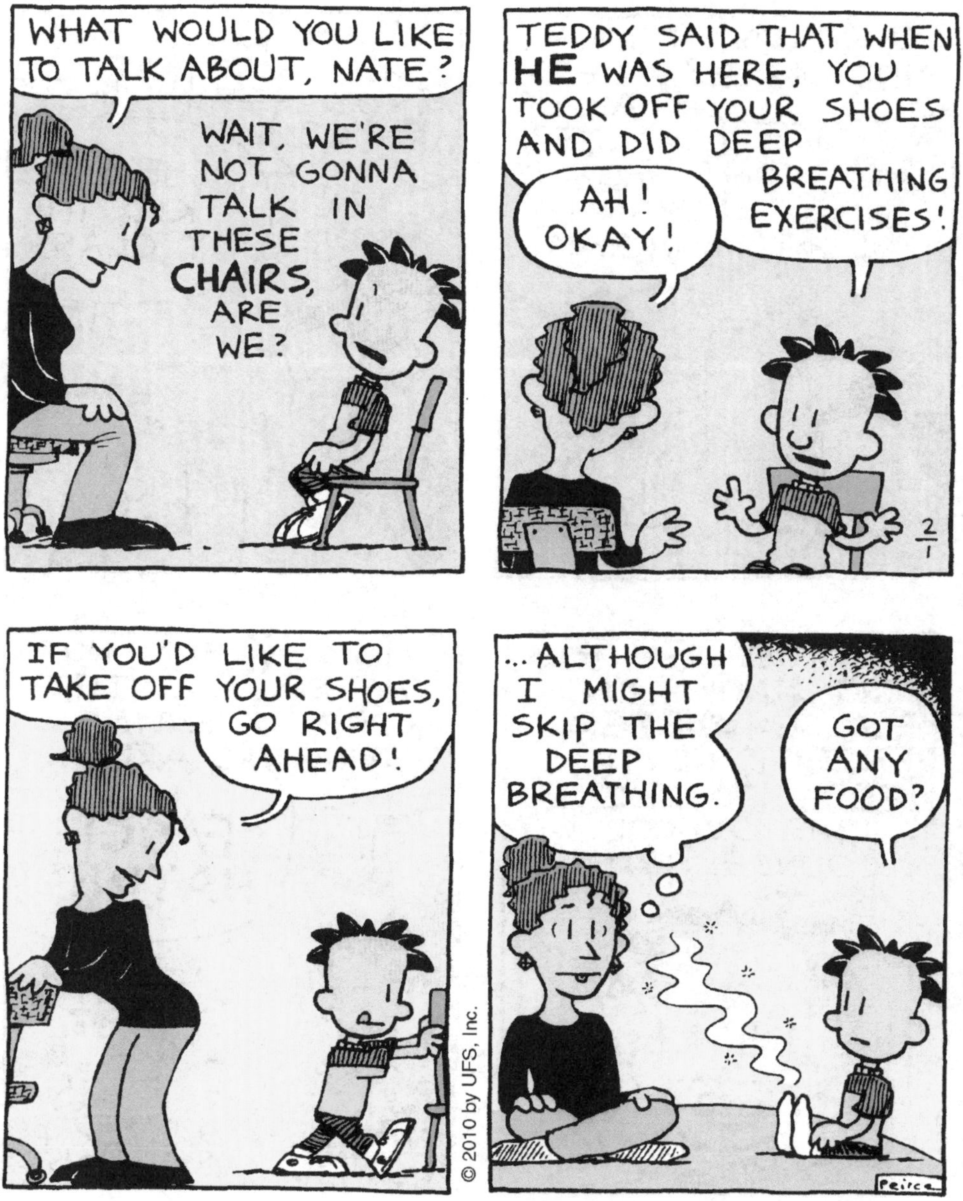
WHAT WOULD YOU LIKE TO TALK ABOUT, NATE?
WAIT, WE'RE NOT GONNA TALK IN THESE CHAIRS, ARE WE?
TEDDY SAID THAT WHEN HE WAS HERE, YOU TOOK OFF YOUR SHOES AND DID DEEP BREATHING EXERCISES!
AH! OKAY!
IF YOU'D LIKE TO TAKE OFF YOUR SHOES, GO RIGHT AHEAD!
...ALTHOUGH I MIGHT SKIP THE DEEP BREATHING.
GOT ANY FOOD?
PEIRCE

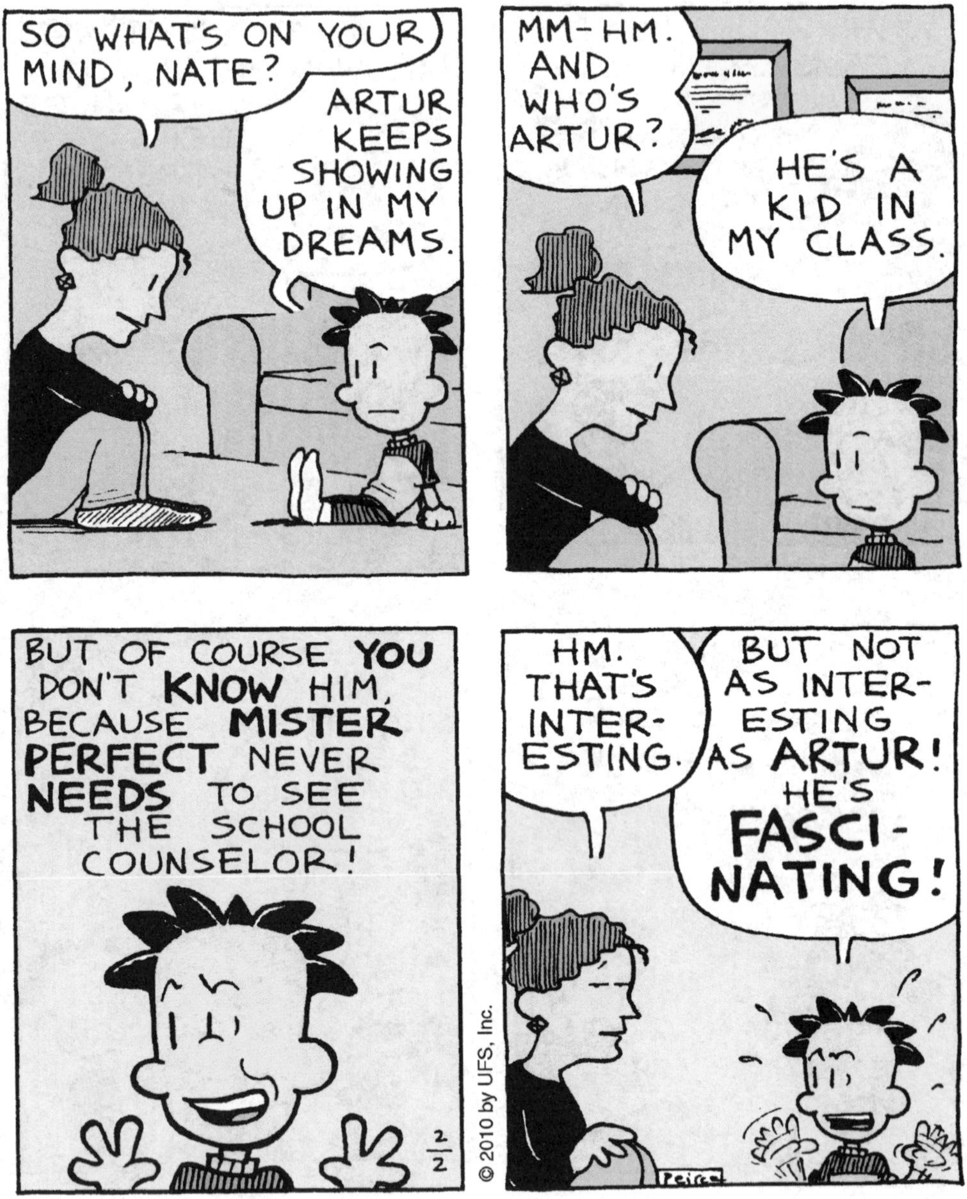
SO WHAT'S ON YOUR MIND, NATE?
ARTUR KEEPS SHOWING UP IN MY DREAMS.
MM-HM. AND WHO'S ARTUR?
HE'S A KID IN MY CLASS.
BUT OF COURSE **YOU** DON'T **KNOW** HIM, BECAUSE **MISTER PERFECT** NEVER **NEEDS** TO SEE THE SCHOOL COUNSELOR!
HM. THAT'S INTER-ESTING.
BUT NOT AS INTER-ESTING AS **ARTUR**! HE'S **FASCI-NATING**!
2/2
Peirce

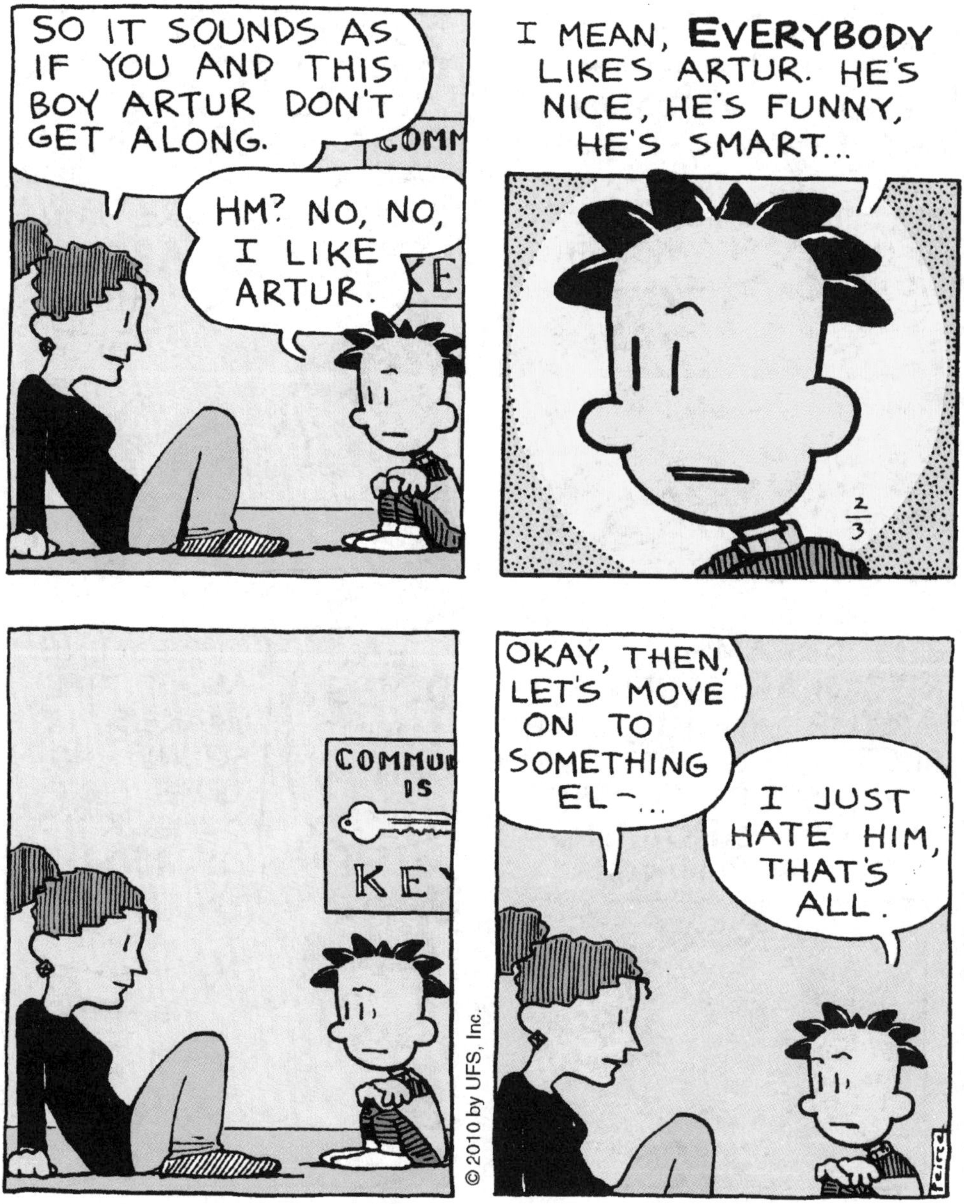
SO IT SOUNDS AS IF YOU AND THIS BOY ARTUR DON'T GET ALONG.
HM? NO, NO, I LIKE ARTUR.
I MEAN, EVERYBODY LIKES ARTUR. HE'S NICE, HE'S FUNNY, HE'S SMART...
OKAY, THEN, LET'S MOVE ON TO SOMETHING EL–...
I JUST HATE HIM, THAT'S ALL.

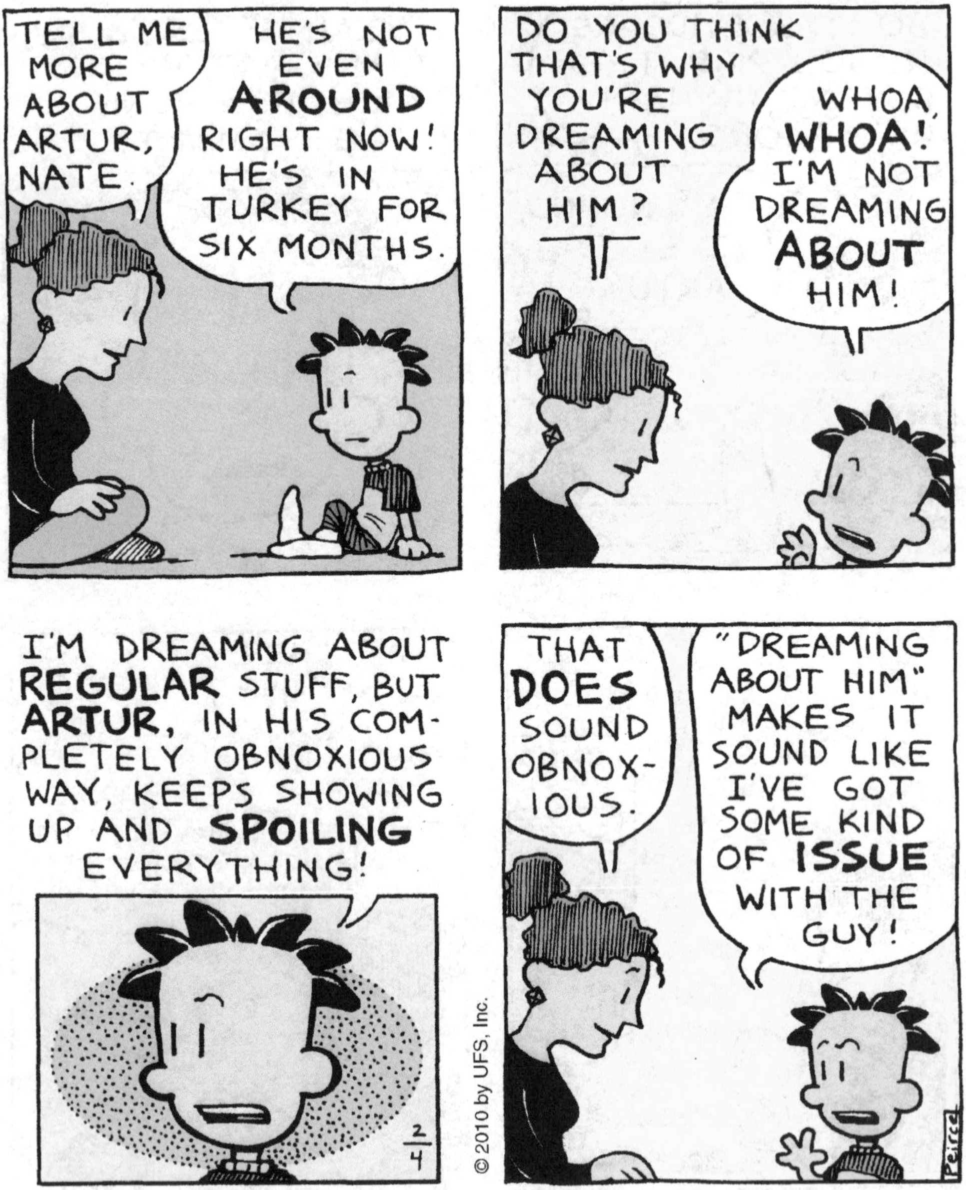
TELL ME MORE ABOUT ARTUR, NATE.
HE'S NOT EVEN **AROUND** RIGHT NOW! HE'S IN TURKEY FOR SIX MONTHS.
DO YOU THINK THAT'S WHY YOU'RE DREAMING ABOUT HIM?
WHOA, **WHOA!** I'M NOT DREAMING **ABOUT** HIM!
I'M DREAMING ABOUT **REGULAR** STUFF, BUT **ARTUR**, IN HIS COMPLETELY OBNOXIOUS WAY, KEEPS SHOWING UP AND **SPOILING** EVERYTHING!
THAT **DOES** SOUND OBNOXIOUS.
"DREAMING ABOUT HIM" MAKES IT SOUND LIKE I'VE GOT SOME KIND OF **ISSUE** WITH THE GUY!
2/4
Peirce

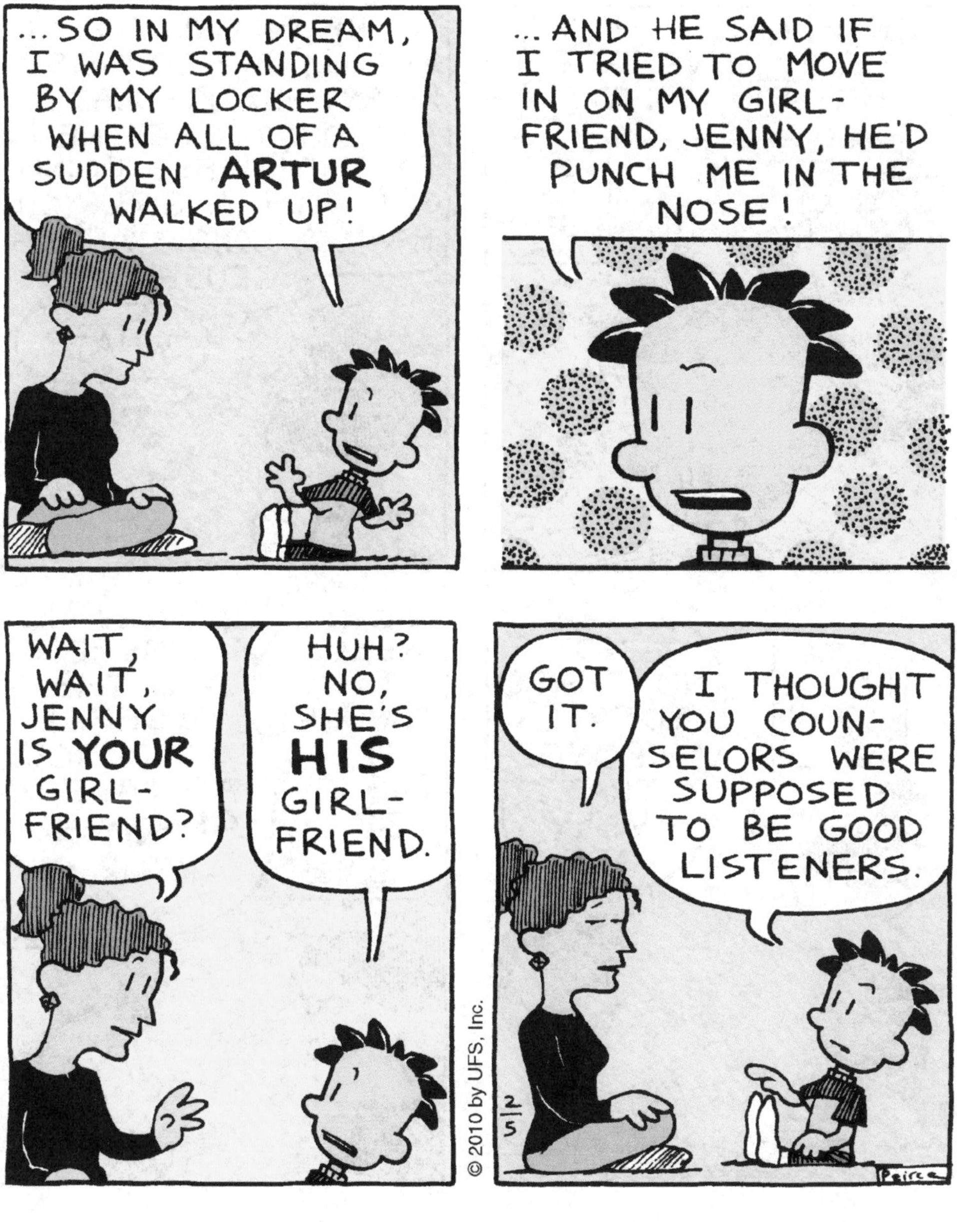
...SO IN MY DREAM, I WAS STANDING BY MY LOCKER WHEN ALL OF A SUDDEN ARTUR WALKED UP!
...AND HE SAID IF I TRIED TO MOVE IN ON MY GIRL-FRIEND, JENNY, HE'D PUNCH ME IN THE NOSE!
WAIT, WAIT, JENNY IS YOUR GIRL-FRIEND?
HUH? NO, SHE'S HIS GIRL-FRIEND.
GOT IT.
I THOUGHT YOU COUN-SELORS WERE SUPPOSED TO BE GOOD LISTENERS.
© 2010 by UFS, Inc.
5/2
Peirce

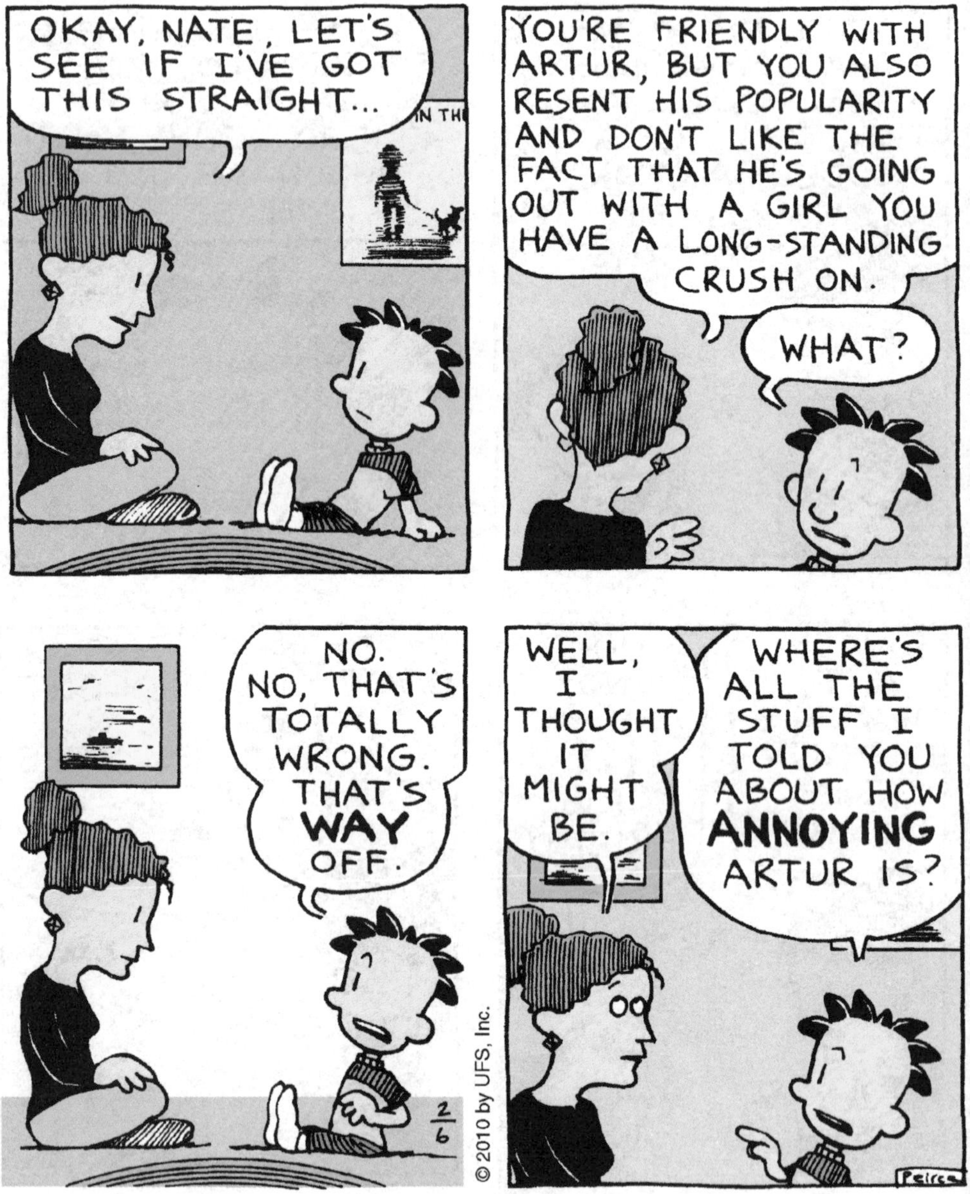
OKAY, NATE, LET'S SEE IF I'VE GOT THIS STRAIGHT...
YOU'RE FRIENDLY WITH ARTUR, BUT YOU ALSO RESENT HIS POPULARITY AND DON'T LIKE THE FACT THAT HE'S GOING OUT WITH A GIRL YOU HAVE A LONG-STANDING CRUSH ON.
WHAT?
NO. NO, THAT'S TOTALLY WRONG. THAT'S **WAY** OFF.
2/6
© 2010 by UFS, Inc.
WELL, I THOUGHT IT MIGHT BE.
WHERE'S ALL THE STUFF I TOLD YOU ABOUT HOW **ANNOYING** ARTUR IS?
Peirce

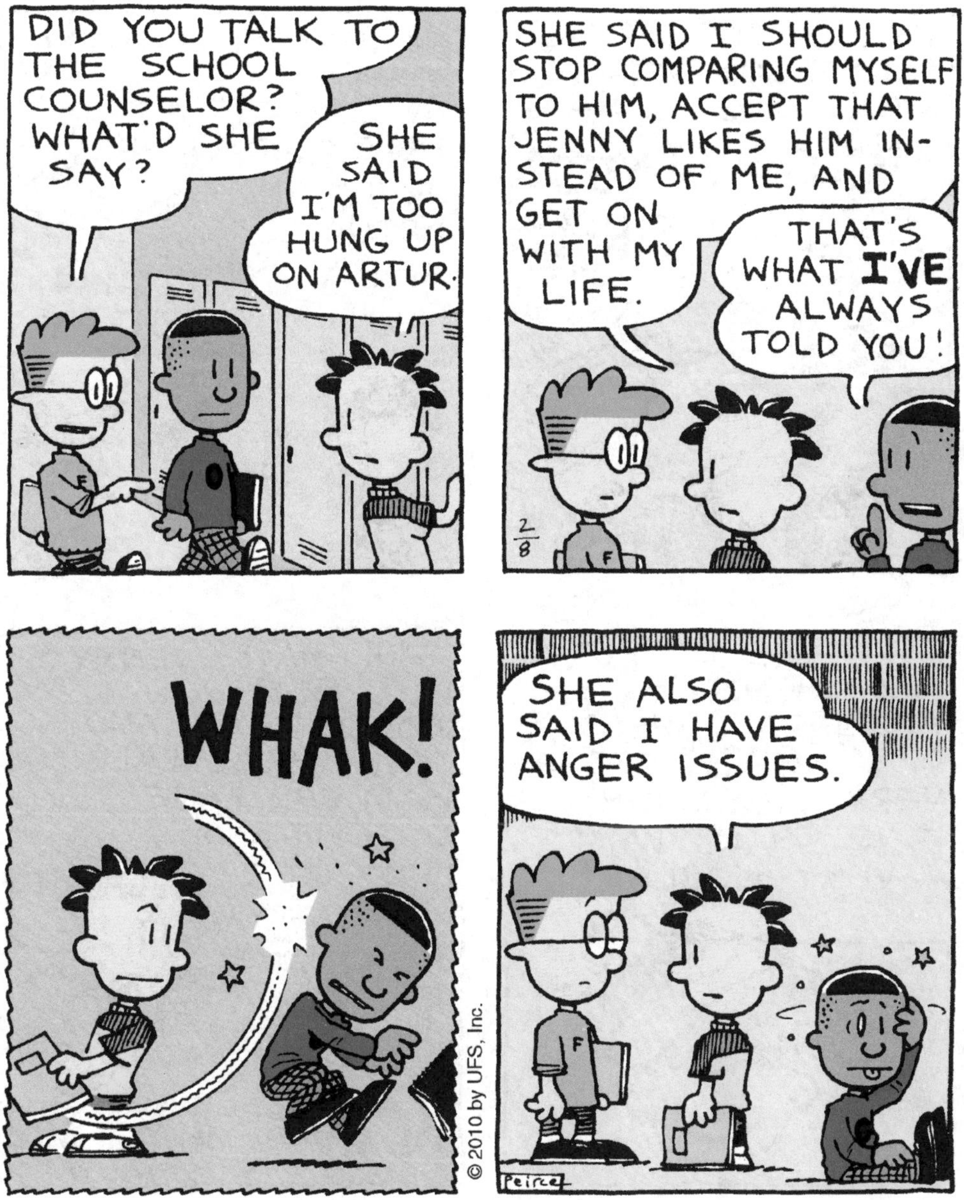
DID YOU TALK TO THE SCHOOL COUNSELOR? WHAT'D SHE SAY?
SHE SAID I'M TOO HUNG UP ON ARTUR.
SHE SAID I SHOULD STOP COMPARING MYSELF TO HIM, ACCEPT THAT JENNY LIKES HIM INSTEAD OF ME, AND GET ON WITH MY LIFE.
THAT'S WHAT I'VE ALWAYS TOLD YOU!
2/8
WHAK!
SHE ALSO SAID I HAVE ANGER ISSUES.
Peirce

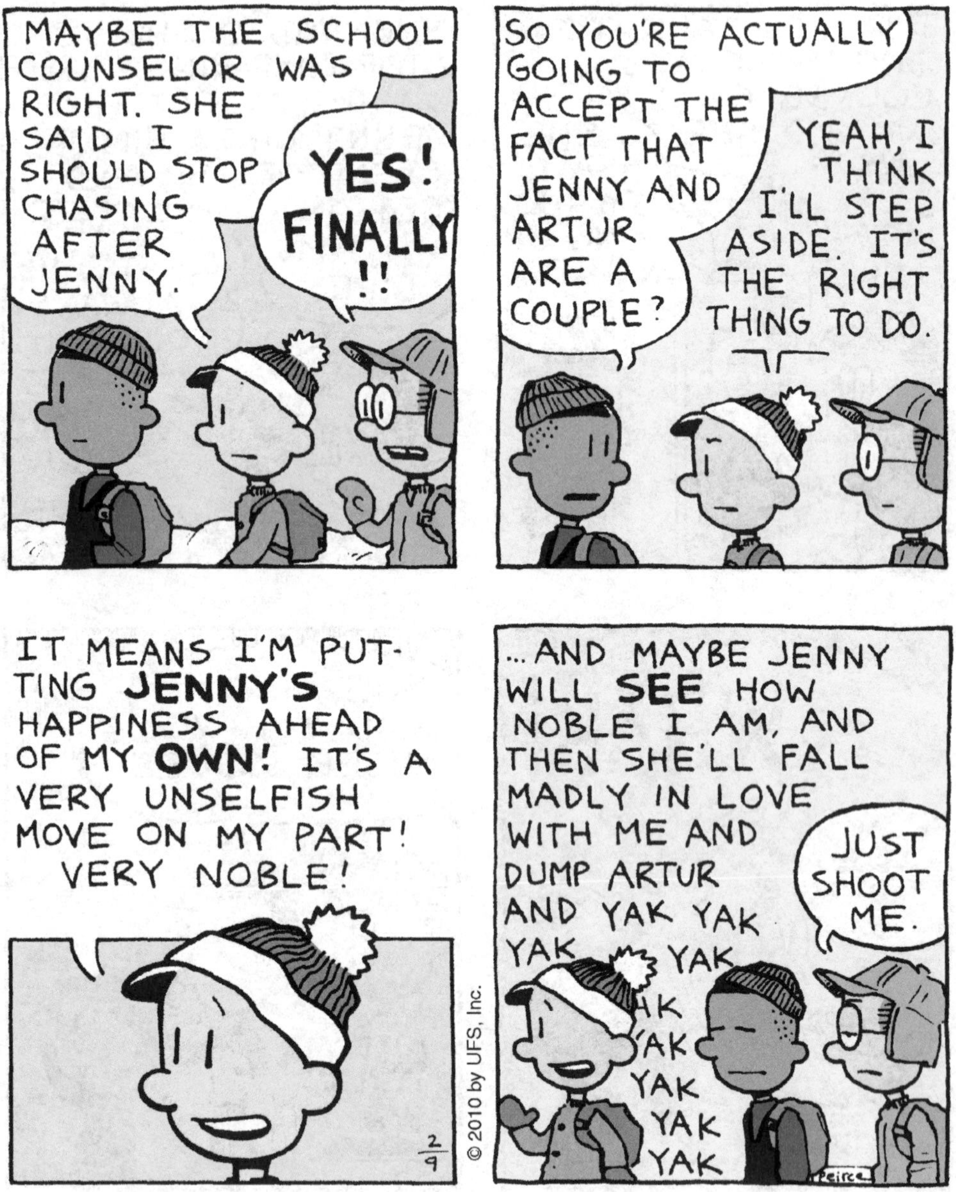
MAYBE THE SCHOOL COUNSELOR WAS RIGHT. SHE SAID I SHOULD STOP CHASING AFTER JENNY.
YES! FINALLY!!
SO YOU'RE ACTUALLY GOING TO ACCEPT THE FACT THAT JENNY AND ARTUR ARE A COUPLE?
YEAH, I THINK I'LL STEP ASIDE. IT'S THE RIGHT THING TO DO.
IT MEANS I'M PUTTING JENNY'S HAPPINESS AHEAD OF MY OWN! IT'S A VERY UNSELFISH MOVE ON MY PART! VERY NOBLE!
2/9
© 2010 by UFS, Inc.
...AND MAYBE JENNY WILL SEE HOW NOBLE I AM, AND THEN SHE'LL FALL MADLY IN LOVE WITH ME AND DUMP ARTUR AND YAK YAK YAK YAK
JUST SHOOT ME.
Peirce

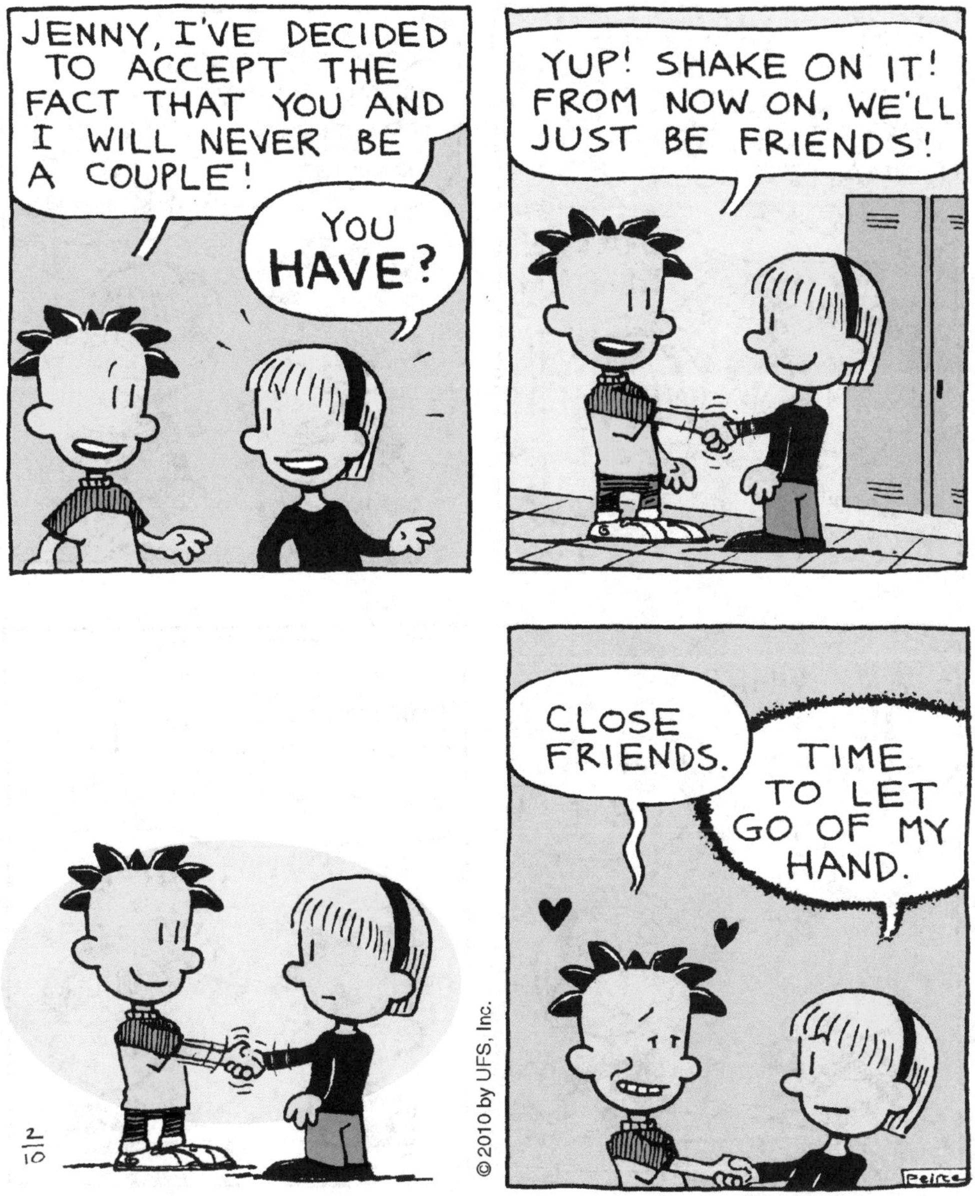
JENNY, I'VE DECIDED TO ACCEPT THE FACT THAT YOU AND I WILL NEVER BE A COUPLE!
YOU HAVE?
YUP! SHAKE ON IT! FROM NOW ON, WE'LL JUST BE FRIENDS!
CLOSE FRIENDS.
TIME TO LET GO OF MY HAND.
2/10
© 2010 by UFS, Inc.
Peirce

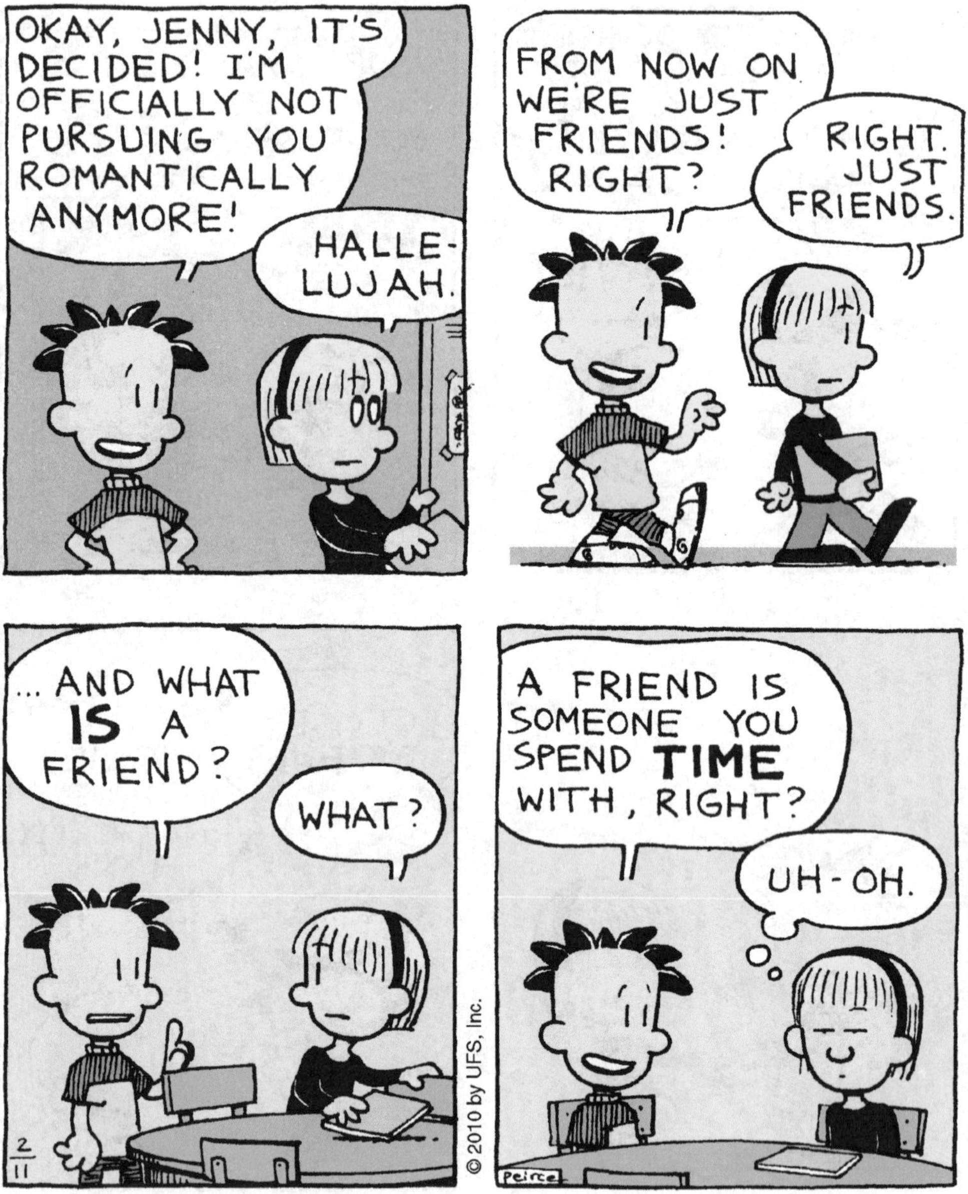
OKAY, JENNY, IT'S DECIDED! I'M OFFICIALLY NOT PURSUING YOU ROMANTICALLY ANYMORE!
HALLE-LUJAH.
FROM NOW ON WE'RE JUST FRIENDS! RIGHT?
RIGHT. JUST FRIENDS.
... AND WHAT **IS** A FRIEND?
WHAT?
A FRIEND IS SOMEONE YOU SPEND **TIME** WITH, RIGHT?
UH-OH.
2/11
Peirce

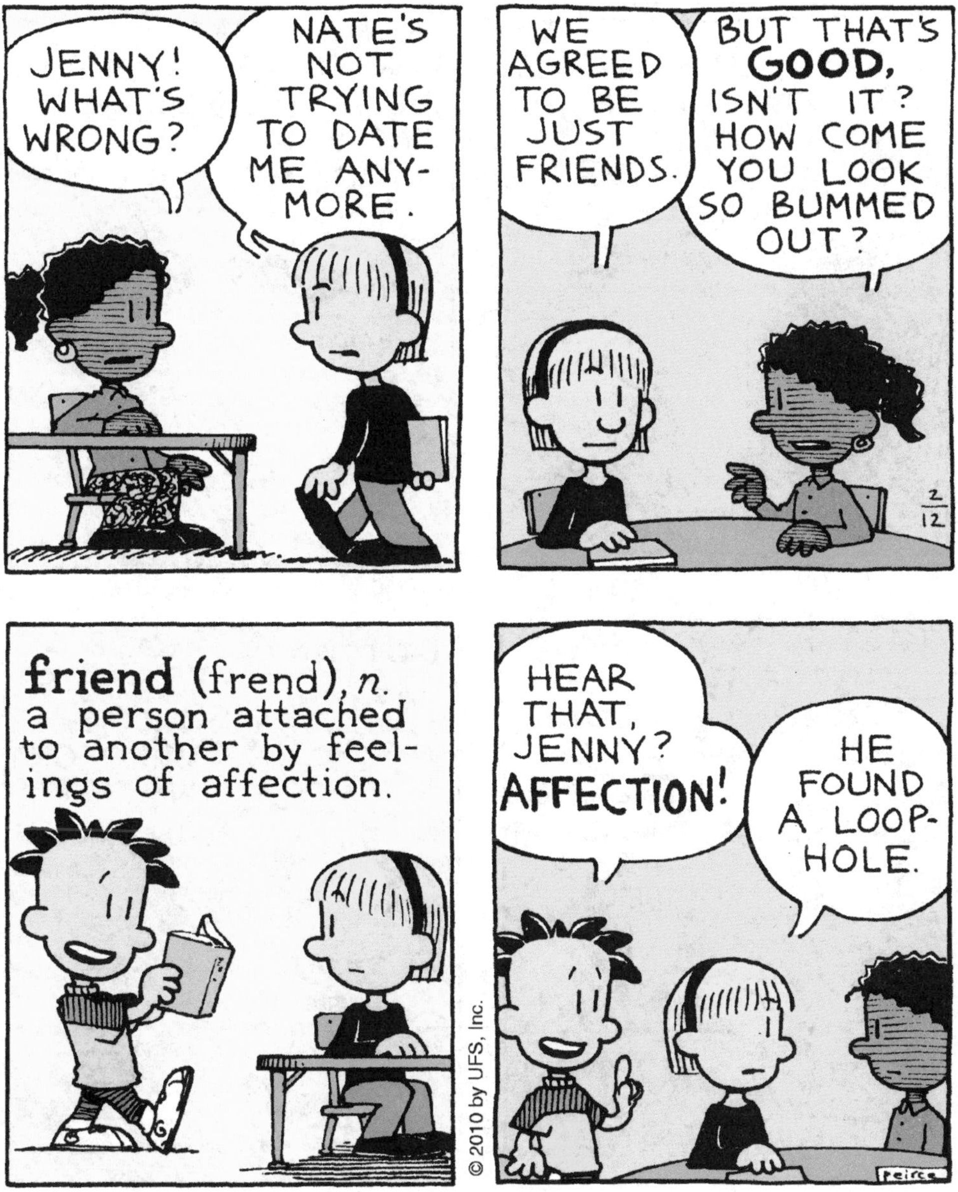
JENNY! WHAT'S WRONG?
NATE'S NOT TRYING TO DATE ME ANY-MORE.
WE AGREED TO BE JUST FRIENDS.
BUT THAT'S **GOOD,** ISN'T IT? HOW COME YOU LOOK SO BUMMED OUT?
2/12
friend (frend), *n.* a person attached to another by feel-ings of affection.
HEAR THAT, JENNY? **AFFECTION!**
HE FOUND A LOOP-HOLE.
peirce

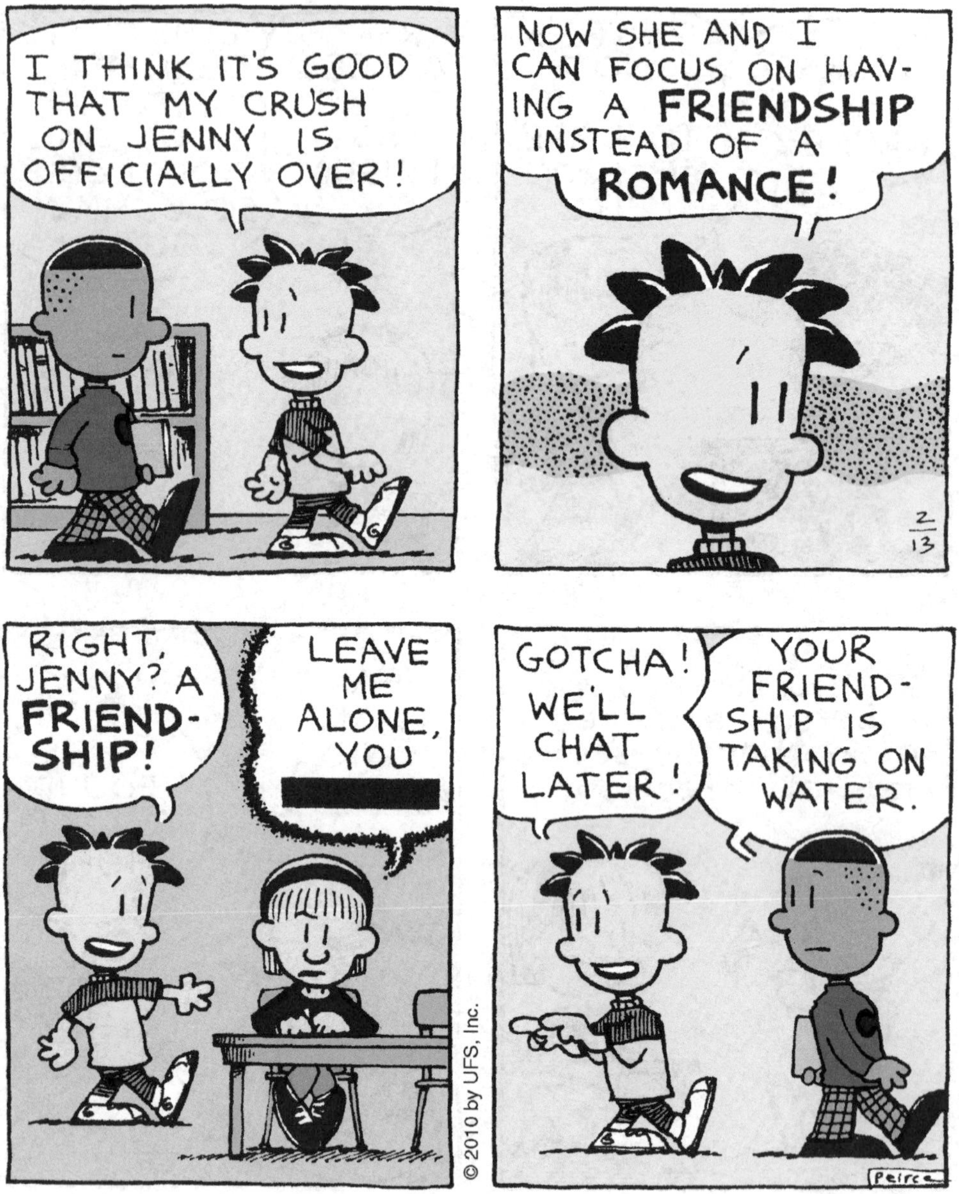
I THINK IT'S GOOD THAT MY CRUSH ON JENNY IS OFFICIALLY OVER!
NOW SHE AND I CAN FOCUS ON HAVING A **FRIENDSHIP** INSTEAD OF A **ROMANCE**!
2/13
RIGHT, JENNY? A **FRIENDSHIP**!
LEAVE ME ALONE, YOU [redacted].
GOTCHA! WE'LL CHAT LATER!
YOUR FRIENDSHIP IS TAKING ON WATER.
Peirce

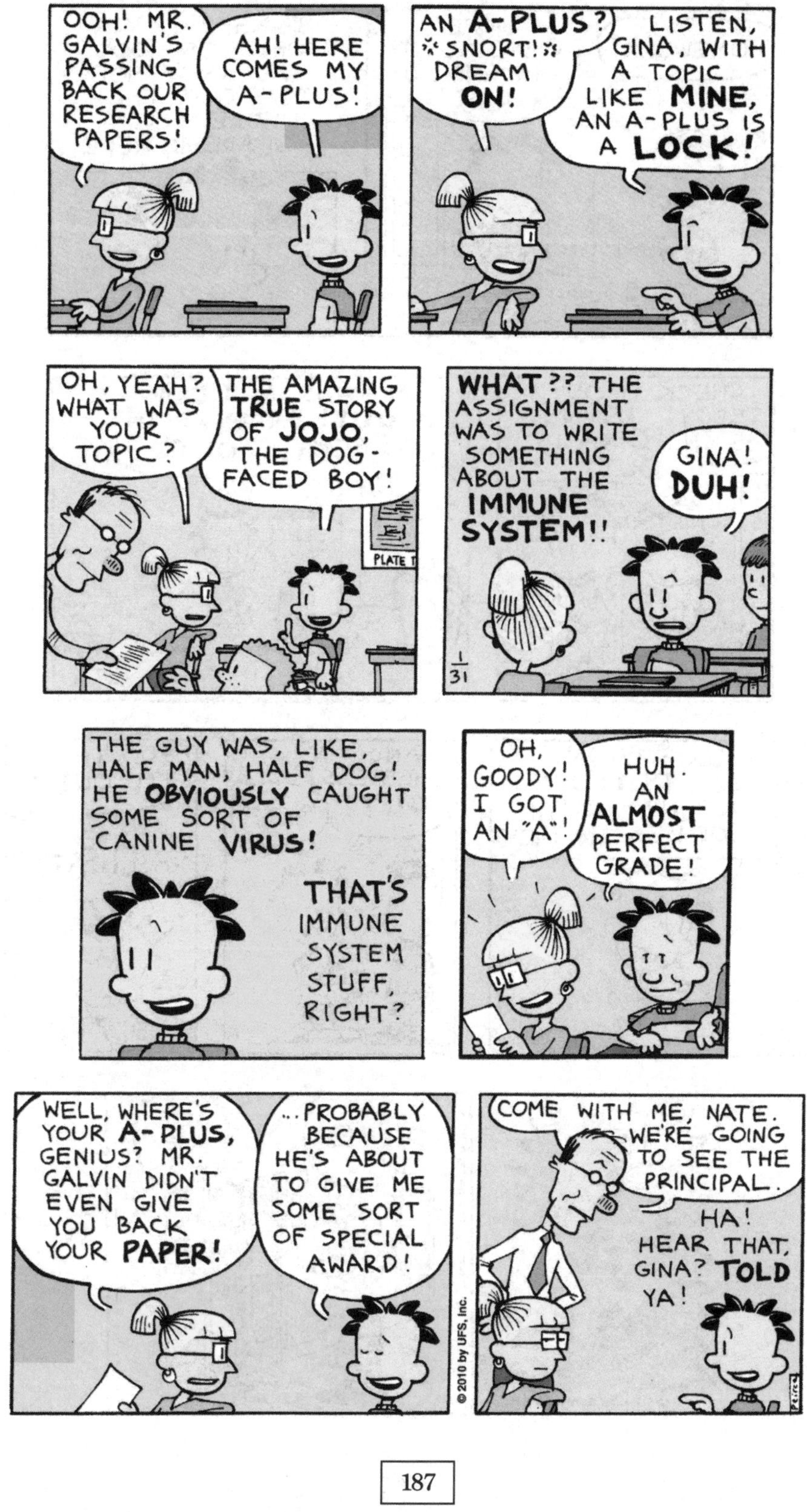
OOH! MR. GALVIN'S PASSING BACK OUR RESEARCH PAPERS!
AH! HERE COMES MY A-PLUS!
AN A-PLUS? *SNORT!* DREAM ON!
LISTEN, GINA, WITH A TOPIC LIKE MINE, AN A-PLUS IS A LOCK!
OH, YEAH? WHAT WAS YOUR TOPIC?
THE AMAZING TRUE STORY OF JOJO, THE DOG-FACED BOY!
PLATE
WHAT?? THE ASSIGNMENT WAS TO WRITE SOMETHING ABOUT THE IMMUNE SYSTEM!!
GINA! DUH!
1/31
THE GUY WAS, LIKE, HALF MAN, HALF DOG! HE OBVIOUSLY CAUGHT SOME SORT OF CANINE VIRUS!
THAT'S IMMUNE SYSTEM STUFF, RIGHT?
OH, GOODY! I GOT AN "A"!
HUH. AN ALMOST PERFECT GRADE!
WELL, WHERE'S YOUR A-PLUS, GENIUS? MR. GALVIN DIDN'T EVEN GIVE YOU BACK YOUR PAPER!
...PROBABLY BECAUSE HE'S ABOUT TO GIVE ME SOME SORT OF SPECIAL AWARD!
© 2010 by UFS, Inc.
COME WITH ME, NATE. WE'RE GOING TO SEE THE PRINCIPAL.
HA! HEAR THAT, GINA? TOLD YA!

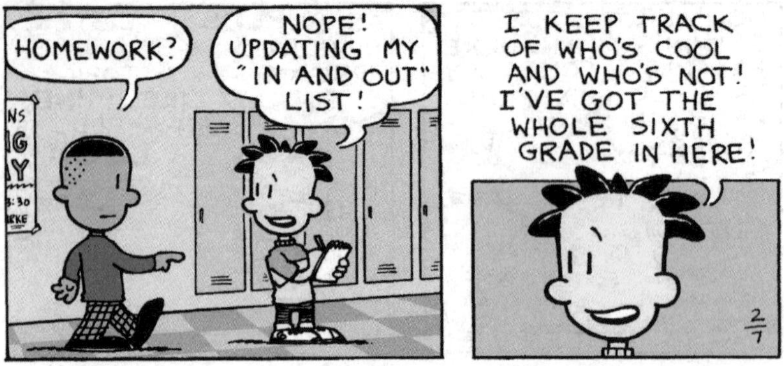
HOMEWORK?
NOPE! UPDATING MY "IN AND OUT" LIST!
I KEEP TRACK OF WHO'S COOL AND WHO'S NOT! I'VE GOT THE WHOLE SIXTH GRADE IN HERE!

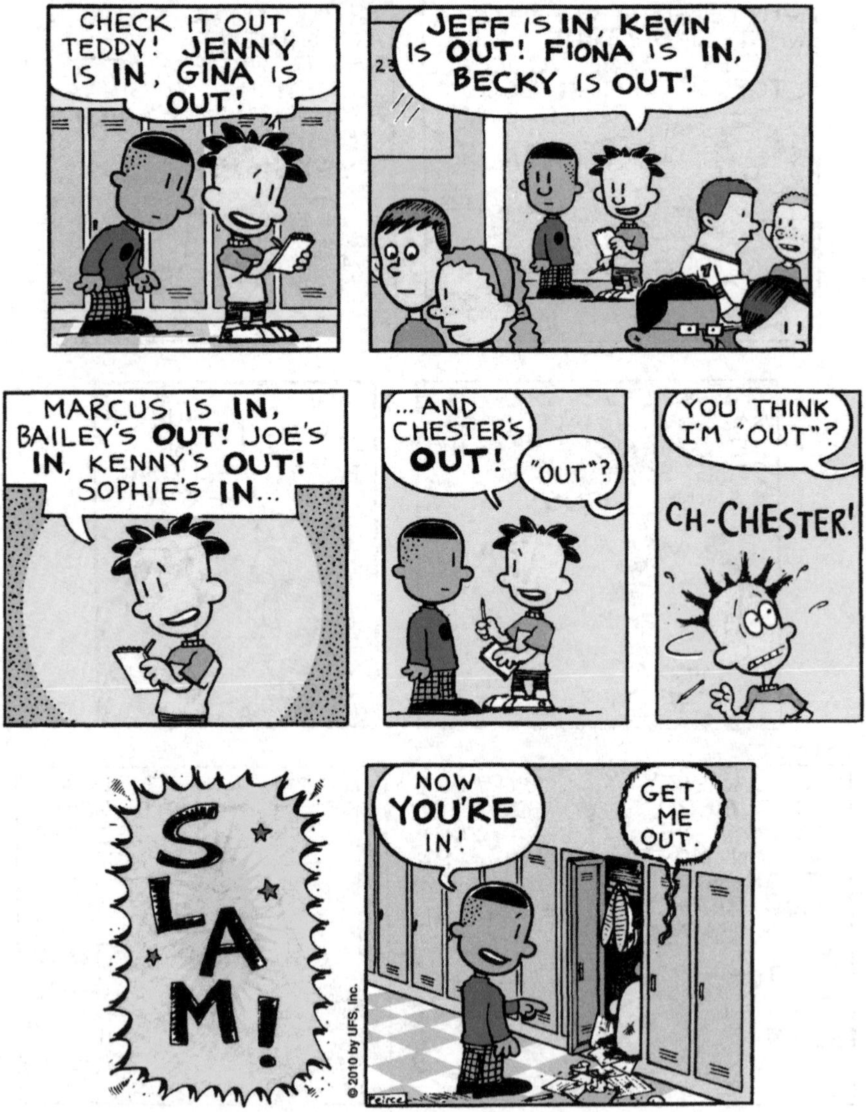
CHECK IT OUT, TEDDY! **JENNY** IS **IN**, **GINA** IS **OUT**!
JEFF IS **IN**, **KEVIN** IS **OUT**! **FIONA** IS **IN**, **BECKY** IS **OUT**!
MARCUS IS **IN**, BAILEY'S **OUT**! JOE'S **IN**, KENNY'S **OUT**! SOPHIE'S **IN**...
...AND CHESTER'S **OUT**!
"OUT"?
YOU THINK I'M "OUT"?
CH-CHESTER!
SLAM!
NOW **YOU'RE** IN!
GET ME OUT.
© 2010 by UFS, Inc.

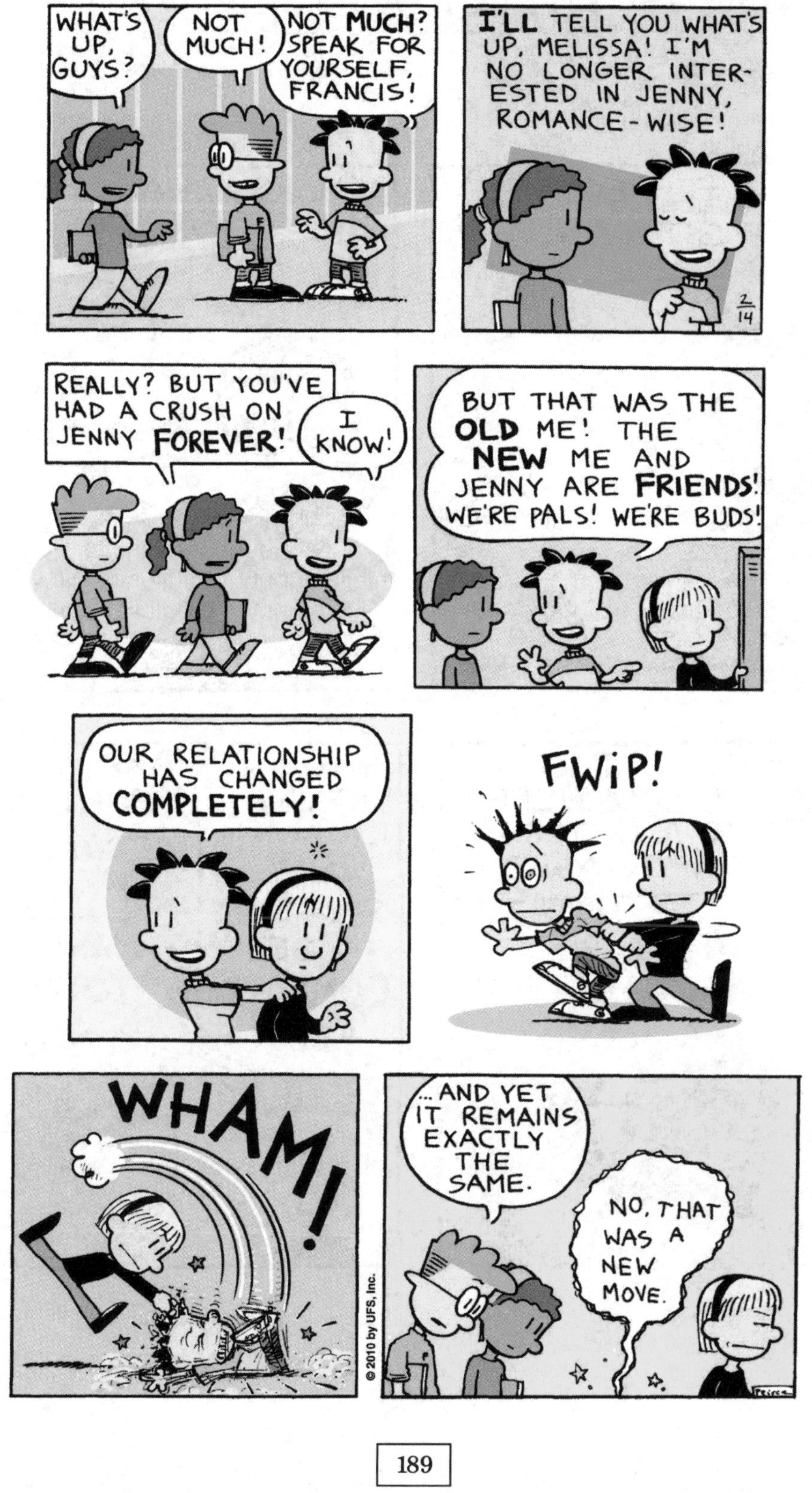
WHAT'S UP, GUYS?
NOT MUCH!
NOT MUCH? SPEAK FOR YOURSELF, FRANCIS!
I'LL TELL YOU WHAT'S UP, MELISSA! I'M NO LONGER INTERESTED IN JENNY, ROMANCE-WISE!
2/14
REALLY? BUT YOU'VE HAD A CRUSH ON JENNY FOREVER!
I KNOW!
BUT THAT WAS THE OLD ME! THE NEW ME AND JENNY ARE FRIENDS! WE'RE PALS! WE'RE BUDS!
OUR RELATIONSHIP HAS CHANGED COMPLETELY!
FWIP!
WHAM!
© 2010 by UFS, Inc.
...AND YET IT REMAINS EXACTLY THE SAME.
NO, THAT WAS A NEW MOVE.

BE SEATED

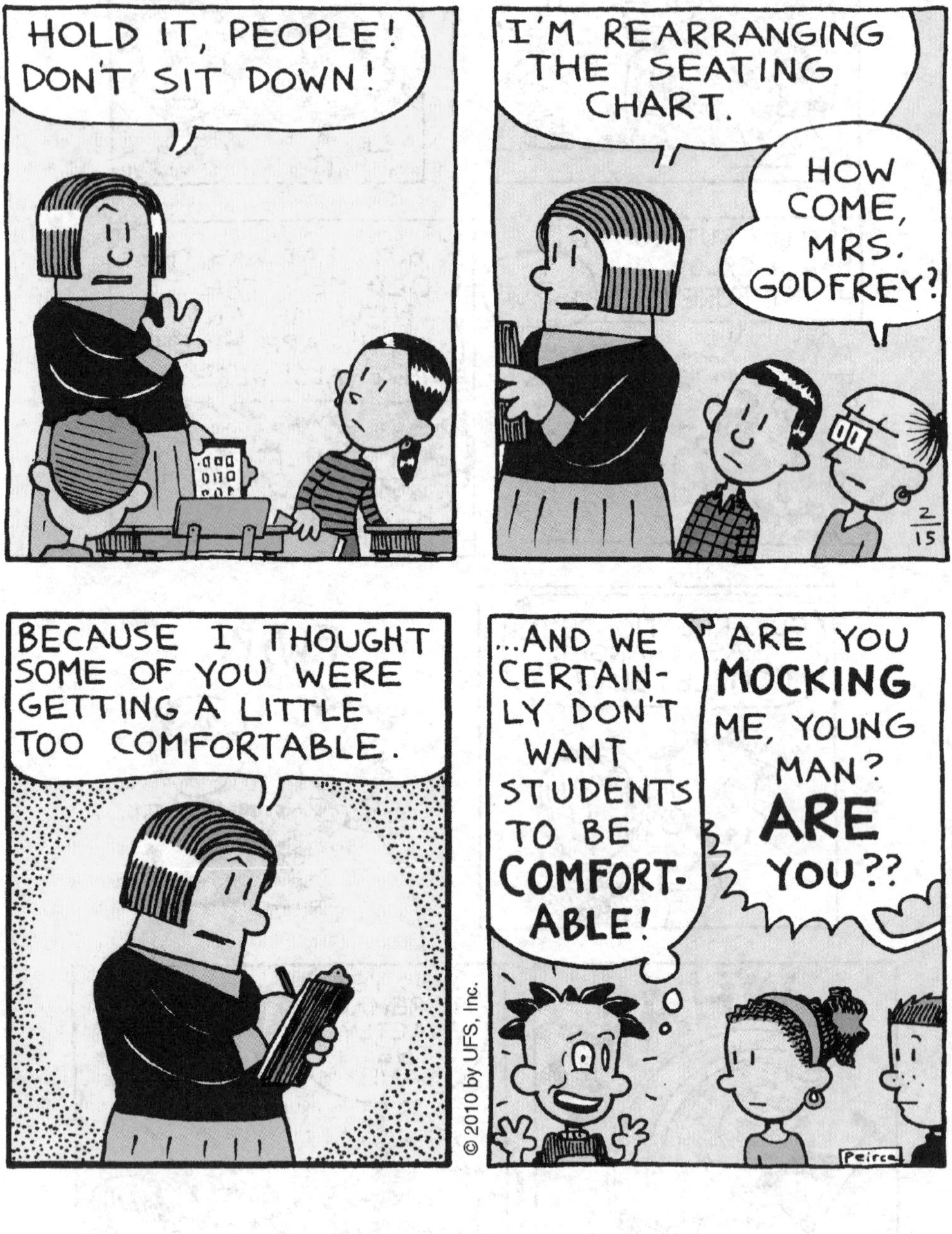
HOLD IT, PEOPLE! DON'T SIT DOWN!
I'M REARRANGING THE SEATING CHART.
HOW COME, MRS. GODFREY?
2/15
BECAUSE I THOUGHT SOME OF YOU WERE GETTING A LITTLE TOO COMFORTABLE.
...AND WE CERTAINLY DON'T WANT STUDENTS TO BE COMFORTABLE!
ARE YOU MOCKING ME, YOUNG MAN? ARE YOU??
Peirce

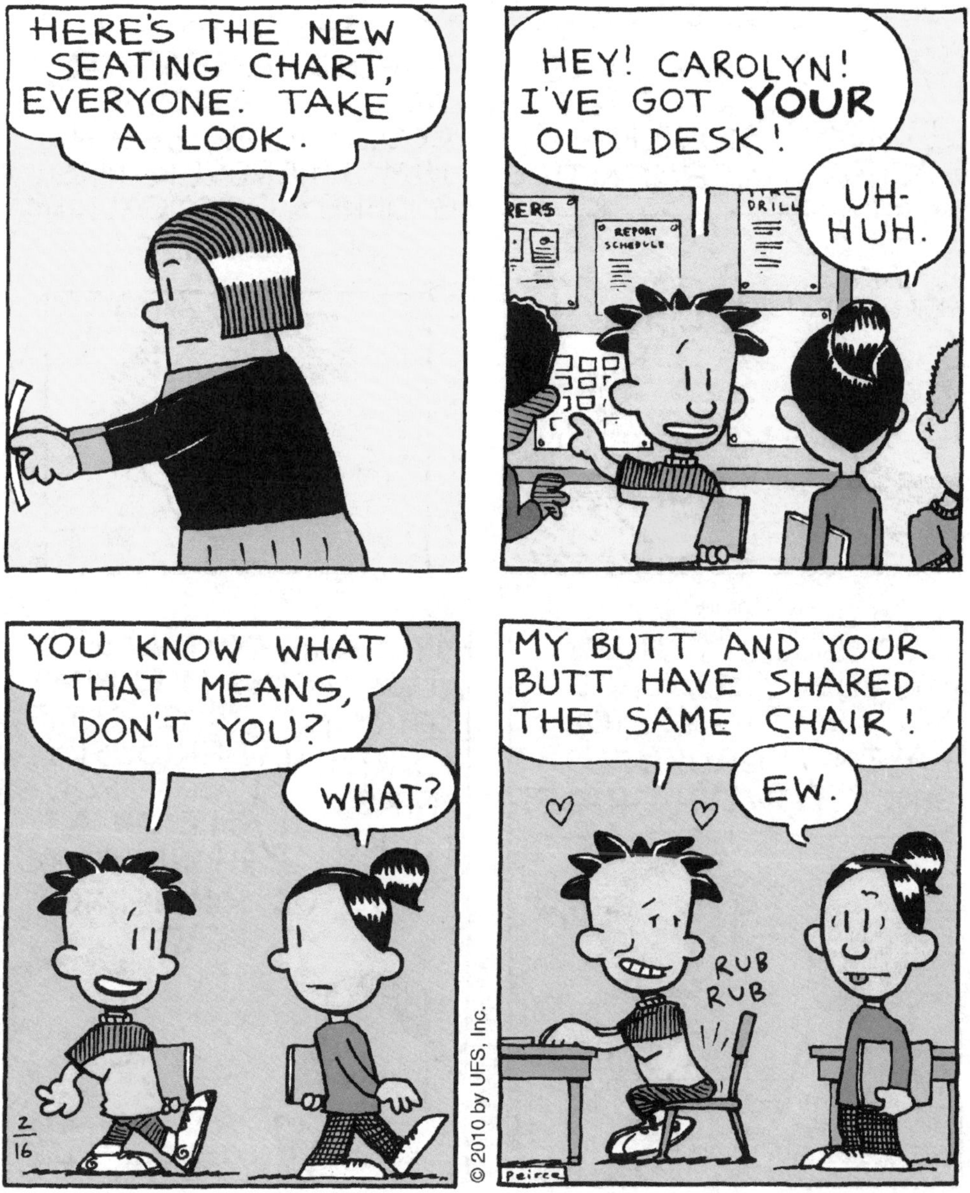
HERE'S THE NEW SEATING CHART, EVERYONE. TAKE A LOOK.
HEY! CAROLYN! I'VE GOT **YOUR** OLD DESK!
UH-HUH.
REPORT SCHEDULE
DRILL
YOU KNOW WHAT THAT MEANS, DON'T YOU?
WHAT?
MY BUTT AND YOUR BUTT HAVE SHARED THE SAME CHAIR!
EW.
RUB RUB
2/16
Peirce

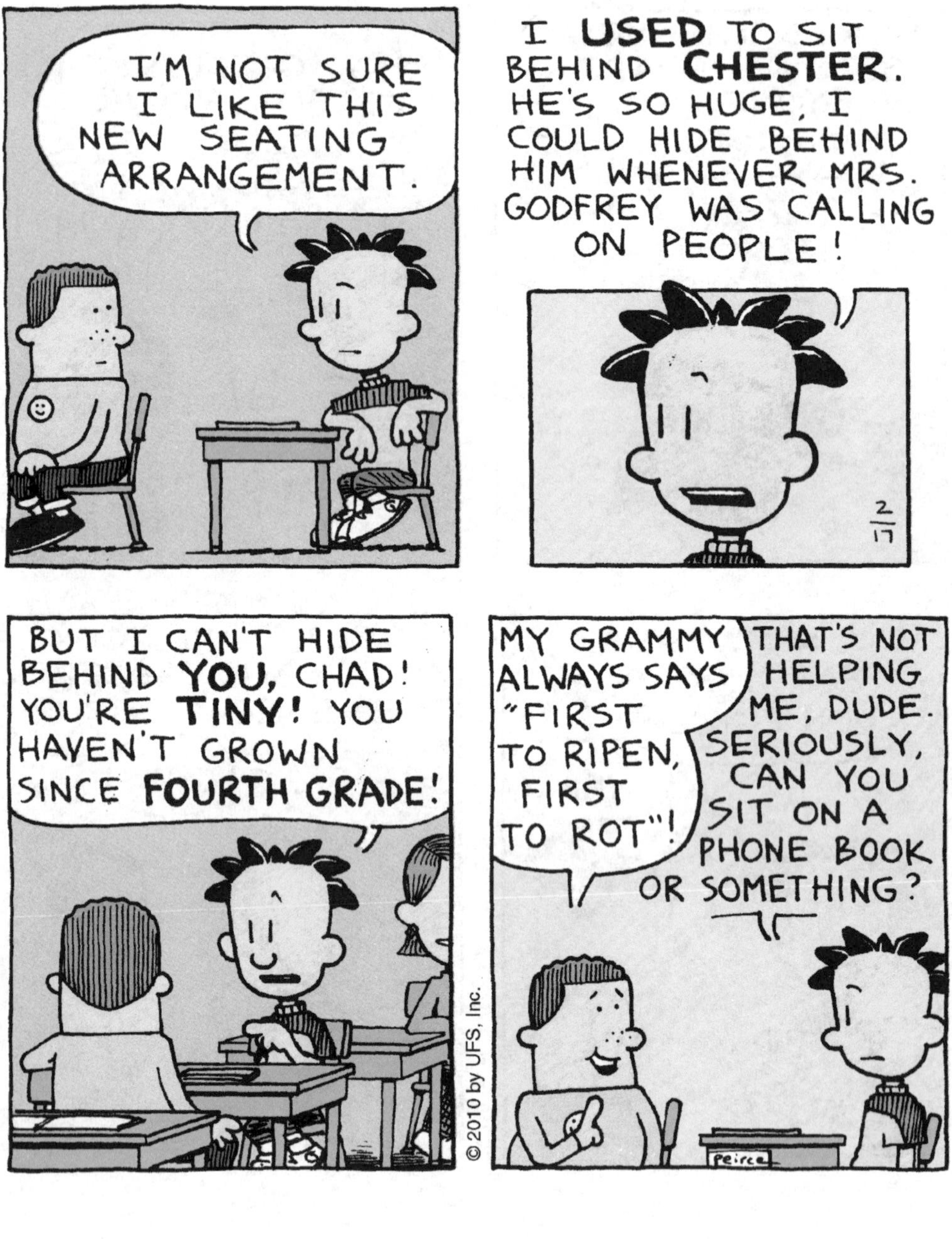
I'M NOT SURE I LIKE THIS NEW SEATING ARRANGEMENT.
I **USED** TO SIT BEHIND **CHESTER**. HE'S SO HUGE, I COULD HIDE BEHIND HIM WHENEVER MRS. GODFREY WAS CALLING ON PEOPLE!
2/17
BUT I CAN'T HIDE BEHIND **YOU,** CHAD! YOU'RE **TINY!** YOU HAVEN'T GROWN SINCE **FOURTH GRADE!**
MY GRAMMY ALWAYS SAYS "FIRST TO RIPEN, FIRST TO ROT"!
THAT'S NOT HELPING ME, DUDE. SERIOUSLY, CAN YOU SIT ON A PHONE BOOK OR SOMETHING?
Peirce

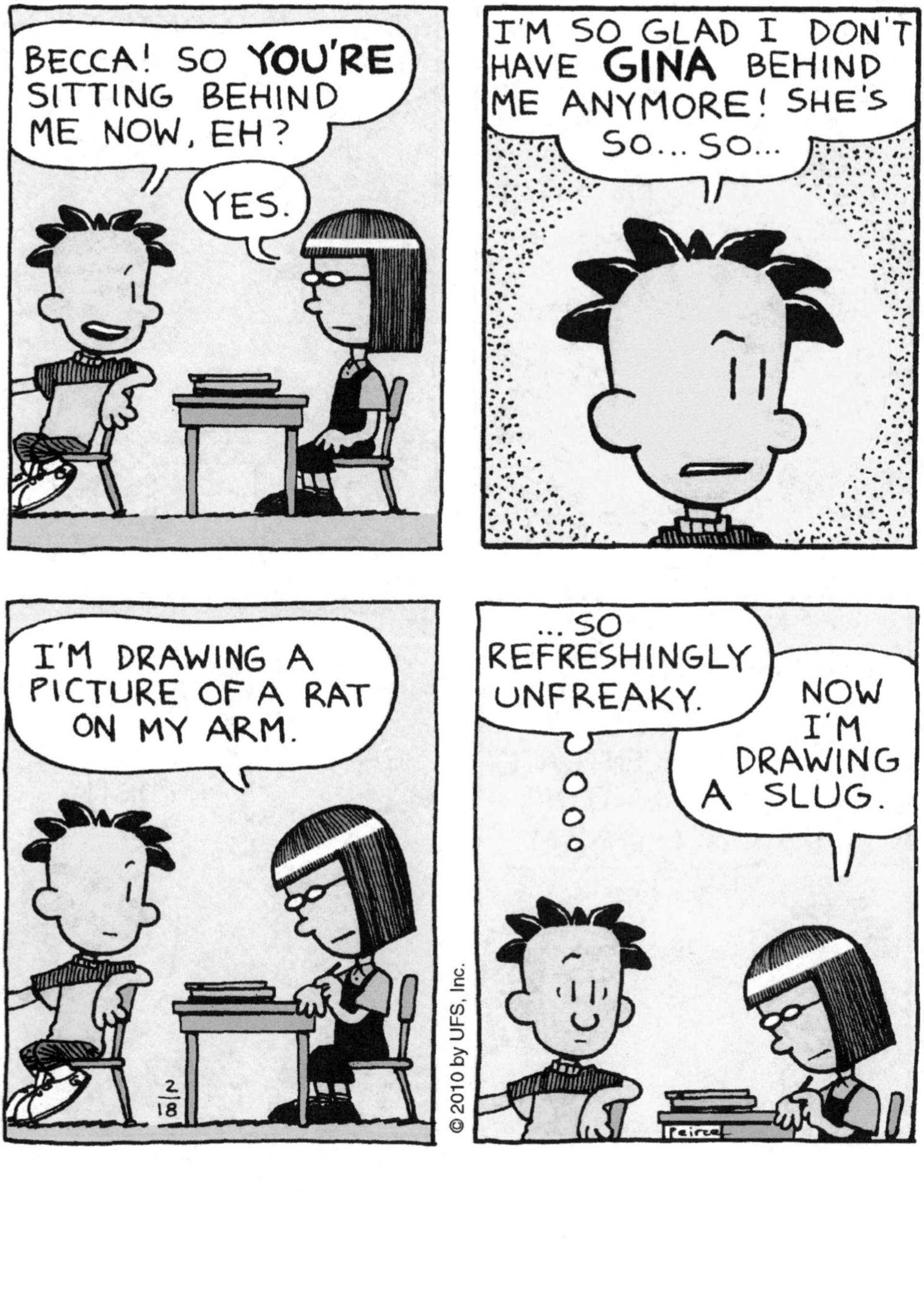
BECCA! SO **YOU'RE** SITTING BEHIND ME NOW, EH?
YES.
I'M SO GLAD I DON'T HAVE **GINA** BEHIND ME ANYMORE! SHE'S SO... SO...
I'M DRAWING A PICTURE OF A RAT ON MY ARM.
2/18
© 2010 by UFS, Inc.
...SO REFRESHINGLY UNFREAKY.
NOW I'M DRAWING A SLUG.
Peirce

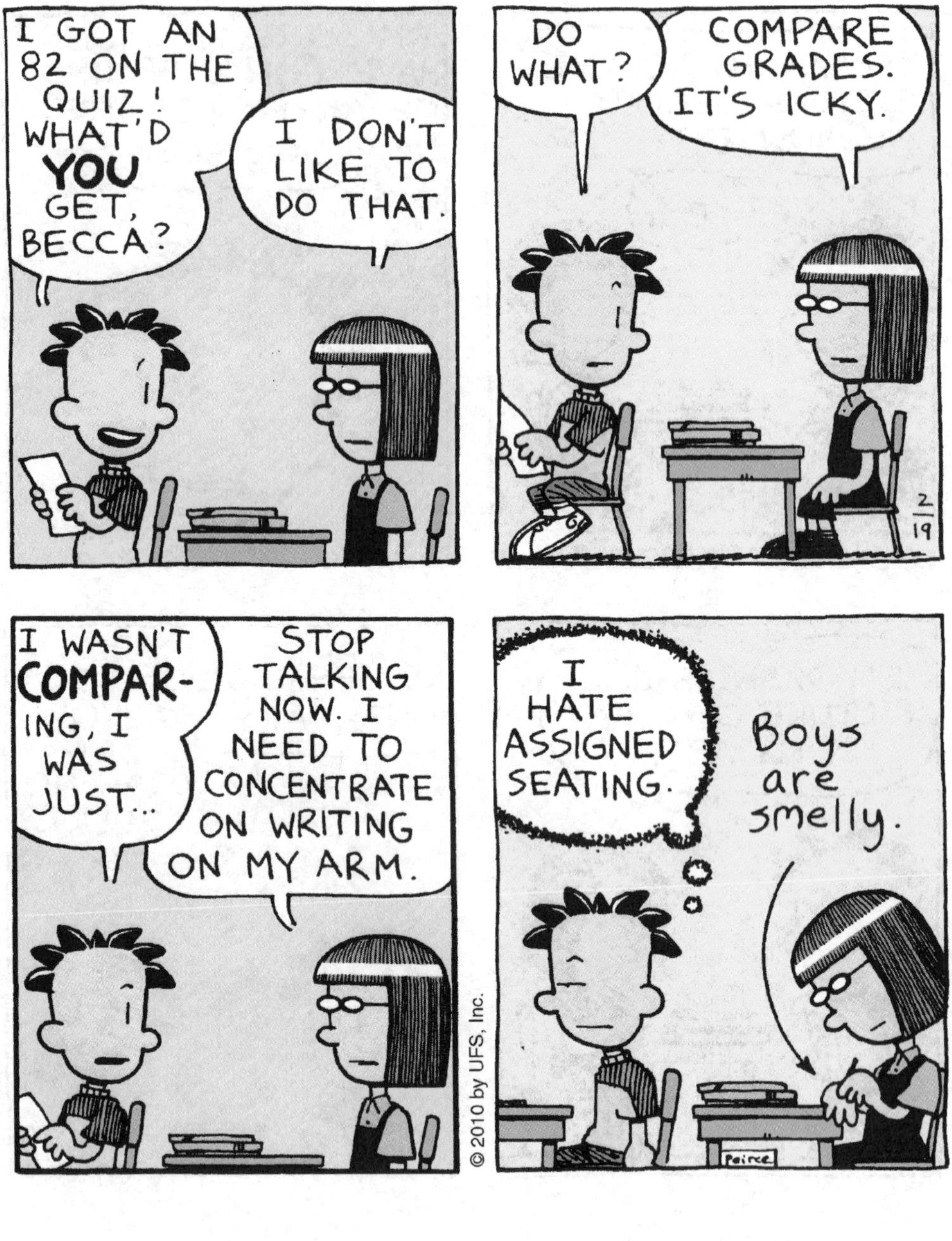
I GOT AN 82 ON THE QUIZ! WHAT'D **YOU** GET, BECCA?
I DON'T LIKE TO DO THAT.
DO WHAT?
COMPARE GRADES. IT'S ICKY.
2/19
I WASN'T **COMPAR-** ING, I WAS JUST...
STOP TALKING NOW. I NEED TO CONCENTRATE ON WRITING ON MY ARM.
© 2010 by UFS, Inc.
I HATE ASSIGNED SEATING.
Boys are smelly.
Peirce

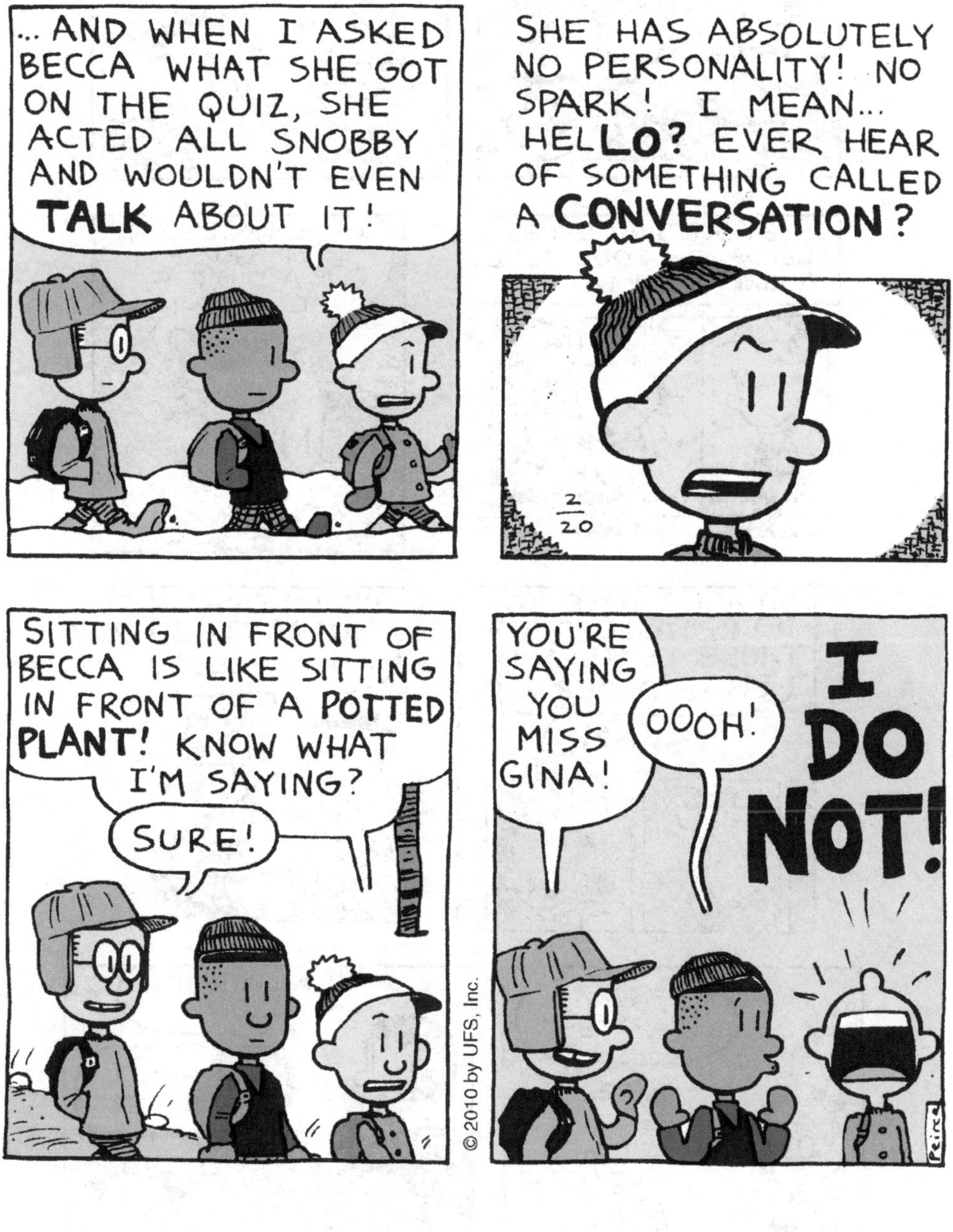

... AND WHEN I ASKED BECCA WHAT SHE GOT ON THE QUIZ, SHE ACTED ALL SNOBBY AND WOULDN'T EVEN **TALK** ABOUT IT!
SHE HAS ABSOLUTELY NO PERSONALITY! NO SPARK! I MEAN... HEL**LO?** EVER HEAR OF SOMETHING CALLED A **CONVERSATION**?
2/20
SITTING IN FRONT OF BECCA IS LIKE SITTING IN FRONT OF A **POTTED PLANT!** KNOW WHAT I'M SAYING?
SURE!
© 2010 by UFS, Inc.
YOU'RE SAYING YOU MISS GINA!
OOOH!
I DO NOT!
Peirce

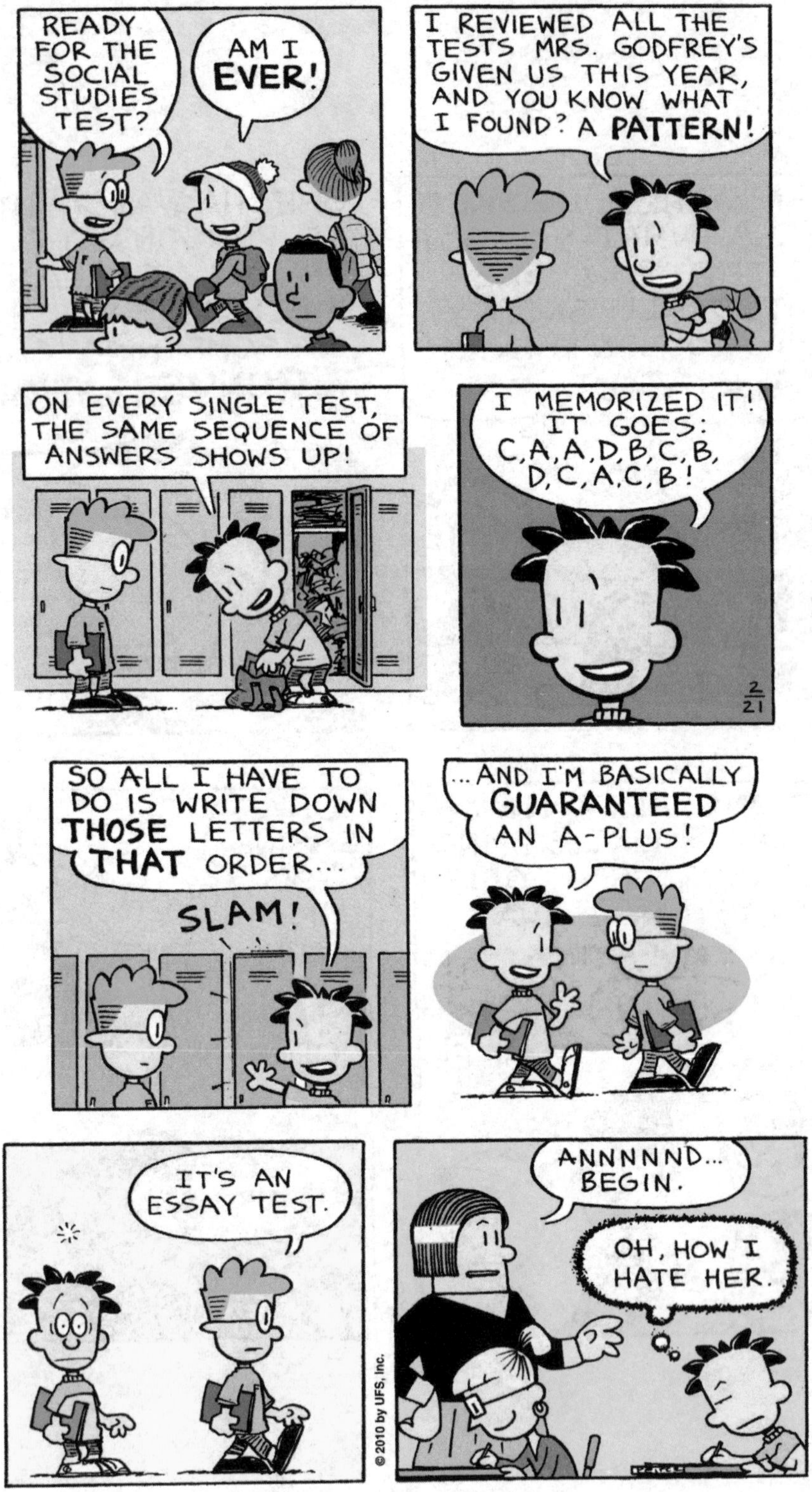
READY FOR THE SOCIAL STUDIES TEST?
AM I EVER!
I REVIEWED ALL THE TESTS MRS. GODFREY'S GIVEN US THIS YEAR, AND YOU KNOW WHAT I FOUND? A PATTERN!
ON EVERY SINGLE TEST, THE SAME SEQUENCE OF ANSWERS SHOWS UP!
I MEMORIZED IT! IT GOES: C, A, A, D, B, C, B, D, C, A, C, B!
2/21
SO ALL I HAVE TO DO IS WRITE DOWN THOSE LETTERS IN THAT ORDER...
SLAM!
...AND I'M BASICALLY GUARANTEED AN A-PLUS!
IT'S AN ESSAY TEST.
ANNNNND... BEGIN.
OH, HOW I HATE HER.

WHAT'S YOUR POINT?

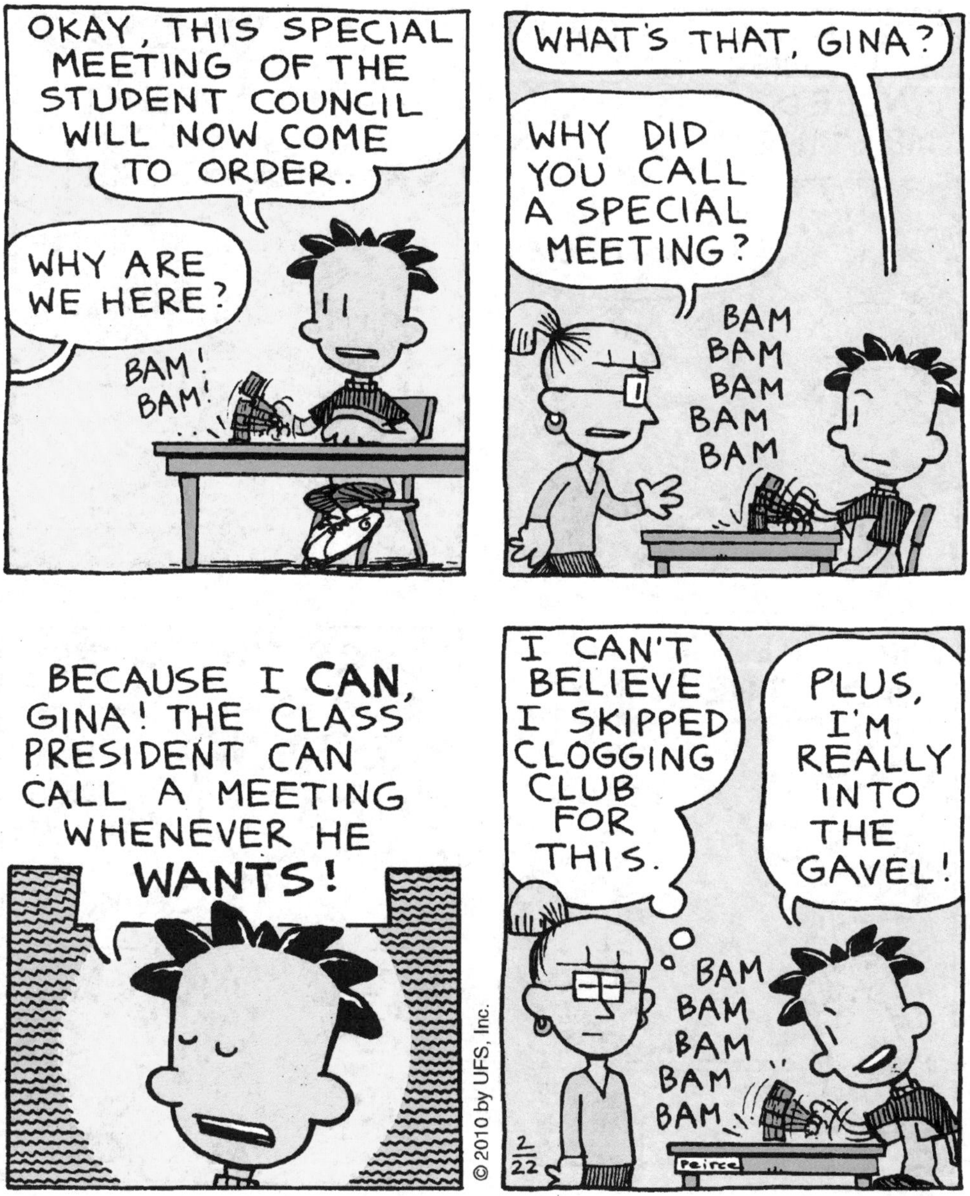

OKAY, THIS SPECIAL MEETING OF THE STUDENT COUNCIL WILL NOW COME TO ORDER.
WHY ARE WE HERE?
BAM! BAM!
WHAT'S THAT, GINA?
WHY DID YOU CALL A SPECIAL MEETING?
BAM BAM BAM BAM BAM
BECAUSE I **CAN**, GINA! THE CLASS PRESIDENT CAN CALL A MEETING WHENEVER HE **WANTS**!
I CAN'T BELIEVE I SKIPPED CLOGGING CLUB FOR THIS.
PLUS, I'M REALLY INTO THE GAVEL!
BAM BAM BAM BAM BAM
Peirce
2/22

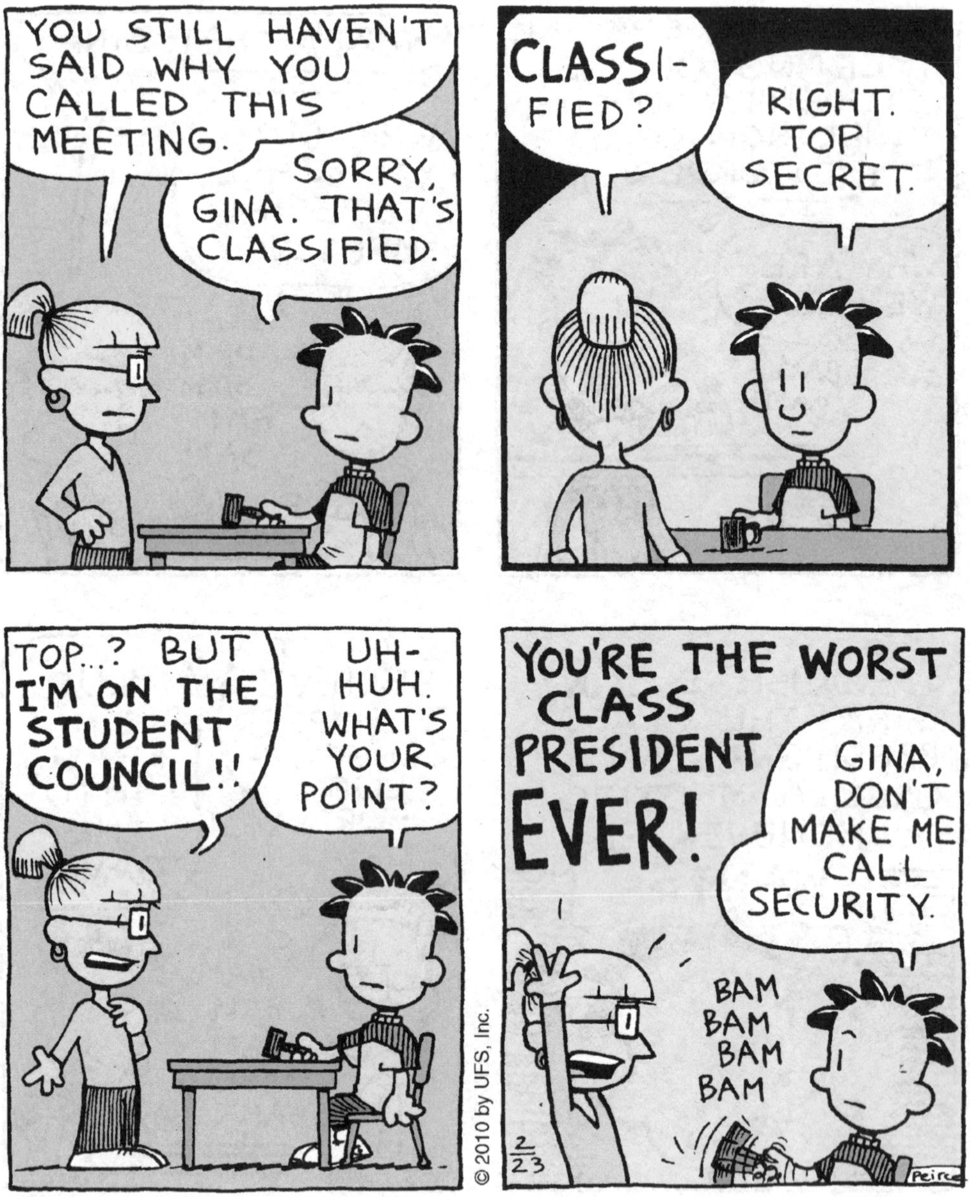
YOU STILL HAVEN'T SAID WHY YOU CALLED THIS MEETING.
SORRY, GINA. THAT'S CLASSIFIED.
CLASSI-FIED?
RIGHT. TOP SECRET.
TOP...? BUT I'M ON THE STUDENT COUNCIL!!
UH-HUH. WHAT'S YOUR POINT?
YOU'RE THE WORST CLASS PRESIDENT EVER!
GINA, DON'T MAKE ME CALL SECURITY.
BAM BAM BAM BAM
2/23
Peirce
© 2010 by UFS, Inc.

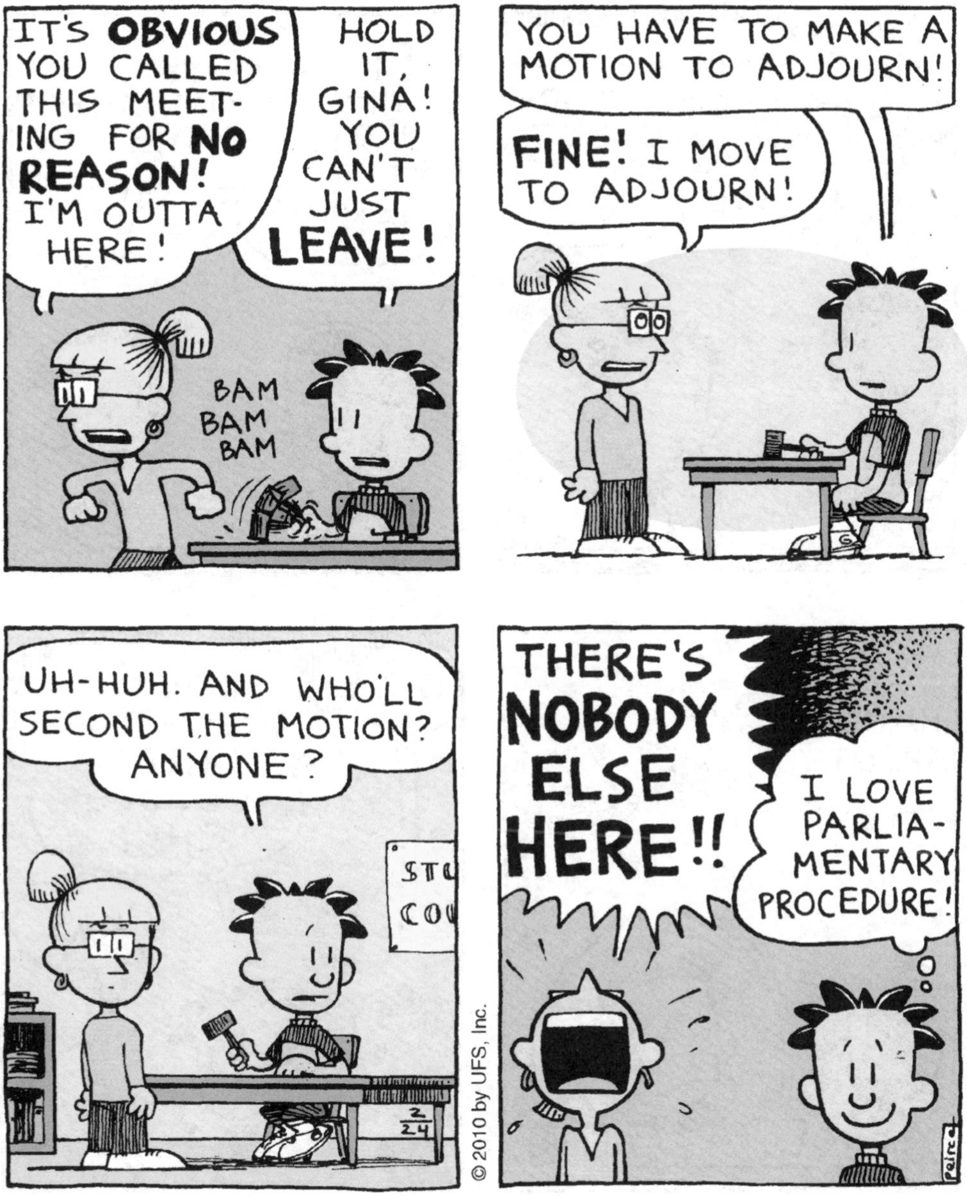
IT'S **OBVIOUS** YOU CALLED THIS MEETING FOR **NO REASON**! I'M OUTTA HERE!
HOLD IT, GINA! YOU CAN'T JUST **LEAVE**!
BAM BAM BAM
YOU HAVE TO MAKE A MOTION TO ADJOURN!
FINE! I MOVE TO ADJOURN!
UH-HUH. AND WHO'LL SECOND THE MOTION? ANYONE?
STU
COU
2
24
THERE'S **NOBODY ELSE HERE**!!
I LOVE PARLIAMENTARY PROCEDURE!
peirce

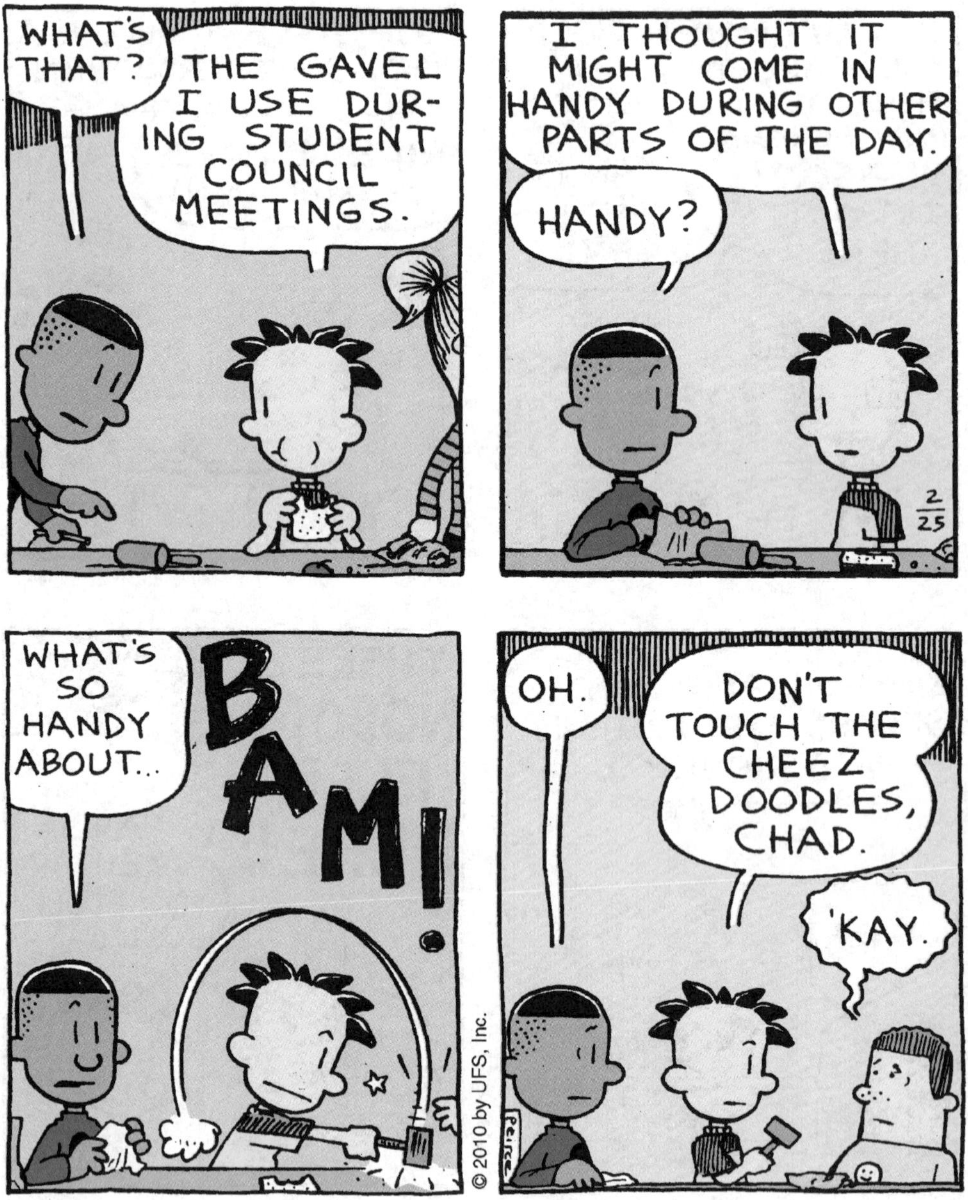
WHAT'S THAT?
THE GAVEL I USE DUR-ING STUDENT COUNCIL MEETINGS.
I THOUGHT IT MIGHT COME IN HANDY DURING OTHER PARTS OF THE DAY.
HANDY?
2/25
WHAT'S SO HANDY ABOUT...
BAM!
© 2010 by UFS, Inc.
OH.
DON'T TOUCH THE CHEEZ DOODLES, CHAD.
'KAY.
PEIRCE

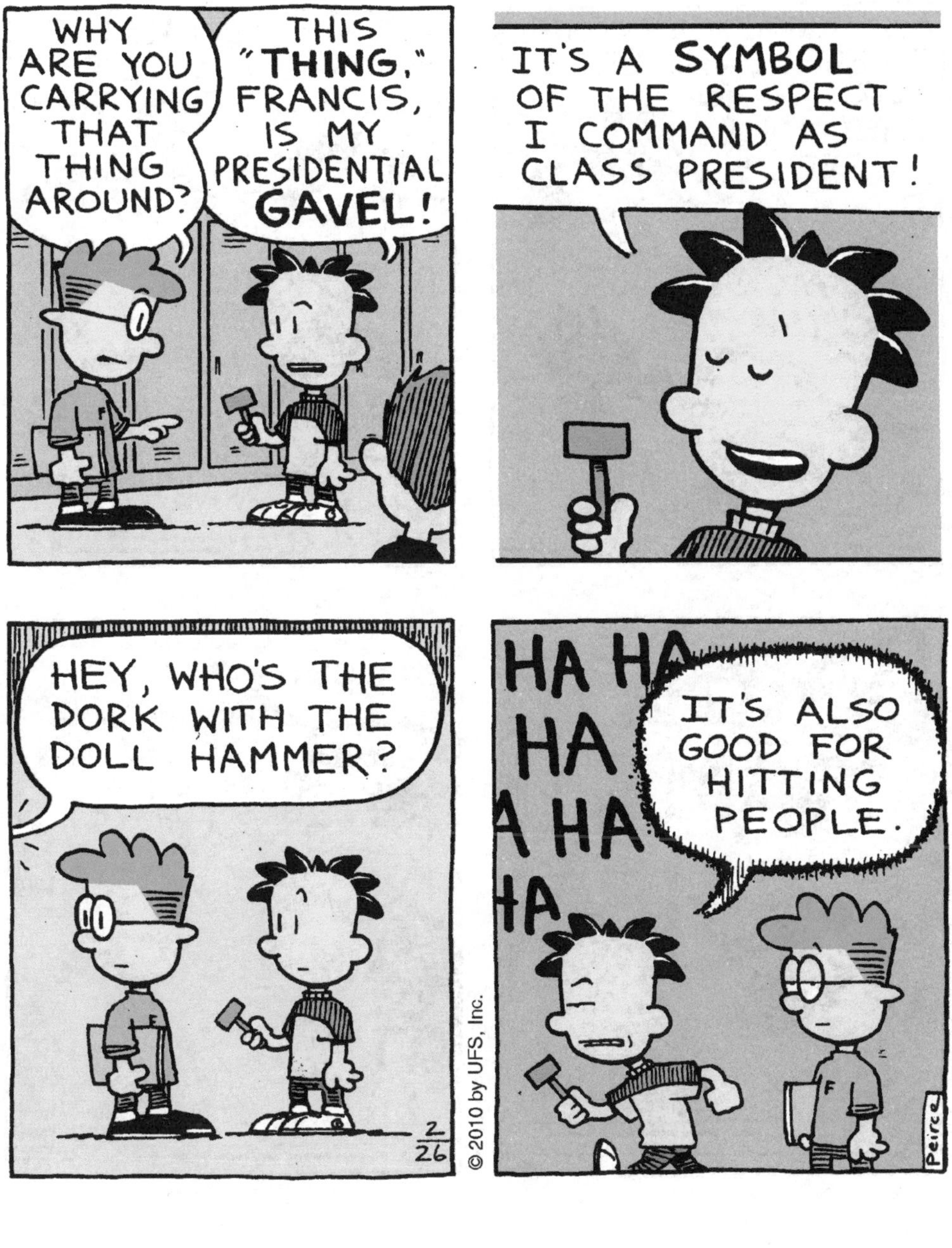
WHY ARE YOU CARRYING THAT THING AROUND?
THIS "THING," FRANCIS, IS MY PRESIDENTIAL GAVEL!
IT'S A SYMBOL OF THE RESPECT I COMMAND AS CLASS PRESIDENT!
HEY, WHO'S THE DORK WITH THE DOLL HAMMER?
2/26
© 2010 by UFS, Inc.
HA HA HA HA HA HA
IT'S ALSO GOOD FOR HITTING PEOPLE.
Peirce

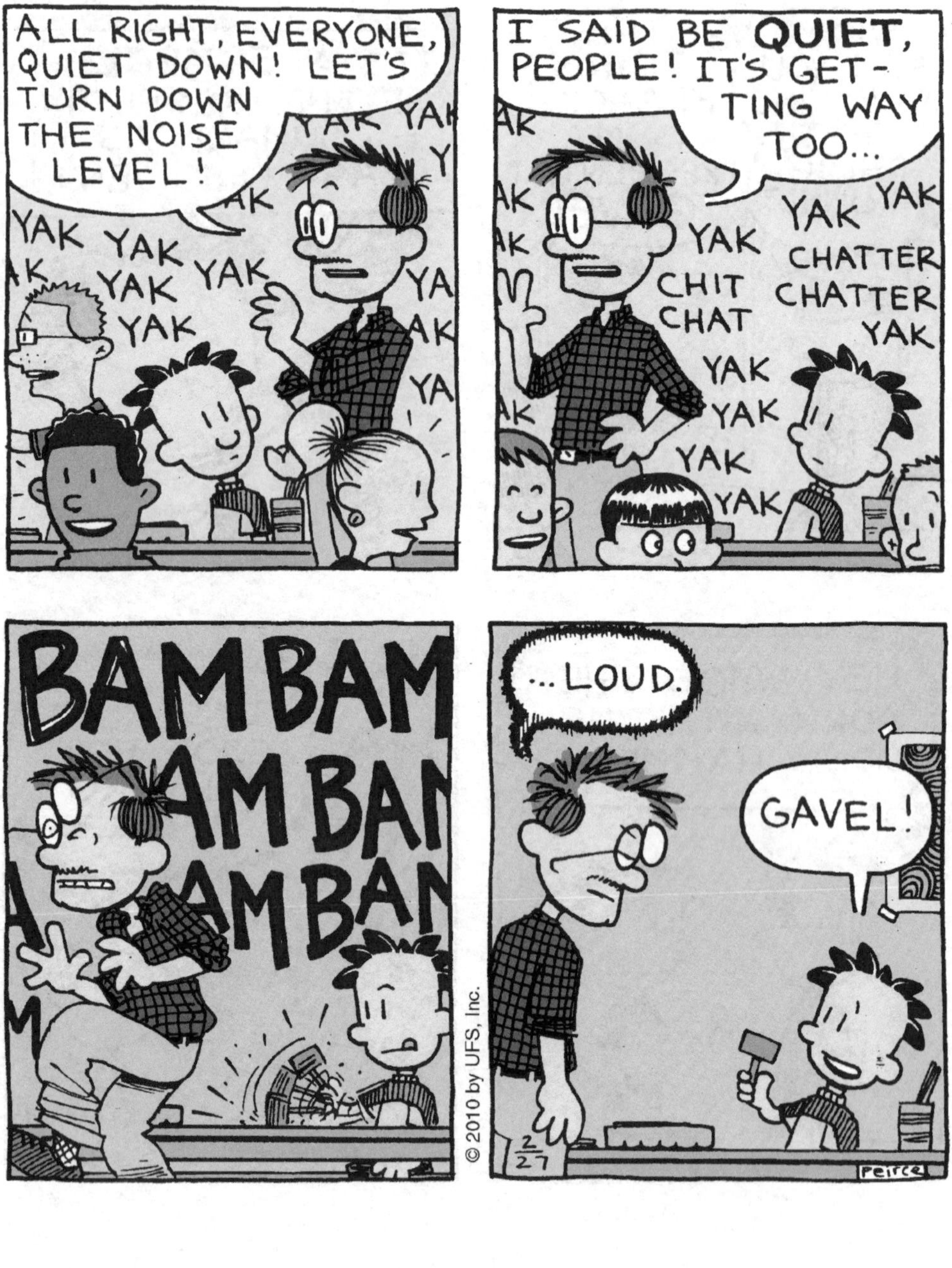
ALL RIGHT, EVERYONE, QUIET DOWN! LET'S TURN DOWN THE NOISE LEVEL!
YAK YAK YAK YAK YAK YAK YAK
I SAID BE **QUIET**, PEOPLE! IT'S GETTING WAY TOO...
YAK YAK YAK CHATTER CHATTER YAK CHIT CHAT YAK YAK YAK YAK
BAM BAM AM BAM AM BAM
...LOUD.
GAVEL!
2/27
PEIRCE
© 2010 by UFS, Inc.

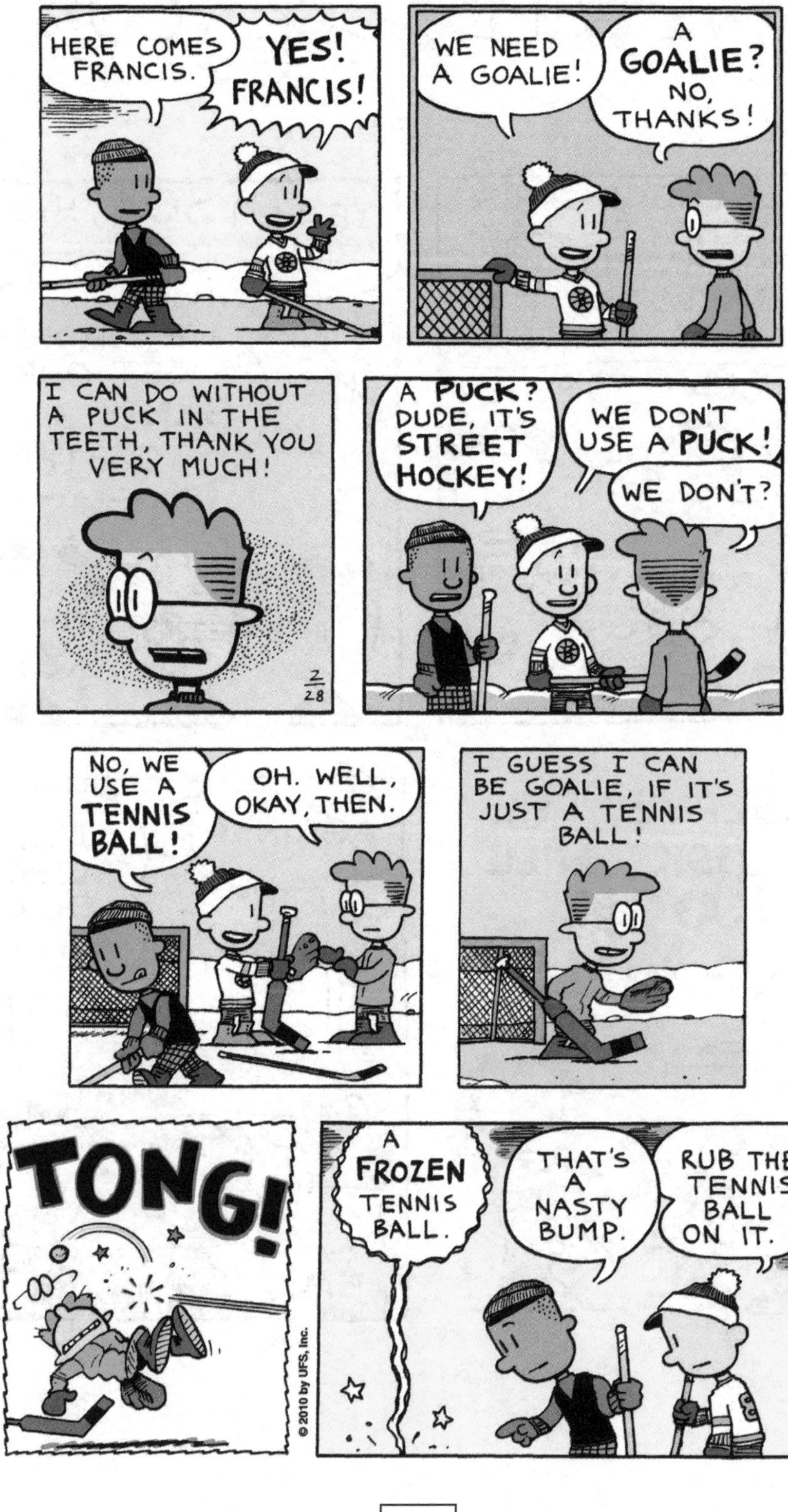
HERE COMES FRANCIS.
YES! FRANCIS!
WE NEED A GOALIE!
A GOALIE? NO, THANKS!
I CAN DO WITHOUT A PUCK IN THE TEETH, THANK YOU VERY MUCH!
A PUCK? DUDE, IT'S STREET HOCKEY!
WE DON'T USE A PUCK!
WE DON'T?
NO, WE USE A TENNIS BALL!
OH. WELL, OKAY, THEN.
I GUESS I CAN BE GOALIE, IF IT'S JUST A TENNIS BALL!
TONG!
A FROZEN TENNIS BALL.
THAT'S A NASTY BUMP.
RUB THE TENNIS BALL ON IT.

WE WILL ROCK YOU

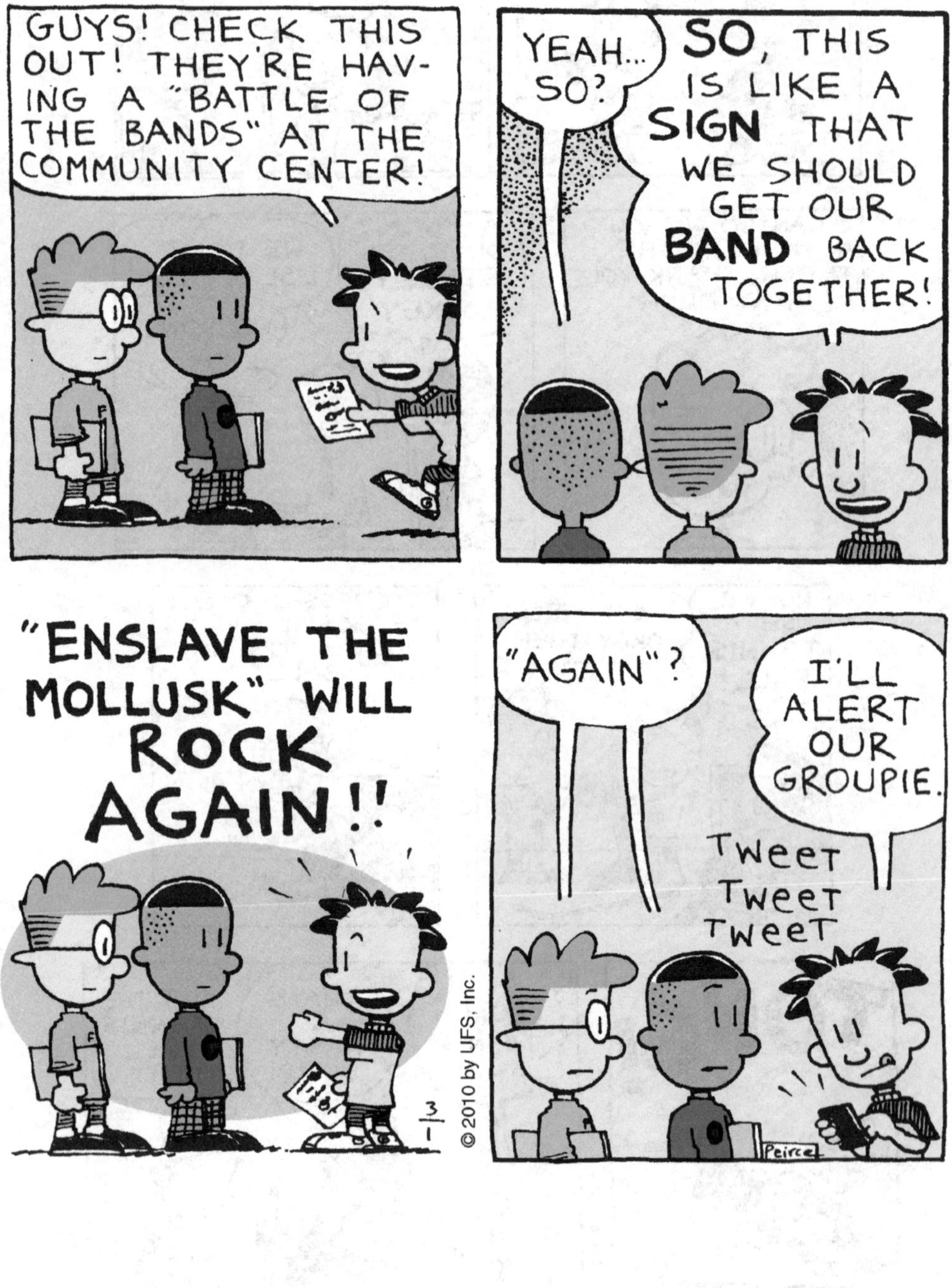

GUYS! CHECK THIS OUT! THEY'RE HAVING A "BATTLE OF THE BANDS" AT THE COMMUNITY CENTER!
YEAH... SO?
SO, THIS IS LIKE A SIGN THAT WE SHOULD GET OUR BAND BACK TOGETHER!
"ENSLAVE THE MOLLUSK" WILL ROCK AGAIN!!
"AGAIN"?
I'LL ALERT OUR GROUPIE.
TWEET TWEET TWEET

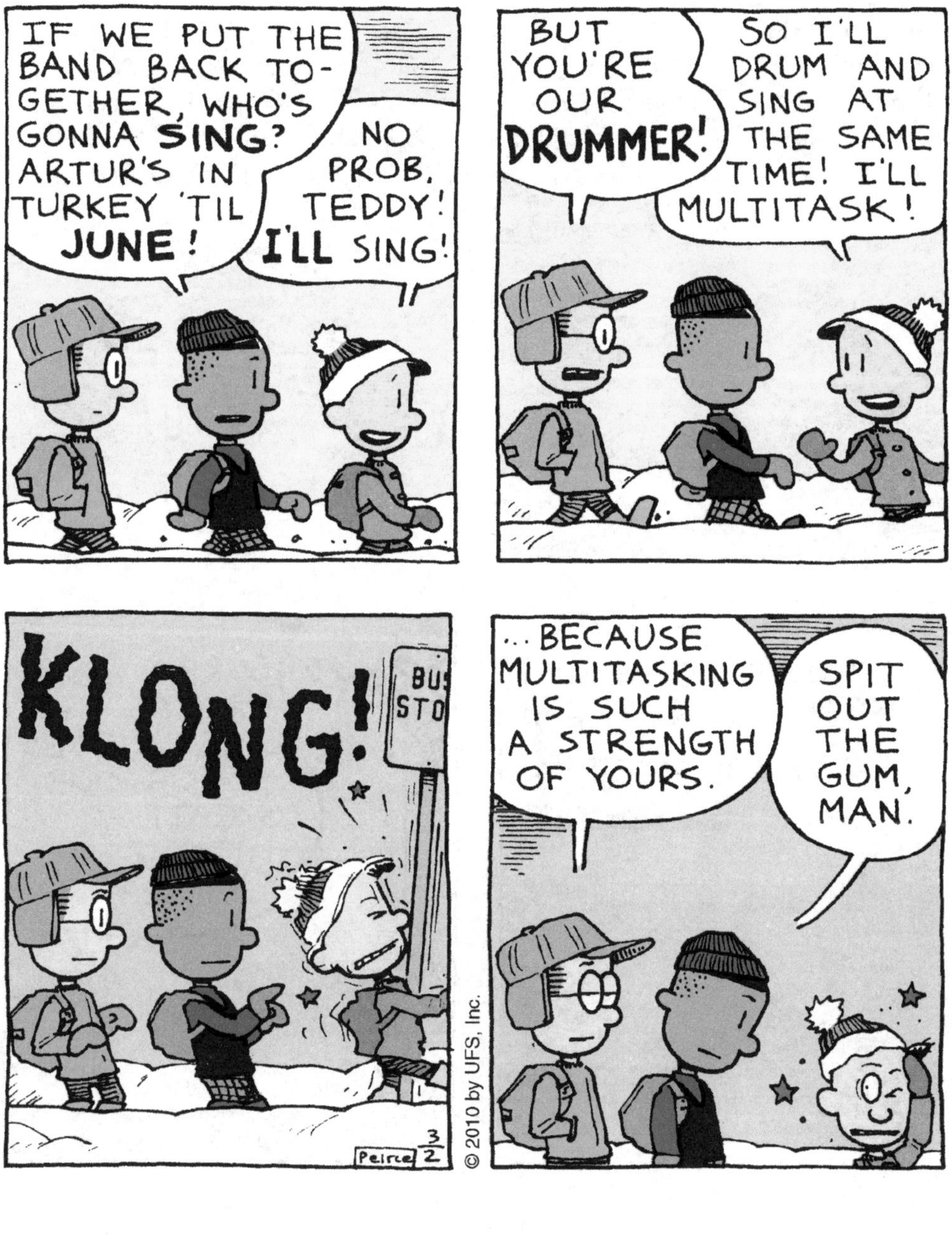
IF WE PUT THE BAND BACK TOGETHER, WHO'S GONNA SING? ARTUR'S IN TURKEY 'TIL JUNE!
NO PROB, TEDDY! I'LL SING!
BUT YOU'RE OUR DRUMMER!
SO I'LL DRUM AND SING AT THE SAME TIME! I'LL MULTITASK!
KLONG!
BUS STO
...BECAUSE MULTITASKING IS SUCH A STRENGTH OF YOURS.
SPIT OUT THE GUM, MAN.
Peirce 3/2
© 2010 by UFS, Inc.

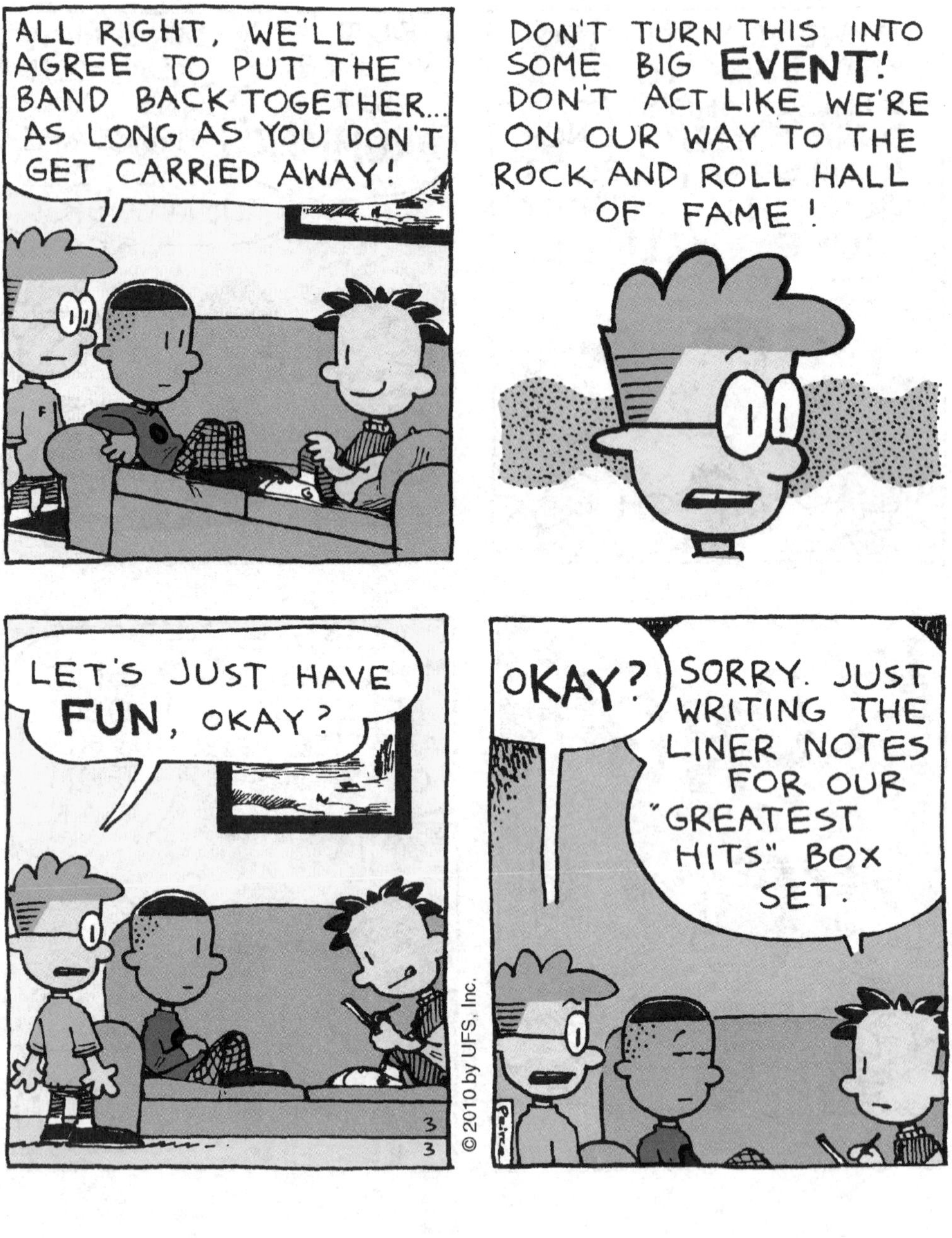
ALL RIGHT, WE'LL AGREE TO PUT THE BAND BACK TOGETHER... AS LONG AS YOU DON'T GET CARRIED AWAY!
DON'T TURN THIS INTO SOME BIG EVENT! DON'T ACT LIKE WE'RE ON OUR WAY TO THE ROCK AND ROLL HALL OF FAME!
LET'S JUST HAVE FUN, OKAY?
OKAY?
SORRY. JUST WRITING THE LINER NOTES FOR OUR "GREATEST HITS" BOX SET.

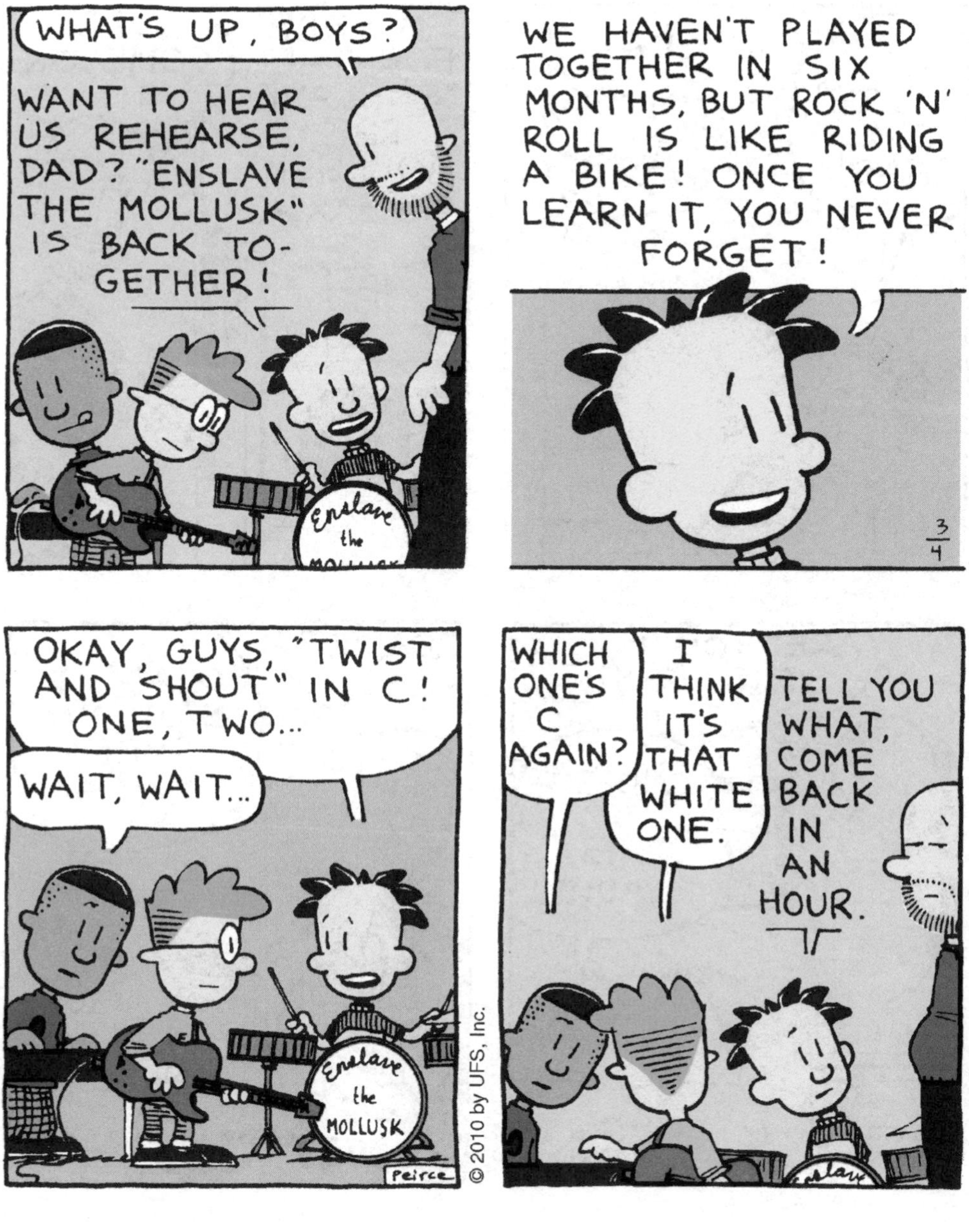
WHAT'S UP, BOYS?
WANT TO HEAR US REHEARSE, DAD? "ENSLAVE THE MOLLUSK" IS BACK TOGETHER!
Enslave the
WE HAVEN'T PLAYED TOGETHER IN SIX MONTHS, BUT ROCK 'N' ROLL IS LIKE RIDING A BIKE! ONCE YOU LEARN IT, YOU NEVER FORGET!
3
4
OKAY, GUYS, "TWIST AND SHOUT" IN C! ONE, TWO...
WAIT, WAIT...
Enslave the MOLLUSK
Peirce
© 2010 by UFS, Inc.
WHICH ONE'S C AGAIN?
I THINK IT'S THAT WHITE ONE.
TELL YOU WHAT, COME BACK IN AN HOUR.

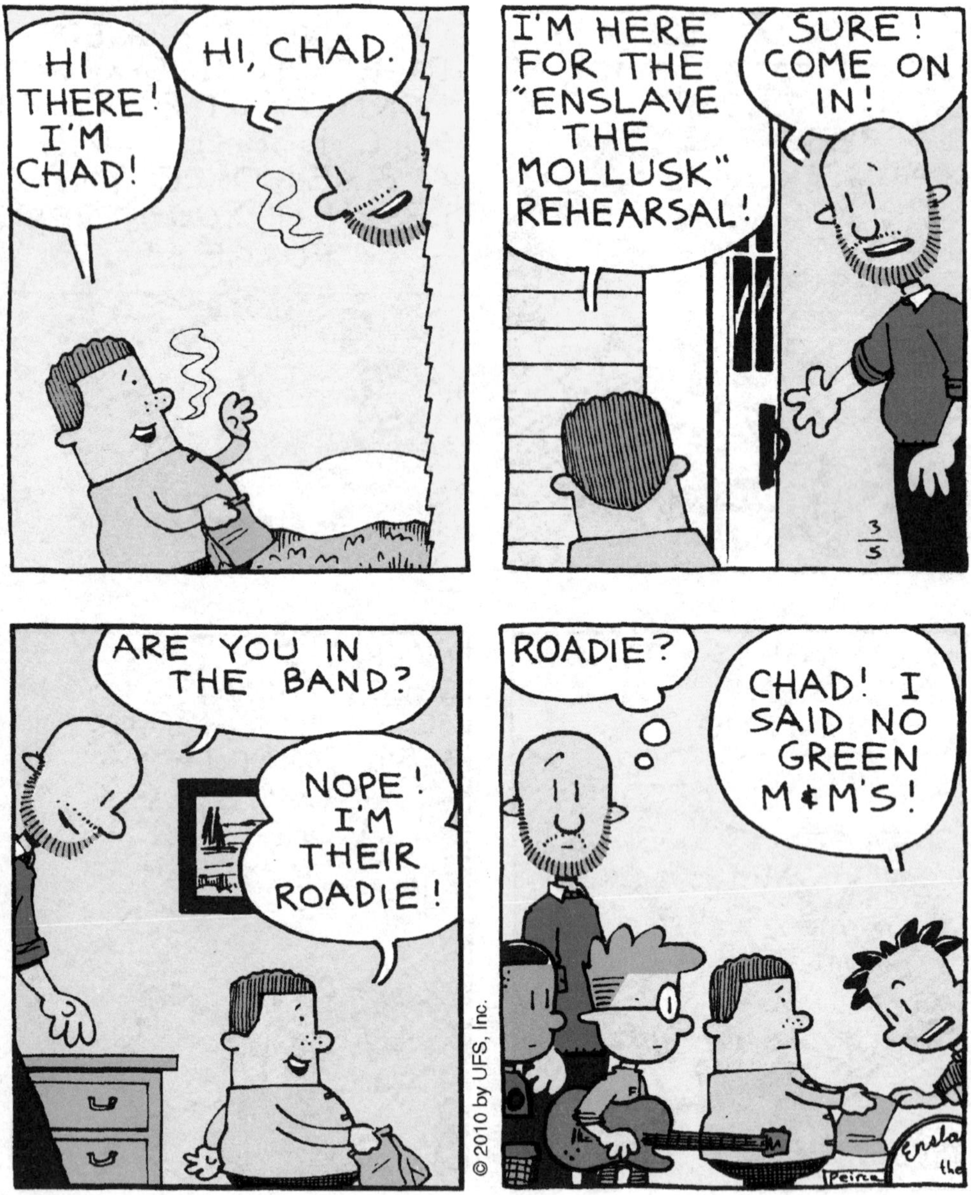
HI THERE! I'M CHAD!
HI, CHAD.
I'M HERE FOR THE "ENSLAVE THE MOLLUSK" REHEARSAL!
SURE! COME ON IN!
ARE YOU IN THE BAND?
NOPE! I'M THEIR ROADIE!
ROADIE?
CHAD! I SAID NO GREEN M&M'S!

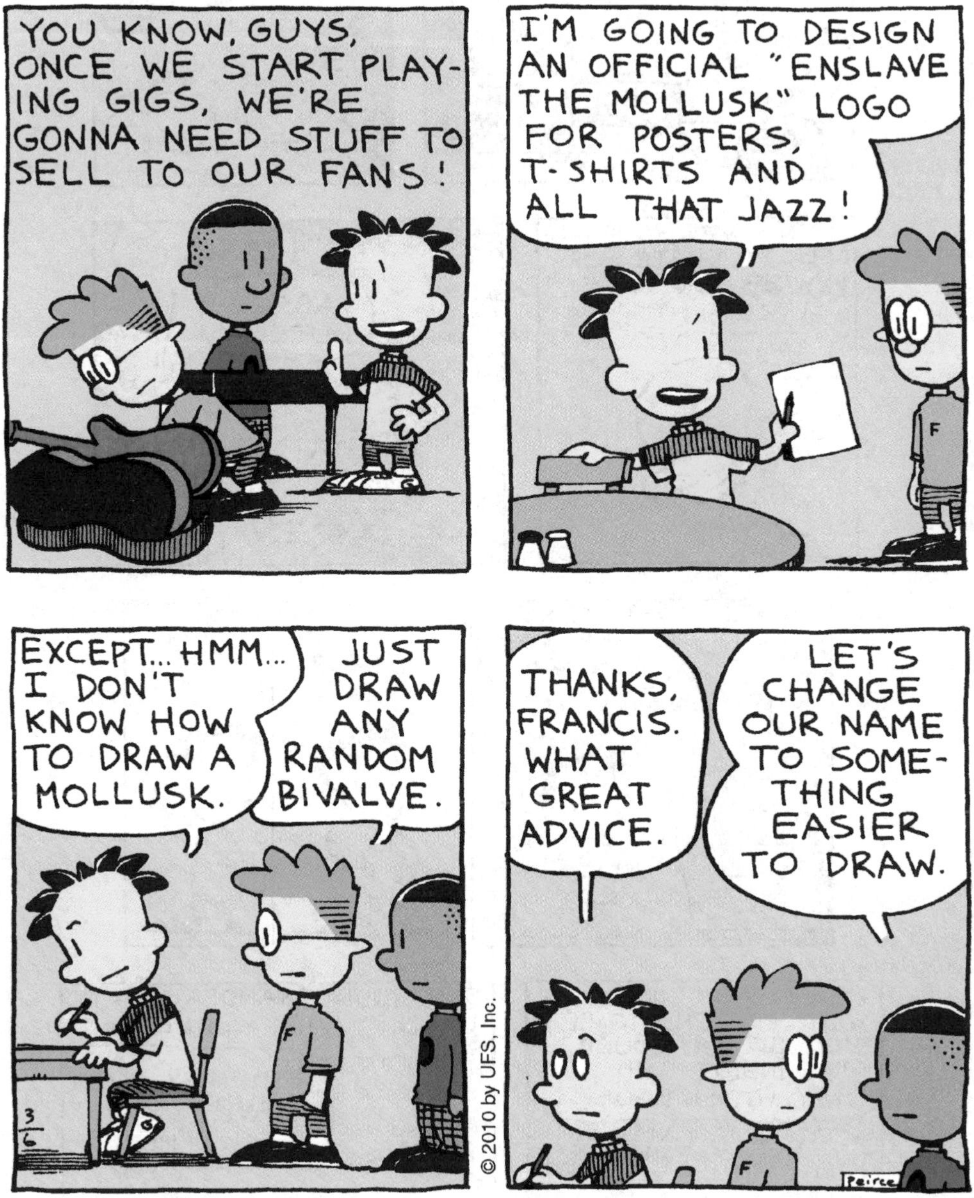
YOU KNOW, GUYS, ONCE WE START PLAY-ING GIGS, WE'RE GONNA NEED STUFF TO SELL TO OUR FANS!
I'M GOING TO DESIGN AN OFFICIAL "ENSLAVE THE MOLLUSK" LOGO FOR POSTERS, T-SHIRTS AND ALL THAT JAZZ!
EXCEPT... HMM... I DON'T KNOW HOW TO DRAW A MOLLUSK.
JUST DRAW ANY RANDOM BIVALVE.
THANKS, FRANCIS. WHAT GREAT ADVICE.
LET'S CHANGE OUR NAME TO SOME-THING EASIER TO DRAW.
3/6
Peirce

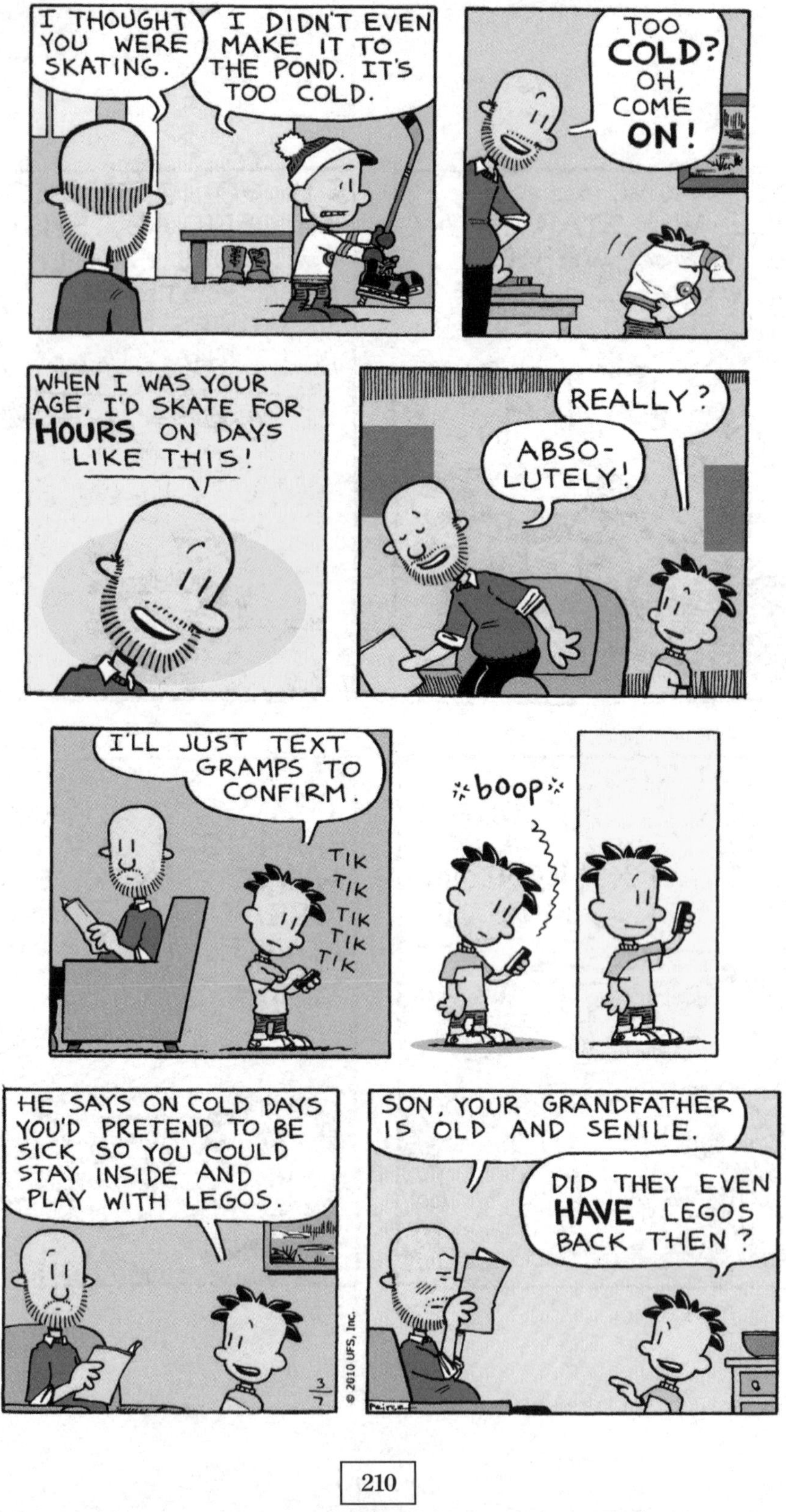
I THOUGHT YOU WERE SKATING.
I DIDN'T EVEN MAKE IT TO THE POND. IT'S TOO COLD.
TOO COLD? OH, COME ON!
WHEN I WAS YOUR AGE, I'D SKATE FOR HOURS ON DAYS LIKE THIS!
REALLY?
ABSOLUTELY!
I'LL JUST TEXT GRAMPS TO CONFIRM.
TIK TIK TIK TIK TIK
boop
HE SAYS ON COLD DAYS YOU'D PRETEND TO BE SICK SO YOU COULD STAY INSIDE AND PLAY WITH LEGOS.
3/7
© 2010 UFS, Inc.
SON, YOUR GRANDFATHER IS OLD AND SENILE.
DID THEY EVEN HAVE LEGOS BACK THEN?

STUCK ON NATE

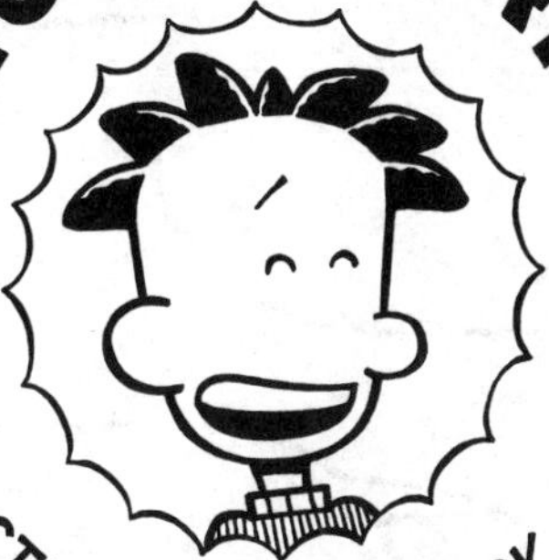

BONUS ACTIVITIES TO CRACK YOU UP!

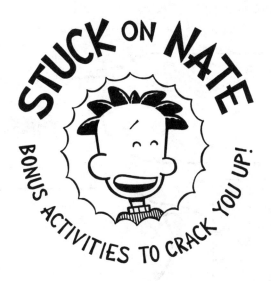

CAPTION ACTION

Ready, set, write! Come up with cool captions for Nate's sketches.

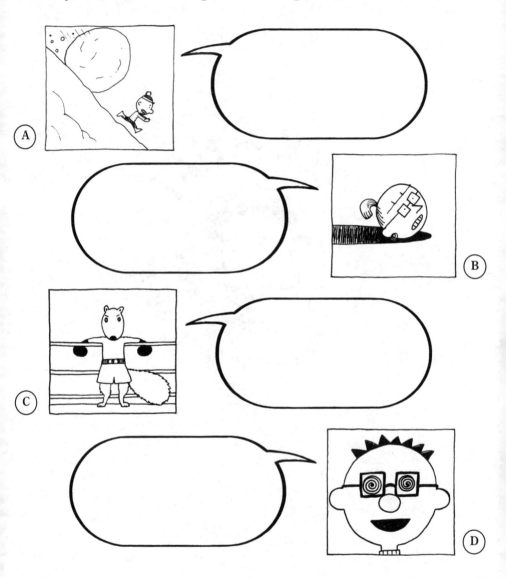

EXTRA CREDIT! Match each sketch to the original comic.

Comic A goes on page _____.

Comic B goes on page _____.

Comic C goes on page _____.

Comic D goes on page _____.

FAST FORWARD

What's going to happen next? It's up to you!

A

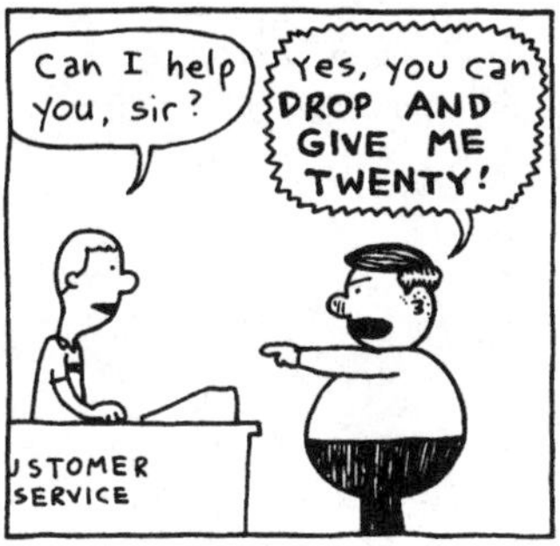
Can I help you, sir?
Yes, you can DROP AND GIVE ME TWENTY!
USTOMER SERVICE

B

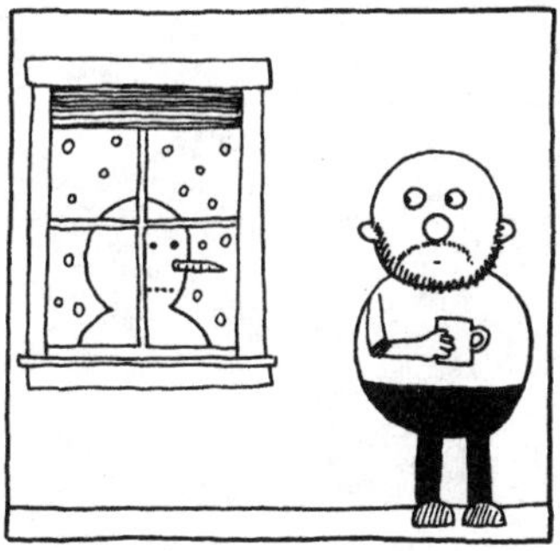

C

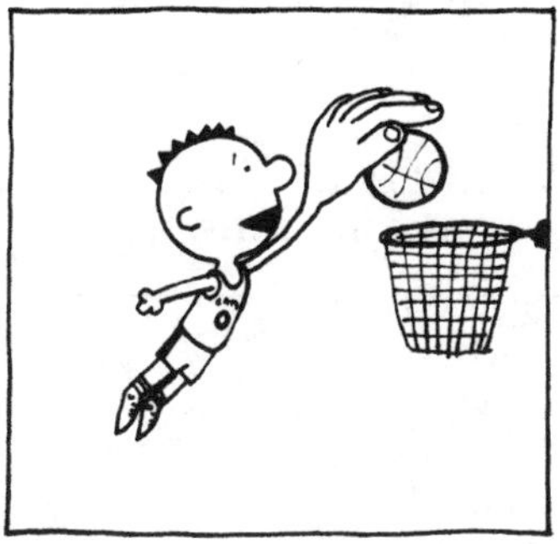

Bonus: Can you match each sketch to its Sunday strip?

Comic A goes on page ____________.

Comic B goes on page ____________.

Comic C goes on page ____________.

Answers: A: 62; B: 210; C: 98

ALL ABOUT YOU!

Nate loves sports, Spitsy (most of the time), and Jenny.

How about you?

NATE

YOU

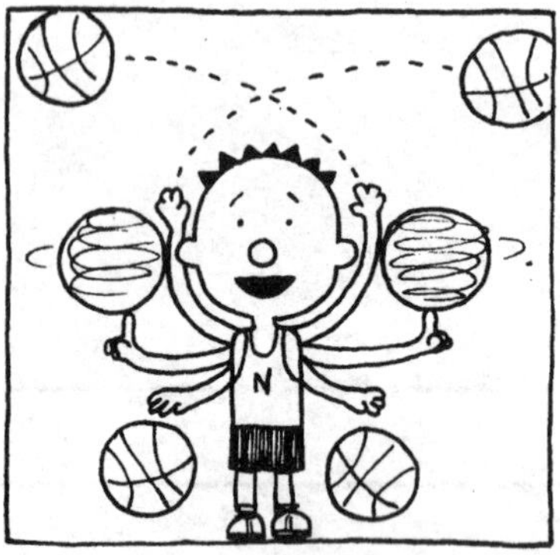
N

Favorite sport

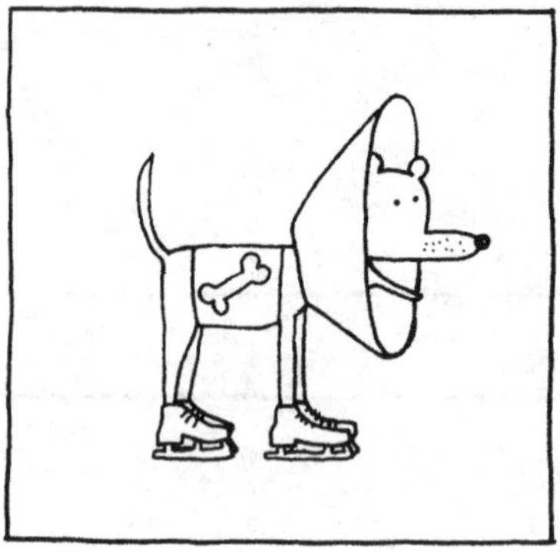

Favorite animal

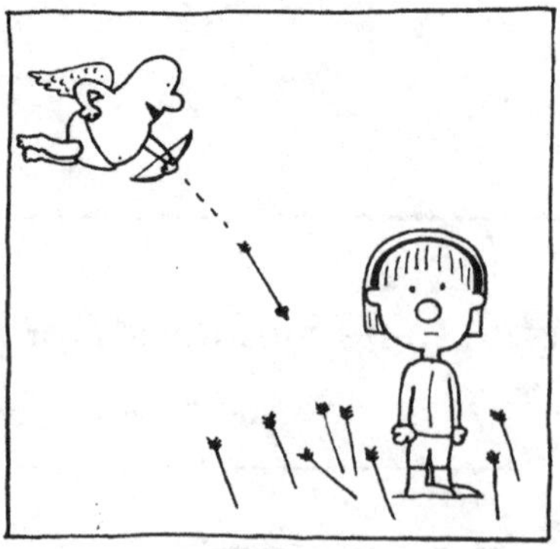

Favorite friend (or crush!)

BRAIN BOWL

Nate's brain is
filled with trivia!

Now write down all the things running through *your* brain.

LIVIN' LARGE!

P.S. 38 is pretty small. Everyone knows everyone else. So whenever a new kid shows up, it's a major event. Especially when he's got a name like **THIS**:

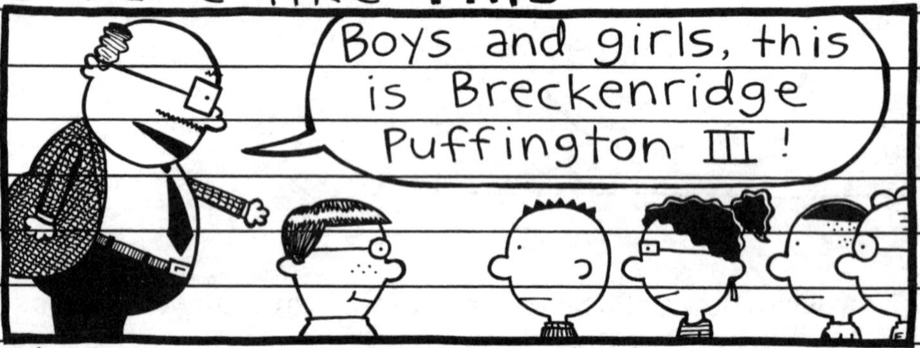

Boys and girls, this is Breckenridge Puffington III!

Anyway, Principal Nichols asked me to be the kid's "buddy," so it's my job to help him make friends...

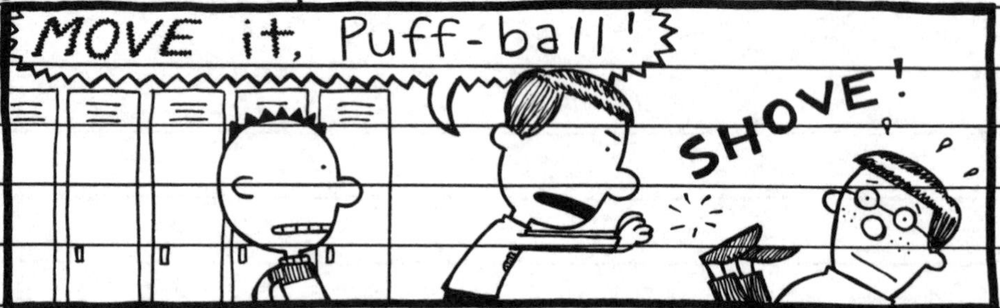

MOVE it, Puff-ball!
SHOVE!

... and to show him around the school, which is falling apart. That's what happens when a building is one hundred years old.

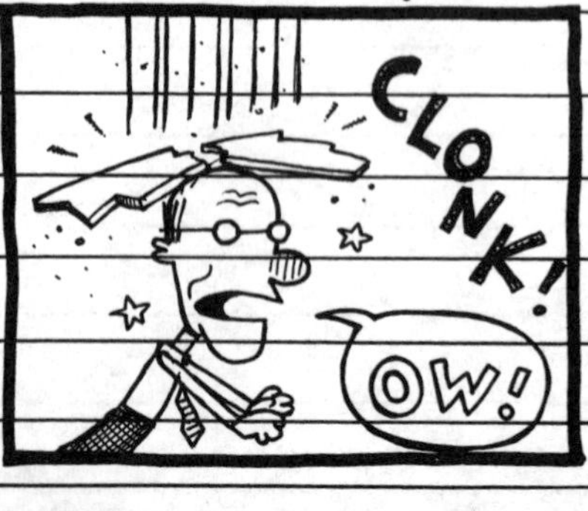

CLONK!
OW!

Yup, I said one hundred years old. So P.S. 38 is going to throw a gigantic **BIRTHDAY PARTY!**

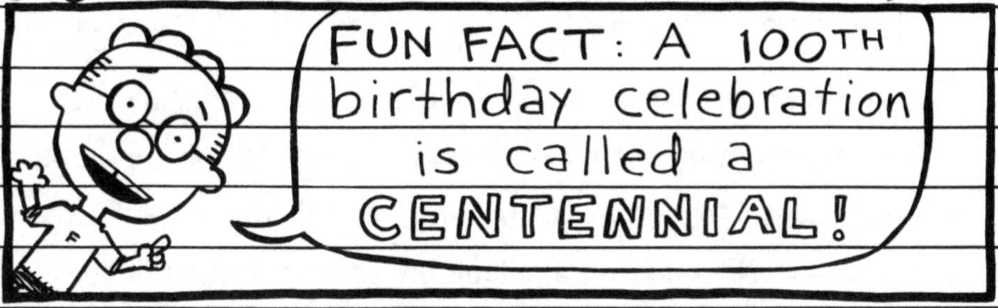
FUN FACT: A 100TH birthday celebration is called a CENTENNIAL!

Actually, Francis, they haven't even decided yet what they're going to call it. But they're promising us plenty of food, fun...

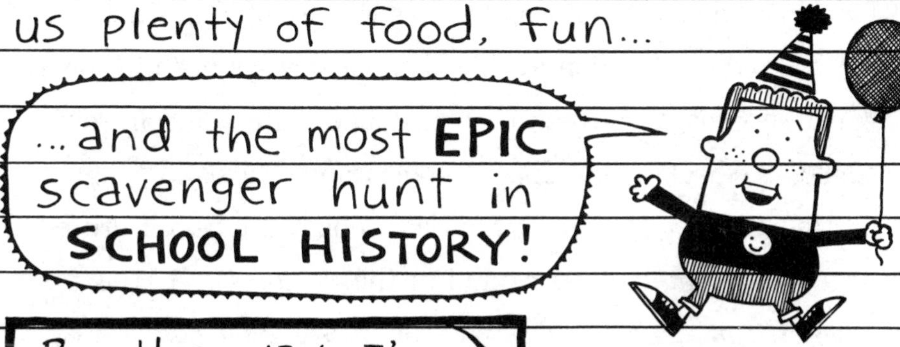
...and the most EPIC scavenger hunt in SCHOOL HISTORY!

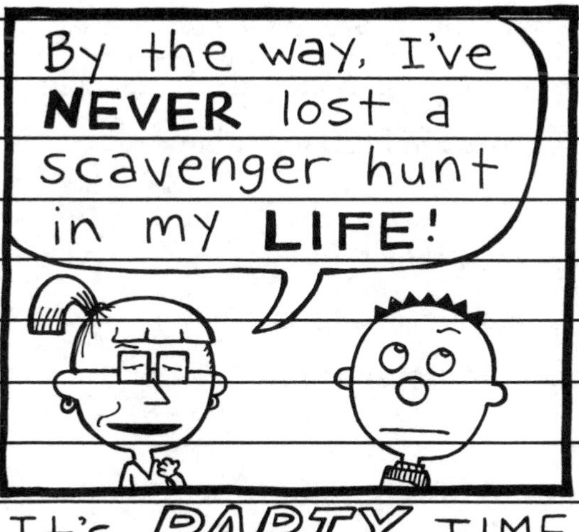
By the way, I've NEVER lost a scavenger hunt in my LIFE!

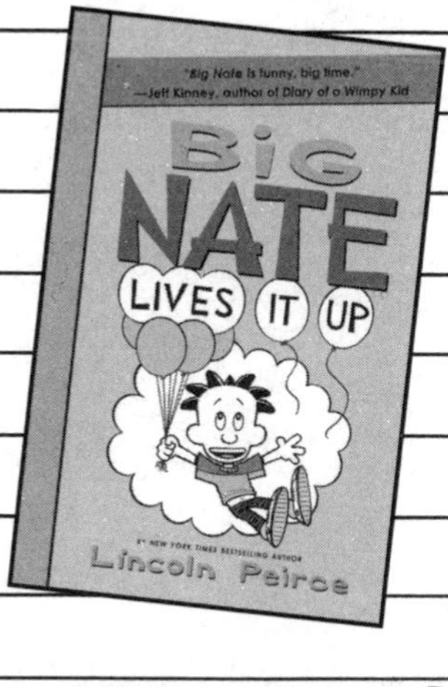
"Big Nate is funny, big time."
—Jeff Kinney, author of Diary of a Wimpy Kid
BIG NATE
LIVES IT UP
Lincoln Peirce

It's *PARTY* TIME!

Read ***BIG NATE LIVES IT UP!***

Lincoln Peirce

(pronounced "purse") is a cartoonist/writer and *New York Times* bestselling author of the hilarious Big Nate book series (www.bignatebooks.com), now published in twenty-five countries worldwide and available as ebooks and audiobooks and as an app, Big Nate: Comix by U! He is also the creator of the comic strip *Big Nate*. It appears in over three hundred U.S. newspapers and online daily at www.gocomics.com/bignate. Lincoln's boyhood idol was Charles Schulz of *Peanuts* fame, but his main inspiration for Big Nate has always been his own experience as a sixth grader. Just like Nate, Lincoln loves comics, ice hockey, and Cheez Doodles (and dislikes cats, figure skating, and egg salad). His Big Nate books have been featured on *Good Morning America* and in the *Boston Globe*, the *Los Angeles Times*, *USA Today*, and the *Washington Post*. He has also written for Cartoon Network and Nickelodeon. Lincoln lives with his wife and two children in Portland, Maine.

For exclusive information
on your favorite authors and artists,
visit www.authortracker.com.

TEDDY RATES ALL THE BIG NATE BOOKS!

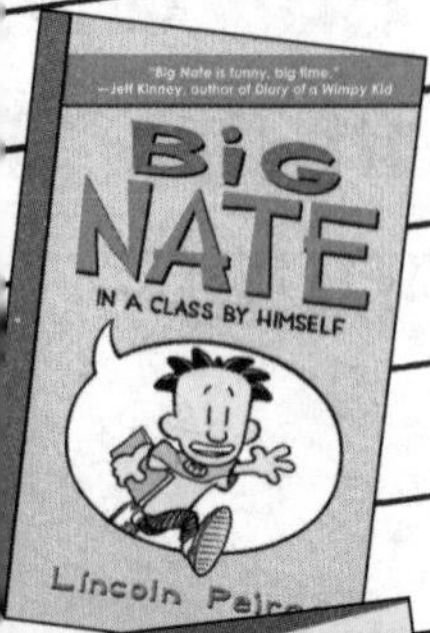
"Big Nate is funny, big time."
—Jeff Kinney, author of Diary of a Wimpy Kid
BIG NATE
IN A CLASS BY HIMSELF

Grade: A

Comments: My fortune cookie says Nate is destined for detention!

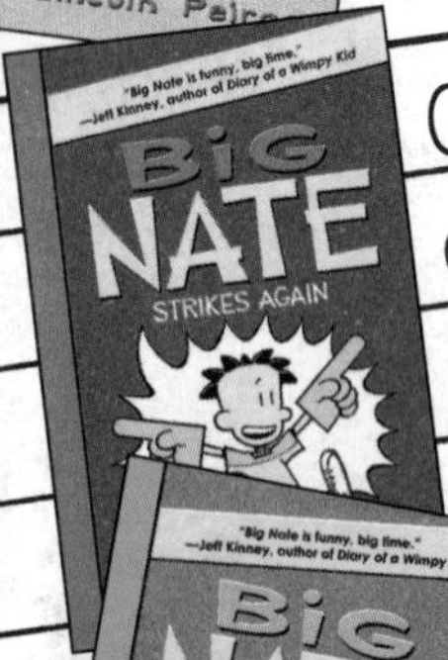
"Big Nate is funny, big time."
—Jeff Kinney, author of Diary of a Wimpy Kid
BIG NATE
STRIKES AGAIN

Grade: A

Comments: Nate and Gina are partners? Even I couldn't come up with something that funny!

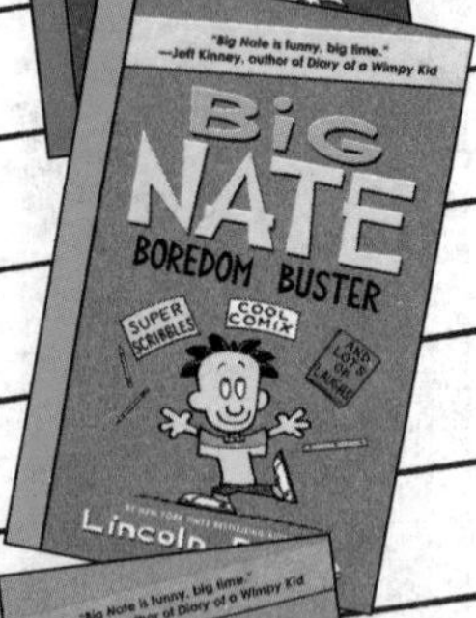
"Big Nate is funny, big time."
—Jeff Kinney, author of Diary of a Wimpy Kid
BIG NATE
BOREDOM BUSTER
SUPER SCRIBBLES
COOL COMIX
AND LOTS OF LAUGHS

Grade: A

Comments: Better than a bag of Cheez Doodles!

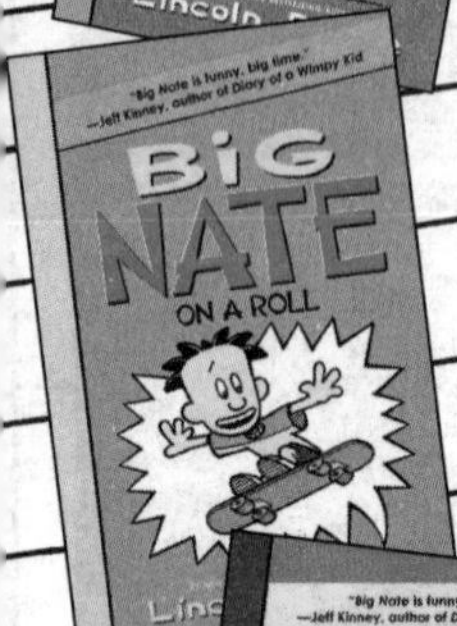
"Big Nate is funny, big time."
—Jeff Kinney, author of Diary of a Wimpy Kid
BIG NATE
ON A ROLL

Grade: A

Comments: I get warm fuzzies thinking about our Timber Scout fund-raiser. Ha!

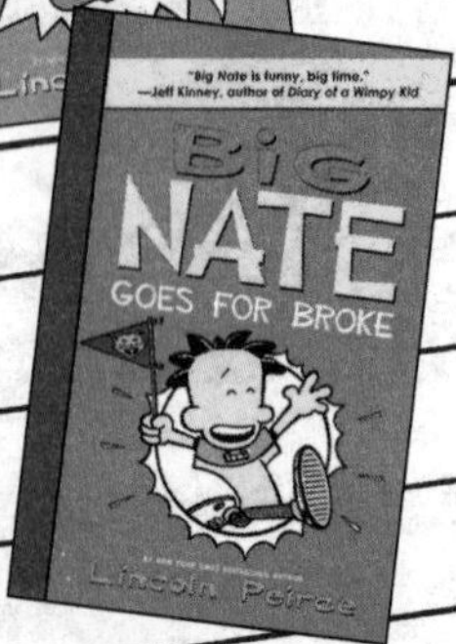
"Big Nate is funny, big time."
—Jeff Kinney, author of Diary of a Wimpy Kid
BIG NATE
GOES FOR BROKE
Lincoln Peirce

Grade: A

Comments: P.S. 38 is ready to put an end to Jefferson's seven-year winning streak! We rock!